Dedicated to the littlest Rhea, who loved wolves the most.

Cover Art: Leigh Graphic Designs (leighcoverdesigns.com)
Editorial Queen: Amanda
Proofreader: One Love Editing

CONTENTS

RAISED BY WOLVES

HUNTED BY WOLVES

LOVED BY WOLVES

AFTER THE END

RAISED BY WOLVES

BLOODLINE - BOOK 1

RHEA WATSON

EWAN

"Soren, get off your fucking phone."

"That's rich—coming from you." Slumped on his barstool across the table, the blond wolf shifter kept his eyes on the screen, thumbs flying. "I'm in the middle of a conversation."

Lucian leaned over to steal a peek, moss-green gaze briefly illuminated by the phone's max brightness setting.

"He's texting his mum," the Brit growled, settling back in his seat with a flick of his eyebrow, followed by a huge chug of stout. I stared at him for a beat, just waiting for the leather-clad wolf to take it back, but when he slapped his mug down and smeared the bubbles from his beard, I closed my eyes and sucked down a deep, calming breath.

Of *course* Soren was texting his mom.

Of fucking course.

Sat in a pub at the crest of the southern wastes in our newly combined territory, a franchised location that had branched off from the wildly successful Farrow's Pub in Soren's lake tourism empire, conversations all around us but silence at this hipster barrel-top table, three stubborn alphas tucked away in the corner…

Of course he was talking to his mom instead of us.

Fuck *me*. I could have gotten so much work done in the two hours our asses had been stuck in these stupid chairs, all hard angles and aesthetically pleasing but grossly underwhelming in terms of comfort. Not like the biggest season of the year for Redwood Grove was about to kick off or anything—the one that would rake in the serious cash. Nope. I was here, not talking and nursing a weak bourbon while Lucian drank the entire pub dry and Soren texted his mom.

Could this night suck any harder?

I cleared my throat, fingers coiled loosely around the glass tumbler, its ice nearly gone, the bourbon too cheap to actually *enjoy*. "*You* were the one who planned this—"

"Yeah, because it's how normal wolves bond." Dressed in a navy button-up patterned with tiny pineapples, Soren Acker was the preppiest of our surly trio, going so far as to rock a pair of dark khaki shorts like it was still the height of summer and not late September. He swept a hand through his dirty-blond locks, smoothing back that long on the top, shaved on the sides cut. "They go to the bar and drink a lot, share stories, talk, laugh, scope out the females, and then go for a run." He finally clicked the little button on the top of his phone, then set it on the table, his bottle of Belgian beer downed ages ago and not a refill in sight. "But *you* two..." The alpha's pointed glance between Lucian and me had my inner wolf's hackles rising. "You two antisocial assholes managed to turn this into a night of drinking and staring at the table, so I figured no one would notice if I stared at my phone instead."

For fuck's sake. I kept *my* fucking phone out of sight despite it buzzing away in my *fucking* pocket all night long—

I bit the insides of my cheeks, consciously trying to soothe my inner wolf. Of this new pack, he and I had the biggest issue with Soren and *his* wolf, but no surprise there. Close in age with an original territory that was established and self-sufficient without mine, he was direct competition.

A palpable threat.

We were all alphas, sure, but the innate *need* to seize top spot, claim the pack throne for ourselves, didn't go away just because as men we had combined three neighboring territories into a massive new one.

And blaming *me*—plus Lucian, but we had known the English bastard wouldn't say more than five words total going into this disaster—for the failure of this pathetic attempt at *bonding* was horseshit.

Just as I was about to snarl something back, Lucian guzzled the rest of his stout. Noisily. Aggressively. All of it in one go, looking more like a Viking tossing back a horn of mead than a modern-day shifter, a lone wolf, a solitary alpha from England who had somehow ended up in our neck of the Canadian wilderness fuck only knew when. According to Soren's dad, one day the silent, brooding wolf was just *there*, content to live alone in a log cabin deep in his territory within the western woods, distant and unobtrusive, barely noticed by the rest of us. Sure, he was still an alpha, huge and terrifying to behold, but not a personal threat.

Yet the way he pounded his empty mug down, green eyes flitting between me and Soren, sober and in control, annoyingly calm, quashed what would have been one of many heated exchanges between us.

"Let's run."

My inner wolf whined, animosity forgotten at the thought of finally *running* again, free and unchecked, wild to the bone. I grimaced, fighting the way his excitement reverberated through me, adrenaline suddenly spiked and hands slapped with a giddy tremor. It had been way too long since I unleashed the beast, and my inner wolf, my companion for life, had grown surly and frustrated as the summer dragged on. Unfortunately, my life needed the man right now: logical, cautious, calculated, *focused*. The wolf had to be caged to survive and thrive this first year as a one-third alpha of a new pack, with a huge new territory and new businesses to manage.

Tonight, the man just wanted whatever the hell *this* was to be over, so, fuck it—time to run.

Soren tapped his phone screen and squinted into the light. "It's barely nine o'clock—"

"Good enough," I growled, then shot back the remainder of this shit whiskey and stood. Seconds later, more chair legs scraped across the plank-wood flooring, the others rising and tossing cash onto the table to pay for our tab. Despite owning this territory, it was still a human's world; supernatural and shifter communities remained in the shadows, secret and the stuff of folklore, outnumbered but never overpowered, living alongside them but not *with* them. The best way to really make it was to buy shit: buildings, restaurants, spas, *land*.

That was exactly what I had done the last ten years.

Still, even real estate titans needed to pay for drinks in pubs that didn't belong to them. If anything, the Acker property development group that licensed this fucking franchise should have covered our drinks, but here we were, forking out cost plus tip.

Unfortunately, Farrow's Pub was the only bar that wasn't a total dive this far south in our new territory. When we had planned these little bonding outings, scheduled right before the business seasons kicked off in our respective industries, we agreed that it ought to be in a neutral space.

Lucian claimed the western woods ages ago. Soren's family had controlled the lake and its surrounding forests to the east for generations. I had the middle ground, with a luxe village that I had rebuilt with my bare hands and capital in the last five years at the foot of a priceless mountain range that opened us up to skiing and winter tourism.

My original territory brought the Swiss Alps to middle-of-nowhere Canada.

The rich and famous flocked to my upscale spas and luxury hotels and pristine million-dollar chalets.

After assessing the summer's haul, Soren's lake industry of boating and cottages and campgrounds paled in comparison.

I was the power player here.

And that really fucked up the dynamics among wolves, especially three alphas.

So, here we were, way down south, just before the land turned barren and scraggly and useless, on the cusp of the no-man's-land between us and the conniving shifter pack to the south.

And the east.

And the west.

They all wanted what we had.

And with Soren's pack numbers down to single digits, the original alphas retired and his siblings spread across North America, he needed me to protect his precious lake industry, just as I needed his reputation to maintain the grip I had on all I'd built.

Lucian had land, resource-rich and fertile, and next year we planned to scatter tiny cabins throughout for glampers to rent and take selfies in at exorbitant prices.

So, you know.

He contributed too.

Sort of.

Mostly Lucian brought strength, physical and psychological, a powerful alpha in his own right who, for some unknown reason, bailed on his English pack and decided to live the hermit life here.

We all had vital resources that ensured the security of this new pack, but figuring out how to interact as alphas who lorded over a pack of three definitely had a fucking learning curve.

Hence we were here.

In this pub where our drinks weren't covered and *way* too many local high school humans occupied the booths, jailbait females undressing me with their eyes as I stalked for the exit.

Outside, in the crisp night air, gravel crunching underfoot and maples swaying with autumn-dipped canopies all around the parking lot, it was easier to just *breathe*. For a beat, I reveled in it, let nature wrap her arms around me. Let the breeze ruffle my hair. Let it fill me, consume me, drive me.

Despite dealing in luxury, the core of my business stemmed from the natural world: the mountains skied and shredded each winter, the full pine trees around the village bedazzled with lights as soon as November hit, the ponds with water like sapphires and red berry bushes and lush, *green* green grass that required less maintenance than one might expect...

Wolves thrived in the natural world. Mother Nature lived in our hearts until we eventually left this world behind, destined for the stars.

But I had pushed *this* life to the side for years, so focused on building Quinn Enterprises into the megalith it was today.

I didn't have the *time*—or the energy—to stop and smell the goddamn roses anymore.

But here, just for a beat, I closed my eyes and let the outdoors in, let the wilds call to my soul.

Until Soren and Lucian's heavy footfalls crashed across the parking lot. Without a word, I fell in line beside them, my polished oxfords taking a dusty beating as we crossed the gravel to the main road. Not a car in sight, the handful of locals in this nothing town in bed an hour ago, Farrow's Pub the only form of quality nightlife until you hit Redwood Grove.

Then you were in my den of sin, and I had *plenty* to offer those who craved some after-hours fun.

We crossed the two-lane country road in silence, carrying on to an open grassy field across from the pub. Bypassed the pathetic playground, the rusty slides and broken swings a little *too* reminiscent of my childhood, then into the forest beyond. As one, we clawed our way through more maples, dogwoods and hawthorns, alders and birches, eventually abandoning the well-walked trails for the wilderness. What would have taken humans forty minutes to cover took us ten, deep in the darkness, in the soaring trees and tangled landscape.

At a small clearing, Lucian was the first to stop, moonlight slanting through the broken canopy. As soon as he wrenched his old leather jacket off, followed swiftly by that bargain-store white cotton tee, the rest of us followed. Off came my freshly ironed charcoal dress shirt, the tailored black slacks, the silk boxers that cost more than Lucian's entire outfit. I wrapped my Cartier in my shirt, then tucked it all in the awaiting branches of a leaning old red alder.

Hardly the first time I had seen my fellow alphas in the nude; clothes never survived the shift. While we all shared a shifter's sculpted physique, muscly and toned, defined and built for physical dominance, it was when our wolves came out to play that I noted the most obvious differences.

We shared some traits, sure, all three of us enormous black wolves by chance, reminiscent of Alaskan timber wolves. Soren, unsurprisingly, was the fluffiest, his fur pristine, his eyes like glittering copper in the night. He moved with this annoying *bounciness* that had made my inner wolf want to fight him when they first met, just a little too exuberant and happy-go-lucky for either of our tastes. He still carried himself like a wolf who had wanted for nothing: never faced starvation, never stared down the bleak promise of a long, dismal winter. Carefree, sweet, extroverted, he hadn't changed since his alpha parents handed him the deed to Redwood Lake and all its properties, then sailed into blissful retirement last year.

Not even the stress of a summer season with two new alphas nosing into his affairs had dampened his high—pampered—spirits.

Super fucking irritating, honestly.

To my right, Lucian's enormous form blotted out the moonlight. Biggest of the bunch, he came with an abundance of scarring from tip to tail. Up his front legs. Around his neck, puncture wounds lingering with every shift. A chunk missing from his upper lip. Battle-hardened, his black fur was coarse, peppered with dark grey and a little patchy in some areas—like a rival had ripped it out.

When I had initially locked eyes with his wolf's golden gaze years back, I thought the scars might be from a fated mate. After all, as far as I knew, only your fated mate could well and truly scar a shifter.

But none of us had been lucky enough to ever *find* the females chosen by Lady Fate, so that theory went down like a lead anchor.

Some other fucked up shit must have happened to him, and he sure as hell wasn't ever going to talk about it.

Where Soren was like an eager pup despite being older than me by two years, Lucian was slow and steady, his wolf form cautious with every step, quick to pause and sniff, ears always up and on high alert.

My wolf and I…

We were somber. Quiet. Distant. Aloof. Calculating and focused. Work smart, not hard. Utilize the fewest moves to behead the queen.

My head of glossy black hair mirrored my wolf's fur, thick and pure obsidian. In my eyes, I had always been midnight, while Soren was the dawn. Lucian…

Lucian in his wolf form was a haggard sunset after a hellish day.

Like many shifters, our inner beasts reflected the human side we showed the world—but somehow we three got along better as wolves than men. As soon as the shift was over, air steamy from the heat of transformation, we greeted each other cordially, reacquainting ourselves with each other's wolves through sniffs and licks and low growls, tails wagging *just* enough to suggest the beginnings of a true pack bond.

Fucking *finally*.

Unprompted, we took off together. Bonded packs could communicate in shifted form; not with words, per se, but through images and scents, emotions and feelings rippling through the shared connection. Tonight, I vaguely sensed Soren's exhilaration as he tore through the forest, that heated excitement undercut by Lucian's caution. He brought up the rear of the group like he needed to see us at all times—or maybe to stand guard from an ambush. Either way, I maintained my usual position in the middle, tempering Soren's puppy energy and Lucian's stormy mood for something in between.

Almost.

Given it had been way, way too long since I let the inner beast free to stretch his legs, a bubbly pleasure rumbled in my chest, paws hitting the ground hard and true, lungs filled with damp forest air. We all pushed ourselves, almost as if our inner wolves sensed they had ground to recover after such a forced outing at the pub. Together, we headed northeast, cutting through dense patches and over ravines without breaking our strides, sending little critters skittering along branches and bigger game fleeing into the shadows.

Wolf shifters bonded best through running. It was tradition by now in our collective history, something we all knew would forge friendships and dampen strife. Tonight was no different. Through the faint pack bond, the awkwardness lifted, floating through the canopy and into a moonlit sky.

Sometime later, we detected the first whiff of the wolf pack that had moved into our new territory. Lucian had already mapped their movements last month; based on the piss and other scent markings, they had come from the south and now occupied a substantial stretch of our southeastern domain, even branching into vicious Hawthorne territory further eastward. He estimated they were headed north and taking the long way around, maybe swing up through Hawthorne lands into the northern territories for the springtime thaw. For now, as winter crept closer, they had hunkered down here, basking in our territory's fertility and its abundance of wildlife.

Hardly a threat, standard wolves. Sure, their familial packs bred unbreakable bonds, but they weren't in direct competition with shifters. We all wanted one thing: resources. Shifters were just more complex in their desires. Land. Wealth. Strength in numbers. Social status and political ties in the human world. All that was reason enough to explain our influx of rivals, other packs pushing toward our new territory as my resort village took off and the lake tourism that Soren's family had cultivated for decades met similar spikes in popularity—mostly by proxy, frankly, the village feeding the cottages and shoreline bars during the off-season.

Wolves wanted food and shelter and a mate to call their own.

Which…

I suppose we craved too—a mate to call our own.

No female had ever called to me before, however, not in the way that fated mates were supposed to, which meant I was stuck with these assholes for the foreseeable future, mateless and buried in work.

Just the way I liked it.

If I'd had a mate, I wouldn't have built Quinn Enterprises from fucking nothing to the powerhouse it was today.

The newly settled wolf pack was easy enough to track, but we did so together, vaguely sensing the anticipation of finding our quarry through the bond. We threaded through the trees and underbrush in a standard V formation, Lucian at the rear tip, Soren and I spread to the left and right. Sniffing. Sneaking. Hunting. We had never chased down an elk or a moose together, but if we bothered, we would probably do a half-decent job. Despite being three hardheaded alphas, our wolves worked well as a team.

Unfortunately, that didn't carry over to our human selves.

And it probably never would.

Unsurprisingly, the pack had hunkered down near the bubbling stream that cut through this section of forest. Descended from the deep pools in what was once my mountain territory, the water had lost that rank, foul scent that tainted the inner caves, smelling like your usual natural spring all the way out here. The wolves, meanwhile, had that musky canine scent mixed with dirt and tree bark, the air colored by the blood of their most recent kill. Soren and I slowed as one, a calm seeping through our tentative bond, the hyperfocus of tracking making it that much stronger.

Camped along the stream, the wolf pack was fourteen strong with a springtime litter of four. Some dozed in the shadows of the tree line. Others frolicked with the pups, fat and plump little ones who had thrived over the summer months, and a profound longing suddenly pounded through our bond when the smallest pup yipped.

His brother had nipped too hard.

Ouch.

Little ones, be careful.

We needed little ones of our own to really cement pack claim on the territory. For now, we were just three alpha males aggressively defending a massive stretch of land. We needed to start a bloodline with mates, females who would birth heirs and forge an unbreakable legacy.

Then no one would dare challenge us, no matter how brutal their pack customs.

In time, other lone wolves would flock to our strength, and again the pack would flourish.

That was the endgame.

And we were barely off the starting block.

Soren made the first move, creeping out of the shadows in a low crouch, ears up, his interest in the pups palpable. Stronger than anything I'd ever experienced between us, in fact. Probably saw them as fucking playmates. I huffed, pawing at the dirt briefly, hesitant, and then padded after him. Lucian tiptoed behind us, ears up and alert, practically vibrating as he tuned in to our surroundings.

Hidden downwind, the pack scented us at the last second, right when we were almost on top of them. Wolves shot up on the other side of the stream, eyeing us warily, hackles raised and tails low. Normally they'd charge strange wolves in their territory, but something ancient and primal in their coding must have warned them a fight with us would be pointless.

Never mind that we were roughly the size of grizzlies, wolf in every way that mattered except the enormous pawprints we left on this world.

The alpha pair rose from sleep together, side by side, male and female, parents and leaders of this pack, scenting us, watching us from the darkness of an old maple. Only after the female turned and trotted into the woods did the male follow, silently urging the rest to follow. Pack babysitters—young males and females—corralled the pups and led them away, and we three watched them go, envy prickling in the bond, faint yet somehow irritating enough to set my teeth on edge.

Just as the last swishing grey tail disappeared, the shadows *moved.* Darkness took on a life of its own, crispy fallen leaves fluttering down and sprinkling the forest floor. A figure soared, taking on the shadows, swathed in them, expertly hidden—best of the whole pack, in fact. Near where the alpha pair had dozed, it swelled, hidden even to my keen night vision.

Until it wasn't.

Until it was just *there*, huge and unassuming—a wolf silhouetted against the trees.

Nothingness twanged through our pack bond, all of us transfixed on the figure creeping through the darkness.

She emerged a few moments later, hesitantly strolling into the moonlight.

Fierce blue eyes drank us in, practically neon they were so luminous.

That...

Roughly the size of a male black bear, smaller than us but obviously *way* larger than her pack, that... was a shifter.

Living with wolves.

Actual wolves.

Curiosity suddenly hummed in our bond, but I barely felt it, the sensation like a fly buzzing in your ear.

Her scent struck with her next step, slamming into me like a hurricane. *Roses*—but not overly sweet. A subdued floral that struck from every side, the direction of the winds be damned. Subtle and soothing. Calm and quiet. Not flashy. Not showy. Not the type to announce her presence, to hog the spotlight or demand the world on one of my silver platters.

Beautiful.

I breathed deep, images of late springtime blooming across my mind's eye. The comfort of sprawling on your back on a blanket of lush green grass, sometime in the dwindling afternoon, a picnic consumed, wine drunk, not a care in the world.

Nowhere to be but *there*, with her, watching fluffy white clouds amble along—

Grey.

She was grey, not midnight like us, but a stunning light grey that darkened to black at the root. Her snout and the tips of her ears were also black, a rainbow of shades, and then her eyes. So fucking bright and inviting. Curious. *Cautious* as they swept over the three males sizing her up from across the watery divide.

Wind rustled through the trees.

The stream bubbled and gushed, trickling along the forest floor, keeping us from *her*.

This female.

Who smelled like roses.

And felt like peace.

Springtime sunshine and stillness and sitting at the end of a dock, feet in the water, beer in hand as the sun dipped behind a hazy horizon—

I blinked out of the strange stupor, every nerve on fire, head empty, heart hammering.

Mine.

And then charged straight for her.

2

SOREN

Whoa.

Who was that—and why did she smell like sunbathed cotton and laundry fresh out of the dryer? Pine freshness and baked bread and breakfast on a snowy day, pancakes stacked high and everyone dressed in flannel.

Why did she *feel* like closeness and comfort?

Like *hygge*?

Like laughter and bonding and familiarity—

The forest blurred around her, melding with her grey-to-black ombre fur, leaving only her eyes, bright like blue neon, like pristine sapphire marbles mined deep in the Redwood mountains.

I mean. Did you… mine for sapphires?

Whatever.

Because those were *it*. Sapphires, the sort a goddess might wear on a crown of starlight.

Never seen eyes so beautiful before, so startling, so intense and bright, oozing intelligence and calculation as they darted back and forth between us.

Brave little she-wolf—staring down three alphas without her tail tucked between her legs. In fact, she rose to her full height as she

16

surveyed us from the other side of the babbling brook, nose twitching, scenting us in the dying breeze.

At the first splash of Ewan's paw in the chilly water, I lunged. Sprang forward just a beat behind him, headed straight for her, for this wolf shifter we'd found surrounded by wolves—honest-to-goodness *wolves*. Not shifters. *Canis lupus*, a whole pack of them slinking through the trees, disappearing into the shadows with their pups in tow.

Ewan reached her first—because of course he did—but I was a close second, Lucian bringing up the rear like always. But each of us fought to get in her face, greeting nose-to-nose, breathing deep, soaking in the scent of this stranger. This she-wolf who still hadn't flinched, who didn't cower or tuck tail and flee. In fact, her hackles rose, making her seem bigger—though still dwarfed by a trio of alpha males—and her tail suddenly shot straight up, full and thick, her scent suddenly muskier, and it trembled with a tense interest that I *swore* jumped from her to me.

Yeah. I *did* feel it—I felt *her*. Her frantic curiosity and her excitement, a giddiness purposefully stamped down and restrained, like she was fighting with herself—fighting for control.

The only reason I'd be able to catch a whiff of her emotions, her innermost feelings, would be if she were a part of our new pack.

If she was—

Oh.

Oh wow.

Wait.

Wait.

Was she my *fated*?

I stabbed my nose into the thick, luscious fur at the base of her neck, sniffing deep, tail wagging, interest spiking.

Yes.

Yes, that had to be it.

This brave little she-wolf was *mine*.

I'd waited all my life for my partner, the female Lady Fate deemed worthy of me—and me of her. An alpha's mate, strong and brave and true. The mother of a new bloodline, caring and soft and supportive. Mom and Dad had set such a beautiful example of *legit* fated mates for me and my sisters, forging a legacy of love for the rest of us to aspire to. So far, my younger sisters had either bonded with their mates or flocked to other territories for university where they might *find* their mate.

And I had stayed here to maintain the Acker traditions, to carry our virtues and values into this new nameless pack.

But I'd expected to do that alone, the only two wolf shifters left in our territory these jagweeds on either side of me—and they were nosing at her.

At *my* girl.

And I sure as shit wasn't fated to *them*.

Lost in her cozy scent, I barely noticed what Ewan and Lucian were doing—until Ewan's inky-black figure crept down my mate's body, sniffing a little too intensely, almost aggressive as he rounded to her rear. *Rage* pounded through me out of nowhere, my wolf and I exploding on the inside, vision misted red, heart hammering a war anthem.

How *dare* he be so... so... so *pushy*?

How dare he shove his nose at what was *mine*?

Mine, mine, mine, *mine*.

Snarling, I bodychecked him away, but the alpha came back swinging, snapping at my face, teeth big and sharp and dangerous. I'd never been in an actual fight before with another wolf shifter; sure, I had chased rivals out of our territory with Dad more times than I could count. Scared off looky-loos. Wrestled with my sisters and their mates. But if Ewan wanted a fight, I'd give him a damn good one.

Only as soon as we got into it, snapping and growling and tussling, shoving each other away from the female, there was Lucian —taking all her attention for himself. After Ewan knocked me on my side and tried to go back to her rather than lunging for my throat, I caught *my* mate sniffing at Lucian's snout...

And then *lick* it.

Her tail wagging.

Her eyes bright.

Nope. Nope, nope, nope—*baby, you're mine.*

So, I shifted the scopes from Ewan to Lucian, to the massive scarred wolf who usually kept to himself. I had no issue forming a pack with him as co-alpha because, at the end of the day, he just wanted to hermit deep in his territory. He had no interest in gaining wealth, status, and privileges like Ewan; Lucian had always been a physical threat, a monster lurking in the dark, but he wasn't competition.

Until now.

Until I barreled into him, teeth bared, and he didn't move an inch.

It was like tackling a block of granite. Ewan joined the brawl a moment later, coming at him from the other side, clearly hell-bent on claiming the female for himself.

I mean, who wouldn't?

She was breathtaking in every sense—and we hadn't even seen her shifted yet.

Much to my surprise, Lucian fought back like a true warrior, light and nimble on his paws despite his immense size. Obviously his scars had come from somewhere, but Dad and I always assumed he had *lost* all those fights—*that* was why he was so grizzled and gruff.

Maybe not.

Maybe you learn something new every day.

We scrambled around the riverbank, snarling and growling, fur flying and teeth snapping, one claiming the upper hand for a *second* before the other two knocked him down. Sometimes Ewan and I were on the same team, sometimes me and Lucian, sometimes both of them against me. Anytime one male got too friendly with this female, the others ripped into him. Blood splattered the forest floor like some grotesque abstract painting, the air scented by a metallic sharpness. Our injuries healed fast, but they still *hurt*. Whimpers punctuated the brawl. Blood stained my tongue.

And in the middle of it all, my fated mate.

Literally. Bumped and jostled by our huge bodies, she stayed put, oddly determined to ride this out. I should have been focused on getting her to safety, but apparently I couldn't turn my back on Lucian *or* Ewan for a second before one of the other black wolves, alphas to their core, tried to steal what was mine.

When we crowded her a little too close, surrounded by alphas with no room to breathe, the little female finally snapped. Hackles way up, every individual fur standing on end, she snarled at all three of us, whirling around, flashing her teeth, lunging—shrieking, almost.

I retreated two steps.

Never in my life had a female besides my mom cowed me.

But this one was... tough.

Wild.

Savage, really, all teeth and growls and nips at our faces and front legs to separate us—to check our stupid alpha male crap before it got out of hand.

Her frustration tickled the nape of my neck, featherlight and wispy, those neon blues laced with confusion.

She didn't understand what was happening, and I didn't blame her one bit for finally putting an end to it.

Strange that Ewan and Lucian *also* listened to her.

No one but an alpha's fated mate could *properly* put him in his place—

Suddenly, she shifted. With the fight quashed and the three of us separated, she turned from wolf to woman in a flash.

And I fell just a little in love.

Because...

Wow.

Just...

Wow. Thank you, Lady Fate.

Small like her wolf, she still rocked a stunning hourglass figure, steam rising off her olive-toned skin from the heat of the shift.

Despite the curves, her ribs were a little too prominent for my liking; did she eat enough with these wolves?

Well. That wouldn't be an issue going forward. Not in my house.

Her deep, panting breaths drew focus to a pair of weighted breasts and pebbled pinkish-brown nipples. The odd freckle dotted her torso. Rounded hips and strong legs.

Hair. Body hair—everywhere. Unshaven legs. Armpits. A nest at the crux of her thighs. Women in my past, shifters or otherwise, were relatively hairless, and my mate was… not.

And I kind of dug the look?

Sort of… amazon of the wilds, more wolf than woman. Her hair hadn't seen a cut in years either; it spilled all the way down her back and over the curve of her ass. Thick, wavy, and tangled, it fell like a warm bronze waterfall. Full lips the same hue as her nipples. A square jaw and sharp cheekbones. Hollow. She needed to be fed, needed to fuel her powerful body with more than what the woods had to offer.

Grey-blue eyes, lighter and almost transparent compared to her inner wolf, but no less striking.

Silence blanketed the forest. Even the stream had quieted, a hush descending, as though every natural element held its breath while she sized us up in her human form, fingers loose, knees bent—ready to fight *or* fly.

Lucian shed his wolfskin first.

Ewan and I followed.

And without a word, all eyes locked on her, we pounced on our delectable prey as *men*, lusting after more than a good, deep sniff…

3

LYSSA

The last time a man touched me, he hurt me.

Deeply.

And he never touched me like this—never with wonder in his eyes, curiosity in his fingertips.

I knew it was wrong the moment he stole my first kiss—*not meant to be, not my other half, not like my alphas*—but I was so young at the time. Lonely. Desperate for human connection and needy for the embrace of a mate.

I tried to stop it back then when it felt wrong, but not like this. Not with the snap of my teeth and the rage in my soul.

He carried on until he was finished.

He wasn't mine.

I wasn't his.

He pushed me away when it was over. Called me a whore, the insult spat on beer-soaked breath.

He threatened me.

I broke his nose.

Then his arm.

Then his *other* arm.

Then I left him there, behind the bar, next to the filthy metal dumpster he'd pinned me against, and never saw him again.

Rarely ever thought about him, this not-mine male who stole something from me almost ten years ago—he barely crossed my mind until now.

Until three males turned from wolves to men and *touched* me.

This had to be a dream, right?

This wasn't real.

There were no others like me—only wolves and humans, then me in the middle. A freak. An abomination. Demon-born. Devil child. Possessed. Garbage.

Mistake.

For once, I didn't feel like any of those things. I felt... special.

Wanted.

Only I couldn't bask in that because... I couldn't think straight. Could barely *see* straight, struggling to find myself in the middle of three huge males, their hands everywhere, their body heat stifling, their eyes penetrating. Never mind the suffocating bliss of being surrounded by them; shock pulsed through me with every ragged beat of my heart.

There were more like me out there.

More human-wolf *freaks*.

All my life, twenty-six long years, I'd thought I was the only one.

Even if *I* struggled to understand, they seemed to know what they were doing—what they wanted. So close. So *hot*, fire licking low in my belly, scorching up my back and flaring at the nape of my neck. The only reassurance came from Kira, my inner wolf companion's whines persistent and insistent, her yips excited, the sort we howled for the return of a hunting party.

Her interest melded with mine.

We both wanted them to touch me, hands everywhere, but only if they didn't go nuts again. I had no clue what triggered the fight, but the forest had gobbled up enough of their blood, the dirt drenched in it—and their bodies showing no signs of the attacks.

Just like me.

We all healed in a flash.

I'd watched wolves bleed out and fade away over the years—but these males acted like it was nothing.

Because it was.

My kind was indestructible, but did that come from darkness like they always said—or light?

Good or evil.

I had no idea.

All I knew for certain was that I didn't want them to stop *touching* me. Sniffing me. Scenting me as no human had ever done before.

I liked the big one at my back. He had a calmness about him even after the brawl that called to my heart. Bearded, scruffy, dark brown hair and eyes like moss in springtime, he was a mountain of a male who soared over me—who crouched to run his nose down my shoulder to my neck, breathing me in, marking me with the brush of his lips. The first graze of teeth along my throat unleashed a storm of eager little bumps all over my body, nipples painfully erect, and I arched into him with a soft moan, surrendering to the sensation.

To his slow, firm exploration of my flesh.

The blond stole my attention when he snatched my hand and sniffed the underside of my wrist, brows furrowed like he was determined to drown in my scent and my fluttering pulse. When he had taken his fill, he kissed my palm, robin's-egg-blue eyes locked on mine, handsome mouth quirked in a way that made my belly squirm pleasantly. He then kissed the top of my hand, then each of my fingers, a wickedness about him despite his beauty— mischievous, maybe, like the tricksters in all the old stories I wasn't allowed to read but *always* did.

Despite that, he was tender. Gentle.

I liked that too, just as much as I liked the mountain man nipping at my earlobe, his huge hand wandering down my thigh— something hard and insistent nudging into my back.

The third male, like the sun, was too breathtaking to look at for more than a few seconds. Like the black-and-grey adverts I'd once seen in a subway tunnel, he was model handsome, destined to sell clothes or watches or colognes. With thick, tousled midnight-black hair, he made my heart thunder.

Made Kira howl the moment our eyes met, fleetingly, desperately, his like a dark, layered hickory bark.

He was the first to drop to his knees before me, dragging an openmouthed kiss along my outer thigh, up, up, up, until he reached my hip. His hand delved between my legs, and the first brush of fingers in my cleft sparked a brighter, sharper pleasure in my belly.

But it was too much.

It was *all* too much.

All three males were very *there*, in my space, touching me, kissing me, licking and nibbling at my skin. Their scents crashed and twined, threaded together into a distinctly masculine, musky smell, but there was so much more than that. Clashing scents, distinct but entangled, unique to each man—only I couldn't tell them apart. For some reason, that kicked off a panic deep in my being; I needed to know who was who, and I *needed* to assign a scent to a man.

As if that would help me know him better.

Detect good from bad, dark from light.

Scents were so telling, way more clear-cut than words, and I couldn't read a *thing*—

Kira allowed me one panicked heave before we traded places, the woman retreating inside the wolf. I was always braver with her in the driver's seat, more confident in my abilities, in who I *was*. That hadn't always been the case, but nearly a decade in the North American wilderness, roaming the continent with my pack, had changed things.

In this form, we had faced down grizzlies and mountain cats and all manner of vicious beast. As a human, I... Well, I rarely fared so well.

The males reared back, their shock at the change rippling down my spine. Strange, to feel someone else's emotion; this was a first, and the low growl rumbling in Kira's throat suggested neither of us was comfortable with it. I tried to make a hard left between the model and the blond, the gap between them barely wide enough to scoot through, but they were just as fast as me—just as nimble on their feet. Fully grown, I had become *better* than the wolves around me. Faster. Tougher. Keener. With humans, I smelled deeper, saw clearer, stood stronger.

But these three matched my every move, blocking any escape with chiseled male bodies—cut, muscular, *sculpted* bodies unlike any I'd ever seen before. In fact, this was my first brush with full nudity besides my own; the man at the bar had stayed dressed—just whipped out his dick for the main event.

Collectively, these three had nicer dicks.

Bigger.

Fuller.

Thicker.

And no wonder, given they would have towered over that drunk coward, bigger in every sense. Broad. Bold. Defined in their own ways. Beautiful.

So, *so* beautiful that just the sight of them calmed my pounding heart.

There was something about them...

They reminded me of angels.

I tripped over my own paws at the thought, Kira's interest and mine a distraction that allowed the blond to block an opening by the thickets.

At the old farmhouse, there were so many pictures of saints and *angels*, the loveliest creatures in my living memory, exquisitely painted, always so handsome, smiling serenely...

Maybe these three were angels.

And if that was so, did that make *me* an angel?

A firm hand suddenly smoothed over my side, large and strong, heavy as it settled between my shoulders. I whipped back and snapped my jaws on instinct, *just* missing the biggest one's rugged torso.

"Stop," the blond barked, hands up, chest falling hard with every breath, "just don't touch her—"

"Clearly she's fated to all of us." Oh. Mountain Man had an accent, different from the blond—like the people in historical movies about ancient Rome. *British.* The word came back to me out of nowhere, and I huffed, pleased to remember *something* of the civilized world despite the chaos. Mountain Man was British, his voice soft and velvety, rich and low like dark chocolate.

No. Not that. Horrible stuff. One Easter a nun had given me a bar and *oh.* No. Never again.

I lacked the vocabulary these days, so used to communicating with a glance or a growl.

He...

His voice was beautiful, *period,* just like him.

Meanwhile, the blond sounded local, earthy and cozy and familiar.

"That's *bullshit,*" the model rasped, his eyes shimmering like his wolf side suddenly, a sunset on fire, and his commanding voice deepened to a snarl. He then blinked down at me, and the hickory bark returned. Our gazes locked and tangled, and Kira and me... We padded closer, lost in him. Model Man tore his eyes away first, then stabbed a hand through his hair. "Oh, *fuck...* No."

I flinched at the curses, briefly assaulted by memories I had stuffed down years ago: the scent of leather in the air, the taste of soap on the back of my tongue, the sensation of a square bar *shoved* down my throat. Another huff and a violent shake, ruffling out my fur, scared the mental pictures away.

Fated.

That word meant something.

Stirred something.

Made me and Kira happy—and I had no idea *why.*

"That... makes sense," the blond muttered slowly, scratching at his clean-shaven jawline, sculpted like a marble statue.

"Three alphas," Mountain Man said, sounding like he was trying to diffuse the tension with a calm tone and an inoffensive posture.

In the pack, lesser wolves licked at muzzles and whined, quick to submit if it meant avoiding a fight. These males handled it differently, almost like they were *constantly* on the verge of a brawl. Not good. Not a strong pack. "We weren't fated for mates of our own... We're here tonight for *her*."

"No, no, I don't..." Model Man flexed his hands in and out of fists, then pointed at me, expression *angry*, like it was all my fault. "I'm *not* sharing my mate. I'm not. She's *mine*."

"Seems like you don't have a choice, Ewan."

Ewan. Huh. I liked that—

Ewan lunged at the blond with a snarl, and I rolled my eyes, Kira and I instantly unimpressed that we were all in a fight again. Despite what had seemed like an even temper, the blond swung back, clocking this Ewan in the jaw, snarling just as savagely, their eyes like their wolves and their movements ferocious.

Okay. *Don't like that.*

"Enough." Mountain Man kept his warning low and dangerous. No bark. No flash of teeth. He didn't need to be loud to command the space, and I backed away from the bloody, panting pair who glowered at each other with locked jaws and trembling fists. In my experience, *true* alphas stayed calm, only lashing out as a last resort.

Still, he wasn't *better* than his companions, because he had charged right into the fight minutes earlier, taller and broader and scarier than the others. Scarred. Probably a whole lot stronger too.

The thought of his *strength* sent another shiver of interest down my spine, and I padded to his side—then plopped into a prim seated position, my snout reaching his shoulder, ears roughly jaw height on this enormous male. They perked up, alert, and I fought for just a measure of his control in this scenario, in a scene that I still wasn't sure was real or not.

I'd been dead asleep when they first arrived.

Maybe this *was* a dream.

"Well, what now?" the blond demanded, strong shoulders heaving as he chased his breath. He swiped his hand under his nostrils, smearing blood across his skin, then snorted the rest back with a grimace. "We can't just leave her here... She's living with *actual* wolves."

Hey.

I growled low at his tone—like living with the pack who had taken me in as a pup, who had cared for me, fed me, kept me safe from harm time and time again, was a *bad* thing.

Three pairs of eyes suddenly darted my way, and a sinking feeling settled in my gut, like falling through the ice and *struggling* to crack the surface again.

Like getting swept away in the river's raging current, lungs about to burst, back crashing over rocks.

I longed to be near them—longed for their hands in my fur, on my human flesh, between my thighs again. Longed to smell them one by one, really get a grip on each.

But I didn't like the direction this conversation was headed.

Here comes the current. Why can't you breathe?

"Little she-wolf." The blond male crouched somewhat to meet my eyeline, his head cocked and his smile kind. "Shift back for us." *Shift?* What did *that* mean? "Let's just talk—"

No. I bolted to the left, then zig-zag-*zigged* around Ewan and leapt over the stream. Talking never did any good. Talking led to trouble—to beatings, to locks on closet doors with you on the inside. Talking hurt.

I didn't want to talk.

I wanted to *feel*—and I needed to find my family.

Needed to make sure the pups were safe.

Make sure they hadn't moved on without me.

Low growls and deep, gravelly barks nipped at my heels, followed by the thunder of paws tearing across the forest after me. Ears tucked flush to my skull, I charged headlong into the trees, screeching for my pack, Kira and I both panicked and confused and lost.

And three snarling males *right* on my tail.

4

LUCIAN

What a night.

From awkward thumb-twiddling at the pub to *this*.

I took a long drag of my cigarette and reveled in the burn, in the cinders scorching the back of my throat, then let it all out in an exhale that felt more cleansing than it should. Ass half-asleep, I shifted from cheek to cheek, my beat-up jeep jostling side to side at the movement. Seated on the hood, I gave it an affectionate pat; Ewan despised my firstborn. *Hated* it with every fiber of his being— likely because it didn't come with a luxury brand name or some pretentious hood ornament. Tonight, I was the pretentious ornament, smoking away, three ciggies down and two left in the pack.

The bastard might hate my ride, but this creaky, groaning, secondhand vehicle had transported our mate back to civilization.

Couldn't wait to hear his prissy views on it now with her scent all over the leather upholstery.

Inhaling another lungful of fire, I eyed the outlet mall warily. Stuck in the middle of nowhere off the highway in the desolate south end of our territory, the combination of cast-off shops ran twenty-four hours a day, seven days a week, all year long. No holidays.

Ewan had bought it on the brink of bankruptcy two years back for a steal.

It made him a small profit, supposedly, and tonight it would supply our mate with everything she needed to survive a few days, clothed and groomed, before the flood of online deliveries started pouring into Redwood Grove proper.

After a quick check of my phone—no messages, as usual, and nearing three in the morning—I twisted around to check on our she-wolf through the windshield. Right where we left her: slumped in the back seat, buried in my leather jacket and sulking up a storm. Arms crossed. Petulant. Silent.

Her pouty lower lip *did* things to me—made my inner wolf frisky.

We had hunted her for over two hours before the final takedown, this little female fast on her paws and wily as a fox. Despite the wolf pack we found her in only entering our territory last month, she knew the ins and outs well, capable of turning on a dime to avoid capture. Her size was an advantage tonight in the tangled undergrowth, as was the fact that Soren, Ewan, and I had never properly hunted before. Sure, we'd done the obligatory pack run here and there to forge a connection, but this was new.

And we were rusty.

Sloppy.

Barely capable of taking down a deer, honestly, never mind an adult female wolf shifter.

In the end, a rabbit warren tripped her up—that was all we needed. Quick as she was, we overpowered her tenfold. Shifted back to men, we took turns carrying her snarling, snapping, seething wolf form through the forest, then spent another forty bloody minutes coaxing her to shift. Could hardly waltz out of the woods carrying a wolf the size of a black bear, after all.

The security footage of *that* would certainly have done the rounds on the internet, fueling all those—correct—conspiracy theories about the secret supernatural world living alongside humanity.

While we three had clothes waiting, our mate was without—and touting a struggling nude woman would be even worse than a human catching sight of her wolf form. So, I put her in my jacket, fed her skinny arms through the sleeves, and zipped her in. It drowned her, but she could *just* pass it off as a dress.

Good enough for now.

Our mate was strong though. Capable. Intelligent and adaptive.

My inner wolf loved her already.

Wanted pups with her *already*.

Sentimental old fuck.

I felt it the moment I first scented her—connection, desperation, want and desire unlike any that came before. It cut me off at the knees. Made my heart pound and my mind race. Made me impulsive, drawing on my most base instincts to *take* what was mine.

Only she wasn't *just* mine.

She belonged to Ewan and Soren too; no wolf would turn on his packmate, his fellow alpha, for anyone *but* his mate.

And we had no idea who she was.

Where she came from.

How long she had been living with feral wolves.

Stubbing the spent cigarette on my wrist, taking the burn with a grimace, I tossed the butt aside without tearing my gaze from her beauty. Hard to look away from, my mate. Silvery-blue eyes, like ice stretched across a cobalt lake, so much depth lurking below a frosty exterior. Square face. Full lips. Hair—*so* much hair, and not just trailing off her head. Olive-skinned like me, naturally curvy but could certainly do with a bit more meat over her bones.

She hadn't said a word yet. Not when we captured her, dressed her, or manhandled her into the back of my jeep. Small and silent—I felt that. I rarely said much anymore. Why waste the energy on ten words when two would do?

At this point, however, I was *dying* to hear her voice—*aching* to know whether it suited her body.

For she looked utterly wild, even as a woman.

Her inner wolf had been so fierce putting us squabbling fuckwits in our place; her voice would no doubt possess the same gravitas.

For she was a she-wolf alpha, and power flowed through her veins.

That voice could probably command armies—

Fuck me. Easy to surrender to the what-ifs tonight. I pinched the bridge of my nose and faced the mall again, the stretch of cracked concrete they called a parking lot dotted with eight cars—likely all employees at this hour. Given my mate had to be shared between three alphas, three wolves of equal rank within this misfit pack, I had to be on top of my game. Stay sharp, or Ewan would talk his way into hoarding a bigger slice of the pie for himself, and Soren would fight for what was left, his power drawn from an unbroken line of alphas.

She was *mine*, same as them, but the competition had already started—first blood marked its beginning, and even if we'd all calmed down a little, behaved more like civilized men, the end was a long, long way off. Despite working together to claim her in the forest, the battle for dominance continued. Not with teeth and claws, spilled blood and torn fur, but with who had possession of her.

Who touched her.

Who pressed a hand to her lower back.

Who opened the car door for her.

I had no choice but to man the wheel, the jeep fussy with any other captain, but Soren and Ewan shoved each other over who got to sit in the back with her.

Ewan had won that tussle, knocking Soren aside with an elbow to the ribs and a swift kick to the knee.

None of this would be easy. Combining three separate wolf territories into one was a challenge in and of itself. Crowning three alphas from different packs and expecting them to get along?

Fucking *nightmare*. Now we had a mate to squabble over—and that was the fiercest fight of all, this prize valued far above the rest.

Worth it.

I'd waited my whole life to find my fated mate, thirty-six long years of strife and sorrow, heartache and loss. This was nothing compared to that. *This* made all those gruesome years worthwhile.

Jaw clenched, I scoped out the parking lot perimeter, assessed entry and exit points, busied myself with defensive work to drown out the flood of memories—the ocean of blood tied to my previous pack's legacy.

Don't get too attached, old boy.

Grateful as I was that Lady Fate had *finally* unveiled my fated mate, I refused to get *too* invested. My inner wolf already loved her, but loved ones leave. Always. They died right in front of you, in your arms. They hurt you. Betrayed you. Scarred you inside and out.

I... couldn't do that again.

I wouldn't survive it.

Of course she deserved comfort and protection. She deserved a mate who would watch her back and provide all she needed. That little she-wolf was safe with me.

But she'd never have my heart.

Never.

Then she would never find a way to rip it to shreds—toss the broken bits around like bloody confetti.

After confirming *again* that this location was, in fact, secure, I checked my ancient flip phone, then growled, narrowed gaze on the mall's main doors.

"Come on, you twats."

They weren't shopping to fill an entire wardrobe—just bits and bobs, enough to tide her over for a week at most.

Suddenly, the jeep's creaky back door opened, followed by the sound of bare feet slapping concrete. I whipped around to discover my mate had broken through the lock mechanism—ripped it clean off—and was now sprinting across the parking lot, headed for the chain-link fence at the rear perimeter.

A fence she scaled and hopped over like it was nothing.

Fuck.

I was up in a flash, inner wolf howling for her, calling her back, begging her to *stop*. A dull ache throbbed between my eyes courtesy of his distress, but I shoved all that aside and charged after her. The fence kept the forest at bay and was more a nuisance than a true obstacle. I jumped it without actually touching it, landing hard on the other side, eyes fixed on her as she scrambled through the birch grove.

Quick as she was in her wolf form, I outpaced her on two legs, closing the gap between us in seconds, hot on her heels, snarling when she wrenched off my jacket and tossed it in a thorn thicket. Her hair flowed like the tail of a blazing comet, catching on branches, ripping, giving her away to any other pursuers. Fully naked again, I predicted my mate was about to shift, adrenaline whispering through our bond, faint and subtle, the connection between us almost as tenuous as the one I shared with Soren and Ewan.

My inner wolf panicked at the thought, whining and snorting, clawing up my lungs, desperate for her to *stay*.

"*Wait,*" I called, staggering to a halt, fighting my inner beast's terror—resisting the urge to just tackle her and throw her over my shoulder. "Please don't go."

Brunette mane swishing down her back, she slowed from a sprint to a jog—then stopped abruptly. Kept her back to me, her shoulders heaving, her calves twitching from the exertion.

Fuck's *sake*. I longed to call out to her, but I didn't even know her name. None of us did. She-wolf. *Mate.* She remained elusive to us, more of an idea than a physical being, and I fucking *despised* that.

This wild woman of the woods hadn't said a word yet, not when we explained the importance of fated mates in the shifter community. Not when we introduced ourselves. Not when we insisted she was *beyond* safe with us. Her eyes were the most expressive thing about her, facial features locked in a guarded sulk, posture rigid and arms always crossed.

None of us could even hazard a guess at how long she had been living with wolves, but from the look of her, the raw energy she gave off, the flawless way her wolf side handled three massive males without flinching...

She had been wild for a long time.

And all of this was new. Scary. *We* were new and scary.

Of course she tried to run again.

Even as my inner wolf descended into madness, regressing to puppyhood, plunging into a black hole of fear and panic that he was about to lose his fated mate for *good*—dramatic bastard—I held up my hands and took a deep breath. Quieted my hammering heart. Surrendered to the calm inside that was still there, buried beneath the paranoia, dusted with the chaos and trauma of my past.

This is now.

It isn't then.

"I know it's frightening," I told her, injecting a gravelly rumble into my tone, relying on the baritone to lull her, *call* to her as a true alpha calling to his mate. "You're unsure. You want to go back to your pack, right? You love them."

Even if they weren't shifters, those wolves belonged to her. For all we knew, that pack was all the family she had in this world—and we had ripped her from them in a single night.

She fidgeted, flicking her long—too long—nails with her thumbs, then slowly peeked over her shoulder and nodded. Good. No words still, but this was progress. Relief trickled through my veins like ice water; my inner wolf didn't trust it.

"Please don't go," I begged. I had *never* begged. Never yielded until the bitter, bloody end when there was no one left but me and the fire. Perhaps I ought to do it more often, because my fated turned the rest of the way around, then dragged her hair over her shoulders, shielding her curves from my wandering eye. Blinking hard, I refocused on her face, not quite her eyes, but close enough for her to know it wasn't a challenge or scare tactic—just a need for connection. "We search our whole lives for our fated mate. It doesn't make sense, but you and me..." I gritted my teeth, still uncertain how I felt about sharing her with *them* but rather aware now wasn't the time to snarl about it. "You and Soren and Ewan..." We needed the pack strong. We needed a bloodline. We needed *her*. "It's destiny. It's written in the stars."

I motioned in the general direction of the parking lot with a strangled laugh, struggling as all shifters did to come to terms with the concept now that it was staring me in the face.

"It sounds ridiculous, I know." I licked my lips, pausing when her thick, unkept brows shot up in agreement. "Just... cheesy as fuck. I get it. We know. We understand. But fated mates make each other whole. When you find your fated, you... you aren't alone anymore. You never have to be alone again. Please." I pushed my luck with a step toward her, which she immediately countered with two steps back. Fair enough. Patting the air, I softened everything about myself, my inner wolf finally settled now that she hadn't bolted. "Please just try."

If she really was an absolute newcomer to the shifter ways, I couldn't begin to imagine what was going through her head right now. We had a lifetime of knowledge behind us, raised in this culture, brought up on stories of love written in the stars. Yet for this little she-wolf, all she had was three burly alphas stealing her from her family, forcing her to shift, shoving her in a car and racing into the night.

She had three men insisting she belonged to them because some mystical entity made it so.

Surely she felt the bond, but given her response so far, she didn't understand its significance.

That would fall to us to explain—to not fuck up by being a bunch of pricks who wouldn't stop fighting with each other for a speck of her attention.

"No one is going to hurt you, I swear." Hand to my heart, I ducked to meet her eyeline, holding those grey-blue orbs—melting into them, suddenly struggling to keep thoughts straight, fighting to form every persuasive word. "And if they do, if they *hurt* you in any way, I'll fucking kill them." Just the notion had me fired up, inner wolf baring his canines, hackles high and anger flowing. "I swear that too."

The growly undercurrent of my vow brought heat to her cheeks, pink and adorable and so very *there*. Because of me. Because of my intensity and savagery. Clutching at her hair, my flushed fated rocked her hips side to side, as if taking a beat to consider things, then meandered a half step closer.

Good. *Very* good.

"We'll keep you safe, warm, and secure," I promised, wants that spoke to shifters and wild wolves alike. "There'll be lots of food. You've only seen a glimpse of our territory, but it's so beautiful."

Well and truly *stunning*. I had roamed quite a bit before settling on the western woods of Redwood Grove, and never before had I experienced such *vibrant* seasons. Spring, summer, winter, fall— they were like postcards here, idyllic and untouched by modernity. Wildflowers in the spring. Thriving orchards in the summer. Crisp autumn leaves and fluffy, snowy, starlit winters. It was the region's best-kept secret, frankly, that, as Ewan and Soren pushed its tourist potential the last few years, was slowly getting out. Was it any wonder we had rivals who craved a piece of it?

"Mountains, the lake, the forests"—my chef's kiss whooshed right over her head—"all so vibrant. And it's yours too. This territory belongs to you because it belongs to *us*, your fated mates."

I hadn't spoken this much in ages. Mouth dry. Throat raw with emotion and effort. I felt winded, which was a bit sad, and drained —but her second teeny, tiny step forward made it all better.

"Just... try," I rasped, my inner wolf brightening at her next step, followed by another, and another, until we were only a few precious feet apart. "For me, for them, but also for yourself. If it's torture, we'll discuss what should happen—what's best for all of us, including you."

The she-wolf stilled suddenly, cheeks hollowed, cobalt gaze a million miles away. Head bowed and brows scrunched, she appeared to be considering the offer seriously. In the silence that followed, one that dragged on for a fucking eternity, the distant rumble of highway noise picked up, late-night commuters going to and fro. Forest critters scrambled along birch branches and grumbled their discontent at our intrusion.

Yet I waited with bated breath, refusing to rush her, refusing to say another word until she gave *some* kind of decision.

A pale pink tongue flicked out, sweeping her lower lip, and, arms crossed, she padded toward me—then past me, headed back for the parking lot. *Desire* pounded through me as she breezed by, my inner wolf snarling and yipping, demanding I grab her, kiss her, mark her, *fuck* her—right here and now, before the others had the chance.

The man knew better.

Sort of.

Tensed, I eased out of the way so that we didn't even accidentally nudge into each other, then strolled along behind her. With her hair parted over her shoulders, she offered a spectacular view for the walk back: her perky round ass jiggling with every step.

My inner wolf huffed and stomped, clawing at my insides, hungry for a taste.

I gritted my teeth, trying and failing to not admire her nudity, the curve of her thighs and the sway of her hips.

Until she dug my discarded leather jacket out of the brambles. After picking out the thorns, she slipped it back on and zipped it up, the hem nearly at her knees, and pride bloomed in my chest once more, billowing like a nuclear cloud—because she was wearing *my* clothing. Not Ewan's luxury labels. Not Soren's cozy contemporaries. Me. *Mine.* It doused her in my scent, proclaimed to wolves far and wide that we belonged to each other, but her natural scent still sang loudest.

Apple blossoms. This little she-wolf smelled like apple blossoms in full bloom, the cherry-pink and white petals splayed wide, sweet and potent, basking in the sunshine. Yet she also had an earthy quality to her, like dirt and moss—she was both woman and wolf, wild to her core. A floral musk unlike any I'd ever scented before, coaxing images of apple orchards to my mind's eye.

Night in the dead of summer, a bonfire flickering, a pack gathered around it to toast marshmallows and sausages. Happiness. Laughter and chatter and safety, not a care in the world.

Peace.

This she-wolf's scent brought me peace, every whiff a treasure.

And she had no idea.

Not a bloody clue.

Which seemed… cruel.

To *both* of us.

We scaled the chain-link fence together, slower this time. I offered to help her down, but she ignored my outstretched arms, totally oblivious as she hopped off and landed barefoot on the sad strip of grass. Relief and frustration suddenly plucked at the weak bond I shared with the boys, and I spotted them by the jeep, by the still-open shredded rear door. Right. Probably looked suspect—

"What happened?" Ewan demanded, his tone an overt challenge to me as the she-wolf and I strolled back to the scene of the crime. Both he and Soren had about twenty shopping bags shared between them; so much for just buying the bare necessities.

"We needed a breather," I remarked, inner wolf bristling at his attitude. The man kept things slow and smooth, my velvety drawl proof that I wouldn't rise to his level. Still, I couldn't help the hand hovering between her shoulder blades, not exactly touching her, but close enough that the cool leather brushed my palm here and there. *Familiar* enough that Soren and Ewan's hostility crackled through our bond—through the connection that had always felt more like a whisper, now a poignant murmur.

Arms crossed again, unaware of our collective inner turmoil, the jealousy brewing in every corner, our fated mate merely drifted toward the open door, as if sensing where she belonged—for now.

"A *breather*?" Ewan repeated tightly, clearly annoyed at how casual I sounded. My smirk certainly didn't help things either.

"To clear our heads."

"Couldn't have fucking texted that?" the black-haired shifter growled, plastic bags rustling as he jostled them through a dramatic throwing of his hands. "Thought we'd lost her again."

Unusually quiet and overloaded with his own set of shopping bags, Soren assessed the situation with an uncharacteristic scowl; Ewan wasn't the only one who didn't buy my white lie.

And I couldn't give two shits about that, honestly.

Let them think whatever the fuck they wanted. She was here, safe and contained, and that was all that mattered.

"Well, we're back now," I muttered, about to hoist the little she-wolf into the jeep until she scaled the beat-up old bastard herself, her movements nimble and beautifully fluid. Once she was in and seated, I slammed the door and patted it, offering the other two males a thin smile each. "Ready to go."

Amidst teeth-gnashing and suspicious glares, I hopped into the driver's seat and lilted to the side to dig the keys out of my jeans pocket. At the back, Soren and Ewan shoved the shopping bags in without a word, the pack bond tense enough to trigger a niggling headache between my eyes.

The she-wolf sunk into the back seat, our eyes briefly tangling in the rearview mirror before she slumped out of sight, arms crossed, sulk firmly in place. I took a steadying breath, then turned the jeep on, ignoring the creaks and squeals and protests of the engine, the exhale of tarry black exhaust with its rumbling start.

We had our fated mate back in our possession, sure, but as we peeled out of the parking lot, headed for home in a stony silence, I had a feeling this wouldn't be the last of our troubles *keeping* her.

5

LYSSA

"And, yeah, here we are, back in the foyer..."

Arms crossed, I padded down the stairs, tiptoeing along on bare feet that were almost an insult to this spotless house, so clean and sparse it was like a museum. Over Soren's blond head, which weaved side to side with his bouncy descent in front of me, I spotted Ewan on his phone at the front door, shoulders back and brows knit, glaring down at the screen. To his left, a loitering Lucian; the huge alpha leaned against the wall and fiddled with a black lighter, flickering it open and snapping it shut—much to Ewan's flinching annoyance. His mossy green gaze locked on me immediately, and I tugged at his leather coat still wrapped around my naked body, self-conscious and *very* aware of his stare.

Very aware of *all* of them—in a house that was supposedly theirs but lacked their scents, feeling cold and barren despite the natural touches. After driving far from my beloved pack, the alphas hustled me into an enormous lodge at the edge of a lake, planted a little way down a peninsula that jutted into still, dark water. Soren came alive as soon as we stepped inside, rambling on and on, chasing his breath, almost like he had to fill the silence.

Apparently they had started building this place in the spring, using a combination of sweat equity—my new phrase for the day, the definition explained by Soren so slow and basic that he must have thought I was stupid—and outside contractors. At this point, the headquarters of the Redwood wolves was complete. Barely furnished, but more than livable. Modern. New. It smelled clean and fresh and untouched, full of light woods and grey stonework, timber beams and raw elements; they had collected all the natural pieces of their territory and built a home out of it.

Well, a house.

This didn't feel like a home.

Top-of-the-line appliances littered the space, high-end finishes around every corner. You walked into a sprawling foyer from the front door, empty and spotless, with a wide set of stairs dead ahead leading up. To the left, a huge room for socializing: a massive open kitchen with a marble island—Soren talked a *lot* about the fine details, whether I looked like I was listening or not. In the same space sat a live-edge dining table—another new term for the day— that was big enough to seat twelve. Beyond that, a sunken seating area around a stone fireplace that stretched to the ceiling. It overlooked a wraparound porch with views of the lake and surrounding forests.

Huge windows *everywhere*. The light must have been gorgeous in the day.

The first floor also had a guest bedroom, bathroom, and Ewan's office, which only had a glass desk in bubble wrap for now and a chair that still needed to be built.

Upstairs, the wood floors, stone accents, and massive windows continued into four bedrooms, one for each male plus a guest, then a sprawling master suite that none had claimed.

According to Soren, the suite was mine now, with its king-sized canopy bed and nothing else, its ensuite bathroom so pristine that I refused to touch anything—refused to even tiptoe inside because a little wolf who smelled like dirt didn't belong there.

I didn't *want* to touch anything.

Didn't want to give them a reason to reject me.

Shun me.

Insult me and beat me and dump me in the forest.

All my life I'd thought I was a monster. I took the venom hurled my way as a pup, absorbed it, believed it—when, really, there was a whole community out there like me. Living. Laughing. Falling in love and building families and having *normal* lives.

Shifters.

I was a shifter.

Not a demon.

Not a possessed woman.

A *shifter.*

The revelation hurt—made me desperate to fold in on myself and sob until there was nothing left.

I still might do that.

Because…

I…

I just…

I had found my people, my *mates*—supposedly—but I didn't feel whole.

My insides were still broken and warped. Damaged. I missed my pack. I didn't understand why Kira and my own *body* yearned to be near these males. Sure, they had explained fated mates in the car, talking over each other and correcting each other and *bickering* with each other. These males weren't family like my wolf pack; they were three unconnected wolf shifter alphas who had allied themselves for the sake of their new territory.

That made sense.

Strength in numbers and whatever.

The rest?

Too much. *So* much information that it was falling out my ears, refusing to stick, refusing to make sense.

I wanted to scream.

Cry.

Fight.

Run.

But I'd gone back with Lucian because his words—his velvety voice—called to something deep inside me. Deeper than Kira. Deeper than my fears and desires.

Now that we'd crossed *that* hurdle and moved on to the next, however, it got hard and scary all over again.

"Okay, so, that's the general tour." Soren clapped his hands together, halfway between me at the bottom of the stairs and the others near the front door. He looked back and forth in the silence that followed, then cleared his throat. "We're... We're going to head out now, but, uh, I'll be back for breakfast around ten, okay?"

I slipped off the bottom step and onto the cool tile. They were... leaving?

Like—*gone*, gone?

Here, all by myself?

Kira processed it faster—and instantly started to panic, making high, squeaky cries and whines like we had our leg cinched in that bear trap again. Her terror was infectious, my heartbeat quickening, my palms suddenly clammy.

"You're all... going?" I asked roughly, my throat tight and sore. Sure, I was a chatty wolf, but as a woman, I hadn't spoken to anyone all year. *Not* an exaggeration. Even as exhaustion drilled into my bones, the thought of them deserting me in this empty mansion had me *wide*-awake and ready to run. "You're leaving me here alone?"

Ewan's head finally snapped up. Lucian stopped fiddling with his lighter. Soren's arms fell limp at his sides. Different as they were, angelic and beautiful but varied, all three males wore the same expression: dumbfounded shock. The air tensed in the foyer, Kira whining low inside me, and I wiped my sweaty palms on the leather, worried I'd said something wrong.

"She speaks," Ewan rumbled when the silence finally became painful. The other two blinked, still staring at me like I'd sprouted an extra head, and heat warmed in my cheeks.

Did they think I was mute?

"I speak." Gnawing at the insides of my cheeks, I ambled deeper into the foyer, positioning myself with multiple exit points if I needed to retreat. "I just think you learn more when you don't."

The males swapped glances, their slack-jawed stares replaced with gritted teeth and—suspicion? A weird, tingly sensation buzzed in my belly, feeling like a betrayal that wasn't mine, making Kira whimper and the hairs on the back of my neck stand up.

Lucian separated himself from the others, tallest of the three with a coarse blackish-brown beard and a calm presence that soothed Kira—but not me.

"What's your name?" he urged, striding forward, those legs so long and strong, and stopping just shy of touching me. One of the other males growled, and he backpedaled enough that they could still see me, his massive body not blocking their view. I swallowed hard, hands darting up to fidget with the zipper clasp thing on his huge, soft jacket. It smelled like him, his scent stronger and more defined than Soren and Ewan for me now.

This alpha smelled like oakwood and the air after a storm, the cozy quiet that blanketed the forest when the scary part was over.

Above all, he reminded me of the alphas in my pack—strong wolves who didn't need to snarl to control us. Just a look was more than enough, a side-eye glance, an unblinking stare that demanded our willing submission.

"Lyssa."

I hadn't shared that with anyone in years, and from the way the alphas glowered down at me, all intense and rough, someone growling low, another huffing sharply, their eyes turning to molten sunlight like their wolves…

Well, I almost wished I hadn't.

Because it must have upset them.

"That's a nice name," Soren told me, his voice deep and rough like sandpaper. He had such nice blue eyes, but they were gone now, replaced with a fiery amber glow that made Kira perk up inside me, her interest, her *excitement*, suddenly palpable in my chest. Made me feel light—like I was floating, soaring like an eagle.

I tucked my hair behind my ears and shrugged. "Thanks."

This was… weird. Life had become so routine with my pack, our dynamics fluid but simple, our world straightforward and to the point. Wolf *shifters* seemed complicated.

More human.

And humans were messy.

I was messy as a woman, and I hadn't spent this long on two legs in *ages*.

"Why are you leaving?" I looked from male to male, shifting my weight between each leg as they continued to just *stare* at me—like they had never seen a female before. Unnerving, kind of, to be the sole focus of their unblinking scrutiny. "This is our… den."

Sure, there were no pups anywhere, but dens were like houses: safe, secure, protected. Only the mating pair and babysitters like me could enter the den, and given they were the alphas of this pack—and I was too, I guess, if I was their mate—then *this* was where we belonged.

Right?

"It's been a long night for all of us," Ewan said as he tucked his phone away, one big hand diving after it into his pants pocket, the other sweeping through his inky-black hair. Of the three, he was the hardest to keep eye contact with, so unnaturally handsome—both as a wolf *and* a man. He made me feel *tight* when he looked at me like that, hot and small and frazzled. The less restrained creature living inside wanted to sniff him from top to bottom, get into all the nooks and crannies, lick him, taste him—make him taste me.

But his masculine beauty was almost intimidating, and I didn't believe for a *second* that some divine being fated him to *me*. Me—the freak. Ugly and unwanted. Wild and dirty.

He and Soren and Lucian deserved to sleep in that big bed in my new room.

I… deserved the porch.

Maybe.

Since I usually slept in the leaves and dirt and snow, it wouldn't really bother me.

"Consider this a gift." Ewan's hickory gaze flicked up the stairs.

"Take a shower. Sleep in a *bed*." I bristled at the shift in his tone, the pinch of his gorgeous mouth, suddenly self-conscious with no idea why. "We all need time to process, and I..." The black-haired alpha flashed his teeth and shook his head, his next words wrapped in gravel. "*We* think it's better that you have some space so it's not so overwhelming."

"I'll be back before you know it," Soren added, his grin boyish and warm. Interest zinged between my thighs, but it didn't make me feel any better about them leaving. As if the conversation was over, Ewan went for the main door, Soren hot on his heels. Lucian said nothing, just pinned me with another one of those long, intense stares that set every nerve on fire.

But eventually he followed the others.

Abandoning me.

Ditching me—after he had asked me to stay.

After he made me feel *safe* enough to go with them.

He had sounded so sincere back in the birch grove.

Was it... a ploy?

A trick?

A lie.

I watched them go, arms crossed and toes curled. As soon as the front door shut, someone out there locked it, the *click* echoing through this massive house.

Kira howled, her song mournful and desperate.

Wet heat plummeted down my cheek, and as soon as I wiped away that first tear, another quickly took its place.

Trembling, I yanked off Lucian's jacket and balled it up, then chucked it hard at the front door before stomping upstairs to my new room.

Alone again.

Always and forever—*alone*.

6

LUCIAN

Just keep moving.

One foot in front of the other always gets you home.

Eventually. Never had my feet dragged before—never on the way back to what had once been exclusively *my* territory. The western majority of Redwood Forest circled away from the lake, past the village Ewan had monetized the last eight years, and around the northwestern part of the mountain range. Thick, wild, dense, and unsafe for even the most experienced human hikers, it stretched on and on to the horizon, our new territory border on the cusp of Hampton, a city dominated by witchfolk some forty minutes up the highway. All this used to be mine, and I patrolled it daily.

Hell, patrols were my life before Ewan and Soren. *Walking,* always moving, always keeping tabs on everything in my domain. Monitoring the borders. Scent-marking at every turn. Declaring *mine* for shifters and beasts alike. Now, I could barely move. Barely put one foot in front of the other, my inner wolf more aggressive with every step away from Lyssa.

Lyssa.

She looked like a Lyssa, small but mighty. Petite and ferocious.

A true alpha female.

My mate—who we had abandoned in the main house. Ewan declared this precious alone time a gift, but none of us really *wanted* to leave her. Indecision and frustration rankled the tentative pack bond as we stalked out the front door and went our separate ways back to separate homes we couldn't give up just yet. The main house, which had been ready and habitable for weeks, was supposed to be the new seat of power within our territory, the heart of our nameless pack.

Yet we stubborn twats still slept in our own homes, well within the confines of the original territories, and until tonight, the thought of using the sprawling luxury estate rarely crossed our minds.

But Lyssa needed a place to call her own, and to make it fair, we stuck her in neutral territory. Tomorrow, we had agreed to discuss how all... *this* would work. After all, no wolf ever prepared to *share* their mate, despite its commonplace in our community. Usually, however, *bonded* males happened upon their mate together. They already had the hierarchy sorted, the dynamic deeply entrenched. Sharing came easier to them. Ewan, Soren, and I spent as little time together as possible despite managing the booming industry around Redwood Grove this year for the first time—to outrageously high profits, apparently.

Like I gave a fuck about money. Even back when I had it, gold in my veins from birth, I never cared for it.

Ewan and Soren bought new cars to celebrate, forever tangled in their one-upmanship.

I hibernated deeper into the forest.

Yet tonight we had agreed to set our egos aside. Tomorrow or the next day, we would discuss what to do about Lyssa—how to share her without triggering a power imbalance. It needed to be fair. A wolf pack really found itself once the alpha female birthed her first heir, and no longer was it a race as to who among us would mate and procreate first. Our mate was here. Just the one. Did it matter who fathered the first pup? Would it change things within the alpha circle? Cause infighting? Jealousy? Wrath and rage and fire—

I couldn't do that again.

It *had* to be fair.

Our lives had just become a whole hell of a lot more complicated —but not for my inner wolf. To him, this was clear-cut and obvious: we had our mate, and she wasn't terrified. *Mark* her. Mate her. Claim her. Period.

He didn't care that Ewan and Soren had rights to her too.

The fucker was *all* animal urges and primal yearnings tonight, which put us at great odds as I trudged along the paths Ewan had installed in *my* forest this past spring. His uppity tourist clientele could now rent bikes and explore the natural splendor in the safer, relatively even areas. Next spring, construction on the tiny cabins started, blinged out with the most modern upgrades and priced to make *bank*—Ewan's words, never mine—for all the rubes desperate to escape city living for a weekend without getting *too* rustic.

The idea made my skin crawl, but I had been a team player from the start—if only to keep the peace. Thus far, despite the rival incursions, not a drop of blood had been spilled in our new territory, and by Lady Fate as my witness, I intended to keep it that way.

Inner wolf? Not so much.

He raked his claws across my insides, snarling and barking, *fighting* me to get back to her. While I breathed easier once we stepped off the paths and into the forest itself, he stayed the course, determined to overpower the logical, rational man.

Determined to let the beast *free*.

No.

I braced on a maple trunk, head bowed, breathing deep to dull the pain in my chest, to blot out the screaming between my ears.

We can't have her tonight—

A lone howl cut through the noise, loud and pure and so, so, so bloody *sad*. My clenched lids snapped open. My head shot up. My inner wolf issued a ceasefire, mesmerized by her mournful song.

Ewan's howls were crisp and sharp, painfully to the point, always with a purpose.

Soren's were playful and layered, ongoing, so used to howling with his family late into the night, the Acker pack a symphony unto themselves.

Standard wolves erred toward Soren's style, singing to one another, guiding lost members home.

This was too beautiful to belong to some *animal.*

My inner wolf took a deep breath, our hearts pounding hard as one, and then howled back, desperate to answer her cry. His intensity struck like a fist to the face, and I crouched beneath the maple, pinching the bridge of my nose, fighting every instinct to stay put.

No. Give her time and space, like we agreed.

But she didn't want time and space.

Her howl resonated like an air-raid siren, sweeping the territory, lulling the noisy nighttime forest and leaving us all in hushed awe of her song.

She was calling us home—searching for her lost mates, perhaps without even realizing it.

No.

No.

We had all agreed—

Another long, lonely howl, sweet as honey and smooth as silk.

I shifted without thinking, tearing clean through my clothes as I transitioned from man to wolf. After shaking off the tattered fabric, I raced back to the new house. Human foot traffic was low and unlikely at this time of night, but most shifters had it engrained from puphood *not* to be seen by humans. Their numbers far exceeded ours; given their penchant for vivisecting what they didn't understand, it was best to stay off their radar. I clung to the shade of familiar trees, brushing against them, marking my scent everywhere, fueled by an unconscious urge to claim territory that by rights was already mine.

Focused, I bypassed the stone walls that enclosed Redwood

Grove, new and luxe, the gates meant to give the chalet village an air of exclusivity. Beyond that nestled Soren Acker's family lake, their legacy built from the ground up at the foot of the eastern mountains. Lost in the shadows, I charged by empty shoreline cabins, midweek and out of season, the plunging fall temperatures assuring lower occupancy numbers.

Which was sort of a blessing.

The new wolf pack had brought humans into the night this summer, obsessed with their songs, some even asking if we could organize tours to see them. Fucking prats. *No*, none of us would lead cityfolk into the wilds so they could Snapchat a real wolf.

Nor would any of us subject the wolves to such a gross invasion of privacy.

Humans and wolves would *stay* separate in this territory.

Still, Lyssa's howls, beautiful and alluring as they were, a song that beckoned to my broken heart, would undoubtedly attract attention.

She needed to learn the ways—adjust to new rules. Adapt. Coexist without exposing us.

Any inkling I had about explaining that to her tonight died as soon as I traipsed out of the brush and down the gravel driveway to the big house. Despite Ewan's *need* to mimic Swiss ski villages in Redwood Grove, we had settled on a western heritage architectural style for our pack's seat of power. Large windows and hand-hewn log exterior. Local grey stone at the foundation and a huge deck wrapping all the way around. Modern elements. Upscale. They could have built the damn thing to look like a fucking spaceship for all I cared; so long as I had been allowed to select the location, I let Soren and Ewan call the design shots.

Let them fight it out, more like.

After months of study, I chose *this* spot at the end of a jutting lakefront peninsula. Easily defendable, the location was strategic. Soaring mountains through the trees behind us. The lake on three sides, the rental cabins further west and not staring directly into our windows.

If some rival pack tried to mount a full-scale assault, they'd have to tangle with the elements first.

From here, surprises were unlikely.

Yet we still hadn't moved into it—hadn't even chosen a date. Our own houses were just too valuable, steeped in too much separate, unique history to abandon.

We were still lone wolves.

United now by fate—by a mate who begged for company.

I could have tracked her by sound alone, that fourth mournful howl echoing through the early morning hours coming from the main deck at the back of the estate.

But it was *smell* that really drove me, the rich scent of apple blossoms thick in the air, luring me to her. Pushing me harder.

As I hunted her around the side of the house, up wooden steps and onto the grey timber deck, there was nothing and no one but *her*. Padding around the corner, I found Lyssa seated in her wolf form on the back porch overlooking the star-dotted lake, the black waters calm and sparkly, the communal firepit fresh and uncharred as the day we installed it. As soon as my claws clacked over the wood, she whipped around, hackles up, eyes a furious neon blue. I hesitated, heart beating wildly, and we locked gazes in an unblinking challenge, two alphas squaring off.

Brave little she-wolf, even now, alone with a strange male—

Lyssa yipped suddenly, the sound playful and puppyish, then pranced over to me with a wagging tail and her tongue lolling out the side. Apparently she had forgiven me for leaving; she greeted me warmly, nosing along my snout, our tails swiping back and forth together, and I nuzzled at her muzzle with a low rumble, basking in her scent. We sniffed each other over, back to front, tip to tail, paws tap-dancing on the deck, our whines and whimpers hardly submissive—no, they were the noises of long-lost mates when they found each other again.

She ducked into a play bow, front low, ass up, tail going, then scrambled down the length of the porch. Giddy for the first time in a fucking decade, I chased after her, nipping at her hindquarters, her fluffy grey tail. My mate returned the gesture with a snap of her teeth, then trundled after me down the porch, back and forth, the chase so bloody *freeing* and fun and youthful.

No way could I walk away now. Fuck what the boys and I had agreed on: I was locked in—smitten.

Enjoyable as it was, I ended the chase by shifting back, desperate to touch skin and not fur, to trail my nose along the tender column of her throat and breathe her in deep. Lyssa bounced a few paces down the deck, then whirled around, her bright blues soaring to mine. She licked her lips with a flash of white canines, then padded a few paces away before transitioning from wolf to woman. Steam spiraled off her skin, her chest rising and falling hard, same as mine, the effort of the shift thickening the air.

Her smile was extraordinary. Pushing her huge, knotted mane over her shoulders, she twirled around to face me, panting, grinning, eyes wild and gloriously free. But as soon as they swept over me, top to bottom, hesitating by my cock before darting way, *way* up to the heavens, her sparkle dulled. That smile faltered, fading first from her eyes, then her sumptuous mouth.

My inner wolf whined at that, fretful and worried, and he tried to shift back against my will, tried to *force* himself out—maybe he thought running around the deck until sunrise was all she needed.

I knew better.

He was staying *right* there, tucked deep inside, the other face of the coin—the other half of my being.

Still chasing my breath somewhat, I crossed my arms and tipped my head to the side, careful not to leer no matter how hard I *needed* to. Hell, my cock was already rising fast at the mere sight of her. Choosing touchy-feely conversation deserved a fucking medal. "Are you okay, Lyssa?"

Bathed in moonlight, her skin prickled when I said her name. "I... No?"

I shoved down the possessive longing in my chest, dominance flaring, that wild, untamed alpha side craving her flesh—my teeth, her neck, one glorious mark to last forever. *Focus.* Behaving like a fucking cave wolf got us nowhere. "That's all right—to not feel all right. I'd be surprised if you were."

"I don't understand..." She tiptoed toward me, rising up and adding a few extra inches to her petite frame. In the short time I'd known her, she did it a lot, almost as if her alpha side demanded she go toe-to-toe with her males.

"Understand what?" My hands coiled to fists the nearer she came, nails gritting into my palms, the pain that was usually so centering barely a blip on the radar. When the she-wolf finally stopped, just a few precious inches between us, I shook with the effort to stay in. fucking. *control*. Without it, I would have snatched her up, tossed her to the ground, and brutally mounted her right here and now. Instead, I grappled with myself, teetering between man and beast, taking shallow breaths to not drown in her apple blossom scent.

Naked, nipples like tight dark pearls, Lyssa licked her lips again, the tease of pink nearly my undoing. "I don't understand..." Her eyes swept over my chest, snagging on the garish scar that sliced across my left pec. "Why I can't control myself."

Trembling fingers hovered between us for a moment, then tentatively brushed my forearm. My sharp inhale gave her some pause but also seemed to embolden her. Lyssa angled her body closer, her touch firmer as she walked those fingers up my arm, over the coarse black hairs, then set out to map every inch of my torso.

And I let her.

Barely.

My scars had always been so off-putting to other females. I hadn't bedded another wolf in nearly twenty years, but the women who occasionally warmed my bed, eased the loneliness, were short-term distractions at best—and scared of me. Unnerved by the rough lines crisscrossing my chest, by the bite marks in my shoulder, the slash up my neck.

Even with a shifter's supernatural healing abilities, flesh capable of stitching itself back together in seconds, a fated mate could inflict permanent damage. We all wanted those kinds of scars, but these were left by a grave betrayal, by accursed power and the claws of my kin.

My *blood*.

And I'd carry them forever.

Lyssa seemed fascinated by them, unafraid to trace them, poke them, splay her fingers wide to fill the hardened pockets of a bite on my side, just below the ribs.

That one hurt like a bitch.

"I-I get that," I said tightly, needing to talk to distract myself or I'd lose it. Stiff as hell, I stared over her head, arms at my sides, and tracked the valleys and peaks of the silhouetted Redwood mountains. "The struggle for..." I swallowed thickly when she plucked one of the hairs on my treasure trail. *"Control."*

"Really?" Her cobalt blues shot up, wide and imploring, painfully innocent, and suddenly those curious fingers found my beard. She stroked the rough scruff at my chin, then up my jawline—

Fuck it.

Snarling, I scooped her into a kiss without warning, arm slung around her waist, hoisting her off the ground as my mouth crashed to hers. Lyssa surrendered with a squeal, lips slightly parted, and I seized the opportunity to claim her, once and for all, tongue darting into her mouth.

She tasted sublime.

Like the fresh peach juice Soren stocked in the fridge.

And she felt so fucking perfect, curves crushed to my chest, her hands in my hair, her lashes fluttering, fluttering, *closed*. I cupped her ass with my free hand and lifted her higher, desperate to feel her heat locked around me. My inner wolf howled triumphantly, his song so raw, so victorious, that I figured this was *right*—

But we had agreed.

Me, Soren, and Ewan... We had promised to discuss *this*, her, what it meant to share a mate.

Was this a betrayal of my fellow alphas?

I reared back, uncertain. Lyssa chased after, fisting my hair and scaling my body like a palm tree, legs curved around my torso and ankles locked.

My inner wolf growled. *No.* This wasn't a betrayal. I wasn't a traitor. This wasn't like the rest of my story... She was my fucking fated mate—and not even a silver stake could stop me from claiming her.

Our kiss descended into madness, falling hard and fast, like we couldn't get enough of each other—like we needed to *consume*, not just claim. With a low, possessive snarl, I backed her into the nearby wall, pinned her there with the weight of my body, and cupped her perky ass in both hands. Just as I was about to snag her wrists and trap them against the stonework, Lyssa planted her arms back and shoved. Her strength surprised me, almost as ferocious as her kiss, and we stumbled, then tumbled to the ground when she pushed again and again, refusing to be caged.

This time, my back crashed into the too-solid surface, quite literally hitting the deck. In a tangle of tongue and teeth, lips swollen and eyes wild, we wrestled for top spot. Hands everywhere. Nails raking flesh, she broke the kiss first to bury her nose in my beard, then down my jaw, breathing deep and moaning, marking herself with my scent.

But Lyssa wasn't the only one with *needs*. I nipped at her shoulder, dragged a rough openmouthed kiss over her collarbone, eventually sucking one pebbled nipple between my lips. Even the slightest pressure there had her whimpering, the air stained with womanly desire, musky and thick. My ramrod straight cock all but chased her with every position change, the pair of us rolling around the deck, her on top, then me, then her, snarling and baring our teeth. Sniffing. Nibbling. Kissing. Branding each other in our scents.

Strong as she was, tough and durable, small but nowhere near made of glass, the tussle lasted as long as I let it. Eventually, when I couldn't take the teasing a second longer, I flung her over and trapped her against the timber. My hand cuffed her delicate throat, pinning her, muscles flexed and tensed when she tried to fight her way out. Lyssa responded with a flash of teeth and a wolfish gaze, her eyes neon. Draped over her body, I locked onto those bright blues and flashed a feral grin, unblinking, daring her to best me. Alpha to the core, this little female *tried*, refusing to back down, refusing to submit—and failed. Miserably. I chuckled, free hand sweeping down her center, between the valley of her breasts and straight to the raven curls between her thighs. She flailed again, struggling beneath my heft, and then sagged with a huff.

Then a whimper.

Then a long, girlish whine, her thick dark lashes fluttering ever so sweetly. I cocked an eyebrow, my smile all teeth.

"You think that puppy shit works on me?"

A blush the shade of a red delicious plumed in her cheeks and plunged straight down to her navel, and Lyssa's eyes narrowed briefly like the calm before the storm. A beat later, her faux submission vanished, replaced by a struggling, snarling little she-wolf whose raw power paled in comparison to mine. I tightened my hold on her neck, her pulse thundering against my fingers, and stroked my other hand up and down, relishing the heat, the inferno raging just under the surface.

She managed one swipe with those clawlike talons, *barely* missing my cheek as I ducked out of the way, and my next squeeze of her throat came as a warning. While she settled somewhat, I didn't trust my fated for *one* second; if I gave an inch in this fight, she would clock me upside the head and take a mile.

I'd only met her a few hours ago, but of *that* much I was certain.

Tempted as I was to get lost in her eyes, Lyssa's heaving chest steered me southward, down, down, down her exquisite blush. I kissed a blazing path over one breast, then popped back up to swirl my tongue around the other nipple—fair's fair, after all. Her hips bucked and her breath hitched, lower lip snagged between her teeth, and my inner wolf rumbled with interest, keen on hearing what other noises she made.

All of them.

I needed them—now—almost as desperately as I yearned to

explore every inch of her body. Skin darkened by the odd mole or freckle, this she-wolf was perfection.

Then I reached her thighs and…

Well, lesser men might have fled, her curls wild and untamed, but this was where her scent was the strongest, rich and musky, a siren song I couldn't ignore. Abandoning her throat, I smoothed both hands over her hips as I delved between her thighs, shouldering her knees, spreading her, unfazed by her shy hands tugging at my hair, her wordless mewls attempting to steer me elsewhere.

This was what I craved: her molten center, folds slick with desire, the heat buzzing in my lips, making my mouth water.

No hesitation.

I didn't ask for permission.

I *took*.

I claimed.

And I bloody well *conquered*. The first sweep of my tongue over her magnificent pussy made her sing, lower back arching, heels gritted into me.

"W-wait," Lyssa whimpered, squirming in my grasp, unable to shake me no matter how hard she tried. "What are you—*oh…*"

I stole her breath with a precise sweep of my tongue across her clit. Her body quivered. Her inner thighs trembled. Her hips bucked against my greedy mouth, and I finally just devoured her. Worshipped at the altar of Lady Fate, stroking her with my tongue, arms snaked around her thighs. One spread flat across her mound, pinning her jerky hips down against the porch, while the other splayed her nether lips open for better access. As soon as my tongue found a rhythm, fucking her to her heart's content, my thumb did its dark work at the helm of her pussy, toying with her clit.

She preferred the back-and-forth stroke, her body sagging whenever I dipped into little circles. Every so often, the she-wolf attempted to wriggle free, begging me to stop even as her muscles clenched, her body tightening deliciously, her skin stained with pleasure.

And when she eventually came, soaking my tongue with liquid gold, with pleasure that tasted sweet as her apple blossom scent, the woman—not the wolf—howled into the night.

Had Ewan and Soren heard *that* too?

Did they *feel* it as I did now, my fated mate's ecstasy dosing my blood, shivers plunging down my spine with her body's every sensuous pulse.

At the sound of her hapless moan, followed by skin slapping to skin, I pushed up on my elbows, looming over her as she gasped and panted, her hands in her hair. Sweaty, flushed, desperately chasing her breath, Lyssa read as a woman satisfied, but I needn't *guess* at that. The rumors were true: as my mate, I'd felt a whisper of her climax's delicious tingles flutter in me.

"Wh-what just happened?"

And she had no clue. None at all. *Fuck*. Growling, I folded over her for a moment, fighting the desire to pounce and plunge deep into her sweet heat, claim her beautiful pussy with all the savagery the innocence of her question demanded.

"Did it feel good?" I rasped, head still bowed. Her body shuddered beneath me.

"Uh, yes?" Lyssa cleared her throat. "It... felt very good."

"You..." Licking her climax from my lips, her desire no doubt glistening in my beard, I eased up and locked eyes with the beautiful she-wolf. A slight quirk of my brow had her flushing scarlet. "You came, little wolf..." Without warning, I thrust two fingers into her pussy, slow and cautious at first—but her body *took* almost selfishly, engulfing all I had to offer in the most exquisite hellfire, her eagerness forcing a groan from me that harmonized with her moan. "You *came* all over my mouth." Stroking her inner walls, I tipped my head to the side and grinned. "And you taste utterly divine."

Her thick dark lashes danced for me, fluttering across her cheek as she sank onto the porch, hips rocking, hands twisting in her hair. Concern cooled the wildfire blazing across my flesh, and I withdrew just for a moment, about to ask after her comfort—but my fingers came out bloodless.

She...

My inner wolf snarled.

Had some male touched her before me?

Before *us*, the alphas chosen specifically for *her* by Lady Fate?

Arousal smeared over my fingers, but not a drop of virgin's blood.

Disappointment rippled through me. My inner wolf had an even tougher time digesting the notion that this Lyssa, this shifter living with wild wolves, had had a life before tonight. It both was and wasn't my business what she had done with her body, who she had given it to. She was mine now—*ours*. If another male sniffed around her, horned in on what belonged to the alphas of this territory, we would rip him to pieces on principle.

So, I let it go.

All of it.

Virgin or not, it didn't matter.

All my life I had longed for a mate, someone to stand by my side without question, and now she was here. Never again would I stare down the horrors of betrayal and heartache alone, so, really, who gave a toss if she had bled already?

Nibbling along her inner thigh, I stroked her soaking folds, massaging her, flicking my thumb over her clit, determined to make her climax thrice more before the night was over—until suddenly little Lyssa clamped her thighs around my head and *rolled* us over. My back hit the timber planks *hard*, and I landed with a grunt, only a touch humiliated that a she-wolf had bested me. The position change came out of nowhere, but it left her straddling my face with the most sublime view of her pussy, the perfect angle to lick her straight into paradise.

Before I could palm her ass and steer her to my mouth, Lyssa shuffled back, stretching wide to accommodate for my far broader frame. She even braced on my chest, inching backward, looking over her shoulder like she was reversing out of a parking spot— stopping only when her backside nudged my almost *painful* erection. I hissed sharply, hips bucking of their own accord.

With an oddly steadfast twinkle in her eye, she busied herself with the mechanics—and I just sat back to watch. There was nothing sexier than a woman who seized control of her own pleasure, and my fated mate seemed determined to have an equal role in our first union. One hand planted on my chest, oblivious to my scars, she lifted her hips and peered between her wide legs.

Grabbed my cock.

Fisted it, more like, hard and insistent and oh *shit, fuck* me—

I sucked in a harsh breath between my teeth the moment her heat engulfed me, slick and fiery, a tightness overtaking the head of my cock that I wasn't sure I could withstand. Pleasure tugged low in my gut, balls tight and on the brink of detonation as she inched down, taking me slowly with her swollen lower lip snagged between her teeth. Hands trembling once more at the restraint, at the control I exerted over every bloody cell so that I didn't just take her by the hips and spear her, I steadied my mate by the waist but let her set the pace.

Lyssa took all of me, right down to the hilt, but let out a breathy cry as soon as she touched down. Panic sliced through the hazy pleasure muddling my brain, and I sat up quickly, one hand cradling her cheek, the other on her thigh.

"Did I hurt you?"

A chuckle fell from her lips, almost incredulous in a way—a little sarcastic, maybe. Lyssa shook her head, then steered my hand to her breast and away from her face.

"Not even a little."

Good.

Because…

She was hurting me, her cunt slick but so *fucking* tight I could barely breathe. Still, confident as she had sounded there, the bravado faded fast while she studied us where we joined. An overwhelming heaviness leaked into our fated bond, a connection not strong enough for me to really *feel* the true weight of her emotions, but enough that I clued into the fact that she was struggling.

That, quite possibly, this was still very new to her even if she had done it before.

I allowed her a beat, watching her smile plummet from confident to half-hearted, before wrapping both arms around her and drawing her into my chest. This time, she came without a fight. Lyssa nestled in, her head tucked safely under my chin, her arms folded between us. Briefly, we bathed in each other's scent, savoring the skin-to-skin, our shifter fire shared and cozy.

Feet planted on the timber, I set the pace to start. Nothing more than gentle thrusts, hips bucking, our bodies rocking. Good as it felt —fucking nirvana, honestly, to be balls-deep in my mate—I kept her in mind. Shoved the growly, possessive, desperate beast in me to the bottom rung on the ladder of priorities. Her comfort came first. If she suddenly wanted to stop, I'd respect that, ready to walk away with the worst case of blue balls in the fucking history of the world.

Slowly, Lyssa started to move with me. Back and forth, up and down, she cuddled into my chest while meeting my slow, gentle thrusts, and only when she ground back harder did I respond in kind. It could have been minutes, could have been hours, but eventually every buck jostled her, jerked her around, and my thrusts became a pounding that had my little she-wolf moaning and writhing and raking her claws over my chest.

Eventually she shot up, hands on my shoulders, eyes closed and lips slightly parted, then threw her head back to the moon. I fucked her with earnest, no longer capable of being gentle even if I tried, and my mate *rode* me, tits bouncing, skin flushed, her cries and moans worthy of the angel choirs of heaven.

She was a vision.

And when she came again—a goddess. Lyssa folded in on herself when her pussy danced and spasmed, cheeks on fire, eyes wide and starlit.

"*Oh!*"

One syllable. One word. *Oh.* And I was fucked.

I might not be head over heels in love with this she-wolf, but as of that moment, she was *mine*.

Fingers gritted into her hips, I pistoned into her, overwhelmed, lost in a black sea of desire where nothing else mattered but *relief*.

Pain slashed through the darkness, bringing with it a flurry of light and ecstasy—

Lyssa had marked me.

Lost in her own climax, she had slashed her nails across my right shoulder, fierce enough to inflict real damage. Four bright red lines glared up at me when I risked a peek, and that finally tipped me over the edge. My rhythm faltered, stuttering off to a few rough, harsh bucks, and I jerked into her with a snarl, spilling myself as the pleasure went nuclear. The aftermath slithered through my veins like shock waves coursing through a city, and I lunged up, the world tinged red, totally tunnel-visioned on her neck.

Hand fisted in her hair, I plunged my teeth into her flesh as we writhed together. Piping hot blood spilled over my teeth and down my throat, and I held on for as long as I could, marking her, declaring our union for all to see.

Sanity seeped in slowly, drips and drabs of control entering my system again. At Lyssa's whimpery moan, her insistent rocking and her fingers buried in my hair, I dislodged and tried to blink the stars out of my eyes. A part of me expected to find her furious that I had taken such liberties, marked her somewhere so obvious, but the she-wolf just collapsed into me with a long, languid sigh. Cradling her in my arms, I sank onto the deck, still buried inside her, cock at half-mast again, and kissed her sweaty forehead. She responded with a lick and an open-mouth kiss to my neck.

My shoulder still throbbed from her nails, the four stripes hot and sore. Although my heightened healing had already sealed the wounds, they would scar if given by my fated mate, same as my bite on her throat.

Time would tell.

If by tomorrow we still wore each other's brutality, we belonged together.

And I'd have to contend with Ewan and Soren, the pair bound to be fucking *furious* that I had acted without consulting them.

Beyond that, I'd also have to come to terms with the fact that once again, there was someone in my life, destined for my inner circle, who could break me.

Snap me like a bloody twig and toss the pieces into the fire. Watch me burn. *Laugh* through my screams.

My inner wolf growled at the thought, long and low, the memories getting his hackles up.

Enough. Just enjoy the moment.

With a deep, cleansing breath, I closed my eyes, blocked out the stars and the moonlight, and just held her.

Regretting nothing—but dreading the fallout still to come.

7

SOREN

"So, where is she? Let me see my new daughter."

"Mom." I rolled my eyes as she tried to peer into every corner of the laptop screen like she was searching for Lyssa in some sad *Where's Waldo?* landscape. Seriously, she got like this every time one of us kids found our fated mate—which was… kind of nice, I guess. In fact, if it were anyone else, *any* other situation, I would have shared my parents' giddiness, but that wasn't the vibe. At all. Not only was my fated mate some woman of the woods who had been living with wolves—which hadn't fazed Mom and Dad at all—but I had to share her with two other alphas. Not my beta. Not someone lower in the pack hierarchy who I could pull rank on. Two equals.

Also a nonissue, apparently, from the way they reacted to my story of last night's craziness.

My sisters—all six of them—would give the reaction I wanted when I eventually called them: incredulity and shock and frustration and just a glimmer of hope for an amazing fated connection. This fairy-tale response from two wolves who'd had a smooth courtship *and* a perfect fated mate marriage was just… nauseating, especially on so little sleep.

"She's not actually—"

"Oh, I know, I know." Mom waved me off, totally dominating the webcam view with Dad barely peeking around her in the background. "You're not *married*—it's just exciting! *Min lille ulv*, I've been waiting for you to find your fated for *years*. Of course it happens when I'm not there."

I slumped in my office chair, elbow propped on the armrest, then worked my thumb up and down my forehead as Dad chuckled. *Min lille ulv*—my little wolf. Man, she really *was* excited to whip out *that* after all these years. Since I had four years on the next Acker pup, I'd been their only little wolf for a good while, and apparently Mom was feeling nostalgic suddenly on her luxury cruise down the Portuguese coast. As autumn inched toward winter, my parents were living it up overseas, having just wrapped their walking tour of Italy, on two legs and four, now destined for the Canary Islands before jetting over to Africa. They planned to explore the whole continent over the next eight months—prove *wolves* were king of the jungle, not lions, or whatever.

Weird, but it was *their* retirement.

They had worked hard all their lives, raised seven pups, and made a small fortune even after divvying some of it up for inheritances—let them do whatever they wanted now. The business was in good hands back here.

Relatively speaking. I'd shoved all the paperwork piles out of the way and tidied as best I could before the video call, nowhere near as meticulous as Dad at organizing my workspace. Still, despite the messiness that had followed me from puphood to alpha status, officially the lone Acker wolf left in Redwood Grove, I managed to keep us afloat.

More than that.

This past summer had been our most profitable yet, the cottages rented months in advance, the watersports a big draw, the music festivals held on the lakeshore luring in a young, hip crowd for the first time in *years*.

The festival had been Ewan's idea.

Douchebag. At no point would I share the numbers—or that it

had been the best-received event of the season, with sponsors already beating the hell out of each other to snag a spot for next year.

Even with a new partner—partner*s* if you counted a reclusive Lucian doing whatever he did all day in the forest—*I* drove the Acker legacy now.

And it was *good*.

And the new pack was… fine.

Ish.

What I wouldn't do for alphas who knew how to hold a damn conversation—

Or laugh.

Or do anything a normal wolf did on their off time.

But, whatever. Bigger fish to fry now with Lyssa and the issue of mating and starting the bloodline and who gets first crack at her and just so—much—extra—*crap* to deal with suddenly.

"Look, Lyssa isn't… here," I interjected, cutting off Mom's rambling as she veered into wedding territory—her favorite form of escapism, having planned three weddings for Acker she-wolves already. She sank into her seat, finally allowing Dad, an alpha who was basically my twin—just thirty years older—a chance to get in on the conversation.

"What? What do you *mean* she isn't there?" Yikes. Mom's Norwegian side always reared whenever any of her brood threw her for a loop, accent sharpening, pale cheeks flushed pink. She smoothed the white-blonde wisps away from her face, barely touched by age, same as Dad, and fidgeted with her bun. "Is she with Ewan?"

Dad arched a dirty-blond brow, arms crossed, his shirt hilariously floral and definitely chosen by the she-wolf at his side. "Please tell me she isn't squatting with Lucian in that—"

"No, no, guys." My next frustrated huff had Mom's eyes narrowing like she could scent my next move through the screen. Uh-huh. Pretty much how I expected this conversation to go once we got over the exciting stuff. "We put her in the main house alone… Just to give her some space to decompress." Even a million miles away, the unimpressed crinkle of Mom's nose had me wilting into the chair. Should have had this talk on a smaller screen, my office monitor top-of-the-line and *way* too big for the desk—maybe that would make her slightly less intimidating when pissed. "Look, last night was a lot for all of us. We just needed to, you know, breathe and process in our own space, and she didn't have a space, so we left her—"

"Tomas." Crap. Despite my thirty-four years, Mom's crisp, no-nonsense voice still made my heart beat faster. My inner wolf, described by my sisters as a literal ray of sunshine, actually cowered a little at the subtle—dangerous—shift in her tone. One of the downsides of pack life: you *always* obeyed your alphas, even when you became one yourself. Mom turned away from the screen, offering me a stern profile as she glowered at my frowning father. "Speak to your *son* about how one treats their fated mate."

Awesome.

My sisters would have peed themselves laughing if they felt the panic tightening in my chest. All our lives, they teased me about being the golden child, the firstborn son, *perfect* in my parents' eyes. Maybe they were right, maybe not, but I'd always been a good wolf who rarely put a toe out of line.

They were the ones who tested boundaries, not me.

I wasn't a troublemaker, but as Mom sat back, dressed in airy white linens and wearing a scowl that could cut diamonds, I felt two inches tall—and five years old again after I'd shattered one of her glass dolphin figurines while roughhousing indoors.

Clearing his throat, Dad shuffled closer to the monitor. He exuded the calm, controlled patience of an alpha who had run a strong, successful pack all his life—my idol. The wolf I most admired.

And he looked totally unimpressed with me.

"Soren." He steepled his fingers and held them to his thin lips for a moment, eyes flickering like he was rooting out the right words. "Let me get this straight."

I nodded. "Shoot."

"You three… *wolves*—" He wanted to say idiots. *Soooo* badly, he wanted to call us out. "—stole your fated mate from actual wolves."

Another nod. "That's the gist."

"Whisked this wildling away from what appeared to be her pack," he continued, slow and steady, laying out all the pieces for us to connect. Ugh. I hated when he did that, because once the puzzle was complete, it spelled out what a complete and utter asshole I'd been. "Even if they *were* just wolves, you took her from her family in the dead of night."

"Uh, yeah." Heat brewed under my collar. My inner wolf, meanwhile, derped around inside like this conversation wasn't even happening.

"You kidnapped her—stole her from everything she knows."

"I mean, I guess. We don't really know her story—"

"And then," Dad pressed, tone sharper, "you stuck her in a big empty house—"

"It's mostly furnished—"

"And left her *alone*." He paused to let that sink in, as if I hadn't beat myself up over the decision a thousand times already. "Without her new mates."

"Uh… yeah." No denying it. None of us had wanted to walk away from Lyssa, but at the time, in the heat of the moment, it *felt* like the right thing to do. Only my inner wolf hated me for it and I hadn't been able to sleep and my stomach had twisted itself into an irreversible knot that was still giving me hell. I scratched at the back of my neck, smoothing the nervous sweat, then swiped a hand through my hair like I was still in control—because I was an alpha, just like them, who had been forced to make the tough call. Hindsight came easy when it was all said and done. "She… howled for us, but we agreed to leave it—"

"Soren *Mikael*—" Double crap: middle name spelled doom. "—Acker." Mom shoved Dad aside and took over the entire screen again, glowering at me through a crystal-clear connection. "She cried out for you, and you *denied* her?"

My inner wolf whimpered, forever and always cowed by his mother. Most shifter clans were patriarchal, but Mom called the shots with the Ackers; Dad had always been happy to let her, more than capable of stepping in when things took a turn for the dangerous. If only he'd do that now and spare his *only* son from virtual homicide—

"Yeah, Mom, we did that."

"I love you, *min lille ulv*," Mom hissed, anger-articulating what had always been a term of endearment, "but I need a *moment*."

She then shot out of her seat and stalked off-screen, a door slamming seconds later. Dad could have left me to ruminate in my failings, but he just pulled the chair up to whatever surface they had mounted their laptop on, probably a cabin writing desk on the luxury liner, and then planted his elbows and folded his arms, one on top of the other. Unlike Mom, his expression hinted at empathy —which I didn't deserve.

"Look, Soren, she's being dramatic."

"She's right though," I insisted weakly. "It was such a dick move. I should have gone back. I... I wanted to, but I'm trying to get on the same page as Ewan and Lucian, so I... went home to, you know, *not* sleep."

I glanced at the clock in the top corner of the screen. About fifteen minutes to go before my shift at the main house started. Ewan was such a workaholic that just the *thought* of rearranging his meetings on such short notice put him in a tailspin, so I had volunteered to take the morning leg. Unfortunately, that only cemented his theory that because he had the most money and the biggest investment portfolio, my work mattered less than his— somehow. Yeah, with summer over, our focus *had* shifted to Redwood Grove proper to prepare for the upcoming autumn and winter seasons. The entire village would double in size each weekend, tourists and celebrities and politicians fleeing north for the region's beauty, luxury, and privacy.

But Redwood Lake was a year-round establishment, what with the maintenance of a dozen rental cabins along the shoreline, plus the few bars and restaurants scattered throughout our territory owned by the Acker property development group. My work wasn't any less important, but somehow Ewan Quinn always made me feel that way.

Seriously, *Lucian* should have played babysitter all day.

Not like he did anything but patrol the territory.

Which, yeah, had *merit* or whatever, especially with other wolf packs nosing at our borders, but he could spare one stupid day to make sure our mate was okay while Ewan and I took care of the real Redwood Grove business.

Not that I didn't *want* to visit Lyssa.

Last night, after the emotional and physical whirlwind of scenting my fated mate, things hadn't played out as I'd always imagined.

She wasn't what I'd always imagined.

In the cold light of a new grey fall day, I... didn't really know what to do with myself when it came to her.

And that wasn't how it was supposed to be with your fated, right?

"Fated mates is a beautiful concept in *theory*," Dad stressed, reading my mind like always, even as our pack bond continued to disintegrate. Now that I'd formed a pack of my own, I would slowly lose that innate connection with my parents and siblings. A few of my sisters had already gone through the process, married into new packs with their mates. It sucked. I loved my family more than anything—but this was for the best. This was for the *future*, and with Lyssa, the future was now.

Dad must have seen the fear in my eyes, because when he spoke next, his tone had liquified to melted chocolate. "But, listen, my boy —it isn't always easy. It's not like the stories. Take your time. Get to know one another. Don't expect things to fall into place without any work."

"Sorry, but isn't that exactly what happened with you two?" My scoff might have been out of line, but Tomas and Mari Acker had the best marriage *ever*. We held all our relationships up to their standard and put potential partners through the wringer because my sisters and I knew exactly how *good* it could be. Why settle for anything less?

"Not always," Dad told me with a patronizing chuckle. "Your mother and I had rough patches, even being fated. It's about the time and effort you put into each other... *That's* what you get back."

I gnawed at my thumbnail, contemplative, then frowned. Lyssa had been sullen and standoffish after the initial meeting. We were all on a high after scenting each other, but then things got weird and competitive. Honestly, we probably scared her off with all the snarling and fighting, but then she made it worse by running and sulking in the back of Lucian's barely functional jalopy the whole way back to Redwood Grove, hardly responsive when we had explained the situation.

Nicely, too, me and Ewan on the same page for once.

And Lucian, while silent and standoffish, had possessed the same calm energy as my dad, which should have helped.

It didn't.

It should have, but nope. I walked away confused and torn and aching to touch her again, yet also keenly aware this she-wolf was *not* who I had expected.

"Now, you left her alone, correct?"

Lady Fate, give me strength. "Yes, Dad, I already told you—"

"And you figure she's still there," Dad carried on, eyebrows creeping up his forehead, looking dangerously tan after lazing around Italy the last two months. "Alone. In the main house that, let's be real, isn't as homey as you three think."

"Uh—"

"After you kidnapped and then abandoned her..." He tipped his head to the side, eye twitching, waiting for me to clue into his thoughts like I used to. "You left her alone—and now just assume she stayed there all night, after trying to escape *twice* already?"

I blinked at the monitor. "We..." *Shit.* I shot up, then hunched down, left eye right in the camera and taking up the whole picture. "Gotta go."

"As you should."

"Love you—kisses to Mom. *Bye*." I stabbed the disconnect button, grabbed my sweater off the back of the chair, and hightailed it out of my office cabin at the rear of what had once been the heart of Acker pack property, a short walk from the lake and tucked away from the tourists. Inner wolf rambunctious at the thought of seeing her again, I drew from his Energizer Bunny battery and sprinted through the maple grove, belly howling for breakfast, and *prayed* that today I'd just be a fated mate babysitter—not the fated mate hunter.

8

LYSSA

The sound of clinking cutlery and whumping cupboard doors jolted me from a short, fitful sleep.

The hiss of bacon landing in a hot pan had my eyes snapping open.

The scent of fatty, cooking pork made my belly *howl*.

Determined as I'd been to not sleep in this huge bedroom after Lucian left around dawn, my body refused to crash anywhere else. Yeah, I had slept on dirt and rocks and pinecones for years. Snow and dead leaves and frostbitten grass—but nothing beat a brand-new, never-before-used, *massive* bed just for me.

Not that I made use of its size—not really. Instinct forced me to sleep with my back to the headboard, pillows piled high around my balled-up body, protected from every side. Sucking down a gulp of bacon-scented air, I punched through the pillow wall by my face. A dull grey day greeted me from the sliding glass doors to the left of the bed that opened onto a private balcony. The sight of the timber decking there had heat curling in my belly and licking south, tingling between my thighs at the memory of Lucian driving me into identical wood planks just one level below.

Scratching at my knotted mane, I pushed onto my elbow with a sniff and a yawn. Had he come back? Was he downstairs now—cooking me a feast?

Maybe. That bacon really overpowered every other scent in a scentless environment.

I hadn't wanted him to go.

But I guess my pack's alphas never cuddled after mating.

He gave me more than expected: pleasure, comfort, security, and, worthy of another mention, *pleasure*. My last rutting hadn't been anything like that. No pain with Lucian. No regret. No wrong feeling in my belly. Kira hadn't snarled the entire time, her hackles up and her teeth bared. This had been... wonderful.

Fairy-tale-level stuff, the type Reed and Nikki used to fast-forward through in the movies—reminding us it was sinful before marriage.

This was *glorious*, and no one could tell me otherwise.

But he left.

At first light, he kissed me deep and changed back into a wolf, then trotted into the forest without a backward glance.

Ignoring the deep hunger gurgles, I stretched out, smashing the rest of my pillow barrier, and twisted this way and that, flexing deliciously sore muscles. For the first time in a long time, I woke up *stiff*. Contented but achy in a way that was almost... satisfying?

Weird.

After rubbing the sleep from my eyes and scratching the dried drool from the corners of my lips, I slipped out of bed, out of fresh white sheets and a crumpled duvet, the four-poster style reminding me of the old movies—of kings and queens, princes and princesses, who had dark, heavy wood furniture and a bed just like this.

Almost like this. The wood here was light and angular, the corners sharp, the tones soft. Smooth to the touch. Polished.

The second I was upright, my bladder demanded emptying, and while tempted to just squat next to the bed and claim *my* sleeping spot, I padded into the ensuite bathroom. Used a *toilet* like any regular human and way too much toilet paper to wipe.

So much softer than leaves.

So much nicer—

I've been in the woods too long.

Kira whined, low and half-hearted, like she didn't see the problem with it. Of course she wouldn't. As her, we peed to mark our territory. Here, it all went away with one flush like it had never happened.

Not a bad thing, really.

Washing my hands with lavender-scented soap, I scrutinized the redness on my neck, breath catching when the individual teeth marks crystallized as I leaned closer.

In the height of bliss, my body on fire and the world all starlight, I had slashed at Lucian—driven by this primal urge unlike any I had ever experienced.

Mark him.

Claim him.

Make him yours.

Had he felt the same way? Was that what fated mates did to each other during pleasure?

Nothing had ever scarred me before—and I'd once fought a grizzly to defend my pack. Way up north, just a teenager, I went toe-to-toe with some big, burly, angry male who wanted to steal our pups. Make a meal of them.

Not on my watch, sir.

I'd ripped his throat out in the end, but only after he got a bunch of deep lashes in my sides, scored up my underbelly.

All that healed, and his claws were *scary*.

Lucian's teeth, while white and straight, were just... normal.

But he had marked me.

Maybe even scarred me.

What did that *mean*?

Kira made happy noises at the sight, all puppyish and soft, her excitement meant to inspire me—I wasn't so sure. These three males might be my fated mates, whatever that actually meant, but I didn't have to *trust* them yet.

This had come from one of *them*.

The warmest, safest alpha of the bunch, sure, his immense size maybe intimidating to others, but he had also abandoned me after he did this. Left me alone when I was sleepy and vulnerable—again.

So, Kira could shut up and let me feel my feelings.

Some good, some bad, most a mishmash of the murky middle.

Pain sizzled under my skin when I brushed a finger over the lingering red bite, and I hissed, rearing back and vowing not to poke at it for a while. Still, even though it hurt, it was... a good hurt. A *welcome* hurt. Pride warmed in my chest at every spark of fire, and had the bacon smells not wafted through the vents, I might have stayed all day in front of the wall-to-wall bathroom mirror just to look at it.

But hunger called, and I wasn't the type of wolf to turn down a hot meal.

Naked, sore, and empty, I caught the light on the way out of the bathroom, then beelined for the door, right past the mountain of plastic shopping bags at the foot of the bed. Inside, the clothing smelled fresh and clean, new and untouched, but nude had always been my preference. *This* was my most natural state—and my fated mates seemed to enjoy it.

Besides, despite the miserable grey overcast, warmth coursed from the floorboards, no goosebumps to be found. If it was cozy, why cover up? *They* were naked when they went from wolf to man —maybe it was normal in shifter society.

Arms crossed, I paused on the second-floor landing for a quick scan of my new territory. The south-facing windowpanes overlooked a sprawling dark blue lake, stretching east and out of sight. Cabins lined the shore *way* over there, docks bobbing on the surface, the forest canopy all oranges and reds and yellows, fall in the air.

A beautiful place, just like Lucian had said.

In fact, it had been a long, long time since my pack moved into a territory so abundant in game, so rich and vibrant this late in the season.

Made sense why they'd want to live here.

I gnawed at the inside of my cheek, catching my frown in the window.

Still not completely sure why they wanted to share it with *me*.

Trudging down the stairs into the foyer, I could have followed the path to bacon paradise with my eyes closed—but it was logic that steered me to the kitchen.

Because.

Duh.

Even if these guys *were* wolves, it wasn't like they ate their meals outside in the dirt.

Right?

Nerves prickled my fingertips as I peered around the doorframe, and Kira squealed at the sight of a tall, masculine form with his back to me in the kitchen area, surrounded by marble and granite and white-white cabinets.

Blond hair.

Not Lucian.

I licked my lips, painfully aware that I wasn't as disappointed as I should have been.

Soren made me... *feel*, same as his fellow alpha.

The sight of his broad shoulders alone made my low belly all hot and squirmy, his scent drowned by bacon. Dressed in a light blue sweater and a pair of dark jeans—and, oh, was that an apron? Like what women wear?—he puttered around the L-shaped kitchen with its enormous center island as if he belonged there, managing a few pans on the stovetop at once, the open, airy space ripe with competing scents.

"Hey." I stiffened at his voice's rough morning rasp, the squirmy feeling heating up even as he kept his back to me. He ducked down to pull something out of the oven—oh, *yes*, buttermilk biscuits!—and plopped the pan on the huge marble island. "How did you sleep?"

I blinked, trying to refocus, to *not* spiral into frenzied feeding mode, then tiptoed into the kitchen.

"Good." My answer barely made a sound, the wind knocked out of me when I spotted the enormous spread on the dining table, the sunken seating area beyond that empty, the hearth quiet, the two-story windows on either side of the stonework letting in all the grey light we needed. But the food. The *food*. Strawberries and ham and scrambled eggs and croissants and boxes upon *boxes* of cereal. I snapped my dropped jaw shut and cleared my throat. "Uh, good. Slept good."

"I wasn't sure what you liked, so we got a little of everything today," Soren mused as I crept past the high-end kitchen toward the dining table, arms out, fingers reaching, mouth watering like this was some kind of desert mirage. I'd almost made it, almost *lunged*, when the wolf shifter behind me dropped something with a clang. "Oh, uh, Lyssa..."

Swallowing the flood of saliva, even Kira torn between the spread and the man, I begrudgingly turned around and found him red-faced and gawking—pointing at me with a greasy spatula. Desire tickled the nape of my neck, hot and needy and insistent, a sensation that once again didn't feel like it belonged to me. I smoothed a hand over the heated skin under my hair, shifting my weight from leg to leg, back and forth, surprised to find myself wet between my thighs.

"We... Uh..." Soren glanced skyward with a deep breath before looking me dead in the eye. "Lyssa, you can't..." His vibrant blues plunged to my neck, to the mark left by Lucian at its base that edged onto my shoulder. He suddenly slammed the spatula down on the island, the desire breathing fire over my skin replaced with just *fire*. "Where did you get that?"

I stroked it with a wince, pain making my core clench. "Lucian. He came back."

The alpha's cheeks darkened from pinkish to ruby red, those unassuming eyes stormier than the clouds outside. My response wasn't an accusation, but it seemed he took it as one. Last night, after they left, anger, loneliness, and fear took over. Suddenly it was eighteen years ago and I was lost in the woods all over again, yowling, scrambling, struggling in the darkness and desperately searching for a familiar face.

Crying. Confused and drowning in guilt.

Why can't I just be better?

This morning, I had let Kira out to howl for my pack. They had to be looking for me, *me*, the biggest among them, the toughest, the oldest adopted offspring of the grey-muzzled mating pair. Babysitter. Hunter. Playmate. Snuggle buddy. I did it all.

They... They had to be worried.

Had to be tracking me.

I had called out to them, just a pup again—and Lucian had answered.

Then everything changed.

Then I was a woman, not just a wolf, and when he kissed me, I couldn't stop the avalanche. I let it bury me.

I let *him* bury me.

Soren could have answered. His scent was strongest around the lake; he had to have been nearby.

But he didn't come back.

And he wasn't saying anything now, just staring at the mark, jaw clenched so hard the muscles danced and his nostrils flared and his eyes...

His eyes could stop a polar bear dead in its tracks—send the most dangerous bear out there scampering across the tundra.

I had no idea what to do about that, but I refused to just stand around while he glared, not with a feast at my back and Kira getting frantic, my wolf side overly concerned with his mood shift. So, after flashing a thin smile, I darted for the table and collapsed into the first chair I hit, then grabbed a plate from the stack in the middle.

Wow.

Never in my life had I seen so much food in one place.

While I spent most of the time with my pack, I wasn't completely off the grid either. If we ventured near towns, I'd sneak into a bar or shopping mall just to taste the human experience as the world went on without me. All my clothes for those jaunts were either shoplifted or stolen out of empty cabins or backyard laundry lines, and any food consumed along the way was, again, stolen.

Nothing like this.

Nothing so... *perfect.*

This really was paradise, and as I reached for the plate of honey-roasted ham, I vowed to make the most of it before these alphas realized I was too wild to keep—

Fabric crashed over my face, Soren's scent suddenly all-consuming. Light blue blocked my vision for a beat, and I grunted as he yanked his sweater down and over my head, then got to work on dragging my hair out from under it.

Kira practically vibrated, smitten with the way he smelled like bonfire smoke and sleepy summer sunsets, then, in the next breath, like ginger and allspice and nutmeg and a fresh-baked pie, cinnamon buns cooling and waiting to be frosted. I shoved my arms through the too-big sleeves with a flash of teeth, too focused on the food to deal with the nonsense of being naked or not.

Did he think I was cold?

I burned just as hot as him, his fingertips brushing the back of my neck, the squirmy feeling reigniting in my belly. Hunger won out, however, no matter how fascinated my body seemed to be with his.

"Redwood Grove might be our territory, but it's still mostly humans," Soren told me, sounding tense but like he was trying to play it cool—casual. I nodded absently, too distracted by the ham to care. "You can't walk around naked anytime you're not in your wolf form... It's a precaution. To humans, our kind doesn't exist."

I grunted again before dumping the entire plate of ham onto mine, then ripping into the perfectly seasoned, *perfectly* cooked flesh with a long, desperate moan. Both hands put to work, I shoveled food into my mouth, occasionally lashing out to grab a biscuit or a strawberry, rumbling happily as I gorged.

So. Good.

So. Goooo*ooooooooood.*

"Lyssa, slow down."

I ignored Soren's playful tone, bristling a little when he nudged my shoulder.

"Seriously—be careful." His chuckles landed like silk butterfly wings, but I didn't stop. Didn't slow. Didn't even bother to take a breath as I scarfed as much as possible before someone stole it. The alpha suddenly ducked down into my peripheral. "Come on, don't choke on me now…"

The second he latched onto my arm, I threw a fist, narrowly missing his chiseled face. He reared with a warning grumble, but I countered with a warning of my own, my snarl turning his eyes from that rich blue to a violent amber. As soon as *his* wolf eyes appeared, Kira nudged to the surface, my vision suddenly sharper.

"Calm down—"

I attacked instinctively, shooting to my feet and lunging for him. Wolves fought for food, our access to a kill based on the pack hierarchy. I loved my brothers and sisters, my alphas, but I knew where I stood with them, and if someone tried to cut in line, they got the sharp end of my teeth.

I always ate third.

Alpha male and female—then me, then the rest on down to the bottom.

Soren seemed ready, bracing against my attack, and slapped my hands away when I tried to rake my nails across his cheek. Snarls and growls reverberated through the space, and I shoved, kicked, scratched, *bit* to get him away from my breakfast.

Zero idea where I ranked in this new pack, but, hey, might as well establish it now.

Only for all my bark, my snap at his bare muscly forearms, Soren was just stronger. He countered my strikes and barely moved an inch with my shoves, slowly and methodically backing me away from the dining table, from the *food*, until eventually he grabbed both wrists, whirled me around, and bent me over the island.

Then blanketed me with his body.

I'd thought Lucian was a mountain.

And he was.

But I hadn't given this blond alpha enough credit: he was all muscle, no softness, no weak spots. He deftly dodged my backward kicks, his warning growls still low and civil, while mine got squeakier and wilder the longer he had me pinned. After tossing my head back, aiming for his nose, the wolf fisted my hair and shoved me down so that my cheek touched marble for the first time ever.

Kira snarled—but her aggression was directed at *me*, her ire burning up my esophagus and scorching the back of my throat.

Like *I* was the one who had stepped out of line.

He was trying to take the food!

"You aren't there anymore," Soren growled in my ear, his breath falling gentler than mine, the heat between us suffocating, both our hearts thundering—mine between my ears, his through his chest draped over my back. He was so *heavy*, but I didn't want to escape the pressure…

I wanted to bask in it.

Bathe in his might.

More.

Forced up on my tiptoes, I still had enough freedom to wiggle my backside into his front, into something rock-hard and insistent thrust between my cheeks. He drew a sharp breath, and I found myself hungry to push his temper just a little higher—eager to spar again and find him on top of me, but face-to-face so I could glare into the storm clouds and watch them shatter.

Soren eased just out of reach without loosening his grip, one hand in my hair, the other pinning my left wrist to the island, his body as immovable and resilient as the marble below.

"You don't have to *fight* for food," he told me thickly, harshly, sounding more and more beastly by the second. "It's not a competition here."

Oh.

Oh. Maybe that was just a wolf thing.

I mean, yeah, we fought for food at the farmhouse, but that was a different story; if someone snuck candy in somehow, it was an all-out war to get a piece of it. My alpha wolves, meanwhile, made sure we all got a piece of the kill no matter what, even if we snarled and snapped and bullied each other aside in the process.

Maybe shifters just... didn't.

Humiliation churned in my belly, shame burning in my cheeks, and I managed a stiff, silent nod before Soren finally withdrew. As soon as I had an inch of leeway, I shoved off the island and darted around him, back to the table without delay. A numb fire spread throughout my body, tingling in my fingertips and toes, making my head light and my hands shake.

You're such an animal, Lyssa.

Sometimes I still heard those words in Reed's voice; today it was mine—all mine.

Seated with near-perfect posture this time, I returned the rest of the ham to the shared wooden board in the middle of the table. Still trembling, I scooped some scrambled eggs onto my empty plate, then added a croissant and a few strawberries, jaw clenched so tight it ached. When Soren appeared with the bacon, crispy and fatty and greasy, I grabbed a handful without thinking, scorching my palm in the process. I barely flinched, used to swallowing the pain, and dumped it on my plate, then wiped the grease on the cloth napkin under the fork and knife I'd been ignoring. It was soft and purple like a plum, and I ruined it with greasy fingers, just like I ruined Soren's breakfast feast by going full wolf.

As the alpha settled across from me and went for the breadbasket, zeroing in on a pumpernickel bagel, I shoved forkful after forkful of creamy scrambled eggs into my mouth, unsure of the green bits but taking the risk because I owed it to him after... *that.*

"Why were you out there with them?"

The inevitable came after I'd devoured my first, second, and third plates of food and was deep into the fourth, determined to eat as much as I physically could. Food was never a guarantee; no telling if this was an everyday thing or a one-off.

I flicked my gaze up, mouth full of ham, then returned to my plate. Why I was with the wolves... was a heavy question that I didn't feel like answering. Not now. Not today. Not tomorrow. Probably not ever. My origins with the pack wasn't exactly a story I liked discussing *or* reliving.

"Lyssa?"

Kira whined at the way he said my name, so familiar, so warm and gentle. We both wanted to get lost in eyes the color of a clear sky on a summer's day, *blue* blue, so blue they couldn't be real. The alpha across from me in a plain grey T-shirt with muscly arms and strong, veiny forearms, his blond hair swept back and out of his face, shaved at the sides, lush and full on top—he reminded me of a movie star.

A specific one whose name I didn't know, but I'd seen him on a huge billboard once, *Captain America* scrawled in big block letters beneath his strong, stern face.

I focused on the food, on filling a stomach that had always felt bottomless.

"Lyssa, please look at me."

I gave him that much, burning a hole in his forehead as I carried on chewing. Soren allowed me a moment, staring, the warmth slowly dying like a candlewick on its last leg. The frosts returned, as they always did, while he buttered his bagel and *waited*, his huff nowhere near as patient and understanding as Lucian's responses to me.

"As your fated mates, we have a right to know that kind of stuff," he growled before taking a massive bite of the buttered bagel, that handsome frowning mouth suddenly sprinkled with little brown pumpernickel crumbs. Soren brushed them away with the back of his hand, then sat taller. If he expected me to cower under his unflinching gaze, the blue darkening again, sprinting toward his amber-eyed wolf stare, this alpha would be waiting a long time. "I mean, we know nothing about you. We don't even know how old you are—"

"Twenty-six," I told him before popping a baby strawberry between my lips. If these wolf shifters wanted the basic stuff, they could have it. Do what they wanted with it. No one could hurt you with a number. After I swallowed, tongue bathed in the berry's tart sweetness, I nodded at him with a thrust of my chin. "You?"

"Thirty-four." He demolished the rest of the bagel with his second bite, scrutinizing me with one eye slightly narrowed, his tone cautious, quiet—almost like he was plotting his next move. When he swallowed, the generous bulge in his throat bobbed in the most distracting way. "Were you always with them?"

Right back at it, huh? All that tense calculation for nothing. I stabbed my fork around my plate, trapping the last scrambled egg bits on the spears. This wolf had no tact, no game. Not that *I* could coax information out of someone through a conversation: teeth and claws were more my speed.

Oh.

Oh no, I hoped they didn't do that.

Please don't beat it out of me.

"Is it... Did you find them recently?"

I resisted the urge to lick my plate clean, instead settling for my fingers, which would smell like honey-glazed ham for the rest of the day.

Not that I was complaining.

"Lyssa, please." Soren settled back into his seat, his restraint around all this food pretty impressive. Wasn't his wolf dying to gobble up every last bite? Kira was too distracted with *him*, but usually we had a one-track mind around mealtime. "This is important. It matters."

His hard edge roused my hackles. Lucian had been patient and compliant. Scarred and grizzled like an old bear after a lifetime of battles, that huge alpha hadn't once pushed. He... seemed to understand. He acknowledged my worries, my confusion, and then kissed it all away.

Soren glared.

And waited.

He seemed to be trying to school his expression to something softer, but I almost *felt* his frustration, all staticky and sharp and tingling down my spine. It rubbed me the wrong way, and I responded in kind.

Teeth gritted, I grabbed the orange juice jug and shoved my nose into its open top, breathing in the scent of fresh-squeezed deliciousness. Years had trickled by since I'd had real, fresh, pulpy juice, and I chugged it straight from the glass pitcher, eyes locked on his, challenging him again in an effort to distract him.

It got me nowhere. His frustration ramped up, the sensation unsettling as it whittled deeper into my bones and made the air thick. Made Kira growl, once again at *me* and not him, the traitor.

After downing half the jug, I set it aside and sank into my chair, belly bloated and sore as I folded my hands over it. "You first."

"Excuse me?"

Kind of annoying that even his frown was gorgeous. Were all shifters as breathtaking as my mates, or was this—what was the word?—*karma* for the life I'd lived?

"Show me your deepest wound," I ordered, snapping at him for emphasis. "Come on. Let me see." This wolf had no wounds. Lucian had scarred me with his bite, but he wore years of violence on his skin. Soren looked pampered and clean and strong. Supposedly still my fated mate, still beautiful, but he struck me as... soft. Not physically, but on the inside—his heart, maybe. Earnest. Sweet. Not naturally confrontational. Easily flustered when things didn't go his way. Maybe he needed a lesson in disappointment. "Tell me your worst memory, the one that stings the most," I snapped again, barking at him now. "Come on. Show me. Let me see it, stranger I met in the woods last night. Show me your *scars*."

He sputtered back some nonsense, dark blond lashes fluttering, brows knit deep. Shock suddenly whispered down my back instead of the itchy frustration. Not sure which I preferred, honestly. When he gave me nothing, no answer, no trauma, I went back to eating, stuffing myself again, afraid that after this conversation, food portions might not be so generous.

"Okay." Soren scratched at his clean-shaven cheek, then coiled both hands around a coffee mug that had stopped steaming a while back. "I get it. Tell us when you're ready."

I looked up with a huff, eyes stinging, the cavernous space around us blurring until I blinked things back into focus. Kira whimpered, finally focused on me again, sensing the overwhelm, the weight of it all crashing down from every side—the ice cracking under our paws.

"I don't know much about fated mates," I muttered, fiddling with my nails, full to the point of nausea, a thick burn creeping up my throat. "But mine kidnapped me. They took me away from my family." I licked my lips and sniffled, hating the tears, hating Kira's panic. I hadn't cried in forever, and I wasn't about to here, now, over something as simple as a curious wolf. "The least they can do is show a little patience."

My pain isn't yours just because fate said so.

"You're right." It stung that it took so long for him to say something, but once he did, his rumble soothed me like a balm. Unfortunately, as I smeared a bit of croissant around my plate to soak up the leftovers and he drummed his fingers on the table, his words hadn't changed anything. Tension still blanketed the dining area, the sunken living room, the soaring stone fireplace, and the enormous windows. Such a beautiful place.

Why couldn't it be easy?

Soren ate the rest of his breakfast in silence, only occasionally glancing my way, his distance purposeful and palpable. Kira whimpered for attention, but I swallowed her cries, refusing to beg.

By the time he wiped his mouth on the back of his hand again, napkin ignored, plate cleared, the fight in me was gone. Hackles down, embers smoldering, I watched him stand, expecting more.

Something.

"Just leave the dishes," he told me gruffly, gathering his into a neat stack. "I'll load them in the dishwasher later." Soren then glanced back at the massive windows backlighting his broad figure, making his shoulders even wider, his waist more defined, his silhouette divine. "I need to check out the work they did in the basement wine cellar... Ewan had some complaints. I... You can go anywhere you want in the house, but please don't go past the end of the driveway or off the porch. This is new territory for you, and we don't want you to get lost."

Didn't want me to get lost?

I tucked my hair behind my ears, head bobbing when he arched a prompting eyebrow.

I was already lost. I'd been lost since birth.

Couldn't get lost-*er*, right?

"I'm going to stay," I told him, hating the effort it took to speak suddenly, every word labored. "Lucian said... to try, so I will. I promised."

"Sure, uh, good."

"Yeah."

"Okay." Soren downed the last of his cold coffee, then added the mug to his dish pile. "I'll be in the basement."

"Yup. Wine cellar."

"Yup."

And then just like, gone again.

Alone again.

Wishing I had done different, been *better*.

And knowing that no matter what, they would always leave. I'd drive them away with my wild. Walking around naked and brawling over food—clearly I was even too much for *shifters*.

Same as before.

Same as always.

One by one—gone.

It was only a matter of time.

9

—————

EWAN

"Keep up, Lyssa."

I tightened my hold on her forearm as we rounded the corner, headed up the Redwood Grove high street at a steady clip. Today *so* wasn't the day for this—but when did I ever have time for non-work activities? Rarely, and they were always scheduled months in advance, Jocelyn managing my social calendar with an iron fist. Every outing had a purpose, something to gain, something to benefit: connections, donations, sponsors, politicians to pin under my thumb.

This little jaunt offered none of that.

But a deal was a deal. Soren had kept an eye on our flighty fated mate all day, extending his morning shift when bullshit arose on my end. Not that he'd needed to do much: Lyssa had wasted away the hours snoozing on the back porch by the lake. As soon as the sun conquered the clouds, apparently she was out there in wolf form, sprawled like a giant grey floof. Fortunately, midway through the week on the brink of October meant foot traffic around the lake and occupancy of the Acker rental cabins was down; her secret was safe, but I'd still lectured Soren about letting her do whatever the fuck she wanted—at risk to *us*, I might add.

He hadn't taken kindly to it, but when did he ever? We seldom agreed on anything, and the management of our fated mate was no different.

Well, we begrudgingly accepted *one* aspect of all this: we needed her mated as soon as possible so no rival packs could steal her—bag themselves an alpha she-wolf. Lucian had gone ahead and done so already, the fucker, mounting her this morning while the rest of us stuck to our agreement.

I'd never felt *anger* like I had back when Soren broke the news.

It rippled through our slowly solidifying pack bond, fierce enough that the blond alpha flushed and snarled at the sensation.

Once the mating and marking was over with, she needed to get pregnant. Fact. Not the most romantic way to go about it, and under normal circumstances there wouldn't be so much pressure, but we had to really stake our claim on this territory—establish a bloodline, start a legacy, build a strong pack no outsiders would *dare* challenge. The Acker pack had done that decades ago, but then the pups grew up and the elders retired, leaving only Soren behind.

And now we had this mess to deal with: a fated mate for three alphas who only ever saw eye to eye in business.

I mean, Lucian hadn't even *been* there for the awkward, stilted pregnancy talks as Lyssa got dressed for tonight's appointment. True to hermit form, the asshole was out on patrol, monitoring our borders, roving the mountains, circling our territory in a single day like he was our only line of defense.

Which had left Soren and me to... talk.

Hardly my favorite activity in the world, especially with a pampered wolf born into a peaceful legacy—but never mind.

I glanced back when Lyssa lagged again, those grey-blue marbles darting around, wide and curious, taking in the beauty of the village I had personally rebuilt. Before I came along and realized its potential, Redwood Grove was just some hick town at the foot of the Redwood mountain range. After buying run-down buildings and waning hotels, investing *all* my savings into a gamble, this place was a destination. A ski village. A winter getaway. Reminiscent of

Aspen or Vail, inspiration drawn from villages in the Swiss Alps, we had log chalets and brick inns. Five-star restaurants and cobblestone streets. Pine trees perfect for snowy evening strolls and blooming flower boxes on every windowsill in the spring. High-end boutiques. World-class spas. Cozy burger bars. Parks and a bustling village square. Pedestrian-only paths.

Quiet now that the summer hubbub at the lake had died down, everything would ramp up again soon, the rich and famous—supernatural *and* human—flocking here for privacy during the holidays, our village bylaws especially strict with paparazzi behavior. Politicians and CEOs found solace in our luxury chalets, and as fall bled into winter, there were a million activities and events to prepare for.

And here I was, the wolf who owned most of the public buildings, the man who helmed the real estate company that built those exquisite chalets, the shark who seized control of the slopes—escorting his fated mate to a fucking hair appointment.

Beautiful as she was, my fated mate was a mess by society standards. Hair down to her perfect ass, all scraggly and knotted and angry. Eyebrows that needed a tweezing. Leg hair that had never seen a razor under her leggings. Nails long and sharp enough to sculpt glass. I had never envisioned my fated mate before—she was more of an idea than anything, a *feeling* in my chest—but apparently Lady Fate decided mine was to be raised by wolves, and despite dressing her up this evening, she definitely *looked* the part.

Still. The black leggings clung to her strong but too skinny legs nicely. The purple cotton tee was one of the basics Soren had grabbed, the unimaginative fuck raiding a department store at the outlet mall while I dropped a few grand on essentials from a pricey boutique. Apparently, Lyssa favored the simplicity of cotton—which was... fine. At least she'd opted for *my* jean jacket find to give the outfit a touch of class, elevate her from mall rat to the cool girl who didn't care about beauty standards.

Flats instead of heels. Hair everywhere. Luscious pink lips slightly parted and eyes devouring Redwood Grove—my creation, my monster, my greatest achievement and the start of *my* Quinn legacy. She stood out like a sore thumb with hair like that, but tonight's appointment would fix that. Once Rosa was finished with her, Lyssa would look like an alpha's mate—*that* was priority number one. A matriarch *no one* would question. Powerful. Stylish. Confident.

And, you know, pups—they mattered too.

Bloodline. Legacy. Pack security. All that.

Lucian might have been quick to mount her, but as we headed down the little side street toward the village's premier salon, I struggled to wrap my head around it. Yes, she was our fated. No denying it now, not with his mark still blazing on her skin. Yes, I felt alive touching her, even through the jean jacket's dense fabric.

Yes, my inner wolf, usually so stoic and standoffish, had been whining and pawing at me all day, desperate to get back to her, making it damn near impossible to focus.

But I couldn't just… fuck her.

I couldn't.

In the heat of the moment, I'd wanted to taste her last night—spread her pussy lips and lap at the altar of fate. Now more in control, the man in charge again and not the wolf, things weren't so simple.

I needed connection.

Sure, I had a new model on my arm at any event with photographers, but I rarely took them to bed after—not unless I was shit-faced, and I had too much responsibility to get shit-faced at *every* bullet point on my day planner. The empire couldn't run on whiskey. Only a fucking moron would risk it all for liquor and a quick lay.

If she wasn't pregnant already, I'd have to give it a go sometime soon—Soren and I had tersely agreed to that much. So, in theory, Lyssa and I ought to spend quality time together. This could have been quality—but I didn't have the time. With a six-o'clock conference call looming, I needed to deposit her into hands I could trust, then get back to business as usual.

Because, frankly, I was still too shell-shocked to process the fact that I had a fated mate.

That we had found her in the woods less than twenty-four hours ago.

That she also belonged to two other males I *barely* tolerated.

So, while beautiful, her scent like a subdued rose garden, I couldn't handle the emotional fallout right now.

Therefore, work took priority, and the rest would just have to wait.

Same shit, different day. Nose to the grind. Push, push, push, *push*. That was how I'd survived the collapse of my life before, and that was how I'd survive the uprooting of it now.

Simple.

We stopped just shy of the Grove, an upscale salon situated at the foot of a three-story brick building, its storefront matte black with the name in a gold-plated serif font, the *O* shaped like an apple. Hackles rising when a few passing males checked out Lyssa's cute little ass, I tugged my mate closer and ducked down to center her focus on me and not the serene high street shops around us.

"The man who runs this salon is a warlock," I told her. Supers and shifters seldom ran in the same circles, but Redwood Grove had space enough for the both of us—so long as the supernatural folk knew their place. This was wolf territory, and any attempt at a magical coup would end in bloodshed. Given my mate had no clue what a *shifter* was when we first found her, I expected her knitted brows and crinkled nose, lips bowed in a beautiful arc. Exquisite. Perfection. So pouty and tempting and *ugh, focus. And not on her fucking mouth.* "Ethan Perry is safe, and you can trust him. I do, Soren does—" Lucian had a *thing* about warlocks and usually just glared. "—so you can too."

Her confusion tickled the nape of my neck like a creeping frost. This linked emotion shit was a double-edged sword: it meant we were forming a bond just by proximity, but it was also a fucking distraction. Because the second my inner wolf sensed her discomfort, he was up in arms and snarling, determined to find the culprit and make him *pay*.

Fuck's sake.

"Ethan runs the salon and these two boutiques." I motioned to the shoe shop beside us and the clothing boutique on the other side of the salon. While I technically owned the land and the buildings, Ethan Perry had transformed these locations into a well-oiled profit machine since he signed a lease three years ago. Not only that, but he wasn't an asshole like most warlocks. No shifter prejudice. Just a family man with a mind for business. A solid member of the new Redwood Grove elite. "This evening you need all of... this—" A pointed glance at her hair made her flush. "—taken care of."

Frowning, Lyssa twisted out of my hold, strong for such a little she-wolf, and then fussed with her unruly mane. "Why?"

"Because you look like you belong in the forest." I flicked my wrist, bringing the face of the diamond-encrusted Piguet around. Twenty minutes to go before the conference call for the Thanksgiving market, followed by another meeting about Halloween events shortly after, then a quick weekly check-in with my Toronto investments. Vancouver tomorrow. London after that. New York next week. Hong Kong negotiations on the back burner while legal went through contracts. I sniffed, cheek twitching when another gentle wave of Lyssa's apprehension washed over me. "And you're not *in* the forest anymore, so..."

Snagging her arm again, I steered her toward the Grove, only to be met with *instant* resistance, the she-wolf planting her feet and ripping free again. Fear sprinkled her uncertainty, and I rounded on her with a gentle sigh, really crouching down to meet her eyeline— not to control her this time, but to comfort her.

Hopefully.

"Lyssa, no one is going to hurt you in there. I would stay, but I have a few calls I can't miss, and my office is only around the corner. You'll be so busy, and in such good hands, you won't even notice the time fly."

While the owner and his wife were of the supernatural variety, the stylists and makeup artists employed at the Grove were human —a non-threat if I ever saw one. Not only that, but they were all women. Every last one of them. Not a male to be found once we crossed the threshold, and that was *exactly* how I liked it when it came to my fated mate.

Apparently.

I'd never been jealous before Lyssa.

But even *thinking* about Lucian now, that hulking hermit touching her, kissing her, thrusting into her and spilling his seed, possibly even creating the firstborn pup in our new pack—

Fuck.

Fortunately, I had mastered control years ago.

If I hadn't, I'd burn this place to the ground just to keep her to myself.

We might lack the emotional connection I craved, but she was my fated mate. *Mine.* And that carried more weight than she would ever know.

Already men had checked her out as we marched through the village. While rough around the edges, my fated mate was exquisite. They sensed it, even as humans, and if another alpha wolf caught her scent, he'd feel it too.

If we left her unmarked, she'd be fair game for *him* to steal in the dead of night. Not a chance in *hell*.

"I like the way I look." She gathered all three fucking feet of that dark caramel mess over one shoulder, absently picking through the tangles. Her cheeks hollowed suddenly, forehead creased with worry—oh. Wait. No. Not worry. The glint in her eye was very much a challenge. "Am I ugly?"

"What?" My blood ran cold. "No. It's..." *System reboot.* Blinking fast, I sifted through my scattered thoughts, rooting out the most appropriate response for when a woman asked *that*. "Lyssa, you're beautiful—but you're the mate of *three* alphas now. You have to present yourself to the world as such. Does that make sense?"

She pursed her lips for a moment, and my inner wolf and I let out a collective sigh of relief at the stiff nod that followed. While she still didn't seem thrilled with the idea, at least she didn't fight me as I guided her toward the salon's main doors. Ripping one open came with a whoosh of vanilla-scented air, warmed to perfection—for humans—and the background hum of the usual soft indie radio station. As soon as I got her in, I felt comfortable enough to let go; even if she wanted to bolt, my little she-wolf was too taken with the salon to bother.

For now.

And I didn't blame her—the place reeked of luxury. High-end finishes. Black furniture with gold accents. White marble floors. Dark floral wallpaper behind the oval mirrors. Ivory shampoo stations.

Ethan had designed the place. I approved the plans. We built it from the ground up into a ridiculously popular salon that was usually booked six months out.

They made an exception for me, of course. Tonight, my fated mate could have whatever her heart desired. Hair. Makeup. Nails. Waxing. Eyebrows. Tanning. I had no fucking idea what vajazzling was, but if she wanted it, Lyssa would have it. Hell, she could pierce her fucking ears for all I cared—my credit card was already on file.

"Ewan!"

A familiar voice drew my attention to the nearby front desk, and Rosa Perry darted around the onyx brick in a flash of bouncy red ringlets. Short and curvy, green-eyed and sweet, the redhead epitomized the perfect Irish witch—only she was Canadian through and through, same as me.

Dressed in the salon's customary all black, the witch sauntered my way in a pencil skirt and a silky blouse that crept all the way up her throat like lace ivy. Last time her husband and I had met for drinks at the Chalet, he told me she felt self-conscious about not losing the baby weight as fast as she would have liked, but she looked marvelous as always.

Lovely, yes, but way too docile and submissive for my taste.

Just right for Ethan, who doted on her as lavishly as I planned to with my forever mate.

Still, Rosa Perry was a nurturer, always meant to be a mother and nailing it in that department already—which was why I had requested she supervise *everything* that went on tonight with Lyssa in my absence.

"So good to see you," she gushed, arms out and hands landing daintily on my shoulder like butterflies. We eased in for a chaste peck on each cheek.

"You as well," I rumbled back, suddenly struck by the scent of minty arnica when we touched, my inner wolf snorting and wheezing at the assault. "How is little—"

A wall of bronzy brown elbowed between us, accompanied by a snarl and a *shove* that sent Rosa stumbling back in her dangerously high heels. The receptionist gasped, the noise jerking me back to the moment before I drowned in Lyssa's scent. Set firmly between me and Rosa, my fated mate flashed her neon blue wolf eyes and lunged for the witch—

"*Lyssa.*" My hiss did nothing to stop her, so I grabbed her arm and hauled her back toward the front of the salon. She fought me the entire way, a wildling in my grasp, until I pinned her up against the glass window that had to be triple-pane or it would have splintered like a spiderweb.

Her every heaving breath was all teeth, all madness and crazy and wild. Absolutely *infuriated* that she had caused a scene the second we walked in the door, the Redwood Grove gossip grapevine on fucking *fire*, I smothered her body with mine and clamped a hand around her throat—not too tight but firm enough to get her attention, trying my best to block the view of what went on between us from the stunned salon staff.

She snarled.

I growled back, low and dangerous.

Our eyes locked. We both stilled, neither backing down, a challenge thickening the air.

"Remember where you are," I whispered heatedly. "We're not wolves here, Lyssa. Do *not* expose us."

The tension eased out of her limbs, her taut throat softening beneath my palm. Blinking furiously, she gave herself a little shake —then looked up at me with the disassociation of a woman who had just blacked out.

"I…" Her lips parted for a shuddering breath, and I loosened way up on her throat. Not completely, but just enough for her to know I could take her down in a *second* if she lost control again. Fuck's sake. Trembling little fingers ghosted along the underside of my wrist suddenly, setting my blood on fire and making my inner wolf howl. Lyssa seemed not to notice the annoyingly instant effect she had on my body from the faintest of touches, her greyish-blue eyes still darting around, acclimating to the environment as her body settled.

Fuck. Fated mates was going to be more difficult than the old stories suggested.

"I-I saw her hugging you," she whispered with a frown, cheeks flushed a dull pink. "I don't know what happened. She—"

"*She* is married," I said flatly, "to Ethan. They just had a baby. *She* doesn't want me—*I* don't want her. Calm your inner wolf or we're going…" *Home.* I nearly said it, but that house wasn't home—not yet. "Or I'm taking you back to the house and locking the door."

Terse as I was with her, my inner wolf was doing some stupid happy dance around inside, giddy at the thought that his mate, our girl, was *jealous* over someone as harmless as Rosa Perry. The green-eyed monster had plagued *me* for the first time in my life and I'd barely known her twenty-four hours. It was only bound to get worse the more time we spent together and the deeper our connection grew.

Assuming our connection grew at all.

Not all fated mates were best friends and lovers.

Some of them just… co-existed.

And I didn't do crazy chicks. Too high-maintenance. Too much work.

But… a fated mate *should* be protective of her mate. We belonged to each other, marked or not.

Curious.

Frustrating.

A bit tedious and overwhelming and *exciting*—

Her nostrils flared and her eyes snapped to neon blue. Lyssa's upper lip peeled back, her canines sharp and white, and the moment I caught a whiff of Rosa—amber and honey, soft and rich and cozy —I cuffed her around the throat again and pressed closer.

"Enough, Lyssa." When the neon faded, not gone completely but enough to tell me the woman could subdue the wolf, I seized that moment of calm and whirled around, shifting my grip back to her arm. "Right, who is doing her hair?"

Across the empty salon, a petite blonde in a pixie cut—wearing a fucking corset and leather pants, good *grief*—tentatively raised her comb from behind her chair. Good. I'd requested Ethan have the place empty so Lyssa got all the care and attention she needed, but now, with the handful of employees gawking at us and Rosa rubbing her shoulder, it was just awkward.

"You"—I squeezed Lyssa's arm—"go sit over there." Keeping my voice low, I then pointed to the blonde's station, which appeared to be set up for some serious de-matting. "In her chair. Don't move. Do what she says, and for fuck's sake, *behave.*"

My fated mate stumbled a few steps forward when I gave her a nudge, then glared over her shoulder at me. Other wolves cowered before a powerful alpha. We were born, not made, the right to rule pumping through our veins from the start. Non-alphas sensed it. They feared it. They respected it—most of the time, anyway. And if not, alphas were *more* than capable of putting troublemakers in their place.

Lyssa didn't flinch. She didn't cower.

So, she was a *true* alpha. Not some she-wolf who got the title by default from her mate—a queen who had been born, not made, to rule. What flowed through me was also in her, pumping with every fierce beat of her heart.

Her eyes narrowed, straddling the line between wolf and woman. We held eye contact for a long beat, the tense awkwardness simmering throughout the salon, until I finally tipped my head to the side and purposefully softened my glare. An alpha fated mate was going to be... complicated. Not one to take orders. Lyssa was chess, not checkers, and required a more skilled hand to play.

Finally, with a huff and a low, barely audible grumble, she crossed her arms and marched stiffly across the marble tiles, head down as she passed Rosa, not stopping until she found her stylist. The tiny blonde gave her a wide berth and gestured to the chair with her comb, the instrument trembling, and Lyssa plopped gracelessly into it.

And the salon finally breathed a little easier.

For now.

I kept an eye on my mate for about a minute as the stylist puttered around her, setting up trays and organizing her station, and when Lyssa stayed put like a good girl, I finally rushed to the real victim here.

"Rosa." I swooped in and herded her to the side, out of the receptionist's earshot, the woman tapping away at the huge touch-screen monitor, expression blank. Ethan's wife followed dutifully, her face almost as red as her hair, and guilt plucked at my heartstrings. "I'm so, so sorry about that."

"Did I do something wrong?"

"She's my fated," I told her in a heated whisper as we loitered in front of a product stand, the shelves black and the wallpaper behind it an apple tree full of golden fruit. The witch blinked at me, processing the news, and then frowned.

"Oh." Her eyebrows shot up, realization dawning. "Oh. That makes so much more sense. Congratulations?"

"Yeah, thanks." I smoothed a hand down my rumpled suit, then over my hair, annoyed that Lyssa had caught me off guard. "We found her last night. It seems she's literally been raised by wolves, so her manners are... questionable."

My inner wolf growled, like he was pissed I was badmouthing Lyssa to another woman, but whatever. Even he couldn't deny she needed an etiquette seminar. At the very least, Rosa appeared to understand and accept the outburst for what it was: a jealous wolf claiming her mate in front of a perceived rival. The rest of her employees were human, unfortunately, which made the whole thing look insane.

My gaze fell to her shoulder, which she was still massaging, wincing every so often, and I mentally clocked myself upside the head for ignoring the more important issue here. "Did she hurt you?"

"What?" Rosa snorted, then hid her mouth behind her hand like she'd just cursed at me. "Sorry—no. Not even a little. I'm fine."

Sure. Witches and warlocks were built sturdier than humans, but they paled in comparison to shifters. "Again, I'm so sorry. What *they* must think after that, too. She'll be better, I swear—"

"Ewan, it's fine. I'll do a mild memory modification spell once you leave—make the girls remember the night a little differently. We're good." Rosa peeked over her shoulder at a sulking Lyssa, chin on her fist and eyes clenched shut as the stylist attempted to brush through her hair. "Is she... Is she fated to Lucian and Soren as well?"

"Unfortunately," I muttered tightly. The Perry coven—all two and a half of them—had been very supportive of the new pack, proud of our unification efforts and eager to see the territory secured from the more violent packs at our borders. Still, she didn't need to look so smug about my disdain for sharing a mate. Squaring my shoulders, I checked the time again—late as fuck, of course— and shook my head. "Please just make her look the part. She doesn't act it yet, but we'll get there."

"Easy." As the salon's manager and head makeup artist, Rosa could no doubt work literal magic on my mate. The witch scrunched her red ringlets with both hands for a moment, considering my girl from a distance, and then rounded on me, forced to look way up even in her heels. "Ewan, she's so pretty. Once we get the hair under control, it'll be nothing. I swear I'll take care of her."

"I don't know how to thank you—"

"By not stressing out," she insisted with a chuckle. "I think she's just nervous. Doesn't look like she's seen shears in a few years."

"Decades, more like." I checked the time again with a grumble, then nodded to the Employees Only door behind the reception block. "Ethan in?"

"In his office, yup."

"I'll just have a quick word." I gave her wrist an affectionate squeeze followed by another chaste kiss on the cheek before breezing through the place like I owned it.

Because I did.

I blew by the receptionist and through the employee door, which opened to a tight hallway with the staff breakroom at the end, then a set of dark, narrow stairs to the right. Taking them two at a time, I fired off a quick text to Jocelyn that I was running behind—my fox shifter assistant had already predicted this would be a nightmare, and she'd better not fucking *gloat*—and to start the Thanksgiving street market meeting without me.

Phone tucked back in my jacket pocket, I then sprinted the rest of the way to Ethan's glass box in the sky, needing the warlock to be completely in the know.

All the while praying to Lady Fate that Lyssa could keep her shit together for the evening of pampering ahead.

10

LYSSA

Ugh. I scrubbed at my tired eyes, then smoothed my fingers over razor-shaped brows, still thick—just tamed. How often did women do this? Was it a regular thing? Once a year? Four hours after I arrived at the Grove and we still had makeup to do. The first hour went to untangling my hair, which set my scalp on fire, then the second hour for wash, condition, rinse, *repeat*. Repeat, repeat, repeat.

Usually I just splashed around in the lake or whatever, ran my fingers through my hair, and called it a day.

This was... a lot.

Another hour to cut and shape. A fourth to style and blow-dry and tweeze my stupid eyebrows.

And now I was here, in a well-lit private room alone. Ten o'clock had come and gone—no Ewan, no end in sight. Kira had dozed off ages ago, bored out of her skull and in no mood to suffer with me. Seated in yet another comfy leather chair in front of another huge mirror, I had to give credit to the tiny blonde who tackled my unruly tresses—this looked good.

I guess?

Chopped to about halfway down my back, my hair had a light,

fluffy look to it now. It was soft. Silky. Unnaturally straight. Fell nicely with all the layers. Framed my face well. No tangles. No matted chunks. Just—pretty girl hair.

Even before the forest, pretty girl hair was a luxury beyond my reach.

And now I knew pretty girl hair stank of artificial coconut.

Not a bad smell in small doses, but I was drowning in the stuff.

It all seemed like a lot of work. I had walked into this expecting the haircuts I used to get as a kid: lob it off with a pair of blunt scissors, ruffle it out, done.

Maybe this was just what an alpha's mate needed. Ewan— beautiful, breathtaking *Ewan*—had insisted I look the part. Why did it matter? Was there a specific look, specific outfit, specific hairstyle, that declared *alpha's mate* to the world?

Did I... not look like that?

Obviously not, or you wouldn't be here.

Not only did I lack an alpha mate's style, but the other women in the salon made all-black *work*. They were chic—one of many new words I'd learned in the last four hours—and glamorous. I was... in leggings and a T-shirt. With the unpleasantness of my arrival quickly forgotten—like, suspiciously fast—some had actually complimented my jean jacket, gushing over the label on the tag, but that meant nothing to me. It was just a stupid jacket, something I wore so I looked bothered by the autumn chill.

None of this stuff mattered. Scattered across the black vanity in front of me was an army of brushes, clean and floral-scented. The gold frame around the oval mirror? Pretty. The palettes of makeup? Smelled nice. Lots of colors. But—it didn't *matter*.

Food mattered.

Family mattered.

This was fluffy nonsense, but it had seemed important to Ewan —even Soren agreed I needed the makeover before we parted ways —so I was here, trying to fit in once again.

And once again, struggling.

I stiffened when the door behind me creaked open, and in the opening stood the woman I had shoved away from my mate.

The woman who had been doting on me all night with freshly brewed herbal teas and offers of whatever treats I desired. After munching on crumbly biscuits and weird hard cheese, I turned down the rest, still full from breakfast.

Still guilty from... attacking her.

Her mirror reflection's sweet smile had me sinking into the chair.

I shouldn't have shoved her.

She had her own mate—she and Ewan were just *friends*.

But I couldn't stop myself.

Couldn't think.

Just... acted, letting Kira call the shots.

"How are you doing, Lyssa?" Rosa tipped her head to the side, leaning on the doorframe, effortlessly beautiful with all her curves. Well fed. Plump. She exuded kindness like my fated mates did strength. "It's been a long night so far. Would you like a break?"

Woven into the shame and disappointment was the discomfort of being waited on. I didn't need someone to take care of me. I was a grown wolf. I could fend for myself.

But it was kind of nice, I guess.

"Uh, no, I'm fine." I tracked Rosa and her tight red curls in the mirror as she slipped inside and shut the door, bringing a cloud of amber and honey with her. Before, that scent had triggered me, egged me on, made my mouth water with *fire*. Now, it belonged to her, the woman who had cared for me all night, and its cozy comfort made me feel even worse. "Thank you."

"No problem." She grabbed a stool and tugged it toward me. "So, I'm going to—"

"I'm really sorry about before," I blurted, the chair spinning a little too fast when I kicked round to face her. Feet planted to stop from going in a full circle, I dropped my gaze submissively, *hating* how I'd reacted earlier—because now I just felt stupid and childish. Obviously it wasn't a human thing to do, to attack a woman for saying hello to her friend, and all the humans had been so *shocked* at the time, maybe even a little scared of me.

They got over it fast, but still. Not good. *Terrible* first impression.

Rosa just smiled like I hadn't tried to rip her throat out. "Oh, honey, I understand—"

"I'm really sorry I hurt you." If I could take it back, I would, but life had taught me nothing was ever that simple.

"You didn't." Rosa winked as she brought the stool right up close, then took a seat. "Promise."

I did though. I threw my weight into that shove, witnessed pain flash in her deep greens like lightning across a furious black sky. I *saw* it. I hurt her. Yet she continued to dote on me.

She and Ewan must have been good friends.

Or maybe he and her husband were allies.

Whatever the reason, Rosa had lied to spare my feelings—and it wasn't right.

"I just..." I swallowed hard with a wince, throat too dry, tongue too big. "I don't know what happened."

"Shifters are very protective of their mates," she insisted as she got situated on the stool, heels up and over the golden ring at its base. Rosa said that so naturally, like it was just fact. My pack alphas protected each other, but I'd never seen the rage I felt in my *soul* over a simple touch. Once she found her comfy groove, Rosa straightened and brushed her hair back over her shoulders, her smile brighter than the lights sparkling around the mirror. "It seems like you're new to this."

Her words—her *truth*—hit like a landslide. "Yeah, I guess."

I was new to this. New to shifters, to fated mates, to a civilized world where a haircut took four hours.

I was new to it—and already bad at it.

"Want to know a secret?"

Head bowed, I peeked at her through my lashes. Rosa's cheeks dimpled, and she leaned closer.

"Lucian, Ewan, and Soren—they're all new to it, too," she whispered, head bobbing when my eyebrows arched up. "Yeah. Those three are used to being lone wolves, and now they're a pack of alphas. And, real talk, no shifter has met their fated mate until they do. You're all just fumbling around in the dark, suddenly hit with this, uh, *visceral* but also very spiritual connection to a stranger." She patted my knee gently. "So, don't be too hard on yourself, okay? You're all just doing your best."

Oh.

I thought—

My eyes watered, and I blinked back the rush of emotion, nodding through a sniffle. Rosa gave me a moment to compose myself, fluffing her hair in the mirror, then grabbed hold of my chair's armrests and eased me around to properly face her.

"Okay." She clapped her hands giddily. "Tell me about your current makeup routine."

This stuff was a *routine*? Kira snored deep, deep inside, absolutely no help. "Uh, I… don't."

Lips pursed, Rosa nodded slowly. "Like, you don't have a routine, or…?"

"I've never worn makeup."

Heat flared across my entire face when she zeroed in on it, scrutinizing every hair, every pore.

"Well, you don't *need* to wear it, so that's totally fine. Makeup is just for fun," she said brightly. Rosa then stood, roughly my height in her heels but drastically shorter if she took them off, all hips and boobs, womanly and full. "To keep it short and sweet, we'll go over the basics tonight." She nudged the stool back to the wall. "And then we can make another appointment later to learn some fancy looks? Ewan hosts a lot of parties, so it might be nice to have a couple options in your back pocket. Would you like that?"

I nodded shyly, palms slick with nervous sweat at the thought of Ewan throwing *parties*. Parties full of pretty people, probably, who looked chic and glamorous like these ladies—and then there would be me. *Me*. Like this.

I needed all the help I could get.

Or… I could leave.

I had given Lucian my word that I wouldn't, that I would at least try.

But this was a lot. I had finally found *shifters*, beings like *me*, and I just couldn't…

There were so many rules. What if I blew it? What if they realized I wasn't like them?

I thought I had family before, and they left me in the woods.

What if—

"So, first, we're going to clean and moisturize your face," Rosa said, butt to me as she rooted through one of the vanity's lower drawers. "It's really important to take care of your skin, but then…" She twisted around for another long look at my features. "I think it's different for shifters. Your bodies do a fantastic job at taking care of you already. Just make sure if you wear makeup, you wash it off properly before bed."

"Okay." Why did I sound like a shy little mouse? Why did this have to be so complicated? Biting on the insides of my cheeks, I watched Rosa gather supplies in the mirror, wishing Kira would wake up already and go through this with me. "Ewan said…" A quick sweep of her exposed skin showed no marks or pocks. Weren't witches branded by the Devil? "He said your husband is a warlock?"

"Uh-huh."

"And you're a…" I swallowed hard, another bout of nerves wetting my palms. "A witch?"

"You betcha." Rosa kept her back to me as she lined up a trio of small jars on the vanity, each with a different colored cream inside. Kira didn't stir at her confirmation, which had to mean she wasn't… bad?

No pointy hat.

No warts.

No crazy teeth or cackling laugh.

"I've only ever seen witches in movies."

Rosa giggled. "Well, don't believe everything you see in there."

She finally pivoted around with a wet wipe. "Is it okay if I touch you?"

"Uh, yeah."

No one had ever asked before.

They just *did*. They took and touched and hurt without question.

This witch approached with a calm energy and a gentle caress. She moved my head side to side tenderly, feather-light, like dandelion fluff billowing over the field—kissing your cheek. Her wipe smelled like lavender, and as she cleaned my face with all the kindness of a mother nuzzling her pup, I struggled to keep my eyes open. After four hours of pain, the hairstylist tiny but rough, this was paradise.

"I heard stories about witches when I was little," I admitted, voice thick and subdued, Kira snoring away. Rosa grinned out of the corner of my eye.

"Oh yeah?"

"Do people..." I sucked in a sharp breath as Rosa moved away, done with the washing and on to the moisturizing. Her hand hovered over the three glass jars, and I swore her fingertips *glowed* before she selected the one with the pink cream in the middle.

"Do people what?"

"Do people ever..." The words shriveled on the tip of my tongue, suddenly tasting sour. When she returned, I closed my eyes and tipped my head back, offering my face for whatever her tender touch might bring. The cream smelled like roses, so light I barely felt it as she swept her fingers over my forehead. "Do they ever call you, uh, a demon?"

Much to my surprise, Rosa snorted. She smoothed her fingers across my cheeks, her breath cool and minty. "I mean, no. Humans have their own lore about our connection to Lucifer, but it's not true." She dabbed at my lips. "Why?"

I curled my hands to fists and said nothing.

"Lyssa." Rosa smoothed the cream down my neck, careful even when she didn't need to be. "Have you ever met a demon?"

I shook my head, suddenly hot all over. Before, my eyelids had grown heavy from her touch. Now, I refused to open them—refused to see the pity in her eyes for this poor dumb wolf shifter who knew nothing about her world, raised on lies and violence.

"Well, good." She was behind me suddenly, and I flinched when both hands settled on either side of my head, thumbs massaging around my temples. "They can be really nasty. Would not recommend."

"They said I..." Kira snorted awake, as if *finally* sensing my distress, and a warm, comforting weight settled in my chest. "They said I had a demon in me. That... Kira was a demon."

"Kira?"

"My wolf."

The massage stopped, and then Rosa was back in front, a little *too* in my face if she knew anything about wolves, those big emeralds searching, maybe seeing more than she should. Crouched with her hands on the chair's armrests, her neat red brows creased.

"Who said that to you?"

Fear slithered down my spine. Was she angry with me? All the sweetness was gone, replaced by a hardness that could be anger *or* concern—or maybe both.

You ruined it again.

First Soren, now Rosa. I seemed to have a knack for taking a nice moment and pooping all over it.

"No one," I whispered, shaking my head and ignoring Kira's mournful howl. "Nothing. It's nothing. Never mind."

Her frown said she didn't believe me, but she left it at that, once again respecting not to touch without permission. No poking and prying. *Respect.* That was new.

And so was everything else she had to show me. Rosa moved on like the demon talk hadn't happened, directing my attention to the mountain of makeup on the vanity. She took her time explaining the differences between foundation and concealer, never once making me feel stupid for not knowing anything about anything. When the makeup tutorial eventually wrapped, she told me she was going to do a basic day look tonight, something light and natural.

"Just enough to accent your beauty—never hide it."

Cool. Like I knew the difference. Hands twined on my lap, the awkwardness forgotten and Rosa just as bubbly as she had been from the start again, I let her do her thing. Kira passed out almost immediately, obsessed with the witch's gentle touch, the amber and honey no longer a threatening smell—one that signaled a potential rival for *our* mate—but a soothing one.

"So," Rosa started as she swept a soft makeup brush over my closed lids, "you got three fated mates in less than twenty-four hours, eh? That's a lot to juggle."

I shrugged. Maybe it was—who was I to say? If ten were the average, I wouldn't have a clue.

"Have you ever had a boyfriend before?"

I shook my head. Reed probably shot boys who so much as glanced at his daughters. Besides, I wasn't one of the mating wolves in my pack, so even if males nosed around me when I went into heat, we weren't a *thing*. It didn't work like that in the woods.

"No? Really?"

"I've mated," I insisted, hoisting two fingers and sinking into the chair—only for Rosa to gently nudge me upright, needing a canvas with good posture, face fully in the light. "Twice. But the first one was really bad." Honestly, that drunk human shouldn't even count. He had made me bleed. Stolen my purity. *Nothing* like Lucian. "It hurt a lot."

The feathery brush disappeared, and I cracked one eye open, then the other when I found Rosa frowning down at me again.

"I'm sorry, honey," she murmured, followed by a squeeze of my shoulder. Now it was my turn to frown, because what did she have to apologize for? *I* chose that male. I followed him outside behind the bar. *I* didn't stop him.

And *I* broke his stupid face.

"Was the second time with one of your fated mates?"

Fire pooled in my belly, sex clenching at the memory of his mouth on mine. "Yeah. Lucian. He made me feel really good."

"Well, that's great." I caught Rosa's grin just before closing my eyes again, letting her get back to work as she added, "You take your time, okay? Don't rush. Don't feel pressured. You, er, *mate* when it feels right, and if you want to stop, your mates will respect that."

I gave her a teeny, tiny nod in response—which was a lie. Like I could *stop* around those three males. Anytime I was with them, it was a battle between my heart, my body, and my head. Throw a needy Kira into the mix and everything got so muddled. I felt things I'd never experienced: need, desire, longing—yearning, maybe. But then a whole bunch of familiar heartaches too, like frustration and anger and that fidgety, flighty feeling that made me want to run and never look back. Discomfort around strangers. Fear that they would reject me, toss me out alone again.

Fear that my pack would never find me.

Fear that I wasn't enough.

That I would *never* be enough.

And it had only been *one* stupid day. Would it get better—or worse?

"I don't know how to be an alpha's mate," I admitted, face hot as I eased out of Rosa's reach. She stopped working on my eyes immediately, but I kept them closed, worried if I opened them, the emotion thickening in my throat might leak out. "I don't know how to be *one* alpha's mate, never mind three." Finally, with a little prodding from a sleepy Kira, I peeked at the witch with a sigh. "Can you… help me?"

Rosa blinked those thick full lashes back at me, her makeup flawless, the liner sharp and flicking up at the ends. "Oh, I—"

"You just seem to know so much more than I do." Obviously, best-case scenario would be to handle this by myself. If I had grown up with wolf shifters instead of wolves, maybe I would know what was expected of me.

And what to expect from them.

But here I was, just a pup lost in the dark, trees soaring like mountains and curious eyes stalking me from the shadows.

"Of course," Rosa said warmly. "Look up for me, honey." I complied as she got back to it, sweeping color—or something—

under my eyes. "I'll do my best. Witches and shifters are different, I guess, but love is universal."

I tried not to squirm at that word. *Love.* Never had it carried much weight in my world. I loved the aging pair of wolves who found me, but that couldn't be what she meant. Love was the stuff of fairy tales, princes and princesses defeating the dragon and sharing their first kiss. Fireworks and rainbows and one *person* forever.

But I had three.

And love couldn't start with a kidnapping, right? Being stolen from your family and forced back into the world that had rejected you long, long ago...

Maybe fated mates didn't fall in love.

Maybe we were just a pack destined to find each other, mate, and protect our territory.

That wasn't so bad, actually. No different from my wolves.

"What do you think of Redwood Grove?" Rosa asked when she eventually moved on to my face, finishing my eyes up with mascara that made my lashes feel too heavy, too *there*. "Have you seen much of it yet?"

"Just the house and the lake." I did my best to avoid the mirror now, not wanting to catch my reflection until she was finished. I owed her a genuine reaction, not one built over time.

"Oh, I love the lake." Rosa blended something along my nose with her finger, sighing wistfully, her smile almost permanent and a little too beautiful. Were all witches lovely, or just her? "Ethan and I go kayaking there every summer. Lots of inlets to explore, a couple caves... Redwood Grove is unlike anywhere we've ever lived." She paused, easing off and letting the light spill across my features for a moment of scrutiny, then got back to it. "I'm sure your mates will show you around soon. They all have a special area they like best. Lucian is usually in the western woods. Soren's family has run all the business by the lake for decades, then Ewan has the village and..." Rosa licked her lips and cleared her throat. "And the mountains." Her eyes locked with mine. "You be careful if you go up there, okay?"

"Why? Are there bears?" The thrill of the hunt suddenly made my mouth water. "Or mountain lions? I've killed both before."

"Oh." Rosa faltered, her smile seeming forced as she swept a big fat brush over my cheekbones. "Well, uh, good for you."

Uh-oh.

Had I made it bad again?

Before I could throw out something normal, some human activity like, uh, hiking, she showed yet another small mercy and carried on talking.

"No, no, it's just... there's a stream," she told me, deep in her work, so focused on my face that it was kind of unsettling "It's from mountain runoff, and it feeds through the range, then down into the valley. We think it's cursed." She huffed and rubbed her thumb along my hairline. "There's old magic there, and even Ethan doesn't know what it is, but I wouldn't go near it. It has a really harsh energy, and this *smell*, and just..." Another lingering moment of direct eye contact. "Keep your distance, even if you're with your mates. They know not to mess with it."

"Got it." It wouldn't be the first time I'd happened upon a ditch or gulley or pond that smelled off. Never faced a *harsh energy* before, but if it smelled like danger, like sickness and death, I knew enough to steer clear. "No mountain stream."

"Gull River is the official name." Rosa returned to the vanity briefly, then came back with the biggest brush so far and—blush? Was that blush? Or holding powder? Ugh. Too many new terms today. "We've done some poking around... The magic is confined to the range, so don't be scared of the lake or brooks in the forest. Just be safe is all I'm saying."

Oh.

Well.

That was nice.

No one had ever worried about my safety before. Reed and Nikki were great at telling me why the thing that had hurt me was *my* fault, and my alphas had the greater good in mind—always.

Kira stirred inside me, her lazy yawn and toe-spreading stretch

117

teasing my muscles. Hours ago she had used my body like a puppet and gone for Rosa's throat. Now, we both leaned into the witch's touch, savoring her attentiveness, her gentleness, as she finalized my makeup with the big brush, dusting my face with powder that smelled like lilacs.

"Okay, done." Rosa stepped back to appraise her work, her curves blocking the mirror, and then nodded. "Basic day look —achieved."

She then swept aside, and the full weight of this stranger's reflection hit like an avalanche. Not only was my hair tame, but my brows had shape and definition, same as my cheekbones. My lips were soft and womanly like hers. My eyelids shimmered with a golden brown that didn't scream in your face. Subtle, the liner there to enhance, not distract. Pretty. My lashes had never looked so full and healthy before.

Rosa had made my eyes pop.

Made my skin glow.

Gave my face more definition. She muted my freckles and hid the big pores on my nose.

She...

She made me a cool girl.

A *pretty* girl.

"Do you like it?" And she had no idea, her tone cautious, her body language shifting from confident to hesitant. I slipped off the chair and went in for a much closer look, practically shoved up against the mirror as I absorbed every detail.

Only women in magazines and movies looked like this.

I had never thought...

I was never the cool girl. Never the pretty girl. Just the wild girl —the demon girl who belonged to no one but the trees.

Eyes stinging and throat tight, I whirled around and grinned. "I *love* it!"

"Oh—" Rosa let out a long breath. "—good, I was worried maybe—"

I pounced before she could get the rest out, flying across the tiny room and dragging her into a hug.

"Thank you, thank you, thank you, *thank you*," I whispered frantically, buried in her red curls and squeezing much harder than I should. *For everything.* Not only had she made me beautiful, but she had been so patient with me. Forgiving. Kind. Thoughtful.

What had I done to deserve three mates and this witch?

Seriously, was this a dream?

Something this good would never last if it wasn't. *Never.*

Might as well make the most of it now.

I crushed her to me until something cracked. Rosa inhaled sharply, and I scrambled back, Kira's whines upping the staticky panic buzzing in my chest.

"Oh, no, I'm so sorry—"

"It's fine," Rosa insisted, wincing as she massaged her collarbone. Had I fractured it? My mates seemed to be able to take my strength like no one had before, but maybe witches weren't built the same.

You did it again.

Three times in one night.

You ruined it.

"Rosa, I—"

She held up a hand, stopping me when I tried to swoop in and fix it, her smile bright but a little broken. Oh no. I'd really hurt her. I—

"I'm a mom now," she said as she shuffled over to the vanity, opened a drawer, and pulled out what I could only assume was a wand. Witch holding a polished oak stick? Yeah. Definitely a wand. Had to be. She then angled its tip toward her right shoulder. "Seriously, I have all the healing spells memorized."

Curiosity sparked, I cocked my head, totally fixated on the wand. "Can I... Can I see?"

Magic.

Spells and sorcery and all the scary stuff Reed had harped on and on about—used to heal. To *help.*

Rosa glanced toward the closed door, then winked. "Don't tell the humans."

"Promise," I whispered. Kira stood alert inside me, uncertain but interested—then in awe when nothing more than a word murmured in a language I didn't understand fell from Rosa's lips and the room lit up a rosy pink.

Right then and there, I knew that everything Reed had drilled into us kids was a *lie*.

I wasn't a demon.

Magic was super cool.

And most of all, I wasn't doomed to die alone. Not a freak. Not possessed. Not *garbage*. There was a whole world out there with creatures just like me, different and powerful and strange, and I owed it to myself to explore that.

To not run, just this once.

To stay and build.

To be brave. To let others in. And finally, *finally*, to live.

Yeah.

Sure.

Easier said than done, right?

11

LYSSA

Okay.

Okay.

Don't panic. You tried your best.

Why was it that when Rosa did my makeup, I looked fresh and vibrant and young and *cool…*

But when *I* tried to do the exact same thing, following her very detailed instructions, I looked like a clown?

Or a troll.

Or some crazy swamp monster.

Tossing the biggest brush of the bunch onto the bathroom counter, I leaned closer to the mirror and crinkled my nose at the painted *thing* staring back. My eyeshadow had no subtlety, just smears of dark brown dirt over my lids. Clearly I still couldn't color inside the lines, my gloss past my lip line, and I guess *Mulberry Kiss* wasn't my shade of blush, because it made me look really sunburnt.

Not cool.

Not pretty.

Just a mess.

"Kira?" I tipped my head side to side, angling it this way and that, hoping that maybe from another point of view, the last two hours of work and rework had been for *something*. "Opinion?"

Nothing. She passed out the second I'd dumped my new makeup bag on the counter and kicked the door shut. Yeah, an empty, echoey house meant there was no one around to witness my shame, but it felt safer attempting this behind closed doors.

Attempt failed.

I looked ridiculous.

Scowling, I smacked the faucet and cupped my hands beneath the lukewarm stream, then hunkered down to splash away the evidence.

Two days after three alpha males turned my world on its head, I'd just wanted to look nice for Ewan. I mean, he had paid the outrageous bill at Rosa's salon for all the services spent turning me into someone presentable, and he hadn't even gotten a chance to reap the rewards.

Whatever those were.

Anyway—something held him up at the office that night, and after twiddling my thumbs for another hour with Rosa like the last lonely kid waiting to be picked up from daycare, I went home without him.

But not alone. Ethan and Rosa had driven me back to the house, the short time spent with both of them confirming their Perfect Couple status in my brain. She was short and curvy, he was tall and lean. He looked at her like she was the sun, him her gorgeous full moon. The warlock called her Rosebud, and she blushed up a storm, pushing at him playfully, all giggly, seeming ten years younger as soon as he showed up.

Good guy.

Told me I looked pretty—like a real alpha's mate.

As soon as they left, I had washed it all off. With nobody at the house and bed calling my name, I scrubbed my face raw. Went to sleep alone, surrounded by pillows again. Woke up to another breakfast feast from Soren, but he hadn't stayed.

Some plumbing emergency in a few of his cabins had called him away.

And Ewan didn't show.

And neither did Lucian.

But as soon as I crushed the last crispy slice of bacon in my mouth yesterday, the doorbell rang, and on the other side: Rosa. Wonderful Rosa with a makeup kit just for me and a million romance movies for us to devour in the basement cinema room. We ate, watched, and talked about boys all day—about romance and respect. She showed me how to use the high-tech TV and connect to the internet on the packaged laptop someone had left for me in the foyer, *finally* allowing me access to a digital world that had always been off-limits at Reed and Nikki's house. I mean, yeah, I'd seen and sampled some technology over the years, but poking at the odd tablet that was bolted to the counter and impossible to steal at big box stores hadn't exactly prepared me for the high-tech world humans had created while I lived in the forest.

We cooked two meals together. Watched the sun set over the lake. Drank hot chocolates with a *tiny* splash of cinnamon-flavored liquor after dark.

Kind of annoying that I had spent more time with a witch than my fated mates, but after watching, rewatching, and then dissecting all those romance movies, I was at least slightly more confident in how I ought to carry myself.

Maybe.

Thoughts, feelings, and emotions remained muddled, sure, but things were a little less scary today.

Again, Soren had popped by for breakfast, but after learning he needed to supervise the wintering of his cabins, I told him to go. We weren't rolling in carefree conversations like me and Rosa anyway, still stiff and quiet and uncertain in each other's company, and if he had other obligations, might as well just get on with it.

The alpha had sounded frustrated to leave, arguing with himself, furiously texting someone throughout breakfast, until eventually he disappeared, same as before. Alone again, but this time I had *purpose*.

I refused to mope around the house and wait for one of these males to entertain me. I didn't need a babysitter. I didn't *want* one of them watching me, making sure I didn't get into trouble.

I wanted to make moves.

In all the movies, one half of the couple always made a move, some grand romantic gesture that turned their sweetheart to mush. A speech. A gift. A surprise. *Something.* I could do that. Yeah, those couples were fictional, but they weren't better than me. Not smarter or more resourceful. I could do... something.

It wouldn't be *I Love You* in skywriting out the butt-end of a plane, but I had the element of surprise on my side.

None of these males seemed to expect anything from me.

Soren was wrapped up in work yet close enough that I saw him every so often across the lake—we even waved once, me on the back porch nursing a tea that tasted like twigs and grass, him on the shoreline surrounded by humans given their clumsy gait. That had been nice. A little dose of connection today for us, a strange comfy coziness warming in my belly at the sight of his huge smile and enthusiastic wave with both arms.

Lucian was... somewhere, doing something, refusing to show his face back at the house.

Ewan was at work in the village, but it was *finally* lunchtime. People took breaks midday to eat, and since Rosa and Ethan had pointed out his office building the other night, I knew *just* where to find him for the big gesture.

Which was ruined now. I straightened, eyes shrouded in black like a raccoon, water dribbling off my chin, and then nudged the metallic faucet off. The makeup was supposed to be the surprise. I'd stroll into his office all dolled up, proof that his efforts hadn't gone unnoticed.

I mean, Rosa had told me how firmly he ordered the salon staff to take care of me. He demanded they make me comfortable, keep me safe, and watch my stress levels.

Nice, I guess, but it would have been even better if he had stayed.

Or shown up at the end.

Or poked his head through the front door yesterday, just for a couple minutes.

But never mind.

Men are stubborn idiots, Rosa had told me as we picked apart the counterintuitive actions of the romance hero in one of the afternoon films. *Shifter alpha males are even worse.*

So, maybe he was just stubborn.

Maybe that was normal.

I didn't *like* it, but, based on the movies and Rosa's sage wisdom, we all had to adapt a little to make this work. Change. Grow. Be better versions of ourselves.

Whatever. It sounded like a lot of work, but everyone seemed really happy before the credits rolled, so... worth it?

Groping a hand down the counter, I eventually found the makeup-smeared towel amidst the chaos, all the brand-new products—including a shredded plastic bag of hair elastics—Rosa had dropped off yesterday scattered everywhere like debris after an explosion. Once I'd dried off and rubbed the raccoon eyes away, I took a long, hard look at myself in the mirror, clean-faced, hair in a ponytail.

For the first time in her life, the woman staring back at me fit in. She *belonged*. Sure, they tamed my hair and plucked my eyebrows and made me wear clothes, but that was nothing compared to what others had done to change me in the past. Kira and I—we had a house, a territory, and three handsome mates. Even Ethan had congratulated me on finding them, so enthusiastic, so expressive, so hopelessly in love with *his* forever girl that a bit of it had rubbed off on me.

For the first time ever, I wasn't totally alone. Sure, right this second it was a party of one, but there were creatures out there like me. Shifters. Witches. So much more, probably.

My eyes narrowed, and I pointed a warning finger at the girl in the mirror. "Don't mess this up."

With all that in mind, I wanted to be a good fated mate—and despite the knowledge boost from Rosa and her movies, I still wasn't sure how to do it. The mating pair in my pack had each other above all else. They hunted together, reared pups together, and snuggled together.

Protect. Procreate. Eat first.

None of that mattered here. Shifters were *way* more human than I would have guessed, with jobs and responsibilities that weren't about finding food and holding temporary shelter. Humans ran the world, and we just lived in it. *I* had to change. The wolf-girl in the mirror—*she* had to become more human.

With a deep breath, I rolled my shoulders back and stood tall. "You're an alpha female now. You can do this." Lower lip snagged between my teeth, I tugged my shirt's neckline to the side, admiring the marks left by Lucian. Sure, the color had softened to a dull pink, a few shades brighter than my complexion but subtle enough that you might miss it at first glance. "You've mated. *You* are the alpha. You can make moves when stubborn boys *don't.*"

I stepped back, frowning at my uncertain reflection. Great pep talk, but I wished the fancy clothes Rosa and I had ordered online yesterday were already here. Ewan was so stylish, effortless, and beautiful, and here I was in snug faded denim and a teal crop top. At least the black coat on the bed had the same designer label as my jean jacket; that counted for something, apparently.

Clothes had never mattered before.

Not until him.

Soren dressed casually, like the males I had seen at bars or on the subway. Lucian's dress style remained a mystery because the jerk hadn't come back, but Ewan was all *class,* his scent accented with rich leather and effortless control.

I... looked like a mall girl today.

And that was fine.

It was a start.

Just a start.

Swallowing thickly, I snatched the mascara and leaned back over to darken my lashes. Tricky as it was not to smudge or accidentally ink my eyelid, I managed better this time, and when it was over, my eyes were... okay. Fine. Brighter surrounded by all the black, and that would have to do for now.

"Kira, we're going out." My inner companion snored almost passive-aggressively. I smirked. "We're going to see Ewan."

She lurched awake inside me with a long, needy whine that sent shivers down my back. Rolling my eyes, I ducked out of the bathroom as she paced about, her giddy energy hurrying me along, then grabbed my coat and slipped it on as I padded along familiar empty hallways and staircases and landings. After two days, I knew the place backwards and forwards, capable of navigating it with my eyes closed if necessary. I'd sniffed all the corners, brushed up against the stonework, scent-marked and explored and made it mine.

With or without my mates.

The only spot that gave me some pause was the front door. After squishing my feet into a pair of slightly uncomfortable flats, I hesitated in front of it, heart suddenly hammering. This was the first time I'd walk out it alone, about to stroll through my new territory—*alone*. Maybe they trusted me. Maybe they thought I would keep my word. Whatever the case may be, I refused to break that trust; I had promised Lucian to try. My mind might still be a mess, all of this confusing and overwhelming, but if I didn't make an effort now—when fate dropped everything I'd ever wanted into my lap, seemingly out of nowhere—then I would regret it forever.

Let Soren, Ewan, and Lucian do what they thought was best.

Fate may have brought us together, but *I* called the shots in my own life.

And for now, I *chose* to stay here and tough it out.

To stumble and fall and get back up, just like I'd done countless times before.

To make an effort—to make mistakes.

To show these stubborn lone alphas how it felt to be part of a real *pack*.

If, by the first snowfall, it was still confusing and overwhelming and frustrating, if I was still alone and spent more time with Rosa than my mates, I'd leave. Head west. Reconnect with my wolves. We walked the same route every year, every season. Shouldn't be too difficult, right?

Taking a deep breath, I unlocked the door and slipped outside, then crept down the front porch steps. Gravel crunched underfoot as I marched along the empty driveway, an autumn-dusted forest ahead, mountains looming above the orange, red, and yellow canopy. Sun out full blast, the air had that perfect fall chill. Ethan might have driven me home the other night, but I'd already memorized the route; a short drive would be a quick walk for a wolf. I headed west, eyeing the paved path that cut into a treed area, maples dusting the roadway with fallen leaves.

As soon as I stepped off the gravel, someone exhaled on the back of my neck.

Lyssa.

My vision sharpened to Kira's, nostrils flared as I sucked in a breath, ready to scent out whoever had snuck up on me—

Nothing.

I whirled around to nothingness. Scowling, I slashed at the empty air, ignoring Kira's snarls, and then rubbed my neck.

"Who…?"

Lyssa.

There it was again—my name whispering over my skin, tickling my sides, making my ears buzz. So soft, so serene, like the midday breeze was calling to me. With no one at the nearby lakeshore and Soren's guys puttering around the cabins way up and across the shimmering blue, I rounded on the forest. Stalked to the tree line and glowered inside.

"Hello?"

The forest answered with rustling leaves and chattering squirrels. Nothing unusual. Just trees and brambles and unearthed roots. Rocks, dirt, yellowing moss.

"Soren?" Creepy. Very, very creepy. The hairs on the back of my neck stood straight up as I padded between a pair of birches, knees bent, hands up, ready to attack if necessary. "Lucian?"

Lyyyyyyssaaaa...

I scrambled out of the forest with a panicked gasp, Kira's hackles up, her canines bared.

That... sounded like a woman. Still airy and breezy, the voice had a higher pitch, a seductive purr that only a female could pull off.

Lyssa.

My name crashed through the trees louder this time, clear and distinct, more like an actual voice.

"What?" I barked, scenting the air, searching for footprints, listening for the crash of an unwieldy figure battling their way to me. Nothing. Same as always, the smells and sounds familiar, comforting.

Kira urged a retreat. She and I had never gone looking for trouble, but as a team, we were *great* at finishing it. If she thought we should go, I'd be a fool not to listen. Arms crossed, I stalked out and headed for the main road again, lake to my left, forest to the right, house behind me—

Lyssa, come home.

For a second, my feet grew roots. I couldn't move. Couldn't think. Honey on the breeze. Apple blossoms in the air. Pressure between my shoulder blades that slowly turned me around. My chest tightened as soon as I laid eyes on the mountain range—which made no sense.

"Stop," I growled, fight pumping through my veins, Kira *right* there, ready to shift in a flash, attack and tear whatever this was to pieces. Trembling, I closed my eyes. Took a breath. Then another, and another, and another.

All was well when I opened them again. Same bright, sunny fall day. Same ripples on the lake. Same faraway human workers in khaki uniforms around Soren's cabins. Same massive house of stone and wood, grey and brown, with its huge windows—my den. My new home.

It was all the same.

But it *felt* different.

Somehow. Just another feeling I couldn't describe, the words beyond my growing vocabulary.

And when I finally turned away, stalking down the main road and eyeing the rustic wooden sign—*Redwood Grove Village This Way*—it felt like someone was trying to make me stay.

Their hand on my shoulder.

Their grip tight…

But loosening with every step, eventually fading away. No more honey and apple blossoms in the air. No one calling my name.

Just the rustling leaves and little forest critters—and my pounding heart—to keep me company all the way to the village gates.

12

EWAN

At exactly 12:17 p.m., chaos erupted outside my office door. What was usually a quiet lunch hour descended into a symphony of snarls and growls, heels on hardwood, and Jocelyn's firm objections met with whumps, thumps, and clunks.

I peered around my huge monitor, wolf on high alert, chopsticks in one hand as I typed an email with the other, not even looking at the screen, barely processing the words as they flowed from my fingertips. A few seconds later, the door crashed open and Lyssa stumbled in, disheveled, her neon blue wolf eyes darting around and Jocelyn hot on her heels.

"I'm sorry, Mr. Quinn, I tried to stop—"

"Jocelyn..." I set my chopsticks down on the maki platter I'd only *just* dug into and gestured to a panting Lyssa. "Meet Lyssa, my fated mate." My inner wolf immediately ditched the piss-poor attitude of the last two days, howling victoriously at the sight of her *here*, in our domain, in the throne room of my empire. "Lyssa..." Those scary bright blues snapped to me, the she-wolf's teeth bared. "Meet Jocelyn, my assistant."

And just like that, the drama vanished. Jocelyn nodded knowingly, smoothing her strawberry-blonde bob and fixing her

131

rumpled tartan pantsuit, all cigarette leg cut and sharp hemlines for the jacket. Effortlessly stylish, my fox shifter PA, rocking a pair of heels that gave her five-foot frame a substantial number of extra inches. Lyssa, meanwhile, looked adorably relaxed in the jeans and crop-top combo, a smidge of belly on display, the black jacket yanked down her shoulders.

"Right. Yeah. Should have guessed." Jocelyn then thrust her hand out for Lyssa, and, breath finally caught, my fated mate merely stared down at it, her neat brows furrowed as she fidgeted with her jacket cuffs.

"You're meant to shake it, Lyssa." I tipped my head to the side, biting back a grin. "It's a human greeting."

Teaching her how to be civilized would get old fast, but there was something stupidly charming about the way her cheeks flushed before she attacked Jocelyn's tiny hand with gusto. She grabbed hard, shook firmly, and maintained intense eye contact the entire time. My assistant's smile turned forced the longer it went on, and her tawny gaze darted my way, begging for help.

"Jocelyn is a fox shifter," I insisted, easing out from behind the monitor and rolling my chair along the massive glass desk. Usually I hated interruptions, especially during a rare bit of downtime, but my inner wolf zoomed around inside, driven by her rosy scent, and his enthusiasm was infectious. "She's my right hand at work... My number one lady."

Both women turned on me, Lyssa's confusion gritting into me through our faint bond like tacks on a corkboard, her lips ever so slightly parted to the point of distraction. Jocelyn, meanwhile, shot me a *What the fuck, dude?* look that made me clear my throat and backtrack.

"I mean, number one lady... professionally. Not, you know, in, uh..." *Fuck.* The explanation didn't seem to appease my fated mate, who had already demonstrated her short fuse when it came to other women, but just as a low growl rumbled in her chest, Jocelyn saved the day.

As usual.

"How can you be this *hot and* this *socially inept?"*

I'd heard the sentiment in one form or another over the years from that fox more times than I cared to admit.

"Don't fret, pet," my assistant drawled, bumping Lyssa with her hip. She then turned her snark on me, the twinkle in her eye pure fox sass. *"He* should be worried about *me* stealing you, honestly."

Lyssa blinked away a few shades of wolf-eye, suddenly looking very small and *very* out of place just over the threshold of my office. "Uh, okay?"

"Jocelyn strictly mates with females," I clarified. A sharp jerk of my chin in the general direction of the fox's smaller, messier kingdom outside had her slowly backing out the door. "Thank you, Jocelyn, that'll be all for now."

Her knowing smirk had my hackles up, but for all her teasing and button-poking, she always followed orders.

Rare in her kind.

"Have fun, kids."

Helpful as Jocelyn had been with Lyssa so far, offering advice and shouldering more of the professional burden the last few days with my head a total dumpster fire, I'd also been walking on eggshells around her, careful not to mention *fated mate* unprompted if I could help it.

She had one once.

A male fox from her clan near Sudbury, their fated connection sparking as kits. Best friends. Soulmates. High school sweethearts. Prom king and queen nominees.

A bear shifter killed him just before they finished the twelfth grade.

The fucker swept through their territory on a cleansing mission, his prejudice and hatred of *lesser* shifters rooted deep.

She survived.

Her fated didn't.

We met years later in Toronto just as I wrapped my business degree. Having only recently turned my back on the Quinn pack shitshow, I craved companionship. She needed distraction and purpose. I wanted to build an empire. She had been willing to work for pennies and a roof over her head.

We'd shared studio apartments and penthouses alike, until I finally gifted her a Redwood Grove luxury chalet once the village took off. She had stood by me through thick and thin, a true friend, a hard worker, a loyal PA, and I took care of her as best I could in return.

One day, the bear shifter who stole her forever would meet the business end of my fucking teeth.

For now, however, I had my own messy forever to sort out.

Lyssa flinched as soon as the door clicked shut, trapping us in a confined space together. Sure, the wall behind me was a solid block of window overlooking one of many village parks. Years ago, I had insisted the designer create a bright, airy workspace, drawing on Scandinavian aesthetics so that nothing felt cluttered. This was more my home than my *actual* house; it needed to be breathable.

But it was still just a room.

Me and her, alone.

Her scent *strong*. Roses. Not the sweet fake stuff used in perfumes and lotions, but roses as old as *time*, lush and rich, the sort Aphrodite might weave into her crown.

My inner wolf breathed deep, the *whoosh* followed by a growl and then a skull-splitting howl that rattled in my gritted teeth.

"Lyssa," I said tightly, battling the urge to stalk around my desk, hurl her to the ground, and fuck her raw. Mark her up with my teeth and my scent and my seed. I stayed put instead, forcing a smile as my vision sharpened, the wolf clawing his way to the surface. "Hi."

Swooping her wispy caramel flyaways behind her ears, her hair in a swishy ponytail today, she strolled closer—*too* close, given the swift and violent freefall of the animal in me I'd always been able to control. Denying females came easy before. Even if they were drop-dead gorgeous, really bendy, and great for my brand, I rarely went beyond kissing.

I mean, maybe the occasional blowjob. A screw every couple of months, both of us aware it meant nothing.

A wolf had needs.

But as she meandered toward my desk, taking in the walnut bookshelves, the black bar cart on wheels with its sharp edges next to the door, the two-seater couch and the glass coffee table and twin armchairs with no frills to my right, she damned me.

By doing fuck all, my fated mate had me wrapped around her *fucking* finger.

No. You can fight this.

You're better than this.

Squaring my shoulders, I threaded my hands together and nudged my half-eaten maki platter aside. "Look, I'm sorry I didn't take you home the other night." If she could stop nibbling her lower lip and taking everything in with wide, curious eyes, that would be fucking swell. "Things took a turn here, and I had all this new bullshit to deal with, and… it's been kind of hellish putting out the fires lately, you know?"

Of course she didn't know. This she-wolf lived with wolves; the corporate jungle meant nothing to her.

Just as it suddenly meant nothing to my wolf, who had been absolutely *raging* the more time we spent away from her. Plagued with heartburn whenever I chose work—stressful but familiar— instead of her, he fucked me over. Hard. Never mind that I needed to ensure the first big village event of the fall season went off without a hitch, especially after Soren's success this summer, but there were dozens of other investment businesses to check in on, plus general Redwood Grove shit to deal with at the hotel and nightclub I owned, the slopes my company managed, and all the other properties I landlorded over.

The world didn't stop spinning just because I'd found my fated mate.

Seriously, she had two other assholes to pick up the slack when I was busy, but apparently they were shitting the bed too lately.

Which was just… great.

Of course *I* had to fix the broken behind-the-scenes fuckery so this train didn't completely derail.

Story of my goddamn life.

She finally stopped her aimless wandering on the other side of my desk with its matte finish and exceptional organization. Every drawer had a purpose. Every pile a meaning. The only thing out of place was lunch, and I usually demolished that in two minutes flat.

Today, it lingered.

And caught the attention of a she-wolf.

Lyssa pointed to the six rolls at the edge of the plate. "What's that?"

"Unagi," I told her. Jocelyn always organized the rolls by my preference, transferring them from takeout containers to china dishware, the chopsticks my personal onyx pair. Eel was next on the list, and I'd eventually work my way around to the salmon special rolls at the end. "It's an eel roll. Would you like to—"

She stole a piece and popped it in her mouth before I could even get the offer out.

Lyssa stiffened, nostrils flared, and a blink later her eyes watered.

"Yeah," I said, slow and deliberate, watching her cheeks tint red again. "I like a lot of wasabi..."

Gagging, the she-wolf then had the audacity to spit the mouthful onto my hardwood floor.

"*Lyssa.*"

"Sorry," she muttered, head bowed—maybe in response to my snarl, more likely to hide the way she frantically rubbed her lips on her sleeve. "It hurt my mouth."

Whether she yielded to my no-nonsense tone or not, she seemed embarrassed, all the gusto of her arrival deflating like a pinpricked balloon. Okay. *Don't... push it.*

We had agreed to be patient with her. Teach her. Encourage her. Shape her into the alpha female Redwood Grove needed.

Lucian, Soren, and me—holed up in a group text chat, gossiping about her like teenagers. Fucking ridiculous.

"Here, let me get you something to drink."

I'd barely made it up and over to the hidden minifridge, designed to blend with the black cabinets around it, when the bar cart rattled, and I whirled around to find my fated mate—my classy, wild fated mate—chugging *bourbon* straight from the crystal decanter. She slogged back about eighty bucks' worth before she slammed the thing down and coughed, eyes watery again.

Wasabi to bourbon.

Interesting choice.

Eyebrows up, I crossed my arms and watched her struggle through the aftermath of her brilliant decision-making, then squatted in front of the minifridge and fished out a water.

"I understand it *looks* like root beer," I mused as I lobbed the unopened plastic bottle her way. Lyssa caught it one-handed, still coughing, and hurriedly cracked it open. "But it costs more than some people's monthly salary. Please don't... chug it."

She nodded and wiped at her eyes before guzzling the entire bottle in a single go.

Messy. Messy, messy, messy.

And still I wanted her.

Craved to run my nose along her inner thigh and taste her molten core.

Needed to bite and mark and fuck.

Ugh. Fated mates was such a fucking nightmare. Shifters spent years trying to master the beast within, and all that hard work shot straight to hell as soon as our soulmate entered the picture.

"This is a nice surprise, but I have a lot of work to do," I told her, trying to set firm boundaries for her *and* myself as I marched back to my desk. My inner wolf snarled when I planted my ass in the leather chair, heartburn prickling up my esophagus in seconds, but I plastered on a smile and ignored him. "Not to be rude, but is there a reason you're here? Is everything okay at the house?"

Is Soren being an oblivious dick again?

Barely recovered from the wasabi-bourbon incident, Lyssa gently recapped the decanter, then set the crystal bottle back on the tray with all its friends. She then mumbled something incoherent under her breath, so quiet and so muddled that even my keen hearing failed to catch a single word.

"What was that?"

"Big romantic gesture," she blurted, blushing as she threw her hands up and faced me. Her gaze flew around my office, snagging on the ten-foot window wall behind me, finally greyish blue again, her wolf probably licking her wounds deep within. "Like... Like in the movies."

Wait.

What?

Movies... Rosa had shared her plans for a girls' day yesterday; I guess they binged movies. Fair enough. Media was a simple way to introduce Lyssa to the modern world if she lacked experience. But —big romantic gesture?

"I thought I could show up here, looking pretty, makeup and hair and, you know, stuff, that you, uh, paid for the other night," Lyssa went on, rambling so fast I could barely keep up, "and you would be surprised and we could, I dunno, be... together, and..." With a huff, she folded her arms and stared at the floor. "I tried to look nice."

"Oh." No one had ever turned me to jelly before, but that babbling speech really took the wind out of my sails. I softened, feeling like the world's biggest asshole. "You *do* look nice."

Clearly she had put effort into her look, wearing a bit of mascara, her hair up, her outfit coordinated.

And she had done all that for *me*.

She and Rosa must have watched chick flicks; what else would plant the seed of sweeping romantic gestures into her head?

Here I was, grumbling and grousing about all the work on my plate, when my fated mate went out of her way to do something she thought I'd like. Surprise me at work. Show up around lunchtime looking cute.

And all I gave her in return was an awkward *You* do *look nice*.

Fuck.

Idiot.

Such an idiot. My wolf was right to roast me.

Jaw clenched, I shot up and rounded the desk, halving the distance between us—then forcefully planted my feet so that I didn't straight-up tackle her. I mean, she looked so disappointed and put out and defeated.

Not good.

Not *right*.

I ought to make it better, make it go away. I had no fucking idea how, but pouncing on her probably wasn't it.

"You're beautiful, Lyssa," I told her roughly. "You don't need to try."

She padded closer, eyebrows up in surprise, fingers at her sharp jawline. "Really?"

"Yeah." Now that the stylists had tamed some of the wild out of her, our girl had the build and beauty to walk world-renowned runways. Wasn't it obvious? I mean, there were *mirrors* at the main house, right? Our contractor hadn't left them out?

"I'm beautiful... even to you?"

What the fuck was that supposed to mean? Of course to me. If she peeked inside my stupid hulking caveman brain right now, she'd either run screaming in the opposite direction... or she'd be into it. "Uh, to me?"

"You look like that—" Lyssa motioned up and down my body, then to herself. "—and I look like... this. I just thought..."

Dangerously within reach, I went for her, but only to capture a few coarse wisps of her hair that had escaped her ponytail, snagging them between my thumb and finger, rubbing them thoughtfully. "Fate designed us for each other. I..." Not *I*. Apparently Lady Fate didn't think I deserved a mate all to myself. My inner wolf gave no reaction to the thought, but a low growl rumbled in my chest, still *pissed* that I had to share. "*We* think you're breathtaking."

Those gorgeous slate marbles plummeted to the ground as pink bloomed in her cheeks. Despite her adorable shy smile, I retreated, releasing her hair and folding my arms, eyes on the ceiling. *Fuck.* Shifters craved a mate all their lives, but no one ever told you just how much it screwed with you as a person. The beast in our chest—no problem. Apparently that soft fuck was a love at first sight guy, but that didn't vibe with the man. Sure, as a woman Lyssa was a stunning physical specimen. Modelesque face. Nice-sized tits. Hips bony but still wide enough to start our bloodline.

And she seemed willing to learn, adapt—more so than the rest of us, anyway.

But the physical wasn't enough for *me*.

Totally unfair to dump my bullshit baggage on her. What did I expect, that we'd be best friends and partners in crime after a couple of days? I'd barely seen her, and my wolf wouldn't let me forget it, claws out and ready to fuck up my lungs if I didn't play this right.

"I *am* sorry I haven't been around much," I admitted, heat gathering at the back of my neck—*shame*. I knew it was wrong... knew to feel guilty about it. Being away from her was torture, but burying my nose in work had numbed the pain for years. It would always be my go-to. "I'm... used to working all the time. It's just... force of habit, I guess."

Lyssa tipped her head to the side curiously, very puppyish in her expression. "Even when you have a pack?"

My jaw clenched, but I shoved down the sea of simmering rage. "The Quinn pack is literal garbage. Most of them are dead or in prison at this point." I softened only because the news seemed to upset her, my mate leaning away from me, her confusion and sadness and fear prickling in my gut like fingers tapping guitar strings. Not quite playing it yet—just testing the waters, teasing the tautness. "Sorry. *This* isn't the Quinn pack... It's my old one. I've been keeping busy to forget since I was a pup. I left my—" *Family.* They were my family, for better or for worse. I'd been destined to rule them, but who the fuck wanted to lord over ashes? "I left them, it, because they were... bad."

She licked her lips and nodded, sporting the same dense concentrated look Lucian did whenever *he* mulled over heavy shit. "Okay."

"I work to provide for my employees," I carried on, gaze flitting in the general direction of Jocelyn's desk outside. It wasn't just the fox shifter under my jurisdiction, but supers, shifters, and humans alike got their paycheck from Quinn Enterprises these days, and unlike my father and his father before him, I wouldn't fuck this up. My people's money was a guarantee, even if I had to go without. "And now, uh, I also work for my new pack."

For you.

Lucian and Soren could fend for themselves. Alphas and lone wolves, those two dicks didn't need my support.

But Lyssa…

She had nothing and no one.

This season, *my* season, needed to be the most profitable yet, especially if there were pups on the horizon. My bloodline deserved the best.

"Should I work?"

"Only if you want to," I told her with a shrug. As soon as those heirs rolled around, she'd be singing a different tune. People thought bears were maternal, but wolf moms would burn the world for their young.

At least, normal ones would.

Mine… drank. A lot.

"I don't know how to do anything," she admitted after a brief pause, as if that was news to me.

"That's okay." Right. Kind of unfair to assume she had zero skills. This she-wolf had survived in the wild for fuck only knew how long, which made her intelligent, resourceful, strong, and adaptable. Brave too, but we'd already seen proof of that. She was here, after all, facing this fated mate stuff head-on while the rest of us pretended it was business as usual. "We'll find your strength. You just need some time to figure out what you like."

Curious as I was about the wild wolves, I had already put a pin in that particular line of questioning; Soren told us it was a no-fly zone anyway. *Obviously* he had bulldozed straight into it with no tact, in true Soren form, expecting everyone to cater to his wants and needs. When she trusted us more, *I* would take the lead there, rooting out the truth so she wouldn't feel ambushed and immediately on the defensive.

For now, all this was really eating into my lunch hour.

"Lyssa, maybe we can table this for a later—"

I stilled with a sharp breath when she went for my tie. Just—out of nowhere, her fingers coiled around the strip of dark green silk. She used it like an anchor, stabilizing the rocky seas, then a fishing line, drawing her prey in.

Me. With the slightest of tugs, she prompted me forward.

And I went like a fucking whipped pup, her rosebud scent intoxicating, her touch curious.

"I like your outfit," she murmured with a sweeping study of my frame. I blinked down at her, at this she-wolf who had manipulated me physically with zero effort.

"Uh, I—what?" Seriously, it was just black slacks and a grey dress shirt, tie loose, sleeves jerked up to my elbows. My jacket hung over the back of my chair, worn only for meetings, and usually I kicked my shoes off for lunch. Still on today, the leather glossy and expensive. She... She liked *this*? This did it for her? "Thanks, I guess."

"I tried to dress nice for you," Lyssa remarked, perhaps without thinking, because a second later, she snapped her full lips together. Her cheeks then hollowed like she was biting at them, but her fingers stayed clamped around my tie despite embarrassment plucking at the paper-thin bond between us.

She had tried to look nice for me.

Showed up at my office during some downtime to surprise me.

Ugh. My inner wolf stamped his paws impatiently, like he was just *waiting* for me to finally feel shitty about my behavior. And I did, okay? I fucking *did*. She made all the effort, I made none.

No wonder Lady Fate thought I was unworthy of a mate all to myself.

She'd be miserable with just me.

"You don't have to do that," I blurted, voice cracking like a puberty-racked fuckwit. I swallowed hard and forced a tepid smile, drinking in her outfit with a nod. "I mean, yeah, you look great—you just don't have to dress a certain way for me. Not, er, unless you want to. I... I..."

I like you best when you're naked.

"Anyway." I swooped a hand over my hair, then nodded over my shoulder toward my desk. "I should get back to it."

She eased closer, her other hand suddenly leaping to my collar—stroking it, like the crisp edge and the soft fabric was a totally foreign concept. The second her finger grazed my Adam's apple, Lyssa did that fucking *thing* women do, catching their tempting lower lip between their teeth, only she paired that with a longing look that sliced clean through the control I'd spent decades mastering.

The rest of the Quinn pack gave in to the animal, let impulsivity and violence rule their lives.

I chose a different path.

But with Lyssa—the path blurred.

Fuck. I finally snapped. Snarling, I slammed my mouth to hers, scooping her into a feral kiss as she gasped. One hand clawed possessively at her lower back, yanking her against me, while the other fisted around the base of her ponytail and tipped her head back to deepen the kiss. Claim her *properly* and thoroughly, my fucking fated mate who belonged to two others.

But first and foremost—she belonged to *me*.

And she tasted like upscale bourbon.

Lyssa kissed as I'd expected: like she had been raised by wolves, all teeth and raw strength. No holds barred. No shame. The social constructs for women in my world—gone. She let me bend her over my arm, kiss her deep and rough, all while her nails, trimmed now but no less deadly, slashed at my clean-shaven cheeks, cut into my hair and down the nape of my neck.

But I fucked it up.

"*No.*"

Just like I always did.

I ripped away and put a few feet between us, not stopping until the backs of my thighs met my desk—not until I nearly plowed right through it, *needing* the space or I'd succumb to the beast again.

My wolf snarled, fire scorching up my windpipe.

Yeah, yeah, I get it.

What touched me more than that, however, was the shock tearing across Lyssa's features, followed by hurt and humiliation, their collective sting reverberating in my chest.

"Did I do something wrong?" she asked breathlessly, her words on the cusp of a wobble. Teeth bared, I slashed my hands through my hair again, then viciously shook my head.

"No, *no*—not at all." *Fuck's sake, you fucking coward.* "No, it's me, Lyssa." I stabbed at my chest to drive the point home, really knuckling into the bone. "I-I just like to know a woman better before... *this*."

Flushed and panting, a hand to her heaving chest, she took a step back. "Oh."

My wolf snarled, equally useless at reading the nuances of her faltering expression. His irritation melded with mine; we wanted to *know* our mate, read her with a single glance.

This was... confusing.

For everyone.

"You did nothing wrong," I reiterated, fists tightening at my sides as I battled to regain the control suddenly slipping like sand through my fingers. "Seriously. It's me. It's my issue."

"But don't you feel it?" Lyssa whispered, her hand smoothing up her throat, then down as if to rest over her feral heart. I tracked every move, every twitch, the hunter in me shaking off the dust.

"Feel what?" I growled back. Voice deeper, raspier, it took on a wolf's edge that caught her attention. She brightened, eyes alive again, all the confusion and insult fading away, excitement flickering like fireflies. I knew that look: it wasn't the first time I'd seen a wolf scent her prey—zero in on it, ready to take it down. *Checkmate.* "I've felt a lot in the last few days—"

"It's like an itch," Lyssa insisted, stressing the sentiment with a low, girlish whine as she tugged at her shirt. Then, without warning, she yanked her jacket off and tossed it aside, then fanned her swanlike throat, all graceful and long and beautiful and *fuck*. "When I'm around you three, there's this *itch* I can't *scratch*." She might have whined again, but the sound spilled from her lips so frustrated and needy, like she was in *heat*. Hell, maybe she was. "And then with Lucian, once we mated, the itch got better. It calmed down, and I don't understand—"

Wolf *right* at the surface, I stole her words with a hard, all-consuming kiss, the kind that made my mate stiffen—then *fight*, all teeth and claws again, all snarling she-wolf and ferocious goddess.

Yeah, I felt *it*. Of fucking course I felt it. If Lyssa was in heat, I'd been burning in hellfire from the moment I first set eyes on her. The fire had never touched me like this, scorched through my veins and exploded in my chest, but that was supposedly the way with fated mates: we couldn't help ourselves. The connection was instant, visceral and otherworldly, like Lady Fate had brushed her tender hands across our hearts and we were done. *Fucked*. Destined to mate and build a pack, a legacy, a bloodline.

But as good as she felt against me, as deeply as her scent called out to me—I still wasn't a fan of fate deciding who I slept with.

So. Fucking. Good.

But the logical, rational, calculating part of me switched off, my inner wolf locking it away. For now, I was a man at his base programming, desperate for flesh and fucking and *conquering*. Hoisting her onto her tiptoes, I marched my fated back, easily dominating her smaller frame no matter how fiercely her mouth tangled with mine, and I didn't stop until she slammed into the bar cart. With a snarl that Lyssa greedily devoured, I reached around her and shoved everything off—all the expensive crystal, the pricey liquor, the glittering diamond-studded tray crashing to the floor.

Spurring me on.

"I *feel* it," I hissed against her mouth as I scooped her onto the cleared cart, then roughly parted her thighs to accommodate for me. My fingers attacked her jeans rough enough that it was a wonder they didn't shred to ribbons, ripping at the button and yanking down the zipper. "I feel it every fucking second we're apart, but I try to control it." I nipped at her lower lip, the fire in my marrow gone nuclear when her neon blues, her she-wolf gaze, her *truest* self, snapped to mine—looked deep into my soul, challenging and daring and utterly fearless. Wrenching her jeans down her hips, I flashed my canines as I growled, "We have to control the beast, Lyssa."

"Why?" she shot back breathlessly, ripping at my tie until the knot loosened and the dark green silk fluttered to the ground.

Why?

I fumbled over the question.

No fucking idea why.

In the moment, it didn't make sense. *This* was how we ought to live, our wild sides *right* there, primal and powerful, ancient energy sizzling over our skin.

So, I answered with another snarl, then pulled back to fully rip those meddlesome jeans from her body. They soon joined my tie, followed swiftly by damp cotton panties that I resisted bunching up and shoving at my nose—breathing her in where her scent was *strongest*.

Because why waste time on that when I could have the real thing, the bush between her thighs the only part left wild after the salon trip.

And I wanted it.

Wanted *her*.

All of her.

Right. Fucking. *Now*.

"Wait." Lyssa planted her hands on my shoulders as I lunged, barely stopping me, her protest beckoning to the civilized man buried somewhere deep inside. I glowered into the neon as I sank to my knees, just a believer kneeling at his goddess's altar. A sharp quirk of my brow had her sputtering the rest. "I-I don't want you to be mad at me after. We can get to know each other more first—"

"Do you want me to stop?" I rasped, guiding her legs open by her calves, struck with a waft of musky roses, her center calling me home. Her slick folds glistened in the sunshine spilling through the windows behind me, practically a spotlight for what I craved most in the world right now.

But I waited.

Painful as it was, I held back and fucking *waited* for her to answer my question.

If she wanted me to stop… I wasn't sure I could, but I would put up a damn good fight.

Gripping the edge of the bar cart, Lyssa licked her lips and swallowed hard. Heat gathered between us, turning my office into a goddamn sauna, the silence only making it worse. Her pants slowed. Her eyes flickered between wolf and woman. I braced for the worst—

She shook her head.

"No. Don't stop."

Her whisper fell like thunder, and I attacked, a predator claiming his prey.

An alpha claiming his true mate.

I'd stood at this bar more times than I could count, drinking and ruminating and scheming—but never had I imagined wrenching my mate to its edge, tossing her legs over my shoulders, and devouring her molten core like a starving man. The rosebud scent lingered, yet she tasted like a sweet summer wine, something sparkly and light and deceptively intoxicating. Desperate for a proper taste after days of denial, I lacked finesse at first, my tongue sweeping in broad strokes, sampling all I could, committing Lyssa to memory.

Only when her whimpers and moans misted over me like spring showers did I find some tact—lick with *purpose*. Using my thumbs to part her luscious lips, I finally took my time and tested every inch of her, an ear out for when her breath snagged, when she keened, noting every time her hips bucked without her consent, body taking over and surrendering to pleasure.

Minutes passed between her thighs that felt like hours, breath scarce—not a single fuck given if she smothered me right here and now. I'd die happily between my mate's thighs.

All that time, she accepted my ravenous mouth so sweetly, so innocently, gasping and whimpering and moaning, rocking her hips ever so slightly.

When she came, my mate turned violent. Snarls echoed around my office as her pussy pulsed through a climax, dancing along the finger I'd used to stroke her inner walls right at the end, something extra to hurl her into the black. She tore at my hair, lashed out with her claws, her movements stilted and jerky and rough.

I'd never felt more fucking accomplished, honestly. Years of real estate success and financial gain paled in comparison to milking a vicious climax from my mate.

Smirking, I sat back on my heels and wiped her desire from my mouth. Cock so hard it hurt, I couldn't look away from her if I tried, Lyssa's eyes hooded and dark, her lips parted with every ragged breath, her chest dancing in uneven beats.

"How a-are you all so *good* at that?" she purred before letting her head fall back.

And good thing, too, or she would have witnessed the rage surge, jealousy roiling in my gut.

Right. Lucian had tasted her before me. Of course he would have gone down on her.

Fuck. I hated being second. Fucking *hated* it.

I shot to my feet, jaw set, heart determined, and Lyssa slowly straightened as my fingers flew down the buttons of my dress shirt.

"Oh, little she-wolf," I rumbled, ripping my shirt down my arms and hurling it aside. I then went for my belt, nowhere near gentle as I wrenched it open. "You should know..." I tugged my slacks down just enough so they wouldn't get in the way, then fisted my cock beneath my briefs. "I'm the fucking *best* at that."

Fear darted through her grey-blues just before I claimed her lips again. I kissed her deeply, tongue-fucking her mouth so that she tasted her own heady pleasure. Her thighs parted without prompting, beckoning me home as I stepped between them, her wetness staining my black briefs, soaking through to the bastard beneath who was officially captain of this ship. Snarling, I scooped her up and slammed her to the wall next to the bar cart. Lyssa grunted on impact, one arm thrown snugly around my neck, her other hand threaded deep in my hair.

Our eyes fluttered open together, lost in each other's gazes, then widened as I plunged into her. Fisting the base of my dick, I steered into her heat like I'd done it a hundred times before, sinking down to the hilt, filling her, stretching her, unable to tear myself away from her fucking *eyes* as she blinked hurriedly—then closed them, head back, mouth open, surrender in her moan.

Possession in my growl.

Desperate as I'd been to mate with her from the very start, I took my time. Sure, I'd fallen far from the composed CEO of Quinn Enterprises, a man who had his shit together no matter the circumstances, but I refused to turn this into mindless rutting just to appease *fate*. Steering her legs higher, I wordlessly urged her to lock her ankles behind my back. Before I indulged in my first deep thrust, I kissed her, caressed her high cheekbones, her sharp jawline, her delicate throat. We wiggled her out of her top and bra together, followed by my undershirt, and then I nuzzled into her neck.

Bathed in her scent.

Closed my eyes.

Moved as one.

I'd felt so frantic before, so out of control, that this should have been a rough-and-tumble fuckfest, Lyssa on all fours while I pounded her from behind. Yeah, that still sounded appealing as hell, but for now, this felt... right. A slow grind. Deep and intimate, sensual in a way I'd never experienced before. Just rocking together, her heels digging into my back, me never once withdrawing fully now that I had her.

It turned feral over time. Frenzied. From the way I eventually slammed her into the wall, fast and furious, the entire building must have known somewhere someone was getting his rocks off. But it wasn't like that. We couldn't help ourselves—couldn't maintain the sweet, steady pace, not when Lyssa flashed her teeth over my temple and my hands turned bruising on her thighs.

Alphas weren't flowers and sunshine.

We were savage.

Shifters at their prime.

Apex predators who took without question—I'd just never had another alpha match my ferocity. For her size, Lyssa gave as good as she got, and when she splintered apart in my arms, pussy shuddering over my cock, my name falling from her tongue like a hymn, she slashed me up *good*. Down my right bicep, she branded me with four brutal lines, the pain of her mating mark nudging me into oblivion without my fucking consent.

As pleasure tore through me, starting in my gut and exploding outward, I went for her neck—then her shoulder. Even blinded by bliss, my wolf howling, singing savagely to our mate, I knew better than to mark her somewhere so fucking *obvious*. Lucian had left her with a scar that required effort to hide, half on her neck, the rest at the crook of her shoulder. I clamped down further along her other shoulder, visible only when she was naked or in a tank. Spilling my seed inside her, I staked my claim on this she-wolf with a muted roar, the echoes reverberating between us—making the walls shake, the floor tremble, the earth quake.

Maybe not.

Maybe that was just how it felt in my soul to mark Lyssa.

When the world stilled, I licked the spilled blood away, marveling at my bite on her flesh. Her healing abilities had already kicked in to seal the wounds, now pink and waxy. If they disappeared in the next minute, the next day, the next month, she wasn't mine and she never had been—which meant I must have a brain tumor or some shit, because how I felt around this she-wolf wasn't normal.

It stayed, same as the slashes on my arm. The pain dulled to a throb, and as I eased away from her sweat-slick body for a proper look, I wished the agony lasted. I wanted to feel it, feel *her* on my skin for as long as I could. Of course, my body wouldn't allow that, but her mark soon matched mine, healed but not, forever carved in flesh, binding us as mates.

And you still know jack shit about her.

The thought came out of nowhere like a sledgehammer to the face. Frowning, I set a weak-kneed Lyssa back to the bar cart, then gently pulled my spent cock out of her and went for my crumpled shirt. A lukewarm calm flooded my veins, putting out the fire, quieting the storm.

Itch scratched, apparently.

Was this when the guilt set in? The uncertainty? Now that the beast was mollified, my wolf sleepy and spent and satisfied at fucking last, was it time for the man to take over again?

You know, and fuck everything up?

Regret. Doubt. Fear. Annoyingly human characteristics that affected all shifters, try as we might to deny it.

A sniffle cut off the impending spiral. My fingers slowed their rapid-fire buttoning as I glanced Lyssa's way—then fell limp at my sides when I realized she was fucking *crying*.

Crying and trying to hide it.

Shit.

Shit fucking shit *fuck*.

"Lyssa?"

She waved me off, head ducked so that if I only had human ears, maybe I would have missed this breakdown. Unfortunately, wolf ears heard *everything*, and as soon as the first glossy tear swelled and spilled, I was fucked. No turning back. Impossible to ignore a crying woman, but it was a billion times harder when she was your mate.

My heart stumbled into its next beat, tripping over itself and face-planting, splintering into painful little shards. The tortured howl of my inner wolf resonated in my molars, and I rushed to her side, half-dressed, my office stinking of sweat and sex, remnants of *us* smeared on the bar cart. She tried to keep me away, the hand planted on my arm strong and insistent, but I steamrolled her physical objections to crouch *right* in her space.

Doubt spread like a forest fire.

Had I been too rough?

All things considered, our first mating had been gentle and

passionate. It felt like fucking fireworks. Our bond had strengthened today, sure, evidenced by the way her haunting sorrow dripped down my spine suddenly, but in the heat of it all, I swore Lyssa had seemed… happy.

I mean, she came.

Hard.

Marked me.

But was I as fucking oblivious as Soren? As distant as Lucian?

"Are you going to leave me now?" Lyssa choked out, that horrible question followed by a hiccup and a gasping breath. My inner wolf finally shut the fuck up, switching from panicked howls to warning rumbles, reminding me not to screw this up.

"W-what?"

Awesome. So articulate and comforting. *Idiot*.

"Lucian hasn't come back," she told me as she finally, *finally*, lifted that waterlogged gaze to mine. Cheeks burning bright, Lyssa's emotional storm sprinkled through me, the sensation just a fraction of what had to be raging inside.

"Lucian hasn't…" My brows deepened, pleasure-addled brain slow on the uptake.

Oh my fucking *fuck*.

He mated and bailed.

That dumb fucking neanderthal British *hermit*—

"No, blue eyes," I whispered, sweeping the loose hair from her face, her ponytail sagging low, just as brutalized as her lips. The lower one wobbled, and I brushed my thumb across it with what I hoped—please, please, *please*—was a reassuring smile, something to make her feel secure in this mess we had made. "I'm not going anywhere."

The universe used that exact moment to fuck with me: my phone buzzed on my desk, always set to vibrate, as a call came through. We both stilled. My fingers twitched, used to answering on the first ring.

Lyssa's gaze fell.

My inner wolf growled.

And I stayed put.

Let it go to voicemail.

Just this once.

Lyssa looked up again with a small smile, and I perched on the bar cart, barely enough room for both of us, the wood groaning under our combined weight.

"Come here," I rumbled, gathering her spent body under my arm. While stiffer than I expected, my mate shuffled close, threw a leg over both of mine, and nestled her forehead into my throat. Bit awkward, but for a wolf who never cuddled after sex, it was a start. "Look, Lucian is…"

I closed my eyes, teeth gritted, pissed that, on principle alone, I now had to defend that dick to everyone outside our alpha trio. Unity, strength, and a healthy bloodline made a shifter pack, coven, or clan truly thrive, which meant I couldn't shit-talk Soren and Lucian to anyone but Soren and Lucian. Exhaling the frustration away, I peered down at Lyssa, lips brushing the top of her head with every word.

"He's more of a lone wolf than the rest of us. He patrols the territory. Does his own thing." Liked to carve weird shit out of driftwood in his shack. "I'm sure he's not doing anything to hurt you." I rolled my eyes. "But, you know, sorry he's being an asshole."

Lyssa nodded, then had the gall to slug back two full nostrils of snot—and wipe the rest on my shirt.

Gross.

"Uh, but I *do* have a lot of work to do today," I told her after a quick glance at the minimalist white-and-black wall clock hanging over my office door. It had no numbers, just the two hands, and ticked along soundlessly. According to said clock, my lunch hour was nearing its end—and no one gave a shit that I had my fated mate at work with me today. The show must *always* go on.

As Lyssa hardened to stone at my side and struggled to slip away, my inner wolf beyond unimpressed with me, I figured maybe the show needed an intermission every so often.

Yeah.

Just to keep it running smoothly.

"*But,*" I stressed, snagging her ponytail and gently tipping her head back. My mate stilled, her eyes swimming with rejection again. "How about you stay and, uh, hang out with me while I work?"

Lyssa sniffled, neck arched but taut, like she was straining against my touch. Her frown prompted a nod toward the couch.

"Over there." Her gaze slid in its direction. "I'll put a movie on my laptop—something you didn't watch with Rosa but maybe you still want to?" Against my better judgment, I let her ponytail slip its noose, and Lyssa slid off the bar cart, naked and looking thoroughly mated as she mulled over my offer, my mark prominent on her shoulder. "You can watch. I'll work. We'll be together. How does that sound?"

I'd never invited anyone to loiter in my space while I worked; she had no clue what that meant. Even Jocelyn got the boot if she wasn't crucial.

Lyssa twitched out of reach when I went for her tearstained cheek, wiping the wet away herself as she nodded.

"Okay."

"Okay." I stood and finished buttoning my shirt, purposefully ignoring the snot-smear near my armpit, and then scrunched up my sleeves. "Good."

Before I could delve into what movies she had already watched with Rosa, Lyssa's stomach roared.

Not just a rumble. Not a gurgle.

A straight-up, *I'm starving,* hangry bellow that echoed throughout the lands.

Her wide eyes snapped to mine, and, smirking, I crossed to my desk and stabbed the button on the intercom in the corner.

"Jocelyn, can you bring the takeout menu book in here?"

"Are you dressed?" the fox vixen drawled back, voice crackling through the speaker.

"Yes."

"Completely?"

As Lyssa tugged on her shirt out of the corner of my eye, I growled and leaned closer to the triangular speaker. "*Yes.*"

"Like, I refuse to ever see your dick again—"

"*Jocelyn.*" Fucking fox had walked in on me once without knocking as I got changed for a run. Not a wolf run—just a jog around the village, something I did regularly since the early days to both keep an eye on progress and make sure everyone saw my face. Redwood Grove might have a mayor, a city council, a municipal government, but unofficially, I called the shots.

And it was best they didn't forget it.

"Yes, Mr. Quinn, right away" was her chirpy sign-off before the faint hiss of her chair wheels rolling across the hardwood outside.

Fantastic.

Just what Lyssa needed to hear after mating.

I rounded on her, an apology raring to go, only to find her shimmying into her jeans, torn panties forgotten amidst the shattered crystal around the bar cart, bra somewhere, her nipples pointy and distracting through her shirt—and her savaged lips quirked.

Was she... *grinning?*

Humor?

Was that...?

Did she enjoy Jocelyn snarking at me through the intercom?

Thank fuck. I'd have a serious case of emotional whiplash if I had to deal with a crying mate and then a fuming, jealous, raging mate in the span of two minutes.

Rumpled and flushed, the she-wolf no longer felt like an invading presence in my personal space. Just like that, an emotional connection sparked. Our bond strengthened. Our connection sharpened. In time, we'd share feelings with ease, as natural as breathing. Fated mates were supposed to be effortless.

But as good as the sex had been, as beautiful as I found her, I still knew nothing about this wild creature who had spit half-chewed maki onto the floor. For the sake of our future, for the longevity of our bond, I needed more.

This was a good start though.

And I could finally stop imagining myself slitting Lucian from nose to tail now that I'd also left my mark.

Another earthshattering belly roar made her red like a cherry tomato.

"Hungry, blue eyes?" I rumbled, chuckling at her shy nod. "Yeah, me too. Let's get you *fed*."

With Redwood Grove's impressive selection of eateries, a good five hundred dollars' worth of takeout for us to feast on over the next few hours should suffice.

Because no matter how busy, distracted, and intense I would inevitably become during the upcoming fall and winter seasons, at the end of the day, whether we shared that deep emotional connection or not, only the best for *my* fated mate.

13

LUCIAN

As dusk stretched across the Redwood valley like a soft, shadowy blanket, I turned my back on the main house and trotted into the northeastern woods, headed for the mountain range without delay. Having sniffed the perimeter of the estate, plus the shoreline, the storage cabins, and the roadways leading up to our mate's home, I left knowing that not a single rival wolf had slipped into our territory and skulked around Lyssa. No strange scents. No markings besides those by my fellow alphas.

Nothing out of the ordinary.

All was well.

Lyssa was safe.

The same couldn't be said for our territory at large, and now that I'd secured my mate's den, it was on to the next issue, all the while breathing easier knowing she was—

Whump.

Deep beyond the tree line, a rock pelted me in the head.

Hard.

Shifted in wolf form, I staggered into a nearby birch, pain blooming behind my eyes, then snorted and huffed and shook my head. Whipped around with a snarl. The forest was quiet tonight, kissed by autumn and growing cooler by the day. Decay crept into the trees, the bushes, the brambles. Migratory flocks prepared for their journey south. Squirrels fattened up for the months ahead.

And some bastard had just thrown a bloody *rock* at me.

Scanning the sleepy landscape, I searched, searched, searched—until my narrowed gaze landed on the culprit.

My heart sang as Lyssa crashed between twin maples, naked, beautiful tits bouncing away. Having charged clear through a spiderweb, she slashed the whispery webbing from her hips, which I could have watched for *hours*, their sway hypnotic. With an eager whine, I pranced toward her, tail and ears up, hackles raised with interest, then stilled when I finally got a proper look at her face.

Oh.

Oh no.

Furious didn't even begin to describe that expression.

Fucking hell.

"Where have you *been?*" she shrieked, on the warpath and headed straight for me. Little feet and claws scrambled along branches and into burrows, the forest creatures I knew so well fleeing before this raging she-wolf.

Where had I been?

Here, there, and everywhere, frankly.

A miserable eight days and nights had dragged on since I last saw her—since I slipped away at dawn after marking my exquisite fated mate. All this time, I had been on patrol, in a perpetual loop around the territory. At peak anxiety, I pissed and scent-marked my way around the lake, mountains, and forest, even down to the barren southern stretches, determined to *scream* that any neighboring wolf twat who came near did so fully aware that this land belonged to another.

I had a mate to protect now.

For all I knew, she could already be carrying our pup.

Soren and Ewan were so busy with work that they rarely bothered, leaving the brunt of patrol duty on *my* shoulders. The Hawthorne pack to the east had clawed up a tree in our territory recently, a clear declaration of their intent to push in and stake claim. The Ashwood jokers to the south were rarely so bold, more like coyotes than wolves, but lately they'd pissed closer and closer to the dividing line between our territories, as if testing the waters.

None of that was okay.

The life of an alpha was a one of *war*. Conquest. Bloodshed. Violence. It always had been and always would be, even if we established a strong bloodline through the fuming she-wolf barreling my way. Soren and Ewan just didn't understand. They treated this like a game, both born to established packs with legacy bloodlines. Strength in numbers. Ancient roots. Aggressive ties to the land. Our territory was new, huge, and thriving.

Valuable.

Ripe for the plundering if we didn't remind nearby packs that all this land, this vast, sprawling, prosperous empire, belonged to *us*.

Those two were just pups about it.

Which left me to do the heavy lifting.

And had kept me apart from my mate for far, far too long.

Sensing the need for words, I swapped the wolf for the man. Heat billowing around me after the shift, the transition making every shifter burn bright, I held up my hands and backpedaled a few paces when she didn't slow.

"How... did I not scent you?" Given all I did was patrol and sniff and mark, I should have realized I'd picked up a tail. Lyssa's glare intensified from a boil to an inferno, and she stiffly swiped another rock.

"I stayed downwind!" She then hurled the stone at me, *barely* missing my right ear—perhaps on purpose, perhaps because I flinched just out of reach. My inner wolf whined, desperate to crawl on his belly back into her good graces, and when she finally stopped, Lyssa planted her hands on her hips and stared me down with the might of a true alpha. Chest heaving. Breath racing. Teeth bared. What were once bony hips now had a fullness to them, a week of consistent meals doing wonders, her ribs no longer so prominent. When she caught me scoping her figure, she maneuvered herself into my eyeline with a snarl, then jabbed an accusatory finger my way. "Why haven't you come back?"

"Please don't be cross with me." I softened my tone despite my wolf's hackles shooting up, this time indignant, not excited, that our mate was ripping us a new asshole. Very few held an alpha to the fire—not without serious consequences. Yet here she was, obliterating my defenses. "I've been patrolling our territory all this time—"

"I've been *alone*," she stressed, her voice cracking and my heart breaking. I schooled my features at her adorable little foot stomp, like a pup throwing a tantrum, and tried to focus—to not get distracted by her exquisite body, her tempting curves, her luscious form. After all, my mate was clearly distressed; she deserved to have her grievances heard. Lyssa speared both hands through her tamed hair, layered and rich like aged honey atop a chocolate spread, then crossed her arms, eyes suddenly glistening. "Soren and Ewan just work all the time, and when they check on me, it's like they're babysitting—making sure some dumb pup hasn't shoved a fork into an electrical socket, or whatever. And you..." Back was the rigid thrust of her finger, and despite the good ten feet between us, I swore I *felt* her stab the dead center of my chest. "*You*. I thought you were *better*. We're mated!"

While my mark still shone brilliantly against her olive skin, another of my fellow alphas had marked her in my absence as well. Crisp, clean lines on her flesh, a little way down her shoulder, easily hidden beneath a shirt. Rather matter-of-fact and to the point.

Probably Ewan.

All this time, I'd reasoned that the benefit of sharing a mate with two other alphas was so she would never be alone. Soren and Ewan rarely left the civilized parts of Redwood Grove, keeping to either the lake or the village. In theory, they could be around all the time. Sure, that meant their connections to our mate would flourish in my absence, strengthen and thicken and grow faster than the one Lyssa and I shared, but it was a sacrifice I had been willing to make to protect *all* of them.

They were supposed to *be* there for her.

But apparently not.

Fucking useless wankers.

"Lyssa," I started, forcing the frustration from my voice—because it wasn't meant for her, not by a long shot, "I just want to keep you safe."

"Packs keep each other safe," she snarled with a disappointed shake of her head. She then gestured to the landscape around us, to the blanket of fallen leaves at our feet. "But this isn't a pack. It's just... a bunch of wolves in one territory." Not wrong there. "And they work and sleep and eat, but there's no connection. No community. No *family*." My mate sucked down a shallow breath, her pain resonating in my chest like the last ripple of an echo. "It's an insult to call *this* a pack."

Her words carried a knockout punch. My wolf whimpered, both of us realizing what a huge mistake we'd made. These last eight days, he and I had both been *so* anxious, so vigilant, constantly on the move, exhausted but determined, protective mode on overdrive.

And for what?

To hurt her?

"You're right."

This wasn't a pack. Stealing our fated mate in the dead of night and dumping her in the heart of this new territory did *not* a pack make. Marking her meant nothing. Even fated mates without territories marked each other. It was just a symbol, akin to flashing a wedding band when some drunk hit on you at the bar. Sure, it was reaffirming and magical in its own right, one of the rare wounds in our long lives to ever leave a scar—but that wasn't the point.

"And I'm so *lonely*," Lyssa told me, almost like she hadn't heard my surrender. Her watery eyes darted about, every sniffle another dart to my heart, her hands trembling until she curled them to fists. "You three took me from my family, *my* pack. A *real* pack—we spent all our time together. We played and slept and hunted. We sang and grew and raised pups. And now I'm *alone*, and I hate it."

Wet spilled down her cheeks with the next blink, and I resisted the almost violent urge to tackle her and wipe the sorrow away, lick her clean—hold her. Make her feel so *good* again.

Lyssa took care of it herself with a growl, the heat sizzling under my skin through our fragile bond a stark reminder that this wasn't just sorrow. Tonight, *rage* drove her too, and we three bastards had no one to blame but ourselves.

"I *hate* this, Lucian." She rubbed her runny nose on her arm. "Ewan lives in his office, and Soren just works on his cabins. They leave me the basics and *go*. Rosa visits more than them, but she isn't pack. She isn't *family*. *We* are supposed to be." Her watery gaze soared to mine as she motioned between us, those orbs a startling bright blue, almost glowing in the descending dark, she and her wolf in this rant together. "Why didn't you come back?"

Because I'm afraid.

Fear and regret and a past full of blood drove my every action for more than a decade now.

And no one could know. If they knew, they'd pry.

If they knew, they'd question my ability to be the alpha I needed to be—for her, for Soren and Ewan, for our future children.

Say nothing.

I shook my bowed head, shoulders rounded, palms open— contrite, almost a little submissive here in the forest where no one else could see. After failing to swallow the bitter lump, I cleared my throat and choked out, "I'm sorry, Lyssa. I'm so sorry."

"Words mean *nothing*." Stung by her venom, I looked up sharply, and Lyssa gave me a chilling once-over, almost like she was deciding right here and now if I was even worthy of being her mate. "Action. That's what I want—"

Nodding, I turned on my heel and stalked off, mind officially made up.

"W-where are you going?" Her voice broke again, rejection and longing staining every syllable. *Nowhere, little mate.* I faced her, marching backward through woodland I knew every inch of, confident that I wouldn't fall.

That *we* wouldn't fall.

"To get my things," I remarked. A strange buoyancy coursed through me at the thought, resolve no longer feeling steely and cold, but bright and peaceful, like sunshine bathing a field of summer wildflowers. Unfortunately, as the physical distance mounted, my emotional shift struggled to reach her—barely even touched her, actually, given the way she crossed her arms and scowled.

"All of it." Not like I had much in the log cabin I built myself, alone and broken, all those years ago. It would take twenty, maybe thirty minutes to shove all my shit in boxes and bags and load them in the jeep. "I'm moving into *our* home—tonight. Now. You won't be alone anymore... Promise."

Maybe I could even take a few nights off just to spend time with her.

Do nothing but *be*.

Let Soren and Ewan shoulder the burden of patrolling our territory borders for fucking once.

Confusion twisted Lyssa's features for a moment, then lifted at her slow, cautious nod. Her defensive posture softened, arms falling to her sides. "Oh. Okay. Well, uh, *good*."

"I'll be home soon, little mate," I called, veering right to cut through the woods, around the village, and into *my* domain. "If I take longer than an hour, feel free to throw something bigger than a rock at me."

My wink and grin made her nipples pebble and her cheeks color, and then I was off, sprinting, shifting midstride into my wolf and tearing through the forest at full speed.

Determined, at long last, to finally come home.

14

SOREN

"Uh, pretty sure this was supposed to be my room."

I poked my head out of the cavernous walk-in closet, all the super-organized built-ins screaming *Ewan* loud and clear. At the moment, however, it was my crap filling the shelves, and I quickly shoved another balled-up sweater anywhere it would fit. Loitering in the bedroom doorway was the wolf who had designed the place, selecting a floor plan for his domain with lofty high-ceilings and a stonework hearth, along with this insane walk-in beside the ensuite.

Jaw clenched, Ewan glowered at me from the threshold, his suit clean and pressed, collar stiff, tie all the way up. The guy had no idea how to relax, and apparently the Redwood Grove Thanksgiving Market required him to look like a douchebag city CEO with a stick shoved so far up his ass you could probably see it when he talked.

A long black trench completed the ensemble, paired with a red wool scarf hung artfully over his broad shoulders—Jocelyn's handiwork, probably. Like wolves needed *scarves*, but the weekend had been unseasonably cool for humans, so it was cool for us too.

He was probably roasting under all those layers.

The thought made me smirk.

I strolled out of the walk-in, noting the suitcase at his feet, and shrugged. "Well, you snooze, you—"

"If you say *lose*," Ewan growled, jet-black hair swooped back like the soapy villain from a CW drama, "I'm going to punch you in the face."

Bring it. I flipped him off. He flashed his teeth, his sunset wolf eyes taking over, a snarl vibrating deep in his chest.

I mean, yeah, this technically *was* supposed to be Ewan's room. Mine was the basic suite down the hall; this one was closer to Lyssa, and none of us thought this stubborn wolf would ever leave the village. He had a chalet all to himself with a stunning mountain view, every appliance top-notch, every finish marble or, I dunno, solid gold. Of the three of us, I figured Ewan would be the forever holdout, refusing to move into the main house until we eventually forced him.

For the good of the pack, or something.

But here he was with a suitcase.

Color me surprised.

Still. He was the last to arrive, and he hadn't done a damn thing to claim the space besides being overly anal with the contractor about that closet, so whatever. I took it. *I* wanted to be closer to Lyssa. Lucian already had the room beside hers, so this was the next best thing.

Ewan had snoozed—fair's fair.

He just wasn't used to losing.

"You want something?" I said after I ducked back into the closet. Contrary to him, I'd scent-marked the pants off this space, my sheets already on the bed, my clothes stinking up the shelves here. My toiletries were unpacked in the bathroom, and I'd rubbed my scent glands over just about every square inch in my wolf form. This was *mine*. Wolves respected claimed territory—in theory. Ewan, however, lingered in the bedroom doorway, his scent crisp and sharp, earthy but with a hint of city, just like the man himself. "Don't you have some stupidly expensive wardrobe to unpack elsewhere?"

Silence greeted me, and I rolled my eyes before shoehorning my suitcase into one of the lower compartments, then stalked out to face him. A step *inside* my bedroom now, Ewan scanned the room with narrowed eyes and a tight jaw, its clench suggesting he was very aware that I'd staked my claim.

"Full house now," he remarked stiffly, zeroing in on the huge piles of books I still needed to organize and load into the—once again, this guy, just buy regular furniture—enormous built-ins on either side of the hearth. Arms crossed, I pursed my lips and nodded. While his presence always made me bristle, my inner wolf was a dopey shit who just wanted us both to shift so he could harass Ewan's wolf—who rarely put up with our antics for long but entertained them to a point. The man? Not so much.

"Yup. Gang's all here."

Sniffing, Ewan made a show of gracefully unbuttoning the clasps on his leather gloves, then removing them a finger at a time. "How did you know to show up?"

Shit. Yeah, he saw right through me.

Because I hadn't planned to move in yet either—not until we all agreed. But then my guys pointed out that they had seen a beat-up jeep in the driveway. With the Acker rental cabins prepped for the winter, my crew was about to get cut in half, and we'd been having a farewell barbeque at the lodge before I sent the seasonal guys on their way. One had spotted Lucian lugging boxes into the house, and it took all of two seconds for me to realize his game: once *again* he had jumped the gun and made a move on Lyssa before the rest of us.

No discussion.

No forethought. Just—boom. Moved in. We had all agreed to give our mate space to settle. She needed to decompress after leaving the wolves and the woods, but apparently a week was more than enough time. I'd wanted to be more involved, really dive into what made her tick, but anytime we were together, it felt like... hanging out with a stranger.

A stranger I was supposed to mark and make babies with.

Who I was supposed to share my alpha responsibilities with.

Who I was supposed to fall head over heels in *love* with.

And it just didn't feel like that yet. Sure, I still cooked her breakfast most days, but conversations were stilted and awkward and quiet. I had no idea what to talk to her about since pop culture references flew right over her head and we clearly had way different upbringings. She always looked at me like she *wanted* something, this bitter longing tickling our faint bond, but I had no clue what to make of that.

We got along fine waving to each other from opposite sides of the lake. She liked napping on the back deck in the afternoons, so as I'd prepped cabins for the last week, we still saw each other most of the time. Wave. Smile. Repeat.

But that was just getting sad.

"You think I don't know when my mate needs me?"

Ewan squinted at me for a beat, then scoffed. "Bullshit."

"Your assistant told you we moved in, didn't she?" Tit for tat, dick. Ewan maintained that suave air as he slipped his gloves in his trench's pockets, then squared off with me, shoulders back, wolf eyes blazing.

"No. She didn't."

My snort made his cheeks pink, annoyance prickling in the pack bond. Seriously, if that fox didn't manage his social calendar and force him outside every so often, Ewan would have grown roots at his desk by now. How *she* figured out that I had hauled all my junk over this afternoon, my own cabin now empty and dusty as hell, was beyond me, but she probably had feelers out all over the territory. Was it just *me* that tipped her off, or had the fox known about Lucian too?

Lucian who had repeatedly acted without discussing anything in our group chat.

Not the first time he'd pulled a stunt like that, but I hoped, for the sake of leading this pack with as little drama as possible, it was the last time he took me and Ewan by surprise.

For a wolf who rarely talked, the guy was good at making moves.

"Frankly, I'm surprised you're even here," I told Ewan after the silent glaring match got boring. "Don't you have a fair to lord over?"

"Thanksgiving Market," the black-haired alpha corrected tersely. "And that *fair* is raking in tourist dollars, you asshole."

I rolled my eyes. Big deal. This past summer had been my most successful yet; Ewan had a lot to live up to if he wanted to make even a fraction of the lake industry's net profit. Before I could fire that little tidbit back at him, Lucian's hulking figure materialized in the doorway out of nowhere, making both of us flinch. Silent but deadly, Dad had always dubbed him. Point taken.

"Where's Lyssa?" he demanded. Dressed in nothing but a pair of slouchy shorts, barefoot and bare-chested, scars out in the open tonight, he shouldered by Ewan into my space, his dark greens darting between us like *we* had the answers.

I motioned to my disheveled bedroom, books everywhere and bed only half-made. "Clearly not in here."

"In her room, I assumed," Ewan added when the biggest among us growled. Lucian scratched absently at his coarse beard, gaze sweeping the space like I'd been lying—maybe hiding her in my fancy new walk-in.

No one had come down to greet me when I'd rocked up to the house about an hour ago, which was fine: Lucian had been in the shower, and Lyssa's pine-fresh scent bathed every inch of the place. This was *her* home now, and we were just living in it. Given the time of day, I just assumed she was sprawled on the deck, soaking up the last of the afternoon sunshine in either her wolf or woman form. The plan was to sniff her out properly once I'd sort of unpacked.

"No," Lucian snarled, everything about him tight as he jabbed a finger in the general direction of her room. "She's not there. Not swimming in the lake. Not on the porch. Not on her usual trail in the woods."

"But—"

"I checked," he snapped, steamrolling my objection with a glare that would make Medusa proud. "She's *gone*."

"I'm sure you just didn't look right," Ewan insisted as he

wrenched off his scarf and tossed it on my messy bed, followed swiftly by that trench, his suit jacket, and his tie.

Didn't look right?

Was he for real?

Lucian was the best tracker among us. Best woodsman too, despite my childhood here at Redwood Lake. If he couldn't find her and he looked like *this*, pissed and concerned and, frankly, a little terrified, I had no reason to doubt him.

His mishmash of feeling suddenly pounded through our pack bond, confusing and conflicting, like hesitant nails on a chalkboard. The other two seemed to share a deeper connection, because Ewan suddenly snarled like he'd been poked with the business end of a cattle prod.

My wolf whined, then yipped sharply, demanding action— demanding I do something to make the unease churning in my gut go away. He ignored my flicker of jealousy over *them* being bonded deeper as alphas and me stuck on the outside, focused solely on our mate and her whereabouts.

Her well-being above all else.

That was how we'd survive this thing.

Tension radiated through the house as we peeled off to find her, searching high and low, even in the basement wine cellar with its tricky lock.

Nothing.

Eventually, all roads led back to her bedroom, and we huddled just outside the open door, wolf eyes bright, teeth flashing with every word, our voices guttural as all our beasts tried to claw their way out. *They* were better trackers, even with a shifter's keen sense of smell in human form. If we wanted to find her fast, the wolves needed to take over.

"What the hell?" I grumbled, yanking my sleeves up to my elbows, my long-sleeved grey sweater way, *way* too hot for this. "Didn't she want us here?"

"I wouldn't be surprised if she just left," Lucian rumbled back, massive shoulders filling the doorway, all that muscle blotting out the weird crystal chandelier thing Ewan had chosen to hang over the master suite's four-poster bed. "You wankers haven't given her *any* attention. She's waited long enough."

"Okay, calm down." Dramatic British dickweed. I held up a hand to settle the snarling alpha when he glowered my way. "You moved in last night. Chill. We're all as bad as each other."

"She came *crying* to me about how you bailed on her after mating," Ewan added, his wrath hissing along our bond, accented suddenly by a splash of the ol' green-eyed monster from me. Why didn't Lyssa confide in *me*? Why Ewan? The wolf didn't elaborate, fortunately, fixed on Lucian's jugular. "Where the fuck have *you* been?"

"On *patrol*," Lucian sneered, to which we both rolled our eyes. Of course. Lucian was *obsessed* with boundaries and borders. Sure, now was a critical time for our pack, the connection between us fragile, the territory massive for three wolves to defend by themselves, alphas or not. But there had always been enemies at our doors. For as long as I could remember, outsiders wanted Redwood Lake. They wanted to capitalize on its rich potential, which my family had done for decades.

So, yeah, other packs were a real threat, especially when ours was hanging by a thread, but it didn't require twenty-four-seven surveillance. We could handle those Ashwood wolves to the south with our eyes closed, and, from Dad's stories, the Hawthorne pack to the east were all bark and weak bites when it came to squaring off with anything stronger than humans. Seriously. Not a problem.

"Well, *I'm* working as much as I can so our kids grow up spoiled, happy, fat little trust fund babies," Ewan growled, unbuttoning his dress shirt cuffs, then jerking one sleeve up his muscular forearm. He turned on me as he worked the other, goading me, challenging me, daring me to take a swing when he drawled, "What's your excuse?"

"My work is just as important as yours." Seriously, this *guy*. Such a pretentious douchebag. "Just because I'm the closest to the house doesn't mean I'm solely responsible for watching her. We agreed that she needed to decompress—"

"She doesn't need to be monitored like a child," Lucian snapped.

"Well, apparently she does, because now we're *here*." Ewan threw his hands up, pacing side to side, one wall to the other, his caged fire sparking in all of us. We needed to run. Needed to let off steam, bond as alphas—as males who needed to set ego aside for the greater good.

Because right now, we sucked at it.

This was why I never organized social stuff for us. Growing up with a million sisters, it was nonstop action in the Acker territory. We always had friends from nearby towns crashing at our place, sleepovers frequent, boating trips standard, dozing under the stars around a bonfire just a regular Saturday night. Trips to the bar with fake IDs. Milkshakes at the coffee shop overlooking the water. Now that everyone but me had moved on, my parents retired, this place was a freakin' ghost town, and Ewan and Lucian weren't exactly the wolves to breathe life back into it. Both were hermits, no matter what Ewan said: one lived off the grid, the other in his office.

Anytime I attempted to change that, they dug their heels in and bared their teeth.

At some point, you just gotta walk away.

"Maybe she's with Rosa," I suggested, tempering my tone as best I could, hoping that might deflate the escalating tension. As wolves, packmates could calm a fight before it started with body language alone, emotions shared and felt deeper in our shifted form. As men, the nuance and subtleties really screwed us.

"Why is that *witch* more involved with our mate than we are?" Despite taking his frustration out on us, Lucian sounded just as disappointed with himself. I had no clue what he and Lyssa had done last night after he moved in, but since he lost her less than twenty-four hours later, it couldn't have been all that significant.

Probably movies.

She seemed to like movies.

I looked to Ewan for backup, only for my inner wolf to snarl and bark when I caught the asshole on his phone. Of course.

"Can you put your phone away?" I asked tightly, resisting the urge to yank the damn thing out of his hand and chuck it at the wall. Seriously, it was like those two had shared a womb.

"Fuck off. I'm texting Rosa."

"You should just *call*, you millennial prat," Lucian snarled. He then lunged for the phone, only to be met with Ewan's elbow, then shoulder, as the wolf shoved him back. Rubbing my crinkled forehead, I closed my eyes and let out what should have been a long, refreshing breath—but it did nothing. The tension stayed like a cancer, infecting our chances of bonding as alphas.

But, real talk, *this* was why I never asked either of them to hang out anymore.

We couldn't do anything, say anything, without starting a stupid fight over nothing.

How we were going to live in one house without mauling each other was beyond me.

The scuffle grew louder on the other side of my tightly clenched lids, the sounds of snarls and clacking teeth and bodies colliding with the walls rising alongside my frayed temper. Just as my eyes snapped open, frustration at a boil, all of me tight and my inner wolf pretending not to notice as the storm turned cataclysmic, a door slam echoed through the house.

Wham.

One solid crack of thunder that stilled all of us. Nothing rippled through our bond for a few precious seconds, like we were on reset mode, and then we were off. Tearing through the second-floor hallways, we sprinted for the landing, shoving and elbowing each other, fighting to get there *first*, to investigate *first*—to be the one to call the shots.

True alphas always charged into the fray ahead of their packs.

They set the tone.

They led by example.

And apparently three alphas had zero idea how to delegate,

because Ewan's elbow literally broke my nose when he flung it back. Pain exploded through my face as we all rounded the corner and trundled down the small set of steps to the staircase landing, but I managed to nail him with a dead leg, making him stumble and snarl while I overtook him, only Lucian between me—

Between me and whatever made the foyer *reek* of blood.

Lucian's massive frame stopped suddenly, and I plowed into his back, forcing the wolf down a few steps. Panting, I glared over his shoulder—and then zeroed in on what had made that horrendous *bang*, its shockwaves still crashing through the house.

There, just inside the front door, stood our mate.

Our bloody, naked, filthy mate, mud caked up her calves, glistening red in her tangled hair…

A dead moose at her feet.

A massive, full-grown adult male *moose*, the largest in our territory.

The second she spotted us gawking midway down the stairs, she lit up like Canada Day fireworks, eyes bright neon, her teeth a startling white, sharp canines apparent in her savage smile.

"Happy Thanksgiving!" Lyssa cried as she threw her arms up, then gestured down to what I could only assume was her kill like she was a presenter on *The Price is Right*.

Uh.

Uh.

My inner wolf yipped, the sound high-pitched and playful and way too grating for the bloody crime scene leaking across the foyer tile. Swallowing thickly, I peeked around Lucian to get a proper read on his expression, because our bond was just a screechy shell-shocked whine right now.

Yup, just as thrown as me.

A quick glance back showed Ewan staring with his jaw on the floor, lost for words—*finally*. At least someone here knew how to shut him up.

"All my mates are home," Lyssa said brightly as she lugged the enormous carcass inside by the antlers—that thing had to be pushing a thousand pounds, easy—and left a river of bright red blood in her wake. My wolf stilled at the flood of iron in the air, his interest making my mouth water.

Come on, man, focus.

Like we needed to get weird and wolfy *now*, when... *this* was happening.

After hauling her bloody friend deeper into the foyer, a panting Lyssa stepped back with a nod, dusting her hands off, and then beamed up at us on the stairs.

"All the more reason to celebrate, right? Everyone's here."

Her joy tickled my chest, faint and barely there, like a ghost toying with my ribs. Lucian exhaled sharply, probably because her emotions hit him harder, and Ewan had finally picked his jaw up and stuck it back in its perpetual clench.

"Is..." I licked my lips, voice hoarse, and pointed at the carcass. "Is that a moose?"

Lucian slowly looked back at me like he was worried I had a brain injury, and Ewan huffed at my back. I mean. *Duh* it was a moose, and despite the dick behind me breaking my nose—already healed, mind you, and more than a little bloody—I was well in control of my faculties.

But no one else was *talking*.

"I meant to go for that really old male I've seen around," Lyssa admitted, hands on her hips, breasts jiggling with every giddy breath, "but this guy kept charging me, and I was like... fine, I guess it's you today, buddy."

Lucian set the pace, padding downstairs with Ewan and me at his heels, all our wolf eyes out, beasts *right* there, spurred by the smell of a dead animal—by our mate covered in the blood of her kill.

"You... took him down alone?" Ewan managed, sounding both impressed and a little intimidated. Same, bro. Same. Lyssa shrugged as he crouched beside the moose's ginormous antlers.

"Uh, yeah."

The light in her eyes dwindled the longer the silence dragged on, her proud smile faltering, faltering, *gone* as three idiots just stared at the moose—at the huge aggressive asshole who had no issue charging wolves the same size as him whenever he saw us, who Lyssa had stalked, hunted, and killed all by herself. Like. That throat was lunch meat. Minimal suffering, maximum *dead*, our mate had *huntress* in her DNA.

She was so proud of herself—and slowly losing confidence with each passing second.

Say something.

Anything.

Actually, no.

Say something less stupid than what you said before.

"I'll get my skinning knife." Lucian saved the day, his posh English accent smooth as silk, all rumbly and deep in a way that made Lyssa blush. He then swept over and kissed her cheek, hard and assertive like it was the most natural thing in the world. My mate folded into him with a soft smile, lashes fluttering shut as if to relish the moment. To his credit, Lucian didn't grope her in front of us. His hands didn't wander. His teeth didn't drag across her skin down to her neck. He didn't make a show of his physical connection to her: just a kiss, then a murmured "Well done, little mate."

And there it was—intimacy.

My wolf whined, jealous for the first time in his whole derpy life, desperate to have what *they* had. Easy. Simple. A kiss on the cheek and a whispered compliment—leagues ahead of where Lyssa and I found ourselves.

I resisted the urge to junk-punch him as the alpha jogged by, taking the stairs three at a time, off to get his skinning knife. Ewan, meanwhile, remained crouched near the moose's head, admiring the fuzzy antlers, the tuft of light brown pelt, like he had never seen one before.

"Holy shit, Lyssa." He eased back on his heels with an incredulous laugh, missing the way she flinched at the curse word. "You... I'm so impressed." Ewan peered up at her in awe, eyes a coppery sunset. "I don't think I've ever taken down anything this big before."

"Once a city wolf, always a city wolf," I told him, the insult a gentle underhanded toss—because it felt easier, way more natural, to jab at Ewan than say how I *actually* felt about Lyssa's accomplishment. So, yeah, I'd just poke at him; better than standing here, blood weeping toward my bare feet, like a tongue-tied jagweed.

Ewan's eyes narrowed, and he offered a hint of teeth with his rumble, then hauled the carcass toward the door at the far end of the foyer, just under the landing. Since the weekend was a national holiday, my workers either home tonight for Thanksgiving or at the village for Redwood Grove's kind of pretentious Euro-inspired outdoor autumn market, it made sense to get the dead, bleeding body out of the house and onto the back deck. There, we could skin him, break everything down, and maybe *finally* put the firepit to use —roast us a haunch, or whatever.

Lyssa watched him go, arms crossed, expression unreadable. I breathed deep, her scent muddied by the moose, the blood, everything, and tried to tap into her emotions.

Nothing.

Just... a flicker of pride, our bond clearly the weakest of the bunch.

Awesome.

My inner wolf growled.

Yeah, yeah. No one to blame but myself.

Alone in the foyer, we glanced at each other, and Lyssa brushed the blood from her cheeks with both hands. On the cusp of another awkward conversation, I finally rolled my shoulders back and took charge—became the alpha mate she deserved.

The confident Acker alpha I had been all my life but somehow forgot about as soon as she appeared.

Sidestepping the blood puddles, I sidled up to her and draped her in a one-armed side hug. Not exactly the most romantic gesture, but maybe we just weren't there yet, no matter how crappy that made me feel. I tugged her close, hating the way her body tensed, and ran my nose across the ridge of her skull.

"This is amazing," I whispered. "You're incredible, Lyssa." When she eased away to blink those neon blues up at me, I grinned. "Seriously. I'd need a pack to take that thing down."

"I… wanted to feed my mates," she said with a frown. "That's what mates do, right?" Before I could answer—I mean, really, what the hell did I even know about being a fated mate?—she pressed on, more like she was rationalizing with herself than me. "The movies are all, dress sexy or walk around naked in front of your man, or, like, rent out a restaurant or bake a cake. I don't… I'm naked all the time anyway, and I'm not sexy." *Beg to differ.* "So, I just thought this was better." Lyssa fidgeted with her nails. "I've watched my alphas for years. They're just wolves, I know that now, but they're bonded. They hunt for each other—make sure their mate eats first. I thought, you know… Why not?"

"Yeah, you nailed it." *Smooth.* Suave as Lucian and confident as Ewan. My inner wolf huffed, then growled, super unimpressed with me. "I mean, uh, you did a great job—is what I mean." *Damn it. Talk like a normal guy and not a stammering teenager.* "Lyssa…" I stepped in front of her and crouched down to meet her eyeline, gathering both her hands together for a quick, affectionate squeeze. "This is *exactly* what fated mates do. They look after each other. And you just made sure we're all fed for, uh, at least the rest of the weekend." Four wolves, one moose? Yeah, it'd be gone by Monday. "Seriously, we're all so proud of you."

Her eyes shimmered with unshed tears, which made my inner wolf panic because neither of us knew if they were happy or sad tears. They caught the light of the crystal chandelier overhead, giving the neon blue an ethereal glow, and she suddenly sniffled, head tipped, then locked onto my gaze.

"Are you here to stay now? Not come and go—*stay?*"

I nodded fast, my inner wolf practically holding a knife to my throat. "Yeah, definitely. I think we all are."

Couldn't speak for Lucian and Ewan, of course, but I had a

feeling if one of us was here permanently, the rest would stay out of pure spite.

If we didn't kill each other first, Lyssa officially had three males in her home.

While the thought gave *me* anxiety sweats, her lips bloomed into the most breathtaking smile, and suddenly her hot, naked body slammed into mine. Shorter, slimmer, she still packed a punch with that hug, noosing me around my midsection and squeezing like she was giving the Heimlich.

I loved every second of it.

Until I noted the *two* bite marks on her shoulders.

My wolf faltered at that.

Jealousy reared its ugly head again, but I forced myself to stay in the present, to enjoy the happy little bubble she had created. Rage, upset, frustration—longing. So. Much. *Longing*. The bouncy, happy-go-lucky shit inside had been *waiting* for this moment, this hug, same as me, but as usual, human emotions had to ruin it.

But Lyssa didn't seem to notice.

And this was awesome pack bonding for *all* of us, Lucian's footsteps echoing upstairs, Ewan with the moose outside—me ready to season the crap out of that gamey meat once we got it all dissected. Sure, we'd squabble and argue, but Lyssa clearly wanted us all here.

This was *good*.

So, with a deep breath of her scent, I let it go. Tucked the jealousy aside. Pushed the frustration down. Reminded myself that it wasn't all about *me*—but us. *We*. We needed this to get stronger as a pack, so, whatever. Lucian and Ewan had marked her—*whatever*. My time was coming.

Our time was coming.

Right?

"Come on," I urged, retreating from her death grip—but then snagging her hand when the wounded look in her eyes came back. Our fingers twined together so naturally, and I led her toward the kitchen, serenaded by my inner wolf's victorious howl. "Let's check my recipe books—see if we can find some awesome spice rub for moose."

Lyssa nibbled her lower lip for a moment, her eyes a striking grey-blue again, her wolf gone, the woman back at the helm. She scrutinized me as she followed, her steps slow and cautious at first; then, with another dazzling smile, she too seemed to let it all go, bouncing along after me, practically skipping like a pup, naked and bloody and filthy…

And, in my humble opinion, really, really *happy*.

15

LYSSA

"Have fun with Rosa, little mate." Lucian swooped in, bringing with him an earthy masculine musk that made my toes curl in my boots and Kira *purr*. His firm kiss warmed my cheek, then my neck, then, just as goosebumps exploded from head to toe, my forehead. That was his pattern: cheek, neck, forehead—then a rough, biting claim of my mouth. I tipped my head back, eyes fluttering shut, totally prepared now after a few days of practice for what was to come. Lips parted, I allowed his tongue access to mine, only to immediately turn the tables, thrusting into his mouth, asserting *my* dominance over a wolf a head and a half taller than me and broad, thick, and strong as a mountain.

He growled, the sound rumbling in his chest like his jeep's engine, and I tore away when his arm snaked around my waist, crushing me against his naked figure.

Against taut muscle and sweeping planes and brutal scars. So many scars. Angry slashes that had hardened over the years, his past a mystery, his old wounds lingering—but not like the mark he had left on my shoulder. No, that stayed soft like normal skin. It tickled when I brushed it, same as Ewan's, and tugged at something delicious in my belly.

Lucian grimaced when any of us so much as glanced at the reminders of his old life. They hurt him. Our marks... did not. Not mine, at least.

"You can come too, you know," I mumbled, words smothered by his greedy mouth. Giggling, I finally planted my hands on his chest and shoved; the force would have sent a human flying, but Lucian just eased back with an arched brow and a dangerous twinkle in his eye. Chasing my breath, I nodded toward the Redwood Grove village. "She said it's fine."

With a huff and a low grumble, Lucian let go, then fixed my rumpled outfit, me fully dressed, him gloriously naked—risky, given how close we were to the road, the forest skimpier than usual in the October sunshine. Ground blanketed with fallen leaves, canopy open to a clear blue sky, it was the perfect day for a hike or a run.

I was destined for a boat of sushi instead.

Apparently. *Apparently*, they served big platters of those weird rice and raw fish rolls on boats, which made zero sense, but if it worked for Rosa, I was game to at least try.

"It's important for you to foster friendships outside of your mates," Lucian said gruffly as he smoothed the creases out of my black coat, grinning. "I'll be right here at two thirty to walk you home."

Even after all my mates had come home, the house noisier than usual, bustling with energies and scents and noises that made me and Kira *very* happy, Soren and Ewan still worked. They had full-time jobs that were vital to the success of the territory, and I might not like it, but those jobs mattered to them. So, I mean, I *guess* they mattered to me—and I *guess* I could put up with them being gone all day if it meant they came home every night. Of the two, Soren was the one who showed up for dinner lately; three days since the Thanksgiving weekend and Ewan was onto the next big project in the village, which kept him away until midnight sometimes.

Not great, but progress.

And Lucian only left to patrol if I had someone else to keep me company—*real* company, not just another body to exist with in the same space.

He had no idea how much that meant to me.

"Be safe out there," I told him, more out of habit than necessity. In the movies, women seemed to say that to their men before they trekked into the wilderness. My new territory was busier than any I had lived in before, with bears and mountain lions, moose and elk, foxes and badgers, rabbits and mice. Strange to find them so close to humans, but the richness of plant life—and therefore prey—must have made it worth the risk. Lucian planned to do a patrol sweep of a single mountain while I lunched with Rosa this afternoon, and from experience, the greatest wild predators out here were no match for a shifter.

I also figured he knew to steer clear of cursed Gull River, Rosa's warning popping into my head anytime I saw the mountains.

"I always am, little mate."

Largest of our fragile pack, Lucian was the least of my concerns when it came to safety. He was battle-tested; he wore it on his skin. A survivor, just like me. After stealing another fiery kiss, the kind that marked me just as deeply as his bite, my mate sauntered into the forest as I watched the sway of his perky backside. Back and forth. Bouncing taut butt cheeks—replaced with furry hindquarters when he shifted. Despite his size, Lucian's black fur melded with the shadows almost instantly, and he trotted into the wilderness without a backward glance.

Like he was confident in me.

Which… felt good.

Because he was less confident living with Soren and Ewan, and vice versa times two. No one had said as much, but besides the noise and energy and *life* in the house now, there was also tension. Most packs only had a single alpha male, so I wasn't surprised to watch three of them bicker and snap and bare their teeth over nothing.

But they were all my mates, so, really, they had to just get over it. Find a way to coexist—or I'd throw more than rocks at their thick skulls.

Hardly romance heroine behavior, but those ladies only had to deal with *one* soulmate. I had three, none of them human, and as the loneliness burrowed deeper into my bones last week, things needed to change. No more drawing inspiration from film: I went with my gut, letting instinct drive me as it always had in the wild.

And now my mates were home. Not exactly the most seductive of moves—throwing rocks and lecturing and hauling in a dead moose—but it *worked*. Our fated mate journey now included a full weekend of feasting on slow-cooked, fire-roasted moose meat; sunning on the back porch with Lucian, snoozing the afternoons away; swimming in the lake with Soren between video calls with his many, many sisters; and quiet evenings reading in the sunken living room with Ewan, him buried in work files, me trying to muddle through one of Soren's worn paperback thrillers. Then three days of normalcy after Thanksgiving.

A lifetime ahead.

Kind of daunting, actually.

For now, I tried not to think about that—*forever*—and focused on how having my mates in one place softened my tummy knots and made Kira bouncy and flirty, her good-mood vibrations infectious. So, even though I'd rather work on the connection between me and the alphas, Lucian was probably right.

I *should* have other friends.

I'd never really had friends before; not outside of a pack, not outside of the farmhouse—nothing. Once Rosa had heard about my horrific experience with Ewan's spicy rice roll eel thing, about how embarrassed I still felt, she offered to take me for lunch at an actual sushi restaurant, with a table reserved in the back, out of sight, where I could safely explore this weird food Ewan seemed to like without anyone judging me.

After tightening my ponytail, fixing what Lucian had ruined, I made a beeline for one of Redwood Grove's main roads, headed for the bike path paved alongside it. As soon as I stepped beyond the trees, however, I *swore* I heard my name.

In a woman's voice.

Again.

Whispered on the wind, it enveloped me, cradled me, beckoned me back to the forest. Kira snapped out of her lovey-dovey bubble just long enough to snarl and bare her teeth, and I whipped around, glaring through the trees for the source.

Nothing and no one. Just the trees, the fallen leaves, the squirrels and their bushy tails sprinting along branches to avoid a predator's gaze.

She didn't call me home this time, but every step I took toward the village felt like a challenge for the first little bit, like trudging through huge snowbanks on two legs. Arms crossed, head ducked, I bore down against the gale suddenly ripping down the road, swirling orange and red around me, screaming through the forest, slapping me in the face with bits of dust and debris.

Lyssa.

"Stop," I growled. No clue who that was directed at. I'd never heard voices before, not even as a priest stood at the end of my childhood bed and splashed me with holy water, my wrists and ankles in restraints. Never heard anyone inside my own head but Kira, and knowing now for sure she wasn't a demon, I liked to think I was sane.

Maybe just hungry.

Yeah.

My belly gurgled when the village stone walls came into view, then the open wrought-iron gates and the cobblestone streets inside. As soon as I crossed the threshold, the wind died down. *She* disappeared, my name no longer stuck on the breeze.

Weird.

But there was magic in Redwood Grove. Heck, I was officially becoming fast friends with a *witch*.

Maybe the forest called to everyone, or maybe it played favorites.

Lucky me.

Whatever the truth may be, I planned to keep my mouth *shut*:

Wild and all, my mates seemed to accept me. I couldn't risk some stupid voice ruining that. No way.

With plans to meet in front of Rosa's salon, I strolled through the adorable village at a steady clip, sticking to the high streets that were off-limits to cars, surrounded by luxury shops and upscale restaurants that meant nothing to me but, *ugh*, smelled delicious. Every so often, my reflection glinted out of the corner of my eye, caught in a shop window or metallic sign. Dressed in a pair of fitted jeans, a slouchy pink tee, and my black jacket, I looked... good.

Normal. Fewer awkward glances from humans when I wore clothes like this, though the leering men still made me bristle.

Hated the boots with the added heel. They weren't even that high, nothing compared to Rosa's scary shoes, but my calves *despised* them the second I stood up. Lucian had promised I'd adjust when I whined about it. We might have left the house as wolves, these very clothes in a pack strapped to my back, along with a handful of now pocketed cash for lunch, but he had helped me style things a little in the woods, artfully draping the relaxed-fit T-shirt, tucking it so that it hung right.

He did a good job there.

Maybe he was right about the boots.

Maybe—

I rounded the corner and spotted my new friend in front of her salon, as promised, her mane of flaming curls impossible to miss...

Just like the baby in her arms.

Oh?

Oh.

Oh!

Kira exploded inside me, frenzied, barking and pacing and desperate to get out so she could sniff that chubby little *darling* in Rosa's arms from top to bottom. Eyes wide, smile wider, I sprinted down the street, unfazed by the stares of nearby humans, and skidded to a graceless halt in front of them both. Swathed in a black wool tunic, Rosa flinched away, holding her pup protectively to her chest.

"Lyssa—"

"You brought your—" *Don't say pup.* "—baby!"

Rosa popped her dark sunglasses on her head, beaming, my squeaky squeal obviously not as offensive to her senses as it would have been to one of my kind.

"Lyssa, meet Aster Perry," the witch said, shifting her little bundle of absolute *joy* to her right hip, closer to me so that I got a true whiff of her scent. Honey and amber, just like her momma, with a splash of baby powder. Chubby cheeks pink in the fall chill. Smooth, probably *super*-soft red curls poked out from under her purple cap, and she had the most beautiful huge hazel eyes—a mix of her parents right there, Ethan's gaze brown and Rosa's that startling emerald. Dressed in a teal jumpsuit that was just *too* precious, her shoes the sweetest beige blobs I'd ever seen. Rosa tucked a curl away from her pup's forehead, looking absolutely smitten with the little one as she added, "Our sitter had a thing today, so I hope you don't mind—"

"She's *amazing*," I gushed, Kira's excitement vibrating in my words, the rest of me shivering with an intensity that made Rosa frown. "Can I hold her?"

The witch twisted away from me, lips opening and closing as she stammered—probably searching for a polite way to turn down a wolf seconds away from frothing at the mouth. Couldn't blame her there, but *ughhhh.*

"Please, please, please?" I held up my hands, fingers wide and weaponless. "I'll be so gentle." Aster's enormous eyes darted warily across my face. "I was the pack babysitter for all the new pups. I know how to be gentle with babies. Please, Rosa? Please, please, please?"

"Uh…" Rosa glanced at the tinted windows on the second level of the salon's brick building, probably way up to Ethan's office, then nodded. "Okay, sure. Just… be careful."

She passed her pup over slowly, not fully backing off until I had the little munchkin secure in both arms, both hands engaged. Aster weighed nothing, just like the actual pups I looked after while the others disappeared for a hunt. My alphas had trusted me with their offspring for nearly a decade, my first role in the fledging pack that of a caregiver and protector. My size kept larger predators at a safe distance, and I had the best eyesight of the bunch. I even taught the yearlings how to look after their baby brothers and sisters, harsher with them when they didn't take care. Whether they knew that or not, my alphas trusted me to keep the next generation safe.

A huge responsibility, one I had accepted and cherished.

Just as I imagined Rosa would give her life for this bundle of *sunshine*. Aster didn't seem sure what to make of me at first, stiff and silent as I readjusted my grip. Usually I cared for babies as Kira, used to holding precious puppies in my mouth. This was the same concept, just with my hands: don't squeeze too hard, and don't drop them on their head.

"Oh, what a little chubby *puppy* you are," I cooed once I had her where I wanted her, this teeny witch baby on my hip, my one arm around her back, the other supporting her squishy bum. As Rosa watched on, I took a big whiff, running my nose from Aster's wind-kissed cheek and up to her hair, reveling in a scent that said *friend* now.

Just as I was about to kiss her temple, the pup found my ponytail over my shoulder, grabbed on with a surprisingly firm grip, and *ripped*. My head jerked, more out of surprise than anything, and Rosa rushed forward, cheeks flushed, looking totally mortified.

"Aster, *no*." She reached over to pry her mischievous little one from my arms. "I'm so sorry… She just hit her six-month milestones, and that's unfortunately one of them."

"No, no, it's fine," I insisted, bouncing in place, distracting Aster with a silly face so that she loosened her tiny fist. "She's strong, but it doesn't hurt." My giggle made the tiny witch smile, and I used that distraction to tug my ponytail away, then toss it over my opposite shoulder out of reach. "Puppies bite too hard all the time, and we tell them off for it." I wrinkled my nose and went in close, my baby-talk voice the same I'd used on foster siblings a lifetime ago: stupid and squeaky enough that even Kira winced. "They just have to learn boundaries, don't they? Don't they?"

Aster huffed a spit bubble of approval, her adorable mouth quirked up.

"Yeah, I just wish she had worked up to pulling that hard. I swear she's torn chunks out of my scalp."

I looked her way as Rosa laughed, about to remind her that she had more than enough hair to spare, just like me—only to pause when I finally noticed the dark, shimmery eyeshadow over her lids. Still bouncing little Aster gently on my hip, I cocked my head to the side and frowned.

"I thought you said dark and heavy was a nighttime look?"

That wasn't a subtle face of makeup, her foundation blotting out her freckles, her eyes a smoky black with grey highlights. Below the huge black scarf that nudged right up to her chin, a stylish but thick wool tunic draped from her shoulders to her knees, fitted plaid trousers poking out the bottom meeting up with another set of sky-high heels.

Weren't we just going to lunch?

Rosa flushed bright red, even through all that face goop, and then let out a strangled laugh.

"Sometimes you just want to look fancy, you know?" the witch mused, staring dead into my eyes, her smile fractured.

Huh.

Weird.

"Sure." I nodded quickly. "I get it."

I didn't, but Rosa's fashion sense far outweighed mine. Even her diaper bag was a classy soft leather, looking more like ritzy luggage than a bag to haul baby stuff around in. Maybe it was a *thing*, dressing fancy for something as simple as lunch with a friend. Ignoring the hot flood of *You're still not good enough* curdling in my belly, I went back to Aster, kissing her little hand with a hum.

"Oh, I could just eat you up," I whispered, nipping at her cheek without an ounce of teeth while the pup squirmed and chuffed happily in my arms. "Om, nom, nom, *nom!*" Sensing how a mother might take that, I straightened, serious and focused on Rosa again as I said, "I won't. Never. Promise."

She chuckled weakly. "Lyssa, I didn't think—"

"I'll kill anyone who looks at her wrong, Rosa, I swear." I scowled at a pair of men strolling along the opposite side of the street. "I tore a moose's throat out last weekend. It'd be easy." Back came the baby voice as I booped Aster's adorable button nose. "Mommy's my new friend, which means I'll protect her young with my life. Won't I? *Won't* I, Aster? Yes." Her little huffs of *almost* laughter made my heart soar. "Yes, I will."

"Wow."

Oh, shoot. Was that too much? I chomped down on my lower lip to keep anything else from tumbling out in front of Rosa, who seemed taken aback.

"That…"

Oh no.

Had I finally ruined it for us?

"Thank you, Lyssa." A huge smile split the witch's face, and she laughed as she readjusted her sunglasses, shoving them deeper into the mess of wild red curls. "That's actually… really sweet. Aster doesn't know how lucky she is."

Ugh, I could have cried. Tears tickled the backs of my eyes, relief making my throat thick and tight, but I did my best to play it cool— to not let on just how much acceptance of any kind meant to me.

"Okay, back to Mama," I crooned. While I could cuddle this darling all day, we had a reservation—and Rosa probably wanted her pup back. I mean, *I* wouldn't be able to stomach more than a few minutes apart from *my* first offspring; I didn't want to be a hog, especially with a new mom.

As soon as I passed her over, however, Aster went straight for those big red curls, one hand tearing into them, the other tugging Rosa's scarf down. Before I could jump in to help, the witch whipped around and gave me her back, sorting Aster herself. Kira whined low, her concern blending with mine, a strangely protective urge swelling in my chest—one that didn't go away when Rosa faced me again, scarf firmly in place, hair out of Aster's wayward fists.

"Ready?" she asked somewhat breathlessly. Sunglasses down, smile like sunshine, she *looked* fine.

But I suddenly didn't *feel* fine.

Even with all these strangers milling around the village on a balmy autumn afternoon, the protective surge wasn't meant for Aster.

No, the sensation targeted Rosa.

And I had no idea *why*.

"Yeah. Bit nervous after that stuff burned my mouth so bad," I babbled, trying my best to ignore the feeling washing over me. "But ready to try something new!"

"Don't worry," Rosa said kindly as we strolled up the cobblestone road. "We'll keep the wasabi way out of reach. Like, four tables away if that's what you need."

Right. Sushi. Lunch. Friend. Conversation. Normalcy.

I tried to focus on that.

Not my name on the breeze again, a mournful cry that only I heard, a beckoning Kira responded to for the first time with a howl, not a snarl.

And definitely *not* my gut instinct, the very same that brought my mates home, suddenly screaming for me to grab Rosa and Aster...

And run.

16

LYSSA

I never swam for fun before. Always with a purpose: crossing a river or fishing in a stream. Battling bears for the salmon spoils. Quenching my thirst.

Here, in sleepy Redwood Grove, as the moon shone bright in the inky-black midnight sky, I swam for fun. Back and forth, round and round, deep dives to the squishy bottom. While officially too cold for humans to brave at this point in October, it was *just* right for a beast who burned like the sun—a wolf shifter who was thought to have a constant fever as a child. Nikki and Reed dragged me from doctor to doctor, demanding they find a cure for my scalding forehead.

Now I knew the truth.

Shifters ran hot.

Our bodies worked hard maintaining the animal within *and* our human sides. Eating seven plates of food in one sitting was normal because this body needed fuel. Not a weirdo. Not a freak. Not a pig. *Normal*. In the three weeks I had been with my fated mates, I missed my wolf pack something fierce, but at least I was normal for once in my life. With my own kind, I learned more about myself than I had

191

in years. Was it perfect? No. Did my mates wander? Always. Were we a real pack yet? No. Not in my opinion.

But it was a good start.

For the first time *ever*, I wasn't an oddball. I fit in. Even with Rosa, her hands full of magic and wonder, I wasn't an outsider.

And suddenly, a strange howl split the quiet night wide open.

Threatened to ruin *everything*—my belonging, my peace, my home.

Headed east in a lazy breaststroke, I stilled at the crisp melody rising above the forest, a howl straight to the full moon that made the hairs on the back of my neck rise along with it. Kira snorted, her intense focus slowing my heartbeat, narrowing my senses.

While we had spent more time together lately, I still didn't know the song of my mates. Sure, *I* had howled that first night. They knew my cry, glimpsed *my* soul. This could be them, but instinct said otherwise.

All three had left the house tonight with Soren and Ewan finally joining Lucian on a nighttime patrol of the territory. Usually my scarred mate did it alone, trotting the perimeter from dusk until dawn, always waiting for one of the others to come back to me before he left, always crawling home exhausted. Knowing tonight would be no different, I cornered Ewan and Soren in the kitchen and stressed how unfair it was that Lucian was the only one guarding our borders.

"Even the wolves take turns," I'd growled, glaring between them, hands on my hips. "Or are you both too chicken to patrol after dark?"

That had done it. If comparing them to wild wolves hadn't lit a spark under their butts, questioning their bravery unleashed a whole forest fire. So, for the first time, all of them had set out around eleven, headed in different directions to secure our territory. Lucian hadn't said a word about it, but from the look in his gorgeous greens, the thinning of his handsome mouth, the indignation shimmering from him to me, he wasn't thrilled to have company.

Probably thought he could handle it alone.

Typical alpha shifter: wild wolves recognized the value of teamwork.

So, while that lone howl could have belonged to one of mine, it didn't feel right. Pack howls stirred something beautiful in you; at least, that was how I always felt howling with *my* pack, connecting across vast distances, singing together to welcome home the hunting party, teaching the pups our chorus.

This song put me on edge.

And when three other unfamiliar melodies harmonized with it, I knew for a fact this wasn't my pack—not the old one, and not this messy new one.

Teeth gritted, I front-crawled for the rocky shoreline opposite Soren's empty lakefront rentals, headed in the general direction of this unwelcome song. Halfway there, a new choir burst into song, three distinct howls cutting across the night sky. North, west, and south, they rang out proud and true…

My mates.

Pausing, I hovered in place just to listen, chest suddenly so wonderfully full. My heart stirred at their harmony, soulful howls dominating our territory. Longing tore through me right then and there, this unquenchable *urge* to be near them forcing my limbs to *move*, to paddle hard for the shore. They might have been communicating with each other, coordinating an attack against the opposing choir, but this was a pack song, the first honest and *real* connection I sensed between the three.

Beautiful.

Haunting.

And for the first time—wild.

My mates were wild in their souls, and that feral side called to me, its intensity—its potential—knocking the wind from my lungs, making my knees buckle as I scrambled up the rocks. Kira answered them, eager and alpha in her own right, her howl bouncing around my skull. Choking me. Forcing me to the ground.

Forcing me to change.

But by the time she appeared, the night had gone quiet. No howls from either side. No critters in the trees. Not so much as an owl hoot. The valley held its breath, war on the horizon.

No.

Shaking out my fur, I dipped into a low bow, then rose to my full height in Kira's body, breathing deep, trying to scent the invaders.

Because that was what they were: *invaders.*

This was *our* territory.

No one threatens my home.

For the first time in my life, I belonged, and no strange wolf would ever take that from me.

I sprinted low and fast through a familiar forest, avoiding human trails and sticking to the underbrush. Thorns and leaves snagged on my pelt, but I briskly pushed east, pausing anytime the invading chorus started up again. Still only four voices.

I... could take four wolves.

Not four alphas, but what was the chance *every* shifter pack had multiple leaders? Ours seemed like an outlier since my mates sucked at working together. If it was normal, maybe they would have gotten along better, modeling *their* alphas' behavior after years of watchful study.

Eventually, I picked up Lucian's territorial markings: claw marks on tree trunks, his fur snagged on bushes, his urine *everywhere*. He had gone out of his way to declare *mine*; this wasn't a close call. If someone sauntered into our territory, they did so knowing it was claimed. My mate was a protector—he marked what belonged to him.

And that included me.

Way, way east, deep in the forest, I found where our territory ended. Lucian's marking was more often, almost every few feet— and then nothing. He had staked out the territory line, and eventually, I found the invaders about to cross it.

Four of them. Males. Smaller than my mates in their wolf forms, but still much larger than wild wolves. Shifters, *not* alphas, nosed at

Lucian's marks in a clearing. Two reddish-brown wolves. One white. One grey like me.

The grey one made the first move.

He crossed the border first. One paw, then another—then he pranced forward like he had every right to be here. In our territory. *Mine.*

For a time, I just watched them, safe in the shadows, downwind and silent. Forest floor cushioned my belly as I sheltered beneath the twisted branches of an old oak, eyes narrowed, body taut, back legs ready to rocket me forward when the moment was right.

The others hesitantly followed the grey wolf, one at a time, until all four crossed the territory line. Sniffed around. Pissed on a scraggly thornbush near a lightning-split birch. Yeah. Not happening here, guys.

They stilled at my growl, ears flicking my way before the rest of their bodies. Hackles up, I crawled out of the shadows, slow and deliberate, giving them one last chance to go before I ran them out.

Shifters weren't the only ones to purposefully cross territory lines. Lone wolves snuck into our pack lands all the time, and my adopted alpha parents had taught me *exactly* how to handle invaders.

Every fur stood on end as I stared the four down. One of the red males bolted immediately, scampering back into his territory, kicking up dirt and leaves he ran so fast. Another warning growl. The white wolf padded back to our border, whining, his head low and ears back. The grey wolf held his ground. *Dared* to growl back at me.

Nope.

I charged. Snarling and barking, teeth snapping and paws pounding, I bullied the remaining wolves across the territory line. Nipped at their back legs and tails, even tore fur if I could. But as soon as Lucian's scent disappeared, I stopped. Retreated. Backed up until it enveloped me again, soaked into my raised fur. Scattered in the trees, my rivals paused and peered back, almost surprised that I hadn't followed into what easily could have been an ambush.

Who knew, right?

Coyotes did it all the time—lured a wolf away from the pack, scampering and whining, looking like an easy meal, then right around the corner, *wham*. Fifteen of the jerks ready to tear the wolf limb from limb.

Standing tall and silent, I stared back. Unflinching. Unblinking. I was an *alpha* now; they were the ones who had to avert their gaze from *me*.

And they all did, one by one, eyes dropping, tails tucking, hackles lowering.

Let them remember I respected territory lines. *Stay out of mine, and I'll stay out of yours.*

They finally scampered into the shadows when my mates broke out in song again. Three distinct howls echoed through the forest, complementary and in perfect harmony. Closer this time, so close I swore their presence danced beneath my paws. Whipping around, I threw my head back and joined in, calling them to me, adding a high, sweet melody to their chorus of masculine cries. Kira had always been a beautiful singer, so much better than my attempts in human form, and tonight was no different. The landscape came alive as four howls met in the moonlit sky.

A pack song.

Our *first* pack song.

Oh.

This was how it felt to be whole.

Eyes closed, I sang into the night for as long as they did, all four of us eventually tapering off when we were close enough to scent. Lucian's oakwood from the west. Ewan like rosewood in its prime from the north. And Soren—he charged through the trees first, almost on top of me suddenly, bringing with him this rush of coziness, cinnamon and nutmeg and quiet breakfasts on a grey day. I sprang up, heart full, vocal cords tuned, and wagged my erect tail *hard* at the sight of his fluffy, bouncy black wolf form.

Amber eyes hastily snapped east, searching the territory line for the invaders, then landed on me again, burrowing deep inside, searching for the woman in the wolf.

He shifted back mid-stride, four paws to two legs in a flash, and it didn't even slow him down. My mate, the only one who hadn't marked me yet, soared to a statuesque man, broad and sun-kissed, dirty-blond hair in need of a good finger-combing. Muscular. *Strong.* Thighs like tree trunks and chest so sculpted it hurt. I whined, eager to touch and taste, and shifted back just as fast, both of us steaming, heat billowing from our skin.

"Lyssa," he breathed, stalking straight to me and grabbing me by the shoulders. Not to snuggle like Lucian. Not to throw down and devour like Ewan. Soren just held me at an arm's length, assessing every inch with clear blue eyes and a full frown that I wanted to kiss away. "What happened?"

"I…" We both glanced behind me as the sounds of a massive wolf crashing through the forest turned from a dull roar to *thunder.* Lucian barreled toward us a moment later, bursting from the shadows, scarred and grizzled, hackles up, the air suddenly crackly with his fear.

I… I felt that.

I felt *them.* Lucian and Ewan more than Soren, but somehow their emotions tickled in my belly and warmed in my chest. Whispered across my skin, sometimes even under it in my veins. Licked down my spine.

No one talked about it, but I assumed it was normal. All this time groping around in the dark, I had to just assume it was a fated mate thing—and if no one freaked out about it, I shouldn't either.

"Little mate," Lucian growled as soon as he shifted back, shouldering Soren aside so he could inspect me from top to bottom. All this touching and *no* kissing, no licking, no desperate heady greeting that Kira and I *both* desired. They should have been happy to see me here; I had defended our territory. We were safe. We were together. This was a *good* thing.

"What are you two doing?" I twisted my wrist out of Lucian's steely grip, then stepped back when Soren lunged for the dirt spattered up my thigh. Easily mistaken for a bruise, I guess, but we didn't bruise. I'd learned that the hard way a long time ago. "I'm fine."

Ewan was the last to turn up, arriving no less dramatically than Lucian at a full sprint and going so fast that he almost blew right by us. The enormous black wolf pivoted and charged back, shifting mid-stride just like Soren.

His anger exploded through me like I'd just stepped on a land mine.

"What are you *doing* here?" Ewan snarled, naked and panting, steaming, the heat of all this shifting crashing, colliding, swelling to fill the clearing. Moonlight caught the sharp angles of his formidable beauty, casting frightening shadows across his face, so much so that I scrambled backward—ready to fight but needing some space.

It didn't matter.

His fire still blazed under my skin.

Between my thighs.

Hot and wanting and *furious*.

"I-I heard strange wolf calls," I snapped back, arms crossed under my breasts, Kira just as unimpressed with all their reactions. Concern. Fear. Rage. We had just howled our first pack song; we ought to be in a huge pile on the ground right now *celebrating*. "I knew that it wasn't you three, so I came to investigate."

"That's not your job, little mate," Lucian said roughly. He sounded like he was scolding a puppy, but he looked away, jaw clenched so hard it flickered, when I glared into green eyes that were usually soft and warm.

"Alphas protect their pack and territory," I argued. My knowledge of the human world was severely lacking, sure. I didn't know much about fashion or sushi or Thanksgiving markets. I could read and write, but my vocabulary still needed time to come back to me after years of silence. Modern technology confused me. Soren's sisters intimidated me despite being so sweet and open, all because I met them through a really bright computer screen. Ewan's angelic beauty threw me. Lucian's scars haunted me.

Pop culture. Adult relationships. Friendship. Makeup. High heels. Toaster ovens. Can openers. Wine cellars. Barbeques. Cell phones with internet.

Not my *thing*. I'd been out of the game for years, and the odd solo trip into a human city or town or bar or library or *whatever* wasn't enough to make up for that.

But I knew how to be a wolf.

And wolves defended their land.

Period.

"You could have been ambushed," Ewan growled, words flying like gunfire—accusatory and harsh and a little patronizing, as if I hadn't *considered* the possibility. This devastatingly beautiful wolf had never even taken down a moose before; frankly, he had no right to lecture me about pack ambushes. "How many were there?"

I sucked in my cheeks for a moment, biting at them to keep from lashing out, then shrugged. "Four."

"Hawthorne pack, from the smell," Soren muttered, scanning the invisible line our rivals had crossed. Wordlessly, Lucian stalked over to the spot where that grey wolf had held his ground before I bullied him across the boundary. He crouched to investigate the claw marks in the forest floor, thigh muscles taut and flexed, shoulders rippling as he brushed over the scratchy lines.

Ewan, meanwhile, wasn't done with me, the weight of his glare tightening like a snare around my neck. "Lyssa, that was so reckless."

"So, hunting a moose is fine, but this—"

"You could have been *hurt*," my mate snarled, sounding—almost —like it would have been my fault if that happened. And you know what? Sure. It *would* have been my fault. I knew how to defend myself, and if I was stupid enough to get seriously hurt in a fight, I needed to rethink my abilities.

But the forest was the *only* place my confidence could stand on its own two feet.

"I'm fine." He didn't get to take that from me. At one point or another since they took me, all three had made me feel small and inferior. Unintentionally, I hoped, but that didn't matter. I hated feeling stupid with them, unable to contribute to conversations, totally lost around the high-tech kitchen appliances. But this? I could handle *this*. "I've chased off invaders before. It's not a big deal."

"Ewan, calm down," Soren barked when the black-haired alpha flashed his canines at me. I bared them right back. This wasn't the wolf who had comforted me when I bawled in his office. It wasn't the man who had marked my shoulder.

This *guy* was...

He was just...

He...

He was a *jerk*.

"No—" Ewan snarled the second Soren went for him, and as soon as the blond grabbed his arm, he whipped around and shoved him. The pair growled and snapped, their eyes similar shades of golden brown and coppery amber. Beautiful. Deadly. Even in this form, they knew just how to strike to make it hurt, pain warming in the meaty part of my right thigh when Soren's knee stabbed Ewan in the same place.

Lucian seemed used to the fighting at this point. Back to us, he crept along our territory's border, sniffing, dusting through the fallen foliage, tossing twigs and rocks this way and that. Trembling, I rounded on my squabbling mates, arms crossed and hip cocked, with Kira sighing irritably inside me, almost in an *ugh, males* kind of way that made my temper climb faster.

"I'm your *mate*," I shouted, slowing the brawl from a frenzy to a lazy shoving match. Ewan side-eyed me, still focused on Soren, still pushing at him, blood dribbling from what was once a split eyebrow, now fully healed. Sick of the display, I marched right in there and elbowed the pair apart, then glared Ewan down just as I'd done to Lucian that day in the forest. Standing my ground, hackles up, fury out in the open, had gotten my point across with *him*. "You're all alphas, but *I'm* an alpha too. I was protecting my territory."

"And what if they had the full pack here?"

Huh. Less inclined to submit to a raging female. *Good to know.* "Ewan..." I motioned to what I now knew to be Hawthorne pack territory. "I wouldn't have shown myself—"

"What if they found you anyway?" he snarled, towering over me, his distress and anger prickling in my palms like stinging nettles. "What if they attacked? What if they tore you to *fucking* pieces?"

Kira let out a noise somewhere between a whimper and a growl, unsure of how to react to *this*, to the furious avenging archangel in my face, his eyes wild and emotions unchecked. Swallowing hard, I held my ground, even when *fucking* triggered a surge of icy lightning in my veins, still conditioned years later to flinch at a word.

"Ewan, enough," Lucian rumbled, his voice impossibly deep and rough as he glowered over his shoulder. While the unspoken warning had Ewan backing up a little, he shook his head, eyes never once leaving mine.

"No, no, *not* enough." His anger hit my cheeks in puffs of hot, sharp air. "She has to understand this shit." Then, without warning, the alpha snatched my forearm and ripped me forward, our bodies crashing together. Desire throbbed low in my core, sprinkled with uncertainty and a fire of my own that sparked in his cheeks. "Do you understand how stupid this was? Lyssa, the Hawthorne pack is strong."

"I'm *stronger*," I growled, struggling to rip free from his hold. The alpha's cheek twitched, and his lip curled.

"You're not. This was reckless—and unnecessary." His fingers temporarily bruised my skin, making Kira grumble, her confusion clouding my thoughts, her neediness making me hot. Why was he *so* angry? Ewan's sunset gaze flicked in Lucian and Soren's directions. "We were coming to handle it."

"I—"

"*No.*" Finally he released me, then seemed to force himself not to prowl after as I stumbled backward. "With one stupid impulse decision, you could have cost three wolves their fated mate. *Forever.* Do you get that?"

I blinked up at him, shock extinguishing the flames in my heart. He… He had been scared to lose his fated mate? Did I really mean that much to him? I mean, *my* body responded to these three males as it had for no one in my life. My heart yearned for them when we were apart. My mind craved conversation and attention… Was it just as fierce for them?

Did he…

Did Ewan love—

"And where would our bloodline be then?" he snapped, his wolf eyes flashing brighter, more dangerous in the way they assessed me. "You think any of us want to mate with another female? Force ourselves for the sake of the pack? You think we want *anyone* else now that we've met you? You—are—*everything*, Lyssa."

My arms fell limp at my sides.

What… was he saying?

"*You* are the most important wolf here," Ewan snarled, "because through you, we claim this territory. It's tenuous now. We have to constantly defend it. But *you*—your pups… And to be so fucking… You risked all our futures tonight. You can't birth the next alpha if you're dead—"

Soren's fist met Ewan's jaw with a thunderous *crack*. The pair redirected their frustration and aggression onto each other, instantly shifting so they brawled as wolves this time, fur flying and teeth snapping. Growls and snarls became the new pack song, swiftly joined by Lucian in *his* wolf form, though from the way he handled himself, he seemed to be trying to break it up. Blood scented the air as he shoved his enormous body between the pair, but that only earned him a few vicious bites, which he returned in kind.

And I just stood there, watching.

Kira silent.

Ewan's words ringing in my ears.

My hot, hot ears. My numb fingers. My shaking knees.

My breaking heart.

He had been so angry... because I put the future of the pack at risk. That was the root of it. Not that I put *myself* in danger for me, but because of my womb.

Because if they lost me, they lost the opportunity to... make pups. Claim this land for good.

That was the main takeaway, right? I understood that correctly?

They don't want you.

I...

They just need a female.

No—

Why can't you do anything right?

Sniffling, I blinked back a flood of tears.

And left.

Marched into the woods, barely feeling the thorns rip into my bare calves, the branches catching on my shoulders and in my hair. Sometime later, Lucian's scent tickled my nostrils, his pounding paws closing in from behind, but I didn't stop. I shifted, let Kira free, had *her* call the shots while I retreated deep inside to nurse my aching heart.

Sprinted back to the house.

I desperately wanted to go south—find my old pack, start over with them wherever they had ended up.

Kira took me home.

I hated her for it, but as I locked myself in my room, shifted back with fiery rivers streaking down my cheeks, I knew I'd thank her in the morning.

There was always a fight in the movies. That one big blow-up between the hero and heroine. Before the credits rolled, they kissed and made up.

We...

We would all make up.

But not tonight.

Tonight, I slid down my door and sobbed into my hands, wishing we could just finally skip ahead to when it was *good*.

And all the while, Kira's mournful howls went unanswered.

17

SOREN

"You okay down there?"

Ugh. Stupid question, because *duh* she was okay. Lyssa might have been hiking the mountain barefoot, putting my lifetime of wilderness prowess to shame, but clearly she had been raised in this terrain.

And, really, I wasn't worried about her physically. She could probably handle what to others was a grueling off-the-beaten-path climb in her sleep. As always, I just needed a way to connect, to bridge the gap between me and the she-wolf who was supposed to be my fated mate.

My lover.

My best friend.

My soulmate.

All that had been modeled for me and more—yet we struggled. *Hard.*

Tiptoeing across a precarious ridge, I peeked over my shoulder and spotted her leaping from boulder to boulder to boulder, nimble and beautiful. Graceful. Lyssa was made for the wild, and we had cut her hair.

But we hadn't tamed her.

Not if last night was any indication.

When she glanced my way, she hoisted a thumbs-up before choosing her next step. The goal was to reach the top; getting there without using the man-made paths carved across the mountain range was just part of the challenge.

Thumbs-up.

All good.

Sure.

She was fine *here*, but she wasn't good.

Last night had messed her up, just like the rest of us.

Ewan hadn't come home after that stupid blow-up. If I had to hazard a guess, he slept in his office; it wouldn't be the first time. Had he been stupid enough to crawl up the front porch in the cold light of a new day, Lucian probably would have ripped him apart for the unending vitriol he hurled Lyssa's way after the territory breach.

That tirade was just so damn *unacceptable* it still made my skin crawl.

Made my inner wolf, usually so carefree and happy-go-lucky, ready to go to war.

But...

A part of me understood him.

Not that I would ever admit it. Not to Lucian and *definitely* not to our mate.

But we had all been alarmed to find her surrounded by Hawthorne pack pawprints, their scents obvious on our side of the territory divide. All three of us had heard the howls on patrol. Coordinated an attack with songs of our own. Rushed across miles to confront the invaders.

And found her.

Our mate.

Alone.

They could have torn her to pieces, just like Ewan said, and for the first time since we begrudgingly unified, our emotions coursed through the pack bond as a roar, not a whisper. Fear. Terror. Fury. Protectiveness surged between me, Ewan, and Lucian—even when we couldn't see each other. We just knew. From a distance, we sensed our mate walking a dangerous road, and that united us.

It had scared the shit out of me.

Lucian's anxiety battered the bond like a hurricane.

And Ewan…

Ewan lost it.

Waking up this morning, I had no clue how to make it better. With Lyssa holed up in her room, her misery scenting the air and smothering the whole house, I took the day off. Played hooky. Asked my distraught mate with her heavy eyes and sullen frown to go hiking with me. I figured some time away from the heart of our screwed-up pack would do her good. She could escape Ewan's scent in the house, but also explore what was once *his* territory.

Maybe get a feel for him, somehow.

See his wolf side in the slate and the stone, the trickling mountain streams and the cold natural beauty.

Lucian had said the plan was a good one—not in so many words, of course, answering more with grumbles and eyebrow raises, but that was just classic Lucian for you. Why say anything at all when a caveman grunt would do? When invited out by our mate, the English wolf declined with more elegance in his velvet timbre than I possessed in my entire body, citing his need for sleep.

Which was fair.

He *had* stayed up all night outside Lyssa's locked door, slumped against the opposite wall, watching, waiting, tense like the rest of us.

I barely slept either, but shifter genes made up for that, allowing us all to function two, maybe three days tops with no sleep at all. Lucian had played the part, but if push came to shove, he could have hiked this entire range twice today without batting an eye, never mind the single mountain Lyssa and I chose. It was almost like he had purposefully held back to give me and her some time alone.

Which…

Kind of made me feel like crap, but whatever.

We had all been living in the same house for nearly two weeks, and I *still* hadn't marked my mate. The wait was torture, but something inside promised it would be worth it. Work always put a dampener on courting plans anyway. I had no idea if she was having sex with the other two, but the house didn't *smell* like carnal depravity when I came home around suppertime, so... Who knew, really.

But our connection was the least developed. Lucian and Ewan already felt flickers of her emotion after a single mating, which left me on the outside looking in. Even with that, it seemed all of us, Lyssa included, wanted our bonds to be further along than they were, and that put the pack collectively in such a weird, frustrating spot.

Like, could we skip ahead to the fun stuff already?

You know, the deep, intense roots to this land and in each other? Communicating with a look. Feeling pleasure and pain no matter the distance between. *Connection.*

My parents said it took work, this fated mate business.

Well, the last three weeks had *definitely* been work, and I was the only one who hadn't really reaped the reward yet.

Not that this outing was...

You know.

We weren't here to bang on a mountaintop.

This was for her.

Her benefit.

Give *her* a chance to breathe and decompress after Ewan's super embarrassing and totally unnecessary freak-out.

Man, clocking him in the face had felt so awesome though. Just really *wailing* on him. I did it for Lyssa, first and foremost, but being able to shut him up with my fist...

Yeah. Awesome.

The brawl that followed? Less awesome. Lyssa had seemed annoyed with our fistfights from day one, but with three males all trying to be top dog, she'd need to put up with a few more before we settled things.

More than a few if Ewan didn't get his shit together.

With Lyssa on my trail yet blazing her own path up the

208

mountain, I scaled the last wall between me and a pit stop, fingers rooting out grooves, the climb fluid and brisk. By the time I reached the small outcropping at the top, I decided on a break. Nearly halfway up the slope, the distended ledge offered a spectacular view of the valley below. Heart beating a little harder than usual from the climb, I strolled right up to the edge, arms crossed, and surveyed our territory.

Redwood Grove was at its best in the fall.

A sea of reds and oranges, yellows and browns, stretched west into Lucian's old territory, then east into mine, curving around the misshapen sapphire lake I so loved, the water glistening and sun dappled. Straight down and a little to the west nestled the brick and cobblestone village Ewan had built up from nothing, once just a collection of shanty houses and a general store—now a thriving tourist attraction and retreat for the rich, famous, and politically savvy. Way, way, *way* south, beyond twisting freeways and the odd town or two, at the forgotten end of our territory, sat the barren wastes, a mesh of tundra and dying forest humans had tried and failed to pasteurize over the years. Mother Nature claimed it for herself with thorny brambles and twisting vines, poisonous weeds and steep drops into the earth.

Not habitable.

If wolves weren't so obsessed with territory, we probably would have just given it to the Ashwood pack clowns down there. But it was *ours*. Useless and ugly, even property investors didn't want it, offers for condo developments everywhere else constantly flooding Ewan's office over the years. They wanted to parcel off the western woods, expand the lake tourism industry to the east. Build into the mountains. Set up retreats of their own.

Nope.

Between my family, Ewan's company, and Lucian, we had bought every stitch of land in Redwood Grove. Now that we could really stake our claim in the shifter world with an established pack and bloodline, not a chance in hell we'd ever sell.

It was all too beautiful.

Too prosperous.

Mom swore trees she had only ever seen in Norway and Sweden flourished over here. Lie, truth, a bit of both—no clue. But anything you planted around the village thrived. This valley had the Midas touch, excluding the southern blip.

Shortly after I started my sweep of the territory from this new vantage point, Lyssa hauled herself onto the rocky platform. Misted in sweat, she looked as though she had gone for a jog around the village—not scaled half a mountain barefoot. Beneath the relentless afternoon sunshine, the nuances of color in her hair stood out. The streaks of light wispy blonde and warm bronze caramel. The rich undertones of dark chocolate. Milk chocolate. *All* the chocolates. She wore it wild and free today, those locks in need of a firm hand, a little tangled, a little wavy.

Perfect.

I preferred this look to high ponytails and tastefully tousled buns.

Tugging at her droopy baby blue tee, fanning herself as she meandered to the cliff's edge, Lyssa looked to the east. My wolf whimpered when we both realized those stunning silvery blues lifted higher than the lake—far-reaching, seeing beyond our territory and into Hawthorne pack lands.

Those wolves had been around since I was a kid. Lots of biker gangs in their territory. Violent. Aggressive. Rumors of criminal activity. My parents were the first line of defense against them, and they had held our territory borders for years. Now that Redwood Grove had overtaken whatever the hell they did for money in their collection of small towns and rural farmlands, the Hawthorne alpha had turned his sights here with earnest.

Last night, his minions tried to push in. Test the defenses of new alphas—unproven and green alphas at that.

And our she-wolf had sent them packing.

Still, from the way her breezy smile flatlined, her gaze darkened, her entire body tensed, last night's victory wasn't a happy memory. Not that I could blame her.

"Hey." I swiped at her, but she was too far down the ridge to make contact. My fingertips breezed by her elbow, the flash of heat between our bodies making her flinch. When she glanced my way—barely—I offered a crooked grin, because being genuine and serious usually made me ramble, and then I made things worse. "Look, sorry about last night."

Her brow arched, and she looked back to our rival's lands, to forests that thinned to fields and pastures—to secret pot farms that were never raided despite being out in the open. Another distressed whine from my inner wolf, and I cleared my throat, head bowed, searching for ways to make this right. She had spoken maybe ten words since I invited her on the hike, and most of them had been directed at Lucian. Dressed in a pair of black yoga leggings and a tee that while obviously too big for her still clung to her curves, stuck in place by the sweat, Lyssa looked gorgeous—and smelled fucking fantastic.

Her scent had turned musky on the hike. Thick. *Wild.*

And it took an embarrassing amount of effort to work around it —to focus on shit that had nothing to do with her body and her beauty and my insane need to plunge my teeth into her skin and make her *mine.*

"Ewan went too far," I told her, and she responded by hollowing her cheeks, offering me her sharp profile and nothing more. Still no words. Still upset. Fair enough. Swiping my hand through my hair, back and forth, I sighed and sat at the cliff's edge, legs dangling over a precarious fifty-foot drop.

One wrong move for a human hiker here meant broken legs, back, neck—everything. A straight plummet to jagged rocks scattered along the mountain's face, plunging into spiny thornbushes for an extra screw-you as you tumbled down, down, down.

A fun jump for a shifter. A challenge for a pup, an inconvenience for a seasoned wolf. When I spied Lyssa studying me out of the corner of my eye, I patted the smooth stone beside me, then waited. Eventually, after what felt like an eternity of tense consideration, she joined me. Seated about a foot away, she twined her legs at the ankles and leaned back on her palms, elbows jutted at an odd angle.

Huh. Double-jointed.

Learning new stuff every day.

"So, I'm not the guy's biggest fan," I started up again slowly, knowing what I had to do but dreading every word of it. On the last video call before their cruise finally docked in Dakar, Senegal, my parents had pushed for coexistence: peace and understanding so that our strengths complemented each other. Made us strong and unified. Yeah, yeah. Logical, sure, but practical? Not really.

Still, I had been *trying* to follow their advice, even when it was hard. Talking that asshole up to *our* mate after he royally dropped the ball? Damn near impossible. "Ewan Quinn can be arrogant and stuck-up. He's judgmental and pretentious. He's a workaholic and likes to lord it over the rest of us—but he's really successful, so obviously he's smart. His assistant thinks he's funny, and she's kind of normal, so take that for whatever it's worth."

I hesitated, fully aware of Lyssa's intense blues burning into my temple, like she hung on my every word. Right here, right now, I could ruin them. Ewan was already on thin ice with our mate, and I had enough anecdotal evidence to prove he was more asshole than wolf.

"But I've never seen him act like that before." I chose the high road instead. This territory needed strong alphas, and infighting would only give our circling rivals an edge. "He's not a raging wolf. He's not... Like, in my experience, he's a dick sometimes, yeah, but I don't think he's *mean*. Or cruel. Just... egotistical."

Ewan and I came to physical blows the most in our alpha trio, but outside of that, he read as calm and collected. Not in the same way that Lucian did, so grounded and wizened and damaged. Lucian oozed a serene energy most of the time, while Ewan was locked up tight, quiet and calculating in how he navigated the world. It made him good at business, but, given Lyssa's mood, *terrible* at relationships.

My mate ducked her chin to her chest, cheeks sunken again, and picked at her nails. Her nails that were too long again but none of us had the heart to tell her to cut them because we picked on her hygiene enough already. Yes, you need to shower daily. *Yes*, you need to floss. Haven't brushed your teeth but headed to bed? Back you go.

Trivial shit in the grand scheme of things, especially when shifter bodies looked after themselves, but they were good habits to make. Eyes closed, I sucked in another lungful of crisp autumn air, the breeze chilly this far up. Kind of regretting the shorts and T-shirt combo I threw on before we left, but I wasn't *cold*. Just marginally less comfortable than I could be.

Focus.

Shaking my head, I looked out to the horizon. "Lyssa, I think he flipped out like that… because he was scared to lose you."

Her head snapped up, and the scoff that followed had merit. Seriously, all that shit about pups and a bloodline…

It was a wonder she trusted any of us today.

"And I think he was scared to feel that way," I continued, "so he, uh, used that bloodline crap so he wouldn't be so vulnerable. We all felt the fear. He just—"

"Who are you, his PR guy?"

My inner wolf huffed and snorted, thrilled to hear her voice again, and I found the she-wolf smirking. Was that… a joke?

Sarcasm?

Nice. Her lips twitched into an even wider grin, and we both chuckled as we took in the valley below.

"I get what you're saying," she insisted, straightening and throwing her head back as a stronger breeze rolled through. It toyed with her hair, made her smile brighter and more natural, but when it died down, the seriousness crept back into her voice, her words rougher, lower, her wolf speaking with her as she said, "But Ewan can tell me all this himself. That's what I want."

"Fair enough." Officially off the hook for fixing *his* mess, I brought one leg up and hooked my arm around my knee, lost in the abstract autumn canvas below. Above, the sun beat down, the sky clear, the winds *there* but not as violent as they could be at this altitude. For a little while, my mind just went blank, surrendering to the moment, to feeling instead of thinking. Unfortunately, that left me unprepared for the thought that sparked when Lyssa shuffled closer, using me to block the next billowing gust.

"Lyssa?"

"Hmm?"

"I'm sorry we're not better fated mates."

Ugh, come on. Brain—mouth. Get it together.

Frowning, Lyssa tucked her windswept hair behind her ears. "What?"

Shit. Yeah, that definitely wasn't a *What?* like she hadn't heard me, but a *What nonsense just came out of your mouth?* kind of thing that you couldn't go back on even if you tried. The kind of *What?* that spelled trouble from a she-wolf if you answered wrong.

"We fight all the time." Might as well just be honest. No taking it back: we kind of sucked as fated mates. Meeting the bare minimum of food and shelter might work for actual wolves, but my parents would slay me if they knew what had gone on the last few weeks. "And we left you alone for ages, thinking that's what you needed. It must have been..." I swallowed hard, my wolf whining, slowly deflating inside at the thought. "It must have been really lonely."

Lyssa scrutinized me for a long, *long* while, nostrils flared like she was trying to sniff out the deception. After Ewan's freak-out, I didn't blame her, but it was literal torture to just sit here and wait.

"It was," she said at long last, gaze cast out to the horizon. Cobalt blue turned near transparent under the relentless sunshine, her eyes watery against the sheen and the wind—and maybe the memory. "I was lonely... and I didn't like it."

"We—"

"Someone left me alone for *good* once," my mate pressed on, and I swallowed all the excuses. They didn't matter anymore. We had hurt her. She had a right to express that without being fed bullshit like that would soften the blow. Finally, her gaze fell to her lap, to her fingers twisting together, to white knuckles that made my heart ache. "I need to know you're all coming back."

Obviously this fear had something to do with the wolves. Someone had abandoned her—then the wolves found her. Or someone had thrown her to the wolves. *Something.* As desperate as I was—as we all were—to push for answers, I let it go.

For now.

Ewan had already lectured me about being subtle.

Some people have actual *wounds on their souls. Don't pick the scabs with a dull butterknife.*

Classic Ewan, reminding me via text that not only had I led a pampered, sheltered, carefree life, but I lacked tact.

And then last night...

Heh.

So much for subtlety.

"Lyssa, we—"

"I know wolves wander," she insisted hurriedly, almost frantically—like she was worried she had said too much or blurted the wrong thing, and now she had to backtrack and make it right. "I do too. I want to roam the territory like *my* alphas..." Her throat rippled through a gulp, cheeks suddenly pink from more than just the wind. "I just need to be secure that you're coming back. That you... want me." What? Want her? Of course I— "Not because of a bloodline, but—"

"We do." I smothered her tangled hands, stilling their frantic movements, waiting until her eyes met mine to speak again. She required a lot of patience, my fated mate, but maybe that was good for me. Good for all of us. Eventually, her gaze darted up, then fell, then back again, and I bit my tongue until they made themselves at home. "*I* do—if that's any comfort."

Her cheeks hollowed again but fattened out a beat later, a tender smile playing across her lips.

"And, look." I angled toward her, tunnel-visioned on her face, her perfect mouth and sharp jaw and high cheekbones. "Pups are a given. We're all mating, you're not on birth control..." Doubt a

215

condom had ever crossed Lucian and Ewan's beast-driven brains when they had her, anyway. "Pups will come, but what I need you to hear is that we could lose this territory tomorrow." I nodded when her eyebrows shot up. "Yeah, it could happen. Life is unpredictable. I'm sure you know that better than the rest of us. We could end up halfway across the country, or, ugh, in some city." Worst nightmare: city life. "So long as I have my fated mate, *that's* all that matters."

She frowned at our clasped hands. "Really?"

"Yeah. Promise."

"You..."

Please hear the sincerity in my voice. We might not know each other well enough to detect the minute inflections, but I had meant every word—and if we had the freakin' pack and mate bond already, she would get that without question. Until then, we were stuck in the dark like humans, forced to rely on tone and expression, on body language and circumstance, and that drove me *nuts*.

Lyssa took a soft breath, eyes closed, and then withdrew from my grasp. I retreated as well despite wanting to smooth my hand across her thighs—venture up, too, so that my touch imprinted on her body, same as the others.

"You don't seem to want me like they do."

Uh.

Okay.

My brain short-circuited, and I put it in a forced reboot before the damn thing fried. Even my inner wolf had no idea what to make of that comment.

"W-what?"

Nice. Elegant as always.

"The pull is there," Lyssa insisted, nothing about her overtly cruel. Still, every word landed like a dagger to the heart, her narrowed gaze sweeping across my face, assessing me again. "The itch is there when I'm with you, but it's like there's a... block. Like we don't know how to be when we're alone."

"I..." The high-pitched siren ripping through my skull joined my wolf's panicked whines, and I shoved a finger in my ear, wriggled it around, and then shook my head. Heart hammering, I glared into the clear blue sky, wondering for the first time if Lady Fate was kind of a sadist. "I *want* you, Lyssa. I was just raised by a strong matriarch and have a bunch of little sisters who I would go to war for..." If some douchebag got up in their faces *expecting* them to spread their legs—with or without their consent—I'd beat him bloody, no questions asked, and then feed him to *real* wolves. "I-I'm trying to be respectful."

Warmth whumped in my chest, unfurling like wildflower petals at the first glint of morning sunshine. Unfamiliar, that sensation— like it didn't belong to me. I risked a glance to my left and found Lyssa flushed and grinning, her head bowed, her private feelings out in the open.

And blooming in me.

The heat dipped into my gut, stronger now, relief sweeping through and taking control.

Right. Not as crappy at this relationship stuff as I'd thought. Cool. Cool, cool, cool.

"I'm just trying to figure out how I feel," I told her, taking in the patchwork blanket of autumn color below. "It isn't just, uh, the wolf that drives this thing."

"I know," she murmured, fidgeting with her fingers again. The flicker of her emotion was just that—a flicker, a dancing flame snuffed out by the wind. Back to reading body language and tone, I guess.

"My parents are fated mates and best friends. They do everything together." They were everything I aspired to be. "That's what I always imagined in a mate."

"And I'm not like them?"

"No." *Shit.* I pulled my focus off the fall canopy and back to her, to her slightly wounded expression and her lower lip snagged between sharp white teeth. "It's not that. We just... Everything happened so fast. Me and the guys barely know how to coexist as alphas in one territory, and then throw in this strong, confident, capable, beautiful she-wolf who is *all our mate*, and we're a mess."

The other two would never admit it, but we had been a mess from the start. Lyssa just shoved us deeper into the red, feelings and dynamics and mating all twining into quicksand—dragging this pack under.

"I... I'm a mess. And I'm sorry." I offered a one-shouldered shrug. "I wish I wasn't, but here we are."

Rather than folding in on herself, buried under the reality of dysfunctional mates and a disjointed pack, Lyssa smirked and swatted playfully at my thigh. "I wish I knew how to use the coffee maker, but here we are."

My inner wolf brightened, and I sat taller suddenly; that was *just* the response I'd needed.

"Woman," I said through a long, dramatic bellow, which made her giggle, "I have showed you how to work that thing like eight times."

"Ugh, I *know*." Lyssa buried her face in her hands with a groan, one that quickly descended into giggles when she peeked up at me. I nudged her with my elbow, chuckling, *beaming*, and she kicked my foot.

And there was the warmth again, burning just a smidge brighter right in the center of my chest.

My inner wolf howled as our mate looked out to the valley, her profile stunning, her laughter music to my ears.

To my heart.

With some of the heavy stuff out of the way, I tried to segue into lighter topics—like just how much I loved fall. Sure, it meant we were back at school as kids, but I had so many fond memories of the season, of the cooldown after an action-packed summer on the lake. Bonfires in the moonlight. Diving into leaf piles. Corn mazes and tractor rides out to the pumpkin patch. Playing for hours with my sisters in a barn converted into a hay-stacked playground. Carving stupid faces into pumpkins.

Man, I had a million stories that might make her feel more at home here in Redwood Grove, but before I could launch into the first, Lyssa squared off with me, one leg tucked beneath her—and her expression almost deadly serious.

Shit.

Had I jumped the gun?

Was there more heavy stuff to wade through?

"Soren?"

I cleared my throat, preparing for the worst. My inner wolf held his breath. "Lyssa?"

"How would you act... if you weren't trying to be respectful?"

She peeked up at me shyly through her lashes, chin dipped, almost demure in the way she phrased such an insanely loaded question.

Instant erection.

Not even a half-chub—my cock shot to full-mast. Desire. Need. Longing. Yearning. *Hunger.*

How would I act?

I'd destroy her.

And then she'd thank me for it.

A composed calm washed over me. Gone was the humor, the giggles, the teasing. In its place, a raw, primal *focus* that rested squarely on her. I cupped her chin so suddenly that she jumped, and her eyes widened as I tipped her head up—and back. Forced her to gaze to mine. Kept her in my thrall, our eyes locked, our hearts beating as one.

"What would I do?" I rumbled, close enough that the hum of her lips buzzed in mine, her short, shallow breaths feathering my skin. "I'd hunt you, Lyssa."

Her eyebrows lifted in disbelief, uncertainty—maybe a little fear. My grin turned feral, and this time I felt her throat dance through a gulp.

"I'd hunt you, and I'd catch you..." I held firmer and forced her head back a little higher, the delectable arch in her neck like a siren song to my teeth. "And then I'd *fuck* you."

Lyssa flinched at that *word*, just as she had time and time again. The second I released her, she sagged with a ragged breath.

"You don't like when we swear, do you?" Had the others noticed she twitched and flinched like someone was about to smack her anytime we cursed? Ewan had a mouth that could make a biker blush, and even though they sounded all prim and proper with that accent, Lucian had refined swearing to an art.

"Bad words mean bad things happen to you," Lyssa admitted as she shoved her mane over her shoulders, folding in on herself by the second. "Or… at least it did. Once."

"Not here." If anyone had a problem with her word choice, they could take it up with three alpha wolves. We may suck as pack leaders, but we'd go to bat for our mate. Don't like what she's saying? Take a hike—or get your teeth kicked in. "Say what you want with us, however you want."

She shook her head ever so slightly, almost like that was meant for herself, a reminder not to break the rules. Shit, what had *happened* to her in a past life?

"No one's going to hurt you," I added, catching her chin with my fingertip this time. Still rocking one hell of a boner, I managed to tamp down the white-hot need inside for this—for making her feel safe. Sure, resisting the call of my mate, especially out here, alone with her, practically in each other's laps by now, triggered a bitch of a headache *right* between my eyes.

Worth it.

One hundred percent.

When her shy gaze found mine, I grinned, the smile reaching my eyes and blazing back into hers. A few droplets of warmth pitter-pattered in my chest, and she sat a little straighter when I let go, faced forward, and—

"Fuck!" And bellowed that *word* loud enough to start an avalanche in the right conditions. Much to my surprise—and delight—Lyssa clapped her hands over her mouth to muffle the most adorable squeal-giggle, her eyes wide with shock and laughter. *Fuck* echoed across the valley, my baritone howl pinging back to us in rounds, quieter and quieter every time. I gestured to the autumn canopy and the blue horizon. "Your turn."

Lyssa shook her head, still hiding behind her hands—but her smile poked out the sides. Right. Not scared. Good. *Very* good.

I did it again, adding an alto to the echoey chorus, then gestured for her to follow.

"*No,*" she whispered, sounding like I had just told her to streak through the village—totally scandalized.

"Come on, it feels good." My soprano *fuck* cracked like a kid on the brink of puberty, which made her snort. Spurred by her reaction, I shuffled closer and wrapped an arm around her, then grabbed both wrists and held her unwilling arms out. "Say it with me…"

I drew a dramatic breath as she side-eyed me, then held it—and held it, and held it, and held it until it hurt. Until finally—

"Fuck," Lyssa whispered. Fire plumed across her face, forehead to chin and beyond.

"There you go." My enthusiastic praise only made her blush worse, but I focused on touching her as much as possible in this game instead. "Now, throw your shoulders back…" I did it for her, already obsessed with the way her body caved to my touch. "Open up those lungs, free that diaphragm… Really breathe *deep.*"

Fighting her smile, Lyssa did as she was told.

"Fuck." A great indoor voice.

"Okay, a little louder."

"Fuck." Sounded like a teacher ordering a rowdy classroom to simmer down.

"Come on, you can do better than that. *Fuck!*"

"Fuck." Maybe you'd hear her across the football field.

"Really give it to 'em, Lyssa—"

"*Fuck!*" We both stilled as her voice cracked across the valley and sent a tiny flock of birds scattering from the trees below. She turned on me, looking surprised but impressed with herself, her huge smile so exquisite.

And so tempting.

So gorgeous—that I just had to kiss it.

She tasted like spearmint toothpaste and promise, like waking

221

up January first with this feeling of untapped potential, the year ahead full of possibilities. I caught my mate with her lips parted, but we fell into a slow, passionate rhythm—at first. At first, it was gentle exploration, tongues shy but curious, lips soft and wanting. Her face was perfect for cupping, for cradling in my palm and tipping back. Her fingers crept up my chest, along my neck, and around into my hair.

At her first *twist*, the wolf in me surged to the surface. At the flash of teeth, the whiff of pain, the hint of *fight*, a true alpha seized control.

And I was gone, kissing her with wild abandon, throwing caution to the wind and claiming her mouth for my own. Lyssa quickly matched my tempo, my ferocity, heat rising between us amidst a chorus of snarls and low growls. When I caught a glimpse of her eyes, neon blue shone back, her inner wolf rising, ready to fight and play and *fuck*.

She climbed into my lap first. Unprompted, Lyssa scrambled over my thighs and straddled me, snagging my lower lip and sucking hard. Claiming the power position—but not for long. I rolled her onto her back, driving her into the stony ledge.

But she was *good*.

Unpredictable, using my momentum to regain the upper hand.

Two could play that game, and I eventually had her writhing body pinned, cradled between her thighs. She moaned and gasped and rocked as I bucked against her center, grinding my aching cock, desperate for my own relief—and hers. Desperate for her climax to imprint on my memory forever: her moans, her cries, her expression as she plunged into oblivion. I wanted it all. *Needed* it.

Needed her.

Now.

Just as I dragged an openmouthed kiss down her delicate neck, she seized control again—hooked her legs around me and spun us over. This time, she planted her hands on my chest and *pushed* like her petite frame could physically overpower mine. Panting, rumbling, I smoothed my hands up the back of her thighs to her ass, then groaned at the way her thick, dark lashes fluttered shut. For a moment, she rocked back and forth, using my shaft, exploring how it felt to brush her clit along its hardness.

And then it stopped.

And her smile turned wicked. No longer the enraptured she-wolf, Lyssa radiated an almost unnerving air of control, of *power*—more than just an alpha. One look and I was lost in her thrall, offering up my throat on a silver platter.

Which she accepted with a growl, her hand closing around my windpipe, her gaze unrelenting as she leaned over me.

"Hunt me, Soren."

My eyebrows rocketed up my forehead, and the last bit of blood circulating my body zipped straight to my dick. Lyssa tipped her head with a sigh, loosening her grip on my throat—but barely. Her lower lip slipped between her dangerously sharp teeth, more wolf-like than any shifter I'd seen before. Animalistic. Primal. The first of our kind.

"Hunt me," she urged again, grinding her hips, using me for the final few precious moments, "if you can."

And then she was off, sprinting across the landing and down the wall, leaping into the abyss with a giggle—then a howl. Not her wolf's howl—no, that was a song I'd recognize anywhere, the only melody to ever tap directly into my heart and control its beat—but a woman's cry. A challenge.

Her absence *hurt*.

I shot up with a snarl, tearing after her at full speed like a bullet leaving a gun.

Even in this form, I scented her on the wind. Pine needles and dryer sheets and fresh-baked bread. She veered left, away from the rock-strewn path we had taken up here, headed into the trees instead. With my inner wolf quivering *right* under my skin, I locked on her silhouette, on her almost careless scamper between saplings and ancient giants alike.

And I wouldn't let her go.

Lucian was the best tracker, though our mate may yet unseat

him. Ewan was just a city wolf—it was time for Lyssa to taste what a wolf raised in the forest could do. It had been *ages* since I did any proper hunting, and it showed. Lyssa put me through the paces, pausing occasionally for me to catch up, to clue into her scent again, but when I did, she raced into the shadows with a shriek, all but *begging* me to pursue her.

Once I found my footing again, I did.

She was fast.

I was faster.

She was nimble leaping over fallen trees and jagged boulders, skirting brambles and underbrush, dodging reaching roots and abandoned animal burrows…

But Redwood Grove was my home. The mountains had never been my territory, but it was now, and it welcomed me like the prodigal son. Lyssa was swift as the wind, agile and free—but she was used to being the hunter.

Not the prey.

That was her undoing.

I eventually broke off from her direct trail and skidded down the steep mountain face—then swung back up and circled around.

Cut her off at the pass, appearing before her between two bowed elms. She staggered, eyes wide with shock, but before she could turn on her heel, I claimed my kill. Snagged her elbow and ripped her back. She crashed into my chest with a grunt, then a growl, wriggling and squirming for freedom, but I soon had her pinned to the tree trunk, trapped in place, blocked—caged.

"Got you," I rasped before seizing her mouth brutally. No cautious, languid pecks this time. No, this kiss was fire and passion, both of us sweaty and panting, growling and snapping our teeth, bodies crashing together.

"But can you keep me?" Lyssa whispered against my mouth. I swallowed the challenge and answered with a hand cuffed around her throat, dragging her onto her tiptoes and easing off just enough that she chased my lips.

"You're not going anywhere."

My voice had never sounded like that before, so gravelly and rough. Sure, it deepened on the brink of a shift, but this sounded darker—more dangerous. Demonic, maybe, from the way Lyssa gasped, her eyes wide and a little frightened.

And that just *did* something to me.

Triggered the predator.

Inside, this tether that had held the beast at bay all these years tightened, tightened, tightened—snapped.

I claimed her with a ferocity that startled my inner wolf—that made our mate gasp and moan and arch against me. My kiss was nothing short of brutal, hard and punishing, deep and domineering, a part of me that had been locked away all my life charging to the surface. A wild thing. An animal.

Lyssa greeted him with a snarl and a snap of her teeth, her hands nowhere near gentle as they ripped down my shorts and briefs. As soon as the cool autumn air tickled my thighs, I went for her shirt, ripping it up her body, forced to abandon the kiss for the sake of stripping her bare. I'd seen her naked plenty since we found her, but Lyssa's figure only became more tempting with time, a temple of worship I was stuck watching from the outside instead of falling to my knees before the divine and making my willing sacrifice.

Huh.

The moment broke—briefly—when I noticed the sports bra.

I'd bought that the first night.

Grabbed it on a whim.

And now she was wearing it…

Something about that was weirdly *thrilling*.

That disappeared too, hastily dragged off and tossed aside to join her shirt somewhere on the forest floor. Perfect breasts bounced and hung with a sublime weight in its absence, nipples like little pinkish-brown pearls. Panting, vision tunneled to what I craved, I dragged my mouth along her jaw, down her neck, nipping and sucking until I reached the pebbled buds. Lyssa cried out when I took the first in my mouth none too gently, and even though she smacked at my shoulder, her body still arched into me in a trembling bow, startled by the flash of pain—yet intrigued by my teeth.

I caught her wrist when she slapped harder, then jumped to her left breast, refusing to give one more attention than the other. Three long, painful weeks of being the good guy, of giving her time and space, of being patient when all I wanted to do from the start was bend her over literally *anything* and fuck her into oblivion...

No more.

Enough.

As I engulfed her perky, soft mound in my mouth, I freed her strong thighs, thicker now after weeks of good eats, from the leggings. Then those simple cotton panties, not made for seduction: practical and purposeful and still somehow so fucking *hot* on my mate. She could wear a paper bag and look like a goddess, but I preferred her like this most of all. Naked. Raw. Beautiful. A woman of the wild who belonged out here—with me.

Her free hand soon found my hair, twining in and twisting hard for a little payback after all the abuse reaped on her darling nipples. Snarling, I grabbed her hips and hurled her to the ground. Lyssa plummeted with a yelp and a grin, quickly rolling onto her belly, seconds from pushing into another blitz.

I pinned her first, crouched behind and shoving her into the crunchy leaves below with a firm hand on her lower back. Even though it upped her chances of escape without them tangled around her ankles, I tore her leggings and panties the rest of the way down, growling in frustration when they snagged and put up a fight. Smirking over her shoulder, Lyssa did nothing to help wrestle them free, biding her time, waiting for the opportune moment to sprint for freedom.

Not today, mate.

Not with me.

As soon as I had her stripped completely bare, I yanked my T-shirt off and hurled it aside, then went for her beautiful hips. Clamped down with both hands. *Yanked* her onto her hands and knees, then blanketed her body with mine. Heat swirled between us, an inferno darting from her flesh to mine, fires spreading and multiplying, intensifying. If we didn't mate properly soon, they'd go nuclear—I was sure of it.

Determined to keep my prey, my savage mate, my tricky girl, I secured my prize by the back of her neck, then peppered her with biting kisses across her shoulders and into the delicate skin of her inner arms. Lyssa squealed and growled, kicked back and squirmed, but I *had* her. My wandering mouth marked up her back with hickeys and fleeting teases of teeth, and by the time I reached the base of her spine, she was trembling. Legs quivering. Elbows wobbly. Breasts dangling. Breath coming hard and fast.

Pussy so slick with need it smeared past her swollen lips and onto her thighs. Desperate as I was to bury my face *there*, lick her until she screamed, taste the source of her musk and devour every drop, I couldn't wait anymore.

I'd die.

I'd just… I'd die without her.

Fucking *fate*.

What are you doing to me?

With a hand still firmly planted on the back of her neck, I steered my cock to her slick entrance, and as soon as the head plunged into her heat, we both stilled. I hissed. She mewled and arched her back, thrusting her ass up for me.

"*Fuck*, Lyssa—"

"F-fuck me, Soren," she whined, stumbling over the word but handling it so much better than before. But the agony dripping with every syllable? Not because of a swear word. "You promised you would—"

I thrust all the way home, right to the hilt, hip bones pounding into the globes of her rounded ass, and the mountainside came alive with our mating song. My growls low, her cries high, pleasure and sex scenting the air.

Before today, I had pictured this moment a thousand times, every night before I fell into a fitful sleep, longing for her, lusting for her, imagining how we might forge our bond over and over again. Each time, it had been slow and gentle.

Not this.

Never this.

But now—there was no other way. This was us, Lyssa and me. We set the tone, and anything less felt wrong. Insulting, even.

Buried inside my mate at long last, I saw stars. Behind my closed lids, head tossed back as pleasure whumped through my limbs, pops of color and light flashed, fireworks pinwheeled—everything was just so *right* in the world.

Lyssa made the first move, bucking back, whining impatiently. Eyes fluttering open, I realized she had clawed into the dirt, her head bowed, body arched before me. She slid the length of my shaft, then pounded back, fucking *me*.

And that just wouldn't do.

Nope.

Not with us.

Growling, I gripped her shoulder with one hand, her hip with the other, and seized control. Set the pace. *Fucked* her properly, roughly, and thoroughly, slamming into her from behind, lost in a haze of fire and stars and her moans.

So—*fucking*—tight.

Was this Heaven?

I didn't believe in it—shifters were destined for the stars, right alongside our fated mates. But, man, this *had* to be the shit humans touted in their sacred books... Pure, uncut bliss.

When her moans turned to whines and whimpers, her pussy like a noose around my dick, I dragged her up. Bounced her on her heels, her sweaty back to my chest, needing to see paradise on fire in her eyes when she came. The bruising hand on her hip quested down between her thighs, and I circled her clit, gazes locked, hips pumping. Her mouth fell open in a soundless scream.

"No, no," I hissed, tweaking her nipple when her eyes clenched shut. "No, let me *see*."

Flames danced in the greyish blue, and I fell headlong into them as her pussy rippled through a climax. Lyssa exhaled a jumbled, breathy mess of nonsense, not a single coherent word to be heard, but I understood it. I nodded, teeth gritted, thumb back on her clit to really draw it out. *I know, I know.*

She twisted around to kiss me like she was *grateful*—but then her gratitude turned painful. Agony ripped across my chest, down my right pectoral, and I broke away with a snarl.

"Mine," Lyssa growled, her nails bloody, my chest permanently scarred. Four glorious slashes wept red for me, for us, and I lost it.

Fucking *lost* it.

Frenzied, overwhelmed by the need to secure my mate, I shoved her back to the mountain. Blanketed her with my body, driving harder and harder until I came apart at the seams. Pleasure ruptured through me like a volcano on fucking overdrive, but in the shadowy haze streaking my vision, instinct steered me to her flesh.

Not her neck or shoulders.

No, those were taken, and for the first time, those marks didn't inspire jealousy or rage.

Because mine was the best and brightest of all. I sunk my teeth into the dip of her waist, puncturing skin, bathing in blood. Binding us forever. Over the ecstasy flooding my veins, the primal howl of my inner wolf, I vaguely heard her cry out.

But I definitely *felt* her come again, her pussy clenched tight, taking my seed deeper with her body's every spasm. As my hips jerked through the aftershocks of a climax on steroids, I peered up at my mate just as she glanced back over her shoulder. Our gazes met, clashed—issued a challenge that we *both* won.

"Mine," I snarled, offering her a bloody smile that made Lyssa moan and bury her face in her arms.

Finally.

We belonged to each other properly.

No longer the odd man out.

Bonded.

As the beast retreated and the man scrambled to steer this runaway freight train, awareness of her pain—her comfort—came in dribs and drabs. Not only was her side slick with blood, the mark sealed but *there*, I had fucked her on an unforgiving surface. Pounded her hard and fast, furious and dominant.

Even a shifter needed a beat after something like that.

With a little nugget of guilt hardening in my core, I eased out of her and sat back on my heels.

"Lyssa, are you—"

My mate sprang up, nimble as ever, bouncy and frisky as she scampered a few paces forward and then whipped around. She crouched, eyebrows up, my seed dribbling down her thigh and my mark blazing on her waist.

"Hunt me, Soren," she dared again, smirking, bold as brass and unfazed by the brutality of our mating—and then shot off into the trees, her laughter echoing over the mountainside.

Just like that, the beast was back.

The alpha in my blood roared.

I tore after her with a growl, hot on her trail and more than ready to prove that *I* was a wolf who kept my word.

Hunted. Caught. *Fucked.* Repeat—apparently.

My mate was in for quite the afternoon.

18

LYSSA

Soren's searching song echoed through the mountain.

I slowed, panting, and answered him with a teasing howl, head thrown way back, voice bouncing off the grey stone above, around, below—everywhere.

He sounded closer this time.

Ears up, tail up, hackles up, I listen to my wolf song reverberate through the mountain passages, winding corridors and steep drops and huge caverns. Abandoned dens and winter stockpiles of clean, stripped bones. We weren't the only creatures slinking around in the darkness, but Soren and I were probably the only ones here for fun.

Another deep, rich call from my mate rippled up the passageway, coming from behind and washing over me so that my hackles stood higher, ears perked harder, interest zinging from the tip of my snout to the pads of my paws. Snorting my excitement, I trotted off again, making sure to brush against the stone around me, leaving a very clear scent trail for him to follow.

My mate had pursued me into the night, the entire mountain range his hunting ground—his prey a little too willing to be captured.

All afternoon we had played this game. At sunset, I sprinted into an opening in the mountainside, and Soren raced after, catching me —mating with me like it was the first time, not the tenth—in a cave, and then I was off again, deeper and deeper into the range, daring him to keep up. As the shadows grew longer, he claimed me time and time again.

Hunted me.

Caught me.

Fucked me.

Just like he promised.

Not exactly what I'd expected when I woke up this morning, miserable and puffy-eyed, still aching over Ewan's words. Kira had refused to come out, even when I tried to force the shift. For the first time since she made herself known to me at six years old, she stayed hidden. Ignored my emotions, my thoughts, my feelings. Barely reacted to the sight of her mates, sweet Lucian included. Nothing.

Now, our excitement wove together, minds aligned again, spirits one.

Soren had made it all better—also not what I'd expected. When he invited me for a hike, I assumed it would be as tense and awkward as always between us, neither knowing what to say, neither knowing what to *do* when we were alone.

Today had been different.

Fun. Open. Honest.

His explanations and apologies hadn't made up for Ewan's rage, but it was a start for *us*.

And...

I hadn't sworn once all my adult life. Not out loud. Not after the first time all those many, many years ago.

My blond mate made me brave.

And made me *feel*—feel like a shooting star, like a firework, like floodwaters gushing through the forest. This rough, growly, dangerous side of him toyed with my body so deliciously, made me hot and hungry with nothing more than a glance, my belly pleasantly squirmy at the memories. His mark still throbbed, a dull ache on my side, felt even in my wolf form. Meanwhile, my own mark, something that just happened out of nowhere in the blinding throes of pleasure, instinct driving me to wound them, make them mine for all to see, shone like a spotlight.

Like those huge billboards in the city, lit up on all sides, blaring, demanding attention without making a sound.

Relying on my shifted senses, I followed the curve of this gaping corridor until the ground dropped off, then hopped down, down, down the ledges, headed deeper into the mountain. Air thick and still, I landed in a cavern with snoozing bats hanging from the ceiling, their droppings littering the ground in white sticky splotches.

Lyssa.

I stiffened, heart pounding, my name fired at me in a short, fast whisper.

Hackles higher, no longer with the giddy thrill of our game, I scented the air cautiously, expecting to find Soren.

But no.

That wasn't his voice.

And it wasn't in my mind either.

Right?

That...

Lyssa.

Another curt whisper, a hiss, sharp enough that my blood ran cold.

It came from the left this time, distinct, defined, like its owner had... moved.

Like it was circling me.

Whatever it was, whoever it was, it was in *my* territory. The Redwood mountains belonged to *us*, and if something was down here trying to intimidate me...

Well, that wouldn't fly.

Wary, on high alert for movements in the dark, skitters in the shadows, I prowled to the left. Low. Tensed. Wishing Soren had just *found* me already; I had made my movements obvious, rubbing on everything and offering howling hints during what felt like the final hunt of the night. Seriously, he should be hopping down those stony ledges any second now.

Instead, I crept out of the bat cave alone, slinking through a narrow passage and into another yawning cavern.

One that smelled like honey.

Oh.

This is nice.

I paused to really soak it all in, basking in the cozy scent, in the nostalgia—in the memory of a farmer's market when I was fifteen, wearing a stolen thrift-store T-shirt and a pair of cutoff jeans that were two sizes too big. Barefoot. Wandering the stalls, in scent-heaven with all the fresh fruits and vegetables, the raw meat from cattle vendors—and the pyramid of honey in mason jars with red-and-white checkered bows around the lids.

The vendor's wife gave me a jar.

I guess I'd looked sad and hungry enough, this dirty, shoeless teenager eyeing every stall like I hadn't eaten in weeks.

I had. My pack took down a caribou a few nights before, but I never turned my nose up at food back then.

On the verge of tears, touched by a rare glimmer of human kindness, I'd plopped down behind her stall and demolished the whole thing.

Just... scooped the golden nectar out with my fingers and licked every last bit before I returned to my pack with a belly full of honey, having had enough human interaction to last another few months.

Why did it smell like honey in here?

Why not bat droppings and decay, damp rocks and thick, musty air?

Intrigue overtook caution, and at the first trickle of running water to my far left, I moved. Nose to the ground, I sniffed over to a small hole at the foot of the stone wall, then dropped to my belly and scooted through. The trickle turned into a cascade, then a dull roar when I finally clawed out the other side into another enormous cave, this one soaked in light, gorgeous white beams spilling through two jagged slits in the walls, then a circular hole in the ceiling.

Wait.

Wasn't it night?

Where—

Lyssa.

A third heated whisper. Ears up, I searched for its source—but only found water trickling from the ceiling, icy runoff from the peaks working through the mountain to the valley. The liquid shimmered like diamonds, streaking down stone and falling into... a river.

A line of glittering water sloped down the center of the cave, then disappeared under the opposing wall, headed elsewhere.

Was this...?

Was this Gull River?

Rosa's warnings bounced around my mind, and I backed up with a low whine, Kira's hesitance threaded with my uncertainty.

Lyssa, please.

The whisper sounded pained this time.

Gull River was supposed to smell *horrible*. Bad energy. Scary business. Avoid, avoid, avoid.

The water here glistened, starlight in liquid form.

And, *oh*, the honey. Strong and sweet and *rich*. Golden paradise.

I took a step closer, eyes narrowed, nostrils flared.

Was that—apple cider too?

My mouth watered.

Lucian had introduced me to the stuff on Thanksgiving, though the cans I'd slurped from had a teensy, tiny bit of alcohol in them.

This smelled pure.

Uncut.

Honey and apple...

Diamonds and starlight.

That wasn't so bad.

After a quick glance back at the hole in the floor I'd squirmed out of like a bunny rabbit, I padded closer. And closer. Right up to the edge of the stream, then leaned over.

My wolf form stared back; Kira looked beautiful in the spotlights. Grey fur, black at the base. Dark muzzle. Healthy. Eyes bright, bright, *bright* blue. I tipped my head side to side, ears perked.

Hello, friend.

I rarely saw myself as Kira. We were lovely.

And we had been running for ages.

Playing with our mate.

Mating with him over and over again as the sun dipped below the horizon.

We were tired—and thirsty.

It smelled so good. Looked so good.

Couldn't be dangerous.

I dipped a toe, just to test, and pulled back with a whine. *Cold.* Fresh.

Mouth so dry—

I lowered my head, smitten with the starlight, and drank.

Ice trickled down my throat and cooled in my belly, the most refreshing gulp I'd ever tasted.

I went back for more, more, more, more, ignoring Soren's curious yip somewhere nearby.

More.

It was so good—

Until my back legs collapsed.

Until I realized I couldn't... feel anything.

The strength sapped from my limbs, and I staggered away from the diamonds—from the trap.

Lyssa... You're here.

The whisper was the woman again, the one who called to me on the breeze.

Panic exploded inside, my mind racing, frantic, terrified, but my body showed none of that. Sluggish, I collapsed onto my side. Try as I might to move, nothing answered.

A howl from Soren.

I responded with a strangled yowl, then used the last of my energy to shift back.

It's okay, Lyssa.

Claws clicked across stone. I managed to tip my head back before my entire body went numb and tingly—just in time to spot Soren barely squishing through that hole in the wall, his wolf too big, his amber gaze panicked.

Darkness swirled across my vision like a creeping fog.

"Lyssa?" His silhouette soared, warping from wolf to man. Darkness claimed me a heavy blink later, just as his slapping footsteps boomed like thunder. "Lyssa!"

Lyssa, the nameless woman sighed, the world fading away, my mate a distant memory. *Don't be afraid. You're here. Little wolf, you're finally home.*

HUNTED BY WOLVES

BLOODLINE - BOOK 2

RHEA WATSON

1

LYSSA

Wet warmth dragged across my face. Up my cheeks. Over my forehead. Around and between my slightly parted lips. Extra-special interest in my nostrils. I groaned, waking to a world of soft light behind my closed lids. A gentle huff brushed my skin, familiar in a way, like a packmate snoozing beside me, their breath even and deep with sleep.

More wet.

More warmth.

A more persistent exhale.

Was someone... licking me?

I peeled my well-rested lids open—and found Kira's reflection staring back.

Only it wasn't a reflection. My brows furrowed. No hazy shimmer of water. Nothing out of focus. Just intense blue eyes, bright and intelligent and *focused*. Her fur, grey at the tips and darkening to black at the base. A dark muzzle. Black-tipped ears. Full fluffy mane leading down her neck to her shoulders.

Sprawled on my back in a bed of cushiony grass, I reached for her—with my hands. Not *her* nose like I'd done in the past, poking at the spring or the lake, watching the water ripple and the reflection wobble.

Fur.

Warm, soft, thick *fur.* I flinched back when my fingers grazed her snout.

"K-Kira?"

The enormous wolf snorted, misting my face with a much cooler damp, and then did a happy little jump, her enormous paws pounding the earth on either side of my head. The internet called them tippy-tappies; I'd learned that this past month.

It signaled excitement in dogs.

I blinked up at her as she wiggled and huffed, the apprehension in my belly melting away to *love.* Tears welling, I shot up and grabbed her around the neck, burying my face in her fur, hugging as hard as I could. She nosed at my shoulders, at the marks left by Ewan and Lucian, grunting and whining and nuzzling.

Until she stilled.

The hairs on the back of my neck shot up.

Slowly, I let go. Kira whipped around immediately, hackles raised, a massive wall of black and dark grey blocking whatever she had scented approaching from behind. Although her alertness prickled down my spine, I stole a few precious seconds to take in where we found ourselves.

An orchard.

Rows and rows of trees, their canopies lush and green, their trunks thick and hearty. Wicker baskets full of... *apples* at their base.

Strange. I'd always thought apple harvests happened in the fall; I'd stolen more than my fair share when the pack passed by one in the past. The smell in the air, the morning dew on the thick grass, the pinkish-orange sunrise creeping above the horizon—I could have sworn this orchard was in the throes of summer. The air was much warmer than...

Than... *home.*

This wasn't home.

This wasn't my territory. Redwood Grove's orchards were dead, a wasteland to the south where nothing grew. Even my wolf pack plodded through without stopping, the intensity of game tripling further north.

A low growl rumbled from Kira.

Hesitantly, I touched my face. While still damp from her tongue, nothing seemed out of place. Broken. Swollen. Deformed. I'd hit the ground in the cave pretty hard, an intense heaviness coursing through me back then like cement in my veins. Now, I felt... good? Refreshed. *Whole*, in a way that I didn't understand.

Still naked. A quick check of the rest showed everything was as it should be. My nipples hardened when Kira growled again, tension rising like the hairs on my arms, like the little bumps on my exposed skin.

The river.

It had tricked me.

It was supposed to smell horrible, but it smelled like honey and glittered like diamonds.

A *lie*.

And I fell for it.

Kira unleashed a snarl and a snap of her sharp teeth this time, and I whipped around, hopping up and crouching at her side. Her tail stood so erect it quivered, ears perked, hackles high. Lips peeled back, she stared down a figure drifting through the nearby trees, creeping toward us like a shadow through the morning fog...

She solidified into a breathtaking woman as soon as the first rays of amber sunlight hit her.

Wow.

I'd thought Ewan had angelic beauty, but he paled in comparison to *her*. I gulped, holding my position at Kira's side as the wolf soared over me, massive and intimidating with her next warning growl.

But she didn't scare this woman with honey-blonde hair and eyes like gold. She seemed... young. Younger than me, maybe. Late teens, early twenties? A few inches taller than me if we stood toe to toe, draped in a white gown belted with a thin silver band. Bare feet.

Glittering rings on her dainty fingers. A deer pelt around her slim shoulders.

Kira lurched forward—but didn't charge.

We always charged.

I frowned. That had been a bluff—and the stranger called it. Didn't even flinch. Barely even slowed. With a gentle smile, this beautiful creature finally paused beside a nearby tree, maybe ten feet out from me and Kira—from some naked woman and a wolf the size of a black bear—then offered her hand. Palm up and open and empty.

Always the brave one, Kira trotted over, slow and steady but oddly confident in her posture as she approached this ethereal beauty. Still as stone, I watched on, transfixed, unable to look away...

Worried, suddenly, that this was another trap.

Another *lie*.

Kira stopped a few feet off, then leaned forward, sniffing cautiously at the woman's small, outstretched hand.

"What's her name?" the beauty asked, her voice high and clear like Christmas bells. None of our tension, our caution, touched her. She sounded so at ease, that melodious tone a little too similar to the one that had called my name.

Murmured it on the wind.

Cried out to me from the forest.

"Kira," I said without thinking, distracted, sifting through memories and trying to match her to that frantic whisper in the cave.

"Hello, Kira." Her melody softened, like she was speaking to a pup and not a full-grown wolf, an alpha in the making. She tipped her head to the side, smiling, golden eyes locked on Kira's, honeyed waves spilling over her shoulders and fluttering in the breeze. "My name is Idunn."

After another wary sniff, Kira shoved her face into that tiny hand.

My eyebrows shot up, surprise fisting around my heart.

Kira then dropped to her belly and wiggled closer, tail darting back and forth, very much a puppy in the way she greeted this Idunn.

Who stroked her face. Her snout. Her ears.

Every touch—I felt.

Knuckles whispering over my cheeks, in my hair, around the shell of my ear. I swatted at the phantom touch, still on my haunches, still ready to run or fight.

But then Idunn lifted her golden gaze to mine, and I turned to stone again, heavy and frozen, trapped in her eyes.

"You know," she mused, "shifters don't name their inner animals."

I sucked in a harsh breath, trying and failing to so much as twitch my fingers, our eyes locked, mine starting to water.

"She's a part of you," Idunn said gently, and when those beautiful golden orbs dropped to Kira again, I slumped to the side onto my thigh, my hip, then my elbow stabbing into the grass for balance. "Well, I suppose she's more than that." I refused to so much as glance up, refused to look anywhere but Kira's wagging tail—just in case she trapped me again. "She's *you*, Lyssa."

Fear and relief mottled in my belly.

Yeah, that was the voice.

She had called to me over the last few weeks, begging me to come home.

Why?

"Are you an angel?"

Her good-natured chuckle had my head snapping up, and I found her seated cross-legged with Kira's enormous head on her lap. Deer pelt on the ground beside them, her shoulders were bare beneath silver pads bedazzled—another new word courtesy of Rosa —with sapphires.

Sapphires so blue... like Kira's eyes.

"No, sweet girl, I'm not an angel."

I mirrored her position, legs crossed, elbows planted on my thighs, chin on my fists as I watched her fawn over Kira.

And Kira just lapped up the attention, going so far as to expose her belly, tongue lolled to the side, eyes closed.

"Am I dead?"

Did the water poison me? Was this Heaven? Had Reed and Nikki been right all along? My mates had mentioned shifters and stars once, that we lived forever *there*, but I wasn't a star.

I was… here.

Normal.

Still *me*, just in an orchard.

"No, little wolf, you're not dead." Idunn pressed a tender kiss to Kira's snout as she stroked the wolf's belly in broad, circling strokes. "You're chosen."

I felt her peck, her hands on my tummy—but I felt those *words* harder.

"F-for what?"

Her smile widened, but just as she glanced up, maybe to trap me again in her golden gaze, a snarl ripped over the orchard. Then a grunt, a growl, a *bang*, crashing like thunder and clouding up the horizon. I pushed onto my knees, heart hammering, searching for the source, for the reason the darkening sky was at war with itself.

Only to realize… those were my mates.

"Lyssa?"

Lucian. His voice tickled my ear, rumbly and soft, smooth like velvet and warm as afternoon sunshine. But he wasn't… here.

Trembling, I turned to Idunn for answers, but she had already slipped under the safety of the nearby tree, hiding in the canopy's shade and settling there against its trunk, knees hugged to her chest like she was about to ride out the incoming storm. Kira, meanwhile, was up and on the move again, padding toward me, picking up speed with every step—

She jumped.

I braced.

And she dove straight into me, plunging into my chest, filling me up…

The orchard faded away.

The black returned.

"Lyssa?" And Lucian's whisper *cracked* like lightning splitting a tree. "Little mate, please wake up…"

2

EWAN

"Are you sure you don't want us to stay?"

I offered Ethan Perry a lopsided grin, too tired at this point to flash a whole one. "No, no, go. It's late." Almost four in the morning, actually. Beyond the beanpole blond warlock standing on the porch at the front door, his missus loaded little baby Aster into the back of their SUV, the pup still dead to the world. In fact, that tiny witch had slept through this whole nightmare, never once out of Rosa's sight, snoozing away as our pack went up in flames. "I think we're fine... Right?"

"From what we can glean in the ether, she seems okay." Ethan's brown gaze soared upward, almost like he could see through the house to Lyssa's bedroom—to my mate, also dead to the world, limp and lifeless in her bed. "No curses, no magical injury... She's just lost somewhere."

I pinched the bridge of my nose with a frustrated growl. "Fantastic."

"She's strong," Ethan assured me, his tone gentle but raspy, the night taking a toll on all of us. He and his wife had raced over the second I called almost three hours ago, the pair shooting out of bed to help Lyssa. Eyes rimmed with dark circles, he looked just as

248

fucking beat as I felt. "Give her time. I'm sure she'll find her way back. Remember… Everyone who drank from the river before that we know of died." The warlock clapped me on the shoulder, our weary gazes briefly tangled as he added, "This is really promising, even if it doesn't feel that way."

This time, I managed a full smile, thin and heartless as it was, and we said our final goodbyes—for now. If shit hit the fan, he was on fucking speed dial. Ethan had already offered to come back as needed; I'd accepted in a heartbeat, even with Lucian grumbling under his breath about warlock trickery and whatever other bullshit he brought from across the pond.

My inner wolf huffed, frantically pacing around my chest, determined to get back to our mate *now*. The fucker was nowhere near as exhausted as me, alert and hyperfocused on *her*, and it would have been easier to just let him out instead of fighting to keep him in.

But he'd go straight for Soren's throat.

And… that solved nothing.

Apparently.

So, I knuckled at the middle of my chest as I watched Ethan crunch down the gravel driveway, hop in the SUV, and peel away from the house, his shift over.

Bourbon and violet tickled my nostrils as I slowly shuffled around, Jocelyn's natural musk mingled with the liquor she had decided to drown herself in tonight. The fox shifter tiptoed off the stairs across the foyer, swathed in an enormous grey knit, her sweatpants stained and a far cry from the put-together executive assistant she presented to everyone else.

"Are you sure *I* should go?" Arms folded, she side-eyed the foyer staircase behind her. I nodded, so not in the mood to argue tonight. Usually her oomph and snark amused me; now, I just needed her to do what she was told.

"You too, vixen. Good night." I gestured out the open door. "Obviously I'll be taking a sick day tomorrow…" *Fuck's sake.* "*Today*, I guess. Cancel everything and reschedule the—"

"Stop." She raised a hand, meandering right into my personal space with her brows knit and her nose crinkled. Judgy little fox. "Seriously, don't talk about work right now. I got you—but I can stay. Let you guys sleep. I would never let anything happen to your mate."

I gritted my teeth at the wobble in her words, the loss of her own mate ancient history yet fresh as ever given the circumstances. Despite living at the far western edge of the Redwood Grove village, holed up in her private chalet and nursing old heartaches, Jocelyn had blown open this very door in record time after my panicked text, ready to save my mate no matter the cost.

She knew how it felt to lose your fated.

The fear.

The gut-wrenching panic.

The *agony*—and we hadn't even lost Lyssa. She was still here, technically, breathing, maybe even sleeping.

Jocelyn's fated had been dead for years.

I shouldn't have even involved her, but I trusted no one else, no one but her and the Perry coven, to help as my precarious forever threatened to turn to ash.

"I know," I said softly, mustering up a more genuine smile as her eyes watered. "I'd trust Lyssa to you in a second, but *we* have to do this."

Me, Lucian, and mother*fucking* Soren—who had let this happen to our she-wolf in the first place. Outside assistance made a world of difference, especially if there was accursed old magic at play in my mountain range, but at the end of the day, we were responsible for Lyssa. No one else. *Us.*

As soon as Jocelyn shuffled out, I closed the door gently behind her, then slumped into it with a sigh that quickly morphed into a long, frustrated groan. Head hanging, I battled back the memories of the other night, the all-too-vivid flashbacks of the horseshit that spilled out of my mouth after we found Lyssa in the clearing, having just beaten back four Hawthorne invaders all by herself.

Bikers and gangsters and thieves. Sadists. Killers. I knew that fucking pack—because I'd been raised by one just like them. Most of the Quinn wolves were either in a human prison, dead, or in hiding, enemies everywhere, our days of running the Toronto shifter drug trade a distant, painful memory. Still, no matter how fancy a suit I wore, no matter how much *legal* cash I pulled every day, I was still a Quinn in my bones.

Violent. Dangerous. Underhanded. *Killer.*

You couldn't shake that shit.

Legacies were forever.

The Hawthorne pack, our eastern rivals who seemed ready to really test us now, had a legacy steeped in blood and violence.

And Lyssa, our mate, our girl, the future mother of our fucking bloodline and queen of all she surveyed, squared off with a handful of them *alone*—

I'd lost it.

I hadn't meant to.

Hell, I'd barely noticed the venom pouring out unchecked, my inner wolf snarling, raging, yelping in panic.

Just a blur of fear and anger, fists and fury, claws and teeth and *violence* as we three alphas turned on each other, spurred by the visceral turmoil in our pack bond.

I'd fucked up.

Hurt her.

And it was too late to take it all back.

The last thing I had said to her before this Gull River disaster… Hateful. Cruel.

Above all else, a blatant lie.

Yeah, we needed pups ASAP. It was the only true way to cement pack ties and claim this enormous territory. Put down roots. Forge a new legacy.

But we needed *her* more than anything. Our fated should stand above the rest, above bloodline and territory, and I'd ground her into the mud—all because I was terrified.

Fucking coward.

Your father's son.

I snarled and shoved off the door, stalking for the stairs and fighting the flood of memories. My father's son—*fuck* the inner voices. I was his boy by blood and nothing more.

No pup of mine would ever find me with a needle in my arm and a lethal dose of wolfsbane in my veins—all because I couldn't face the consequences of my own fucking actions.

Taking the stairs three at a time, I sprinted up and around the corner, down the hall to the western wing of the house that was finally starting to smell like all of us and not just Lyssa…

Then stopped dead in my tracks, eyes narrowed as Soren sniffed at her open bedroom door.

"What the hell are you doing?"

"I think she's waking up," the blond alpha remarked, squinting into her room, a breath away from crossing the threshold. *Nope.* Fuck no. I ripped him backward by his T-shirt, the stitching torn open, and slammed him into the wall.

"Stay the fuck out," I snarled, *right* in his face, skin humming at the closeness. "You've done enough."

Soren's furious baby blues met my gaze fleetingly, but then he forced them down and away, jaw clenched like he was fighting his dominant urges. Good. He'd fucked up, and we all knew it. He hadn't a goddamn leg to stand on if he tried to pull rank here.

"*Good,*" I hissed, on the verge of adding *boy*—but that one word was enough. The alpha in him snapped, and Soren shoved back, snarling, his eyes all amber and danger now, seconds from shifting. The heat of it burned in my chest, our bond stronger, his guilt and fear and regret churning through the connection as we pushed and wrestled away from the bedroom door.

He should have known better.

Explore the mountain range, sure. Humans did it all the time; we made a mint off the seasonal ski slopes, the year-round hiking trails, the climbers with their little metal picks. But to let her bound around *inside*, unsupervised, was the height of fucking stupidity.

I wanted to kick him out.

Boot him from the pack and call it a day.

But we needed a majority vote to expel a fellow alpha; we'd put that in the fucking charter we signed last year when all this had started.

Lucian had said no. Pissed as he was, he couldn't do it—couldn't banish Soren from our territory, land that his ancestors had worked way before either of us showed up, and cut him off from his fated mate.

Furious as we *both* were, that was just too cruel.

Soren might have carried her home, kicked down our doors well after midnight baying for help, eyes wild with panic, but he had no right to access her fucking safe space now—

"Lyssa?" We both stilled at Lucian's murmur. The grizzled alpha hadn't left her bedside since we laid her in it, naked and unconscious. Not even when Rosa and Ethan did whatever magical nonsense necessary to cleanse the air and poke the ether. Right there, planted, rooted in place, Lucian had barely moved, barely spoken, until now.

Which had to mean—

"Little mate, please wake up."

A deep breath and a feminine groan followed. I shoved Soren into the wall one last time, then cracked him across the face with my elbow as I whirled around and charged into her room.

With that fucking blond right at my heels.

Teeth bared, I turned back to clock him again, repay him for the cheap shot he took at me the other night, but then Lucian inhaled sharply. Relief didn't trickle through our bond. No, shock plucked at the strings stretching between all of us—then *fear*.

Soren forgotten, I raced across the biggest suite in the house, over to the four-poster bed beside the balcony's french doors, the space all white linens and gossamer curtains. Stumbling to a halt just behind Lucian's hulking figure, I was about to ask—then she rolled over.

And opened her eyes.

No more greyish-blue marbles.

Gold blazed up at me, rich and warm like it was fresh out the forge.

My inner wolf fell silent.

I just stared, shell-shocked.

Nestled under the sheets, our mate *seemed* fine, no bruises or marks or scars except those Lucian and I had left on her shoulders...

She smiled. Sleepily. Groggily. Adorably. Smiled and rubbed at her lashes, knuckling the crust out of the corners.

"H-hi," Lyssa croaked. Her voice sounded the same. All in all, she *looked* the same. But her eyes.

Fuck.

Fuck.

Something was so, so, so *fucking* wrong. My fingers twitched toward my pants pocket, toward the phone—my lifeline—I'd use to order Ethan back here immediately.

"Lyssa?" Lucian recovered first, sweeping her bronzy-brown hair from her forehead, his tone gentle but cautious. She blinked up at him, then me, then lifted her head like she was searching for Soren.

Who had also marked her.

Who we couldn't banish after *that*—in theory.

"Yeah?" she rasped back, voice still a little scratchy. Actually, my mouth suddenly felt like a fucking desert too, but I pushed through, folding up my dress shirt sleeves that had been torn down from my elbows during the squabble.

"How... are you feeling?" I asked slowly.

"Okay, I guess." Wincing, our mate sat up and scratched at her head, sighing like she'd just had the best sleep of her life. "Tired. Bit stiff."

The linens fell away, and my caveman brain went straight for her tits.

Which also looked... the same.

Nipples like distracting pinkish-brown pearls.

A floorboard creaked, and the second I caught a whiff of Soren's scent creeping up behind me, I swiveled around to bare my teeth, Lucian up and snarling. We prowled toward him, more than capable of throwing his spoiled ass off the balcony, glaring through our wolf eyes, the promise of violence in the air—

"*Stop.*"

The windows rattled, Lyssa's command strong and certain, almost *final* in the way it quieted the fight. She-wolves could subdue their pups with just a look; Lyssa did it now with a single word—a word that triggered a mini earthquake throughout the house. Lucian and I swapped panicked glances, finally looping Soren into the silent conversation. My fellow alpha eyed the windows even after they stopped trembling, and I slowly looked back when Lyssa cleared her throat.

"It's not his fault," she insisted, her golden eyes heavy, her hands in loose fists—but her curled fingers couldn't hide the way they still shook. Something had just happened. Something way outside our realm of expertise. Something *magic*, just like the gold bouncing from alpha to alpha, desperate and exhausted and pleading all at once. "Don't punish him for... me."

"He should have—"

Lucian nudged me in passing, strolling back to his bedside post again. Teeth gritted, I bowed my head to collect my thoughts and subdue my emotions. Hardest thing about solidifying the pack bond was coming to terms with *everyone's* feelings hitting you at once. In time, we'd find a balance. The sensations would be whispers, not roars, amplified only in a crisis.

Mind you, if this wasn't a crisis, I had no *fucking* idea what would be.

Even worse, Lyssa's feelings were muted now. Lucian's resignation. Soren's guilt. My frustration. All that shit simmered along the invisible ropes binding us, but my mate, the she-wolf bonded forever through my bite and her scratch—she felt distant.

Difficult to read, body language included.

I perched on the far corner of the bed with a sigh, fluffing my hair, then folded over to bury my head in my hands.

Why couldn't things just go *smoothly*?

We'd had maybe a few days of peace since finding her, and now this?

"Lyssa, I'm so sorry."

"It's not your fault," she repeated. With her permission, Soren finally marched across the room and clambered onto the bed opposite Lucian, probably still on alert for another attack from either of us. Dark rings circled his eyes too, the toll this night had taken on him obvious, but that did *nothing* to soften my rage. Lyssa, meanwhile, fidgeted with her fingers, refusing to look any of us in the eye as she said, "The water I drank smelled like... honey. And apples. Like that cider we tried... And it looked fine, I swear. I was thirsty. It was there. I didn't really think—I just drank. Then I couldn't move, and then..."

We three stilled, collective breath held when she tapered off. Not only had her eyes turned to fucking gold, the irises molten, but they seemed to have aged a full century. Wisdom sparked in her dreamy look, our mate suddenly a million miles away. Experience. Heft. *Time.* Lyssa was the youngest here, but the gold... It gave her an unnerving edge, like some immortal—like one of the fair folk with their terrifying electric gazes.

Was that it?

Was Gull River a fae trap?

"Then I woke up here," Lyssa finished a few moments later, quiet, thoughtful. Soren, meanwhile, had a frown so deep those forehead lines might become permanent.

He didn't buy it for a second.

Disbelief buzzed in our bond, and when he stole a peek at Lucian, the oldest among us actually nodded like they were on the same page.

Stupid alpha pack bond bullshit.

Made it so much harder to hate him when I could *feel* him.

A tense quiet blanketed the suite. No one mentioned her eyes. We didn't stare. Didn't even allude that something was off.

How... How did you tell someone that?

How did you manage the fallout?

"I'm going to shower." Throwing back the blankets, Lyssa crawled out of bed, sounding more herself. Lucian lurched forward to brace her, as if he expected her to stumble and fall, but she breezed by, surefooted as always, and locked herself in the connected bathroom without another word.

Gnawing at the insides of my cheeks, I faced Soren head-on, demanding an explanation with nothing more than a lift of my brows.

And the promise of bloodshed simmering through our bond.

Soren shrugged it off, unfazed by my threat, and shook his head.

"The water smelled like it always does," he whispered with a cautious glance at the bathroom door. "It smelled like shit and garbage and sulfur. Like, it looked *fouled*, like a sewage drain or—"

"For fuck's *sake*," I snarled, launching off the bed. "I'll be back in a bit."

Not looking back, I headed for the door and straight out of the house, stripping down along the way, shifting on the porch and bounding for the nearby woods. There was only one truth.

Honey or garbage.

One or the other—but not both.

Time to take a pilgrimage to Gull *fucking* River and make my own conclusions.

3

LYSSA

Folded over against the bathroom door, I sucked down a shuddering breath, eyes closed and stinging with unshed tears. Out there, whispers—I couldn't make out the exact words, but my mates *had* to be talking about me.

About how I drank from Gull River.

About how the windows shook.

Coming to in bed, Lucian by my side, his voice soft and rich, I'd thought it was all a bad dream. Idunn. The orchard. Kira licking my face.

Then the windows rumbled like the surge of adrenaline in my blood shot out and hit them.

And…

Something was wrong. So, so, so very *wrong*. I bet any shifter could feel it the second they stepped in this house, the thick and smothering wrongness in the air. Tension from my mates twisted and twined throughout my body, all three distinct and strong and compounding with *my* emotions so that everything tightened like a snare. My arms, legs, back, belly—all rock-hard and cramping.

I'd lied.

I *didn't* feel fine. Not okay. Not *just* tired.

It went so much deeper than that.

At the sound of footsteps stomping out of my bedroom—Ewan, probably, given the fast, frantic pace and the click-click-click of his fancy shoes—I finally straightened and wiped under my eyes. Not a tear shed yet. I could do this.

Everything's fine.

In a few days, we'd all forget this had ever happened—right?

Kira huffed a snort. I glared up at my forehead. Why was she so... calm?

Usually we were on the same page about everything: food, mates, pleasure, pain, and the hunt. So aligned. So in sync. *She's you, Lyssa.*

Grimacing, I stuffed a finger in my ear and wiggled like that would shake Idunn's voice out, then crossed to the mirror and—

Oh.

Oh *no*.

It wasn't just her voice I needed to ditch.

Her *eyes* stared back at me from my own reflection, golden and burning. My heart dropped, my belly looped, the cramps worsening by the second. No. No, no, no, no, *no*. I pinched and tugged at my cheeks. Smooshed my lips. Pulled a few hairs from my eyebrows. Closed my eyes super-duper tight, clenched hard, and then opened them as wide as I could, glaring into the mirror, shivering almost violently when the gold was still *there*.

"No," I whispered.

Gull River had changed my eyes.

Or...

Maybe it wasn't a dream.

Maybe this Idunn was like Lady Fate, some divine being here to mess with mortals.

I...

Swallowing hard, I pressed a hand to my shuddering chest, over my hammering heart. Was she inside me now? Did Kira have a bunkmate?

Lucian, Ewan, Soren—they must have seen the gold. It wasn't

like my eyes were brown before and now they were just a lighter, brighter, more vibrant shade. No, this was a *change*.

And they hadn't said anything.

They...

Were they afraid?

Freak.

I shook my head, eyes welling, the gold glistening.

Just a freak.

"N-no."

A monster, all over again.

I wasn't—

Never have a family to call your own. Not human. Not shifter. Not anything.

All the old feelings came screaming back. Worthlessness. Otherness. Just when I thought I'd found my *home*...

Sniffling, shaking, I staggered to the standalone shower and frantically turned it on. The powerful stream struck tile, loud and crashing, hopefully drowning out this meltdown.

This *was* my home, those alphas out there my mates. Maybe they could kick me out, reject me for once *again* being different, but until then, I'd stay. Fight. Some stupid river didn't get to decide that for me.

Demon-child, destructive and wanton. Sinful and filthy.

Sure, that all sounded so strong, so brave.

Big talk for a little wolf with knives in her heart, stabbing deeper and harder with every strangled breath.

As the shower warmed, I stumbled back to the sink, gripping the marble countertop with one hand and wrenching on the faucet with the other. Freezing water hissed out, and I scooped it onto my face, over and over again, splashing my fiery flesh with ice until it went numb. Only then could I gulp down a proper breath, lost in the dark behind my clenched lids, water dribbling off my chin and into the sink. Blind, I groped around for the tap and grabbed the handle.

Yanked it too hard.

Broke it clean off.

I shot up with a gasp, Kira's whines harmonizing with the high-pitched siren screeching around my skull. Oh, *no*. Sure enough, there was the cold-water handle, right there in my palm, metallic with a matte finish, slightly crunched and warped from my fingers. No, no, no, *no*.

Okay.

At least the water was off and not spraying everywhere. Glancing warily at the door, I set the broken faucet handle on the counter as silently as I could, the ache in my lower belly sharper now. Had anyone heard what happened? First the windows, now this? Throw my stupid golden eyes into the mix and they had every reason to at least make me sleep on the porch while they decided if I was safe enough to keep indoors.

Arms crossed tight, head bowed, I stumbled into the shower stall and sealed myself in with the glass door. Not great at muffling noise, glass, but it felt less suffocating than the stone walls of a mausoleum. Never again. Never going in one of those awful places *again*.

But maybe you won't have a say in that...

I clamped a hand over my mouth to muffle the wail, then sank to the tile, stuffed in the far corner of the shower and blasted with piping-hot mist. No matter how brave and strong I'd become as an adult, the fear had its hooks in deep.

What if they kicked me out?

Sent me away?

Sure, their marks had turned to scars on my shoulders, my waist —but if whatever had happened to me at Gull River made me a threat, they'd throw me out. Toss me aside like garbage.

Just like Reed and Nikki.

I'd thought they were my family, my *only* family, my whole world, but those two had hurt me so *deep* that I still felt the blade in my back to this day. Outcast. Freak. Monster. No family wants one of those.

I wasn't a demon before; I knew that now. But what if the water had changed me into one? What if Idunn wasn't an angel, just like she said—but a demon? Demons could be beautiful. Lucifer was the most beautiful of all the angels.

No, no, no, no.

Arms thrown over my head, I sobbed into my knees, steam rising, water pounding, blood whumping between my ears. Kira whimpered and paced, giving off a warmth I'd never felt before, not even on my darkest day, in the darkest hour. We had always been terrified *together*. She bounced back faster, sure, always willing to take the first step, but we were a team.

And here she was, trying to soothe me, calm me, the scent of honey faint in the air.

Like... she was on Idunn's side in all this.

I gritted my teeth. Somehow that struck deep: Kira's first betrayal.

As the clawed fist ripped into my lower belly, I briefly wondered —not for the first or last time, probably—if it *had* been a dream.

No. Kira's memories were my memories, and flashes of us hugging, her fur so soft against my cheek, were all too real.

It wasn't a dream.

I was tainted.

Again.

Trembling, I dragged the wet curtains of hair from my face, then jumped at the blood swirling in the water by my feet. Bright red and diluted, it followed the current down the drain. As if my heart needed *more* stress tonight; breathing hard and fast, I clawed up the wall and realized—

Oh.

The blood was coming from me.

But... not from a wound.

Suddenly, the aches in my belly made a little more sense. It wasn't the tension from my mates threading with my own fear and anxiety, churning and twisting into something that made me sick and hurt. No, it was... normal.

I think?

Hazy recollections of homeschool sex ed came to mind, along

with tampon commercials on muted bar TVs, pad campaigns on bus stop billboards. Girls bled when their bodies could make babies. It happened in wolf form too, but usually only once a year, during the breeding season, triggered by the alpha female when *she* went into heat. The rest of the females in the pack followed, but we couldn't mate. We rode it out and snarled at any male who sniffed too close.

At least, that was what I did.

I'd never... bled in my human form.

But it was supposed to happen monthly, right?

Twenty-six years old, fated and mated, and still clueless about *everything*.

Shoot.

I clutched my belly and sank back to the floor.

Darn.

Cried into my chest, rough and ugly, trying to get it out now where my mates couldn't see or hear.

Shit.

Was it supposed to hurt this much?

Fuck.

My heart still skipped a beat just thinking that word.

"*Fuck.*" But given the current situation, the golden eyes and the bleeding and the windows and the tap—it felt justified.

I whispered it over and over again, through the tears and the terror, the anger and the grief, emptying my guts of it, *purging* here, alone, so that when I walked out of the bathroom and back to my mates, scrubbed clean, I could face them without tears.

And like always, keep pushing forward...

No matter what life hurled at me.

4

LUCIAN

"Cigarette?"

I flicked open the carton and offered Ewan first pick of the last three in the pack. Slumped in the wooden chair next to me, the morning breeze ruffling his sweaty black locks, my fellow alpha slid his weary gaze my way, then, with great effort, lurched forward to snag a cig. I grabbed one myself, then tossed the nearly empty pack on the table, lit the end of mine, and offered the lighter to him. He shook his head, sagging into the chair again, preferring just to fiddle with the stick, twirling it between his fingers, the look in his eyes a million miles away.

Bloody waste of a cigarette.

Taking a deep drag, I sank stiffly back in my chair, head tipped, lost in the starless black void above. No one had used this table, these chairs, since Thanksgiving when the whole pack gathered on the deck to feast on Lyssa's kill. Now, we sat here, adrift on a sea of confusion and heartache, waiting for dawn to creep over the horizon in a couple of hours. While I sported the same T-shirt and flannel trousers I'd thrown on when Soren kicked down the front door way back when, a limp and unconscious Lyssa in his arms,

Ewan remained naked, sweaty and dirty from the shift, having just returned from the mountain range some ten minutes ago.

Shell-shocked, he had confirmed what Soren said: Gull River smelled like shit.

Like *always*.

Mother Nature had a way of warding off her beasties, using smell and taste to warn them that this *thing*, this divine creation of hers, would kill them. Gull River was one such killer; Ewan had noted the discovery of dead animals littered around it back when the mountains belonged only to him, and the Acker pack told their pups horror stories that steered them clear of the acrid stream.

With another puff, I glanced toward the second floor, toward the soft yellow light spilling from Lyssa's bedroom windows.

Why would she drink?

What possessed her to crouch at the heart of the monster, where the scent *had* to be foulest, and fill her belly with water that smelled like piss and sulfur?

My inner wolf unleashed a long, mournful howl, our guilt shared, our fears multiplied tenfold.

I should have gone with them. This morning—well, technically *yesterday* morning—Lyssa was in such a shit place after the run-in with the Hawthorne pack...

After Ewan ripped into her, quite unnecessarily, shouting about bloodlines and packs and the future. Absurd. *Yes*, we needed all that and more, but it was far too early to put that kind of pressure on anyone. Our mate had just bullied a handful of grown wolves out of our territory; Lyssa was a warrior, an alpha female who would stand and fight, never flee, and that ought to be celebrated. Instead, he projected *his* insecurities onto her.

His fears.

The same fears that ached in *my* heart like a fucking cancer—fears I kept to my bloody self because that was the proper thing to fucking *do*.

I'd nearly beaten him to a pulp, but Soren had got there first—

and then she left the scene, which meant *I* left, our borders temporarily secure.

Not my usual plan of attack, to turn my back on duty and tend to someone else. In fact, my anxiety had been maxed out ever since, and while exhausted, I hadn't slept after Soren and Lyssa left for the mountains, for the day of hiking and bonding that they both needed. No, I had gone on patrol. Round and round the Redwood region I'd gone, swift and silent, scent marking more than usual, pissing on bushes and scratching tree trunks, reminding *all* of them that we knew exactly where our territory started—and if they crossed it again, the Hawthornes, the Ashwoods, *anyone*, would have a pack of alphas to deal with.

Alphas out for blood, our female included.

Then… this.

My fault for trusting Soren, a wolf with his head either in the clouds, spoiled beyond measure, or in his work. *Mine*. Should have gone with my gut and followed them, tagged along—something.

But Soren hadn't marked her yet, and Lyssa hadn't marked him. They needed a beat away from the rest of us to cement *their* connection, and while it had fucking *hurt* to send her off when she looked and sounded and felt so bloody distressed, I'd done it. For the greater good, I had held my tongue and resisted every impulse demanding I lock her in my room and make her forget everything Ewan said the night before.

Make her climax again and again until all that bloodline talk was just a thing of the past. Distract her with pleasure and food and the company of a wolf who admired her spirit.

Who had no intention of clipping her wings.

But I spent the most time with her already. Soren and Ewan maintained steady employment despite having found our fated mate, despite all of us needing to connect as a pack, which meant they were gone all day. In their absence, if *I* wasn't on patrol, Lyssa and I napped on the back deck or wolfed out in the afternoon sunshine. We swam in the lake and sniffed around the property, chased rabbits and squirrels through the trees. We tried to figure out Soren's bizarre coffee maker together and watched films in the cinema room. Not much to be had by way of conversation, but that was fine with me. Our bond wasn't based on learning each other's favorite color or how many sugars we liked in our tea.

It was deeper than that.

And I'd had the time and space to explore it with her while the others worked.

I... I'd tried to be selfless yesterday.

No more.

Not if it meant she got hurt due to Soren's negligence or Ewan's words.

No. Never again.

Should have been selfish.

Wasn't selfish enough back then and look what fucking happened.

My wolf snarled at the memories of bloodshed and fire, of screams and violence, and I closed my eyes tight, pinching the bridge of my nose as my ciggy smoldered away.

"So, what do we do now?"

I cracked one eye at the sound of Ewan tapping his unlit cigarette on the tabletop, the black-haired alpha also stuck on Lyssa's windows. No reading between the lines there: we needed a game plan going forward, because our mate had come back to us with golden eyes and some unseen energy that shook the windows when her emotion spiked. We all felt it, the shudder, the surge of primal *power* resonating through the room.

And no one had said a word.

Lyssa insisted she was fine, but that was a *lie*. She looked normal —beautiful, scrumptious, mouthwateringly divine—but she wasn't. Something had happened to her. Something beyond the poison of Gull River. Something deeper and darker.

I was terrified for her.

My wolf had loved her from the first night, the first *second* he scented apple blossoms on the breeze and discovered her. As close as we'd become over the last week or so, I felt for Lyssa as my mate. Not my *love*. Not my heart. My mate and partner, the wolf chosen for me by Lady Fate. I couldn't... love. I couldn't risk my soul like that again. Couldn't go through the turmoil, the agony, the crushing depression and loneliness when it all went to shit.

No.

Me and the beast inside adored her—but only he would ever be *in* love.

That was the safest road to take.

But that didn't mean I wouldn't sacrifice myself in her stead. I would *love* her eventually, but I couldn't be in love. The distinction mattered if I wanted to survive this life without getting torn to shreds again.

Yet the lure of her howl, her scent, her voice, her adorable giggles—

"I don't know—"

The sliding door whooshed open behind me, and out crept our girl. Dressed in too-big black yoga pants and a slouchy pink tee, she shuffled onto the deck and left the door gaping, her hair soaked, her golden eyes like floodlights slicing over stormy seas.

Swooping her hair behind her ears, Lyssa padded over to the wooden patio table, hesitantly glancing between us. She smelled fresh and clean, like vanilla bodywash and apple blossoms and a still night at the end of the dock, feet in the water...

But beyond that, beyond the images her scent stirred in my soul, there was also something *off*. My nostrils flared as I breathed deep, the air tinged with—

"I'm bleeding."

Blood. My inner wolf yowled as I shot to my feet, chair scraping over grey timber and slamming into the railing. Panic flowed between me and Ewan, the alpha also up, his cigarette abandoned and mine snubbed out on my wrist. Panic and concern and a splash of anger all threaded together, pounding through our bond sharp enough that it must have roused Soren from his fucking nap upstairs.

"*What?*" Ewan growled. "What d'you mean—"

"Where?" I demanded, scanning her figure up and down, top to bottom and back again, unable to find the source of the iron tinge in the air. Flushed, Lyssa blinked back at us, then slowly gestured to her chest, then down, down, down to...

Oh.

Oh.

Ewan joined her, both of them pointing at her crotch, Lyssa bright red and him stammering incoherently by my side.

"Do you... Uh... That is... When did...?"

Wait. My wolf whined, pawing at my chest, raking his claws across my insides, desperate to get out and scent her properly. Was our mate having her monthly—or a miscarriage? We'd all mated, but I was the first.

If she *was* with child, then it would most likely be mine.

And now she was bleeding *there*.

Choked with *feeling*, with agony from my inner wolf and the thickening scent of blood, my throat raw and burning, I took a deep breath to settle down. After all, there was no guarantee she had even become pregnant with our mating. Ewan's came shortly after, and Soren was only yesterday, so...

Despite the logic, my heart still cracked in two at the mere *thought* of losing a pup, of the pain she would be in if that were true. I glanced at Ewan—then hardened to steel. Because he was suddenly wearing the same fucking expression he had the night of the Hawthorne incursion, right before he lost it.

Eyes a copper sunset, his wolf *right* at the surface, heat swelled between us. He then parted his thin lips—

And I gut-punched him as hard as I could.

Lyssa flinched, mouth falling open, and Ewan folded over with a cough, then a snarl, lashing out to nail me in the balls. I twisted out of reach with a hint of teeth and a warning growl, and when he straightened, cheeks pink and eyes dark hickory again, it seemed the blow had reset him.

Made him think twice about whatever nonsense he had seething on the tip of his razor-wire tongue.

"I... haven't had my, uh, blood as a human," Lyssa admitted

slowly, her uncertainty trickling from her to me, probably to Ewan too. It made my gut flip-flop, while my fellow alpha merely bowed his head and said nothing.

"So, no... supplies, then?" I managed, adrift at sea again, not a clue how to handle this. But it upset her, no matter the cause, and silence wouldn't do us any good. When Lyssa shook her head hurriedly, mine bobbed up and down, slowly switching gears from the golden shimmer of her eyes to the now—to this very painfully *human* problem. "Right. Okay. Why don't we head to the shop?"

Her flush sharpened. *"Now?"*

"Would you rather we waited?"

"I need... stuff." She swallowed hard, throat rippling, and her discomfort ripened in the air, zinging through our bond. "Just got, uh, toilet paper down there for now so I don't ruin my underwear."

Ewan made a face out of the corner of my eye, nose wrinkled, lips downturned, and I resisted the urge to punch him again. *Grow up.* Honestly.

"Well, off we go, then." I knew fuck all about women's cycles beyond basic biology but might as well figure it out as we went along. No sense standing around out here at five o'clock in the morning, the crescent moon reflecting off the water, the trees whispering—gossiping about us. "Chemist's open twenty-four hours in the village."

"The what?"

"The pharmacy—"

"Let me get some clothes," Ewan growled, sidestepping my colloquial phrase, the few lingering in my vocabulary after all these years, and shoving by. He stalked around the head of the table, barely glancing back as he added, "And *I'm* driving."

He then went for the open sliding glass door, grumbling about my shitty jeep, and disappeared inside. Lyssa and I watched him the entire way, our postures mirroring each other—arms crossed, shoulders slightly rounded, drained but ready for the next round. However, before I could whisper a teasing jab about Ewan's vehicular snobbery, our mate shuffled after him and climbed into the darkness of the sunken seating area inside without another word.

My inner wolf whimpered at the anxious energy buzzing from her to me, our connection flaring suddenly—then going silent.

"Fuck." Tense, I glared briefly at the jagged silhouette of the Redwood mountain range, then trailed after the pair, wishing this night from hell would finally just *end* already.

"Okay, so..." I clapped my hands and rubbed them together, woefully ill-prepared for the sheer volume of feminine sanitary products claiming nearly an entire aisle in the twenty-four-hour village pharmacy. From the wide-eyed look on my mate's face, she appeared equally uncertain, situated between Ewan and myself, seeming very small but for once not entirely out of place.

Ewan, meanwhile, glowered in the opposite direction. Even if I couldn't see the full extent of that stink-eye, I felt the rage in our bond, noting the way his jaw muscles leapt and flexed—all because some cunt down the aisle by the *sexual enhancement* stock was checking Lyssa out.

Some twat who looked like he had just crawled out of the Chalet, Redwood Grove's premiere—pretentious as fuck, just like its owner —nightclub. Sporting sunglasses and a rumpled suit, a coffee in one hand and a box of condoms in the other, the whelp had the gall to stare at our girl.

Ours.

Openly, obviously, even behind those dark shades. My inner wolf snarled suddenly, and in an instant, Ewan's wrath twined with mine. We might have all been on shaky ground right now, fated mates far more complex than any of the elders had ever let on, but one thing was certain: outside males who stared too long lost their eyes.

As I sidled closer to Lyssa, seconds away from tossing an arm around her shoulder and flashing my teeth, Ewan faced the pup completely. No more glowering profile: he stared back, meeting those sunglasses head-on. His low, rumbling growl made Lyssa stiffen, but then she crouched to scrutinize a weird cup thing on the lower shelf, which allowed me to join the glaring match.

No doubt feeling the heat, the lanky little shit who smelled like whiskey, weed, and sweat shoved those condoms back on the shelf and scuttled off.

Good.

Run, run, fast as you can...

Before we rip your throat out.

Satisfied, I redirected my attention where it belonged: this wall of pads, tampons, cups—all from varying brands, all looking the exact same to my eyes but were *clearly* different given Lyssa's palpable indecisiveness.

"I... don't know what I need," she admitted, straightening with a huff. Arms crossed, her hands tightened over her biceps, scrunching the jean jacket she had thrown on after Ewan insisted she wear something *more* than yoga pants and a—quote—raggedy old T-shirt. The notion still made me roll my eyes: Lyssa's outfit was hardly the problem, not with this prick rocking up in designer labels as if we would actually happen upon anyone of importance on our predawn pharmacy run.

For tampons.

Honestly.

Prat.

"What do you usually use?" said prat asked, clearly only half listening, nose up and nostrils flared as he tracked the weed-cloud-whiskey-drenched rich kid through the shop. Lyssa shot him a frown, and he looked back a moment later to catch the brunt of my own unimpressed scowl. "Oh. Right. Never had it... Never mind."

While I once had sisters—loyal, devoted, dead sisters—I was never involved in their monthly regime. All of this was a mystery, which left me standing there like some dozy airhead, just staring, trying and failing to spot the differences between the brand names.

The only thing that differed was price, and that was marginal. Mere pennies.

Rolling her shoulders back, Lyssa strolled a few paces down the aisle, past Ewan, and then seemed to grab a box of heavy-duty pads at random. She read the label, golden eyes flying, gnawed at her lower lip, turned to *me* like I might have the answer, then shoved the box back in its place with a whine.

"I don't *know*."

"Well—" Ewan fished his phone out of the pocket of his open black trench, seeming very much in mourning with the all-black turtleneck and slacks combination beneath. "—the internet has an answer for everything. Hold on."

I rolled my eyes. We hadn't been here more than five minutes and already he had found an excuse to whip out his phone.

"Maybe we grab one of everything." I toed at the metal shop basket beside me, nudging it in Lyssa's direction. "Then you have options?"

At Lyssa's half-hearted shrug, I scooped a shitload of stuff off the nearest shelf and dumped it in the basket. By the time a bell chimed from the shop entrance about a minute later, I had the basket full and considered grabbing a second—because there was still so much *stuff*. So many varieties. Thickness, density, nighttime and daytime, and why did *those* tampons not have a plastic applicator on the box like *these* tampons—

"Way to start the party without me," Soren growled as he rounded the end of the aisle and stalked toward us. Dressed in a pair of sweats and a thin inside-out grey sweater, he felt like nothing in the bond—just the empty hollowness of a wolf running on fumes. His expression was pure frustration, dark and accusatory and brooding, but exhaustion stood tall above the rest, shadowy rings around his eyes, his shoulders rounded. Given neither Ewan nor I were all that inclined to interact with the alpha who had put our mate in danger, we had left him passed out at the foot of Lyssa's bed, snoring away.

At the very least, Ewan *had* sent a text while we idled in the driveway, informing him of the situation at Lyssa's request. She had muttered something about how unsettling it was to wake at an odd hour in a totally empty house—which didn't sit well with me.

But Soren was a big boy.

A grown wolf.

A grown wolf ready to make heads roll, apparently, glaring daggers between me and Ewan, only softening when those bright blues landed on Lyssa—then darted to the wall of pads and tampons.

"*Oh.*" He speared a hand through his dark blond locks, the sides in need of a shave again if he wanted to maintain the punkish air he adopted after his parents left. "Okay, right." Hands settling in his pockets, he glanced down at my overflowing basket, then squatted to root through it. "Uh, I don't think she needs four boxes of ultra tampons, guys."

All three of us turned on her, perhaps without realizing, and our mate went beet red.

"I don't *know*," she hissed, overenunciating every word—something she'd picked up from Ewan, no doubt. But then the aisle trembled, boxes jittering on shelves, bagged stock swaying on hooks. Someone gasped, tremors rumbling underfoot until Lyssa blinked those watery golden eyes, and then it all stopped. Just like that, like the snap of her fucking fingers.

The anger articulating was all Ewan, but *that?*

That was Gull River.

Icy apprehension slithered through our pack bond, making Lyssa's blush worse as she hugged herself—like that would hide the way she shook even now that the shop had stopped.

"Are you..." Soren stood slowly, clearly fighting to maintain a happy-go-lucky energy as we all pretended nothing had happened— that her eyes weren't golden and emotional spikes *didn't* rock the literal foundations of our world. "Are you bleeding a lot?"

Lyssa shrugged again, tears barely contained and shimmering like diamonds under the fluorescent lights.

"Let's just start small and work our way up," Soren said firmly, hands on his hips as he scanned the shelves with a keen, calculating eye. "Panty liners, regular-flow tampons, regular pads, and maybe *one* pack of outliers—something for really light and really heavy days. I mean, we can always come back and restock."

Apparently, he paid far more attention to his sisters' habits than I did mine.

Yet another depressing difference between the Acker pack and my own. Not that I *needed* to know my deceased sisters' cycles, but to this day, the personal details of their lives were a wash. The Hadley pack of London—we were all about power. Wealth. Control. Tabloid darlings and journalistic assassins and aristocratic descendants. Public appearances and net gain and blood feuds and brothers against brothers...

My wolf yelped.

The scars slashed across my body burned.

And I took a step back, eyes closed, breath deep, so Soren could take the lead here. As he fished items out of the basket, I calmed the memories, the tidal wave of blood pounding from every side.

It dulled eventually, but it never disappeared for good.

Not unless I was with *her*—alone, buried deep between her thighs and drowning in her scent.

When I came back to the moment, I found Soren restocking and replacing items at a rapid-fire pace, Ewan glowering at him with that disdainful nose crinkle, seconds from baring his teeth, our bond fraught with tension...

And Lyssa's golden gaze darting between all of us, her frown deepening, her delicate hands balled to fists at her sides.

"I know you guys can see my eyes."

Soren slowed but continued feeding the basket, gingerly adding another soft pack of pads to the mix. Ewan, on the other hand, had suddenly found the floor rather interesting, ignoring Lyssa's pleading gaze, which eventually settled on me.

"Just acknowledge it," she urged, then swiped her thumb under her eyes, catching the damp before it trickled down her cheeks. I gritted my teeth, knowing this wasn't the time or place to really get into it but very aware that if we denied her *again*, she might fall apart.

We might fall apart.

"Lyssa, we... do. We see it," I told her, gesturing to the gold and waiting for the other two cunts to help. No one said anything. Soren stopped loading the basket. Ewan tapped his phone against his palm, cheeks hollow, jaw clenched. The radio played an insulting accompaniment of pop tunes, way too peppy for both the hour and the conversation. The cash register dinged. The bell at the front door chimed. Subdued foot traffic shuffled in and out, the directional flow suggesting they were headed for the ready-made meals in the fridges near the pharmacy counter.

And we just stood around, three dumb twats with a visibly distressed mate.

"I'm still me." Lyssa's voice finally cracked, her words thick and wet. To her credit, nothing rattled this time. "I don't know what happened, but... I'm still *me*."

"Baby, we know that." Soren stood, a box of tampons in each hand, and tapped them together instead of going for her as his eyes implied he might. "We just want you to be okay."

"And we lack answers," I muttered, the discussion quiet enough that *hopefully* any nosy humans missed the key points. "We don't know what to—"

"You're not *you*."

Teeth bared, I faced Ewan slowly, danger in the air, violence in my growl. Our bond grew heated, sparks flying, this fire on the brink of getting out of hand. Yet the black-haired alpha refused to back down, stubborn as *fuck* and seconds from hurting her again.

"You're different," he rasped as Lyssa's eyes watered. "No denying it. We shouldn't tiptoe around it either. Your eyes, the bedroom windows—thinking Gull River smells *good*?" He shook his head, gripping his phone so tight the screen finally splintered. "Lyssa, you made the store shake. You're not *just* you anymore—"

Snatching a few random boxes off the shelves, she marched over to the basket and dumped her haul in. In times like these, tensions high, emotion on overdrive, her eyes would have changed—gone from cobalt to neon, her inner wolf charging to the surface.

Now—just gold. Bright, sparkling, furious liquid *gold* that gave her this divine aura. I almost expected a halo to flare around her head when she rounded on us, glaring Ewan down as she said, "Usually I steal stuff from places like this. I assume one of you will pay for it?"

While the shop didn't quake this time, our fated mate did. Words steady, she saved all the furious shivers for her hands. Cheeks sunken, she gave Ewan a moment to respond, and when he didn't, she turned her ferocity on Soren, who nodded frantically.

"Yeah, yeah, of course—"

"Okay. I'll be in the car, then."

And then she was off, stalking down the aisle and around the corner.

Once again, we just stood there and watched, woefully out of our depth and surrounded by sanitary products. Scenting our fated mate, forced to share her, had already thrown us for a loop; this was another beast entirely.

As soon as the front bell chimed and her scent dulled, Soren and I turned on Ewan, all snarls and teeth and an inferno blazing in our bond.

"*What?*" Ewan's coppery gaze snapped between us, canines bared, invisible hackles straight up. "She wanted us to acknowledge it... She practically begged for it. We should be fucking *honest*. Better than going through all this with rose-tinted glasses." He dodged the squishy package of pads Soren hurled at him with a snarl. "Talking is probably the healthier thing to do anyway—"

"Yes, spectacular job," I growled, rolling my eyes to the high heavens and reminding my inner wolf that no, we couldn't brawl in a human establishment, "you insensitive *cunt*."

"And *I'm* the asshole, right?" Soren shook his head, then crouched by the basket. Blond brows furrowed, he sifted through the products and pulled out duplicates in the stormy silence that followed, our bond a mess, tempers piqued, teeth out. At the end of the aisle, an exhausted woman rounded the corner, looking like she had just finished a night shift at the Redwood Grove veterinary hospital in her pink paw print scrubs—only to stop when she spotted us, backpedal, and disappear.

Fantastic.

Scaring the villagers was hardly on my to-do list this morning.

I looked between my fellow alphas slowly; *both* had royally fucked things up in the last forty-eight hours. While Ewan had more strikes against him, Soren was the cause of our current predicament. Ewan couldn't watch his fucking mouth. That blond pup refused to accept an iota of responsibility...

Enough.

If I stayed here a second longer, ruminating, fuming, I'd snap.

Stab one of them with... something.

Without a word, I left, preferring to pour my energies into *good* —not violence. Across the small, mostly empty parking lot outside, Lyssa perched on the hood of Ewan's black Benz, arms crossed, head bowed. She snapped up as I approached, my steps loud on purpose, and then slid off the pristine luxury S-class sedan, a private jet in car form, something that had cost Ewan over two hundred grand to purchase outright, and then another couple thousand to have delivered all the way to Redwood Grove. His newest baby— now imprinted with the outline of Lyssa's ass on the hood, her body heat warming the exterior.

"I..." She toed at the concrete when I finally stopped in front of her. "I don't have the keys, so..."

Not to this beast, and not to Soren's sky-blue BMW at the other end of the lot, the SUV dust-painted and mud-splattered, a far cry from Ewan's precious darling.

Didn't matter. From what I could see, her tears had dried, leaving only bloodshot eyes and pale cheeks in their wake. Before she could mumble anything else, I snagged her arm and yanked her against me, enveloping her in a bear hug from which there was no escape.

Not that she tried. With a shaky huff, Lyssa snaked her arms around my torso, still trembling a little, and then—

Ah.

Wow.

That—

That was a firm grip.

Wincing, ribs on the verge of fracture, I just rubbed her back and took it. The soothing rhythm eventually made her ease up, and I hastily filled my lungs before the next assault.

But it never came. Always a fast learner, my Lyssa.

"You're different, little mate," I whispered into the top of her hair, shrouded in her apple blossom scent. She stiffened, then tried to wriggle away, but I held strong, hoisting her onto her tiptoes so that I could murmur the next words against her temple. "But we're not going anywhere. I'm afraid you're stuck with us... Three miserable bastards who can't get along. I'm so very sorry for that."

She peeked up at me, my quip falling on deaf ears—her eyes watery again.

After lowering her to flat feet again, I grinned and tapped the tip of her adorable little nose.

"Stare all you want," I told her roughly, my inner wolf warming to the new hue blazing at us. "That gold doesn't scare me."

This time, a thick, throaty giggle tumbled from her lips, and Lyssa pushed up again, arms around my neck for another bone-crushing embrace. I gritted my teeth and rode it out for as long as I could, knowing whatever she broke with her new strength would heal in seconds.

"Now," I wheezed, prompting her to loosen up, "should you feel the desire to, I don't know, consume our flesh, or crack open our skulls for the juicy brains, or suddenly crave our blood—"

"I'll let you know right away," my mate promised, the humor in her words strained, perhaps a touch forced. No matter. I appreciated the attempt to make light of circumstances that would absolutely destroy a lesser wolf. *Yes*, she seemed upset with the changes, but she was still here, still standing—still fighting to live another day.

I rather admired that about her.

Lyssa had always been destined to be an alpha's mate—to lead her pack as a strong, confident matriarch, an alpha in her own right.

She would survive this.

"Good, yes, please do," I rumbled back, teasing tone unleashing a storm of gooseflesh across her neck, which I nipped at—made her giggle more earnestly. Still, as we folded back into a simple hug, holding one another, supporting each other through this fallout, I struggled to keep my own fears at bay.

Yes, she would survive whatever that fucking river had done to her, but would *we*?

And how long would it take for those golden eyes to rip her away from me—this alpha female destined for bigger, better things among the stars?

This she-wolf who smelled like apple blossoms...

And suddenly looked a little too much like a living goddess.

5

LYSSA

As soon as the Perry coven's black SUV pulled onto the end of our driveway, Rosa right up against the wheel and looking extra tiny in such a huge vehicle, I shot off the porch steps and raced across the gravel. Rocks flying, footsteps pounding, Kira whining, it was chaos inside and out, and I sprinted so hard, so fast, so head-on for the SUV that Rosa was forced to slam on the brakes, dust whooshing as it came to an abrupt stop. Engine still rumbling smoothly, I veered around the front and ripped open the passenger-side door, heart in my throat, fear prickling at the nape of my neck—fear that I'd yank the thing clean off, just like the tap.

"Whoa, honey, hold on," Rosa insisted as she scrambled to put the SUV in park. Sprawled in the seat, I slammed the door shut and rounded on her.

"Something's *happened* to me."

The witch finished ensuring we wouldn't roll down the driveway, then settled back in her seat with a gentle smile. "Lyssa, it's totally normal to—"

"No, not *that*." Heat exploded across my face; after a two-hour power nap, I caught Soren just before he left for work and begged him to call Rosa over—to help with all this bleeding stuff. None of my mates seemed to know how to handle a female's period now that I had the support products, so he had been all too happy to get the witch on the phone. And here she was, dressed down in a flowy purple linen jumpsuit, black flats, and a leather jacket that smelled as expensive as the inside of Ewan's car. She came—but she wasn't here to tell me about bleeding. No, the laptop someone had left for me weeks ago would re-educate me about *that* this afternoon; the internet was an awesome place. Kind of scary, sure, but full of useful information, a virtual library that I hadn't taken as much advantage of as I should.

But I didn't need the internet to teach me how to put a pad in my panties, so, you know, one crisis averted—the other still very much ongoing.

Panicked at the knitting of her red brows, I stabbed a finger toward my eyes. "No, *this.*"

Rosa looked up slowly, then stilled with a sharp breath when she inevitably—finally—noticed that my eyes were no longer the grey-blue they had been their whole lives but *gold.*

"Oh." She opened and closed those full lips a few times, blinking fast, clearly struggling. No, no, *not* good. "Oh, *gods*, what—"

I burst out crying before she could finish that thought.

Kira grumbled as once again hot wet streams spilled down my cheeks, my throat raw, my head full of thick, cottony fog. I *never* cried. I'd cried more in the last three days than I had in *years.* Crying didn't solve anything. Crying alerted predators to your presence—told them you were weak or wounded, that they could come take advantage of you in the dark.

Now, it felt like *nothing* set me off, just a gentle poke and I was gone.

Why?

"I-I'm a *freak* again," I wailed, furiously wiping at my cheeks, hating that every tear I smeared away was soon replaced by three more. "They w-won't *want* me anymore."

Still facing me, Rosa slumped in her seat with a deep breath, then straightened. When she put the car back in drive, I stopped wiping the tears and snot just long enough to notice Lucian on the front porch, his beard trimmed to scruff, his arms crossed—his expression more than a little concerned. Apprehension slithered down my back, foreign and hot like it didn't belong to me, and as soon as he stomped down the front steps, Rosa reversed out of the driveway and headed for the main road.

"Okay, okay, deep breaths, honey," she said as we peeled away from the peninsula my mates had built our home on, headed for familiar tree-lined roads that eventually led to either the village or the highway. Eyes forward, the witch reached over and patted my thigh—with two bandaged fingers.

"What h-happened?" I muttered, still catching my breath from the recent explosion. Rosa immediately withdrew, chuckling weakly as she got both hands back on the wheel.

"Oh, caught them in the door this morning like a total idiot."

Huh. I frowned, sitting up straighter and brushing the last of all that weakness from my face. Didn't she know all the healing spells? That was what she said the first night—when I hugged too hard and *hurt* her. She was a mom now, which meant she had them memorized.

So...

Why bandage her fingers like a human?

Not for the first time, a protective wave crashed over me, the hairs on my arms standing upright, Kira warbling her shared concern. Instinct told me, *again*, to grab this witch and run far, far away from Redwood Grove, but that didn't make sense. The gut feeling that had always steered me right before must have been on the fritz, because every part of me knew *this* was my territory. I'd marked each of my mates, still wearing their bites on my skin. I wouldn't leave. I... Maybe I *couldn't*.

Especially after Gull River.

Ugh, *no*.

Just catching glimpses of the mountain range through the trees, the canopy falling and burying the forest floor in an autumn-colored blanket of dead leaves, made my stomach turn.

Rosa bypassed the village, however. Whizzed right by the main wrought-iron gates and the grey stone wall surrounding it. She headed into the western woods, the foliage denser here, the road narrow and barely two lanes. Silent, her emerald gaze distant, her enormous red mane piled on top of her head like a beehive, she steered us around tight curves and winding paths, down steep hills and past the start of hiking trails, eventually stopping at a lookout point. Slowing the SUV way down, she pulled off the road onto another gravel lot, the trees cleared, and then eventually stopped at a low stone wall. It fenced in the cliffside, but seated so high up meant you could see clear over it into the gorge below, the trees slanting down the hill, a tepid waterfall slinking over the rocks.

"Okay." She cut the engine, unbuckled her seat belt, and faced me. "One... You are not a *freak*, and you never were."

I pursed my lips, only now aware that I hadn't bothered with my seat belt, and then pulled the visor down to block out the glare. While overcast, today was one of those cloudy but obnoxiously bright fall days that made your eyes tired and your skin red.

"Not a freak in the shifter sense, but—"

"*Two*," the witch pressed on, ticking these off on her fingers, "fated mates are forever. They'll always want you—" I scoffed. "—even when you're in a fight. *Even* when you want to rip each other's faces off you're so spitting mad..." Rosa arched an eyebrow, almost daring me to argue. "Seriously, you won't always like each other. You'll push buttons on purpose just to start a fight. You'll get annoyed over the little things. That's life. That's how relationships work—but mates will always *want*."

Maybe. I jabbed my thumb at the spot between my eyes where a teeny, tiny, *sharp* little headache had suddenly started. Even if fated mates were supposed to want each other until the end of time, destined for the stars or whatever, this felt... new. Strange. Were there stories about one fated mate turning into a monster? What happened then?

Why would anyone want a broken toy?

Rosa turned the engine back on briefly to lower the front

windows, allowing a crisp, cool breeze to filter in. "Now…" She angled toward me again, expression serious and voice way more intense than usual. "Tell me *everything* that happened at Gull River."

My belly looped, flashes of fear bolting down my arms. "I know you said to avoid it, but it was… It was different. It smelled like honey, and it looked like diamonds."

The witch paled suddenly, even her freckles fading away, and she nodded, gesturing for me to continue with a roll of her hand. "Okay, from the beginning. Be as detailed as you remember."

Details she wanted—details she got. Bat droppings, sticky and white. The darkness of the mountain corridors. The mineral tinge of wet rocks. The oppressive air. The sharp whisper. The apples and honey and starlight. The freezing water quenching my thirst. The numbness. Soren, panicked and frightened, shouting my name.

The heavy black sweeping over me.

The orchard with its dawn-kissed sky.

Kira on the outside.

Idunn.

The thunder.

Her eyes—my eyes.

The tap. The windows. The store shelves trembling.

Lucian wheezing when I hugged him—like I'd crushed him, same as her.

By the time I finished, Kira had gone as quiet as Rosa. Mouth dry, I sat there *waiting* for this witch to say something that would make it all better—to explain it away with magic, simple and easy, like this happened all the time.

But she didn't.

She disappeared inside her own head, gaze downcast, frown deep, and with every silent second, my inner turmoil ramped up until I *felt* the blood pulsing between my ears, decades of cruel voices at the back of my mind screaming insults that I'd long forgotten—

"Are you sure the woman in the dream said her name was Idunn?"

Rosa's cautious whisper shattered it all, subdued the fear—brought me back to the moment. Licking my lips, the best I could do was a stiff nod. Yeah, never heard that name before; *Idunn* wasn't one I'd forget.

With a deep breath, Rosa finally sat up and brushed a few rogue red curls from her face, ready to meet my golden eyes again.

"I could be… wrong," she started slowly, cheeks flushed when I inched toward her, hanging on her every word, "but Idunn is a goddess." She pursed those full lips for a moment, then cleared her throat. "A dead goddess, as far as we all know."

"Great." I rubbed my sweaty palms on my leggings. "Awesome. I have the same eyes as a dead goddess—"

"It's not unheard of for spirits to visit dreams," Rosa told me, her voice soft, her smile sweet as she stilled my fidgeting with a simple touch of my wrist, her skin cool but comforting. "And, look, Idunn was a goddess of youth and fertility. She's nature based. She… She grew the apples that gave the old Norse gods immortality. In all the stories, she's kind and good and sweet, maybe even a little naïve. Don't be scared of her."

I snorted and pointed at my eyes again. Sorry, maybe goddesses were totally normal for witches, same as demons and angels, but how could I *not* be terrified of a celestial being with infinite power? That was how it worked, right? Gods and goddesses… They ranked above us mere mortals.

False idols.

Nope. Just another lie, apparently.

"Maybe she chose you from the afterlife for a reason. Maybe you inherited some of her gifts." Rosa leaned closer and squinted, peering into my eyes like they held all the answers. When she eased back with a sigh, it was clear they didn't. "I don't know. Gods are fickle. I'd never presume to speak for them, even the dead ones."

This… was really happening.

I was dreaming about a dead goddess.

I had her eyes.

And Kira was just *fine* with it.

No. No, no, no, no. Not again. Not a freak *again*.

"Can you help me?" I struggled to choke the words out louder than a whisper. If Rosa feared dead goddesses, then it seemed wrong to rope her into this. At the end of the day, it was *my* problem, but what the heck did I know about monsters and magic? A big, fat *nothing*. "Please? I keep making the walls shake."

Rosa's round cheeks hollowed for a few seconds before she nodded, and from where I was sitting, it didn't *look* like I had twisted her arm. That was... good.

"Yes, but we should really tell—"

"*No one*," I blurted, lunging across the SUV, practically in her lap as I grabbed at her arms. The witch winced, and I reared back just as fast, terrified I'd hurt her worse than before. Hands in fists, I stuffed them in my lap. *Stay. You're stronger than you were before. Remember that.* "Please, don't tell anyone about Idunn. Please. It's our secret until... I can control it, or, or, or it goes away."

The crinkle of her eyebrows mimicked the voice at the back of my head: this was here to stay. No *way* I'd wake up tomorrow with my old eyes, suddenly back to normal, no longer stronger than my mate or capable of making the windows rattle.

One could dream.

Dreams never got me anywhere before, but Redwood Grove and the three alphas who ran it had felt like a dream since they found me...

Maybe miracles were possible.

Maybe that was the one thing Reed and Nikki hadn't lied about.

"But—"

"*Please*, Rosa." If she needed me to fall to my knees, I'd do it. Go against every instinct and grovel at a witch's feet. "Please."

Her defenses fell, expression softening, her sigh full of surrender.

"For now," the witch told me, firm and solid, sounding very much like a mama with every word, "we'll keep it between us. I'll help however I can, but we'll have to wait until after Samhain."

"Saw-what?"

"Halloween," she clarified distractedly, eyes on the gorge ahead, unfocused and out of reach. Loosening my fists, I threaded my hands together and slumped in my seat. Right. Halloween. We weren't even allowed to *talk* about it as kids, spending it in prayer, warding off the devil on *his* night. Having been out in the world, my existence peppered with trips into cities and whatnot over the last decade, October 31 just seemed like another human holiday, one created to sell a buttload of candy.

Not a bad thing. I'd once sat on a bench in some suburb, watching kids in costumes run door to door, the night full of laughter and fake screams.

Maybe witches and shifters did it different, this Samhain. Ewan was currently deep into organizing a Halloween bash at the village nightclub he owned, the thirty-first falling on a Saturday this year—a cash cow, he had dubbed it, whatever that meant.

"So, why do we have to wait?"

"The night is sacred to witches and warlocks, but it can make our magic a little manic," Rosa insisted, fussing with the curly red beehive piled on top of her head. "I just don't want to taint whatever you're experiencing with my power. After, you and me will get to the bottom of it. Until then, I'll research—"

"And tell no one," I reminded her. Rosa shot me a sidelong glance, grinning.

"And will tell no one."

"Not even Ethan." He was too close to Ewan; if he thought I was in danger, he'd probably go straight to my mate with all this, and I couldn't risk them finding out yet. Couldn't risk them looking at me differently—more differently than they already did.

Rosa's throat danced through a gulp. "Even Ethan. Promise."

Keeping secrets from your mate didn't feel good; for once, I could speak from experience. I owed her so, so, *so* much. "Thank you."

Her head bobbed up and down stiffly. "Yeah, of course. In the meantime, you have to work on being calm. If something happens when you get upset, you might expose yourself."

"I…" *I've already done that. Twice.* "I'll do my best."

"And if anyone asks, you're wearing gold contacts—for the aesthetic, or whatever."

"Contacts?" *Aesthetic?*

"Lenses," she said with another distracted wave, "to explain your eyes."

"Right." Yet another thing for the good ol' internet to explain in more depth later. Before I could get another word out, my belly rumbled. And not just a demure gurgle, but a straight-up lion's roar, so loud and proud that it was a wonder the ground didn't shake. With all the dull cramping a little further south, I hadn't even noticed the usual hunger pangs, but there they were, screaming for attention. Kira huffed, unimpressed that I'd let it go on this long, and, cheeks burning at Rosa's giggle, I pressed a hand to my stomach with an apologetic shrug.

"I take it you haven't eaten yet?"

"Nope."

"Right." Rosa turned the key, the SUV humming to life, and then pressed the button to roll the windows up. "First stop, drive-through breakfast burritos, then I'm taking you home—and then it's straight to bed." As she twisted around, looking out the rear window to reverse, she patted the top of my hand once, twice, three times with those bandaged fingers—which still didn't make sense.

And still set off a protective alarm bell deep inside me.

"Because, honey, in the nicest way possible"—Rosa wrinkled her nose at me affectionately—"you look like you really need to sleep."

"Oh, thanks." I patted my cheeks and smoothed my brows as we eased away from the edge of the empty lookout point. "Do you like it? The bags under the eyes and this pale, sickly complexion? I call it Menstrual Chic. You should take a picture—put it in your makeup book."

Rosa snorted. "Definitely first-page caliber."

Rather than heading into Redwood Grove, we took the highway south to a McDonald's just on the side of an off-ramp. The drive through was slammed, but we eventually made our way up, and I let Rosa order for me.

Six breakfast burritos, a muffin, and a pumpkin spice drink *thing* that tasted the way Soren sometimes smelled—homey and warm, cinnamon and nutmeg and autumn spices that made my heart sing. Rosa nursed a coffee, insisting she had already eaten, while I scarfed down the mountain of fast food on the way home, and by the time she pulled into the gravel driveway, my belly had finally stopped howling.

Always taking care of me, this witch.

We hugged, me holding on longer and tighter than I should, before I hopped out and padded back to the front porch. While my lower belly still ached, the cramps dull but ever present, the rest of me was more alert. Hunger crushed, panic soothed, I could actually *think* clearly as I waved goodbye to Rosa and slipped inside.

Huh. Empty house. No mates, not even Lucian's snores to serenade me as I trudged upstairs. Off to work, on patrol, business as usual—like my world *hadn't* flipped upside down.

Again.

Not sure how to feel about that.

Gnawing on the inside of my cheek, I checked each bedroom, just to be sure the oppressive quiet was real and not a figment of my imagination. Sure enough—nobody.

Fine.

Sleeping the day away worked for me; by the time I woke up, hopefully from an Idunn-less nap, at least one of them had to be home.

And then I could show them just how normal I was despite the gold eyes and the bursts of emotional earthquakes.

My bed, however, was not as I had left it.

No, someone had made it, tucked the linens in tight, realigned the pillows—and left a gift at the head. Kira sniffed warily as I climbed onto the huge cushy mattress, and I crawled over, then settled on my knees, head tipped, staring at the velvety blue rectangle, then the sealed beige envelope beside it.

"Card first, right?"

If she could swing it, Kira would have shrugged, equally perplexed as I slid a finger under the sealed flap and ripped into it.

Oh. Not a card.

Just a single piece of thick paper—with *Quinn Enterprises* written across the top in fancy letters, surrounded by stars and other celestial graphics.

> *I was an ass. Please, forgive me.*
> *E.*

His handwriting was as beautiful as the man himself, but as I sank onto the mattress, scowling at the elegant cursive, the words just didn't resonate.

He had been *more* than an ass.

I tossed the card aside and went for the blue box, cracking it open to find a gold bracelet inside. Little sun and moon charms dangled off the delicate chain, stamped with diamonds—maybe? All this looked straight out of those romance movies I'd relied on so heavily at the beginning, and in those, the heroine was always deeply touched by the display.

Oh, he *thought* of me.

Oh, he bought me jewelry!

Yeah, the bracelet was nice—impractical, but still nice.

The card was... lackluster.

Did he think *this* counted as an apology for screaming at me the other night? Instead of celebrating my win against a rival pack, he had shredded me to pieces in front of the others, suggesting all that mattered was my ability to birth heirs—so the pack could maintain our territory.

And at the time, I'd fallen for it. All of it. Heartbroken and insecure, I took his words as fact.

Soren had smoothed out some of the damage the next day, but *Ewan* needed to fix the rest.

Face-to-face.

I grabbed his stupid little note again, reading it a few times, and then crumpled it up as the windows shuddered. Kira whined, an insistent reminder to *calm down*, but I couldn't—not with this beef between us. Ewan had been the bluntest of my mates in the pharmacy, so much so that it sent me running again.

Now, with some of my worries quieted, it was on to the next problem.

Apparently.

Because our connection today felt strained and distant—and if I was supposed to play it cool, not get emotional or upset or whatever to hide what could be stupid magical dead goddess powers, then we had to sort this out.

Today.

Now.

No time to let it fester into an infection.

Tossing the crinkled paper ball aside, I snatched the jewelry box —just like in the movies, this thing—then leapt off the bed, marched out of the house, and headed straight for the village.

Straight for my mate who thought a couple of words and something shiny was enough. To a mate who always carried himself like he had all the answers.

Well, this alpha male was about to learn how it felt to be *wrong*.

6

EWAN

"Yeah, yeah, I'll make a few copies and collate the packets before the —" Jocelyn stumbled into my office doorframe, her back blocking the view—but not the heady scent of roses descending over the entire floor like a fog. "Oh, uh, hi. How are you feeling?"

Lyssa shouldered by, not as brutishly as she had the first time but still rough enough to put a fox in her place. "Doing great, thanks, Jocelyn." She then grabbed the door and closed it in my assistant's face, the very same assistant who had been with me all night during the chaos but *still* managed my professional world this morning with an iron fist like nothing had happened.

Like we weren't operating on maybe a collective hour of sleep between us.

Seated at my desk, I wheeled my chair out from behind the monitor and arched an eyebrow, seconds away from grabbing my phone and shooting a scathing message to the two dipshits who ran this pack with me. Because, I mean... Why the *fuck* was she here and not in bed? Not only had she been fucking poisoned by Gull River, no matter how *good* she pretended to be now, but she was either on her period or in the midst of a miscarriage. Given the symptoms, the former seemed more likely, but the latter made me *ache...*

Whatever the reason, my girl ought to be in bed for the rest of the day while someone waited on her hand and foot.

The sight of her standing there, fuming, unleashed a storm of emotions that I so didn't fucking need right now. Dressed in the usual yoga pants, T-shirt, black jacket combo, to outsiders my mate looked like she was headed to the gym.

The one thing out of place: a Tiffany box clutched in her fist, the one I'd put a rush order on and called in a shitload of favors yesterday to have it expedited up here at breakneck speed.

Hair wild and trundling down her back like a shaggy caramel waterfall, Lyssa hoisted the blue velvet rectangle. "What's *this?*"

Fire ripped through me, her *wrath* scorching my own feelings, the first real reminder of our bond all morning. Fantastic to feel her again—but I'd rather it not be her rage making me break out in sweats. Usually waltzing over my office threshold pushed all the bullshit aside. No matter what was going on out *there*, in here, I was in control. Confident. Assertive. Focused. *Alpha.*

For the last two hours, distraction and uncertainty were the driving forces. I had to read emails twice for the first time in fucking ages just to digest the content. Hell, I even ordered Jocelyn to rearrange my schedule, probably pissing off a few of the organizers for next week's Halloween bash, but what-the-fuck-*ever* —I wasn't in the headspace to deal with the usual shit today.

So, when Lyssa demanded to know what *this* was, I just blinked at the Tiffany box, cocked my head, and replayed the demand in my mind.

Had I... heard that right?

"Did you open it?" I drawled, sounding snarkier than intended but too wiped out to care. My mate jostled the box, probably unaware of the tens of thousands I'd dropped on it, how precious the stones in all the little pendants truly were.

"Yeah."

"Then I think it's pretty clear what it is." After wiping the sweaty sheen from my forehead, I threaded my hands together and tapped them on my desk. "Do I need to explain how jewelry works, or—"

Lyssa hurled the damn thing at me with a snarl, that velvet rectangle soaring like a fucking blue missile. I barely caught it before it slammed into my face, her aim dangerously accurate, the force behind the throw a cause for concern.

Wolves were strong, male and female, but that…

It hurt to catch.

"You think you can, what, *buy* my forgiveness?"

All the blood drained from my face, prickling down to my chest as I gawked back at her. "I… No. I just didn't have time to—"

"To respect my feelings?"

My inner wolf raked my insides like he agreed. We had been in a feud since the run-in with the Hawthorne pack at our border, which was a fucking *joke*. He felt the same way I did about our mate squaring off against four strange wolves from a vicious pack. Sure, not quite as malicious as the Quinn pack in their heyday, but still dangerous.

My mate crossed her arms and glared, waiting for me to say something, *anything*. I bristled at the thought of her expecting me to grovel, but maybe she was right.

Maybe I needed to spend a little time on my knees, because as visceral as my fears had been that night, as frustrated as I'd been at the pharmacy this morning while Lucian and Soren babied her, I could have chosen my words better.

Instead, I'd taken the maelstrom inside out on her.

But women liked gold and diamonds and pretty things to dangle off their bodies.

I'd actually taken a ton of time picking the *right* piece. Her ears weren't pierced, so no earrings, and none of the necklaces in the private buyers catalogue *fit*. The sun and the moon, the delicate golden chain…

It suited her.

Lyssa was the truest wolf I'd ever met, the most connected to our primal side, our rich, rooted past. But she was also the motherfucking *sun*; her joy, her pride, the night she took down that moose for Thanksgiving and hauled it all the way to our front door... for *us*. She was the spark under our pack's ass. Her fire would unite us—forge a new legacy.

A good legacy.

A *strong* legacy.

But my reasons for selecting the piece inside this box, which I set cautiously on my desk, would probably fall on deaf ears if I tried to reason my way through this.

Still though. I had to *try*. "Lyssa, I just thought—"

"You should have talked to me," she said thickly, voice on the brink of a wobble even as the rest of her turned still and severe as stone, "and *not* like you did at the border the other night." *Fuck.* "Do you know how much that hurt? All the things you said? Is that what you really think—that I'm only good to start a bloodline?"

My blood ran cold, and I scrubbed at my face with a groan. "*No*, of course not."

It was just... a part of her.

And to ignore it, to pretend we all weren't highly aware that this she-wolf was the key to starting our bloodline, was bullshit.

Not exactly the most politically correct approach, but...

But I guess I'm willing to hurt her.

I glowered up at my forehead, at the frat-boy tone my inner monologue adopted—the tone that always reminded me just how fucking stupid *I* was being, not everyone else.

Maybe not about the core of my argument, but definitely the approach.

Lyssa shifted her weight to one leg, hip cocked, her golden stare intense—and kind of unnerving "Well?"

"I *am* sorry for that," I started, selecting my words as carefully as possible. "What I said... It was all fear, and—" *Fuck it.* "—a little truth." I raised a hand when Lyssa sputtered. "You *are* our fated." This time when she stared, unblinking and intense, I met the gold head-on and refused to back down. "We'll never want another like we want you. There is no better mother and matriarch for this pack and territory than *you*. Lady Fate designed you that way—"

"I'm a person first," she gritted out, then shook her head with a huff. "Or, you know, shifter, wolf, whatever. But I'm not a label or a thing—I have feelings and wants and my own desires."

With a deep breath, I slowly stood and planted my hands on my desk, balancing precariously on my fingertips. Fights like this were unheard of in the Quinn pack: civil and conversational. Reasonable. Rational. My pack had always been about blame, about who was responsible for the fuckup and who was about to get walloped. We tossed responsibility around like a fucking hot potato, fought for *ourselves*, sometimes literally, and hoped that at the end of the day, someone else looked guiltier in our alpha's eyes.

My dad was a mean drunk, and, even totally shitfaced, packed one hell of a right hook.

So, yeah, deflection had been a way of life for the Quinn kids, and it fucking followed me all the way up here.

Because, looking back, I did the same thing with Soren and Lucian.

Always them, never me.

And it had to stop.

I couldn't bring this disease into our pack—to my mate and whatever pups we had in the future.

Brows knit, I hung my head, shame burning all over. "You're my mate, Lyssa, not a walking womb." I straightened and stared deep into the gold, my wolf and I finally in a ceasefire, the vicious heartburn easing a little. "I'm so sorry I made you feel that way. What I said—how I said it—was uncalled for and beyond rude."

"And wrong," Lyssa growled. She then sucked in a sharp breath, eyes darting around my office. I joined the hunt, bracing for something to shake or rattle or—

One of my pens trembled in the coffee cup Jocelyn bought me the first Christmas we spent together. Just a silly old University of Toronto mug from the campus store.

I'd never drank from it.

And it always had a home on my desk, even as my tastes and style refined over the years.

One pen of the bunch shuddered, nothing more, but the air

thickened around us, her scent sharper, stronger, more intrusive than ever before.

"And... wrong, yes," I said slowly, still eyeing the pen.

"Okay." Her arms finally dropped, body language open for the first time since she had marched in here. "Ewan—" *Fuck*. Wildfire consumed me every goddamn time she said my *name*, and it was really starting to piss me off. "We're both alphas. Me, you, the others —we're the mating, uh, pair times two."

"Quad," I muttered, which made her eyes narrow.

"Whatever." She fidgeted with her hair, tucking it behind her ears, exposing that sharp jawline as it rippled through a clench. "Alphas are equal in the pack. Don't you ever speak to me like that again. I won't take that from *any* of you. If I want to defend my territory, I will."

All that lusty fire turned to rage at the thought. Gritting my teeth, I looked away—to the bar cart where we first mated and where she sobbed after, desperate for companionship, needing just *one* of us to stick around. How far she'd come in just a few short weeks.

No matter how out of line I'd been the other night, I couldn't have her running into stupid situations—alone—where she might get hurt. Unfortunately, if I harped too hard on it now, she'd resent me. The sentiment made the angry flames snap and spit, made my inner wolf pace and snarl, but that didn't change the fact I needed backup for this conversation.

Soren and Lucian had better agree: our mate could *not* charge into the wilderness alone against an unknown number of foes. No way. Not a chance in hell.

I squared my shoulders and changed tactics.

"What happened to your eyes?"

"I don't know," she said a little *too* fast. A gulp and a shrug followed, her anxiety prickling at the nape of my neck like TV static. "Side effect of the river?"

"Why did you drink?"

"Because it smelled good, and I was thirsty." Lyssa stiffened when my eyebrows rocketed up my forehead. "It's that simple."

Gull River did *not* smell good. I had scented it out on my first trip to the unclaimed mountain range years ago, and while it was a blemish on my newfound territory, I accepted it because it was *mine*.

That and there was nothing I could do to change it. Ethan and I had talked at length about Gull River, mulling over the source of its poison, about why some animals drank and died while others turned tail and bolted. Lounging in our usual VIP booth at the Chalet, my shot girls feeding us bourbon all night and security keeping the ritzy rabble at bay, we had discussed curses and toxins, magical and natural alike, but at the end of the day, it was just talk.

No clear answer.

No insider knowledge from the only warlock I had ever trusted.

Who never sneered down his nose at me because I was a shifter, some beast the magical folk considered lesser.

Gull River had been fouled and sullied and fucking *gross* from the day I first found it until this very morning when I trekked out there to confirm.

It didn't smell like fucking *honey*.

And if that was what Lyssa scented inside the range, then she ought to be banned from there too.

I nearly said it, but instead—

"Lyssa, twice now in as many days, I thought my mate was at risk of *dying*." Her anger finally dulled from a dagger to a butter knife in my chest. "You understand why that might make me protective, right? Maybe an overprotective asshole, but I *will* protect what's mine... and I won't always do it nicely. You need to hear that."

Cheeks sunken, Lyssa glanced back at the door, then down to her shoes, voice hard as she said, "Protective of me—or the territory?"

Both. Couldn't say that though. Not now. Not today or anytime in the near future. I held my tongue, not trusting my stupid mouth to keep the truth where it belonged. Lyssa finally looked up expectantly, waiting for me to soothe her worries, her anxiety prickling at the back of my neck ramping up to little acupuncture needles. Teeth gritted, I swatted at the invisible sensation, glad to be feeling her again but *annoyed* that we had only mated once and the cross-contamination of *feeling* hit so hard already.

Our staring match dragged on, her begging, me withholding, until finally my mate headed for the door.

Fuck.

Fuck.

"Protective of you," I insisted roughly, making her pause well within reach of the doorknob, seconds from storming out and leaving us hanging. Before her, I would have let it go—let the opposition think whatever they wanted so long as it was clear that I'd won. Now, it needed to be quashed or I would feel it, literally, all day. "We don't really have a choice anymore, right?"

Lyssa wheeled around, golden eyes narrowed again yet somehow screaming *What the fuck did you just say?* loud and goddamn clear. One step forward, two steps back: that was the Quinn way in relationships. My parents had been fated, sure, but crime and booze and money soured the bond shortly after I was born. The pups that followed? Fucked. Born into chaos, their destinies set in stone.

"I'm just… trying to be honest with you," I told her, tongue tangled around the words—around the honesty. "I could lie. I lie to everyone." Bright and squeaky as my holier-than-thou persona, I was still a Quinn at heart. "I built all this…" I gestured at the wall of windows behind me, out to the parkette littered with pine trees, Halloween décor already hanging from the boughs. "I built it on hard work, sweat and tears and blood, sure, but also on a few lies and false promises along the way."

Hell, that was practically the Quinn creed.

But I wasn't the only shark to spin the truth for gains. My professional world was pretty on the outside and rotten on the inside; I usually tried not to let the rot stain my suits.

"I'm doing my absolute best to be totally honest with *you*," I pressed on, only now realizing why I had been such a mess since I met her. I'd never freaked out on a woman before. Never exposed myself. Never peeled back the layers. My fated mate deserved that, not only because Lady Fate deigned it, but because Lyssa was a blank slate. A good she-wolf. The same old shit just wouldn't and— given how she'd called me out this morning—*couldn't* fly with her. "And you may not always like it. Sometimes the truth is ugly, but no one else gets this. *That* is a choice I *can* make. Fate put us together for a reason, but *I* choose when and with who to share my heart. Honesty? That's from the heart. It fucking sucks. It makes me feel…" *Wrap it up, asshole.* "Anyway. I choose to be honest with you. I think we're all learning we can't always control how we act around our fated mates. It's irrational and frustrating, but this… The cold, honest truth? That's all me."

I held my breath despite needing to gulp it down by the lungful, that rambling speech taking a lot out of me. My inner wolf stilled when her cheeks hollowed again, but we both breathed easier when Lyssa bowed her head, hands on her hips, in a thoughtful quiet. No fire licked across my bones. No anxiety stabbed at the back of my neck. Nothing from her but a contemplative calm that threw me for a fucking loop, because arguments *never* went like this.

It wasn't two parties laying out the facts from their perspective, acknowledging them, and then conceding on certain points. No, it was a duel to the death—and then someone got fucked over *hard*.

Her golden gaze lifted slowly. Fuck's sake—so intense and penetrative. Sometimes pups shed their bright blues as they aged, growing out of their birth color into something more settled. My eyes shifted from dark, dark brown to copper when I changed from man to wolf, but this was different. This was… magic.

Accursed or not—that was the question of the day, wasn't it?

And none of us had a clue what to do about it.

But that hue was impossible to ignore. Couldn't pretend it wasn't there, not when it gave Lyssa an unnervingly ethereal beauty now, like she could see down to the soul and beyond.

People who had met her before today would know something was off. Normally Ethan would have been my go-to about anything outside the physical world, but this felt different—and private. This was pack business for now, and I went with my gut.

If anyone asked, our mate was trying out cosmetic contacts.

Because...

They were...

In?

I shook off the gold, hyperaware of it but refusing to let it dictate our interactions, then extended my arms. "Hug it out?"

She might have sighed like *I* was the one who stormed in here and hurled a Tiffany's box in a snit, but Lyssa agreed with a stiff, quick nod. Darting around my desk, I was on her in a flash, scooping her into a hug that felt lukewarm at best. Her arms slumped around my torso, locked at the wrists and not exactly squeezing, but at least she didn't bail. I ducked down to bury my face first in her hair, then her neck, dick twitching with interest, blood surging.

Her scent was so much *stronger* today than yesterday, the roses headier, the musk more apparent—a louder, bolder siren song to my inner wolf. Trembles shuddered through me when I caught him at the last second trying to force the shift, desperate to sniff her for himself.

"I *am* sorry, Lyssa," I murmured, voice deeper and rougher, growly and beastly and fucking *stay in there, you asshole*.

"You can be honest with me," she whispered back, sounding annoyingly in control and not like her wolf was trying to stage a coup. "Doesn't make you free of consequences—honesty isn't an excuse to be a... a... *jerk*."

"You're absolutely right. Fair enough."

"But if you can just talk to me like this," my mate pressed, "and not through a stupid note or with gifts, then I'm good."

"Heard," I growled back, finally caging the beast even as her scent drowned me, imprinting on my suit, in my hair, across my skin. Warmth blossomed in my chest, the sensation coming straight from her, and Lyssa squeezed tighter. I returned the pressure, nuzzling in deep, throwing caution to the wind and succumbing to the rosy deep.

We stood there for ages, holding each other, almost like we needed the other's strength to process the day.

I mean, Lyssa should have died.

Gull River should have killed her.

But she was here, in my arms.

That was quite the fucking victory—and it was time to treat it as such.

Question it another time.

When we finally eased apart, I swooped her hair behind her ears, noting the dark rings around her golden gaze, the impact of her body's turmoil obvious. *Please don't be a miscarriage. Please just be her period.*

Miscarriages were extremely rare for shifters, but not impossible.

With the river—

No.

No, it was probably just her period, and clearly her three mates sucked at their end of the baby-making bargain.

"You look tired, blue ey—"

She sucked in a sharp breath when I stopped, both of us aware that she *wasn't* blue eyes anymore, that my pet name didn't apply.

Fuck it.

"Blue eyes," I finished properly, softening my tone, my touch, *everything*—because she would always be my blue-eyed mate. Always. "Want to nap on the couch?"

Lyssa rolled her shoulders back, shaking off that little hiccup—one of many—like a fucking champ. "No, I want my bed."

Possessiveness flashed through me at the thought of her considering that room, that bed, in *our* house, hers. The beast in me wanted to lash out, pin her to the wall again, fuck her until she screamed.

I kissed her cheek instead, followed by a gentle peck to her lips.

We hadn't mated again since the first time; interactions around the house were all so tepid and uncertain, the four of us maintaining a frustrating level of social distancing like we were still figuring out this coexistence nightmare. Despite the longing looks, the blushes, the suggestive lip bites, Lyssa seemed more focused on her mates getting along—doing shit together without fighting—when, really, this minx probably wanted to jump our bones.

All our bones.

Because she had been *just* as eager to scratch that itch.

And yet—nothing.

It was driving me *fucking* insane.

"Go home, then," I rumbled, tipping my head toward the door. Lyssa nibbled at her lower lip for a moment, then arched an eyebrow.

"You going to be there for dinner?"

I frowned, knowing it would disappoint her and ruin this cozy bubble we found ourselves in, but still saying it anyway. "No—not tonight."

I never *did* dinner anyway; there was always so much to do here.

The workday didn't stop at five for the *real* workaholics.

After patting my chest, kissing my cheek, and staring deep into my eyes until my inner wolf whimpered, Lyssa headed for the door.

I went for my desk and grabbed the jewelry box.

"Hey." She glanced back, then whirled around to catch the velvet rectangle when I lobbed it her way. As Lyssa hugged it to her chest, I nodded pointedly at the blue, adopting a stern, no-nonsense alpha stance as I growled, "You'd better be wearing that when I *do* get home."

Rather than bristle at the domineering tone, Lyssa smirked, then sauntered out the door with a torturous sway in her hips.

Alone again, the exhaustion hit hard. Heaviness whittled into my limbs, and rather than going for my chair, I trudged over and flopped onto my couch.

Stretched out, just to alleviate the dull ache in my lower back.

Closed my eyes because, you know, the sun was suddenly a little too bright.

Let the heaviness take over—

And then, minutes later, boom—dead to the world, snoring away.

7

SOREN

"But these are Halloween classics." Freddy, Mike, Jason, Ghost Face —gang's all here, literally in the palm of my hand. I motioned to the DVD boxset with a dramatic flourish. This baby had been a part of the Acker pack legacy since I was a kid. Dad shared my love of cheesy horror movies, and we had watched this set so many times over the years, slowly initiating my sisters one by one into the ring, that it was a miracle any of the discs still played. Corners frayed, ink faded, the girthy box set moved with me to this house—and given Halloween was only a week away, it was time for the psychotic stars of the season to make a new pack debut.

And, I mean, where better than our basement cinema room?

When if not on a freakin' stormy Friday night late in October? *Seriously.*

"I don't want to be scared though," Lyssa protested. Swaddled in blankets and sweaters and obnoxious wool leggings, my mate had tucked herself into the far corner of the mammoth wrap-around sectional, comfy, hormonal, and ravenously eyeing the movie marathon spread I'd organized earlier on the coffee table.

She had no idea what my sisters and I would have done to watch these classics in a room like *this* when we were kids. For years, we fought for the best seat in front of the tiny TV in the living room, and even when Dad upgraded our tech, it was still a brawl over who bagged the spot where all the acoustics hit just right.

While Ewan might have had a firm hand in designing the pretentious upscale accents of this cottagey mansion, I had pushed for the *perfect* cinema suite. Windowless. Black walls and ceiling. Old-school movie theater carpeting so ugly it insulted Ewan's sensibilities. Screen that stretched an entire wall with the most expensive sound system we could squish into the budget. The enormous couch hugged three walls, big enough for twenty—and meant for a huge pack to enjoy.

I'd designed this place with my future pups and their friends in mind.

Lyssa had used it the most so far. Rosa came in at a close second, frequently here for girly days, chick flicks galore. Lucian wasn't exactly a TV guy, but film and television was a quick way to update our mate on the modern world, which meant he put up with it. For her, he sucked it up.

We all made concessions for Lyssa, even more now after Gull River, her eyes still a soul-piercing gold, her period—not a miscarriage, thank Lady Fate, after the pregnancy stick read negative for any baby hormones in her system—wreaking havoc on her mood this week, her sleep fraught with dreams that made her cry out and sweat and moan and gasp.

Me and Ewan carried on working, yeah, but we did what we could—*all* of us—to cater to her *especially* hard this week. Whatever she wanted, she got. Specific meal? I had that covered. Treats from the village? Ewan came home with it in droves. Jaunts down south just to *move*? Lucian escorted her on top of his usual excessive patrol schedule.

"They really aren't that scary," I argued weakly, tapping the box set and motioning to the screen. "We—"

"She's made her choice," Lucian said gruffly. Scratching at his dark brown beard, trimmed and neater than I'd ever seen it, he glanced between us with a *sigh* like he was *over* this discussion—and very clearly in Lyssa's corner.

"We watched these when I was a kid. Like, they're *funny*, not scary."

"They're horror movies." Lucian pinned me with a menacing look. "Enough."

My eyes narrowed right back, inner wolf pacing around, uncomfortable with the tension. Seated in the middle of the sectional, legs spread wide like he had a thirteen-inch dick that needed the breathing room, Lucian was usually a go-with-the-flow wolf. Historically, *Ewan* was my main opponent, but I guess when it came to Lyssa, the British dickweed was ready to go to bat, even using his *words* tonight rather than communicating with caveman grunts and eyebrow raises.

"But if it's scary..." Lyssa drew the blankets up to her chin, eyes rounded as she studied the box set. I shook my head, willing my excitement to rub off on her.

"It's really not."

"Not if you've seen it a million times," Lucian interjected again, and we quickly resumed our glaring match, waiting for the other to back down. We'd been at this for ten minutes, ever since the food arrived, and, *no*, I refused to fold—not again. *No one* wanted to do any of my usual October traditions. So far, the guys had shit all over my suggestions, and then Lyssa would side with the majority. Once again, *I* was on the outskirts, even after we'd mated. Definitely a crappy feeling, and not one I expected to go through after marking and being marked by my fated mate.

Seriously, wasn't it supposed to get easier, not harder?

With Ewan bogged down in next week's Halloween-bash nightclub preparations, the Chalet forecast to rake in tens of thousands as rich kids flocked north for *the* premiere party of the spooky season, a Friday-night movie marathon seemed perfect. A little time to bond as a group, the most obnoxious alpha absent, and with the storm, the moody October ambiance—Halloween movies were a given. I'd come up with it this morning, offering to order pizza, wings, cheese sticks, lava cakes, popcorn...

Lucian sucked at food stuff. The guy couldn't cook to save his life, nor did he have a clue how to organize a chill hang in a basement.

This was my gig.

My *thing*. The first themed night anyone had agreed to so far.

No one wanted to carve jack-o'-lanterns, and the guys laughed off my suggestion of taking Lyssa on the wagon ride out to the pumpkin patch down south so she could pick her own. Caramelizing apples? Nope. Decorating the house for the zero trick-or-treaters headed our way next Saturday? Hell no. Group costume suggestions? Get *out*.

Lucian had given me hope this morning that just *one* Acker fall tradition could finally happen—and now this?

This was *bullshit*.

Yeah, the new pack wasn't the Acker pack. We had to make our own traditions, forge our own path—whatever. But my old pack had fun traditions. The kind to endure through generations. Pack-bonding activities that strengthened our connections. And, frankly, it was really starting to piss me off that no one wanted to try *any* of them. I had worked hard all day to be out of the office at a reasonable hour. Ordered the food. Organized it on the table in the center of the sectional. All my bases covered. Beer chilled. Pop fizzy and cooled.

I pulled my weight for this pack, yet time and time again, the two grumpiest assholes on the planet outvoted me.

And my mate just rolled with it.

I kept waiting for Lyssa to realize all this was important to me—but nope.

"Babe, trust me, they're really good—"

"Stop pressuring her." Lucian looked about two seconds away from punching me, but the feeling was mutual. I groaned, pinched the bridge of my nose, then redirected my frustration onto him, our alpha bond sizzling with it.

"*You* stop being a *wuss*." I patted the box set again, determined to plead my case—determined to *win*, just this once. "Halloween movies are a cultural staple. We all did this kind of stuff in October growing up—"

"Strong disagree," he rumbled, his mouth twitching like he was fighting back a grin—like suddenly this amused him.

My inner wolf rustled up a growl, but almost because he felt like he *had* to. All packs had that one wolf who soothed tension by being a clown; of course I got stuck with him.

"Can you seriously, for once, just—"

"Soren, you're throwing a fit over a bloody *movie*." Never heard the guy talk this much. Our fated mate had put us all through the ropes lately, made us reexamine who we were as wolves and alphas, but with Lucian, her presence made him vocal. *Very* vocal. Unfortunately, he had always seemed happy in his little hermit bubble, and arguing about this—just a *bloody* movie, apparently— had his hackles up and his eyes like golden honey. He jerked his chin toward the blank projection screen, all teeth as he added, "Stop being a *child* and just put the *fucking* Lion King on already."

Ugh. As soon as Lyssa spotted the cover art online for the world's most recognizable kids movie, she jumped and squealed and pointed; it was the only film she remembered from her childhood, and instead of all these gorgeous, hilarious, gruesome classics, she wanted… that.

Cartoon lions.

"But…" I hoisted the box set one last time, my inner wolf whining like he could smell defeat. Lyssa finally tore her gaze from the stack of pizza boxes, brows knit, our connection shivering with want—want for something *else*. Lucian, meanwhile, slumped into the couch and glared, waiting for me to grow up.

Fine.

Fine.

Scowling, I tossed my beloved DVD collection onto the couch, then rustled around with the laptop connected to all the tech.

Roughly a minute later, the movie started up, and the recessed lighting dimmed.

And I bailed.

"Soren?"

My mate called to me just outside the door of the cinema room, the basement hallway dark, her voice wanting, her concern like an ice pack plunked squarely on my chest. Sighing, I leaned back through the doorway.

"Be right back."

This was supposed to be a group hang, and with me as the organizer, it seemed shitty to leave.

But I needed a second to *breathe* so I didn't snap.

Neither of them deserved that.

Lyssa just wanted to watch a movie from her childhood, which we still knew nothing about, but the memory seemed to make her happy. And Lucian... That bastard was just sticking up for our mate. Obviously he wasn't chomping at the bit to watch a stupid cartoon, so, yeah, couldn't exactly snarl at *him*.

But couldn't they see I was just trying to build fun pack traditions?

That this mattered to me—and it should matter to them?

I stomped all the way upstairs to grab a beer from the kitchen fridge, ignoring the ones I'd left chilling in the wine cellar. While my inner wolf had always been a goofy dufus despite being destined to rule as an alpha, he delivered when it *mattered*—we had that in common. After my colossal screw-up with Gull River, I just wanted to distract everyone.

Make it better.

Make it *fun* and seasonal and cozy.

Make this place feel more like a home, not just a house we all slept in, unsure how to interact, uncertain what to do with each other. I mean, it sure as hell wasn't sex. Despite the desire thickening in the air anytime Lyssa walked into a room, all three of us stayed polite—like finally we were ready to *not* step on each other's toes.

311

The vibe was weird.

Something had clearly happened to her in the mountain.

The Hawthorne wolves had howled along our eastern borders twice this week. Work, duty, connection, protection, *feelings*—it was a lot.

Why wouldn't they let me *fix* it already?

I could.

I threw a great party.

Cracking open the bottle, I tossed the lid on the kitchen island and trudged back to the cinema room, where I found Lyssa and Lucian scarfing down pizza, half the meat lover's supreme already gone. With the excitement of what could have been an epic movie night extinguished, I hunkered down in the far corner, appetite dead right alongside my original plans, and nursed my beer as the movie's opening montage played out. Lyssa couldn't look away, shoving food in her mouth and barely blinking, still buried in cozy blankets, happy as a clam and focused on the screen.

And Lucian—

I flinched when I glanced his way and found the alpha staring *directly* into my eyes. A few cushions over, we had enough of a gap between us that if one took a swing, the other could dive out of the way—maybe. But his glare had softened. As he chewed a massive mouthful, tomato sauce in his beard, grease smeared across his white tee like he had wiped both hands there instead of taking from the mountain of napkins, it wasn't anger flowing between us.

But disappointment.

Disappointment in me, my behavior, my sulk at the far end of the couch.

But he didn't get it—how it felt to be constantly put down by Ewan, overruled by them both, and boxed out of the decision-making.

If he did, he would have gone along with my plan—been on my goddamn *side* for once.

Head cocked, I flipped him off. The alpha rolled his eyes and grabbed two slices of pizza, sandwiching them together as he relaxed into the couch to watch the movie. He grinned when Lyssa pointed out baby Simba, so absolutely smitten with her that even *this* was tolerable.

I sipped my beer in silence, a little disappointed in my behavior too…

But determined to build seasonal pack traditions for us if I had to drag all of them kicking and screaming into the fun.

The next holiday season in December would be better. Not scary. Family oriented. Tons of stuff to do around the village. Loads of Acker traditions to float.

I needed to strategize. Suggest stuff casually—and sell Lyssa on it first.

But if Ewan and Lucian pushed back, if they refused to so much as drive around the suburbs just to look at the lights and decorations, I'd fucking riot.

8

LYSSA

"Can I see some ID, please?"

I blinked up at the enormous man in black, distinctly human—I'd started to notice the difference in posture, complexion, and temperature the more time I spent around my mates—and attractive in a TV-show villain sort of way. Blue-eyed and bald, he wore a fitted suit and a wool cap, steely and stern as he asked clubgoers for identification. Having shuffled through the line that wrapped around the red-bricked building for the last thirty minutes, I'd watched this unfold time and time again.

Stupid to think he wouldn't ask. Well over the legal drinking age, I should have breezed by. Instead, I stood before him, a head shorter and gawking, then groped at my empty purse. No ID. No phone. No nothing that people on TV had when they went to places like the Chalet. Still, while the nightclub scene might have been totally foreign, bars were old news—and I'd been sneaking into them since I was fourteen. Usually a smile and a flutter of your eyelashes did the trick if anyone questioned you.

"Uh…" Not this guy. I didn't even bother to try; Kira probably wouldn't let me fake flirt with another male now that I was marked and mated with our fated. The thought made my stomach all topsy-turvy anyway, and I licked my lips as I gestured to the red doorway down the brick corridor behind him. "I'm here for Ewan Quinn. He... We..."

Ugh, what did we even call ourselves to humans? *Hello, the wolf who owns this place is my fated mate. Step aside, human.* Yeah, not going to fly.

Probably.

Just as I drew a breath, about to *try* and pull rank somehow, a gruff interjection cut me off.

"You Lyssa?"

I flinched when the second bouncer joined the conversation, the pups he had been questioning when I initially stepped forward slinking away, tails tucked, IDs rejected. Just as tall as his colleague, he was leaner, his skin a rich onyx and his eyes a warm chocolate brown.

The warmth frosted over a little in the silence that followed, and I hastily nodded, struggling to speak—to sound calm, cool, and collected like the *teenagers* on the shows I'd streamed to prepare for tonight.

"She's good, man." The second bouncer swatted at the first. "Boss said she might drop by a few weeks ago—has a VIP room reserved for her if she ever showed."

My face lit up like a firework as the pair scrutinized me, like they were trying to decide *why* I deserved such special treatment. Kira's unimpressed huff slipped out *my* nostrils, and I swallowed hard when they frowned, waiting, waiting, *waiting*—

Then disbanded and let me pass, already on to the next people in line.

A cold, shaky feeling washed over me as I scurried by. Not very alpha-like, quaking before club security, but one day I'd find my confidence.

Rosa kept telling me that, anyway.

Put us out in the wild, deep in the forest in the middle of winter, and those two would be *dinner*. Here, they radiated predator—and I *had* to stop feeling like prey.

The hairs on the back of my neck stood up.

Kira stilled.

I stopped just a few paces from the entrance, all that security stuff falling to the wayside.

Eyes roved my back, up and down, side to side...

Someone was watching me.

Kira snarled as I twisted around, searching, scanning my surroundings for a source. It couldn't just be the bulbous cameras mounted on the walls; a mechanical eye wouldn't make my entire body erupt in goosebumps or douse my blood with adrenaline.

For a Tuesday night, the Redwood Grove village was really *alive*. Nestled in the trendy high street area, flashy restaurants and packed bars surrounded the Chalet on all sides, people milling from one locale to the next, the nightlife bustling when everywhere outside these walls would have been dead hours ago. Just past eleven, the place felt like a major city, not a cozy hamlet at the foot of the mountains.

Must be something in the water—

I shuffled aside as a group of males barreled down the corridor, okayed by security and headed for the door like a pack of wolves— moving as a unit, glancing at *me* as one, totally in sync.

Gnawing at the insides of my cheeks, I stood taller and ignored them. They weren't the first males to leer inside the village walls, and they wouldn't be the last. *They* didn't set my body on fire though.

Wait.

My belly looped and my heart sank.

Oh. Right.

Those eyes boring into me from nowhere probably belonged to the same dead goddess who had turned mine gold.

Stupid.

Of course she was watching me—from the inside of my skull, no doubt. I dreamed about her every night.

Well, I dreamed of the orchard. The endless rows of apple trees. The sky pink, her world beautiful and empty and lonely. *She* hadn't made direct contact in a few days, her whisper occasionally on the breeze, encouraging me to try an apple. Sometimes I caught her out of the corner of my eye, flitting between trees like a ghost, but anytime Kira and I charged over to investigate, she was gone.

"Snap out of it," I muttered, fluffing my soft waves as a couple locked in each other's arms sauntered by, their hips swaying in unison. Shoulders back, I followed them into my first nightclub—

Overwhelmed. Instantly.

Oh.

Oh.

Kira stiffened again, both of us plunged into a deer-in-headlights daze at the assault. Lights dimmed, music blaring, scents clashing and mingling—sweat and beer and liquor and perfume galore. The couple ahead of me veered left, and I just followed along blindly to the free coat check booth tucked into a corner just off the main door. Slowly adjusting to the intensity of it all, the music and the smells and the *bodies* everywhere, I peeled off my black coat and swapped it for a ticket stub with the smiling woman behind the counter. Stepping aside for the next in line, I shoved the slip of paper inside my purse and pressed back against a stone wall, just breathing—processing.

Thank goodness I'd come today and not Saturday. While Rosa had my costume covered, Halloween scared the pants off me—and not for the usual spooky, horror-y reasons. Here, just four nights from now, the others and I would attend Ewan's big October 31 bash.

And I didn't want to make a fool of myself.

Like I was doing right now.

Just a fawn on the ice, legs everywhere, panicked and bleating for her mama to rescue her.

So, to avoid *this* happening on a night that Ewan had been preparing for the second his Thanksgiving market wrapped weeks ago, I had decided on a trial run. Lucian and Soren were both out on patrol tonight, hopefully squashing the beef from our movie night last Friday. Alone at the house with nothing to do, head full of TV moments just like this, I took a risk.

Did the bare minimum makeup-wise.

Washed and brushed my hair.

Put on a form-fitted red dress, sleeves to my wrists, the neck scooped but not showy. Added a pair of black stockings and one of the fancier pairs of flats I owned. Ewan's bracelet dangled from my wrist.

I'd thought...

The articles online said this would be a good club outfit, but as I tugged the creeping hemline down my thighs, glowering at the male by coat check who brazenly checked me out and then seductively licked his lips, I realized it wasn't enough.

Once again, *I* wasn't enough. The women here—they were *sexy*. Short-short dresses. Cleavage out. Sequins and sparkles. Black and sleek. Smoky eyes. Red lips. Sky-high heels. Bare legs that were waxed and shiny and perfect.

I felt overdressed and out of place.

But at least my monthly blood had wrapped up yesterday. Hard to pull off such a tight dress all bloated and achy and grumpy.

You can do this.

Purse strap cutting across my figure like a security blanket, I made a firm little nod before striding deeper into the club. I mean, I'd done the hair, makeup, and outfit all by myself. Got out here and waited in line like everyone else. Made my way inside, now almost adjusted to the sensory overload.

I was twenty-six and mated.

I could walk around a nightclub, for goodness' sake.

Still, when the place offered a literal road map, I flocked to it like a moth to a flame. Designed to look like a park trail map, an enormous landscape hung on the wall of a log-wood corridor, the final frontier before I hit the main club. Arms crossed, I quickly studied the layout of the Chalet. First level: dance floor in the center, bars and booths on all sides. Second level: private VIP rooms that seemed to overlook the dance floor below if I had read the sigils right. Third level: booths, pool tables, bars. Rooftop patio: closed until spring.

Right.

Let's do this.

Much like our house, the interior kept up with the club's namesake, stone, wood, and other raw natural elements everywhere. Only the wood was dark, the floors black, and the stone had a rough coarseness to it that could probably draw blood if you hit it right. Outside the log corridor, *bam*, the dance floor was just *there*, a few steps down from the perimeter seating and bars, mostly full of dancing, writhing bodies. A heady sensation washed over me, this scene so *human*—not wolf at all. Kira retreated, unimpressed with the music's volume, the colliding scents, the ogling males.

I padded forward, past the railing that wrapped around the dance floor, then down the two steps onto the glittery black tile. Out of the corner of my eye, a male strode toward me, only a couple of inches taller and brimming with confidence.

Our eyes met. His hazels widened, then ducked, almost like he *knew* not to mess with an alpha she-wolf.

He pivoted fast, weaving back through the crowd alone.

Good.

The wrought-iron balcony above would have provided the best vantage point, but something told me I'd learn best *here*, in the thick of things. Not only did I want to look the part for Saturday, but I needed to *act* the part.

I had no clue how to dance.

No idea what to do with my feet, my hands, my hips.

But nudging through the crowd wasn't exactly the learning experience I had hoped for; everyone moved differently. Some jumped. Some writhed. Some bodychecked—mostly males to other males. I managed to find a partially open space in a corner, arms still crossed, and swayed to the deepest beat coming from the speakers.

Was this it?

Was I... Was I doing it?

Rosewood suddenly tickled my nostrils, rising above the rest, dominant and insistent, demanding my attention. The hairs on the nape of my neck stood on end again, but for a *way* different reason. Kira stirred the moment we scented our mate, her low whine urging *connection*, and I hastily tucked my loose waves behind my ears, searching for him in the crowd—

And finding him well above it.

Descending a spiral staircase nearby, Ewan emerged from the shadows like a fallen angel, all dark beauty and sharp angles and raw *power* as his hand ghosted the iron railing, his steps slow and deliberate, his hickory gaze locked hard on me. Effortlessly stylish in a pair of black slacks and a simple crisp white button-up, he blew all the males here out of the water, females glancing his way, gravitating toward him like he had this unearthly pull.

A pull I understood.

A pull that immobilized me, trapped me in the corner of the dance floor, the rest of the club elevated around me, railings at my back and a wall of humans at my front.

I'd needed to elbow my way through at first, dancers crashing into me with their wayward arms.

Ewan glided on *air* here, totally in his element, the crowd parting for him. Strong, confident, *utterly* alpha, it was like no one else existed as he cut through the dance floor, not stopping until he was practically on top of me. Kira shivered inside, eager to scent her mate, taste him, *bite* him like he and the others had done to me, give them a feel for *my* teeth.

I just stood there, her excitement slicking my palms and making my belly squirm, gazing up at him and feeling kind of small all of a sudden.

Cornered.

Caged.

Pinned by his dark, dangerous beauty and a smile sharp enough to cut glass.

"Hello, blue eyes."

My sex clenched with interest, hot pleasure twisting in my core. Even though my eyes were far from blue these days, I *loved* that he still called me that—loved the way he growled it, possessive and assertive, like only *he* could say it and anyone else who tried would feel his wrath.

Hands easing gracefully into his pockets, he tipped his head, dark gaze sweeping over my body and making Kira even more antsy.

"What are you doing here?"

Right. The super-embarrassing reason I'd done all this.

"I wanted to get a feel for the place," I told him. All around us, humans shouted over the music to be heard. Ewan set the tone, speaking at a normal volume, and I followed his lead, capable of reading him just by watching that sinful mouth—but also hearing him fine despite the roaring beats. "Kind of nervous for Saturday."

My mate huffed a chuckle. "Why?"

"My bar experience is... not this." I waved a weak hand around, the jingle of his bracelet on my wrist snaring his attention. Cheeks warm, I tucked my hair behind my ears again, keenly aware that he was tracking the movement of the gold strap, the diamonds catching the light with every rustle. "I don't know how to dance, or how to—"

"Let's fix that," he rumbled, low and dangerous, his copper wolf eyes sliding back to mine, his body angled closer. I swallowed hard, flustered, the *itch* suddenly back.

"We don't have to if you're busy." He was always busy. Always working, even at home. As persistent as the itch was, flaring like gasoline on the fire the longer he looked at me like *that*, I hadn't come to the Chalet for him. Sure, Soren had spilled that he'd be here every night this week, monitoring the club and preparing for the Halloween party, but the goal hadn't been to catch his eye.

Get him down here.

Make him smile like that, oozing temptation and sin. Lucifer was said to be so handsome—

"I think I can take a break," Ewan rasped. "Come here."

He caught my hand and jerked me to him, whirling us around at the last second so I faced the sea of grinding strangers. Masterful, totally in control where I had struggled to walk in the front door, Ewan snaked his arm around my waist and yanked me back, molding me to his chest, his hips, his thighs.

"*This* is how couples dance at the Chalet," he whispered in my ear, lips caressing my skin with every word. Back to chest, we mirrored plenty of pairs around the dance floor, I now realized, but they couldn't feel like *this*—like their entire body was an inferno from a single touch. His large hand smoothed down my waist, my belly, all the way to my thigh. The other pressed me back to his hips, which started a slow, easy sway that I couldn't help but follow. Mouth dry, I drifted back and forth, keenly aware of his body thrust against mine, the way his much bigger frame cradled me, his knees bent to make up for the height difference.

Kira retreated, just as she had when we all first mated, leaving me to what was *mine*. No distractions from the inside—nothing but my own body reacting to his, my skin tingly, my head empty. No thoughts. No whispers. No stupid apple orchards. Just—*feeling*. Him. Me. His hands on my hip, my thigh, his wicked mouth brushing my ear.

"That's it," he murmured with a hint of teeth, the sharp nip making my nipples stiffen. "Just like that... Easy, right?"

Flushed and flustered, the heat under my skin blazed south without delay. Somehow, Ewan's arms left me feeling... safe too. After his blow-up in the forest, I hadn't thought that would be possible. Lucian made me secure with nothing but a look, just a flick of his green gaze in my direction and *bam*, everything was right in the world. Soren wavered, sometimes a steadfast support, others surly and distant and pouting—usually when he didn't get his way.

Ewan?

Ewan had become my wild card.

But here and now, in his arms, I could fight a whole pack by myself.

That was how he made me feel.

And I might not trust the feeling, but it was… good. Nice.

Like we'd found ourselves again.

Breath whooshing across my cheek, his mouth leaving a trail of barely there kisses at my jaw, Ewan snagged my arm and brought it up, a snarl rumbling between us at the way the diamonds glittered. The charms jingled, suns and moons alternating, slipping over my red sleeve and up my forearm.

"Looks good on you," he whispered roughly, his words all grit and gravel, his mouth hot and my core pleasantly twisty. Ewan brought my arm closer, my hand limp in his grasp, then dragged his parted lips up over the bracelet and straight to my palm. Desire zinged from where his lips pressed *straight* to my low belly, and I muffled a moan, focused on my breathing, on keeping calm.

What if I made the room shake with *other* emotions?

What if it wasn't just anger?

What if, when one of my mates made me explode, a building collapsed?

My tempered breathing only seemed to excite him, and he threaded my hand back into his hair, stretching me, arching my body over his as that dangerous smile found my neck. Kissed it. Nibbled and licked and sucked while my lashes fluttered and struggled to stay open.

I'd missed this—the itch.

Ever since my mates came home, we were all so careful around each other. Eager as I was to let them mount me again, anytime, anyplace, forming a pack bond was *crucial*. Without that effortless connection, we still weren't strong.

And if those Hawthorne wolves taught me anything, it was that we needed *strength*. Cooperation. Support and wordless communication. Trust and transparency.

We did better lately, my mates on their best behavior around me most of the time, the fights fewer and the snarls subtler.

But we still lacked a few key ingredients.

So, with Gull River and my golden eyes and my stupid monthly bleeding, plus three stubborn mates who almost *refused* to work together, my focus had been elsewhere. Desire fell to the wayside.

Oh, but it felt so *good* to let it back in.

Like my body was *alive* again after stumbling around in the dark for way, way too long.

When the song bled into something faster, I tried to pull away. All around us, the humans moved differently, jumping more, smiling and laughing and singing along to lyrics I'd never heard before.

Ewan just swayed faster, blanketing me with his scent, and tucked me deeper into his embrace.

"Look at them," he rumbled against my temple, one arm crossed possessively over my torso, his free hand snaking up my chest to my throat. Our hips rocked in perfect unison, his interest hardening against my backside, his words taking on a wolf's growly edge. "They're all here for something... Upstairs, they can drink in the quiet. Talk and flirt, negotiate their courtship. They can even *fuck* in the private rooms if the males pay us enough to look the other way." My breath hitched at the thought, pulse pounding beneath his hand. "But down here? It's all about the hunt. You know the *hunt*, don't you, blue eyes?"

"B-better than you." Trapped in his thrall, I stumbled over the feisty retort, the alpha in me a little too happy to roll on her back for him. Ewan chuckled, sounding—*feeling*—very much like a predator who had run down his prey.

"Those girls in the big groups—just here to have fun." He steered me around the dance floor by my chin, each word nibbled under my ear. "The pairs? Looking for men to buy them drinks. Compliment them. Worship them. The males circling—on the hunt. Prowling. Searching for weakness..."

He gripped harder, the pressure on my windpipe sparking the alpha in me again. I turned my face into him, our noses brushing, our skin touching, breaths mingling.

"If one of those little human shits *touches* you," Ewan snarled, "tonight or Saturday or any time after, any-*fucking*-time between—I'll break his hands."

A smitten whimper slipped past my lips, making his dick harder, more insistent as his hips ground against me.

"If one of these staring females touches *you*," I fired back, capturing *his* chin and forcing *him* to meet my eyeline, "I'll break her nose."

My mate flashed his canines. "Naughty girl." He slipped my hold as his fingers gritted into my thigh. "Behave yourself."

"If you can do it," I glared at a blonde whispering to her companion and pointing at Ewan, the want in her eyes *obvious*, "so can I."

Totally oblivious to the female's attention, my mate clucked his tongue at me, the sound followed by a chastising nip at my throat—then a harder bite over my dress where I still bore his mark. His hips bucked harder, more determined, more dominating, the beat of the music be damned, and as I finally surrendered to the black, eyes closed and lips parted, I wondered if it was against the law to mate *right* here on the dance floor. I mean, he could just pull up my dress, rip down my stockings, and really—

"Hey, guys—sorry."

Ewan stilled with a growl, and my eyes snapped open when Jocelyn's voice popped our bubble.

No, no, no, no, no.

Sure enough, a quick glance over my shoulder, and there was Ewan's stylish assistant in a burgundy romper and black stilettos. The look transformed a fox shifter shorter than me into a giantess, her short at the back and long at the front white-blonde bob sharp, defined, and curtaining her foxy features as she leaned over the railing with a grim smile.

"Mr. Quinn, I'm afraid they need you upstairs."

Ewan's snarl made her flinch and me sigh.

"Can't it wait?"

Jocelyn arched a white eyebrow, and my mate disengaged completely. He tucked me back in the corner where he had found me, eyes stormy and mouth no longer sinful, the twist of his lips stiffly apologetic.

"I'll be right back, blue eyes," he insisted, stealing a hard kiss before disappearing into the crowd again. His arrival had been like the seas parting. Now, his disappearance had a lot less fanfare, my dark angel disappearing into the shadows again without a backward glance. People ducked out of his way, sure, but it was because he stalked through his club like a bullet, ready to plow through anyone who didn't *move*.

Safety net gone, I folded my arms, shoulders hunched, and suddenly felt way too alone and exposed out here—

"Come on, wolfy." Jocelyn leaned over the railing to pinch my sleeve and steer me toward the nearest set of stairs. "They don't need *me* up there." The fox grinned when our eyes met, her warm browns chasing away how raw Ewan's sudden absence left me. "Lemme buy you a drink."

Relief thawed the ice water in my veins, and I hurried up the steps after her toward one of the bars in a quiet corner. Perched on leather stools, I let Jocelyn take charge with our drink orders. Sure, I'd tried beer and cider before, but my palate, like my fashion sense, just wasn't sophisticated enough for Ewan's world.

In the end, she ordered herself a martini and me a margarita with half the usual amount of tequila, promising me the next could be stronger if I liked it. Pleased to have company, I took a beat to scan the Chalet from a different viewpoint, all these pretty humans looking like they well and truly *belonged*.

"Everyone here is so…" *Flawless.*

Lean legs crossed, Jocelyn snorted as she slid my drink over. "Wasted?" She then scooped up her martini, the glass and the olives and *everything* just like on TV, and took a quick sip. "Yeah, kind of embarrassing no one can hold their liquor, but that's the Chalet crowd for you. Just rich kids who want to get tanked and haggle over drink prices. Like, the *worst*."

"I-I was going to say"—I poked at the rosemary sprig sticking out of my glass, voice dropping—"*intimidating*."

Another snort. Jocelyn's features then softened when she realized I was serious, and she patted my arm, her nails a sharp french manicure—only they were black on the bottom, not pink, with a crisp white line on top.

"Girl, they're just humans."

"I know, but—"

"And you're a *wolf*," she added with an arch of her brow. "An alpha wolf. You're so above them."

"But..." I gestured to my outfit. "I don't look it, and everyone who sees me and Ewan will know it—"

"Fuck them." She downed half her glass and set it on the napkin with a scoff. "Seriously. *Fuck*. Them. They don't know *anything*. You could wear a plastic bag and still be better than them, so let it go, wolfy. Be who you are, and fuck what the rest think."

Before I could thank her, not entirely boosted by her little speech but still appreciating the effort, Jocelyn hoisted her glass for a cheers. We clinked drinks, and I tried my first tequila-based cocktail.

Not bad.

A little... sour-sweet for my liking, but the rosemary smelled familiar, and the lemon had a pleasant zingy bite that made me come back for more.

"Jocelyn?"

"Yeah?"

"Can you... tell me what to expect for Halloween?" I nudged my glass around the countertop, drawing shapes in the condensation. "After everything with the river, and..." I pointed to my eyes, knowing she saw them but was too polite to stare. "And *these*... After everything, I just don't want to disappoint anyone. I'm good at the wolf stuff. I'm... less good at all this."

The fox's burgundy lips dipped into a luscious frown, the kind that caught the bartender's eye and kept him loitering.

"Halloween is *fun*, Lyssa," she insisted, oblivious to the male—all the while eyeing a pair of females chatting at a nearby high-top table. "And I don't think you could disappoint those assholes if you tried. From what I've heard, *they* need to step up, not you."

Once again, the sentiment was great—but the landing didn't stick.

Jocelyn sighed as I guzzled the rest of my drink, then snapped at the bartender and pointed to our empty glasses, flashing two fingers and angling herself toward me, her back to him.

"Okay, sure. I'll give you the breakdown, behind the scenes and front of house. You'll go into Saturday knowing how the sausage is made."

I frowned. "Uh, what?"

"Never mind, never mind." She propped her elbow on the bar, chin on her fist, and patted my arm again—not like she was *better* than me, but in a way that felt oddly reassuring. "You think of any questions, just cut me off and ask."

"Got it."

As Jocelyn kicked things into high gear, firing information at me left, right, and center, I glanced around quickly for any sign of Ewan.

Nothing.

Not even a whiff of his rich rosewood scent in the air.

Ignoring Kira's disappointed sigh, I slowly sank into the rhythm of Jocelyn's husky voice, committing all the details to memory as best I could, determined to go into Saturday night *totally* prepared…

And confident as an alpha with three mates should be.

Of course it was raining.

And not just a spring showers type thing, but a *we angered the clouds and now they want to punish us* downpour. Sheltered beneath the brick corridor that led to the club's main door, I squinted into the grey wall, then braced when the wind changed direction and blew it straight at me. Misted with just a taste of what was pounding the village, I wiped my cheeks on my jacket sleeve, then flinched when thunder cracked overhead. To my left, a group of huddled females roughly my age screeched, the drunkest in their pack seated and slouched against the wall, mumbling about street meat under her breath.

Lightning flashed a few steady beats of my heart later, the storm right over us and slowly headed north. Midnight had come and gone without Ewan, and once Jocelyn shared that it was always a late night at the Chalet since the nightclub didn't close until three, I decided enough was enough.

My mate had taught me how to dance.

The females here had shown me how to dress.

Jocelyn had given me a tour of all three levels, front and back of house.

As of this moment, I had a fairly good idea of the layout and expectations of a place like this, which settled the anxious static in my belly. Kira had retreated deep inside for most of it, bored to tears without her mate for company, Jocelyn's rundown of the upcoming Halloween event thorough but a bit dry despite the liquor involved.

Even now, tequila warmed my chest, four drinks deep, two of them with the full portion of alcohol, but I was still in control. Not wobbling in heels. Not crying in the bathroom. Not vomiting in a stall—and definitely not sitting on my butt outside, ignoring my friends and mouthing off to the increasingly annoyed bouncers.

Jeez.

Humans were messier than I thought.

Another thunderous *boom*. Another chorus of shrieking females. The lightning came faster this time, turning the empty cobblestone street ahead white, the storm hovering. I felt for Lucian and Soren on patrol tonight; whenever weather like this hit, the pack and I hunkered down somewhere dry—or as dry as possible, anyway. All of us in a pile, warming and comforting each other, pups near Mama while the thunder kept them awake and shivering.

My mates had to keep moving tonight, keep marching the

perimeter. Soren might trot back if things didn't ease up, but Lucian would walk the whole territory no matter the conditions.

I… I wanted to have something ready for them when they got home.

Something hot and comforting, delicious and soothing.

But cooking wasn't exactly my forte.

Throw it in the microwave? Fine. Eat it raw? Perfect.

Simmer and season and baby on the stove? *Nope.* But I'd try.

Hot chocolate was always a nice treat on a night like this.

Kira stretched inside, toes spread wide, her stiffness carrying to me. She sniffed, each *whoosh* tickling between my ears, then grumbled; even she didn't want to go now, Jocelyn's bland tour sounding better than a trudge through the storm.

Lips pursed, I watched a male jog by in a drenched suit, his briefcase a useless umbrella. Ugh. This… was not going to be fun. Head down, I stepped out of the shelter.

Instantly soaked.

Right down to the bone.

Great. No point in rushing, then. I was used to the rain and had never caught a cold. Still, as I plodded down the cobblestone street, the lure of all the soft, warm light spilling out from bar windows was beyond enticing.

Only I had no money.

No ID.

No nothing to barter with for another drink somewhere else— and I couldn't keep dropping Ewan's name like that was currency, right?

Arms crossed, I pushed onward, headed for the main gates but not in a hurry. The village grew dark and empty the further I walked from the high street neighborhood, store windows black, only the odd light or two on in the low-rise condo buildings. Every so often, an automatic porchlight flashed as I passed a chalet, probably triggered by motion. Fewer and fewer humans crossed my path, the sights and smells drowned out by the rain.

The sounds muted by thunder.

A light flickered on behind me, sparking in the corner of my eye. Kira growled low, confused and alert. Frowning, I glanced over my shoulder. The row of nestled bungalows faced a small park, and that particular light had already brightened when I passed, then turned off on its own.

Motion sensor again.

Triggered—again—even though I was five houses down.

Strange.

The hairs on the back of my neck rose.

My vision sharpened, Kira nudging to the surface, both of us scanning the one-story chalets, the vacant stretch of nature across the street full of pine trees and winding stone paths, garden beds brimming with late-season blooms and a few fake tombstones for Halloween.

Nothing.

Thunderstorms always played tricks on you. Made the shadows dance—made scary sounds out of nothing more than raindrops.

But one street over came a sound the storm *couldn't* fake: feet splashing through a puddle. Behind me.

I spun around, eyes widening as lightning lit up the narrow roadway.

The *empty* narrow roadway, the corner grocery closed, the spa beside it silent.

"Idunn?"

Run along home, little wolf.

For the last week and a half, I'd heard the dead goddess in my dreams. Tonight, she whispered through the rain, voice sweet and high and clear, shimmering all around me, slinking down my body in heavy icy droplets.

Another splash, feet charging across a puddle, loud and a little too obvious at my back. Kira snarled as I whirled around, senses on high alert, on the lookout for danger and finding none.

Go home, Lyssa.

"That's what I'm trying to do," I gritted out, barely moving my lips, unwilling to let whoever was watching catch me talking to myself. At the next splash, striking like the storm's heartbeat, I jogged down the street, my own feet pounding through puddles, the sewer drains beneath the sidewalks gurgling as I passed.

Two distinct sets followed me.

Or...

Or the storm was playing tricks and the tequila had hit harder than I thought.

No. I swore those were—

One behind me.

One everywhere else, sometimes to the left, to the right, motion-activated lights flicking on when I was nowhere nearby, illuminating a whole lot of nothing. Between her snarls, Kira whined and nosed at my insides, desperate to come out, to swap places and *hunt*.

I kept her right where she was, refusing to let whatever was happening scare me.

Ewan owned this village—mostly.

And I was his mate.

And I wasn't about to be run out of it by thunder, lightning, and rain.

And more splashes of puddle water. Eventually, I darted through alleys and between houses, zipped and turned and backtracked. I'd lost predators before—not because I feared their claws and teeth, but because I just couldn't be bothered to deal with them.

Tonight, I didn't want to water the streets of Ewan's village with blood.

Home, little wolf.

"Shut *up*," I hissed, skirting around a dumpster and slowing at the mouth of an alley, officially lost. All this darting around, turning on a dime—no idea where I'd ended up, but the neighborhood was still soft and subdued, sleepy and still.

Except for the feet in puddles.

I took a deep breath and blinked the rainwater out of my eyes, vision sharp—and narrowed on the shadowy alley across the street. A street for cars this time, pavement not cobblestone, the gap situated between two dark cafés with hanging flowerpots and pumpkins at their doors.

Oh.

Oh *no*.

This was what they'd wanted. It or they or him or *whatever*—the *thing* I kept hearing?

It had herded me.

Make noise to the left, I went right.

Splash around behind me, I pushed forward.

"Stupid," I whispered, rolling my eyes as I poked my head out and looked up and down the road. Empty.

But the shadows across the street suddenly moved.

A black cloud eased away from the café door, dropping low and creeping along the side of the building, then darted into the alley.

Okay.

This wasn't the storm.

Kira's snarls stopped. Her growls dulled. We became one, hearts beating together, thoughts aligned, staring down the grizzly without fear. Enough was enough.

I was a wolf.

An alpha.

Wild to my core.

You don't scare me.

A strange darkness smothered that alley. I paused at its opening and squinted into the black, unnerved that for once, the night *wasn't* my friend. Iron scented the air, and as soon as I crossed the threshold, my breath fogged.

Footsteps ahead.

I broke into a sprint, charging into the inky cloud, hissing when my knee clanged off something metal a few paces in. Aching, I pushed harder, relying on my sense of smell, tracking the metallic tang, the frost sharpening, swelling, *hurting* the deeper I ran.

Still nothing.

Light returned like a beam of sunshine slicing through the grey fog after a storm. I slowed. Ahead, this alley emptied into the village square, silent tonight but well-lit with enormous iron lampposts.

Someone drew a breath just beyond the exit, right around the corner. Teeth gritted, I charged.

And—

"Oh!"

Crashed right into Ewan's steely chest. My drenched mate swept me up, chuckling, his smile positively wicked as he thrust me back into the alley and pinned me against the brick.

Shock echoed through me.

"Hello, blue eyes," he rumbled, snagging my wrists and trapping them against the wall, holding me captive in his powerful grasp. His midnight-black hair, usually so stylish and full, curtained his dark beauty, softening some of the sharper angles of his face, and he peered down at me with copper wolf eyes.

Victory pulsed between my thighs—a sensation that didn't belong to me—and my heart hammered as Kira cautiously withdrew, my world suddenly upside-down.

"W-what are you doing here?" Had he been following me? Was this… a game? Pups played predator and prey all the time; was it as simple as that?

Had it been my mate all along—and the storm up to its usual tricks?

"I needed to say good night before you went home," Ewan whispered, ducking low so that his sinful lips caressed mine with every word. Each flutter of skin to skin quieted my racing thoughts, his rosewood scent, complemented with a musky sandalwood cologne, muted by the rain but still ridiculously alluring. He snapped his sharp teeth at the tip of my nose, a rumble vibrating in his chest, and my body bucked off the wall without my consent, arching into him, into the memory of his intimate lesson on the dance floor. Without warning, he licked a raindrop from the crest of my upper lip, his touch fiery and distracting. "I'm sorry work is so… busy."

What?

Oh. Right.

Distracted by the chill in the alley, the darkness to my left, and, most of all, *him*, I gulped, skin on fire, heart a drumbeat, and shook my head. "I-I get it." His obsession with living in his office was the *last* thing on my mind right now. Lost in his wolf eyes, I struggled to think, to form simple *words*, never mind a coherent sentence. "Were you... Did you f-follow me?"

Ewan's grin was all pearly whites and bad-boy allure. "You're not the only hunter in this pack, darling."

He kissed me hard, *finally* closing the distance between us with his hungry, laughing mouth. It was a kiss to claim, to possess, dominant and rough. His tongue thrust between my lips in seconds, teasing mine, coaxing it to forget everything that had just happened.

Begging for me to accept that it was just the storm playing tricks.

Still trapped against the brick, my hands curled to fists, and I moaned, surrendering to his brutal good-night kiss a little too easily. Most days it felt good to conquer, to pull my weight with all these males who towered over me. I was the better *wolf*, through and through, but my mates were really good at making me feel like a woman.

Just a woman—desired and coveted and *wanted*.

Wildfire jumped from his skin to mine, burning away the autumn frost in the air. A good-night kiss should have been quick and fleeting, a promise for more to come tomorrow, but Ewan barely gave me room to breathe. He couldn't get enough, his yearning pluming in my belly, tainting the pleasurable clenches, turning them electric like the hum of a farmer's fence. Before I could even try to escape his hold, my mate shifted his grip, pinning both my wrists above my head suddenly and clamping down with one hand.

My eyes snapped open. I glowered into the merciless sunset blazing back, his free hand skimming my drenched figure, our kiss rain-slick and a little desperate.

He found the hem of my dress with a snarl. Yanked it up to my hips. Attacked my stockings so that they *ripped*, louder than the clap of thunder above. Lightning swiftly lit up the alley, chasing away the last of the creeping shadows. I glanced left, just for a moment; nothing there but brick and concrete, a metal dumpster with the lid open and a door to one of the cafés with no handle.

Stupid storm.

Playing tricks.

Dealing *lies*.

When darkness fell again, I submitted to the moment, to Ewan's powerful hand between my thighs, beneath my underwear, stroking me, massaging me—

Fucking me.

I clenched my eyes tight, still struggling to *think* the word, but that was what his fingers were doing: pumping in and out of my slickness, our kiss slowed, breaths crashing. He groaned with every plunge, working me inside and out, toying with the tender bud at the peak of my curls, the one that made my belly squirm and my thighs shake.

Whimpering, I tried to wiggle free. Needed to—*touch*. Stroke him. Maybe even taste him. Ewan and Lucian had tasted me, knelt between my thighs and licked me into paradise.

I… could do that.

Did it feel the same?

From the way they reacted to my cautious touches before, it had to.

Only my mate had his own plans tonight. On the brink of an explosion, the kind that bled like lava through my whole body, dragging with it a white-hot pleasure I had never experienced before Redwood, before *them*, Ewan withdrew.

Didn't let go of my hands, mind you. No, he kept them trapped against the brick, stretched above my head, claimed and captured, his grip like steel anytime I twisted and squirmed. He wrenched down his slacks. Freed his shaft. Fisted it, glaring at the rigid length, not realizing that with every rough pump, he was teaching me what he liked—what I could do to him if he would just let my hands go. I licked my lips, eager to do to them what they did to me.

Eager to make them *burn*.

Almost against their will—a surprise every time.

But then he speared me with that impressive shaft, slamming me hard into the wall, impaling me to the hilt. A twinge of delicious pain swept through the mounting pleasure, and my moan tangled with his snarl, our bodies *home* in each other. He stretched me. Filled me. *Fucked* me, right there, right in the open. In the rain. Beneath the booming thunder and the brilliant flashes of lightning, we *finally* mated again.

Ewan, pounding me furiously.

Me—taking it. Him. All of him. Hands bound above my head, I had no choice but to submit, even when I wrapped my legs around his torso. Pulled him closer. Stabbed him with my heels. Nothing I did slowed him or made him pause.

My mate had me, claimed me, until the glorious, almost *violent* end. Bliss ripped through me during a symphony of thunder, multiple *cracks* rattling the village, the lightning show that followed as I squealed and writhed the sort you'd expect on Judgment Day— the world ending, angels descending, demons clawing out of the pit.

Stark white seized my vision, taking over no matter how fast I blinked, the pleasure of our coupling intense and all-consuming, gobbling me up and spitting me out a mumbling, rambling mess.

I bit him this time.

His shirt was in the way, the undershirt beneath that muffling my teeth, but he still hissed and snarled and bucked harder, not stopping his brutal claiming until—

Ewan stiffened all but his trembling hips, then exhaled my name against my neck like a prayer.

A painful prayer.

Like it *hurt* him. I ducked my head to the side, the alley coming back into focus slowly, pops of white light still sparking behind my lids whenever I closed them. Panting, I nuzzled at his temple, his soaked and slick hair, whimpering, whining for his attention.

Ewan released my hands and kissed me again, cupping my face, cradling it gently, his lips tender and mine sore. When the thunder rumbled this time, it did so somewhere else, the storm moving on, leaving only the rain to slowly put out the fire.

"You know," I murmured between kisses, "I think I'm going to need to change my definition of a good-night kiss now…"

Grinning, Ewan nipped at my neck with a playful growl, then lowered my feet to the ground. Right into a puddle. Rainwater flooded my flats as we untangled and adjusted clothing, hair, everything. My stockings were toast, and I ripped them the rest of the way off, then tossed them in the general direction of the dumpster. My panties, meanwhile, were too cold and wet to put back on, but their survival after Ewan's assault earned them a spot in my purse instead of the ground.

Lower lip snagged between my teeth, I watched Ewan tuck his shirt, his black brows furrowed, his movements rough and stilted as he wrenched his zipper up and moved on to the belt.

"You're not coming home with me, are you?"

My whisper carried over the pitter-patter of rain, and Ewan slowed, buckling his belt without glancing up. Eyes down, chin tucked—that was answer enough. Frustration plunged down my spine like an icy finger, accented with disappointment and regret.

None of it mine.

All his.

Mates… felt things. They felt each other. None of my three had explicitly taught me that, but Rosa had said it was a thing when I asked, and the more we mated, the more time we spent together, the stronger the sensations became. Kira snorted, mildly unimpressed that he felt like that—frustrated and disappointed in himself, upset that, *no*, he wasn't going to walk me home in the rain…

Why go back to the club if that was how he felt?

Why?

She didn't understand, but I was starting to.

Sort of.

"It's… okay." I caught his chin and forced him up, throwing some of my new brute strength behind it to get this stubborn alpha to look at me. "I know Saturday is a big deal. I'll just see you at breakfast."

It wasn't okay. A party *wasn't* a big deal in my books—but it mattered to him. More than the others, Ewan's job was his life and his passion. It might wear him out, but he didn't seem miserable doing it.

He put his all into this side of himself.

So…

I wanted to be a supportive mate. The others teased him about it, and not always in good fun, which meant he *needed* someone in this pack to believe in him.

I'd want the same, honestly.

But I would rather have him at home.

This alpha with his hickory gaze and jet-black hair—he risked a disconnect from the pack if he never showed up.

And, sure, wolves roamed solo all the time. Sometimes wolves left *my* pack and never returned, full-grown adults ready to start their own families far away from ours. But the mating pair? They wandered. Papa left for days, weeks sometimes, and then showed up out of the blue like he had been with us all along.

A few weeks ago, I told Lucian wolves wandered—that all I needed was confidence that my mates would come home.

Maybe that would be enough for a wild wolf, but as the days passed, I was starting to realize that wasn't enough for me. I wasn't *just* a wolf. Shifters needed more than the basics. Food, shelter, family—it was a start, but now I craved *more*. Connection. Conversation. Laughter. Learning. Movie nights and sushi lunches and napping all together on the deck. Hikes into the forest and strolls through the village.

Togetherness. I needed more.

And they were trying.

I couldn't leave them now, not after mating and marking—and definitely not after whatever happened at Gull River. But if we didn't push beyond the basics soon, especially with Ewan, things would nosedive fast.

It's only been a month.

I swatted at the nothing beside my ear, unsure if that comment came from Idunn in the rain or my own thoughts rolling around my skull—but it was fair.

And annoying.

A month in the wild might as well have been a *year.*

My mate fixed me with a long look, eyes heavy and muddled, beautiful mouth arced in a frown so sorrowful that I just wanted to kiss it away.

He did that instead, kissed me deep and slow, cradling the back of my head with one hand and stroking my cheek with the other. Wildfire sparked. Kira howled. Thunder grumbled way up north.

"You stay in bed in the morning," Ewan whispered against my lips. With a soft breath, my eyes fluttered open to warmth and promise, his gaze straddling the line between man and wolf, the hickory rimmed by coppery fire, almost *glowing.* When I arched a curious eyebrow, he smirked and eased back, then tapped me under the chin with his knuckle. "I'll bring you breakfast there, blue eyes. Give you a taste of my hollandaise, a little smoked salmon and eggs benedict, eh? Just me and you—we'll eat together."

I had no idea what hollandaise and eggs benedict were, but my mouth watered at the thought of him climbing into *my* bed with food—though the moan that followed was kind of embarrassing.

"Yes, *please,*" I said shyly, cheeks heating when my rumpled mate chuckled.

"It's a deal." He stole another toe-curling kiss, then murmured right in my ear, breath hot and tickly, "And a promise, blue eyes."

Fingers entwined, we strolled out of the alley together, snuggled close and heads ducked against the chilly downpour. Ewan led me through the village square, then reoriented me, steering us back to the main roads and pointing me in the direction of the front gates. Thankfully, he didn't insist on walking me home—as if Gull River had stolen my fight or ability or smarts. Lucian would have. Soren might have offered. But Ewan didn't. If he escorted me home and then left, back to the village for another few hours of work, that would have been confirmed these males assumed I couldn't take care of myself out here anymore.

We kissed goodbye one last time, then went our separate ways, him back to his world and me to mine. Just as I crossed through the gates, Redwood Grove village at my back, I heard it again...

Feet clomping through puddles.

Boots, actually, given the sound and the echo, the huge *splash* that came with it. Kira perked up from her post-mating snooze, and I turned slowly, proof that whoever and whatever might be watching hadn't startled me.

After all, they couldn't hear my racing heart.

Right?

Nothing. Again. Just an empty two-lane road leading in and out of the village lined with blocky green shrubs, little lights that looked like golf tees dotting the curbs.

I cocked my head. *Listened.* Just the rain and the wind and the thunder drifting across the mountains. Tires rolling over wet pavement further inside the village. Light glowing from the depths around the entertainment hub.

Nothing here. I turned away, headed out—

Splash, splash.

No. Not nothing. *Something* was toying with me.

And it wasn't the storm.

Ewan wouldn't...

My next breath fogged, the temperature in freefall.

With a low growl, I darted into the foliage along the stone wall that circled the village. Stripped down behind the bushes, ditching my clothes somewhere they wouldn't be seen from the main road.

Let Kira free.

Then ran all the way home, swift as the wind, Idunn's voice in my ears—urging me to go *faster*.

And—*please, please, please, little wolf, heed my warning*—to lock the door behind me.

9

LUCIAN

"We don't have to go if you're not feeling it."

I wasn't feeling it, but when had I ever been in the mood for some capitalist human holiday inspired by the same magical folk who made my hackles rise and bloodlust soar?

Never.

Not when I was a pup.

Not when the Hadley pack warlock betrayed me.

Not now, Halloween in general so bloody commercialized, all shiny and pretentious and destined to be packed full of pissed, sloppy humans tonight at Ewan's club.

Lyssa had been a bundle of nervous energy since dawn, rousing me and the others from our, oh, hour or two of collective sleep. Soren and I had patrolled until the wee hours of the morning, while Ewan had practically lived at the Chalet all week in preparation for tonight. Had we been humans, we would have been *the* most miserable prats—more miserable than usual, anyway—operating on literally no sleep. Instead, our shifter bodies allowed us to function on only a few hours, hauling ourselves out of our separate beds as Lyssa crashed around in the kitchen.

Bless her. She so wanted to whip up a feast as effortlessly as Soren did most mornings, but the stove really was her nemesis.

After a meal at the ass crack of dawn, Ewan headed into the village—no shock there—and Soren joined Lyssa and me for a morning forest run as wolves, then a brisk swim in the lake, then a game of Go Fish at the coffee table in front of the enormous sitting room hearth.

After lunch, the blond alpha left for Redwood Grove proper.

He... had promised to help Ewan prepare for the party.

Strange, the thought of those two coordinating *anything*, but business management in a public place surrounded by humans meant they couldn't snarl and pound on each other if a disagreement arose. Apparently he had sensed some distance between Ewan and the rest of us lately, and ever the happy little pup, Soren had found a way to lessen that.

Which made him a better wolf than me.

Like I'd ever *willingly* go to a nightclub, *especially* the Chalet, unless my mate was in danger.

Before today, that was the only reason I'd drag my surly ass into the village, past the doormen, and into a club meant for humans ten years my junior.

Unfortunately, all my firm stances and noble intentions went out the window for Halloween, Lyssa's energy off the charts. Our usual afternoon nap never came despite eating a massive breakfast and lunch *and* afternoon tea. Be it excitement or nerves, I couldn't get a proper read on her. Even my wolf struggled when he tussled with hers, both of them frisky and bouncy and all over the place, vocal and a little rough in their play.

I hoped it was excitement.

Sort of.

Excitement was harder to dampen, but as the sun dipped below the horizon, this was my last chance to alter the course of what was bound to be a truly hellish night.

"No, no," my mate called from the bathroom, the objection

followed by a burst of water, then the *clunk* of the metal tap closing. "I really want to go."

Muffling my growl, I rolled my eyes and flopped back on her unmade bed, arms outstretched, feet on the floor—*dreading* what was to come. Sensing Lyssa's minxy wolf half wasn't going to have an encore anytime soon, my inner wolf had already retreated as far away as he could, equally horrified at the thought of spending the night at a club. So loud. So smelly. So... drunk and human and *fucking* Halloween. Soren had been hyping the holiday up all week, and that paired with her pleasant visit to the Chalet Tuesday night really cemented our mate's opinion on things.

Rosa had her costume sorted.

Ewan had reserved a VIP room for the pack, which was bound to be stocked with only the finest champagne and liquor and snacks money could buy.

Soren had promised to teach her dorky dance moves.

Yeah. I really only had a few bargaining chips left.

"Are you sure you wouldn't rather stay in?" I floated, upping the English charm, voice as velvety as I could swing before it got ridiculous. "Cuddle right here..." I popped my head up just as Lyssa poked hers into the doorway, and my feral grin turned her cheeks crimson. I patted the bed, smoothing a spot by my side *just* for her. "Spend some *quality* time together, little mate... Just the two of us, all alone—"

"I know what you're doing," she insisted, pointing at me with a playful frown, her eyes narrowed and cheeks still flushed—nipples pebbled through her T-shirt, braless and ripe for the plundering. Even if tonight wasn't dreadful as *fuck*, in my opinion Lyssa needed some downtime after days of restless sleep, her nights plagued with fits loud enough for the rest of us to hear and feel all the way in our own beds.

Two nights ago—she screamed.

Nearly six in the morning, the sun cresting the horizon line, and the most terrifying shriek I'd ever heard ripped through the house.

Dragged me out of bed. I'd crashed into Soren on the way to her bedroom, a groggy-eyed Ewan bringing up the rear, and it took all three of us to shake her from the nightmare.

When she came to, she insisted it was fine.

Just a dream.

Just a *lie*.

She passed out as soon as her head hit the pillow again, silent and unnervingly still.

All three of us loitered outside her bedroom door until we heard the toilet flush a few hours later, our mate officially up, then scattered before she caught us.

At the time, I would have given anything to curl up beside her in this massive king—hold her, fight the nightmares for her, banish all of it with my touch and kiss and murmurs.

And from the feeling in our bond that morning, thick and morose and heavy, the others felt much the same.

Yet we still slept in different rooms, in our own beds, longing and heartache shivering through the collective bond every night, touching me even if I was miles away on patrol.

Given all that, Lyssa really ought to stay in.

Talk about it. Unload onto one of us, so maybe, just *maybe*, she could have a good night's sleep again.

Mind you, perhaps she just needed a distraction—and a huge obnoxious costume party in the village offered precisely that.

Bloody *hell*.

"Haven't the faintest idea what you're talking about," I purred before sitting up and slowly peeling my shirt off, flexing all the muscles most males didn't even know existed. I then tossed it aside innocently and fanned my neck, making sure to roll my shoulder a bit too. "Rather warm in here, no?"

"Stop tempting me."

Speaking of bloody tempting, there stood my fated mate in the bathroom doorway, hands on her hips, wearing nothing but a too-big tee and a pair of black frilly knickers. Good *grief*. How did she expect me to allow her to leave the property, let alone this fucking room, dressed like that?

"Oh, little mate," I growled, prowling upright, looming way over her and that delicious pout. "I've only just begun—"

"Well, put a pin in it, wolf!" Rosa suddenly barreled into the bedroom, jerking both me and my mate out of our hazy, flirtatious tug-of-war. As soon as I saw her, the witch's scent detonated like a bomb, heavy on the honey and amber, warm and cozy and innocent. How I hadn't noticed it before, never mind the obvious footsteps slapping over the hardwood, was kind of pathetic.

Sporting a pair of stretchy pants and a turtleneck jumper, in all black today for her beloved Samhain, Rosa had a face full of silver makeup, looking like a sea nymph ready for a night on the town, and her usual mane of red curls stacked around her head in massive rollers. She tossed her armful of laundry bags on hangers at Lyssa's bed, a little too at home here for my taste, and then beamed up at me. "Your mate and I have a lot to do and not much time to do it in. Keep it in your pants, mister."

Biting back a scowl, I offered a deferential nod and bowed out of the fight, odds stacked way against me now. While I loathed most of her kind, Rosa was... fine.

Pleasant.

A nurturer who had taken Lyssa under her wing the past month —which I *supposed* put her in my good books. My wolf rarely bristled in her presence, unlike her stick insect husband. Ethan Perry smelled fake, his smiles too wide and his eyes too calculating, and it fucking *infuriated* me that he had someone as rational and logical as Ewan Quinn under his thrall. Even Soren had taken a liking to him, connected by proxy now that we were a united pack, and that just...

Ugh.

Definitely not my favorite person, that warlock, but from the way Lyssa bounced out of the bathroom and into Rosa's arms for a hug that nearly tackled her to the ground, this witch was one of *her* favorites.

I'd respect that—until the witch and her husband inevitably gave me reason not to.

"*Rosaaaaaa,*" my mate squealed, the pair spinning around at the end of the bed. "I just finished cleaning my face!"

"Then we are officially ready for Samhain costumes," the witch fired back, Lyssa's energy lifting her, both suddenly giddy and giggly and falling all over themselves.

"I love your makeup."

"I'm basically doing the same for you, but in gold."

"*Oh!*"

"It'll go great with your eyes."

"I can't wait to see our outfits!"

Fuck me. My wolf padded closer to the surface, smitten with our mate's eagerness, in love with her smile—touched by their friendship. *I,* on the other hand, teetered on the brink of a ruptured eardrum given the pitch and volume of this conversation. Before I could ask what, exactly, Rosa intended to do with my mate, their joint costume scheme a coveted secret, Lyssa skipped over, grabbed my hand, and hauled me toward the door.

"Time to go," she insisted, sounding as confident and certain as I'd always wanted for her. The thought made me smile; Lyssa was born to be an alpha, a leader, a matriarch. As males, we *could* impose our will. We outnumbered her. Outweighed her. But... Lyssa had an *energy* in her soul that no one could tame. This she-wolf was on par with the rest of us, an equal in every sense, and I knew that with some time and support, she would find her strength in our world.

Unfortunately, I hadn't expected it to be wielded against me as she tried to literally shove me out of her bedroom.

"Right. Why?"

"It's a *surprise,*" she stressed for the millionth time today, darting behind me and shouldering into my back, really bearing down to get my stubborn ass out. "I want you to be—" She grunted at the effort. "—really surprised when you—" Another grunt. "—see me tonight."

I peered over my shoulder with a sigh. "But—"

"And I hear you have a costume to work on anyway," Rosa added from across the room, arranging the clothing bags into separate piles on the bed, smirking at me when our eyes met. Mine dipped to her wrist, exposed when her sleeve had scrunched up at some point —revealing a smattering of purplish-green bruises. The moment she caught me staring, she hastily tugged the fabric back down and focused on her organizing, all the teasing humor gone.

Odd.

Shifters couldn't bruise permanently, any marks left healed in seconds, but those without supernatural healing abilities could. Witches and warlocks, however, relied on balms and potions to mend their wounds *almost* as instantaneously as we did.

Was that fresh?

Had she run into trouble on the way over here?

"Yeah," Lyssa growled, really giving it her all and barely moving me an inch, "I-I want to be surprised by *your* costume too."

I rolled my eyes. Like I had an *actual* costume for this ridiculous night, some stupid outfit that I put time and effort into. Ewan and I had already agreed over breakfast the other morning: black suits all the way, and should anyone ask, we could say we were the night personified. Simple. Easy. Straightforward. The bastard then asked if I needed to borrow something, which had earned him a scowl. A lifetime ago, I wore and abruptly discarded suits finer than anything in his overpriced wardrobe.

Three had survived the transition to the wolf I was today: black, charcoal, and light grey.

"Out, out, out," Lyssa ordered, and I finally gave in, shuffling through the doorway as if she were pushing me along with every step, her newfound strength from before seemingly absent. As soon as I faced her again, about to tell my mate not to get her hopes up in terms of costume creativity, she pounced. Literally. Lyssa jumped up at me, hooked an arm around my neck, and hauled herself up for a kiss. Hard and a little manic, her mouth made me forget, just for a moment, about the night ahead. Scooping her off her feet, I crushed her against me, bending her backward to deepen the kiss, tasting and claiming and marking her with my scent. Her giggles eventually shattered the moment, and I begrudgingly set her down, inner wolf just as riled as my fucking cock.

"It'll be worth it," she said breathlessly, flushed and adorable as she backpedaled into her bedroom.

Fuck. *Fine*. I'd... pretend to have fun tonight.

Because as long as she was happy, so was I.

Smitten, I tapped the tip of her nose, unable to stop my lips from matching her grin. "Little mate, you're *always* worth it—no matter what you wear."

"Oh, good line," Rosa called, not looking up as she sorted her bags but smiling to herself all the same. Lyssa, meanwhile, buried her blushes behind her hands and finally tiptoed out of reach. Behind her, the witch straightened, and an icy finger slicked down my spine when she leveled her wand at me. "Goodbye, Lucian. No peeking—because your mate is gonna knock you on your ass later."

She winked, then flicked her wand at the door.

Which slammed in my face with a *whoosh* and a *bang*.

Grumbling, I dragged myself away only after listening to my mate giggle and bounce around on the other side of the door for a few moments. All right, all right. Let it be a surprise. This was the first time Lyssa had been able to dress up for any of us, and clearly she wanted to make the most of it.

Fine.

The least I could do was put on my suit.

Which was a little big, actually. Not by much, but it used to hug my frame better.

Clearly, life as the forest hermit didn't exactly lend itself to maintaining the bodybuilder physique I'd been known for back home.

Dressed, hair brushed, beard combed, and cologne spritzed, I eventually departed without a farewell. The Perrys' black SUV sat parked out front, which meant Rosa would drive my mate to the village in a few hours when the Halloween party launched.

And that left me plenty of time to grill Ewan's security team, scope out the club for myself, and scent-mark the perimeter.

Halloween always spelled trouble in this part of the world. From children to full-grown adults, humans leaned heavily into the shenanigans the night promised. Supernatural folk tended to go a little wild as well, shirking the secret *living together but apart from humanity* thing we did for the sake of our survival.

All for this fucking night.

If my mate was going to be surrounded by all sorts, humans flocking north for the party of the season alongside witches and warlocks driving down from nearby Hampton to get pissed at the club and then head to the Redwood forests for dark Samhain sabbats—then we couldn't take any chances.

Before this party started, I personally would bulletproof the shit out of that building.

And if anyone tried to stop me, I'd put them through a fucking wall.

10

EWAN

"Happy Halloween, wolf."

Struck by the scent of yew and mint, I grinned and braced for the inevitable clap on my shoulder, Ethan's greetings always the same. Leaning on the thin black railing that lined the second-floor balcony, I'd been lost in the moment for a little while, mind racing, thoughts pinging, mental checklists flying.

It was finally here.

Redwood Grove's exclusive Halloween Bash at the Chalet.

In the last twenty-four hours, my nightclub had become unrecognizable. Starting with the jack-o'-lantern and skull chandelier hanging over the dance floor, timed to erupt with confetti at midnight alongside an explosive DJ set, we had dressed the building like a haunted house—but classy.

Spiderwebs in corners, grotesque face illusions in mirrors, Halloween puns on the bathroom doors. Carved pumpkins with flickering candles at the bars. Themed drinks and appetizers. A militant private chef managing our kitchen. Costumes were mandatory. Tickets cost a small fortune to keep the riffraff college assholes from Hampton out. Guest DJs from all over North America had flown in and rented chalets from me for this one night, allowed to play any set they wanted so long as they had mixes with Halloween classics.

Kind of a mindfuck to hear *Monster Mash* whumped from the speakers alongside heavy dance beats, but whatever.

The clap landed like a whisper, Ethan known more for his shrewd intellect and business savvy than brute strength. Temporarily shrouded in his scent and magical hum, I straightened and went for his hand, for long, bony fingers that always felt like a bear trap whenever we shook.

"Blessed Samhain, warlock," I offered in return, knowing tonight was sacred to his community. He could have been anywhere else— but he chose the Chalet. He had picked *me*, lending a subtle magical hand to really up tonight's atmosphere.

Those little touches that we added—they'd sell next year's tickets. The unearthly *feeling* shivering down a human's spine when they stepped over the threshold would stick with them. This was only my second year organizing such a big Halloween blowout, but given we'd been sold out for months and only forty minutes in the club was packed with ticketholders and a line stretched all the way around the block for those *hoping* they might be let in at some point, willing to pay the outrageous cover charge...

Fuck yeah, this was going to be a yearly thing. My team dropped a fortune on it, but from ticket sales alone, we had been in the black for weeks. The pricey cocktails and specialty snacks would only further the divide between loss and gain.

While Ethan and I had both stuck to classic tailored black suits, he went a step beyond that, dressed as a... fancy skeleton? Gangly, tall, all limbs and sunken cheeks, Ethan Perry passed as Skeletor on a regular day; tonight, Rosa must have gone to town on that face paint, because the shading was *impeccable*.

He looked legit.

And the top hat?

This guy.

Always willing to go the extra mile for my events.

"Looks amazing in here," the warlock mused, both of us back to leaning on the railing, humans giving us a few feet of space—almost like they *knew* tonight of all nights not to invade our personal bubble. Shifters might not recognize Halloween or Samhain as anything special, but even I couldn't deny the electricity in the air, magic sizzling, thick and heady.

"Thanks, man." I motioned to the chandelier. "Make your kind feel right at home?"

All our supernatural ticketholders organized their admittance through Ethan, a massive group of them bussing over from witch-run Hampton at our northwestern border. Unlike the mass of humans squished on the dance floor and crowding the first- and third-floor bars, Ethan's ilk opted for private rooms.

And good for them.

Cost *way* more, but it got you privacy, space, and security. A tinted window overlooking the club below. Bottles on bottles on *bottles*, all night long, for a set fee.

On weekends, our private rooms averaged a sixty-percent occupancy. Weekdays—forty.

Tonight we were at one hundred, the rooms stretched along the east and west walls of the second-floor balcony, hallways on the perimeter connecting the north and south viewing decks for those who couldn't afford the privacy.

One room, however, was roped off for my pack.

No idea if any of them, giddy little Lyssa included, would make use of it, but I'd wanted the option available. No club attendant either, just in case things took a turn for the scandalous.

"Everyone's really happy," Ethan insisted, his huge smile kind of unnerving tonight with the face paint, his teeth hauntingly white. His faint brown gaze flitted around the dance floor, both of us waiting for our girls to arrive. "This is going to make *waves* over there." We bumped fists without looking, our friendship instinctive at this point. "Next year, these humans will have to fight to get tickets."

While I smirked, my inner wolf huffed, dreading the thought of doing this all over again after such a brutal week finalizing everything. This bash was a *performance*, ten steps above what standard clubs did on theme nights. The chef, the bartenders trained in fire shows, the DJs, the private rooms—it was an art. Throwing a party, the kind people willingly paid a shitload for and still talked about months after, was a fucking *skill*.

Thus far, no hiccups.

My crew knew their stuff.

In precisely forty minutes, the lights would dim so that only the chandelier illuminated the first floor. Fog would roll out. The music would take a turn for the creepy and sexy, and our graveyard-themed hour would commence.

As always, Ethan and I immediately dug into the nitty-gritty business talk no one in my social circle put up with. Stats. Numbers. Profit margins. Some gossip about the dick chef who charged way more than he was worth *but* whose name was a fucking Pied Piper for foodies. It flowed fast and easy between us, so much simpler than conversations with Lucian and Soren—until I scented it.

Her.

Roses in the air, floating high above the standard nightclub scent storm. Over the colognes and perfumes, the BO and the bad breath, the liquor and the chicken-and-waffles circulating the crowds—my mate.

I straightened, nostrils flared, vision sharpening as my inner wolf let go of the alpha male shit we used for the club—and tapped into the alpha *beast* who craved his fated girl more than *anything*. Possessive. Dominant. Wild. My lips twitched, threatening to peel back and reveal canines as I searched the crowd. Beside me, Ethan chuckled and nudged at my arm.

"Scent your mate, did you?"

My low growl and stiff nod was answer enough, and he let me search the first floor in peace, scanning, scanning, scanning—

Found you.

Slack-jawed delight ripped through me, probably *pounding* through the alpha bond and alerting the others that she was here—and she looked fucking gorgeous.

"Lyssa looks like a goddess tonight," Ethan remarked as he slowly straightened beside me, his tone respectful, our minds—no surprise—forever aligned.

And he was right.

My golden-eyed mate was a vision, loitering at the helm of the dance floor, above the crowd near the steps, alongside Ethan's wife.

Their couple's costume *so* obvious now I should have seen it coming.

Lyssa in gold, Rosa in silver—the sun and the moon.

They always said not to look directly into the sun or you'd go blind, but if I did right now, locked on Lyssa, the rest of the club fading away, I'd go happy that *she* was the last thing I saw before the abyss claimed me.

Ethan wasn't far off the mark either: she definitely had a Greek goddess *thing* going on with the toga-length dress cutting off mid-thigh, gold and shimmery beneath the moody chandelier lighting. Golden gladiator sandals looped up her bare calves—had she shaved for tonight? Because those legs *glistened*. Gold rings glinted on her fingers, and she wore a straight-up Statue of Liberty crown, seven golden spikes reaching for the stars, her hair wild and wavy. Soft, too, controlled and styled. Complementary makeup for her tanned skin and ethereal costume, obviously done by the witch at her side. Gold and brown and a beigey-nude lip.

Exquisite.

Lyssa nearly hacked me off at the knees in that getup.

So *fucking* beautiful.

I gripped the railing hard, white-knuckling through my wolf's desperate howl—calling to his mate, beckoning her *here* so we could taste her.

In that, my girl *was* the sun. No question about it. Radiant, her smile lit up the nightclub. She outshone everyone here, males and females alike, and they ought to bow down to her—recognize that Lyssa was the center of the *fucking* universe.

I blinked out of the lovestruck stupor, suddenly *very* aware of Ethan's teasing stare burning into the side of my face.

"Breathtaking," I muttered. Not wanting to leave his wife out, I begrudgingly looked Rosa over as well, in need of a compliment so he didn't think I was a completely whipped wolf.

"What's with her eyes?"

"Contacts," I said without thinking, the lie we as a pack had agreed on coming a little too easily for a friend like Ethan. Even though he and Rosa had been heavily involved the night Lyssa drank from Gull River, we needed to get a grip on her changes first and foremost. She seemed fine—but she wasn't.

And none of us knew how to manage that.

And I'd been so busy *here*...

My inner wolf snarled at the thought. Yeah, yeah, fucked-up priorities and whatnot. *I get it, stop giving me fucking heartburn.*

"Contacts?"

"She saw it on Instagram," I told him distractedly, massaging the burning ache in my chest and taking in Rosa's unflattering silver sheath dress with a frown. "Thought it was cool. I ordered them from some specialty shop in LA."

"Ah." Ethan chuckled, his head bobbing, his skeletal smile unsettling. "Makes sense. She's got a lot of social media to catch up on... Prepare for *that* nightmare while you can."

"Hmm." I cocked my head, still scrutinizing Rosa in that oversized pillowcase. Sure, her hair spilled over her shoulders like a red waterfall, similar to Lyssa's in that it seemed soft and fluffy as a cloud. But that *dress*, those sleeves creeping up her hand and looping around her middle finger. That muted crown. Solid makeup, but clearly she had organized Lyssa's outfit; she could have *rocked* something similar. "How's Rosa feeling about the baby weight stuff lately? I mean, she looks fantastic—perfect pair, our girls."

"Yeah, it's hit-and-miss," Ethan remarked with a sniff, fidgeting with his black bow tie, eyes locked on his wife. "Some days she's fine, sometimes it's a lot of sobbing and stress eating. I just try to help where I can." He then glanced my way, his frown exaggerated by the face paint. "Why?"

"No, it's just…" Shit. Had I just dug myself a hole? "Not to be rude, but she has a great figure."

I mean, hourglass was *in*, and Rosa was all curves, womanly and full. Ethan snorted, blackened brows rising.

"I'm not a shifter, bud. Feel free to tell me my wife is gorgeous—I know she is."

My inner wolf rumbled, mildly annoyed at the potshot, but the warlock wasn't wrong. If a male told me Lyssa had a great figure, I'd have to *really* fight the urge to gouge his eyes out just for looking.

"The costume just makes her, uh…" Hands in my pockets, I left it at that. Even a blind man could see that circus tent made her appear ten times bigger than she actually was, her nipped waist lost, her bountiful curves muzzled.

"Well—" Ethan dug out a pair of black gloves from inside his jacket with a shrug. "—she just knows better than to dress like a whore."

Uh. What… the fuck? I turned away from the girls as he shoved his gloves on and tilted his top hat. "What did you—"

"Have you seen the way some of these humans dress?" Ethan's lip curled as he motioned to the throngs of women in skimpy Halloween costumes. "Despicable." The sneer threw me almost as much as his use of the word *whore*. "Anyway…" Another lukewarm clap on my shoulder, followed by a great white's grin. "Gotta go sweep my moon goddess off her feet. Amazing event, man. We'll do drinks to celebrate next Friday."

Still a little shell-shocked, I managed a nod and a thin smile, then watched his back as the warlock wove through all those so-called whores, politely laughing and bowing if he accidentally jostled any of them, then descended the nearest spiral staircase to the first floor.

That was… fucking weird.

I'd never heard him talk like that before.

As I tracked him below, headed toward our females and towering over many in the crowd, I probed my inner wolf for an opinion. Generally, the beast had an aloof, standoffish approach to just about everyone except Lyssa and, annoyingly enough, Soren and Lucian—but only in their wolf forms. Tonight, however, he was too busy clawing up my lungs, desperate for me to refocus on our mate, to notice what had just happened.

Not great, in the grand scheme of things. Growling, I massaged at the hot twinge in my chest, then returned to her.

To my golden girl—utterly alone as soon as Ethan whisked his wife away, steering her onto the dance floor from behind and whispering in her ear while Rosa giggled and plodded along.

My soft, affectionate grin turned feral: this was a familiar picture, my mate alone by the dance floor, in need of a rakish professor to teach her the seductive art of the grind.

Unfortunately, she wasn't alone for long. Just as I was about to push off the railing and stalk down there myself, she was swept into the arms of another.

A fucking *Viking*.

Blond, massive, shirtless, and muscular, he scooped her up and twirled her around, my mate's expression exploding from startled hesitance to giddy exhilaration in a heartbeat. Warmth pulsed in my chest, her feelings twined with his, touching me, tickling me, coaxing me to… join them.

Fucking Soren. Of *course* he had an actual costume for tonight —and from the look of it, he went hard. Dark linen trousers and a rope belt with a plastic axe hanging from it. No clue what the shoes consisted of, the view obscured from here, but that bare sculpted torso had just about every female on the first floor drooling, even if it was artfully dirt and faux-blood splattered— like he had just returned from battle. He'd shaved his hair at the sides since I last saw him, runes carved into the cut, the long top tousled. Blackened eyes with streaks down his cheeks like war paint.

Yeah, he definitely looked the part.

And Lyssa, her back now to me, couldn't stop *touching* him, her hands all over his abs, his pecs, his biceps. From his expression, the light in his amber wolf eyes, he loved every second of it. Again, a whoosh of molten heat bloomed in my chest, their reunion happy and giddy and overtly affectionate.

My inner wolf held his breath, waiting for *my* jealousy to erupt and reverberate back to them through the bond.

Nothing.

In fact, as Soren ushered her toward the dance floor, all that mattered to me was that Lyssa was having a good time.

That she was happy.

And her smile—brighter than the sun.

Good.

I schooled my features when I realized I was gawking at them like a teenage girl who had just *finally* watched her dream fictional couple share their first on-screen kiss.

Fuck's sake.

Below, Soren marched her to the middle of the dance floor, his huge frame and—for once—imposing presence clearing some space. However, while Lyssa backed into him, as though expecting the type of dancing *I* had taught her, Soren Acker busted out the nerdiest shit I had ever seen.

The sprinkler.

The shopping cart.

Dorky Dad moves galore.

Yeesh.

He really looked the part, seductive and brooding and dangerous, and then *that?*

You blew it, buddy.

Or... not?

Because there was our mate, *howling* with laughter, clapping her hands and mimicking his moves, much to the delight of the crowd around them. Hell, a few of the humans even joined in, the blond alpha effortless in the way he connected to strangers with a smile and a bit of self-degradation.

Dick.

Women *loved* a man with a sense of humor, but, really, that just wasn't my bag.

On the brink of sauntering down there and stealing my mate away, Jocelyn intervened. Costume-wise, my assistant went a half step above me and had thrown on a headband with fox ears on top, all fuzzy and velvety, to pair with her burnt-umber pantsuit.

"Issue in the delivery bay," she told me above the pounding bass, her hand on my shoulder, her mouth next to my ear. I ducked down to accommodate, very aware of how intimate the conversation looked, but Jocelyn was like a little sister at this point. I had *real* sisters—two were in prison, forever loyal to the Quinn code of psychotic conduct, and the third had died of a wolfsbane overdose like Dad. I'd always choose this fox over any of them. "Something with the payment."

"Fuck's sake."

"I know, I know, I *told* them..." She rolled her eyes, positively bristling. It wouldn't be the first time the vixen could have handled a problem on her own, yet they always demanded *me*. One day these pushy chauvinist assholes would feel the sharp bite of her little fox teeth. Scowling, I brushed by her, off to deal with the first disaster of the night that warranted my attention.

As per usual, it was shit Jocelyn could have handled on her own, something I drilled into those thick human skulls before returning to the party. I did a quick check-in with the fussy Montreal chef in passing, then exited from the kitchen doors right into the scheduled graveyard segment of the night. Fog hovered about two feet off the ground, lights dimmed, patrons *loving* it. Slower, more sensual music pulsed from the speakers, the DJ dressed as the devil spinning like this was the party of the year, really selling it, really earning that outrageous price tag—and really setting the mood for seduction.

Following the scent of wild roses, I tracked her back to the dance floor, where I found Lyssa alone, loitering by the railing overlooking the pit of writhing bodies.

No Soren.

No Lucian—but no surprise there.

While Soren had showed up this afternoon to *help* with setup, happily following Jocelyn's orders and doing a lot of the heavy grunt work without question—and most importantly, without stepping on my toes—Lucian had been a handful. Normally he stuck on the sidelines, watching, mapping perimeters and exits, but he had arrived this evening shortly before the bash started demanding security information.

Right in my face, asking about the men I had working the door, the bouncers inside, who the hell were all these *strangers*—fucking nightmare.

I dumped him onto the head of club security, telling them both that Lucian had authority to call the shots and override exterior protocols. Infuriating as it was to have him barking at me an hour before opening, he did it for Lyssa.

So.

Whatever. Let him sniff and patrol—because, really, what the fuck else did he do with his time?

And what had happened in his past that made him so goddamn anal about safety?

At one point, literally ten minutes before we let ticketholders in, he blocked me in a men's room stall and growled that the air in the delivery bay smelled like iron.

Like that mattered.

I told him I'd have someone look into it, breezing by to wash up and get out where I belonged.

Hadn't seen him since then, and I appreciated every blissful second of his absence; the huge wolf really knew how to body-block when my stress levels were at an all-time fucking high.

For now, however, a lull blanketed my schedule.

Technically, I had nothing to do but nitpick and micromanage—as Jocelyn put it—which meant, in theory, I too could do whatever the fuck I wanted.

And right now, I wanted *her*.

Strolling through the fog, I snuck up behind my golden goddess. She stiffened, then relaxed, sinking against the railing, her anticipation suddenly humming in my chest like a beehive.

She'd scented me.

Expected me.

One day I'd catch her off guard properly again.

For now, I relished her submission, her body soft and curvy and fucking *mine* as I strolled up behind and smothered her with my own.

"Hello, sunshine," I rasped in her ear, mindful of the spiky crown about an inch from gouging my eye. Lyssa moaned and arched into me, ass to my front, wiggling ever so slightly, her cheeky smile telling me she knew *exactly* what she was doing down there.

"Hello," she purred as she tipped her head back against my shoulder. I grimaced and reared out of the nearest spike's reach. "Where have you been?"

"Putting out fires." Swooping low to safety, I dragged my lips across her shoulder, over bare skin and gold silk, then up her neck, tongue flicking out to tease her pulse point. If Soren hadn't made it clear, *I* staked my claim on the most exquisite female present, not subtle in the way I snatched her and declared *mine*. One arm snaked around her waist, I let the other wander, stroking her curves, her exposed thigh, even hiking up her dress *just* enough to make her squirm. "But I'm all yours for a little while..."

Lyssa chuckled, dragging her nails over my arm, *gritting* into the suit material. "Really?"

"Yes," I murmured against her jaw. I then nibbled just below her ear, reminding her that while she had claws, I had *teeth*, and I had no qualms in marking her right here and now in front of everyone. No one questioned a bit of blood on Halloween. "Whatever will you *do* with me?"

My mate whirled around—or, at least, she *tried* to, only to stake me in the face with her crown. I hissed and fully disengaged before she took out an eye, and Lyssa clapped her hands to her mouth, apologetic but giggly, then smoothed out the pinprick of pain where a sharp little spike had stabbed my cheek.

"Where's Soren?" I snagged her hand, smitten with her tender care but hungry for something darker, then kissed the underside of her wrist. Face-to-face now, my mate sidled closer, her figure flush against mine—against the erection that had been building since I first spotted her looking like the fucking sun.

"Getting us drinks," Lyssa told me with a nod toward one of the larger bars we had installed just for tonight.

"What a gentleman." Threading our fingers together, I stepped back, then jerked her forward into my orbit again. "Well..." *You snooze, you lose.* Wasn't that Soren's sentiment when he stole my *perfect* bedroom right out from under me? Now I was stuck with his boring, unimaginative space the furthest from Lyssa, wardrobe storage severely lacking. "How about a tour of a private room in the meantime?"

Lyssa tiptoed after me as I backed toward one of the spiral iron staircases. "But Soren—"

"He's a wolf," I growled, ignoring her concerned point toward the bar. "He'll find you."

With that flawless logic, she trailed after me upstairs, through the mass of humans, the stifling costumed crowds, then down the west corridor of private rooms. All the way to the end, past the bathrooms and beside the emergency exit stairwell, I whipped out my personal access card and swiped it over the reader. Tonight, Lucian and Soren had a copy as well—as should this she-wolf.

You know. Later. For now, I just wanted to *enjoy* her, not teach her the nuances of a key fob.

Locks unbolted, clicking and clacking and catching Lyssa's attention, her head tipping side to side like she was in wolf form and listening to a strange noise in the bush.

Fucking adorable.

Eager to prove that despite the danger in my smile, I too could be a gentleman, I nudged the door open and bowed low as it swung inward, gesturing for my mate to pass. Shoulders back, head high like the queen she was, Lyssa sauntered by with an added sway in her hips—then squealed and scampered in when I pinched her ass and snarled, prowling after her like a starved man in sight of his first meal.

Kicking the door shut behind, I gave her just a beat to acclimate to our new surroundings. Keeping with the low-light nightclub vibe, the private rooms were all black—walls, floor, ceiling, black, black, black. Black furniture, two crescent moon couches in the center, leather and luxe, separated by a round coffee table with a tray of pricey champagne already chilled. To my immediate right at the door stretched a buffet table, tonight's Halloween-themed canapés tented under coolers or warmers depending on the type. The club's music thrummed from the corner speakers, muted enough for actual conversation, and Lyssa charged over to the wall-to-wall tinted window, practically shoving her face against the glass to take it all in.

My gaze narrowed, the hunter rising, adrenaline prickling in my fingertips the longer I scoped her figure. Lyssa inhaled sharply, and when she peeked back, her flushed cheeks told me she *felt* the desire —felt the predator eyeing his prey, mouth watering, hackles soaring, instinct about to take charge.

She wet her lips on the casual stroll toward the half-moon couch, golden eyes flitting my direction every so often as she drifted around it, running a finger over the leather. I let her dangle, hands clasped behind my back, let her *guess*—then lunged when that glittery orange-and-black bow on top of a champagne bottle caught her attention like something shiny ensnaring a magpie. Ever the fighter, such a quick little wolf, Lyssa pivoted *just* in time, shoving at my chest when I was nearly on top of her.

"Nooooo," she whined, half-hearted in her attempt to escape my rough hands all over her body. "My makeup—"

"Blue eyes," I growled, palming her ass and yanking her against me. "I'll *pay* Rosa whatever she wants to fix it."

And fix it she would, because the way I kissed her, rough and deep, squeezing her ass like I *owned* it while the other hand cupped the nape of her neck, this golden shimmer and nude lip wouldn't survive the assault.

Lyssa responded like a she-wolf who had no interest in being tamed, all teeth and claws, fierce and fiery. Snarling, I cuffed her neck harder and wrenched her back, fully aware that despite the theatrics, she had already hooked a leg around my thigh, her dress hitched, her hips undulating—grinding on me in search of relief.

"You think you can walk into *my* club looking like that and not expect to get fucked?" I demanded, relishing the way her eyes rounded and her hips stopped, the threat landing hard enough that she gasped. I tipped her head back further, fingers twined in her bronze waves, the other hand cupping her, bucking her over my thigh. "Blue eyes, you're lucky I didn't mount you right where I found you."

Oh, *fuck*. The thought of that—hiking up her dress, yanking aside her panties, and *fucking* her right there over the railing...

Like my dick could get any harder.

Whimpering, Lyssa wrenched me to her by my tie, fisting it with both hands and using it like a leash. Typical. I had her cornered—yet she had all the power. We crashed together furiously, each desperate to consume the other, fire sizzling from her skin to mine and mine to hers. Heat swelled around us, the air thick and suffocating. Hands *every*where. When Lyssa finally pried her mouth away, I had her hoisted up, those bare legs snapped around me, her dress up to her waist and her eyes beyond wild.

Golden *fire*.

"Actually," she whispered breathlessly, her grin savage as she dragged a rough thumb across my bottom lip, "there's something I want to try..."

My eyebrows shot up, every last drop of blood officially in my cock. "Oh?"

She nodded, eager enough to make me second-guess the hellfire in her eyes, then wriggled free. Grabbing my hand, Lyssa escorted me to one of the half-moon couches, then pushed me into it, hands on my shoulders. I surrendered to the intrigue and crashed down, curious, hungry, envisioning her sprawled over my lap with her dress up and panties down.

Lyssa nudged my knees apart, putting them in an aggressive manspread, then slowly—*fuck* me, so slow and slinky—sank to the floor. Kneeling before me, she smoothed her hands up my inner thighs to my belt.

"You're all so *good* with your mouths," Lyssa mused as she brushed those wayward fingers over my cock, featherlight and teasing enough that my hips jerked. Smirking, she didn't stop until she reached my belt. "I did a little research..."

"Did you?" I growled tightly. This exquisite sun goddess nodded as she undid my belt. Goddamn it, I *knew* that laptop would be a worthwhile purchase.

"I want to be *just* as good," my fated purred, my belt open, my zipper next, her smile sinful and her eyes powerful. "Sit back, mate. I want to taste you."

Dead.

Officially dead.

Arms outstretched across the couch, I threw my head back and groaned. Fuck it. No more work tonight.

And if anyone barged through that door right now to interrupt her, I'd snap their necks and deal with the body in the morning.

11

LYSSA

Tonight I learned there was power in kneeling.

I'd never want to totally control my mates, just as I would hate them if they did that to me. No, this wasn't that. It wasn't power and control over *all* aspects of our connection—just this moment. On my knees, cradled between Ewan's strong thighs, I had him. Every inch of him. His attention. His eyes like a sunset on fire, his primal heart right on the surface as I nudged his briefs down. The slightest touch of his shaft made him twitch and hiss, his hands flexing in and out of fists along the back of the couch. His dick sprang free as soon as I tucked the silky fabric under his balls, hard and yearning, reaching for me with a beaded wet pearl at the tip.

Desire made his expression tight.

His teeth clenched.

His eyes almost… pained.

Wow. I licked my lips, fascinated by how *open* he was suddenly, my mate who was always and forever in control. No wonder he and the others liked licking between my legs—because this was exhilarating. While Kira left me to it, her *need* threaded with the excitement pounding in my chest, lightning in my veins and damp between my thighs.

Even though I had mated with all my alphas, I'd never been this up close and personal with any of their manhoods. Sure, I'd *felt* them—intimately. Ewan's was as thick and long as I remembered whenever it speared me, pinned me to the wall and pounded me into paradise. A smooth head. Hefty. Two stand-out veins twining around the shaft. Smooth and relatively hairless, the black coils at the base as neat as the hair on top of his head.

I'd read about blowjobs on my gifted laptop. Always when my mates were out of the house, I turned off all the lights and huddled against the headboard, knees up, laptop on top, and hastily skimmed articles about the mechanics, the how-to, what to expect and how not to gag if he stabbed the back of your throat.

Reading about them always made me feel silly and embarrassed; most of the articles were written for teen girls, *maybe* early twenties.

I was twenty-six this year, twenty-seven in January. At this point in my life, I shouldn't need to *research* blowjobs, but all that background reading came in handy now.

Some women in forums seemed to dislike giving them.

I just wanted to return the favor. Lucian and Ewan had knelt between *my* thighs; fair was fair. Mates were equal in all things—including this.

The internet had told me to mind the head because it was sensitive; Ewan groaned and closed his eyes when I traced its ridge, his hips bucking. My research had also insisted I not grip the thing like I was mad at it, so I tempered my grasp, highly aware of my newfound strength, then licked him from base to tip.

One long, fluid sweep and this alpha male was *mine*.

"*Fuck*, Lyssa," Ewan growled, a hand slapped to his forehead, his face crinkled. I hesitated, worried I had somehow messed this up already, but when he didn't push me away, didn't snap his teeth or snarl or stand up and run, I did it again.

And again, grinning when the fiery sunset crashed to my face and locked on my eyes.

Goodness, the power here was thrilling.

Power had been the name of the game since waking up after

Gull River. My limbs felt stronger, my endurance better, my strength heightened. Still, I tailored that last one around my mates so we didn't slip into a power imbalance. It had taken us *weeks* to find *some* sort of stability in the house, and with my males, it was precarious, ready to fall apart on a gentle breeze.

Plus, I didn't want to scare them away.

Refused to give them yet another reason—on top of the golden eyes and the trembling windows—to reject me.

So, I held back. This evening, shoving Lucian out of my bedroom, I had barely pushed. He seemed to enjoy me struggling, and I liked the way his warm affection resonated in my belly. Win-win. Still, it was a learning process, one that I didn't consider mastered yet. Sure, I had adjusted to my eyes—but not my strength, not the raw, ancient power buzzing in my fingertips.

Not the way plants bowed in my direction like *I* was the sun.

And definitely not the nightmares.

Ever since my first visit to the Chalet a few days ago, my dreams had been full of darkness, cold and suffocating. Shadows hunted me through the orchards now; before, the endless rows of apple trees were just that—endless. Annoying. No escape. Now, something sinister stalked me, its icy breath on the nape of my neck. No relaxation. No sitting around wondering if Idunn would show.

Because she was there, in the thick of it: up a tree.

Hiding.

Terrified, just like me. Anytime I saw her through the foliage, the goddess just held a slim finger to her lips, begging me to keep quiet.

Kira protected both of us. For the most part, she circled me, but if the shadows stretched their cold fingers up Idunn's tree, there she was, snarling and scratching at the bark, bullying them back.

Four horrible nights of that.

Of being hunted.

Never caught—but the world of magic and goddesses was new to me, and I had no idea what would happen if the shadows *did* coil their hands around my neck.

I always woke in a cold sweat.

369

One night, my mates had roused me. Apparently, I'd been screaming.

In the orchard, I couldn't breathe.

Tomorrow, Rosa and I were headed south to really work on this curse. I planned to share every detail then with the one person who couldn't kick me out of the house and turn their back on me for being *different*.

Tonight, I let the rest go and surrendered to the power, to Ewan's raw expressions, to the perfect distraction this nightclub and its private room offered.

After a few more exploratory licks, his skin salty and velvety, I took him completely in my mouth—

And gagged.

Whoops. Too deep.

Eyes watering, I coughed and adjusted—combined my fist and mouth, moving both together to create a rhythm that had Ewan's breath erratic and sharp, his fingers twisting into the leather. Totally in my thrall anytime my eyes flicked up to tangle with his, the alpha occasionally toyed with the ends of my hair, feathered and styled to perfection by Rosa's glamor charm. With all the bobbing, it took some tact not to stab him in the chest with my crown, but we managed. A part of me said to take it off, but this costume was divine—that crown wasn't going anywhere, not with the way my mates complimented me while wearing it.

I nearly took *all* of him after a while, getting used to breathing through my nose, relaxing my jaw, maneuvering my tongue—when the locks clicked and clacked open like they had when Ewan swiped his card. Gasping, I reeled back when the door flew open, and Ewan lurched forward to cover himself. I hastily wiped the saliva from around my lips, wide eyes landing on Soren.

Soren with a beer bottle in one hand and a cup with smoky orange liquid in the other, a skull-tipped straw poking out the top. My blond mate cocked his head to the side, then stepped inside.

"Uh-huh," he said, his voice rough but playful. "Just what I thought."

He then kicked the door shut as I settled back on my heels, Ewan covering his dick with his untucked shirt.

"What's *this*?"

Soren's eyebrow wiggle set my face on fire, and I pressed my hands to my cheeks, mortified to have been caught in the act—but not as guilty as I should be. All of this was sinful by Reed and Nikki standards, but in my heart, having three mates didn't feel *wrong*.

My eyes? Wrong. My strength? Wrong. My connection to a dead goddess? Very wrong.

But not them.

By now, I really believed a divine being had linked us all together —even if I struggled and they bickered and we all fought to connect some days. It was a mess, but it was *my* mess.

And there was no shame in kneeling before my mate to pleasure him while the other watched, right?

Especially when the other looked so *rugged* in that costume. Bare-chested with an axe hanging from his rope belt, Soren was clearly an ancient warrior—and that was about as specific as I could get. The war paint streaking his cheeks and smoky-ing up his eyes had to mean something. Females drooled over those abs, those defined pecs and steely biceps, his forearms oddly powerful.

And he could have been so seductive on the dance floor.

I for one was ready to submit to his prowess.

But my mate had been silly. Goofy. Embarrassing for another female, maybe, but his dance moves made me shriek with laughter. It drew the humans into our bubble, the connections made friendly and shallow but really, really fun.

Now, he was still here for fun, but the way he prowled toward the couches in the center of the room—it was a sinful pleasure. Carnal and devious. Only a sliver of his blue eyes remained, snapping to full amber with a blink and a savage grin. Nibbling my lower lip, I glanced up at Ewan, also sporting his wolf eyes, and when Soren finally slowed, drinks in hand and head still tipped, the alphas faced off with each other.

All teeth.

Snarls rumbling in their chests.

Ugh.

"*You* left our mate unattended," Ewan growled, still covering himself, glowering at Soren like the wolf had beat me to a pulp and left me for dead. Like, come on—it wasn't that serious. "Unacceptable."

"She's a big girl," Soren fired back, sounding just as savage, just as dangerous, his hands tightening around our drinks. "She doesn't need a babysitter." Then, with a deep breath, the rage stoking embers in my lower back eased. He wandered over to the door and set our drinks on the food table, then rounded on us with a smirk, arms crossed, an eyebrow arched. "So, what are we up to?"

I flushed again when his amber gaze settled on me, demanding and pressing and oh, *no*, how was I supposed to resist that look? Did he want full details, or…?

"Soren," Ewan motioned to the door, "fuck off already, or I'll—"

You'll do nothing. Instinct propelled me; I shoved him back into his lazy couch-slouch. Surprise nibbled up my spine just as it flashed in his eyes, and I yanked his shirt up—then got back to it.

Taking him deep on the first stroke, I gripped the base of his dick and found my previous rhythm in a heartbeat. This time, Ewan muffled his groans, his hisses tempered and strained. Soren chuckled somewhere over my shoulder, his surprise threading with Ewan's, brightening up our connection as only Soren could.

Seriously, they were *not* about to start a fight here over nothing. This was really the only way to calm him down, body language and words and expressions otherwise useless. I was mated to *all* of them. They had marked me. I had marked them. We were connected on a deeper level than the usual relationship, and that was that.

It felt wrong to bully one of my mates out just so I could be intimate with the other.

We were all deserving of affection.

Fated mates—in our case, anyway—was a team sport.

Right?

Or was I out of line?

Was this a step too far?

My mated answered for me.

Ewan bucked ever so slightly into my mouth, his hips jerking, and Soren hovered *right* behind me, the heat of his presence suddenly stifling.

"T-take a picture," Ewan snapped after a moment of Soren's loitering. Heat sparked at the nape of my neck, sharpening at the *click* that sounded behind me immediately after. My black-haired mate snarled and lunged forward, getting tangled with my crown and shoving his length down the back of my throat.

"Chill." Soren chuckled. "It was facing me."

Squirming free, I sucked down a deep breath and glanced at Soren over my shoulder. If they could *not* push each other's buttons when I was working around a choking hazard, that would be great. My blond mate slipped his phone back in his pants pocket, then held up his hands innocently. I shot him a narrowed look, all discipline in the eyes but humor in the quirk of my lips, then got back to it, rising higher on my knees, legs spread for balance, and taking Ewan deep enough again to make his groan sound more like a whimper.

A gentle *whoosh* tickled the backs of my thighs, Soren dropping into a crouch behind me. Without a word, he tugged my dress up and over my backside, exposing the drenched white cotton beneath, then traced the stretchy hemline. Refusing to get distracted, I leaned deeper into Ewan's lap, focused on using both hands now, my lips and tongue devoted to the silky tip, to the way his thighs trembled and his moans snagged in his throat every time I swirled my tongue.

Soren snapped my panties, pulling back and letting go at just the right distance so that it *stung*. My warning growl went unheeded, muffled by Ewan's dick, because seconds later, my mischievous mate tore my underwear right along its seams. Haphazardly, with no regard for my limited supply back home—*rip*. Mouth full, I whined and wriggled my hips as he peeled the shredded fabric off, then tossed the heap on the couch next to Ewan. Just as I was about to press pause here, maybe remind my mates it was *their* money I spent every time they tore a pair of my panties, Soren *licked* me.

Front to back, he had ducked down without me noticing and dragged his tongue through my slick, swollen folds, all the way up to cleft of my backside, avoiding the puckered hole there by wandering over my left cheek—nipping hard enough to leave a mark.

My rhythm faltered. I sat up, hands still working Ewan's saliva-slick shaft, then whimpered when I found my mate on his back behind me, spreading me wider to accommodate for him as he scooted between my knees.

I soon lost sight of that smirking mouth; his hands shot up, cupped my cheeks, and hauled me down. My yelp milked a chuckle from *both* of them, the jerks, but any surprise melted away as soon as Soren's tongue showed me he too was *also* very good down there. Like his fellow alphas, he knew me. Knew how to lick just right, the pressure perfect, his fingertips bruising into my hips, spreading me wider. He tasted me inside and out, then up to the crest, to that little button that, *oh*, they all knew how to play.

It wasn't fair—Ewan seemed especially sensitive around the head, but their attention on *my* most sensitive spot made my knees weak and my thighs tremble and my mind blurry.

Imbalance. This was where they had me.

Determined not to be outdone by the skillful mouth lapping between my thighs, I resumed sucking Ewan as best I could—but rhythm escaped me this time. I struggled to focus, to maintain any sort of control as pleasure whumped in my lower belly like it had a heartbeat of its own, sparking, soaring, like electricity on *fire* the longer Soren tasted me.

As if sensing I needed a hand, Ewan rocked his hips into my mouth with long, languid sighs. When my gaze flicked up, I tripped right into the inferno, and all it took was a gentle tap of his one finger to each of my hands for me to withdraw. My mate rearranged them on his thighs, almost for the sake of my balance while Soren shoved me closer and closer to the edge. Ewan then took firm hold of my crown—and *pumped* into my mouth. He went as deep as I could take without coughing, then retreated. Again and again, he thrust into my mouth as he had done my sex.

He...

He...

Fucked my mouth.

Oh. Oh, *no*—that nearly punted me into the black, into that slightly scary moment when I lost all control of my body and lit up with pleasure so bright I swore every time *this* was the end.

"Oh, *shit*, blue eyes—"

Ewan's fingers twisted in my hair, and his shaft pulsed, followed by an explosion of salty warmth that flooded my mouth. Scrambling, I did my best to swallow it all down and not spill a single drop on the couch—on my beautiful costume or his expensive suit. A shiver of delight rippled down my spine, skirting the mounting heat in my core, separate and independent and *his*. Soren groaned between my thighs like he felt it too, Ewan's bright moment spreading through all of us, passing from one to the next like a contagious yawn.

As his shaft softened somewhat, I finally eased back—because I *did* it. I did a blowjob. *Yes*. Pride blossomed in my chest, affection sparking in Ewan's eyes as they straddled the shade between man and wolf, the fiery sunshine setting into dark hickory.

Coolness tickled my thighs, my sex—Soren was gone. He vanished so fast that it made my head spin, but then there he was, kneeling behind me, one hand clutching my hip as the other steered his dick into me. My blond mate claimed me with one rough thrust, me moaning and him grunting as soon as his hip bones slammed into my backside. Goosebumps shivered down my arms; he had taken me on the edge of my own explosion, the pleasure heady and a little painful, *hovering*, my sex aching for release. Whimpering, I braced on Ewan's sturdy thighs, hopelessly full, stretched and stuffed and *oh*. My head bowed, then shot up at his pointed throat clear, both of us highly aware of my sharp crown and his sensitive member.

With a low growl, Soren found his grip: the hand on my hip held tighter, while the other smoothed over my shoulder. A familiar position for us, just like the first time he hunted, caught, and *fucked* me on the mountainside. We'd tried just about every other position the rest of the day, our game ongoing until...

Until Gull River.

But never mind.

This—folded over on my knees, his hands dominating me, his strength pushing me down and bending me to his will—made the heat in my belly spiral.

The first firm buck of his hips made me squeal.

A third hand soon found my body, Ewan's fingers creeping up my throat until he cupped my chin and forced my head up. My midnight mate eased forward, the fiery sunshine back, his wolf eyes boring deep into mine as Soren pounded me from behind. I jostled and jerked, nudging into the couch, into Ewan's spread thighs, back against Soren's strong figure...

But Ewan held me still.

Captured me with that hand cuffed on my chin, with his eyes promising no escape.

It was all too much.

I tried to close mine, scared of the intensity in him, in the fire churning in my low belly, but his fingers gritted into my jaw.

A warning.

A plea.

Please, look at me.

And I did. I forced myself to stay with him, to be in the moment and not in the dark. As soon as Soren abandoned my hip and reached around for the sensitive bud between my thighs—I was done. Gone. The pleasure finally erupted, shooting like sparks from a bonfire, melting my limbs, turning me molten and limp between my mates.

And Ewan held me the entire time.

Made me look in his eyes as I broke apart and blew away on the breeze.

The sensation between my thighs turned sharp and deadly, Soren still teasing and touching and tormenting, even as I whined and squirmed. I swatted back at him, unable to take it, and then they both chuckled again—like they were in on it together.

At least *something* united them.

Apparently all it took was my sexual suffering and they were a team.

When his torturous fingers finally relented, Soren found a punishing pace, slamming into me from behind, both hands on my hips, his teeth gritted and his expression dangerous over my shoulder.

So he had found it too—the power in kneeling.

My mate had his way with me, Ewan's thighs supporting me, his hand under my chin, until his pace faltered and his hips finally stilled. As if my own pleasure wasn't smothering enough, the heat suffocating, the sort you died happy in, Soren's bliss touched me too. Tickled the backs of my knees and skittered up my thighs, zinging right at the bud he had tormented.

Strange that the undeniable urge to bite and scratch at them when I exploded like a dying star wasn't there anymore; maybe marking a mate was a onetime urge, an itch that *needed* to be scratched the first time. From here on out, it was like we could just... enjoy ourselves.

And tonight, I had most definitely enjoyed myself. My mates released me at the same time, Ewan easing up on my chin, Soren sliding out of me. My supports gave way, and I just wanted to sink to the ground—pass out, snooze the party away with Ewan and Soren on either side of me—

"You think it's that easy, baby?" But Soren scooped me onto my knees, my back to his bare chest, his skin a raging wildfire that made me sweat. He nipped at my shoulder, my neck, then licked the shell of my ear. Soren was my sweetest mate—until we mated. Then he turned wild, like a switch flipped inside him the moment we kissed, and I arched into the monster with a moan, exhausted but perking up again at his dark chuckle. "You've got *three* mates..."

Ewan tipped his head to the side, watching us through heavy, hooded lids, casually fisting his shaft, slowly bringing it back to life so that it stood tall and proud.

"It's never going to be just one of us," Soren rasped, his voice dropping to a silky purr. "We *all* want a piece of you—and we're going to take what we need."

Before I could get a word out, he *lifted* me off my knees and plopped me down on Ewan's lap. They both widened my thighs, positioning me over him, arranging me however they saw fit. Limbs weak and shaky from pleasure, I let it happen, breath hitching when the silky head I had showered with so much attention earlier nudged my slick entrance. As soon as Soren released me, Ewan took over, our eyes locked again as he slid me down his shaft, down, down, down, right to the bottom. I whined the whole way; I'd already... *exploded*.

But Ewan's touch, his gaze, his intensity, made the pleasure throb in my belly again, the *need* for release swelling. I steadied myself on his shoulders, trembling, our foreheads finding each other, our breath hot and gusting over each other's cheeks, lips, everything. Across the room was the clink of glassware, and out of the corner of my eye I caught Soren slugging back half his beer, then lifting the lids off the platters, perusing whatever made that *heavenly* meaty scent in the air.

I perked up at that, at the food over there, at Ewan's possessive hands kneading my backside.

He set the pace. I rocked half-heartedly; that first explosion had drained me.

Only... Soren was right.

I *had* three mates.

Three males who needed my attention—and I was the one who insisted they all be in the room at the same time. Sure, we were missing Lucian, his scent strongest outside of the club tonight, but as Ewan rocked into me, lifting my spent body and slamming it back down, I was almost grateful.

I couldn't...

My eyes squeezed shut as I gritted my fingers into the leather backrest. *Oh.* I couldn't do this again. Couldn't... Couldn't have one of them drag me to such blissful heights and toss me into the abyss.

And from the determined gleam in Ewan's eyes, his mouth as sinful as Soren's, that was exactly what my mate planned to do.

Refusing to be a passive participant, I did my best to keep up, whimpering, moaning, growling, totally at my mate's mercy. Every time I tried to outpace him, he smacked my backside or nipped at my throat—let me know that *he* had the power here.

Power I happily surrendered, a little sick of keeping it all to myself.

As we turned frenzied, grinding and rocking, Ewan pumping his hips off the couch just to take me as deeply as he could, I finally threw my head back—and came face-to-face with Soren. A few feet away, my mate loitered behind Ewan, shirtless, pants up, war paint smeared. He nursed that beer, a hand in his pocket, casual and distant to outsiders.

Intense and hyperfocused on me. Just as Ewan had forced me to maintain eye contact, a challenge among wolves but a secret intimacy in our pack, Soren ensnared me. Molten amber blazed bright as a shooting star, and I fell into it willingly, needing the burn.

He liked to watch me explode. My mate had demanded it every time he caught me on the mountain, refusing to let me close my eyes or look away, even if he was behind me. I knew the drill by now—knew better than to fight his command.

Tonight was no different. As the hot, sharp pleasure in my belly reached its peak, Soren stiffened, his knuckles white around the beer bottle. Ewan inhaled sharply, then cursed under his breath as my body succumbed to the ecstasy. Pleasure scorched white-hot, tearing through me without mercy, without compromise, drowning me from the inside out. Soren gritted his teeth, every muscle taut, and Ewan choked my name, fingers bruising my backside.

With a snarl, my black-haired mate stilled, his shaft pulsing inside me, his grip like a steel trap. Pleasure licked between my thighs once more, separate from my own and less intense, and Soren finally closed *his* eyes, Ewan's explosion touching all of us again.

Too hot.

Too intense.

Too much *pleasure*.

I whined and buried my face against his neck, riding it out, loving his snarls as Ewan did the same. Still, even with exhaustion worming into my bones and contentment washing over me like a gentle tide, something was missing.

Lucian.

Sure, the thought of being dragged to such sublime highs one more time, from a mate who knew just how to touch and lick and caress, a mountain of a man so scarred yet so tender, made the heaviness worse. But he should be here.

Soren and Ewan could have erupted in another fight, just another one of many. Of my three mates, these two really liked to beat on each other.

They hadn't.

The night could have taken a steep dive into hostility and tension and alpha males baring their teeth just to get a piece of me— to get *all* of me while his rival had nothing.

But we managed to keep the peace. Each of them had me in one way or another, and in the hazy aftermath, neither had started hurling insults again.

This was good.

This was *progress*. A big moment for our pack—and Lucian should have been here to celebrate. His heart deserved to feel just as whole and happy as mine did right now. When I'd asked Soren about his whereabouts earlier, my blond mate had no idea beyond the fact that he was outside pestering security—his words, not mine —and that he probably wouldn't show his face until the crowd died down.

While that fit what I knew of Lucian, I didn't have to like it.

I wanted him here, with me, on this couch, his lips on my skin and his hands everywhere...

But as Soren handed me the pumpkin cocktail he had originally left to fetch downstairs, the straw tipped with a skeleton skull, some little floating ice cube thing still giving off fog—was it a magic trick? —I lacked the energy to make my case.

Next time.

Lucian would be in the thick of it *next* time—I'd make sure of that.

After sitting up and slurping down the tart liquid, the liquor muted by the zesty mix, I fed an equally sweaty Ewan a sip. My spent mate's face puckered as he shook his head.

"Fuck, that's so sweet."

Not for me.

But I kept that to myself, gulping down another icy mouthful with a grin and a shrug.

"So..." Soren set his empty beer bottle on the back of the couch as he perched next to Ewan's head, *right* in his personal space, determined to be involved, and then smirked when his fellow alpha glowered up at him and I smothered a giggle. "Anyone in the mood for round two?"

12

LYSSA

"I'll be right back." *Wait.* I hesitated in the doorway, fixing my two sweaty, disheveled mates with narrowed looks. Fog kissed the corners of that huge tinted window across the room, and the buffet table to my right screamed my name. Knowing wolves as well as I did, I pointed a warning finger from Ewan to Soren and back again. "Don't eat all the food while I'm gone."

Sprawled on one of the half-moon couches, Soren chuckled—then sat straighter when my no-nonsense expression darkened. Tough as it was to be serious after our first group mating, I held my warning composure like an elder wolf checking a mouthy yearling.

"All yours, baby," Soren insisted. When I looked to Ewan, an eyebrow up, my black-haired mate grinned and raised his hands in surrender. Honestly, the sex had been fun and amazing and great and all that. I still burned bright and hot, the aftermath clinging to me, cloying between my thighs and threatening to stain my dress. But those sausage things under one of the tray covers? I planned to eat all of them. Then the fancy cheese. Then the garlicky spread for those fancy crackers, *then* the cookies shaped like little bats.

Yum.

Great sex *and* delicious food *and* my mates getting along?

Dream. Come. True.

Having staked my claim, I slipped out of the all-black private room, then flinched when the locks clicked and clacked into place as soon as the door shut. How... was I supposed to get back in? A special knock?

Even in this narrow corridor away from the main event, the Chalet struck like a charging bull. The heady smells of sweat and cologne and body odor and liquor. The pounding music. The fog hovering a few inches off the ground, artificial and tickling my nose enough to make me *and* Kira sneeze. Too loud. Too busy. Too —human.

I'd had my club fun for the night. If I had my way, we'd all spend the rest of it in there, separate from the chaos but still able to check on things through the window overlooking the first floor. Heck, if it were up to me, I wouldn't leave that room until sunrise. Sure, Ewan would inevitably come and go; that was expected. So long as he came back, Soren stayed, and Lucian eventually found us, it would be the *perfect* night.

The perfect distraction.

Something wet and thick oozed down my inner thigh, and I squished my legs together as I waddled down the hallway to the women's bathroom. Man, what I wouldn't give to be a witch right now instead of a shifter. On one of our lunch dates, little Aster had spit up all over her onesie, and Rosa whooshed it away with a flick of her wand and a softly murmured spell. *Bam.* Gone. Baby clean. No one had even noticed.

Shouldering through the dark wood door with its glossy rose-gold lettering, I stumbled into a space just as packed as the nightclub itself. Wall to wall females crowded the bathroom, the smells and sounds no less intense here—but the air... different. Electric, humming, like there were fifty Rosas in one place. Swallowing thickly, I glanced toward the sinks, catching the purple eyes of a woman washing her hands, her reflection watching *me*.

More witches?

Rosa had said her kind traveled here from nearby Hampton for the Samhain weekend, dropping a fortune on Redwood Grove's hotels, chalets, restaurants—and Ewan's nightclub. Suddenly self-conscious after a glimpse at my own reflection, my hair a mess and my cheeks a telling pink, I tugged my dress down, feeling almost like that purple-eyed witch could see right through it.

"Babe, you got a tampon?"

A human—something about her smell, her energy, her *look*—suddenly bobbed in front of me, dressed like a bride.

A... dead bride?

Half her face was rotted, but given the smell, it was just makeup.

I blinked back at her. Tampon? *Me?*

I didn't even have a purse tonight.

I came to the Chalet with nothing but myself and a crown.

Throat thick, mouth dry, I shook my head and croaked out, "No, sorry."

"Here, girl." A voice echoed from one of the stalls to my right, and seconds later a packaged tampon skidded across the tile in our direction. "I got you."

"Oh my god, *yes*, you *lifesaver!*"

Half-dead Bride scooped it up and skipped into a stall the second another female slipped out. More electric, bright-eyed women gathered by the sinks, fixing their hair, their makeup, all of them *very* stylish on a night dedicated to costumes. A toilet flushed. A door opened. I zipped inside the stall before someone else claimed it, feeling oddly at peace in here.

Surrounded by female strangers.

The air was different with all those witches, sure, but there was this strange feminine comradery here in the second-floor bathroom. Everyone stunk of booze, of the tart orange drink that I'd guzzled before leaving our private room. But it was nice. Drunk compliments flowed. Laughter. Hand dryers whirring and toilets flushing and heels clacking.

Until last month, I thought the only world I belonged in was the one out there—in the forest, in the wild, with the wolves. There was no room for a freak, an abomination, a daughter of sin and evil, among humans. I was too strong, too fast, too savage.

But as I sat to pee and clean up down below, I fit.

Just a little.

Not completely. Not yet.

Still *so* much to learn—about history and tradition, about blending into both humanity and shifter culture. About how to walk effortlessly in high heels. Seriously. Still on the toilet, toes exposed and tapping in my golden sandals, I bent over a little to gawk at the massive stilettos on the woman in the next stall. How did those things not just totally murder her feet?

But despite the hurdles ahead, I belonged here.

Kira whimpered.

Well. So long as Rosa and I could get Idunn's... *gift* under control.

Who knew—maybe I didn't have any of her powers. Maybe it was a fluke, the windows trembling and the pen on Ewan's desk rattling and... me breaking the faucet in my bathroom.

My mates still didn't know about that, and I just stuck to the other tap, forced to do everything with scalding hot water, the cold officially inaccessible.

I gulped at the thought.

Right here, right now, I belonged.

But that could change.

I had worked hard to keep all this new crazy inside, lying to my mates, pretending it *wasn't* happening—refusing to give them a new, very valid reason to turn me out into the cold.

The longer I sat there, trying to focus on the good but forever dragged toward the terrible, the bathroom quieted. Females filtered in and out, but the crowd eventually thinned to a lone pair of whispering women.

Then... just me.

Alone.

Like always.

Nope. Not tonight, stupid inner voice. Sniffing, I stood and flushed the toilet, then sauntered out to wash my hands, makeup ruined, golden gaze a bit bloodshot. After smearing my hands dry on my dress, I wiped under my eyes, banishing the old sorrow before it *dared* leak out. If I kept up the playful attitude—which would be easy once I was back with my mates—no one would notice.

If I didn't think it, *they* wouldn't feel it.

And then we could just have a fun night like any regular pack.

Hair smoothed, sadness squashed, I stared hard into the mirror —and gold stared back. My first instinct was to insult my new eyes.

Instead, I rolled my shoulders and stood taller, willing the tension away.

That gold looks great with your costume. Very on theme for the sun.

Kira huffed, unimpressed with my attempt at a positive attitude.

I glared harder at my reflection, this time directing it to my forehead as I pointed at the mirror. "Don't you start with me."

She fired back with a teasing yowl, just a little something to let me know she wasn't serious, then stomped around inside, bored and eager to get back to Ewan and Soren.

On the same page, girlie.

Feeling marginally better but still chasing the post-mating high, I left the bathroom—

And was immediately hooked around the waist and ripped back into a body so hard it had to be stone. All the air *whooshed* out of my lungs, like taking a punch to the gut, and Kira snapped and snarled inside my cotton-filled skull, her fury slicing through the shock.

No scent except the buckets of bergamot-accented cologne.

Roughly my height. Thin. Not a physical threat, but—

A hand snapped around my throat at lightning speed, the touch ice-cold and brutal.

"You smell like honey and sex," the strange male rasped in my ear, breathing me in deep, the air around us cooling.

Tinged with iron.

Down the hall, next to the emergency exit door, the shadows shifted and *moved*, just like they had a few nights ago.

"If I bite you," he carried on, crushing my windpipe as Kira fought me, desperate to shoot out and rip this guy apart, "is that what your blood will taste like?"

My vision sharpened, locked on the shadow morphing into the shape of a man.

A man in black.

Skin deathly pale.

A walking corpse in a fitted suit.

Handsome. Grey eyes. Cruel smile.

Coming right at me.

I blinked once, twice—and then the fog lifted.

Goodbye, shock—hello, *murder*. I elbowed back hard enough that something *cracked*, probably a rib, and my captor grunted. Whirling around, I hiked my knee into his groin—and found myself face-to-face with a mouth full of sharp, dazzling white teeth.

Two elongated fangs.

Not fake.

Not a costume.

Vampire.

This night was full of trickery, costumes and sparkles and illusion, but those weren't fake. Those were very, very real. Snarling, I shouldered forward, throwing all my new strength around, and knocked him a few paces back. Also ghostly white and in an identical dark grey suit as his shadowy companion, this buzzed blond staggered and struggled to regain his footing, surprise flashing in his gaze, his irises shaded like a wilted daffodil.

"Don't you dare *touch* me," I sneered. No one but my mates had a right to my body—and even they needed my permission. Kira and I aligned, hearts pounding as one, I attacked. Nails. Teeth. Brute strength. I bullied and pushed and kicked, snarling and growling and snapping.

I was strong.

But so was he.

And fast.

So fast he blurred right before my eyes, in front of me one second, behind the next—then *two* of them on me. I could take one if he just stood still for a beat, but two?

I wasn't strong enough for two.

All my fight, tenacity, confidence—trapped in their steel grips, both of them behind me, one gripping my wrists, the other clapping a hand over my snarling mouth.

So I bit him.

As the pair shoved me down the corridor toward our private room *and* the emergency exit door, I clamped down on that frozen flesh with everything I had.

"*Fuck.*" The hand's owner tried to wriggle free, but clearly he had never had a wolf bite before. We chomped hard and never let up, even as thick, gloopy, cold blood filled our mouths—made our stomachs turn and Kira gag and *ugh* vampires tasted like death. But I held on. Clamped down until my teeth nudged bone. Snarled like an alpha. Didn't even flinch when one of them pounded his fist into my side, right over my kidney. "Fucking wolf *bitch*—"

"Just get her downstairs," the original lurker hissed as they plowed me through the heavy metal door. "Don't break anything."

"Fucking cunt won't let go."

"Well, you'll *heal*, won't you?"

"Fuck off."

"*You* fuck off."

Both of you... fuck off.

We stumbled into a dimly lit stairwell, one giant heap of arms and legs and bodies all moving in different directions. Mouth so full of vampire blood it leaked out the sides, I planted my feet and fought the whole way down, these two throwing everything they had into moving me—their curses suggested as much, anyway.

I'd been in fights before.

Faced scarier foes.

Always alone, sure, but always a *survivor*.

After Nikki and Reed and the two years of horror following my first shift, nothing out there could compete.

Not that I had tangled with a vampire before, never mind two, but if they wanted to shove me out of this building—do it. Outside was *my* territory, and they had no idea what they were in for once I let Kira stretch her legs and bare her teeth in the alleyway behind the nightclub.

What I wasn't ready for, however, was their speed. Again. Once we all struggled down a single flight of stairs, like slogging through quicksand courtesy of sheer wolf grit, the pair paused on the landing, the stairwell suddenly *too* quiet except for my heaving breaths and snarls, and then the world just... blurred. Nothing in focus, we moved so fast my belly flipped, and I finally choked on all the vampire blood.

Gagging, hacking, I folded over when the stairwell finally came back into focus, surroundings crystal clear again, heart in my throat and Kira just as loopy. Blood so dark it was almost purple splattered the concrete and my sandals. Kira found her balance first, snarling, hackles up and lips peeled when the men behind me snickered.

"At least we know something shuts her up."

The one death-gripping my wrists, circulation cut and my fingers white, whipped me around and marched me toward the metal door at the end of the corridor.

"You tell me when the world stops spinning, puppy," he sneered in my ear, even his breath cold. Swallowing hard, I blocked out my hatred for *them* and focused on my breathing, on finding my feet again so that as soon as we hit fresh air, I could cut them off at the knees.

Literally, hopefully, only I had no clue how much pressure you needed to snap vampire bone.

But, hey, always up for learning something new.

As the pair ushered me roughly down the corridor, muffled music pounding away, Kira and I braced for the next attack. The first had happened so fast it was tough to take stock of my opponents, but from the lingering cold damp smeared around my mouth, I knew they bled.

And I knew they *hurt*.

On the brink of the final exit, the duo muttered to themselves in a language I didn't understand, fluid and low with a lot of hard *R*s. I took a deep breath. Kira stilled. They shoved me through the door—and right into a furious Lucian.

My mate took *me* by surprise, never mind the vampires. Dressed in a fitted black suit like Ewan, my mountain man pounced with a roar that lit up the night sky. Savage. Wild. Raw *fury* slammed into me, knocked the wind out of me, jumping from his heart to mine and setting it on fire. He lunged for the vampire on my right, and a gush of cold mist hit me from the side. The other vampire dragged me away, cursing, my skin painted with the blood of his friend.

Silly man.

Didn't he remember I could take them one-on-one?

Drawing on Lucian's wild, fusing it with mine, Kira *right* on the verge of a shift, I twisted my arm, loosening his hold, and spun into him. My fist met his nose *hard*, bone snapping, blood gushing, more curses filling the air. He regained control fast, snatching my wrist, but I ducked under his arm, not caring if I dislocated a shoulder in the meantime, and leapt on his back.

Raked my nails across his face.

Bit into his neck and tore off a hunk of icy skin. Down the alley, Lucian wore a mask of deep purple, vampire blood smeared up his snarling face, his neat beard dripping with the stuff.

"Should I shift?" I called over the fray, legs snapped tight around my bucking opponent.

"*No*," Lucian bellowed back. "Not here."

As if the human population of Redwood Grove *mattered* to either of us; I was ready to let Kira taste vampire flesh, and he sounded more beast than man, his voice impossibly deep—demonic, almost, as he slammed the throatless vampire's head into the pavement over and over again.

Unfortunately, these guys seemed to heal as fast as we did: my nose crinkled when I noticed the gaping wound across the vampire's neck stitching back together, ugly and crude. Lucian needed to bash his skull *now* or he'd have a warrior back at full strength in no time.

The momentary distraction was my undoing. Two strong hands shot up, grabbed my shoulders, and *ripped* me forward. I toppled down with a rough screech, Kira's snarl leaking through, and crashed into the ground. At the last second, I'd tried to cushion the fall, but the impact snapped my wrist, bones breaking with a sickening *crunch*. Agony seared up my arm. I hissed, knowing it was only temporary, and tried to squirm away.

Lucian broke the other vampire's jaw, drowning in a sea of rage, and my vision tinted red for a few seconds until I blinked *his* emotions away.

Not good in a fight.

I looked to him, frantic, hurting, needing this huge wolf to get a grip on his emotions—

The emergency door flung open, clanging off the brick and rebounding into a snarling Ewan and Soren. My mates charged into the fight, wolf eyes out and teeth bared, their anger, fear, and *wild* twisting with mine and Lucian's, the air thickening, the four of us briefly so in tune I swore I heard their heartbeats, felt their blood pumping through *my* veins same as my own.

My fingers tingled.

Heat exploded in my chest, scary and sharp and so *bright* my eyes watered.

A nearby trash can shook violently enough to jostle the lid off.

Dead weeds turned green, soaring out of the cracks along the building's foundation.

"*Shit.*" The vampire on top of me took off, blurring down the alley, his friend at his heels, just two shadows racing for the main streets. Without a word, a shirtless Soren sprinted after them, followed swiftly by Lucian, who ripped off his jacket and tie as he ran, hurling them aside and skidding around the corner.

Groaning, I pushed up on my elbow and rolled my previously broken wrist. While still a little crackly, it rotated in two circles with minimal pain—good enough. What had me more concerned were the weeds that had crept along the Chalet's foundations;

yellow and dead to green and vibrant, one had even sprouted a flower head and a few white petals.

"You all right, blue eyes?" Ewan crashed to my side and bundled me up, his wolf eyes assessing me for damage. I nodded. Technically, I was fine. *Technically,* my body healed fast and I lived to fight another day.

Inside, however, the fear turned to reaching ivy, spiraling around my bones, threading through my rib cage, *strangling* my heart.

Not only had two vampires tried to kidnap me tonight, but I made dead plants grow.

I shook that garbage can so hard the lid popped off.

I—

"I'm fine," I muttered when Ewan's search for injuries got rougher and more panicked. Groaning, I brushed the hair out of my face and—oh. *Come on.* One of them had ripped my crown off at some point. Jerks. Annoyed, I sat up properly and dusted the dirt off my legs, then grimaced when I noticed the ocean of purplish blood splattered everywhere. "Why did they do that?"

"I don't know." Now that he had confirmed nothing was broken or permanently damaged, my mate eased off to send a rapid-fire text, thumb flying across his phone's screen before he locked it and stuffed the thing in his jacket.

Then he was all mine.

Ewan hauled me into his lap, arms steelier and stronger and much, much safer than those blocks of marble with fangs. While I wanted to be strong, prove to my mates that once again I could stand on my own two feet against pack enemies, this was nice too. Just for a moment, the world went quiet. Me and him, alone in a dark alley, the ground damp with rain that must have fallen sometime in the last hour. On the other side of the building, the Halloween crowd chatted and laughed, the dull roar punctured by the occasional girlish shriek. Arms folded into my chest, I snuggled closer, burrowed under his chin and nestled into his throat, breathing in his scent. Eyes closed, I bathed in his support—

In his wrath.

Unlike before, Ewan seemed to be trying to keep his emotions under control—which worked great for me. Not only was I so *not* in the mood for another fear-based lecture, but despite the peace and quiet and comfort, something ancient still buzzed in my fingertips. If *I* lost it, influenced by them or my own feelings, I might expose myself more than I already had.

Make my mates question if I was worth the risk—if they wanted to keep this landmine on their territory. One wrong move and *boom*.

I clenched my eyes shut as hard as I could, shoving down the fear and drudging up the anger. If he felt me like I felt him, let Ewan believe I was *furious* that someone had gotten the jump on me.

Just when I noticed him starting to shake, his grip like a snare and his teeth bared, the emergency door flew open again, and out raced a wide-eyed Ethan, his wand drawn, his ridiculous hat forgotten.

His face paint a little smudged…

I guess he and his rosebud had been having a similar sort of night somewhere private and secluded.

"Where are they?" he demanded as Ewan helped me up. I didn't need the support, perfectly capable of standing by myself, but there was something so *nice* about his arm around my shoulders, cradling me into his chest. Clearly, my mate had messaged his warlock buddy about the situation: Ethan stalked back and forth, wand up, searching the shadows—his brown gaze snagging on the weeds I had…

I had…

Done something to.

Yeah, let's go with that.

"No idea," Ewan rumbled, "but I need to find them. Get them the *fuck* out of our territory."

If he was going to chase those walking corpses, then I planned to be right there with him. Had my stupid wrist been fully fixed, I would have sprinted after Lucian and Soren, more than happy to bully any danger to us *and* the humans of Redwood Grove out. "Ewan—"

The emergency door banged open again, and this time Rosa came trundling out, her huge silver dress hiked in one hand, her wand in the other.

"Lyssa!"

Cheeks flushed, emerald eyes panicked, she rushed straight to my side.

"Take her home and stay with her," Ethan ordered—then flinched, the warlock going pale beneath all that face paint when Ewan snarled. Fire surged between us, his grip tightening around my shoulders, and I pushed against the dead center of his chest, willing *my* calm to trickle into him—soothe the inferno, quiet the storm. As if realizing his mistake, Ethan patted the air between us. "No, no, sorry. If... it's okay, Rosa can protect the house. Make sure they don't, er..."

Much to my surprise, Ewan looked to *me* for an answer one way or another. Head dipped, he tapped the underside of my chin so that our gazes met. No words flowed between us, but the sentiment warmed in my chest. Kira whined, then snorted a response back to our mate, reading him loud and clear.

He wanted my opinion.

My permission, maybe?

No. That was a step too far.

He just needed to know I was okay with that.

Licking my lips, I managed a little half nod, because, yeah, I would go anywhere with Rosa, but I wasn't about to just hide in the house and wait for the males to take care of things.

We were a *pack*, now more than ever before. Mated, fated, we had our own song.

I had a duty to perform for *my* pack and territory.

"Can you spell the gates?" Ewan shifted his attention back to Ethan, his voice just as dangerously low and smoky as Lucian's had been. These vampires had no idea what kind of violent end they were in for, but I wanted to be there when it happened. "Ward the village? *Something?*"

"For sure," Ethan groused back. He shrugged out of his black suit jacket, which he then gently folded and set over the garbage can I'd rustled as he spoke. "Fuck those guys... The Hampton coven *vouched* for them. I didn't want any damn leeches near tonight, and I should have gone with my gut."

"Don't blame yourself," Ewan insisted. "Vamps are slippery assholes." His wolf eyes then narrowed at Ethan. "But let it be clear that I will *not* tolerate them in this territory again."

"Agreed." Ethan jerked up his dress shirt sleeves, wand in hand, his energy... complicated. Just like the witches in the bathroom had changed the air, made it electric and *different*, he and Rosa did too. But Rosa was the cold to his hot, the ice to his fire. She was my honey-and-amber friend, her scent strong and supportive, her physical being radiating the serene majesty of a full moon.

Her husband gave off a strange crackly static that made Kira tense, but from the thin smile he swapped with Ewan, he had already earned the right to be trusted.

The warlock shook his head and swooped a hand over his sweaty dirty-blond hair. "Should have gone with my gut... I'm sorry, but I'll get the village locked down now."

This was all moving too fast without me. Before I could get my two cents in, however, Ewan kissed me—nothing firework-inducing like before, just a firm, hard peck on the lips—and cupped my chin.

"No unnecessary risks, blue eyes," he growled. His arched eyebrow said he wanted me to promise and agree and be a good girl. I briefly clamped down on the insides of my cheeks instead, Kira desperate to hunt vampires.

"I can track them with you—"

"No." Like his word was law, Ewan nudged me toward Rosa—handed me off to the next caretaker. My lips twitched into a snarl, and I grabbed his jacket sleeve, ripping into the fabric and yanking him with me. His eyes flashed dangerously. My teeth bared back.

"Honey..." Rosa's gentle words cut through the mounting tension. If she had *any* sense, she wouldn't put herself between two wolves squaring off, but this witch—the moon to my sun tonight—seemed to trust me as much as I trusted her. She stuck herself right in my narrowed line of sight, not speaking again until we met in a clash of green and gold. "Look, if they were trying to take you... Don't give them what they want. Your home is the heart of the territory, right? You and me are just going to defend it." She rolled her shoulders back and wiggled her red brows. "Seriously. No bloodsucking leeches are getting by us."

Kira grumbled and scratched and paced inside me, her energy trembling through my arms, my legs full of *fight* and ready to run.

But we both knew Rosa had a point.

The house *was* the heart, the throne room, the *whatever* of our territory. I had no idea what those vampires wanted with me besides the fact that I smelled like a dead goddess, but if they were making a play for our land, they'd go for it at some point.

Fine.

I conceded with a stiff nod. Over Rosa's head, Ewan and I traded glances, expressions softened just enough to confirm the fight was over—dead and buried. On to the next issue.

After Ethan kissed Rosa's cheek and reminded her to lock the SUV while we drove, he jogged off with my mate, who seemed to be pacing himself so the warlock could keep up. As soon as they disappeared around the end of the building, I grabbed Rosa's arm and pulled her close.

"One of them said I smell like honey," I whispered, easing up on my grip when pain flashed over her features. "Idunn smells like honey."

Rosa pursed her lips. "Okay, we—"

"And I did that." I motioned to the very alive, very happy trio of thorny weeds growing out the side of the building. "They were dead, and now they aren't, and I don't know what I did, but they—"

"Honey, deep breath." Rosa planted her hands on my shoulders, then sucked down an exaggerated inhale and waited for me to begrudgingly do the same before she exhaled. We repeated that a few times, in and out, in and out, her tone and expression meant for baby Aster, not a grown wolf—but something I appreciated all the same.

Even now, after bullying rival wolves and surviving a vampire kidnapping, this witch was *still* looking after me.

"Tomorrow morning, we're going to tackle this together," she told me, slow and precise—maybe to keep me calm, but maybe because she was still working out my newfound powers for herself. "I've got a few exercises young witches do when their powers start to develop... We'll try them somewhere safe and away from everyone. For now—"

"Home," I finished for her. Rosa let out what I *swore* sounded like a relieved breath, almost like she expected me to fight her on this.

Nope.

Protecting our base made sense—even if unleashing Kira on those vampires would have been more satisfying.

"Home," she whispered back. We then set out together, hand in hand, her wand up and inconspicuous on a night full of magic, danger, and costumes, headed for her and Ethan's SUV parked up the street from the club.

Off to defend my pack's heart—and knowing that if one of those fanged weirdos underestimated us because we were *females*, he was in for one terrible, *awful* night.

13

LYSSA

"Okay…" Rosa closed the driver's-side door as gently as she could. "I think she's actually out this time."

With the SUV rumbling, the windows slowly defogging, Redwood Grove bathed in a bright grey foggy November morning, we both whipped around—and found Aster dead to the world. Tucked into her car seat, fed and fat and swaddled in a pink onesie with squishy little booties and blankets, the tiny witch snoozed away with her head slumped and her lower lip plumped. Adorable. Totally oblivious to the stress hounding me and her mom from the night before, but still very cute.

"Did you leave a note for the guys?" Rosa asked as she buckled herself in, the seat belt's click soft, her effort to keep quiet despite the roaring beast around us almost as adorable as her pup. I shook my head when she glanced up, and she huffed, rolled her eyes, then grabbed her phone from the front console, settled back into the much-too-big driver's seat, and stabbed at the screen. While Ewan was all thumbs on his phone—at some point during my forest exile, the world had evolved from cordless phones being the *height* of communications technology to touchscreen, which, gotta admit, was pretty cool—this witch did everything with her pointer finger and her tongue poking out the side of her mouth.

"I'm letting Ewan know we're going out for breakfast." We both made conspiratorial eye contact as I too slowly and quietly belted myself. The color drained from her cheeks, the same guilt poking at my ribcage. Neither of us wanted to lie to our men, but here we were, sneaking away first thing to practice... magic. Power. *Something.* Ethan had no idea—Rosa promised. My mates were still out hunting vampires, oblivious to the extent of my abilities.

It didn't feel good.

But Rosa had dubbed it a necessary evil for the time being, and I liked that. Not good—but necessary to keep our loved ones safe.

"I'm also telling him to get you a phone already," she added distractedly, brows furrowed deep. "Like, I know you can talk through howls, but it's getting ridiculous that you don't have one yet."

Grinning, I left her to it and watched Aster doze in the rearview mirror, relying on *her* peace to calm my nerves. With Halloween taking a steep nosedive only six hours ago, I should still be in bed sleeping it off. As promised, Rosa had spent the night, but I forced her to get some shut-eye when it became obvious a witch's body couldn't function on fumes like a shifter. Besides, I had it covered without her: no vampire set foot on the main property. I couldn't speak to the rest of the territory, but as soon as the sun's golden rays spilled over the horizon, I did a perimeter sweep of the nearby forest.

Nothing.

No weird smells. No iron. No cold spots. No crunching twigs and rustling leaves that didn't belong.

No Idunn on the wind either, but that was kind of just a small mercy.

Last but not least: no word from my mates. I *had* heard them howling through the early morning hours, coordinating as wolves, their intense focus, their frustration and fury, washing over me in waves—sometimes tidal, sometimes nothing more than a splash.

While I had no idea where they were now, I trusted their abilities.

And, for once, I trusted them to protect each other.

Text sent, Rosa reversed down the driveway and headed out, taking winding roads south. After getting a few hours of sleep, the witch had popped back to her place to relieve the overnight sitter. No Ethan either; we guessed he was part of the vampire hunt, but, really, who knew. With Aster in tow, Rosa had fed her chubby-cheeked pup, breastfeeding at our dining table and demolishing a bowl of cereal I had prepped with my useless kitchen skills while I polished off eight in the time it took her to eat one, and once we tidied up, we hit the road.

The further south we went, the sadder, greyer, and more miserable my territory started to look. Even though most of the autumn canopy had fallen, the Redwood Grove I was starting to know and love was dense. Thick. Packed with tons of trees, foliage, and brush. Game of all kinds. Predators. Bears preparing for hibernation. Reptiles sunning themselves whenever and wherever they could.

Here, the trees turned sparse, and fields of brambles stretched far as the eye could see. Litter peppered the scraggly landscape, the few human towns we skirted sleepy and still on a chilly, cloudy Sunday morning.

Rosa eventually veered off the main two-lane roads, carefully navigating backcountry lanes riddled with potholes, not a house for miles. I had no clue how she decided where to go and when to stop, but she eventually pulled off onto the shoulder, the grass dead and yellow, a whole load of grey nothing ahead. Even the dirt down here had a depressing grimy tinge to it.

I hopped out of the SUV, scanning our surroundings with a frown. My wolf pack had instinctively avoided this as we plodded north, headed for the rich forestry where my mates had originally found us. As Rosa unloaded Aster's car seat, the sleeping pup still buckled in, I prowled into the grey nothingness, runners trampling dead weeds and thorns catching on my sweatpants. Arms crossed, I scoped it out in silence—then tipped my head back and *breathed*.

Kira sucked in a lungful of the almost painfully crisp morning air, both of us scenting out dangers.

No vampires, at least.

No nothing.

Not even my pack. I breathed harder, deeper, really filling my lungs—but they weren't here. And why would they be? Why would they backtrack south where the resources were slim and the ground hurt their paws?

As we did every year, they would have headed west for the winter, then north in the spring.

They… were probably long gone.

They wouldn't wait for me.

Probably wouldn't even look for me.

They were *wolves*. Just wolves. They needed shelter, food, and family. Most of the pack was still there; they'd move on and expect *me* to find *them*, if they spared me a thought at all.

Loss slithered through me like the last rounds of an echo.

Kira howled, calling to her alphas, the yearlings, the pups.

No answer.

We would probably never hear their song again.

But as Rosa's boots tromped closer, I sniffed and wiped the sadness away, pushing it deep down so she couldn't see it and my mates wouldn't feel it.

In her heels, the curvy witch was roughly my height, but our sense of style couldn't be more opposite. While I left the house this morning in sweats, choosing comfort over style in black sweatpants and a brown hoodie, my running shoes new and *not* something I would actually run in, Rosa somehow found the time to coordinate her look. Black jumpsuit. Faux-leather boots. Long charcoal trench coat. Stylish baby bag in the car. Hair knotted in a ballerina bun with curly red wisps spilling everywhere.

She *looked* ready for breakfast on the town, somewhere posh with all the fancy folk who trekked to Redwood Grove for last night's party.

I… still looked like I lived in the woods.

Whatever.

Today wasn't a day for fashion or guilt.

Together, we meandered toward a clump of grey stones, and I hung back, watching Rosa set Aster's car seat on the least pointy of the bunch. She balanced it, then pulled her wand from her coat and softly muttered an incantation under her breath. White plumed from the end of the polished wood, and she drew a shimmering circle over her sleeping pup, one that flared into an orb. It stayed white for a few moments, then turned transparent with a *slight* rainbow shimmer depending on the angle you looked at it from.

"For protection," Rosa noted, tapping the top of the see-through bubble with her wand. She then perched on the boulder beside her super-safe babe—I would tear *anything's* throat out, here, there, and everywhere if they so much as glanced at Aster wrong—and crossed her legs, wand on her lap, eyes on me. "Okay, so, what happens inside you when the, uh, *power* comes out? Tell me how it manifests and how it makes you feel."

I sucked in my cheeks, heat wending down my body and pooling in my toes, the bottoms of my feet tingling like I was about to *run*. Kira, meanwhile, settled deep within, flopped down, head on her crossed paws, ready to ride this out.

Right.

How did it feel? I shrugged and unloaded everything I could think of—everything I could remember from the last week and a bit of *this*. Buzzing in my fingertips. Heat in my chest. Noise in my skull, the rest of the world muted.

It shook the windows—garbage cans and pens and toothbrushes and coffee mugs placed too close to the edge of the table.

And it made me feel… scared.

Alone.

Terrified, not of *it*, not completely, but of the fact that my mates could take one look at the monster I'd become and toss me aside.

Rosa let me talk uninterrupted, nodding here and there, those bright emeralds radiating empathy and care and motherly love so earnestly that it made my throat thick, the backs of my eyes stinging with tears I refused to shed.

When I finished, she took a beat, twirling her wand between her fingers, one hand to the other, and then nodded.

"Right, so, baby witches go through something similar," she told me, slow and gentle in her delivery—but never patronizing. Never like I was stupid. "It's this scary feeling of being totally out of control. In my experience, it's like you literally have no idea when and where your magic will manifest, how it'll come out... We learn to control it at academies or within our covens, and in time we use incantations to shape it and wands to channel it. Sometimes we use intention, just, uh, the *will* to make something happen, but it's rare." Her eyes swept up and down my figure. "But I think if you were blessed by a goddess, even a dead one, you need to practice intention. Much more like fae magic, you know?"

"Uh-huh." Sure. I knew *exactly* what fae were and how their—I assumed—complex magic system worked. Still, even if her last comment sparked more questions than answers, at least I wasn't a universal oddity. At least this was a *shared* experience and I wasn't some freak.

An outcast, out of control and dangerous.

I mean, I *was* out of control and probably dangerous, but it could be worse. Rosa could have grabbed Aster and booked it, terrified, then pruned our friendship back to the root.

But she was still here.

And she *cared.*

"It seems to happen when you're really emotional," she mused, tapping her lower lip with her wand, "but we want it to happen when *you* want it—not just when your emotions are heightened."

I shrugged. "Yeah, that would be nice."

"Okay..." Rosa clapped her hands and stood, and I found myself wishing the twinkling resolve in her eyes jumped ship and landed here—because she looked, sounded, and, somehow, *felt* much more confident in my abilities than I did. "Let's start with the basics."

I swallowed a groan. Yeah, I knew I'd have to *work* to contain whatever Idunn had given me through the river, but nothing had ever come so hard before. I navigated the separate, equally dangerous worlds of humans and wolves on instinct, trusting my gut, trusting Kira, and making moves as best I could. Sometimes it backfired. Sometimes I failed. But I always got back up, dusted myself off, and *learned*.

This…

This was frustratingly abstract.

The basics involved a lot of vague visualization work, with Rosa walking me through what she likened to a meditation practice, circling me, her voice lulling Kira to sleep. Sure, my hands buzzed and the heat flared in my chest. My senses sharpened. My mind cleared.

But nothing actually happened.

And a million years later, tendrils of dull sunshine fighting through the overcast and a sweaty sheen on my brow, I'd had enough.

I clenched my eyes shut and snarled.

Something clattered at my feet.

"Oh, Lyssa, look!"

A quick glance down showed the pebbles I had been toeing at since we arrived had moved a few inches, presumably bouncing along with my frustration.

"I know," I said tightly. "That's what always happens—"

"Let's capitalize on it." Rosa came in close, *right* up against my back, taking me by the shoulders and urging me to close my eyes. I didn't. She waited. The world went on without us, and Kira finally let out an impatient whine. *Just do it already.* So, I did. With everything dark again, I flinched as Rosa gathered my hair over the opposite shoulder, then positioned her full lips next to my ear. "Okay, Lyssa, imagine a well inside you."

"A well—"

"Like a wishing well," she whispered, "like the kind you read about in fairy tales. Do you see it?"

I crinkled my nose. "Uh…"

"Picture it next to Kira. Deep inside, I know you see her. She's you. You're her. And the well is a part of you now too."

Even with my eyelids shut, I managed to roll my golden orbs skyward with a long, irritated sigh. Still, Rosa had gone out of her way to help me—and pouting, throwing a tantrum like a puppy, was just rude. So, I did my best to imagine the picture she painted: Kira, seated primly as always, with a huge stone well beside her.

My wolf snorted—then nosed at the new addition.

"Is it there?"

"Yes," I whispered.

"Good." Rosa took a beat, her breath soft, her scent overwhelming. "Imagine it full of water—but the water is *different*. It looks like what you saw in the mountain."

"Like diamonds," I muttered, "and starlight. Twinkling. Cold. Fresh."

"Yes, that. *That* is your power, Lyssa. That well holds all the power Idunn gifted you, and it will never run dry."

I cracked an eye open. "How do you know that?"

"A hunch." She tapped my chest with her wand. "Eyes closed, you."

Smirking, I did as I was told.

"When you want to call on your power, you imagine the well. You imagine cupping your hands in that cold starlight, in the diamond water, and you imagine sprinkling it onto the earth."

Lips pursed, I *tried*, but putting myself *with* Kira wasn't natural. I couldn't explain how it felt to have this other half trotting around inside—either my mind, my imagination, my body… No clue how it worked. But climbing in there with her, with the well, felt…

"This is silly."

"It takes practice, honey," Rosa told me gently, "or we could all just do it from the start."

Sighing, I retreated inside as best I could without letting Kira out. I imagined the well, the sparkling water. Imagined my cupped hands scooping some of the freezing liquid out and dumping it on the ground.

Kira seemed just as unimpressed—and unconvinced—about all this as me, her feelings tainting my efforts. I withdrew from the mental picture, coming back to the black and the flashes of color behind my eyelids, to the cool November breeze and the deathly quiet of our territory's barren southern tip.

Fingertips buzzing, I sifted through my vocabulary for the right words to tell Rosa this felt stupid—

Then she gasped.

Staggered back, her boots marking every frantic step. My eyes shot open.

Between my feet, a dandelion had taken root. Green stem. Bright yellow head. A splotch of color in an otherwise bleak landscape.

Kira snuffled about, her deep breath whooshing around my skull, our disbelief twined. Trembling, I crouched down and stroked the yellow petals.

The very *real* petals—

"No." I shook my head and stumbled away, hands numb, the buzzing between my ears now. Rosa looked so *proud*, her emerald gaze glossy, her mouth lifted in this maternal smile and her hands clasped at her chest, looking at me like she would eventually look at Aster when she, uh, learned to ride a bike or whatever. Pebbles shuddered across the unforgiving ground at our feet as my frustration surged. *Don't look at me like that.* "I-I don't want this."

"Lyssa—"

"*No*," I barked, shaking my hands out, willing Idunn's touch to just *go* already. The grey day blurred suddenly, and I tugged my hoodie sleeve over my hand, then wiped under my eyes. "I just want to be a wolf shifter. All my life, I thought I was a, a, a *demon*, or a freak, or a mistake. And now I know what I am, and I just want to *enjoy* it." I turned my rage on Rosa, who, despite the gaping distance between us, flinched as if I'd shoved her again. "Is that so much to ask for? That I can finally just *be*?"

Blinking hurriedly, she opened and closed her mouth a few times before her gaze plummeted to the ground.

To the dandelion—now charred and gnarled, black and thin, all the life sucked out of it. An explosion of wispy white seeds littered the ground, but they looked wrong, somehow.

Twisted and warped and dead.

I had done that.

I had made something beautiful, then stomped all over it—without meaning to do either.

What if I did that to a person?

To Rosa?

To Aster—what if *my* power plowed clear through that shimmering bubble around the car seat and hurt her?

What if...

What if, in a fit of emotion, this destructive forest fire inside sizzled along by the invisible strings connecting me and mates—and I did *that* to one of them?

Ewan, Soren, Lucian—in pieces at my feet, their handsome faces contorted, their limbs sucked dry of life, blackened and crooked like the dandelion?

Silent, shoulders rounded and head bowed, Rosa padded over to her stirring pup. She perched on the boulder, lowered whatever she had cast to protect Aster, and then soothed her with kisses and coos and murmurs while I struggled to regain control.

Struggled to keep the dam, well, *dammed.*

"Honey, I know it's scary," the witch admitted sometime later, Aster asleep again and me kicking the ashes of my creation everywhere. "But it's happening. You can't take it back." Sighing, Rosa cast another bubble over her baby and then looked me dead in the eye, her courage back, her presence soothing. "Try to communicate with Idunn in your dreams. See if she can share something with you, and we'll work on controlling it. As long as it takes, I'm here for you, okay?"

Throat too raw with emotion to risk some choked response, I just nodded, arms crossed, vision swimming again.

"Remember, Idunn is a *nature* goddess," she stressed like I'd somehow forgotten. "Fertility and growth and rejuvenation—that's what she's known for. She represents the cycles of life, and she gave her fellow gods immortality, not asking for anything in return. She's good. She's deeply tied to this world. Don't be scared of her."

I lifted my eyebrows. Don't be scared... of a nature goddess?

A *dead* nature goddess who dumped a bunch of her abilities onto me?

Never mind the absurdity of all that... Nature was terrifying. I might have adjusted to it before I turned ten, two long years already spent in the wilderness with wolves, but even then I knew to respect the natural world.

Or it would kill me.

Nature wasn't sunshine and rainbows, no matter what the Instagram posts said.

It was raw and brutal, domineering and dangerous.

Beautiful and wonderful and amazing to watch, to be a part of—but if you didn't have a healthy dose of genuine fear, Mother Nature would rip you apart.

But I kept all that to myself.

"Okay, okay, got it. I can do this. Let's just try again." Headache brewing, exhaustion settling in, I threw my head side to side and cracked my neck a few times, then rolled my shoulders back. "Ready when you are..."

14

LYSSA

I knew where I was before I opened my eyes.

As soon as alertness trickled in and sleep's deep hold loosened, I came to aware of the tepid air, warm but not too warm, the *perfect* summer day. The muted light behind my lids. The leaves whispering in a gentle breeze. The thick, lush grass at my back, tickling my bare arms.

The orchard.

I ended up here most nights, but for the first time all week, my breath didn't fog with that first deep, annoyed exhale. Slowly, I peeled my lids open to a hazy purply sky, streaks of red and pink and orange putting Idunn's world in a perpetual sunrise.

Or sunset?

No idea.

I had tried to outrun the horizon time and time again, but the goddess seemed content amongst the apple trees.

Clearing my throat, I lifted my head, neck sore like I'd slept at a weird angle, then pushed onto my elbows. Love plumed in my chest, spreading to the heat in my cheeks and the warmth in my toes. There, in a tense *down* just by my feet, was my girl. Kira perked up when our eyes met, hers the same startling bright blue as always, mine the curveball in our life. I grinned and patted my belly.

"Hi, beautiful."

She pounced with a puppyish yip, plowing into me and pinning me to the ground, tail whipping around, her giddiness infectious. Before the darkness followed me here, this was how we greeted each other: playful and happy, two old friends reuniting, rolling around in the grass. Wrestling. Chasing. Once, we howled together —just because.

Today—tonight, this morning, who knew in a place where time stood still—we kept our tussles short. Eventually, I sat cross-legged by her side, Kira sprawled in the grass and sniffing the long blades. Rubbing her belly, I scanned the orchard, the rows upon rows upon rows of lush, full apple trees flourishing under a goddess's care. My sigh forced Kira upright, and after another quick glance, we stood together and set off through the trees.

I didn't need to tell her what we were doing, where we were going.

We ambled along in search of Idunn, Rosa's request still ringing in my ears. Find her. Talk to her. Get some *actual* answers for once.

Kira sniffed her out a few rows over. Draped in white silk, sapphires on her shoulder pads and her feet bare, the goddess had a wicker basket by her side and an apple in each hand. She faced us as soon as the wind shifted, toying with her golden waves, her eyes— my eyes—sweeping over both of us.

"Hello, little wolves." She gently deposited her plucked apples in the basket, then drifted toward Kira as the huge wolf padded over to greet her, head drooped, tail low and wagging. Submissive, she acknowledged the goddess's place in our hierarchy with eager whines and licks, and with a placid smile, Idunn stroked her ears, her neck, then cradled her muzzle, murmuring soft words in a language I didn't understand.

The tone told me the words were kind, at the very least.

I hung back, refusing to crawl on my belly for this woman, this girl who looked a few years younger than me but had eternity in her eyes. Arms crossed, I scrutinized the pair's interactions from a distance, relaxing only when Idunn plucked a ripe green apple from one of the low-hanging boughs and offered it to Kira. My wolf licked her jowls and snatched it up. Her roughness, the lack of finesse, only made Idunn giggle, and she tipped her head to the side, radiating calm as we both watched Kira trot in a circle, then hunker down to gnaw at the gift.

Another *gift* from Idunn.

I cleared my throat, pleased to find Kira's eyes still blue when they flicked my way, the wolf gracelessly munching on her prize.

"Seems like the shadows are gone."

Back to picking, cleaning, and lobbing apples into her basket, Idunn nodded. "Yes. Your mates protected the land from darkness."

"Did you know they were vampires?" My eyes narrowed when she fumbled, her toss a little off this time. The apple bounced off the basket's rim and rolled in Kira's direction. Even though she wasn't finished with the first, she lunged and grabbed this second, then did her usual circling before settling in the grass again. Dressed in the flannel nightshirt I wore to bed, enjoying the soft cotton enough to forgo my usual nakedness, I fiddled with the open sleeve cuffs, picking at the button. "Were they hunting me?"

Her calm mask fell away, replaced with a frown deep enough to cause a wrinkle in her otherwise flawless skin. Shaking her head, Idunn went back to the apples, back to picking and cleaning and tossing.

"More than vampires," she said—*almost* under her breath, like she was talking to herself, "to touch us here."

Great. I pursed my lips. Someday, it would be *awesome* if she could just answer a question without being so mysterious and otherworldly. After everything, she owed me that much.

But then again, maybe she just wasn't used to talking to people anymore.

Idunn was here alone as far as I could tell, and when *I* spent ages in the forest, far from civilization, months and months walking on four paws instead of stupid human feet... Heck, *my* conversation skills got a little rusty too.

Sighing, I drifted over to Kira, tugging at her ear in passing, and sat between her and the wicker basket. When Idunn turned to toss her next two apples in, I held out my hands. The goddess hesitated, then grinned and passed them over, each one cool and big and smooth to the touch, then went back to picking while I set them with the rest. Wordlessly, we made a little assembly line, with me sneaking Kira a fresh apple as soon as she demolished the one clutched between her paws, core and all.

Let's try this again.

"Did you give me your power when I drank from the river?"

Idunn chuckled, pacing around the tree and squinting into the canopy. "I was wondering when you would finally ask."

"Well?" I rolled an apple between my hands, keeping it in my lap, waiting, staring. Idunn's rosebud mouth quirked, and she stood on her tiptoes to rip an apple from the depths.

"I did."

"All of it?"

"All that I shed, yes." She handed the enormous apple to me, one that was nothing to her but required both of my hands just to hold. "I took the rest here with me."

Struggling, I dropped the massive green orb and rolled it over to sit beside the basket, worried it would crush its smaller siblings inside. "Why?"

"To keep it safe," the goddess said absently, still scanning the branches.

"From who?"

For the first time since we met in my dreams, Idunn tripped. Her foot snagged on a grasping root, and she crashed into the solid trunk, cheeks pink and hair temporarily disheveled.

Huh.

The winds changed, whipping east suddenly, violent and angry enough that I had to duck and shield my eyes from the debris. The sky darkened. The trees bent. Apples tore free and bounced across the grass.

And then it stopped. Brushing the bits of dust and twigs from my hair, I caught Idunn smoothing her dress, righting her sapphire-studded shoulder pads, and then twisting her hair over one shoulder.

Okay. Not a safe topic, just like me and the wolves. My mates had avoided it for ages, but I knew they'd poke and prod eventually.

I dreaded it.

She probably dreaded whatever made *that* happen.

"I-I don't want your power," I told her, opting to take an adjacent path. Her golden gaze snapped to mine, and I gulped, suddenly feeling very small in her divine presence. "I just want to be a wolf shifter... and be *normal*. I want to mate, make pups, and live in Redwood Grove with Lucian, Soren, and Ewan—"

"That's why you have it, little wolf." Idunn crouched, hastily gathering the fallen apples and tossing them at me, one right after the other, so fast I barely had time to catch them all. Kira helped, shoving into the line of fire and snapping up any strays. When the goddess was finished, the ground cleared and the orchard at peace again, she planted her elbows on her knees and smiled at me. "You have it because you *don't* want it."

"Well, that's..." My mouth went dry, and I focused on getting the last of the apples into the basket. "That's mean of you."

Idunn's laughter tinkled through the orchard like a symphony of Christmas bells.

"No one ever said the gods were *kind*."

Good to know. In no mood to be part of our assembly line anymore, I shuffled back until I hit Kira, then slumped into her massive side like I was cozying into the corner of our giant cinema room couch. The wolf paused her apple feast to look back at me, muzzle stained with sweet juices. She licked at my nose, my forehead, then went back to eating, obviously sensing that I was, in theory, fine. I didn't need to be coddled or babied.

I was just... frustrated.

"Why me?" I muttered, ripping out bits of grass and rolling them into little balls. "How did you... choose me?"

"I knew from the moment you were conceived," Idunn said without missing a beat. My brows shot up.

"Uh, what?"

"The apples started to grow again." She brought one of her harvest to her cheek, cradling it tenderly. "I couldn't make them grow. I designed this world for *me*, for my afterlife, but it wouldn't bear fruit. A barren orchard is so... sad." She wiped the apple on her dress, then scooted back to the foot of the tree and took a huge, crunching bite. The goddess chewed thoughtfully for a moment, then tossed the apple to me. "Then you... They started to grow. I found you in the sky. Or, well..." She licked her lips when I risked a small bite, tastebuds assaulted with the tart sour-sweet tide of a perfect green apple. "I saw your mother, but it was the child in her womb destined to—"

"Did you know my parents?" I blurted, gut dropping. I pawned our shared apple onto Kira, then lurched forward onto my hands and knees. Reed and Nikki didn't even know my parents. I'd pressed them again and again; I called them Mom and Dad for a long time, knowing full well they had only fostered me.

Then adopted me.

Then abandoned me.

No more Mom and Dad for *them*.

Idunn drew her knees up to her chest and planted her sharp chin in the dip. "I know who they are, yes."

"Why did they leave me?"

She looked deep in my eyes, deep enough that my fingers buzzed a warning—*danger, danger!*—and Kira sat upright behind me. The gold in my reflection always gave me pause. It startled strangers and made males *and* females do a double take.

But *her* gold?

It ran so much deeper than mine.

It pulsed with power, streaked with time and wisdom and

sunlight. I had her eyes, yes, but mine were a pale imitation, honestly, just a cheap knockoff of the real thing.

"Are you sure you want to know?" Idunn whispered, the breeze dying, the leaves falling silent. Kira sank down at my side with a long, frustrated whine. *Yes.* We had wanted to know from the start. They were Kira's parents too, after all.

I managed to nod, on the verge of being swallowed alive by her unblinking stare.

Idunn's gold brows twitched up. "Are you sure you want *everything?*"

I nodded harder, and then, finally trusting my voice again, I cuddled into Kira's side and choked out, *"Everything…"*

I jolted awake in my own bed with a gasp, alone and indoors. No Kira to greet me. No Idunn. No orchard. No purple-pink dawn. Chasing my breath, I rolled onto my side and blinked the world back into focus, staring through the frosty glass balcony doors and adjusting to another grey November day. Yesterday, Rosa and I had spent hours along the southern border of my territory, trying again and again to harness all that Idunn had given me.

When I came home in the afternoon, my mates were there too. Not at work. Not… somewhere else. *Here.* They told me they ran those horrible vampires into Hawthorne territory but would be on constant patrol for the next week, in alternating shifts, to make sure they didn't come back.

Then I'd crashed. Hard. If the smell of fresh bread and all this soft morning light suggested anything, it was that I had slept a good fifteen hours, maybe more. Lucian's scent tickled my nostrils with my next deep breath, rousing a sleepy Kira as well, and I rolled away from the windows, searching for him.

Nope.

Gone.

But he had been here. At some point, my quietest, most reclusive mate had scented up my linens—a theory confirmed when I crawled down the side of my bed, exploring it with my nose, breathing him in with a moan, then a soft, insistent whine.

Why didn't he stay?

Why didn't *any* of them just climb into bed with me?

Ignoring the pang of want, I settled back against the headboard with a huff, surrounded by pillows and clean white sheets...

Thoughts of my history—the real one—on the brain.

Now I knew.

If Idunn had told the truth in my dreams, then my parents...

Well, it wasn't what I had always imagined.

Bloodier.

More violent.

A betrayal to shifter-kind, apparently.

Nikki and Reed would have had no clue. Even if they heard the story—all the gory details—they wouldn't understand. They wouldn't *get* that my mom and dad—both of them, no matter how the story was told—were traitors.

Groaning, I scrubbed at my cheeks, then picked the crusty sleep out from the corner of my eyes.

A lot to digest.

A lot to process.

But in the end, their tragic story made me that much more grateful for *my* mates. Yeah, we weren't a perfect pack—but I knew in my heart none of those alphas would ever do *that*.

I drew my knees up, then winced, bladder telling me, no, that wasn't the ideal position right now. Just as I flung myself over, about to head for the bathroom and ruminate on the toilet over my questionable family history, I noticed it.

Them.

Two gifts on my nightstand.

The first was a box with a sleek rose-gold phone on the cover. It smelled like Ewan when I picked it up, like rosewood bark, sweet and heady and *earthy*. No plastic wrap: he had been in there already, it seemed, and when I carefully lifted the cardboard lid, I found the exact phone inside, so thin and delicate and pink that I was too scared to lift it up and turn it on.

All this time, I'd studied my mates on *their* phones. Soren was careless with his, always twirling it, tossing it between his hands, dropping it and hoping the screen hadn't shattered. Ewan handled his like it was an extension of himself, just another limb, effortless, his fingers so beautifully graceful that just watching him text was another reminder that he could easily pass as an angel.

Then Lucian…

He had a flip phone.

He looked annoyed anytime he had to dig it out.

He told me it was indestructible once, then chucked it against the wall and chuckled when it didn't even dent.

Mine looked and felt like it was made of glass.

Someone else needed to program it for me—teach me how to use it. Before my mates found me, I would have returned it, insisting that I didn't *deserve* something so fancy and delicate.

Now, I knew I just needed to be shown the way. One explanation. One tutorial. I'd pick the rest up on my own.

However, the phone wasn't the only gift waiting for me. No, next to the lamp on the white-wood bedside table was a potted plant.

Not regional. Definitely not local. Setting the phone box aside, I picked up the purple ceramic pot in both hands, then sniffed at the bulbous green leaves.

Succulent.

I'd seen them on Instagram a lot. Soren had made me an account I could look at on the laptop—not that I'd posted anything—and agreed it, like the TV shows I devoured, would make for good research into the modern human world.

It did.

Because I knew this was a succulent.

What kind? No idea, but the fat leaves were cute and smelled pretty safe.

Taped to the bottom—a note.

Don't be afraid.

I didn't need to sniff the yellowing paper to know that was Rosa's handwriting, but I did so anyway, relishing the honey and amber, eyes closed, heart slowing, all thoughts of my past life fading. Kira yipped, missing the witch already, and I tenderly tucked the note under my pillow—then eyed the succulent with a frown.

The gesture was sweet. She must have snuck this in while I was catching up on sleep, my mind static by the time we got back from training and my energy *deep* in the negatives. *Don't be afraid.* Of nature? Of myself? Of the power tingling in my fingertips?

All of it, probably.

Lips pursed, I cradled the purple pot in one hand, then held the other over it, closed my eyes, and went back to the well. This time, Kira had her paws planted on the stone rim, peering into the sparkling water with her head cocked like it was speaking to her. I imagined myself there beside her, just like in the orchard. Pictured scooping the water out and splashing it around. Clenched my eyes tight to block out the real-life hum in my fingertips and palms.

Little spikes poked my skin.

My eyes snapped open—the succulent had doubled in size.

Grown aggressive spikes and two red flowers.

Shoot.

Trembling, I set it back on my nightstand, then stumbled out of bed, a little dizzy, Kira's whimpers making it even harder to refocus. Needing the comfort of a familiar routine, I staggered into the bathroom to pee, wash my face, and rinse the stinky sleep breath away. When I came back, the plant was there, minding its own business, huge and spiky and dangerous—pretty, I guess, in its own way with those flowers.

Don't be afraid.

Excuse you, witch friend.

I *would* be afraid of the natural world because fear meant respect. That was the only way to survive. I wasn't *better* than nature. I couldn't dominate it. I respected it.

Just like I ought to respect Idunn's power.

Because it wasn't sunshine and daisies and twittering songbirds on a spring morning...

This was dangerous, powerful, deadly stuff.

I... could hurt someone with it if I wasn't careful.

Nice sentiment, that note, but, yeesh, maybe a little tone deaf.

After straightening out my flannel nightdress, fixing the collar and sleeves, I grabbed the phone box—something that, while new and flimsy, *wasn't* scary—and headed down to the kitchen, guided by the sounds of cupboards closing and dishware clinking, hoping that whoever was home could teach me how to use this thing without breaking it.

And distract me—*please, just distract me*—from the horrors of my family legacy ringing truer and truer with every shaky step.

15

SOREN

Okay, so…

Eggs, toast, hash browns, pancakes, diced fruit, cereal on the table. Check, check, check, check, *check*.

The only thing missing…

My inner wolf did his derpy little happy dance when I ducked into the fridge and pulled out two packets of the good stuff. Thick cut. Extra fatty. One kilo per packet—*bacon*. In less than a minute, the whole house would smell of it, and if *that* didn't lure her out of bed, nothing would.

As soon as I straightened and slammed the door shut, however, there she was in her adorable red-and-white flannel, sleepy and rumpled, hair like a knotted bronze halo around her head. Lyssa's scent flooded the kitchen, overtaking everything I had prepped so far, and my inner wolf paused, smitten, howling for her like she *and* her wolf could hear, desperate to run despite spending hours in the forest yesterday doing exactly that.

November 2 was supposed to be a pack breakfast. Sure, I hadn't explicitly told the other alpha dicks that, but from the sheer volume of food, I was ready to feed us for the whole day in one meal. Lucian, however, was still on his patrol shift, and Ewan popped in here while I was halfway through the eggs and about to start on the pancakes. Stiff, stern, dressed to the nines in one of his standard pretentious suits, he grabbed some sad protein smoothie from the fridge and bounced, determined to get a few hours of work in before his patrol shift started.

And, I mean, I guess that was fair.

Work was his life—but somehow we had collectively decided that for the next week, patrolling our borders took priority. Yeah, we chased those vampires all over the place on Halloween. All night, right up until sunrise, we hunted them through the mountains, into the western forest, around the lake. At one point, the fanged assholes even tried to hide in a locked Acker cabin; I nearly ripped the thing apart to find them, and Lucian noticed their shadowy silhouettes blitzing into the trees at the last second, three alpha wolves right on their heels.

By the time the sun poked above the horizon, muted behind the thick overcast, we had *finally* pushed them into Hawthorne territory. Let those dicks deal with them.

If those dicks hadn't sent them.

I mean, maybe the leeches went for Lyssa because she smelled good—because she did—but the risk of the Hawthorne alpha stealing her before she had her first pup remained. It wouldn't be the first time a rival alpha stole a breeding female from another pack. An *alpha* she-wolf? A way bigger score, because then he could forcibly build a strong, powerful alpha bloodline from scratch even if he hadn't found *his* fated female yet.

So, maybe the vamps had just happened upon her at the club.

More likely though: someone had hired them to take her.

And if we ever caught the bastards, we'd tear them limb from limb. Interrogate them along the way. Stuff them full of wooden stakes until we got a name. Introduce them to their first and last sunrise.

Then we'd kill the guy who sent them, on and on until we could guarantee Lyssa's safety.

For now, since we had no dead flesh to stab, we three settled on constant patrols.

Lucian had demanded the lion's share, all amped and anxious and teetering on the brink of wolf madness. Ewan and I managed to talk him down to sharing the responsibility, our patrols split into even shifts, one right after the other, always allowing for someone to be home with our girl.

So, hell *yeah* I took the whole week off. No work. No lake stuff. No check-ins with the franchise owners of the three Farrow's Pubs in the area. No days spent locked in my office surrounded by paperwork.

It wasn't a one-man show in my professional sphere. We had humans heavily involved in managing Acker properties and investments; it was time for them to prove their worth in my absence.

Some of us, meanwhile, struggled to get their priorities in order.

Because Ewan chose to squish in as much work as he could this morning—and missed *this*, our groggy, gorgeous mate sauntering into the kitchen in flannel that cut off around her upper thighs, sleeves hanging loose and open and a little too long, a box tucked under her arm. All that sleep had done her good: gone were the dark shadows around her eyes, the hollowness in her cheeks, the overall pale and sweaty glow.

She looked refreshed, smiling shyly as she approached, my gaze plummeting to those strong, shapely legs.

Ugh. *Perfection.*

"Morning, babe." I kept my eyes on her as I portioned out bacon strips. Eight a piece should do, right? Noticing her nostrils flare, the wolf in her *definitely* tempted by raw meat, I hoisted a handful of fatty pork with a grin. "Bacon?"

"Obviously."

Man, I loved when she *purred* over good food. A she-wolf after my own heart. She headed toward me, then veered away for the island full of food instead—and that wouldn't do. I lunged after her, memories of her helpless cries in that private room making my cock twitch with interest, then gave her neck a sharp, biting kiss that made her squeal and blush and break out in goosebumps. Lyssa scampered away, darting around the island and rounding on me like she wanted to be hunted.

And if my belly wasn't roaring just as loud as hers, I might have.

No one had christened this room yet, right?

However, before I could take one prowling step after her, Lyssa lifted the box and frowned.

"Uh, so, this…?"

"Ewan grabbed it yesterday afternoon," I told her, tossing one portion of bacon onto the cutting board next to the stove, then counting out the next. Okay, *she* could have eight, but for a male— twelve? "Apparently Rosa reamed him out for not getting one yet. What d'you think? Like it?"

Lyssa already had a laptop; it only made sense that she had a phone too. Kind of shitty that it hadn't already occurred to any of us, but I was so close to her most days that it had never crossed my mind. Even when I worked, I just needed to walk the shoreline to check on her.

And Lucian shunned most tech, so of course that weirdo had said nothing.

Seriously though. A pack song, as great as ours was, could only take the modern-day wolf shifter so far.

"Uhm, I like the color." Lyssa set the box on the marble countertop with a huff. "But I don't know how to use it."

"Hold on—lemme see."

Fourteen slices of raw bacon in hand, I sauntered over, sidling right up behind her, then sniped another kiss. This one crash-landed on her temple, which made my mate giggle, and was less teeth, more nibbling peck. Man, she fit so *perfectly*, her back to my chest, the position even better when she scooted backward and nestled under my chin. For a few seconds, I forgot why I'd come over here, safe in a cloud of our mingling scents, everything else background noise so long as she touched me.

I'd wanted to crawl into her bed last night.

Hold her while she slept.

Stand on guard, protecting our mate from the assholes who go bump in the night.

We all did.

For weeks now, one of us would loiter in front of the master suite's door, hesitating, racked with uncertainty, wanting to go in and cuddle with her but unsure if that was what *she* wanted—if that would be okay with the rest of her mates. After marking your fated, sleeping next to them had to be the highest form of intimacy.

But Lyssa had been through the wringer since Gull River. After Halloween, she clearly needed sleep; no one had the heart to wake her yesterday after she crashed in the late afternoon and just slept and slept and slept. *Again*, we had agreed to give her space to process everything—only this time, she set the tone. If she came looking for company, at least one of us had to physically be there for her, a mate always on call for snuggles and comfort and play-fighting in wolf form. We swore it.

And Ewan went to work this morning.

Dick.

As if sensing my distraction, my inner wolf on a Lyssa high and just *begging* me to shove my nose in her hair, my mate tapped the top of the box. Right. Phone.

I squinted at the picture and the name and all the listed features.

Ugh.

Stupid fancy complicated garbage.

Like, if you pressed the screen too hard—common for a shifter—you'd break it.

I should have been in charge of the phone-buying.

"Of course he got you a phone that can launch a freakin' rocket into space," I muttered, glowering at the box like it was *its* fault and not Ewan's. Lyssa tipped her head back, gawking at me with those wide, golden eyes, and I shook my head. Her grasp on common sayings and social norms had improved a *lot* since we found her, but some shit still flew right over her head. "No, sorry, not literally... It's just stupidly complicated."

I mean, I didn't recognize the model number—was it even on the market yet?

Did Ewan have pull in the tech world too?

This guy.

This fucking guy.

"Here." I grabbed Lyssa's wrist, flipped her arm over, and dumped the stack of raw bacon in her palm. "You do bacon. I'll try to set this up."

"But I can't cook," she protested as I eased us around and bumped her toward the stove with my hip.

"Baby, just don't let the meat get black." From the near-invisible waves rising off the pan, it was definitely hot enough to do most of the work for her. I gave her another little push, then patted the perky globes of her bare ass under the flannel, the first light smack making her squeak and skitter forward—but not fast enough. I still managed to cop a feel with my clean hand, then, in an act of restraint that deserved *all* the rewards, headed for the sink to wash up *instead* of prowling after her, ripping that nightdress up, and bending her over the counter.

Instead, I turned on the tap a little too hard, the metal faucet a breath away from flying clean off, my inner wolf still reveling in the taut roundness of her ass cheek. "Just, uh, flip and flip and flip until it's crispy like you like. You'll need to do two or three rounds—just see how many can actually fit in the pan without overcrowding it."

After drying my hands on my sweatpants, I swiped the box off the island, then dipped around it and headed for the dining table. Slouched in my usual seat, I lifted the lid like I was unmasking some ancient, fragile, priceless artifact, the phone inside so damn sleek and thin and clean…

Yeah, I wasn't the right wolf to do this.

I'd broken so many phones over the years, always by accident, usually because my hands liked to keep busy and tossing a phone around was a good way to do that.

This seemed like the screen would fracture if you looked at it wrong.

Oh boy.

"So," I started, needing to put at least a bit of my attention elsewhere or I would *way* overthink this thing, "how are you feeling?"

"Fine."

Phone out and on the table in one piece, I glanced up. Yeah, she said that a little too fast. My inner wolf whined, neither of us buying it. Since Gull River, her emotions had been even more complicated to decipher than this stupid phone. Despite our bond theoretically strengthening every time we mated, I struggled to read the nuances. Sometimes her feelings hit like a hurricane, others a whisper. After mating and marking, suddenly we shared a common dialect, the connection visceral. Invisible, yeah, but so freakin' beautiful and present.

Now it was... complicated.

And getting Ewan and Lucian to admit that they felt the same as me last night had been like pulling teeth.

But they finally did it.

Gull River had changed our girl, and we still weren't sure if it was for the better. All our lives we *starved* for a fated mate connection, and we'd had it so *fleetingly*. It wasn't easy. It never had been—and that created this steep pit in our collective bond, one we needed to fill soon or it would all cave in.

Maybe?

This was uncharted territory for all of us—for three stubborn alphas who each wanted to act like *he* had the strongest bond with the mate we shared.

For the few words he *did* manage to get out, Lucian insisted we wait. Let the water settle. Let nature and Lady Fate find balance again.

Sure.

Alpha males were *awesome* at being patient.

"How are you doing?"

I frowned at Lyssa's back, blinking out of the downward spiral to the hiss of each bacon strip she carefully added to the pan. "Huh?"

Eloquent as always. Seriously, she had to think I was the dumbest of her mates.

She peeked over her shoulder with an arched eyebrow. "You less grumpy now?"

Uh. When had *I* been the grumpy jagweed of this pack? Ewan claimed that title on the daily.

"Er, what?"

Grinning, Lyssa poked at the sizzling strips with a wooden spatula, then sauntered to the island and leaned over the marble. Even though I couldn't see it, it was way too easy to imagine the flannel hiked up, revealing strong, womanly thighs that I suddenly wanted wrapped around my face—

"You've been really grumpy the last little while," Lyssa said as she pointed the greasy-tipped spatula at me. "Like, kind of tantrum-y when we didn't do your fall activities."

What?

Oh. *Oh.*

Oops.

Thought I had kept my shit together a little better than that.

I mean, with everything going on in her world the last couple of weeks, I thought my grump over literally no one listening to me or taking my suggestions for fall fun seriously had slid by unnoticed.

Damn it.

"I... I just wanted to share..." Okay, how to phrase this without sounding like a total pup. "My parents—"

"Soren, we aren't our parents," Lyssa insisted, shockingly firm for a she-wolf who had yet to share a single iota of intel about her past. I sat up straighter as her phone powered onto the home screen, and Lyssa busied herself with the spatula, smearing the grease around its rectangular head. "We have to make our own traditions."

"I know that," I said slowly, hesitant to say anything at all if it cut her off. Was she about to share her past with me? As Lyssa wiped her greasy fingers on her sleeve, I tapped around the phone's main screens absently, getting a half-hearted feel for what came preprogrammed. Right. Not *that* complicated: all looks, no depth.

427

When the silence dragged on, both of us serenaded by the sizzle and crackle of cooking bacon, I cleared my throat and focused on connecting this thing to the internet. "Look, my parents just have a great relationship, and I'm trying to—"

"Copy it?"

I looked up sharply, a little wounded that even my fated mate couldn't see the benefits of carrying forward a tradition of love, mutual respect, and family time. "No. Reproduce it, maybe... Is it so wrong to want to be happy like they are?"

Ewan's pack had a reputation all the way out here, the Quinns known across shifter circles for their heavy hand in the Canadian supernatural *and* human drug trade. He *hated* them; that much was clear anytime the conversation even tiptoed in their direction. Parents, siblings, cousins, whatever—he wanted nothing to do with them. Lucian was a closed book in terms of his past, refusing to even give us his pack name. Clearly, they had both seen and experienced some shit.

Lyssa...

No clue.

But it obviously wasn't a *happy* childhood, right? I mean, someone had dumped her in the woods.

Yet the Acker pack had a history of togetherness and wholesome family moments—cheesy as it sounded—and no one would let me *lead* in an area where I clearly had *some* superiority.

"No..." Lyssa cocked her head, staring through me, probably out to the two-story windows by the soaring stone fireplace. "But we should make our own happiness, right?"

"Yeah, well, this pack kind of sucks at that. It's like those guys *want* to be miserable."

"Right, and some of us get really testy when things don't go our way." She grinned impishly when I glared at her from the dining table. A teasing tongue poke followed, and my mate straightened to stretch out her shoulders. "I mean, it's like *some* of us have never been told *no* in our whole life..."

Ugh.

She had a point.

I'd always gotten away with lots of crap my sisters didn't. I had ignored it until adulthood when hindsight became just a little clearer.

"Look, babe, I get it." I tapped around the phone's app store, selecting the ones Lyssa seemed to enjoy perusing on her computer. No Facebook—she deserved better than that cesspit. "I was being a huge puppy about the pumpkin patch stuff and the horror movies and whatever." As the first of my choices started to download, I leaned back in the chair and folded my arms, locking onto her golden gaze with a huff.

Shit, that gold—so intense. So fiery. So *different* from the grey-blue I had first fallen for.

But...

She could pull it off. Lyssa's olive complexion complemented the warmth, and her hair—a bright caramel brown in the sun, more bronzy and grounded indoors—really suited the change.

Hard to maintain eye contact with though.

Even her wolf had lost the neon, gold inside and out now. My inner wolf couldn't *stop* staring into them whenever he had the chance, and once again, my human side struggled more than the beast.

Unnervingly intense as they were, I needed eye contact for this.

She needed to *feel* my issue.

"But, uh, you need to have my back sometimes too." I scratched at the fresh, rough stubble on my cheek, then up to the shaved side of my head, finding the prickle of. that short, coarse hair soothing as I stroked back and forth. "Ewan and Lucian are just two different kinds of hermits. They don't want to do stuff—*we* are the social ones. I promise, anything I suggest is actually really fun."

While still grinning, Lyssa hurled my huff right back at me. "I'm sorry... Horror movies are *fun*?"

"Okay, maybe not." Not to everyone's taste, anyway, especially a she-wolf whose only film experience seemed to be cartoons, romance movies, and reality TV. "I just—" I shot up in a panic. "Shit —flip the bacon."

Lyssa whipped around and scrambled back to the stove, hastily turning strips that had suddenly started to smell a little too toasty for my taste.

"Look, I'm not saying you have to agree with every little thing I suggest," I told her, back to installing all the necessary crap on this much too delicate phone. "You obviously have your own opinion—"

"Sweet of you to notice."

"*But,*" I stressed, adding a bit of growl for that snarky tone, "those two will always and forever vote no if it means they have to, you know, miss work or take a night off from patrol or, I dunno, just do something that isn't routine. It really pisses me off. I'm always outvoted because they refuse to try anything new."

"Okay..." She flipped the last bacon strip with some difficulty, then padded back to the island and slumped over it. "Okay, how's this? If *they* don't want to do something, you and me will." Lyssa shrugged, then latched onto a particularly aggressive knot in her mane and ripped into it. "I mean, I think we should all do more pack things together, but maybe Ewan and Lucian just need... time to warm up to that."

My inner wolf and I *both* rolled our eyes, but only my scoff punctuated the bacon-scented air. Eyes sparkling mischievously, Lyssa stopped her hair fussing.

"Is this... another tantrum?" She waggled her finger at me. "Soren, Soren, Soren—"

"It's a tantrum on *your* behalf," I argued lightly, leaning to the side and digging my phone out of my pocket. I then did a deep dive into the contacts page, scrolling through to copy the numbers that mattered for Lyssa so she didn't have to ask everyone separately. "*You* have had to adapt the most out of all of us. You always give in to *our* norms. You're jumping into our lives—" I shot her a cheeky grin. "—and quite flawlessly, I might add. I just think those two assholes..." *Don't pick on her mates in front of her.* "Those *two*... They can step outside of their comfort zones for, like, an afternoon. It's really not that much to ask."

Warmth fluttered in my chest, leaking from her to me in pitter-pattering raindrops for a few seconds—then a whole flood when our eyes met and a smile exploded across her gorgeous features.

"Agreed," she said thickly, and I *swore* her eyes glistened with the light of the pretentious modern chandelier Ewan had insisted be hung over the island. Lyssa then sniffed and went back to the bacon, poking at a few strips with a hand on her hip, for once looking very much at ease in the kitchen. "I'm sorry, Soren—I'll be more open to your suggestions." She fluttered her lashes at me over her shoulder. "Whatcha got for November?"

"Nothing." Stupid boring middle month between fall awesomeness and winter shenanigans. "But December? Hang on to your hat, baby. December is gonna be wild."

Her cheeks flushed a dull pink, the heat in my chest ramping up a notch, and my mate resumed her bacon-poking with a nod. "Can't wait."

As she finished this first round of bacon, then her portion of eight immediately after, I got her phone sorted. Deleted space-wasting apps. Added protective programs to fend off malware and hackers. Gave her all the apps she enjoyed, plus a few my sisters obsessed over. Put our phone numbers, the Perrys, and my family into her contacts list.

"Okay," I said, pushing my chair back and patting my knee when Lyssa dumped a mountain of crispy bacon onto a plate. "Come here, mate, and let me give you a tour."

She practically skipped over and dropped onto my lap like a lead anchor, purposefully throwing herself into it so I grunted. Grinning, smitten with no hopes of ever going back, I wrestled my wriggling, giggling little fated mate up my lap, then tucked my chin into the crook of her shoulder. Once she quieted, I gave her a rundown of her phone, going so far as to turn it off completely and reboot just so she could learn from the start.

Unsurprisingly, she picked up fast. Modern tech was more

intuitive than Lucian gave it credit for, and Lyssa was soon tapping, sliding, minimizing, and using dual windows to navigate the digital world.

All while our bellies grumbled and my inner wolf—hers too, probably—drooled over the feast just *sitting* over there on the island, untouched but growing cooler by the second.

"Okay, tech genius." I patted her thighs. "Up. Let's eat."

Lyssa hopped off and tiptoed away, and just as I stood, my phone vibrated across the table. Scowling, I went for it, fully expecting some bullshit comment in the alpha group thread—only to find a message alert from my girl.

Hi.

Nothing more, nothing less—fucking *adorable*.

I looked up and found her beaming on the other side of the island. Lips pursed, I sent a quick reply.

Hello, beautiful.

Her phone dinged. Her eyes lit up. Her smile got wider, and she hugged the fragile rectangle to her chest.

"Now you can *always* reach us... Even Ewan," I mused, more to myself than her—because, *duh*, of course this instant communication made her happy. All she had wanted from the get-go was pack togetherness.

Shit. Should have done this way sooner.

Before I could apologize, however, Lyssa had already abandoned her phone for the bacon, grabbing a handful and shoving it in her mouth, and I raced over to make sure that I actually got a piece of this big, beautiful breakfast I'd made.

One that we demolished together in about five minutes flat, the platters never making it to the dining table.

A meal we then digested down in the cinema room to one of the mildest horror films in my Halloween arsenal at Lyssa's request.

So big, so excessive, so much *food* for just two wolves that we ended up falling asleep before the movie finished the first act, snoozing the day away in each other's arms.

Her emotions clear and strong and happy.
And my heart very much in love.

16

LYSSA

Bare branches rattled in the breeze, the canopy shed and winter on its way. Beneath a cloudy afternoon sky, cool and dry, I trotted across leaf-strewn ground, over valleys and peaks, up and down and around steep drop-offs into the earth. The western wood was quiet today, its critters nesting, preparing for the long, cold months ahead. Pines soared here, more abundant than around Soren's lake, the undergrowth almost too dense to get through in some areas, even as Kira.

Wild. Untamed. Raw wilderness, with bear tracks leading north and remnants of fox dens everywhere. This place felt as ancient as Idunn.

Definitely Lucian's old territory.

I seldom trekked further west than the village. After all, there was more to *do* there—Ewan in particular, but Rosa and Aster were huge reasons for me to stop at Redwood Grove proper and stay awhile. In fact, this was my first solo trip so deep into the western woods, and I made it my mission to *claim* it, brushing on pine boughs and bare trunks alike. I sniffed and sniffed and sniffed, breathing *Lucian* with every breath.

Tracking his old footpaths.

Following where he would have walked before me, stalking along barely visible grooves in the forest floor as Kira, until eventually happening upon the log cabin my other mates had referenced in the past.

And not always nicely either.

Soren and Ewan weren't kind about Lucian's love of quiet solitude. He hid away from the rest of the world for a reason—his scars told that story, I was sure of it—and that spoke to me. My other mates had family. They had a pack. They had a history.

Lucian and I didn't.

And as I crept closer to the cabin, paws soundless, not a twig snapped or leaf crunched, I felt closer to him than I ever had before.

Good thing, too, because two weeks after Halloween and I was starting to feel like we were losing him.

Like... *I* was losing him.

That night had changed him. Lucian had always struck me as a protector, the wolf who hung back and watched from the sidelines. Not showy. Not overly involved in pack activities. But if something went wrong? *Run*, because he'd be there in a second, calm, cool, collected, and about to unleash the killing blow.

Of all my mates, he was the most anxious about territory borders. Always on high alert, always scoping out exits, always mapping the perimeter—even if we were just sitting on the deck of Soren's lakefront pub near the village, enjoying a plate of nachos and a few beers. He didn't *do* fun outings, just like Soren had said.

In the last fourteen days, I'd spent ten with Rosa, down south and practicing my power.

Trying to control it.

Failing to control it, more like.

But my mates had worked out a system, a patrol schedule that Soren stuck to the fridge with magnets so we always knew where each other was and what we were all supposed to be doing. Lucian and Ewan refused to let me tag along with them, but Soren had started bringing me out for a stealthy hike around the Redwood Grove perimeter—if I wasn't passed out by the time his shift started, recovering from Rosa's draining, and still very much secret, lessons.

No vampires had crossed back into our home. Hawthorne wolves howled every night to the east, but none of us had scented so much as a paw over the territory line. Ewan was almost back to his regular work routine, opting for predawn patrol shifts and then heading to the office straight after, and Soren in wolf form was kind of silly on the trail, not taking it as seriously as he probably should.

But Lucian?

Always on guard, even when he *wasn't* on patrol. Always tense and quiet and alert. Thinking. Ruminating. Present but not.

I missed him. I missed his softness, his subdued smiles. I missed feeling small and safe in his big, burly arms. I missed rubbing my face in his beard while he sighed and let me do it. Kind of hard to be around him, to be *mates* just lounging and enjoying each other's company, when he had slowly morphed into a hunk of hyperalert stone. Since the vampire attack, it was like everything that made Lucian *Lucian* had been stripped away, leaving an alpha—*my* alpha—with a one-track mind.

It didn't do him any good—and it made our connection strained. This intense vigilance drained him and kept him away from me, and I just...

No more.

Nose to the ground, I sniffed straight to his old cabin, then once around its foundations for good measure. Riddled with dead ivy, it was exactly as I imagined: simple and straightforward. A wooden box with a steepled roof and a chimney that had probably seen countless fires over the years. Tall as the average man in Kira's form, I pressed my snout against a dirty glass window, scoping out the inside with a whine.

Uh-huh, just what I thought.

One room—from the lingering smells, he did his business outside like a wolf—with a wood-burning stove, small tables set up for a kitchen area, a bed *just* big enough for him, an armchair with a sheet over it, and then an empty worktable. Neat and not too showy, just like my Lucian.

I huffed, fogging the glass, and then dropped into a sit. My Lucian was currently on patrol, and given the hour, he ought to be *just* cresting the mountain footpaths, on the cusp of his old territory.

Close enough that when I howled, it probably wouldn't take him long to find me.

Despite it being midafternoon, I unleashed a howl that ripped through the western woods. One that danced over the mountains and skimmed the sapphire lake. I called out to Lucian—the others knew where I was and what I was doing and had told me there was no point in trying to tame that, quote, stubborn old recluse—and I tried to make it flirty.

Sang a range of notes. Really put my heart in it.

When it was over, my song echoed through the trees. With a snort, I padded away from the cabin into the middle of what looked like a man-made clearing where Lucian probably split wood—judging by the old stump and the forgotten stack, anyway—and then waited.

He answered six long beats of my heart later, his howl deep and luxurious.

And, honestly, a little strained.

That hurt to hear.

I called out to him again, harmonizing with his howl, and stayed put so he could find me. After all, the hunt-capture-fuck game I played with Soren wasn't meant for Lucian. We both needed security in this world, so here I'd wait, in this clearing, at his old home, until he arrived.

However long that might take.

Our howls threaded together, warmth unfurling in my belly like wildflower petals under the morning sun. Slowly, the song drifted from *come find me* to… well, just a song. A connection between us, a duet for me and Lucian and no one else. When it eventually tapered off, our harmony still reverberating through the forest, the heat in my belly had made itself at home, this low burn that nestled between my thighs, a cozy reminder of what my mate did to me.

While waiting, I shifted back to two legs and tucked Kira away for a while. As eager as she was to sniff and nuzzle and nip at Lucian's wolf form, she'd have to wait: this was a time for words, my heart exposed to him *again*. In the meantime, I studied the crawling ivy that wove around the cabin, crinkly and brown, the plant withdrawn before winter hit.

Ten afternoons in the last two weeks had been devoted to intention work with Rosa, but my power refused to do what I wanted, when I wanted, always coming too hard, too fast, or not at all. No in the middle. Just... a fire hose on full blast with no handsome firefighters to steady it. Rosa was quick to praise, insisting that I was doing *great* every time I killed something or made it triple in size or turn from harmless to lethal.

I didn't feel great.

Sure, things had stopped shaking on a whim.

But that wasn't enough.

Once again, *I* wasn't enough.

Hot from the shift, the air steaming, I strolled closer to Lucian's cabin, then raised my hand. Felt my fingertips buzz. Felt the pulse in my core where this stupid well was supposed to sit. Felt the *energy* in my palm. Eyes closed, I did the thing. Imagined cupped hands scooping diamond water, Kira watching from behind a nearby tree, *very* aware that I was a mess with all this Idunn stuff. I visualized sprinkling the water onto brown ivy. Not a splash. A misting. Just enough to revive it—bring some green back to those leaves.

Heat scratched at the nape of my neck.

My belly flip-flopped.

My palms broke out in a cold sweat.

And when I opened my eyes, the entire cabin was covered in the stuff. Green ivy, sure, but thorny ivy now, thick and thriving like it had taken on a life of its own.

I clamped down on my cheeks, my snarl muffled, my frustration mounting. Kira nosed at my insides, her soft chuffs supposed to calm me, but it didn't work.

I didn't work.

Teeth gritted, I marched over to investigate, finding thorned ivy covering way more of the cabin than it had before. Coarse and angry, it spiraled all the way up the chimney and strangled the opening.

Like it wanted to keep the smoke in.

Smother the house.

I rubbed my face, groaning. Perfect.

Before I could even try to fix it—or, more likely, make it ten times worse—paws thundered across the forest floor. Leaves crunched. Twigs snapped. Lucian's oakwood scent tinted the air. He made no effort to disguise his approach, and I jogged around to the northeastern corner of the cabin, some of the frustration melting away at the sight of his scarred, grizzled wolf charging through the trees. Brambles and burrs snagged on his fur, his eyes almost as golden as mine in this form, and he skidded to a halt just past the tree line, claws raking up the dirt. In a blink, he shifted back, swapping the huge black wolf for my mountain man.

Tallest of my mates. Thickest. Hardest. Scarred and sweaty, his chest heaved through every strangled breath. Black curly hair dipped down the muscular planes, thickening around his lower abdomen to his shaft. Mossy green appraised me hurriedly, frantically, his body tense, muscles taut—beard long and uncared for these days, lips in a thin line.

"What's wrong?" he demanded, voice all rough and thick, pure wolf. The English accent always tickled between my thighs, but the animalistic *rasp* made my breath hitch and my mouth a little too dry. Even now, his rugged masculinity had me weak in the knees. Would it always be this way? Would they *always* stun me with their beauty? In my appreciative silence, Lucian scanned the clearing with a growl. "What is it?"

Naked and hulking, he prowled straight for me—then stopped, gaze lifted over and beyond me.

Oh. *No.* He'd seen the ivy.

Kind of hard to miss.

His frown deepened, taking on a slightly different air. No longer panicked, his expression twisted to outright confusion, the emotion zinging down my spine all itchy and uncomfortable. My mate then pointed at his cabin, opening and closing his mouth a few times.

"Right, what…?"

"Nothing's wrong," I told him as I strolled closer, adding an extra sway into everything that jiggled in a sad attempt to distract him. Somehow it worked: Lucian's layered greens plunged to my breasts, then my hips, then slowly—so slow I felt the burn over every *inch* of skin—up my center to my lips. "I just miss you."

He let out a brisk breath and scratched at the back of his neck. For a few seconds, everything about him relaxed—then tightened again, as if realizing he had let his guard down—when my hands smoothed up his burly chest. Kira whimpered at his frown, and a small part of me hated that he didn't immediately stroke my arms or cup my backside or sling his arm around my waist. Instead, he just stood there, staring down at me and looking as tired as I'd felt after my first lesson with Rosa. "Little mate…" Some of the velvet was back, his voice a salve that could fix the world. "We saw each other at breakfast, and—"

Whatever else he had to say went away as soon as I hugged him. Clinging to his sculpted torso, I held tight, hands locked behind his back, and closed my eyes. His heart beat so *hard*, so fast and firm, and not like it did with the effort it took to shift. This was something more. The heat radiating off his body—*more* than that of a shifter.

Fear. Stress. I felt it in my teeth the longer I embraced him, the weight he had been carrying the last two weeks trickling into me, the dams barely holding. He was still my mountain man, strong and solid, but he had lost some muscle.

Probably because he ate less lately.

So focused on *us* eating, on minding the pack and watching for predators in the dark, that he forgot about himself. Pair that with being constantly on the move—it was a recipe for disaster.

I squeezed tighter. Clenched my eyes harder, stemming the tears. *What are you doing to yourself, mate?*

Finally, after what felt like hours of him just standing there, Lucian hugged me back. Draped his strong arms around me, but not as firm as I wanted.

"You've been so busy," I mumbled into his chest, Kira's pitchy whine-growl telling me we were definitely on the same page about him, "and when you're home, you're not... home."

All my mates were busy, Ewan most of all, but this was different. Lucian had no obligations outside of patrol duty, but lately he was a million miles away, and nothing we did could bring him back to earth.

Another rough exhale tickled the top of my bare shoulder, and Lucian snuggled into my hair, his dick perking up against my thigh.

I kissed the dip between his hard pecs with a grin. "I see you missed me too?"

"Lyssa..." He said my name like it *hurt* him. "I swear it isn't purposeful—"

Once again, I cut off whatever he had to say, head tipped back as I cupped his strong jawline. Strands of grey and white streaked his unkept beard today, oddly bright in the afternoon light. His eyes, my favorite shade of green, were hollow and ringed in shadow.

Sacrificing his personal well-being for me—for my safety, for the territory, for the pack...

"It's enough now," I murmured, steering him back to me when he tried to look away. "*Enough.* You're more than enough as you are, Lucian." I stroked his cheekbones, only just noticing the way his cheeks curved inward, hidden from a distance by the beard. "We protect each other, and you need to let go a little." He reared back, but I followed, gripping hard, fingertips gritting into his face. "*I need you to come home.*"

From the look in his eyes, the argument already at a simmer in our fated bond, Lucian had no *idea* how much I needed him these days.

I needed his calm.

I needed his strength.

I needed his quiet and his support.

I needed *him*—sprawled out on the deck beside me, like before, both of us soaking up the afternoon sunshine as wolves. I needed to be a wolf with him, because of all my mates, *he* was the most wild. I needed walks in the forest and rabbit hunting and drinks in the stream. I needed him grooming my ears and rough play that *didn't* lead to mating—just play. Just fun on four legs.

Idunn's power terrified me. Even with Rosa's support, the energy inside was scary and dangerous. I turned innocent greenery savage and mean. I couldn't control it.

And I just... needed to feel his arms around me.

Needed to feel *safe* again.

Him patrolling and working himself to the bone? It didn't make me feel safe.

Not even close.

Having him so *close*, his breath warming my lips, his eyes locked on mine—it all went quiet. The storm raging inside, Idunn's power churning with my own warring feelings... Gone. Silent. It was just me and Lucian, alone in the forest, surrounded by the nature we so loved and the peace we both deserved. Swallowing hard, I stood up on my toes to kiss him. Softly, gently, our lips *just* touching. He was so warm.

So warm and gentle and *mine*.

His beard tickled my chin, my cheeks, and his hands finally curved possessively over my backside, hoisting me higher as the kiss deepened. Even with our lips parted, tongues caressing one another like old friends, nothing turned frantic. With Ewan and Soren, the chaos came so fast, the want and need and desperation driving us to madness in seconds.

With Lucian, it was like we needed to *savor* each other. Reconnect with each other's taste, scent, and touch.

Still so quiet and calm. He made the frantic merry-go-round in my brain, the one I couldn't get off and glittered like diamonds and whizzed so fast it made it sick—Lucian made it stop.

I closed my eyes and speared my fingers into his hair. He clutched me tighter, lifting me off the ground. His arm slipped under me like a muscly seat while his other hand cradled the back of my head, tipping me back—*dipping* me, just like in the movies—to taste so deep we both moaned. Always harmonized, me and Lucian, our sounds music to my ears.

His desire suddenly nudged harder into my belly, his shaft a thick, solid line of want trapped between us. With a protesting whine, I wiggled out of his hold to stand on my own two feet, never once breaking the kiss, and caressed his shaft with both hands. My mate rumbled appreciatively with the first stroke. Not too hard. Not too rough. The skin there for males was so tender and sensitive; I just ghosted over it, the smear of damp at the tip not enough to turn the whole thing silky.

Nipples pebbled painfully, I snapped at his lower lip, ready to take this from a gentle hello to a desperate *I want you*. Lucian nipped back, his bite fiercer and catching me off guard. Pain tingled in my lip. Want flared in my belly, the air scented with my womanly musk, and through the crack of one eye, I caught his nostrils flare with his next impossibly deep breath, like he was breathing in the rush of wet between my thighs.

"I learned something recently," I murmured into his mouth. My mate snarled, his grip tightening in my hair the lighter I stroked him.

"What's that?"

Ugh. Hard to be the seductress with all the power when he sounded like *that*, velvety yet dark, dangerous and powerful and all *man*.

"I learned—" I eased away from his lips, fluttering my lashes and grinning. "—that I'm *very* good with my mouth…"

As soon as I started to sink, about to fall to my knees before him and take that impressive—and kind of intimidating—dick in my mouth, determined to give it my best try despite the size, Lucian caught me by my upper arms.

Stopped me.

"Little mate, wait—"

"No." I pouted up at him, at his wolf eyes blazing gold just like mine, at the tense line his mouth made as if deep down he didn't *want* me to stop. "Let me. Please... I want to make you feel as good as you make *me* feel."

"But *I* want to use my mouth on *you*," Lucian rumbled. His wicked smirk nearly dropped me to my knees for all the wrong reasons, the teasing lift of his lips an incantation all its own.

"Oh." How did that work? Who went first? Me? Him? "Uh, okay, but—"

"Here." My mate withdrew completely, and panic lanced through me at the thought of him *leaving*. His gaze snapped sharply to mine, and while he didn't say anything, he didn't go far either, settling on the ground at my feet, sprawled on his back. He then patted his chest and motioned up to his devilish smile. "Bring your dripping cunt right *here*, little mate. Let me taste you while you taste me."

Oh. My eyes widened. *Oh.*

Fire ripped through me from top to bottom, and I took a few seconds to process, then consider my options. He seemed to want me to sit down right on his face, arms outstretched and ready to guide me, but squatting on top of him like I was about to pee next to a tree wasn't sexy...

Was it?

Pushing through the fog, desire and primal need making it hard to think, I stepped over him, then slowly lowered myself down to his chest.

"The other way, little mate."

I frowned. What? The other—

Oh. Right. Blushing up a storm, I turned around to face away from him, then perched on his broad chest, a muscular plane capable of supporting ten of me. Then, before I could figure out where to put everything, Lucian grabbed my hips and scooped me up, then literally *lifted* me over his face.

"Go on, then," he growled with a front-row seat to my swollen, aching sex. "Show me what I've been missing..."

Lucian then arched up and *licked* me, and, *oh*, now it was even *harder* to think. The first sweep of his tongue stoked the fires burning within, and I stumbled forward, bracing on his taut abs, thighs already quivering. His dick stood tall at the helm of his tree trunk thighs, and while it would have been so easy, so *good*, to get lost in what he was doing to me, I refused to submit.

No surrender.

Not when images of Ewan's submission danced across my mind, this angelic, sharply beautiful alpha male totally in my thrall.

All because my tongue did that *thing* he seemed to really like.

Shoulders back, I sank over his huge frame, then fisted the base of his shaft and flicked my tongue over the tender tip. Lucian bucked, his thrusts into my body with his powerful tongue faltering for a second. Right. Okay. Two could play at this game. Grinning, I took him as deep as I could, then licked the rest, spreading my saliva to make each pump of my hands smooth as silk.

Despite that skilled tongue being wholly occupied, Lucian's teeth, tongue, and lips *very* dedicated to the task of making me squirm and mewl and *squeal* when he teased the sensitive bundle of nerves I now knew to be my clitoris, he wasn't quiet about it. He devoured me like I was his favorite meal, moaning and groaning and lapping me up with such ferocity that I struggled to keep pace. Still, I could throw him when I swirled my tongue or cupped his balls. He loved the slow, torturous pumping of my hands, but his noises turned tortured when I went faster.

We knew how to undo each other.

How to make the other stumble and fall into our control.

Not a word shared, just an inferno brewing between us, within us, hearts connected. His want swelled through me, punctuated by regret, the emotion plunging in cold icy drops down my spine. Lucian's feelings were just as messy as mine, just as complicated, flowing back and forth, the two of us connected by more than just the physical.

I lost it first.

Quite unfairly, too, because as soon as he slipped two rough fingers in me to stroke my inner walls, his mouth dedicated to only my clitoris, I was *done*. The explosion came hard and fast, furious and fiery as pleasure tore through my limbs. Even with his shaft halfway in my mouth, I howled through the sensation, one hand raking up his thigh, the other gripping him maybe a little *too* tight from his next choked breath.

But that seemed to do it for him, the painful slash of my nails jumping from his thigh to mine, the sensations shared—including his climax. *Orgasm*. I'd added more terms to my vocabulary during my blowjob research, and his hit like a detonation, like a building demolition. *Boom*, pleasure shooting you sky-high, then the fall of *everything* crashing back down.

It touched me too.

Heightened my own bliss, upped it to unsafe levels so that I sobbed into his thigh, barely able to take it, as he spilled himself in thick, hot bursts all over my fist.

But when it faded away and I sat up, it was like I could draw a deep, full breath for the first time in weeks.

Like that first gasp after cracking through the ice, no longer at the river's cruel mercy.

As I shimmied down his body, struggling to spread my legs around his massive shoulders, all I wanted now was to waste the day away here, on the forest floor, cuddled against my Lucian and all the peace he offered. My mate had other ideas, however, and just as I started to climb off, ready to tuck myself under his wing, he caught me by the hips and rolled me. Pinned me to the ground. Climbed up and prowled over so that he blanketed my body with unstoppable muscle and raw masculinity. I spread my thighs for him, happy to let him settle there, and he filled me with a single thrust, already hard again, already wanting for my body. It took me by surprise, so relaxed and hazy one moment, stretched and taken the next. My lips tumbled open in a soundless cry, and I arched up and into him, letting him claim me.

And claiming him in turn.

Lucian bundled me up as best he could. While my back took the brunt of the ground's harsh bite, he blunted it here and there, arms under me, head cradled. After stealing another slow, toe-curling kiss, my mate nestled into the crook of my neck, nibbling along my skin, licking over the scar he had left with his bite. His mark tingled, made me shudder with featherlight waves of pleasure, and I hooked my legs around him, *barely* able to lock my ankles, then dug into his hair for support.

We rocked together, slow and steady. No merciless pounding into the dirt. No biting kisses and brutal hands. It wasn't like I didn't *enjoy* what I had with Soren, nor did I only crave Ewan's intense, passionate lovemaking that always ended with the most delicious aches.

With Lucian, it was just different.

Not better, not worse. Different and sublime and *deep*, our gazes frequently crashing together, locking, gold on gold with his wolf eyes *right* at the surface. Emotion thickened in my throat the deeper I lost myself in his gold. Tears stung the backs of my eyes. I'd needed this, *him*, for so long.

A quiet moment.

A soul connection.

No words. No declarations. Just—*this*.

I closed my eyes and burrowed into him, hiding my face against his shoulder and hearing a declaration with his every thrust. *Need you. Need you. Need. You. Needyouneedyouneedyou.* Because he felt it too, the ropes binding us together thick and sturdy and a little scary. Dangerous, to be so *open* to each other but suddenly so closed off from everything else.

This climax broke me. The pleasure tore me to pieces and scattered me on the wind, the emotional bond my undoing, the closeness my downfall, the *connection* my salvation. I came apart in his arms, pleasure burning white-hot, sobbing again. Too intense.

Too much. Eyes squeezed shut, I rocked and bucked and drove it harder, *taking* all of it even if it terrified me.

My fingertips buzzed.

Diamonds sparkled behind my closed lids, exploding, turning into starlight that went on forever and ever, just like the orchard—to the horizon and beyond. I choked his name, and Lucian stabbed into me one last time, hard and possessive, his breath ragged and his voice rough as he snarled *little mate* back like the burn of a branding.

We held each other tight in the aftermath, almost like if we let go, the other would slip away, sand falling through our fingers and disappearing on the breeze. In time, the starlight faded behind my eyelids, the pinwheels of color dying, leaving only a heavy darkness. It threatened to lull me to sleep, knock me out right here on the forest floor, in Lucian's arms—and I would have let it.

But Lucian stirred, rumbling as he dragged his open mouth up my neck and along my jaw, breathing life back into the fire between us. His interest zinged through me, swelling between my legs again, and I arched into him with a moan, lifting off the dirt and leaves, smoothing my feet down the backs of his strong thighs. Slowly, my eyes fluttered open and met with his mossy greens, his golden wolf gaze tucked away for now.

I stroked his cheek, his untidy beard, missing the gold already.

Resting on his elbows so he didn't crush me, my mate grinned, the feeling of his open affection like a cozy blanket wrapped around us both. His lips parted. He inhaled softly, about to say something—

Then his gaze snagged somewhere else.

All around us.

His smile vanished. He pushed up with a harsh breath, ripping the affection away with him, stealing the blanket that kept us warm and safe and together.

"What...?"

Oh.

Oh *no*.

Fear welled in my throat, nearly closing it for good.

All around us—a field of wildflowers.

Spring wildflowers, mostly white and yellow with the odd stamp of red. Scentless.

Evidence of Idunn's gifts, her power in *my* veins, bloomed as far as the eye could see, dominating Lucian's clearing, surrounding his cabin, flourishing at the deadbolted door.

Lucian pushed to his knees, taking it all in with wide eyes, jaw set and lips in a thin, horrifying line again. All the post-mating looseness—gone. Suspicion panged from him to me, tearing up and down my spine, making my belly loop and bile sizzle in my throat.

"Lyssa—"

"P-please *don't*—"

"Lyssa," he growled, reaching cautiously for the nearest yellow bloom, "what just happened?"

My mind went blank.

Kira fell silent.

I couldn't *lie* to him—not to any of my mates, but especially not Lucian.

But how could I tell him the truth?

He always made a face when Rosa or Ethan came up in conversation, clearly not the biggest fan of magic, so how could I—

Lucian hissed, pain stabbing in *my* fingertip, the very same finger on his hand that had just stroked the flower's stem. While thin and green, innocent from a distance, up close I realized every single one of these stupid wildflowers… had thorns.

Tiny, angry, violent little knives on their stems—and one had just ripped Lucian's finger open. He withdrew and glowered at the pluming red dot at the tip. It healed in seconds, but the dull ache lingered, like a whisper of a childhood wound echoing in me.

No. No, no, no, *no*. I buried my face in my hands, smothering the hot, wet panic before he saw, then rolled over and curled in on myself.

Why was it always thorns?

Why couldn't I make something *nice*?

"Lyssa?" His knuckles ghosted along my arm, and I shook my

head, swallowing an agonized wail, *fighting* for just a speck of my mate's effortless calm.

I mean, what if this had been something *worse* than thorny wildflowers? It had happened without my consent—and it was big. The whole clearing this time. The ivy on his cabin. Thorns, thorns, thorns. Dangerous. Unpredictable. What if ivy had, I don't know, *snaked* around his neck, thorns and all?

What if, in a haze of bliss, lost in our connection, I accidentally smothered him?

Or stabbed him?

Or, or, or, *or*...

Rosa had put so much time and effort into helping me the last two weeks.

And now *this*.

It didn't matter.

I was hopeless—and one day, I might accidentally do something to my mates.

Something I couldn't take back.

Something even shifters couldn't heal from.

"I-I can't control it," I blubbered, coiling into a ball as the floodgates burst. Kira finally nosed at me, whining, panicked but trying her best to be supportive. She was all I had in this mess, and—

"Little mate, please don't cry."

Suddenly, Lucian's enormous body nudged up behind mine. He curled around me, folded over me, protecting me from the world and all its problems with his rough hands and fiery skin and raw *strength*. Sniffling, hiccupping, snotty and wet, I lowered my hands just enough to blink at the ocean of wildflowers, then twist back to him. He... He was still here. I'd expected him to run. To pick through the clearing, demanding answers, furious that I had so *obviously* kept something from him.

"Can't you feel how it *pains* me when you cry?" he whispered when I faced forward again. My mate swept me closer, my hunched back to his scarred chest, and I soon felt his breath on my neck, on my shoulder where he had once marked me. Shoving the fear aside, I tried to just listen to his breathing, to count the even exhales.

"I-I'm not ready to explain yet."

"Why?" he rumbled.

"Because you'll leave." *You'll all leave.*

"Never forget, little mate," Lucian whispered, lips brushing his mark with every word, "you don't scare me."

My chest squeezed, both from my own emotional turmoil *and* his. So tight I could barely breathe.

"No," I murmured, "but the world does."

Lucian stiffened at my back.

He patrolled relentlessly because everything else scared him. His past must have brutalized him—and my mate wouldn't let that happen again. Not to him. Not to his pack. Not to his mate. The world was a bad place for my Lucian...

But maybe now *I* was bad in his eyes. When he realized what had happened, the depths of what I'd become, the weight of all the secrets I had kept, I might eventually scare him too.

And then he would run me out of here, just like those vampires, hell-bent on protecting his territory from a monster.

"I'm here, Lyssa." Lucian cuddled me to him harder now, like that would drive the point home, a powerful declaration that he was *here* for me, by my side, at my back, no matter what. His resolve scorched through me like a forest fire, so hot and insistent that sweat broke out across my brow. Of all my mates, I felt Lucian the deepest, our connection almost soul-level. He readjusted his arm, cutting across my chest, between my breasts, like he *needed* to feel my thundering heart. I closed my eyes tight. He breathed me in deep. When I stole a peek at the wildflowers, the thorns had grown to about an inch.

My eyes dropped to my curled fingers.

Belatedly, I felt the buzz of power.

Driven by *feeling.*

By a depressing resolve.

"I'm not going anywhere," Lucian growled. "I swear it. We'll get through this together, little mate."

I closed my eyes again, squeezing out a few tears.

No.

Not together.

Clearly, I needed more help than even Rosa could give. This might be beyond her skill.

Or *I* might be beyond help.

One day, I could kill the wolf at my back without meaning to.

Nature *wasn't* nice. It wasn't carefree and gentle. It was violent and cruel and unpredictable, and that... was what Idunn had turned me into.

Lucian might not be going anywhere, his promise resonating through me, but Kira howled desperately inside, calling to her mate —like she wanted to *snitch* on me.

Like she wanted to warn him...

He might be here to stay, but after today, I wasn't.

I couldn't.

I had to save Lucian, Ewan, and Soren... from myself. From a cursed she-wolf with no control. From a monster, a freak, an abomination.

And to walk away, to *run* fast and far—that would kill me.

But, in the end... better *me* than them.

17

EWAN

…So, this isnt goodbye forevr.

But it is goodbye for now. It has to be. I hope you all undrstand.

L

The *fuck?*

Naked and sweaty from my recent shift, weighed down by a pleasant full-body soreness after my daytime territory patrol, I shook out the small slip of lined paper, then read it again. Brows furrowed, I squinted at Lyssa's chicken scratch, her misspelled words, and hoped that I had missed something the first time around.

But nope. The bullet points remained the same.

She cared very deeply for all of us.

She was so grateful *we* were her mates.

She looked forward to one day starting a bloodline—but was scared she would hurt us.

And for now, needed to leave.

What.

The actual.

Fucking.

Fuck?

I'd returned to a quiet house, Lucian napping on the back deck beneath a foggy sunset and Soren rustling around the kitchen having just returned from *his* full day at work. Slated for an evening patrol, I figured the blond alpha was about to start dinner—and that Lyssa, her musky rose scent faint in the air, was still with Rosa.

She had told us this morning...

Something about a movie with Aster, a mom-and-baby showing at a cinema in Hampton, the lights kept on in the theater, the sound lowered, the flick decidedly *chick.*

And now this.

Crumpling the note in my fist, I stalked out of my bedroom, cock swinging, naked and grimy and in desperate need of a shower, and barreled through Lyssa's half-closed door.

Empty bedroom.

Made bed.

Lights off and too quiet.

Scowling, I ripped open her walk-in closet door and noted a few key items missing: winter jacket we had recently ordered her for the sake of appearances, some jeans and T-shirts, her underwear and sock drawers completely pilfered.

No laptop anywhere. I reread the note one more time, hoping that maybe I had *dreamed* its contents. Nope. Same shit. I went for her bedside table—no phone either, the charging cord gone. If I called it, she probably wouldn't answer.

"*Fuck.*"

Inner wolf on high alert, sniffing deeply, our hearts pounding as one and his concerned whines melding with the high-pitched screech between my ears, I barreled downstairs and plowed straight into Soren as he left the kitchen, a chilled beer in hand.

"Shit, sorry, man—"

"What the *fuck* have you done now?" I snarled. My alpha counterpart staggered back with his bottle of Belgian brew, and then cocked his head to the side. His wolf eyes flared—and so did mine.

"Uh, what?"

I shoved the note at him, hating the way my whole arm trembled, rage and fear turning foul in my chest. "What—did—you —*do?*"

Soren flashed his teeth as he snatched the crinkly paper, shock pinging briefly through our bond, followed by a thunderclap of fury. We had been getting along better lately, connecting through this more evenly divided patrol schedule. For once, we three males had been a *team*; it wasn't just Lucian shouldering the burden of protecting our territory, but all of us, myself included.

It nuked some of the simmering tension, being a team.

But that flew out the window as I gnashed my teeth and glowered at the fucking *cocksucker* in front of me as he read Lyssa's note.

Because obviously he had done something.

Wasn't it always him?

First Gull River, and now this?

Gone.

"I-I thought she was with Rosa," Soren stammered as soon as his wolf eyes touched the bottom of the paper and snapped back to the top, skimming it a second time, faster, his mounting anxiety buzzing in the nape of my neck. I swatted at it like I'd picked up a bunch of mosquitos and growled when Soren shook his head, both arms suddenly limp at his sides, his eyes blue again—and a million miles away. "She told me this morning... They were... The movie, right?"

Behind him, the sliding glass door separating the living room from the back deck whizzed open, then thunked shut, followed by Lucian's slow, firm prowl across the hardwood. Clearly the flash-bang in our bond woke him, and if he had slept through Lyssa sneaking away—I'd kill him.

Or, you know...

Just punch him, really, really hard in the face.

For now, I centered my wrath on Soren. "Again—what the *fuck* did you do?"

Because I sure as shit hadn't done anything. The two and a half weeks since Halloween had been oddly peaceful. No vampires in our territory—not a whiff of danger around our mate. No Hawthorne wolves testing our borders. Ethan had set up charms and spells and whatever else warlocks did around the village to ensure our humans didn't become prey during some fucked-up leech open season. The guys and I got along better. Lyssa seemed happy to have us all home, cycling in and out but sharing more meals as a pack. Beyond us, she had Rosa, spending plenty of afternoons with the sweet witch, something we all agreed was key for our mate while she developed her sense of self as a shifter.

She deserved—and, frankly, *needed*—at least one friend outside of the pack. Wolves who got too into their own dynamics were just... weird.

Desperate as *I* still was to hoard our mate, I let go—just a little—so she could foster a social sphere outside of *us*.

And I hadn't said anything hurtful lately.

I'd been *very* careful about that, watching my manners, minding my words, a lot of the beef between me and Soren quashed after our Halloween threesome. Things had been going well; with patrol and work and house stuff, I hadn't been this tired in for-fucking-ever, but I liked it. Staying busy like this, balancing the impending Redwood Grove winter chaos, the many, many, *many* events we had planned for residents and tourists alike, with pack duties—it was *good*.

Made me feel... connected, to her, to them, to my inner animal, who got to stretch his legs daily now.

All this made me a more balanced wolf.

And that was... a good thing.

Until now.

Until *this*.

"I don't get it," Soren muttered, beer tucked under his arm as he smoothed out the note. "What does this even *mean*?"

"It clearly means she *left*," I snarled, temper spiking, my inner wolf right there with me and ready for a fight, "you fucking shit for brains—"

"Why would you assume *I* did something?"

"Because it wasn't *him*." I shoved a finger in Lucian's direction as the hulking alpha lumbered up behind Soren, a few inches taller, a great deal wider, and looking annoyed as fuck. "This fucker doesn't talk enough to send her running—"

"That's not fair," Soren growled, eyes narrowed and amber again, all canines as he sprinted to Lucian's defense. The enormous Brit behind him merely looked between us, a strange calm washing through the bond—frosty and dangerous. I swallowed hard, my inner wolf on edge at the sensation, and shrugged.

"Well—"

"What's this?" Lucian rumbled. The air went deadly still, Soren and I holding our breaths, the gravelly, demonic timbre of his tone fucking terrifying. "Lyssa *isn't* with that bloody witch?"

Despite the brewing brawl, I swapped glances with Soren, both of us unnerved by whatever the hell *that* was—some fucked-up monster in Lucian form—and he shuffled out of the doorway and into the foyer, near me but out of arm's reach so neither of us could fling a sucker punch. Quick as he and I had been to fight in the past, we had an unspoken truce to try harder, be *better*, for Lyssa's sake.

Only Lyssa wasn't here, so...

My inner wolf's lips peeled back, ready for a fight with *anyone* right now as a storm of feeling hammered our alpha bond.

Lucian sauntered into the doorway, filling it, glaring between us and demanding answers. That icy calm turned to steel, his resolve to assign someone the blame setting my teeth on edge.

"Look, if anyone scared her away, it's *you*," Soren insisted. While he sounded less confrontational now, those were fucking *fighting* words and he knew it. The blond shrugged when our gazes clashed again, his righteousness undercutting Lucian's steel. "I mean, *you* are the one who runs his damn mouth whenever you're stressed... Any more speeches about bloodlines lately that we should know about?"

"Says the douchebag who let her drink from Gull River—"

"If Lyssa's gone," Lucian interjected, "she scared herself away. It has nothing to do with us."

I rounded on him with a snarl. Had he read the note already? No, it was still in Soren's hand—but he spoke with such confidence, such calm certainty, that it made me want to straight-up attack him. Triggered as I might be, my emotions bleeding into the bond unchecked now, Lucian radiated pure, uncut *alpha*, his energy smothering, his stance tall and strong. His voice's guttural rasp had softened, but he sounded perfectly in control.

"*What?*" I'd kill for control right now. What I got instead was fear and panic and anger, all bundled into some ugly, nauseating brew. Bile sizzled up my throat. My jaw ached from clenching. My nails, trimmed and neat for my mate's comfort, gritted so deep into my palms that a droplet of steaming red *plopped* onto the tile at my feet.

She was gone.

And I was fucking losing it.

And it pissed me the fuck off that I seemed like the only one in a kamikaze tailspin.

Wordlessly, Soren offered me his beer. Still full—one of the Belgian whites he so loved.

Rather than downing it, I hurled it at the wall.

No one moved.

No one acknowledged the glass shattering and the beer streaking.

My inner wolf whined—and I felt even worse.

"Ewan..." Out of the corner of my eye, Soren reached out for me, then quickly dropped his arm. "Take a breath, okay? We're all worried—"

"Shut the fuck up, Soren," I growled back. At no point did I need his *pity*, and the warmth rippling from him to me through our bond only made me even more uncomfortable in my own fucking skin. Quinn wolves had never been touchy-feely. My pack lacked transparent communication and logical discussions and understanding and looking at things from each other's perspective.

Lyssa did that.

Soren too—to a degree.

And it made me feel about two inches tall. I pinched the bridge of my nose, my inner wolf equally unsettled by the olive branch. "Just let me—"

"Gull River changed her," Lucian announced, deftly changing the subject, not an ounce of pity lobbed my way. I glanced up appreciatively, but something told me he didn't do it for me, even if it was a flawless redirect, checking all our aggression and feelings back where they belonged. "She's scared she'll hurt us."

"I..." Soren held up the note with a frown. "What the hell does that even mean?"

It was then that Lucian finally decided to share a few crucial details about *our* mate.

Because—fucking *apparently*—not only could our brave little she-wolf rattle the windows and make grown humans cower with a glimpse of her golden gaze...

But she could summon wildflowers from the earth.

Make them grow strong and tall and spiky.

Breathe life back into ivy that had already retreated for the winter—then double its size.

Rage detonated through the pack bond, Soren and I suddenly on the same murderous wavelength.

All this... had happened *yesterday.*

"And did that not seem like something worth *fucking* mentioning?" I bellowed. This time, I took on the demon's fury, my voice harsh and low. The surge of adrenaline was dangerous, pounding from me to them, adding fuel to a fire that shouldn't get any bigger.

"She's struggling," Lucian countered with a flash of teeth. Stoic as his exterior might seem, there was no way he could take the brunt of two packmates seething at him, raging, absolutely furious that he had kept this fucking secret to himself. His cheek twitched, and the alpha suddenly rolled his head side to side, searching for that satisfying *crack*. "And I respect Lyssa enough to let her share what's happening when she's ready—"

"And now she's gone." Soren threw his hands up, terse exasperation oozing from his every pore, then tossed the note at Lucian's feet. "We could have avoided this, Lucian. You aren't an island unto yourself anymore—we're a goddamn *team*."

"I'm well aware of that—"

"Obviously the gold wasn't the only thing she picked up from the river," Soren ranted on, blowing by Lucian's objections as I started to pace, needing to put this adrenaline to use before my wolf forced a shift and we did something we might regret. The blond alpha stabbed a hand through his hair with a low growl. "She's stopped making stuff shake, so I just thought—"

"We all *just thought*," I snarled. That was the fucking problem: we as a pack had let too much slide. And brutal as it was to admit, we were *all* at fault here. We thought our connections ran deeper than they did, like the thickening bond between us was enough to manage a pack. "We babied her feelings and her, her, her *experience* when we should have gotten to the root of the issue."

"She said we would leave her if we knew the truth."

I wheeled around on Lucian with a scoff. Leave her? Fucking ridiculous. Now that I'd found her, I would *never* abandon my mate —even if something were wrong with her. When we first dragged that wild woman out of the woods, kicking and screaming and slashing her claws, sure, I had my doubts.

But Lyssa was meant for me—and me for her. She was strong, brave, and adaptable. Tough. Brash. Independent. Eager to learn and grow and explore. Impulsive. She needed guidance, needed a mate who would pump the brakes when necessary, just as much as I needed a fated who would put me in my place and drag my ass out of the office every once in a while.

Remind me what *should* matter in life.

And together, we needed time to create that dynamic.

To forge that connection with *all* of us. Unified alphas meant an unbreakable pack—our bloodline would rule Redwood Grove like fucking royalty.

We had been making huge strides lately…

Now this.

"So, what, reject us before we can reject her?" Soren kicked at the note on the floor. "I don't get it—"

"She's not rejecting us," Lucian argued roughly. "She—"

"She's not going *anywhere*," I snapped, then motioned stiffly to the front door. "We're going to bring her home and figure this bullshit out."

"Agreed."

The fuck? Soren and I slowly turned on Lucian, who was already yanking off his T-shirt and tossing it aside, preparing for the shift. Slow to agree to *anything*, this bearded fuck was usually the first to press pause and demand a thorough investigation—know absolutely everything about a situation before diving in.

"Those leech *cunts* are still out there," he growled, tugging his sweats down and booting them off. "I smell them sometimes just over the border… They're hunting her, either for themselves or for another."

"Maybe the Hawthorne alpha," Soren muttered, more to himself than us, but anxiety throbbed through the pack bond all the same, each of us radiating the stuff, muddying the waters and clouding our minds. The blond scratched at the back of his neck roughly, the sensation buzzing in the exact same spot on me, and then bared his teeth. "Lyssa is marked, but she hasn't had a pup yet. In theory, he could still take her… *breed* her for himself…"

Nope. My inner wolf, normally so calm and collected, stoic and standoffish, lost it at the thought. We had no idea who the vicious Hawthorne pack alpha was, but I'd never wanted to find out: I had no time in my hectic life for scum like that, some piece-of-shit drug runner and pimp, all too reminiscent of the old Quinn legacy.

And in my old pack, the gilded shithole I'd been born into—males would have plucked a delectable peach like Lyssa and destroyed her. Not right away. No, they'd break her over time, chaining her with silver like monsters, breeding her again and again to make a stronger army.

I'd seen it happen.

Never been a participant in my cousins' fucked-up games, but the gory details were forever burned into the darkest pits of my soul.

Nope. Nope, not *fucking* happening to my mate.

I stalked for the front door, heart in my throat, inner wolf losing his mind. "We'll bring her back *tonight* and make her talk. Then we'll figure this shit out as a fucking pack."

"Ewan—"

"*No.*" I whipped around and bared my canines, wolf eyes blazing, muscles taut and sweaty, *ready* to state my case with brute strength if I had to. "No more feelings and letting her take her time... We find out the *truth*, and we fucking deal with it, or fix it, or whatever."

The house fell silent.

I straightened, arms falling limp at the assault through our pack bond—this strange, cohesive *whumping*, blood beating, war drums pounding.

A heartbeat.

Our heartbeat.

Soren's cheeks flushed a dull pink. Lucian rolled his shoulders back, eyes closed, one hand flexing in and out of a fist in time with that pulsing rhythm.

This...

We...

I blinked, swapping glances with Soren, then Lucian when he finally came back to us.

Us.

United.

Together.

Emotion stung the backs of my eyes—made my throat raw.

"Okay, okay, no sappy shit," I grumbled before ripping the front door open and barreling outside, the others at my heels. By the time we all trundled down the porch steps to the gravel drive, we were three naked alphas on the cusp of a shift, the air thick, my wolf calmed by the heartbeat of our pack—quieter now, just background noise, constant and reassuring.

A little past the midway point of November and the sun set early. Barely six o'clock and darkness blanketed the landscape, the porch lights activated by our presence, the lake still, the forest unnervingly silent. Bare branches. Birds migrated south. Game big and small already tucked in for the chilly night ahead. Frost tinted the windshields of all three vehicles in the driveway, and our breaths fogged, the ice on the breeze beyond invigorating.

Just the kind of shit to put you in the mood for the most important hunt of your entire fucking life.

"Me and Soren should track her scent," I insisted. The others fanned out on either side of me, wolf eyes reflecting the light, nostrils flared as they familiarized themselves with the natural world. "Lucian—border patrol." The alpha arched a thick dark brow at me. "Just keep circling. We'll cover ground faster apart, and you know our borders best. If something seems off, you'll see it first."

Difficult as it was to give him a compliment for his intense, almost obsessive patrol habits, it wasn't *as* difficult as usual. For once, the Brit's anal-retentive paranoia about safety and borders was about to be a serious asset.

"East," Lucian said in a caveman grunt. "I'll start east." He veered away from us, headed right to the scraggly yellowing grass along the side of the driveway, then paused and glared over his shoulder at me. Those golden wolf eyes—so like Lyssa's, just a few shades duller. Soren inhaled sharply, almost like this was the first time he'd realized it, same as me, and I stood taller when the gold narrowed. "Be gentle when you find her."

I blinked back at him, waiting for the punchline, then remembered that the fucker didn't *joke* about this shit. When I glanced at Soren to help, he just raised his eyebrows and crossed his arms.

Did they seriously think…?

For fuck's sake.

"You assholes really think I'm heartless, don't you?" My inner wolf's snarl tainted every word, the syllables coarse and brutish. "I'm pissed because of the circumstances, not *her*."

I mean, a little bit at her—and I didn't deserve any shit for that. Lyssa was the one who pushed for conversation, open and honest communication, the *truth* at every turn. And here she was, fleeing into the night without so much as a proper goodbye, just some horseshit note left on my fucking pillow.

When no one said anything, the pair just staring, waiting for me to out myself as the insensitive bastard they had seen a few times already, I growled low and threw my hands up.

"*Obviously* I'll be gentle with her. I…" *Love her?*

No. Not quite. It was… too soon. It had to be too soon.

Logically—

My inner wolf snarled, and I culled the internal debate before it gained traction.

Fate was more intoxicating than I'd anticipated, nudging me deeper and deeper into a love-drunk stupor from the moment I first saw my she-wolf emerge from the shadows.

"If not," Soren mused, cracking his knuckles as if to intimidate me, "I'll rip you apart."

I flipped him off.

He growled.

Lucian… smirked.

The fucker actually *grinned*, like he possessed a *speck* of humor, then shifted and trotted along the eastern shoreline. Soren and I mirrored him, paws on the ground in seconds, greeting each other briefly—nosing at each other's snouts, scent-marking our fellow alpha as we never had before—then set out together. I hung back, letting Soren lead; he had spent more time with Lyssa's wolf form, hunting her through the mountain range, which meant he ought to take point.

But that only mattered *if* she was in wolf form.

I scanned the dark, barren tree line as we approached, sniffing deep, my wolf side hyperaware of every little detail.

About ten feet into the forest, Soren with his nose to the ground, his wolf side unnaturally focused and *barely* bouncy, a howl split the night.

Long, loud, and mournful, Lucian's call to our mate stilled my thundering heart. Made Soren shoot upright. Ears perked, hackles high, we both listened to his desperate song. Stiffened during the fading echoes. *Waited* for our mate to answer.

Nothing.

He tried again, longing slicing through our bond like razor wire, his heartbreak so visceral and *real* that it knocked the wind out of me.

Soren dropped into a sit and threw his head back, joining the howl. I added a third voice to the chorus, our tones varied and fluid, the perfect harmony, our message clear...

Please come home.

Our song would carry for miles and miles, rippling through the territory. No telling when she had left or how much of a head start she had on us, but Lyssa would hear the echoes. She'd *feel* this, us, her pack unified and searching.

When the icy breeze eventually carried the last of our howls away, silence answered us.

Lyssa had a beautiful song, high and clear and sweet, the perfect soprano to our range of baritones and altos.

Nothing.

Anxiety plucked at the bond again, like some aggressive asshole pulling a guitar string as far out as possible, *just* on the verge of breaking it, before letting it *twang* back into place.

I snarled and bulldozed into a still-seated Soren, forcing him to move. He smoothed his muzzle down my body from tip to tail, a brief moment of seeking comfort in my fur, my scent, then scampered around me and straight ahead. Nose to the ground, he sniffed furiously, searching for her, then veered sharply to the left.

After a quick glance back toward the house, I followed in his pawprints, praying to Lady Fate that we hadn't lost her tonight for good.

465

18

LYSSA

I knew exactly where our territory ended.

No fence, no marker, no lines in the sand—the scent of my mates just stopped. That was enough to tell me I had come to the northwestern border of the Redwood Grove territory…

I was supposed to be over it and gone ages ago.

But I couldn't bring myself to do it.

Seated on the edge of a rocky cliff jutting out from the forest, the mountain range at my back, the sun set and the nighttime chill settling on my skin, I hugged my knees to my chest and sighed. The city of Hampton glittered in the distance, slowly coming alive after sundown, lit up like a great neon jewel in a sea of darkness. Forest on all sides, it was a beacon, a spotlight—a guiding North Star, showing me exactly where I needed to go.

According to Rosa, Hampton was witch central for the region. About a forty-minute drive north of Redwood Grove, it was the last real metropolis before the province's northern nothingness. It had a human university *and* a supernatural academy, a ginormous shopping mall—all the modern amenities. I'd ambled around it once when the pack settled somewhere nearby, maybe six, seven years back. Clueless. Totally unaware that there were shifters one town

466

over and that many of the people with strange energies and stunning eyes were probably witches and warlocks.

One of them *had* to be able to help me. Rosa had done her best the last two weeks, but her best wasn't enough—not when I was such an unpredictable disaster. Idunn's magic needed taming. It needed a teacher with more knowledge. We couldn't stumble around in the dark anymore.

I couldn't...

I couldn't hurt my mates by accident.

I couldn't maim them, scar them, *kill* them.

Yeah, we shifters healed in seconds, our bodies resilient and strong, but at the end of the day, none of us understood this gift—this curse. What if a dead goddess's power went above and beyond what we could handle? What if, in the middle of a heated argument, I sprouted thorny vines and smothered my mates?

What if, what if, what if, what if?

All the *what-ifs* forced my hand.

No more what-ifs. *Control.* I was an alpha wolf, sure, but I needed to be alpha of *everything* within me. The power buzzing in my fingertips—it had to know who was boss. It had to come and go when *I* ordered it.

Not on a whim.

Not when I was distracted.

Not when I was emotional.

No.

If Hampton had its own private academy for witches and warlocks like Rosa said, then, yeah, I bet someone there could help me.

Lucian's howl suddenly shattered the night. My head shot up. My heart leapt into my throat. So sorrowful. So desperate. A cry *just* for me.

Come home.

Where are you, little mate?

Kira answered, her howl just as frantic, just as devoted.

I stayed quiet. Buried my face in my knees. Plugged my ears

when Ewan and Soren joined in, our pack's chorus so beautiful and layered and deep, beckoning to my *soul*. Not only that, but their emotions ripped through me like a hurricane. Confusion. Loss. Anger. Fear. My note hadn't been enough, but I knew that when I wrote it. If I talked this out with them, they wouldn't let me go.

I knew that too.

This was for the best. It felt heartless, even now, but the blowup would have been much more devastating if I had rounded my mates up and told them I had to leave—but then couldn't tell them *why*.

Our pack song struck deeper, whittling into my marrow, tattooing itself on my ribs. I threw my arms over my head and balled up tighter, fighting it, resisting that sweet, sweet call to just come home. Shivers tore through me, head to toe and back again, and didn't stop even as the howls tapered off, their final echoes rippling across the starry sky.

Kira's frustration blurred my vision when I straightened. Sniffling, eyes watery and throat sore, I zeroed in on Hampton, on the bright lights of the city. The plan had been to get there by nightfall. I mean, I left the house this morning. Hiking out there, even on two legs, should have been a breeze.

But I'd stopped here, hunkered down, butt cheeks asleep, and couldn't move—for hours.

Kira had left me to my thoughts all that time, maybe because she thought I would change my mind. However, as I stood and sighed, dusting my hands on my never-before-worn pants, she let me have it. Snarled and snapped. Ripped up my insides so that my next swallow had a painful metallic thickness to it.

"Stop that," I muttered, emotionally drained and confused as heck. Sometimes this felt like the right decision. Sometimes, like when I grabbed my backpack and slung it over my shoulders, it felt like the biggest mistake of my life.

But I wanted to keep my mates safe.

If we were going to have pups and raise a pack, I *couldn't* be this unstable. I needed to be better.

And I could do that.

I'd done it before.

Changed. Grown. Adjusted to new circumstances—new problems and roadblocks and fears.

I could *do* this.

So, why did every step across the cliff face feel like I was wading through quicksand?

Despite wearing them all day, these hiking boots were more annoying than helpful. They felt awkward and too big, my bare feet better for this kind of journey, but I had prepared for my mates to follow me. Track me. *Hunt* me. These boots? Never worn them before. The jeans, sweatshirt, and winter jacket with its faux-fur-lined hood? New. Scentless. Purposeful. I zigzagged through the territory, crossing streams and marking where I shouldn't—hopefully just enough to lead my mates south.

They were strong wolves. Powerful alphas. Masterful and beautiful and *perfect* for me...

But this was my domain.

And I'd use that to my advantage.

Phone off so they couldn't even track that, I already had a motel in mind, a little dive on the outskirts of Hampton that I had passed with my wolf pack more times than I could count in the last ten years. Pretty sure I'd robbed the housekeeping cart once or twice, maybe even the odd room if I wanted to go into the city. It was cheap and dirty, which meant the handful of cash I'd saved from whatever my mates handed me for lunches with Rosa would go far, but it was also quiet and out of the way. Once I had a room, I'd let them know I was safe.

Hopefully talk to Lucian first, *maybe* Soren...

Ewan would just freak out on me, his anxiety a standout, dancing like electricity through the invisible live wire that bonded all of us.

So long as they knew I was okay and that I *would* come home soon—hopefully—that might curb their efforts to drag me back themselves.

This hurt everyone, but I hadn't *asked* for Idunn's power. I didn't even want it.

I couldn't risk my pack's safety anymore. I wouldn't do it.

This was for the best. Had to move. Had to leave the territory. Get out and find a mentor.

I closed my eyes and took a deep breath, boots on the brink of our territory line. *Just do it. This is for the best.*

Right?

Emotion hammered me the second I put a foot over the territory line. It snowballed fast, just an avalanche of *feelings* as I brought the other foot over too. I swallowed hard, vision blurring, Kira snarling, and sucked down a ragged sob.

This was it.

Outside a territory that I had no idea existed just a little while ago.

Now, leaving it like this was *painful.*

A knife in the back, stabbing over and over and over again with every step. Arms crossed and head down, I stumbled into the ravine and didn't hold back. Tears slicked my cheeks. Sobs bounced off the trees. Kira eased up a little, my distress infecting her, wounding her just as deeply as it did me.

The boots did me some good here, durable and tough, made for the terrain. I felt every step in these stupid things, separate from the natural order, and for now, that was good. Instead of spiraling inward, I focused on the *clomp* of the soles over the forest floor, counting the footfalls and just letting the tears flow.

Get it all out.

My fingertips buzzed.

Dead foliage coiled back to life around me, greenery trailing behind, tree roots nudging out of the ground ahead like they were waiting for me to dust them with... whatever came out in these moments. I pushed harder. Walked faster. Tried to get my breathing under control—if only to stop the thorns and vines twining up the surrounding trees, an ocean of thickets rising on all sides.

A twig snapped.

I stilled. Kira stopped whining and whimpering and growling, her alertness melding with mine.

The forest had been so quiet today, on the decline to winter, animals fattening up and plants retreating, preparing themselves for the snow that would hit any day now.

That *snap*... had been intentional.

And it came from behind me.

With a deep breath, I peered back, scanning the shadows, the foliage, the savage underbrush of my own design.

Nothing.

Shoot.

This was how it had started last time, noises herding me through the village.

Ewan had interrupted the vampires' hunt before, but I didn't scent my mates anywhere. Judging from their howls, they were still back at the house, just a little east of central Redwood Grove.

I was on my own out here.

Alone—yet not.

Tears dried, I started up again, slow and meticulous, the buzz in my fingertips sharpening...

But the plants had stopped growing.

Like Kira, it seemed the magic in my veins was on the lookout, waiting for danger to reveal itself before the next explosion.

Another *snap*, still behind but more to the left this time. An owl hooted somewhere close, the sound followed by the flutter of wings. A beat later, an enormous silhouette zipped above the canopy, my winged friend getting out of here before trouble started.

Right.

Good enough for me.

I shrugged out of my backpack and tossed it aside, followed by my jacket, and then pushed my sleeves up.

"Come on, then," I barked, flexing my hands, finding a strange comfort in the tingling heat gathering in my palms. My vision sharpened, Kira poking through, and it leapt from tree to tree, stone to stone, just waiting for one of those pale, dead jerks to show his face again.

Vampires were predators—and Redwood Grove, with its abundance of humans and wild game, was the perfect hunting ground.

Of course they wouldn't leave for good.

Another *snap*, narrowing my search to a few old maples to my immediate right.

"Show your *face*! I'm not scared of you," I shouted, trembling with the effort it took to keep Kira contained. Meanwhile, about two dozen daisies soared from the frost-hardened ground.

Which was… kind of useless.

I snarled as the wind shifted, preparing for their cold, iron scent to wash over me.

But I was struck by something else.

Something so familiar that it made my knees buckle. Dirt and moss and forest. Wilderness. Blood from a recent kill. *Fur.*

I sucked in a harsh breath, shock coursing my veins, and Kira whined—

A wolf face poked around a nearby maple.

I recognized her right away.

Mama.

She had aged a decade since I'd last seen her, her yellow eyes cloudy, her muzzle sunken, her fur patchy.

But there she was—the wolf who had found me in the forest, abandoned and wailing and so, so lost.

The wolf who, like her mate, had outlived the life span of wild wolves.

The internet told me that.

Wolves had *maybe* fifteen years, but she was pushing twenty.

I blinked back at her, stunned. She limped out from behind the tree, revealing herself, her body frail, her head cocked.

Kira lost it, wailing and screeching and baying for her.

I crashed to my knees with a sob, tears watering the field of flowers around me.

With a low whine, my alpha hobbled forward, and a beat later, her mate followed. He had also seen better days, aged years in just a few months. Tails tentatively wagging, they clambered over the rocky terrain with some difficulty, and I folded over, clutching at my chest, *aching* for them when the rest of the pack made their way out too.

They all slowed, however, when Mama stopped. She eyed me warily, the grey in her pupils a sign that she couldn't see as well as she used to. Shivering, I wiped my face dry and held out my hand for her to scent me better. Kira settled somewhat, but she vibrated with the effort it took to be patient, to let my *real* mama approach in her own time.

She padded forward, then stopped to stretch for me, sniffing my fingertips from a distance.

"I'm sorry I went away," I croaked. We rarely interacted like this, wolf and woman, but she had licked my tears dry enough over the last eighteen years to *know* me. Was she upset I left? Or did she understand, somehow, that my time had finally come to start a pack of my own?

Mama sniffed hesitantly, then retreated. Sniffed and retreated, stretching as far as her long, lean legs would allow each time.

And I waited.

Kira held her breath.

Please remember me.

Finally, her bushy grey tail started to wag again. Slow at first, then faster, recognition sparking in her cloudy eyes, and she limp-bounced toward me with a cry. Gasping, I lunged for her too, desperate to hug her, hold on, and never let go. Instead, I let her lick my face and inside my mouth, nose around my neck and in my hair, learning about this new me, where I had been all this time, through her strong sense of smell.

Since Mama said it was okay, the whole pack followed. Papa whined and snorted and slammed into me, his eagerness to get just a little of my attention all too familiar—exactly the same moves I'd pulled as a pup, just the three of us against the wilderness alone.

Soon, the yearlings squished in to greet me, my field of wildflowers trampled, thorns be damned, the whole pack whimpering and barking, peeing and scent-marking, turning their heightened emotions onto each other.

In this form, even wild wolves were huge, which made the greeting rough and a little dangerous—if I were human. But I took every jostle, every accidental snap of teeth, every growl and rumble and claw swipe with a smile, happy tears streaming down my cheeks.

It soon became obvious that the pack had a new mating alpha pair, one of the stronger greyish-white females, just a pup four summers ago, finding herself a mate from a different pack at some point in the last month and a half. The others submitted to them, tails tucked, ears flush—even Mama and Papa. But they didn't demand the same obedience from me. Didn't pull rank. Didn't try to force my submission.

Because I was an alpha too.

And even if shifters and wolves were *different*, they must have sensed it.

Kira burst free the second I let my guard down. She tore through my clothes and sent my old pack scattering, some even disappearing into the trees. Once I shook off the tattered fabric and kicked aside my boots, they swarmed, slamming into Kira's massive body, the pups from this past spring keening for attention, *this* version of me way more recognizable.

They were so big now.

Plump and well-fed, Redwood Grove beyond kind.

Finally on four paws, I got in on the play. I wrestled with my kin, nuzzled my wolf parents—more parent to me than Reed and Nikki, and definitely more deserving of the title than the *actual* alpha and she-wolf shifters who created me. I greeted the new alphas cordially at first, until we all remembered that the female had been raised by my side. Then it was business as usual, playing, wrestling, bouncing around the trees.

Eventually, we all ended up in a dogpile, spent and sleepy, wolves scattered around the valley clearing that I'd accidentally overwhelmed with greenery. Sandwiched between my dozing wolf parents, the pair dwarfed beside me, I snuggled in, belly to the forest floor, limbs stretched way out in the front and back, muzzle nestled between my front legs. A long, luxurious sigh roused a pair of nearby puppies, and they went back to play-wrestling, boxing each other with their paws, nipping at ears, snapping their sharp little teeth without ever actually biting.

It felt so *good* to be home.

And yet...

Something was missing.

I couldn't feel them—any of them. No shared emotions. No *feelings*. No pain, no pleasure, no hunger. The connection between bonded shifters ran so much deeper, and as I scanned the subdued wolf pack, everyone clumped together and happy, I knew I couldn't do it again.

Couldn't go back to this—to feeling so *separate* from my loved ones.

Snuggled between Mama and Papa, the pair so much older now, weak and frail, like a waning moon...

I ought to be with *my* mates. These two had had each other for way longer than wild wolves usually did. They had a lifetime of togetherness, memories and love and pups.

"Why me? How did you... choose me?"

"I knew from the moment you were conceived."

"Uh, what?"

"The apples started to grow again."

Was it all because of me?

Had I been *more* than a shifter all my life?

And when I left, they aged—turned grey and white along the snout. On the decline.

I whimpered, nosing into Mama's thinning coat, and closed my eyes.

Being here with them now, sleeping and snuggling like we used to, reminded me of how it felt to be with a pack.

And I had my own pack now.

I *wasn't* a wolf, as much as I loved them.

Maybe I wasn't *just* a shifter anymore either, but I belonged with my mates.

Mama and Papa did everything together. He roamed sometimes, but we always expected him to crest the horizon within a few days after scent-marking our territory.

Lucian was Papa.

Soren had the energy and spirit and earnestness of the yearlings, of every new spring litter.

Ewan was the invisible backbone, the strength, the nose-to-the-grind spirit that kept the pack afloat in a human world.

And I...

I made the apples grow.

I made flowers bloom.

I would start a bloodline, a legacy, and make Redwood Grove *ours*.

I have to go back.

This... had been a mistake.

What I was looking for, what I *needed*, wasn't in Hampton.

It was behind me, with them.

This power was still dangerous, unpredictable, and wild as nature herself, but once the secret disappeared, we could figure it out together.

As a pack.

As fated mates.

As a real *family*.

How could I ever turn my back on them?

Fear didn't get to rule my life anymore.

Not now, not ever again.

Careful not to jostle anyone too much, I slowly stood and stretched, toes splayed, butt way up and tail curled. As soon as I'd had my fill, I shook out my fur, then stepped over Mama and padded back toward my territory. No goodbyes. Wolves didn't *do* goodbye.

Halfway up the rocky hillside, however, my ears twitched, clued in to the sounds at my back.

They... followed me.

The entire pack, right at my heels. Alphas at the front, then the yearlings and the pups. Mama and Papa at the rear, slow but steady as they scaled the rough forest terrain, made tougher and less walkable by my burst of raw goddess power earlier.

I waited for them to catch up, the rest of the pack scattered around me, then carried on, leading my family back into my territory. As soon as we crossed the border, I breathed easier again, Lucian's scent ripening, a few tree trunks neatly clawed by Ewan, Soren's burrowing in the dirt deep enough to make trenches. I nosed at the marks, pointing them out to my old pack's alphas, soundless, making direct eye contact with each one.

Look.

Mine.

The pair sniffed and rubbed their scent glands here and there, the male urinating on a few bushes.

They weren't shifters, but they were pack.

And if they stayed, I knew, deep in my heart, that they would defend this territory too.

Weaving through the western woods, I kept an eye out for a good spot for them to settle. Lucian's cabin made the most sense: tucked away from civilization, no humans dared hike the terrain. No bear dens. No nosy foxes. No snakes. No danger around, his alpha presence warding them all away.

Halfway there, that ivy-covered log cabin soaring in the distance, a howl split the night again.

But not a howl I recognized.

I stilled, ears up, every muscle tensed.

The alphas paused too, flanked by me on either side.

A second howl joined the first.

Another stranger.

Then a third.

A fourth.

A fifth, sixth, and seventh.

Head tipped and senses straining, I clocked their location.

East.

My nostrils flared. My claws gritted into the forest floor.

Hawthorne pack.

Snarling, I charged into the night—then lilted hard into a birch when *agony* ripped through my side. A sharp, fiery sting sliced from my shoulder to my left hind leg, so powerful, so *real*, that it took my breath away.

Only a quick glance back confirmed the pain wasn't mine.

It belonged to a mate.

I whimpered, stuck shuffling until the pain lessened. More howls erupted after the last song tapered off, new voices—so many voices.

Another burst of pain, this time across my belly. Sharp and messy like barbed wire.

I zeroed in on this new song, snarling, flashing my teeth.

Ahead, the forest came back to life. Ivy and vines and flowers, leaves unfurling on barren branches. The *power* that usually buzzed in my fingertips hummed now in my chest, Kira's strength *there*— her heart. Her spirit. Her *soul*.

"She's a part of you. She's you, Lyssa."

I sprinted into the shadows, headed east without delay, several of my old pack at my heels.

Determined to punish whoever was hurting one of my mates.

Make *them* hurt just like he did.

Make them suffer.

Make them remember once and for all…

Redwood Grove was spoken for, and to challenge us… was to challenge *death*.

19

LYSSA

I found them in the same clearing as last time, right along our eastern border.

But not just four wolves testing our defenses, tentative and uncertain and probably young.

No, twenty at least—full-grown men *and* wolves, some shifted on four legs, others brooding and naked on two. They didn't bother to hide downwind, to mask their scents billowing into our territory, but why would they? Those howls, their violent pack song, had summoned me here.

This wasn't a secret.

I skittered to a halt, claws gritting into the frostbitten ground, pain slicing across my chest, over my belly, around my neck. My old packmates had already peeled away, bolting back to the western woods when we first smelled the chaotic mishmash of rival scents.

Not that I blamed them.

This was more than they could handle.

This wasn't some lone wolf tiptoeing around looking for a mate or to scavenge from our kill.

This was an army of shifters, big as bears when they turned.

And they had brought their alpha this time.

An icy calm slithered through me when I met his eyes, this huge man at the front of the group. His pack loitered behind him, some snickering, others watching on, assessing me from top to bottom. Tall as Soren. *Almost* as broad as Lucian. Salt-and-pepper hair, short and stylish like Ewan, and some rough facial stubble. Tattoos snaked up and down both arms, across his chest, religious symbols Nikki and Reed would have loved and hated, appreciative of the meaning but not the medium.

At his feet...

My mate.

Lucian, kneeling, naked and in chains.

Silver.

I smelled it in the air, the scent cold like those vampires, but it was the seared flesh that stood head and shoulders above that.

The metal sizzled into Lucian's skin, draped around his neck, his wrists, his abdomen, blood weeping down his torso and painting his thighs. I swallowed hard, muffling the whine, then stood taller, hackles up, posture confident.

Not scared.

I stared the alpha dead in the eye, his a startling neon green, practically glowing in the darkness. Moonlight spilled through the bare canopy, a spotlight on the unfolding horror. He quirked an eyebrow, daring me to attack.

I held my ground and ignored Lucian's growls, his grunts, his barely contained whimpers at the way his skin hissed and oozed and blistered beneath the silver restraints.

I'm not afraid of you.

"Hello, little alpha." The male tipped his head side to side, appraising me with a sharper scrutiny than the rest of his pack. Behind him, wolves snorted and huffed, pawing at the ground, while the Hawthorne shifters in human form crossed their arms— tried to make their muscles bulge. They all paled next to Lucian.

Lucian in pain.

Lucian *suffering.*

Lucian terrified, his fear slicing through my belly sharp as any knife—

No.

I bared my canines and focused on the alpha. Losing myself in my mate, distracted by his agony, was exactly what they wanted.

"I was hoping you'd get here first," the Hawthorne alpha admitted, his voice low and tinged with a smoker's rasp, cigarette smoke on his breath.

"Lyssa, get—" Lucian erupted in a fit of coughing and hacking and wheezing. He folded into the silver with a muffled snarl and heaved a mouthful of blood, then straightened—with *such* difficulty, the weight of those chains tearing through me too—and flashed his teeth. "Get the *fuck* out of here."

The alpha jerked my mate's restraints, burying the silver deeper into Lucian's flesh, and I only then realized he was wearing a black leather glove on that one hand—and clenched a gun in the other. How had that escaped me?

"Let the girl talk, *boy,*" he snarled. Another blunt tug had the silver coiling tighter around Lucian's neck, unleashing a fresh wave of steaming red over his shoulders. I gulped down yet another whine, rage nudging aside the terror in my bones, *fury* thawing the ice in my veins.

How dare they come into *our* territory...

Torture one of *our* alphas...

Make demands and orders and *smile* like this was *funny?*

Idunn's power bloomed in my chest, soft and subtle this time.

Just a reminder that it was there.

Unable to articulate *my* authority on this land in Kira's form, I shifted back.

"L-Lyssa," Lucian rasped, arms limp and pale hands curled over the forest floor. "*Go.*"

I ignored him completely.

Of course he would tell me to leave.

Abandon him to his fate.

Save myself while they ripped him apart.

Not happening.

"You're prettier than I expected," the Hawthorne alpha drawled, that unnaturally bright green gaze sweeping my figure slowly as steam spiraled all around me. "Shame Lady Fate paired you with three failures."

"What do you want?" A few of the sniveling chuckles died. Eyebrows lifted on the men behind him, and the alpha stood straighter—like none of them expected my calm, assertive tone.

Real alphas were exactly this.

We weren't the fire in our blood—not until we gave our enemies the chance to flee, to scamper into the night before we *ended* them.

Looping the excess silver links around his gloved hand, this naked alpha gestured to our surroundings with the tip of his gun.

Handgun.

Smaller than you'd expect for a man his size.

And that was about the extent of my gun knowledge: handgun or shotgun. One was a little cleaner than the other. One filled you with neat holes—the other split your chest wide open.

"My wants are simple." He lazily pointed the gun at Lucian's temple, and my heart skipped a beat. "I just want a piece of the pie, sweetheart."

Land. Territory. Money. *Possession.*

Of course.

Disgust dribbled through me with his next leer of my naked body, Lucian snarling at his feet. Kira, meanwhile, remained silent. Still. Calculating every risk, every reward, of every option—totally on my side. Our hearts beat as one. Now wasn't the time to split the difference; we had to *trust* each other.

My words were hers. Her strength was mine. Our resilience came from each other.

"No." No discussion. No snarky pet names. No clever back-and-forth. I wasn't here for a game of wits. No negotiation. *Get out.*

The Hawthorne alpha ripped Lucian to the ground, the silver

down to bone at his ribs, the air thick with blood and burnt skin. Again, the silver touched me through our bond, caressed me like a fiery ghost. Behind him, wolves licked their lips and men eyed the red pools around Lucian's crumpled figure, scenting a wounded predator and ready to make the killing blow.

I held strong on the outside.

Dying on the inside for my mate.

"You seem to forget, *Lyssa*," the alpha sneered before kneeing Lucian's face, bone *crunching*, nose breaking, "that I have all the leverage here."

"Your vampires weren't leverage enough?"

It was just a working theory that those bloodsuckers came from the Hawthorne territory, sent in to disrupt our pack's growth, but from the way this alpha's face twisted in disgust, *warped* with rage, his pack twitching and flinching and clearing their throats awkwardly—that theory hadn't exactly panned out.

"What the *fuck* did you just say?" Another blow to Lucian's face, this time with the butt end of the gun. Pain flared in my cheek, and I bit the fleshy insides, fighting it, whimpers caught in my throat. "You think I deal with filthy fucking *leeches*?" His wrath spread like wildfire, the shifters behind him suddenly furious, hackles up and an army of bright wolf eyes blazing in the darkness. "Watch your tongue, pup."

All I wanted to do was fall to my knees and crawl to Lucian. Peel that horrible silver off and cradle him in my lap while he healed. Kiss the pain away.

I held my ground instead, battling back tears, shoving down a lifetime of my own pain and suffering—drawing on it instead.

Power hummed in my fingertips.

"Look, you're not getting so much as a blade of grass from this territory," I said frankly. I kept my inflection minimal, giving nothing away, like we were making small talk at a crosswalk before the light turned green. "So, let him go and leave—before things take a turn."

The alpha glowered at me for a beat, eyes narrowing, narrowing,

narrowing, *clenching* shut with laughter. Great hooting howls echoed through the clearing from him *and* his pack, and I folded my arms, hating the way my already stiff nipples pebbled even tighter.

"You smell like honey and luxury, she-wolf," he sneered with another dismissive once-over. "I bet you've never tasted *blood* before."

Fine.

Let him think that.

I lifted an eyebrow, daring him to underestimate me.

I'd killed bigger, smellier, fouler beasts than him before—all by myself, thank you very much.

We squared off for ages, each waiting for the other to break first. The temperature continued its nightly plunge, our breaths fogging, the Hawthorne pack getting antsy.

Lucian bleeding everywhere.

Suffering.

Surviving.

"Counteroffer." He blinked first, gaze landing on my breasts. "Mate with a *real* alpha in exchange for your mate's safe—"

My snarl cut him off, contempt overwhelming the forced calm. Even Kira bared her teeth, the thought of another *male* touching us, rutting into us, biting us and spilling his seed—

I'd rather die.

His laughter lacked humor this time, cold and cruel, the males behind him smirking, his dick hard.

"Fine. So be it."

"Lyssa," Lucian bellowed, seeming to muster the last of his strength to shout at me, "run *now!*"

The Hawthorne alpha lifted his gun—and fired four shots, *bam, bam, bam, bam*, into my chest.

It happened so fast. Too fast. So much—*agony*. Kira yelped over and over and over again. I collapsed and squealed and arched on the ground, pain beyond any I'd ever experienced ripping me apart.

"Silver bullets." Vaguely, over Lucian's roars and the pack's laughter, I heard the Hawthorne alpha call out to me. "Heal from that, bitch."

Hellfire blazed in my chest, the scent of sizzling flesh so much closer now. Eyes wide, mouth locked in a silent scream, I twisted down for a look. Four clean wounds—oozing, my blood darker than usual.

And glittery like Gull River.

My ears filled with cotton, slowly blotting out the chaos. Lucian's pain paled compared to my own, and every breath became a struggle, harder and harder to take. My eyelids refused to stay open. The world went fuzzy and soft—black.

And then it was just me and the well.

No Hawthorne pack. No *crack* of gunfire. No Lucian howling.

Silence.

And *pain*. Gasping, I staggered toward the stone wall, crashing into it with a wail. This dream world, this imaginary place inside of me, shifted in and out of focus, the water twinkling like starlight, filled *right* to the top.

Hurts.

So.

Bad.

It would be easy to just collapse. Let my knees buckle like they desperately wanted—fall to the ground and close my eyes and wait for it to be over.

I gripped the stone with both hands, glaring into the water.

I should be dead.

A soft whine forced my head up. There, across the well, sat Kira —Idunn by her side. Unlike our encounters in the orchard, the dead goddess was all wispy and hollow, transparent, the sapphires stitched into her shoulder pads dull, her eyes a muted gold.

Kira huffed and snorted.

I dipped one cupped hand into the well.

My grip went slack, and my elbow folded. I buckled onto the grey stone, teeth gritted against the agony.

"Be brave, Lyssa."

Kira slunk to my side and propped me up, using her powerful body to support my hips and back.

Blinking hard, I brought the dreamscape into focus and tried again. Scooped the water—dumped it on my chest. Massaged it into the wounds, even though it set my skin on fire. Made me woozy and weak and oh, *no, don't faint.*

My wail echoed through the darkness, a strange fog creeping across this world.

"I know it hurts," Idunn whispered, her voice so very far away as I went for another scoop. "I know, little wolf." She braced against my next sob, her hands flying to her ears, then falling back to smooth over the well wall. "I'm here with you."

Trembling, panting, sweaty and sore, I washed the wounds on my chest. Cleaned the torn, blistered skin. Stuck my fingers inside and scooped out the silver bullets. Flushed the holes. Kira held me the entire time. Idunn watched and nodded and encouraged me to keep going—to *drink* when the agony dulled to a whisper.

And I did.

She had tricked me before with a drink, but this time I gulped it down greedily, dunking my face in the well and taking my fill.

When I pushed up, my arms didn't shake this time.

I could *breathe.*

Best of all, the fog had lifted.

And Idunn was gone.

Kira had stopped whimpering—

One blink and I was back in the clearing. On the ground, on my side, four crushed silver bullets there to greet me. Every shallow breath ached with the dull reminder of pain—but it got easier by the second. Kira huffed inside me, nosing around, poking me, demanding I get up and throw myself back in the ring.

Give me a second.

I needed to just… breathe.

Across the clearing, the Hawthorne pack had been whipped into a frenzy since I last saw them, wolves jumping about and snapping at each other, men hooting and shouting and pumping their fists. The alpha kept his back to me, even more religious tattoos smeared down the rigid line of his spine. He was talking—stoking the pack fire—but I couldn't make out the words. Even as the world came back to me, I struggled to be present.

Until one of the males stalked forward with a lumber saw.

Gave it to his alpha.

Who relinquished his hold on the silver chains snaked around Lucian's bloody frame. He shoved them at another gloved male—then fisted my mate's hair.

Wrenched his head back and spat at his snarling mouth.

Bared his throat.

And started to saw.

Agony ripped through my neck with every strike, and I shot up in a panic, the whole world on fire again.

"Stop! Leave him alone!"

A few of the Hawthorne wolves stilled, surprise flashing from male to male; they thought the silver had killed me.

It should have.

But I wasn't a shifter anymore. I wasn't like *them*.

And I never would be.

The alpha continued hacking through Lucian's throat, his naked body blocking me from my mate, from the gruesome *horror* happening some fifteen feet away.

I leapt to my feet with a terrified snarl. A few of the Hawthorne wolves backed away. The alpha kept sawing.

Pain and terror and heartache exploded through me, twisting and coiling and weaving into one, and I finally just let go.

"Get your hands off of him!"

It wasn't only my voice that clawed through the clearing. No, it was a dozen screams, including mine and Idunn and what Kira might have sounded like if she could talk. All pitches and volumes, demonic and angelic. I lunged forward, arms out, fingers reaching, *power* flooding from them. Tornado-strength winds slammed into the trees and lifted a few of the wolves clear off their paws. Trunks snapped. Debris spiraled. Thunder *boomed* and lightning seared the sky. Thorny vines shot from the earth and wound around legs and necks.

The Hawthorne pack bolted, all twenty-plus of them, screeching and shouting and scampering over the territory line.

I let them go.

I only had eyes for *him*.

The alpha whipped around just as my feet left the ground. I slammed into him like the bullets he fired at me, so fast, *too* fast, tackling his much bigger body, snarling and screaming and cursing him in a language that wasn't mine.

No control.

No stopping it.

The world bled red. Kira's howls faded. Idunn's whispers disappeared on the wind. It was just me and him. Fear flashed in the neon green, and he tried to swing that bloody saw over—maybe stick it in my back.

I ripped his throat clean open with my bare hands.

I didn't *need* a weapon.

I am the weapon.

I then plunged my fingers into his chest. Shredded skin and muscle and tendons. Cracked his rib cage. Dug deeper and harder, ferocious, screaming, my mate's agony turning my throat bloody.

Didn't stop until I reached his heart.

Pulled it out for this alpha to see.

Watched the light leave his eyes.

"Heal from that," I sneered in just the one voice this time, all me but more animal, more savage, "*bitch.*"

Heaving, seething, I lobbed the useless hunk of bloody muscle toward the territory line, dismissive, like tearing out a male's heart was an everyday thing. From the shadows, hunkered down beneath wind-bent trees, the Hawthorne pack watched on—and then slunk away into the darkness.

Silent.

A wave of light-headedness crashed over me, and I frantically blinked the red mist away—left instead with literal red, the alpha's blood splashed in my eyes and across my face. Up my arms and over my breasts. Between my thighs lay a male with his chest ripped open, his insides on the outside. Trembling, too *hot*, I scrambled off his body, falling, collapsing onto my elbow as the inner war drums went quiet.

A beat later, the earth took him.

My fingertips buzzed. My mind went blank—then the ground opened and swallowed this alpha wolf whole.

A gurgle dragged me out of my stupor.

Wet and strained and, *oh*, Lucian—

My mate sprawled on his side, throat slit deep, chains sizzling into his flesh. Tears streaked my cheeks as I crawled to his side, fingers clumsy and burning when I wrenched the silver off. Threw it as far as I could.

"I'm h-here, Lucian," I told him, all the calm, confident bravery from before gone. In its place: the pup abandoned in the forest. Lost. Confused. Terrified. Kneeling at his head, I hauled his limp body into my lap, then clapped both hands over the gaping neck wound, his skin ragged and frayed, his body struggling to heal itself. Snot and spit and blood and tears soaked my face, but I pushed it all down, crouching to nuzzle his sweat-slick forehead. "I'm right here w-with you."

His chest *barely* rose and fell with every hollow breath.

Blood watered the ground.

Scented the air.

Broke my heart.

Eyes shut tight, I went back to the well. No fog this time, my inner world crisp and clear and in focus. No Idunn either, just me and Kira—and then Lucian. My mate at my feet, his faint, fading heartbeat pumping all around us.

I splashed him with diamond well water. Fed it to him. Washed his body clean.

But when we snapped back to the clearing, he was still filthy. Still cold. Still *barely* with me—

"Oh, *good*." I folded over with a sob after peeking under my hands.

The wound had closed.

His chest moved with more purpose now, up and down, up and down. My fingertips buzzed almost painfully as the color trickled into his cheeks, his beard caked in dirt and blood.

The silver had left grooves in his flesh.

More scars for his collection.

No, no, no, *no*.

Weeping, I tenderly smoothed my hands over all the dips, *trying* to fix them like I did his neck, but that just set off a headache like a hundred wasp stings behind my eyes.

Kira whined softly. I ignored her.

She whimpered *louder*, her cry rattling my teeth, prompting me to look up...

Across the clearing, safe on our side of the territory line, stood Ewan and Soren.

Naked. Sweaty. Splashed with dirt and smelling of the southern wastes.

Staring at me.

Gawking at me.

Horrified.

A numb, staticky hum resonated between us—almost like our bond was so overloaded it had no idea what to make of everything. Lucian sucked down a deep breath, his eyes closed, his lips in a thin line, then groaned.

Tears squished out from behind his lids.

His consciousness, his agony, suddenly exploded through our shared connection.

I opened and closed my mouth a few times, torn between him and my other mates, looking back and forth.

"I-I'm sorry."

What else was there to say? All of this... was my fault. They were out here for *me*. They... I... If I hadn't...

I smeared the Hawthorne alpha's blood from my cheeks, weak

and drained and on the verge of collapse. For a moment, I tried to keep it together, tried to reclaim the power and control I had shown our enemies.

But under their wide, frightened eyes, I fell apart. Came undone. Sobbed hideously.

"Ewan, Soren, I…" *Please don't hate me.* "I… I'm so *sorry.*"

LOVED BY WOLVES

BLOODLINE · BOOK 3

RHEA WATSON

1

LYSSA

I jolted awake facedown in the grass.

Shoot. Must have dozed off waiting for Lucian to wake up. Groaning, I planted my hands and rolled over, then wiped the bits of green blades and dirt from my cheek, my forehead—my mouth. Ugh. Usually I came to in the orchard on my back, eyes slowly peeling open to a beautiful sunrise.

Even with them closed, something felt... off.

The air was still today.

Too still.

Too quiet.

Too—

Kira *barked*, abrupt and insistent, nothing like her usual giddy greetings when we reunited in here. My eyes snapped open, and a beat later—*crack!* I bolted upright with a cry, searching for the source, for whatever made a sound like the sky splitting and the earth opening, everything about to cave in.

Smoke tickled the back of my throat, the air dead, the leaves quiet and their branches tensed. Panic spiderwalked the nape of my neck, and I stood, stiff and unsettled, fighting to calm my thundering heart and my racing breath. Hackles up, bright blues intense and focused, Kira barely acknowledged me, her snout skyward and nostrils flared.

"What—"

"*Go*, Lyssa."

I whirled around to Idunn sprinting at us, dressed in the usual white silk gown, her deer pelt shrug clutched in a fist, the sapphires sewn onto her shoulder pads glittering with every stride.

Her eyes...

I stumbled back a few paces.

Her eyes were *pure* gold today. Not just the irises—but *everything*. No black pupil or white sclera. Full gold, ancient as the dawn, terrifying and wild and just as frightened as I suddenly felt.

Something was wrong.

"Let me help—"

"*Go*," the goddess bellowed, the ground shuddering and the trees shivering. Kira whined and slunk behind me, submissive, respecting our orchard hierarchy, but I refused to back down.

"Idunn, what is—"

Crack.

We all looked up sharply. What was usually a rosy pink, streaked with purples and blues and reds, orange and wholesome, a perpetual sunrise on the perfect summer day, now had a green tint to it.

An emerald comet blazed across the sky, straight as an arrow at first, then veering hard to the left—and plummeting straight for us. Stunned, mouth opening and closing, Kira's fear woven tightly with mine, I pointed at it like Idunn couldn't see.

Like the goddess *hadn't* already shed a few tears at the sight.

"What—"

She rounded on me with a gasp. "*Now*, Lyssa!"

And before I could say another word, more than ready to stand between her and *that*—she blasted me with a wave of starlight, bright as the sun and sharp as diamonds. It hit like a charging bull, knocking me off my feet, tearing the wind right out of me, and I plunged into hazy darkness screaming her name.

I snapped awake slumped at the end of Lucian's bed, just as I thought—but instead of gasping in a whoosh of his musky, rugged oakwood scent, it was all smoke, the lingering smells of the summer orchard clogging my nostrils. Blinking the comet's green flashes away, I pushed up with a groan, then coughed the smoky burn into Soren's sweater sleeve, still wearing it, even his cozy scent muted compared to whatever had followed me out of Idunn's afterlife.

It usually... stayed there.

The reality had dipped its toe into my inner well world, but the orchard was the orchard. It was for me and Kira and the clothes on my back.

But it had followed me here, to Lucian's dark bedroom—to me still caked in the Hawthorne alpha's dried blood, my hair crusty with it, with dirt and moss and twigs that snagged earlier on the frantic, silent run back to the house.

"What... the heck?" My voice came out raspy and thick, the weight of the day dropping like a ton of bricks. Kira whimpered, her confusion only muddying the already muddy waters, and I scratched the dried drool from the corners of my mouth.

How long had I been out?

Not long if it was still so dark outside, Lucian's bedroom windows curtainless and north-facing, his room next to mine. Small. Neat. Not much clutter, just like his cabin—everything in here had a purpose. Big bed for a big wolf, a digital clock on his nightstand telling me two o'clock had recently come and gone.

Great.

Finally, as the smoke and apple blossoms cleared from my lungs, Lucian's citrus bodywash took over and made Kira sneeze. Ewan and Soren had carried him back here, more focused on his injuries than what I had just done—to the forest, the mighty trees around that clearing bent and broken, the ground scorched, the animals long gone.

And to that alpha.

Heart ripped out and swallowed by the earth.

What a terrifying way to go.

I closed my eyes tight when I remembered his rounded neon greens full of fear and panic and outrage—then nothing. Just hollow and empty.

Dark.

Still.

Dead.

After scrubbing Lucian down in the shower, washing away the blood and the memories, we put him to bed. The others left to clean themselves up, wearing Lucian's trauma on their skin, and at some point Soren had stopped by as I stood guard at the end of this huge bed. He left me his sweater, a green zip-up hoodie that swallowed me whole.

Comforted me too.

Made me feel warm and small and cozy, safe in his scent.

Now...

Now, I wasn't sure anything or anyone could make me feel safe again.

Not if a goddess—a *dead* goddess—feared whatever that comet meant.

Groaning, I rubbed the more stubborn bits of sleep from my lashes, then crawled up the bed, careful not to jostle Lucian. While responsive and alive, my velvet-tongued mate was still way out of it, trapped in a deep healing sleep. Thick indents snaked his body in ugly trenches, the silver chains leaving strange, unnatural scars that, according to Ewan and Soren, should have healed almost instantly. Silver burned shifters. It could kill if it struck just right or poisoned you long enough, but like almost all other injuries, our bodies would recover.

Lucian's scarred.

Again.

A waxy pink line stretched across his throat, so very *there* as I tenderly sifted through his beard to check. Was this because of me? I bit my lip, hovering over him as he just lay there on his back, still as stone aside from the rise and fall of his burly chest. At the time, I hadn't considered if Idunn's powers were strong enough to heal, but if they could grow flowers and vines from nothing, *maybe* they could mend flesh, close wounds...

Even one as life-threatening as Lucian's, his throat sawed open, his skin flayed and windpipe cracked.

I'd never forget the sight.

Never.

Now, he slept peacefully, our connection quiet, his eyes occasionally flicking beneath his lids. Swallowing a flood of *feeling*, I swooped his hair to one side, desperate to cuddle into his chest and sleep the night away by his side.

Be there for him the *second* he woke up.

A pointed throat clearing startled me, stilling my hand just before I brushed my knuckles over his cheek down to his slightly parted lips. There, across the room in the doorway, were my other two mates.

Our bond blurred and unreadable, distant and fractured.

Clean, dressed, they had finally snuck up on me, soundless and silent, their scents hidden...

And they wanted answers.

Crossed arms. No smiles. No words. The pair just stared, waiting, expectant and present.

Unwilling to back down.

Shoot.

Kira whined, though my panic spiked harder and faster than hers.

Soren motioned toward the hallway with a lazy toss of his head, and I wilted a little, preferring to crawl under the covers and hide.

No getting around it.

I had no clue what they saw back there—but it was enough. I couldn't wish it away or pretend it didn't happen.

Couldn't pretend they weren't standing here now, wordlessly demanding an explanation.

Not a lie.

Not a half-truth.

Honesty.

Ugh.

After brushing a gentle kiss over Lucian's brow, I climbed off his bed and padded out of the bedroom. Ewan took the lead, marching away from my room, and headed for the stairs. I followed. Soren brought up the rear—like they thought I might, what, run? The pair felt more like prison guards than my mates as we drifted downstairs, but I shook that off and ignored the way it made Kira bristle. I mean, I hadn't exactly given them a reason to think I *wouldn't* race out the front door the first chance I got.

We ended up in the sunken seating area. Ewan and Soren settled on different couches, me with a cocked hip against the soaring windowpane to the left of the unused stone fireplace. At least here, I had something more to look at than their stern expressions, their tight jaws and clenched hands and—

Well, I hadn't looked either in the eye yet.

Couldn't bring myself to do it.

Couldn't stand to see what I knew I'd find—fear and disappointment and anger.

Nibbling my lower lip and fidgeting with my nails, I picked the blood out from under them more meticulously and thoroughly than ever before, angled toward the outdoors, to the back deck and the quiet black lake beyond. To the bare forest. To the shoreline opposite—

"Lyssa."

I stiffened, Ewan's tone strangely flat. No wrath. No affection. Nothing in between. Just... my name with no inflection or feeling.

Not good.

The backs of my eyes stung.

Not good at all.

Panic flashed through my limbs, slashing like a hailstorm, and I closed my eyes with a deep breath. Kira nosed at my insides, but her usual comforting warmth barely made a dent in the ice wall forming around me.

"Baby, just tell us what's going on." To his credit, Soren sounded more himself, this earnest wolf from pampered beginnings. He had proven himself a good tracker with me in the mountains and a stable support out in the big wide human world, always wanting to share and show and involve me in his life, always ready to make me laugh. Did he hate me now? Was he heartbroken that I'd kept this from him? I couldn't risk it—couldn't open my eyes and check. When he spoke next, he faltered, desperation wringing our bond. "Please, we're not angry. We're just... concerned."

Liar. Frustration tickled the nape of my neck, hot and scratchy and distinctly Ewan.

Not that I could really blame him for that.

He had a right to feel his feelings, whatever they were and no matter how they made *me* feel.

Sniffling, I finally managed to glance their way. This was it. This could make us or break us. Soren perched on the opposite side of the hearth, on the two-seater couch I curled up in to read the lovingly worn thriller paperbacks he had lent me around Thanksgiving. Ewan occupied the three-seater in the middle, straight-backed and brooding, staring into the dark fireplace, looking exhausted but feeling so fired up it made me desperate to *run*, the adrenaline too much.

They wanted the truth.

They were... concerned.

All these long weeks of building trust and connection, working on our understanding and communication, headed for *love*...

It all came down to this.

One conversation and I'd know if all that had been real—or just a charade, a play written by Lady Fate, one where we each said our lines and acted our role, and when it was over, it was just... over.

"I-I..." *Oh no. Don't cry. Do. Not. Cry.* They didn't need a blubbering she-wolf. My mates needed their fated, their fellow alpha, to be strong. And honest. And *real*.

So, I tried.

I struggled at first, words falling like molasses, my tongue too thick and throat too dry. Kira stayed silent throughout the tale, and I eventually started to pace, sharing all the dreams, all the conversations with Idunn, all the lessons with Rosa. Being hunted the night Ewan and I mated in that alley. The buzzing in my fingertips. The *heat* in my chest. The inferno that came over me in the clearing.

The thrill of killing the alpha—and not feeling the slightest bit guilty after.

When there was nothing left to tell, I finally stopped in front of the cold hearth, out of breath and light-headed. No more stories. No more memories. Just the here and now.

Just today.

Yesterday, technically.

"I was s-so scared you'd send me away." I went for my hair, desperate to fiddle as their wolf eyes drilled into me, unflinching and heavy, but the dried blood was too solid at this point to casually pick through. "My... *adopted* parents were humans, and they were so scared of me when I first shifted. I... They thought I was a monster and a freak and, and, I didn't want that *again*, and I didn't want to accidentally hurt anyone because you..." The room blurred with a fresh batch of tears, and I looked skyward, struggling, heartache out in the open. "You're my fated mates. You're all *mine*, and if I hurt you, or, or, or *worse*... I couldn't..." Sniffing and wiping my snotty nose on Soren's sweater again, I shook my head and tried not to sink to the floor. "I panicked, I guess."

The silence that followed was deafening.

I finally looked up, gaze darting between my mates. Kira's stiffness tightened through me, every muscle taut, every breath hitched.

Why weren't they saying anything?

I appreciated it during my storytelling, but now was the time to say something—*literally* anything.

Folded over, elbows on his knees and chin on his fists, Ewan's sunset wolf eyes burned into the coffee table, then slid to Soren. My blond mate, his eyes amber and warm, met them, and a conversation flowed back and forth that I wasn't a part of—one that didn't resonate in our pack connection.

Nothingness.

Stillness.

Quiet.

I gnawed at the insides of my cheeks and braced for an attack. It had happened before—wolves turning on loved ones and littermates, attacking for one reason or another. Kicking them out of the pack. Forcing them away from their family.

For the first time in a long time, I couldn't read either of them. Not their feelings. Not their emotions, neither through that invisible rope tying us together *or* across their faces.

Then—*fire.*

It blasted through our connection out of nowhere, so sharp and visceral that I yelped and swatted at my arms, my legs, feeling the embers on my skin.

But, no, it was just... divine. Just in the fated bond we all shared.

And I still couldn't read it. Couldn't tell if the heat was good or bad or *terrible*, but life had taught me to expect the worst.

I sucked down a ragged breath, Kira whining and pawing at me, and as soon as my hands started to shake, the windows did too. All two stories' worth of glass shivered alongside me; I couldn't control it. Couldn't stop it. Couldn't turn it off.

Soren was on me in a second. The me from before would have slashed at his face, uncertain and suspicious of sudden movements, of males sprinting into my personal space.

I let it happen tonight, let him crash into me and scoop me into a hug so tight it squeezed the air from my lungs.

The windows stopped shaking, but I still trembled against him, arms folded between us and face burrowed in his strong chest.

"You're not a monster, baby," he whispered roughly into my hair, dried blood and all. "You're our fated mate—and that's that. You don't have to carry this alone anymore. None of us do."

Kira howled, and I went limp against him, *relief* coursing like the first thaw of springtime rapids, breaking through the ice and *pounding* downstream.

"Really?"

But I didn't believe it. Not completely. No one was this selfless, even if some divine being paired us up forever. It... It couldn't be *real*.

Rosewood washed over me as Soren nodded, and Ewan suddenly threaded his arms around my waist. Soren went high, and he went low, both of them steadying me, bracing me, fighting off the trembles and shivers so that when I sagged, weak and exhausted and on the verge of harder, messier tears, I didn't fall.

"Don't leave, blue eyes," Ewan rasped, sounding just as harsh and strained as he'd looked this whole time. But the *fire*. My black-haired mate, who smelled like rosewood and security, was an inferno at my back, encircling me and keeping all the dangers of the world at bay. "Please, don't go."

My face crumpled, warping into what the internet dubbed an ugly cry.

"I-I won't. I p-promise, promise, *promise*."

Was this it—unconditional acceptance?

You know, the thing parents were supposed to give their child?

I had two sets who failed to live up to it, the first betraying each other, the second throwing me to the wolves.

But this...

The warmth and comfort and *strength* flowing between us...

It felt real.

I still didn't trust it, not completely, but, *ugh*, I really wished I could.

And I wished Lucian were here to throw his massive arms around all of us, my mountain man the true embodiment of *alpha*.

For so long, I fought the breakdown, especially in front of my mates. Tears signaled weakness, and weakness in the forest meant you were *done*, but here I wailed into Soren's chest and reached back to fist Ewan's shirt. I groped at them just as hard as they held me, and I let it all out, all the silent suffering, the weight of this secret, the aches and pains of hiding it from them had left on my soul.

The storm took its time to move on, really battering down from all sides—but we held firm. *They* held firm. My mates didn't let go, not even a little, until my sobs turned to hiccups, then shallow shudders, then calm, even breaths. When it eventually stopped, I still sagged between them, hit with fatigue brutal enough that it took real effort to lift my swollen lids and keep them open.

But as Soren cradled my face in both hands, tipping my head up with a smile so warm and soft and gooey that I couldn't look away if I tried, everything got just a little easier.

"You're stuck with us," he insisted, his grin turning playful as he stroked my tear-soaked cheeks, "and if you run again, you'll be hunted, caught, and—"

I kissed him before he could get the last word out. *Fucked.* That was how our game worked, a promise and pact formed between us the first time we mated, but even now, after being with them *both* on Halloween, my embarrassment couldn't stand hearing it out loud.

As Soren and I slowly eased apart, lost in each other's eyes, Ewan retreated. I glanced back to find him pacing, head bowed, brow knit, hands on his hips.

"We need outside help with this."

My knees nearly buckled, but I found the strength—somewhere, in my limited reserves—to stand taller and growl. *Please, no.* While my mates might accept me, flaws and all, the rest of the world wasn't so kind.

Unless they had changed overnight, the rest of the world *hated* monsters.

"What you did in the woods," Ewan pressed when he caught me shaking my head, "was powerful, and if you're struggling—" He spoke up when I tried to talk over him. "—then I think you need *more* than Rosa."

"But—"

"It's time to call in the cavalry, blue eyes." He knuckled me under the chin in passing, followed by a playful tap of my nose. "For all our sakes."

He was right, of course.

I had left Redwood Grove to find someone who could handle my brand of unstable ancient power—but that was just me, by myself, forging my own path. Running off to Hampton alone meant my mates were out of the picture. No one would associate us if something went horribly wrong.

Now...

Now we were bringing *strangers* into our home and my mess.

It... made sense. Maybe. I blinked back at him, at the steadfast glow in his sunset wolf eyes. But... what the *heck* was a cavalry?

Don't run. Don't run. Don't run away again. Don't. Don't do it. It's just a word. Don't run. Just ask him.

"Uh, okay, so..." I tugged at Soren's too-big sweater sleeves, hiding my hands—these unpredictable *weapons*—and crossing my arms. "Sure, but is a cavalry a... doctor?" My cheeks warmed when I looked between them again, knowing that I was out of the loop and way behind and grossly undereducated compared to them. Not an ounce of judgment trickled through our bond. No arched eyebrows or scoffs or eye rolls. Still, the not-knowing part made me feel really, really small. "Or is it a, uh—is it a priest? Because, you know, Idunn isn't a demon or anything—"

"No, blue eyes, no. You don't need a doctor or a priest." Ewan swept in and tucked me under his arm, bundling me to his side and nibbling a kiss onto my temple with a soft sigh. "No, I think, for now, the cavalry is going to have to be... Ethan Perry."

2

EWAN

Today was the day I realized silence could take many forms—and all at the same fucking time. Shock. Fear. Anger. Stiff and tense and uncertain. It all came crashing down around the dining table as soon as I finished sharing Lyssa's story with the Perrys, who thought they were coming over for an impromptu Thursday brunch.

Instead, my warlock friend had just learned that not only was my fated mate harboring the powers of a dead goddess in her fingertips, but that his wife had kept it from him for almost a month. Seated at the head of the table, I straightened my cutlery on either side of my still-full plate, scrambled eggs cold and pancakes fat with all the gloopy syrup they had absorbed. Bacon untouched. Coffee lukewarm. Toast hard and unpalatable. The others had eaten their fair share of Soren's breakfast spread, but I just didn't have an appetite.

To my left with their backs to the windows, Ethan and Rosa digested the news in stony silence, my tale interrupted occasionally by Lyssa to fill in missing details or correct facts I'd misinterpreted earlier. My fated sat at my right, Soren beside her, his arm over the back of her chair and his meal almost as untouched as mine.

Wolves rarely brought outsiders into pack business, but this—after what Lyssa did in the woods—was way above our pay grade. Rosa was lovely and talented, sure, but two magical brains were better than one; Ethan should have been on this from the start.

We *all* should have been involved from the very beginning, from the first tingle of magic in Lyssa's fingertips. The gold *should* have been a giant warning sign that Gull River had unleashed something deeper in our girl, something ancient and primal and really fucking dangerous.

I should have realized...

But it was done.

Time to deal with it and move forward

After all, a part of me understood all too well the need to lie to protect yourself. Hell, Quinn wolves were born with it in our DNA —the manipulative gene, the one that made us lie, cheat, steal, and kill to get what we wanted, when we wanted, and at the least risk to ourselves. Fear made everyone do stupid things. Terrible things. Bullshit things. Things you wished you could take back in a heartbeat. I'd been there myself way too many times since we found our fated mate in the forest. Said things I wished I could take back. Done things that still gave me heartburn, my inner wolf perpetually unimpressed with the way dumbass human emotion drove my actions.

As much as it hurt that she had left, that she hoarded secrets, that she was so terrified she would maim or murder one of us by accident—Lyssa got a pass.

We all fucked up now and again.

Sometimes those fuckups were bigger than others, but if she could forgive me for screaming about bloodlines and mating when I was really just horrified at the thought of losing her... I'd get over this.

Not today, but soon.

Besides, there were way more pressing issues to deal with now than my *feelings*.

After a quick appraisal of Ethan—still mulling everything over, eyes down, dirty-blond brows furrowed, mouth thin—I looked to my fellow alpha. We hadn't dissected our reactions to Lyssa's news yet, but the bond put us on the same page.

We chose *her* over what others might consider a betrayal.

We preferred answers—honest, truthful, thorough explanations for what the *fuck* she had done over Lucian's dying body, with the wind and the lightning and the scorched earth and the fucking *heart* —to accusations.

Ever since we sat down for brunch, something was different about him. While Soren wasn't exactly best pals with Ethan, normally he was polite and friendly, prone to babbling when things got awkward. Today, he was none of those things. Uncharacteristically silent, he stood guard at our mate's side—our mate who could level this whole house, probably, with a snap of her fingers, but never mind. As I shared our current shitshow with Ethan, Soren got right in her personal space, arm slung over her chair, and stared down the warlock with his wolf eyes right out in the open, issuing an amber challenge.

Daring him to lash out.

Tense, quiet, highly alert, Soren Acker adopted some of Lucian's more severe traits for brunch.

And neither I nor my inner wolf had felt the urge to attack him yet.

Apparently we both liked this super-serious, protective, I-will-fuck-your-shit-up-if-you-touch-her side to him. It whumped through our pack bond, this guardian trait I'd never seen in Soren before, and it should have woken Lucian from his healing sleep. After all, it told the pack there was potential danger here—even when there was none, Ethan and Rosa two of the safest magical folk I'd ever met, baby Aster asleep in her bassinet on the couch.

Unfortunately, Lucian hadn't shown his face yet, dead to the world upstairs, recovering from what could have been a massacre, a mutilation and a declaration of war between neighboring packs.

Then our mate went and ripped the Hawthorne alpha's heart out in front of all his tweaker underlings.

Yeah, probably not going to be dealing with *those* sadistic assholes for a while.

Without their alpha, the east would be in chaos, wolves battling to steal his spot. He had no pups, no heirs that I knew of, no established bloodline. By the time the bloodshed settled, our territory would be fucking impenetrable.

But, you know, one catastrophe at a time.

Crunch, crunch, crunch, crunch.

All these different silent energies around the table—punctuated by my mate nervously chomping on bacon. She gobbled up each crispy slice like a rabbit working her way through a big piece of romaine, one nibble at a time, the constant crackle and crunch making my inner wolf antsy. Sighing softly, I reached around the helm of the table for her thigh, latching on and giving it a little squeeze. Lyssa flinched, and Soren sat straighter, both their gazes snapping my way. My brows shot up as she shoved the last bit of bacon into her mouth, chewing frantically, and then went for the next slice on her plate.

Honestly, stress-eating bacon—only a wolf.

And to me, that was what she was: my fated mate, *my* she-wolf, my world. It didn't matter that she had magic in her heart and power in her fingertips; she was still Lyssa.

Still nervous. Still hungry for acceptance and family and *pack*. Her eyes widened as she crammed the next whole piece in her mouth, and, difficult as it was when my nerves were at a fucking twelve, I willed some soothing energy into our bond. She slouched into her chair, into Soren's steely embrace around her shoulders, and chewed slower.

Progress.

Some shuffling at the other side of the table drew me away, and I watched Ethan go for his coffee mug, consider it, then down the rest in one slurpy gulp. He set it aside with a frown, just another bit of porcelain in a sea of platters and breadbaskets and cereal boxes.

"So, this is… news," he said slowly, every word measured. The warlock then squinted across the table at Lyssa, pinning her with a long, unreadable look that made my inner wolf growl low, his hackles up for the first time in Ethan's presence. The alertness pounding through our pack bond lessened only slightly when he directed his attention to me. "I really wish you had told me sooner."

Before I could reason that I had only found out literally a few hours ago, low on sleep and patience, Ethan turned on his wife.

And Rosa flinched.

Lyssa lurched forward, bacon forgotten, and stared down the pair like a mother she-wolf ending a squabble between two pups with just a *look*. Neither witch nor warlock noticed, and I didn't sense much aggression coming from him, but...

"Well, she just knows better than to dress like a whore."

But the disappointed scowl he shot her triggered a memory of that *comment* from Halloween, and my inner wolf growled again while my stomach knotted, distress sizzling between the three shifters at this table.

What—the fuck?

Unaware of the swirling invisible turmoil, Ethan cleared his throat and faced me. "Can we talk in private?"

"This is a *pack* matter," Soren said roughly, his usually bouncy, perky, annoying as fuck wolf *right* there, seconds from forcing a shift if the temperature spiking around us like a burst of humidity suggested anything.

Only this wasn't the wolf I knew, even if his eyes were the same. No, this was the dark creature who had fucked our mate like he owned her at the Chalet—and I actually really liked him. When all this started, the thought of connecting with another possessive, dominant male made me want to blow my brains out. But that night, after I got over his presence and accepted that she wanted us *both* there, I found a kindred spirit.

And if that meant we could share her again in the future without trying to kill each other, great. Extinguishing inter-pack conflict had been the goal from the fucking jump.

Soren flashed his teeth when he next spoke, but only after

waiting for Ethan to show him the courtesy of some brief eye contact. "Whatever you say to Ewan can be said to us."

Like he had a death wish—or, more likely, didn't understand the dynamics of a pack with multiple alphas—Ethan glanced at me for confirmation. Soren let out a warning rumble, which had Lyssa reaching back to stroke his arm still strewn protectively over her chair. Sighing again, I just nodded and made a note to remind him about our lack of hierarchy later.

"Okay, so..." Ethan took a moment to organize his cleared plate, fork and knife on top, and then nudged it aside. In its place sat his threaded hands, long, bony fingers twined, which he tapped on the table with a huff. "If what you're saying is true, and the Norse goddess Idunn gave you her gifts from the afterlife, this is..." He took a beat, frowning, and then shook his head. "Guys, it's *chaotic* magic. Powerful and wild as nature herself—and we need to tread cautiously."

While Rosa was suddenly *very* fascinated with her hands, head ducked and magical aura oddly muted, Ethan twisted around to check on his pup. From the sound of her breath, none of our pack nonsense had roused little Aster. Lyssa, meanwhile, appeared to be hanging on Ethan's every word.

Wild and powerful. Chaotic.

Fuck.

What we'd seen her do so far—that ticked all the boxes.

When he faced the table again, Ethan speared a hand through his hair, then leaned forward and whispered, "We should go to Hampton today." Gaze darting between Soren, Lyssa, and me, he seemed to have gone conspiratorial and quiet for our benefit. "I know several warlocks who could consult on this, and we would need to evaluate her." Then, without warning, he shot up. "Right now, preferably before something else—"

Soren launched out of his chair so hard it rocketed backward and crashed to the ground.

For fucking real though, if this warlock was going to have a more integral role in our pack, he needed to learn not to make any sudden moves in front of predators.

Because suddenly even I was on my feet. Up and at the corner of the table, hovering in Lyssa's bubble, same as Soren, like both of us were ready to take down a viable threat to our mate. My inner wolf seethed, my vision sharpening as he pawed at me, desperate to break free and show Ethan *exactly* what he thought about an outsider whisking Lyssa away to the regional heart of witchfolk.

With teeth and claws and savagery.

I braced on the table, battling the inner monster, *fighting* to maintain control—because I could fucking handle things with words, not violence.

This time, anyway, and only for Ethan.

Who seemed to have realized his mistake, slowly sinking into the chair, submissively dropping his eyes and raising his hands.

"Sorry, no, no, no one would *hurt* her—"

"I'm not leaving." Soren and I glanced at Lyssa, still seated, still frowning at a subdued Rosa. Our she-wolf mate cocked her head to the side, reminiscent of her wilder side when she heard something strange on the trail. She then licked her lips and refocused on Ethan, strangely calm after her prickly anxiety had risen like floodwaters through our bond in the last twenty minutes. Now, she sounded and felt certain, grounded, hopefully bolstered by our unflinching support. "I'm not going anywhere while Lucian is recovering. No. Not leaving the territory."

Soren's amber gaze darted to mine, and fire licked through the pack bond, an intense *want* humming between all of us at the sound of our mate staking a claim on her land, her mate. She called the shots in her life—and it was actually pretty fucking *hot*.

"Fair enough..." As Ethan lowered those wide, weaponless hands, a thought occurred to me out of the blue: he could cast without a wand. From what I understood of warlock magic, the wand only channeled their power—made it neater. If he had wanted to subdue the situation, he could have.

He could have hurt us.

Stunned us.

Set us on fucking fire.

That thought had never come to mind before—but it made my inner wolf bare his teeth, lips curled and snarls plentiful.

"In the meantime," the warlock continued, watching warily as Soren and I settled, "let's just talk." Crossed arms resting on the table, he zeroed in on Lyssa. "Can you make plant material grow from, uh, scratch, or do you need a seed of some kind?"

My mate glanced between Soren and me, then shrugged. "I don't know. I can't tell if I'm reviving something that's already there, or if I'm..."

"If you're conjuring something new?" Ethan finished for her with an arch of his brow. She nodded frantically, and he took another thoughtful beat before recentering on her, oozing *predator* as he looked her over. "What's the biggest thing you've grown so far?"

My hands curled into fists under the table. His tone was soft and pliant, but his body language, his expression, suggested this... excited him? Down the table, Soren *cracked* something noisily, either his knuckles or his neck or jaw or *something*, and Ethan blinked hard, waiting on Lyssa, then seemed to compose himself better.

Is this a mistake?

"I made ivy cover Lucian's cabin," my mate admitted, "and it doubled in size. Lots of wildflowers once, and then the, uh, wind stuff from last night was... new."

To her credit, Lyssa appeared fine with this line of questioning.

But what did she know about *this* kind of shark?

That was *my* area of expertise, and as much as I enjoyed Ethan, he was one of them. Friendly, unassuming, good-natured, and slow to anger—he was still a shrewd businessman. An investor with a Midas touch, same as me, and a warlock determined to squeeze a profit and maintain the luxury lifestyle he had built for his girls in Redwood Grove.

Was that happening here and now?

Was he—

I closed my eyes and sucked down a deep breath, steadying the rapidly spiraling thought pattern before it got out of control. *No.* Ethan Perry was a good man and a friend. He was here to *help*. This paranoia and suspicion—all fueled by my inner wolf's general distrust of anyone outside our inner circle and Soren's new protectiveness clanging obnoxiously through our bond.

"Is there any chance you can show me?" Ethan moved the last slices from the pumpernickel loaf to the demolished smoked-salmon platter, then cleared a space in front of Lyssa for the empty basket and tapped the wicker rim. "Make something grow? I just need to gauge if what you have is more like witch magic, or—"

"Rosa said it's like fae magic, right?" My mate redirected all eyes to Rosa with a tentative smile and a prompting bob of her head. The witch did nothing, said nothing, her cheeks nearly as red as her mane, loose and open today like a fiery halo. Ethan went for her hand under the table—presumably, I couldn't see—and that milked a nod out of her.

Concern went off from Lyssa's end of the pack bond like a bomb, which only further upset my inner wolf and made it damn near *impossible* to concentrate on anything else. *Mate in trouble. Mate need help. Kill the threat.* Our inner wolves never used words to communicate, but his frantic pawing and whining and snarling and the ache behind my eyes anytime I wasn't looking at our girl spoke volumes.

"So, intention-based magic rather than commanding it with incantations," Ethan mused quietly. Lyssa continued to stare at a flushed Rosa, same as the tensed blond alpha beside her, but Ethan appeared lost in his thoughts. I knew the feeling, but clearly his wife was… uncomfortable. "We can work with that." And he either didn't notice or didn't care. "Lyssa, let's try to conjure something in the basket here, just to get a baseline."

Same as the whore comment on Halloween, this was a new look for the warlock.

Rather than doing as instructed, my mate stood abruptly and marched out of the room, Soren right up her ass. Frowning, I watched the pair go; she was a far cry from the bloody, filthy, sobbing she-wolf of a few hours ago. Showered and a little more rested, her nap fitful and short-lived, Lyssa opted for maximum comfort in a nondescript dark blue hoodie and a pair of grey sweats. Thick cotton socks with snowflakes on them—something Soren had scrounged up, no doubt—and her still-damp hair in a sloppy bun.

No designer labels.

No finesse or true *style*.

And she was so fucking *perfect*—just like that.

I never would have entertained that in a lover before, but then again, I hadn't been in an actual relationship since my early twenties, and that was a fucking disaster. Disillusioned by the chaotic Quinn pack, broken over my dad's suicide and pretending not to be, destroyed that so many of my kin had set their lives on fire with a batshit smile on their face…

Yeah, not exactly a solid foundation for romance.

The others who followed—flings and hookups and mutually beneficial partnerships—all paled in comparison to her. Even if they weren't mine, I held those women to such high standards all for the sake of my public image: reformed bad boy turned filthy-rich CEO and real estate titan.

Lyssa could wear that exact outfit every fucking day of her life if she wanted. She could go to premieres on my arm and cocktail parties and wherever the hell she desired dressed like that, and a part of me, one that had been so small and insignificant before, now growing stronger by the day, knew I'd still look at her like she was the sun.

"Ewan." Ethan's curt whisper jolted me back to the moment, my mate gone and Soren with her. The warlock shuffled toward my end of the table, leaving his wife behind as his voice once again dropped to a barely audible whisper. "This is dangerous stuff. We need to *very* closely monitor her from here on out to keep not only Lyssa safe, but you three as well—the village, shit, *everything*."

I blinked back at him, inner wolf snarling. Lyssa wasn't

dangerous; she was just untested. Shifters struggled with their strength and their inner beasts at a young age, and to me, this was just that. She had new abilities, but my fated mate had proven herself adaptable and brave.

She would overcome this.

I needed Ethan's *help*, not his paranoia.

"Ethan, she—"

"I'll need you to keep a diary of her progress, how she's doing, all that," the warlock pressed, eyes darting between me and the doorway as footsteps echoed from the foyer. "Daily updates. Any little thing that you can think of, whether it seems significant or not. It's all important, and you *need* to keep me informed."

He retreated as soon as Lyssa strolled back into the kitchen, her potted succulent from Rosa clutched in both hands, Soren at her heels. I spared them a quick glance, but the brunt of my scrutiny fell on Ethan.

My... friend.

Who wanted me to spy on my fated mate and then feed information back to him instead of speaking to Lyssa himself.

No. My wolf balked at the thought; that was just too personal, too invasive in pack life. Whatever Lyssa thought relevant, she could share.

Because it really wasn't my place—not unless everyone decided *again* to coddle her and spare her feelings when the truth was more important. If she seemed like she was hurting herself to *spare* us or whatever, then, sure, I'd call the warlock.

For now, he should speak to her directly.

After all, they weren't strangers. His wife was Lyssa's best and only friend outside of the pack. It wasn't *my* job to play intermediary.

Right?

Clearing her throat, Lyssa made some space on the table next to Rosa at the far end, then tenderly set the potted plant down.

Echeveria elegans, a desert plant with bulbous green leaves that grew in a rose pattern. Rosa had brought it to the house after Gull

River, almost like a bouquet of flowers humans gave each other in the hospital after an accident or surgery. I cocked my head to the side, frowning, because... I didn't remember that thing having thorns.

Or red flowers.

Or being quite so big.

With a deep breath, Lyssa squared her shoulders, threw her head side to side, and wiggled her fingers. She then shot Rosa a shy glance, but the witch focused on the succulent, cheeks still red as her hair. Silence blanketed the room again, thick and tense, Soren looking like he was ready to leap over the table and tackle the damn thing if it put one fat leaf out of line.

The air sizzled with *power* a beat later, electric and ancient. When she had made the windows shake and the pharmacy shelves rumble before, it was just a *whiff* compared to what we all felt now, her gifts undeniable. Golden eyes lost behind her lids, she held her hands over the pot, and while there was no wind this time, no crackle of lightning, there was this fucking *energy* surging all around us, stronger and brighter and *different* to anything I'd felt from witches and warlocks.

My inner wolf howled.

Flinching, Soren winced and rubbed at his ears like his wolf had done the same.

A heartbeat later, the succulent tripled in size, growing so fast and furious, sprouting thorns and more leaves and six fresh flowers —until the purple ceramic splintered. Lyssa scrambled away with a gasp, breathing hard, cheeks flushed and hands behind her back.

And Ethan was... smiling.

Beaming like a proud papa about to break out in a round of applause.

Again: what the fuck?

He wasn't usually like this.

Apprehension trickled through our bond, pitter-pattering like the first few hesitant raindrops before a storm. It made the hairs on my arms stand up and my inner wolf frantic; he *hated* when Lyssa was scared, so much so that he was willing to take on all the fear for himself. But the storm was quieter now, less cataclysmic than it was this morning after she popped the lid off Pandora's box and changed our world forever.

Back then, however, she had only *told* us.

This was showing.

Her golden gaze flitted between Soren and me, our bond muddled with her uncertainty, her desperation, her *need* for something just out of reach.

Acceptance, maybe. That was the obvious one.

Soren stared at the shattered pot for a long beat, then up at her like he was seeing her for the first time—like *this* was the moment he finally scented his fated mate. The same bouncy, insistent, heady energy as that fateful night in late September pulsed from him now, the peppy wolf back, the protective, steadfast guardian faltering as he gawked up at her.

The last display of power had been terrifying.

This was different.

And even if Soren—an alpha wolf—looked like a smitten kitten, soft and mushy, I felt it too.

Want.

Need.

Desire.

The same unstable, uncontrollable, unstoppable *pull* as the first night pounded into me like a hurricane, taking the power of her inner storm and boosting it from zero to a hundred.

Lyssa's cheeks sparked with color, all this palpable *attraction* sizzling from us to her, threading into one desire, one want, one need.

Her.

If it weren't for Rosa and Ethan, I'd have shoved everything off the table, thrown her onto it, and mounted her right here and now.

Never been so fucking attracted to her. A growl slipped out, one that Soren matched and then some. Her scent deepened, a heady rose garden threatening to permanently unlock the *wild* in my chest.

This power, these gifts—Lyssa wasn't just alpha she-wolf quality anymore. She would one day be the mother of our pack, but after Gull River, she could be queen of *all* wolves.

And she was ours.

Just ours, here in Redwood Grove, nestled in this valley, away from the rest of the world.

My heart wanted that—cozy, quiet peace. With her. *Our* goddess.

"That was..." Of course Ethan had to ruin it, but the warlock would have had no idea the subtle shift that had just taken place between us three. All this time, me and the guys—we were scared *for* her. Scared of what Gull River had done, that she was hurt and vulnerable.

Yeah, that was still there. She feared herself, and that had to change, but we would do whatever we could to support her on this journey.

She wasn't a monster. Not a freak or an abomination.

Not really a wolf shifter anymore either.

Ours.

Just ours.

Soren rumbled, ambling closer, and I shot out of my chair, death-gripping the corners of the table, eyeing her with an intensity that made her moan. Just a little one, barely more than a trembling gasp, but it set my body on fucking fire.

"Ah, Lucian. So good to see you up and about."

Everything came crashing down at Ethan's slightly awkward announcement, like he was just *begging* our packmate to cut the tension with his brooding, stormy presence.

I blinked the rolling fog of desire away, zeroing in on that huge figure in the doorway.

Soren's arms dropped to his sides.

Lyssa inhaled sharply.

He...

More scars.

No.

No, he didn't deserve *more*. Why the fuck was there a line across his throat and pale red circles where silver chain links once lay?

"Lucian!" Lyssa squealed his name, the carnal pulses coming from her flatlining to giddiness, to sheer, unadulterated joy, and, most of all, *relief.*

We all felt it.

But Lucian was the only one to snarl.

The fucker stalked away, his emotions messy and unreadable but very obviously not *good.*

Shock rippled from the three of us, followed by a sharp and visceral *ache* from Lyssa. She took off after him, a little slippery in those fuzzy socks, and Soren lobbed me a frown at the sounds of their retreating footsteps. I shook my head and stabbed a hand through my hair.

In the history books of our pack legacy, this meal would be dubbed the What the Fuck Brunch, because, seriously, what the *fuck—*

A bedroom door slammed upstairs, the echo banging through the whole house.

A moment later—knuckles on wood, Lyssa calling the shitbag's name, begging him to open up.

Fury slammed back and forth in me and Soren's alpha connection, hopefully powerful enough that it hit the English asshole upstairs too.

Because if he just slammed the door in our girl's face…

I'd fucking gut him.

I abandoned brunch with a snarl, inner wolf seething, off to investigate this next clusterfuck with Soren stalking after me.

Seriously though.

What the *fuck?*

3

SOREN

As soon as I opened the driver's-side door, I heard the fire alarm screaming inside the house. *Beep, beep, beep, beep.*

"Shit."

Abandoning my baby blue BMW and the pile of work crap on the passenger seat, I bolted up the driveway, leapt over the porch steps, and barreled through the front door—only to be met with a faceful of hazy smoke.

"Shit." I pivoted left and sprinted into the kitchen, immediately locating the problem. "Shit, shit, shit, *shit.*"

Forgoing gloves, I ripped open the oven door, instantly assaulted with a *whoosh* of much darker, thicker smog, the air scented with scorched crust. Teeth gritted and inner wolf panicking, I swallowed the burn and yanked the blackened meat pie out with my bare hands. Hurled it on the island. Kicked the oven door shut, the fire alarm still blaring through the house.

The suspiciously quiet house.

Had everyone left? I'd been gone *literally* two hours—just to do a little officey shit that I felt kind of guilty about dumping on my guys with such short notice.

But, like, I hadn't gone far. I was just up the way—a stone's freakin' *throw*.

Why the hell was something cooking if no one stuck around to watch it?

My wolf huffed a sigh of relief: at least nothing was actively on fire.

Yet.

Burns still healing, I grabbed the pie with two towels this time, marched to the back doors and elbowed one open, then chucked this disaster on the deck. *Dealing with* you *later.* Back inside, I darted around the first floor, opening doors and windows and babying the nearest fire alarm, willing the smoke to just filter out on its own and refusing to call the fire department to clear it out faster.

Using the front door like a giant fan, I glowered in the general direction of the kitchen. Right. Who had attempted to cook while I was gone? Ewan had patrol duty, focusing on our eastern border just to be safe. Lucian still hadn't come out of his room since this morning's tense-as-heck brunch, and the last I saw, Lyssa had been sitting against his door, curled up and miserable, all of us clueless about why he was being a massive dickweed.

Lyssa or Lucian.

One of those two had tried their hand at the oven. Usually I handled food. I made lists, did the grocery shopping, got the best deals on fresh fish straight from the distributor, bartered with Redwood Grove's overpriced butcher, and did the lion's share of the cooking.

I liked it.

I liked providing for my pack. I liked making dope-tasting food. I liked the look on my mate's face when she bit into a perfectly seasoned, perfectly rare steak.

However, I wasn't *always* home for mealtimes, and, really, it wasn't fair that I did *all* the cooking.

Enter our freezer, stocked with frozen crap so simple a pup could prep it. Peel the packaging off and toss it in the oven, set the timer and leave it…

Shit.

Like that meat pie.

Hearty. Simple. Foolproof.

And someone had let it burn. *Hard.*

"Hello?"

The fire alarm finally shut off on its own, and I popped my jaw to give my ears some relief.

"Soren?"

Lyssa. My inner wolf whined, then barked, demanding I leave the front door and find her *now*—because she sounded so small and sad and broken, her feelings suddenly *flooding* our connection like an avalanche.

Shit, shit, shit.

I booked it upstairs and shoved the panic aside as best I could—because, seriously, how much more horseshit did we have to shovel in a single freakin' twenty-four hours.

Whipping around the corner on the landing, I sprinted down the hall, headed straight for her bedroom, only to skitter to a halt, shoes squeaking over the hardwood, when I zipped by Lucian's open door. Was that hermit finally open to visitors?

I understood some of his moodiness. He'd never seemed to vibe with magic or witches or whatever. Always in a mood when the subject came up. None of us—besides Lyssa, probably—were *thrilled* to have an outsider managing pack matters, but if it helped our mate feel more secure in her new abilities, whatever. Let Ethan Perry do his assessment and scribble out a treatment plan. We could take it from there.

But Lucian also wasn't the type to storm off and tantrum like a pup.

That was... kind of my move.

Occasionally Ewan's.

Ruffling the smoke out of my hair, I marched into my fellow alpha's bedroom.

His... empty bedroom.

I staggered to a full stop. Bed stripped. Shelves empty. All the lights off, the yellow glow from the porch lights spilling through the windows. Lucian had the simplest, neatest, most organized bedroom because he had zero crap to fill it with. No lifetime of memories like me and no obscene wardrobe like Ewan.

The only thing left in here was the stripped mattress and its simple wooden frame.

Well, that—and Lyssa.

"Uh…"

Blanketed in shadow, Lyssa stood at the end of the bed, *barely* touching it. "H-he's gone." Slowly, she lifted her waterlogged gaze to mine, the gold painfully bright in the early November nightfall. "I w-was making supper and he… He *left*."

Shock danced between us, twanging through the bond, and the best I could manage was a stunned blink and another scope of the room. I mean, yeah, definitely looked like he cleared out. Nostrils flared, I breathed deep, his scent lingering, all oaky and foresty and earthy.

There—but fading.

"Is it because of m-me?"

"I… don't know what's happening," I babbled, fully aware I needed to say something the longer she stared, *begged* for comfort, yet struggling to find the words, "but I don't think—"

Too late. She burst into tears before I could finish. Embarrassment burned from her to me, heating the nape of my neck as she gave me her back. Face buried, shoulders hunched, Lyssa hiccupped and whimpered into her hands.

My inner wolf howled, the sound forlorn and desperate and way more mature than I expected from him.

And my heart…

My heart broke, not only for her, but for *us*. After nearly losing him to the Hawthorne pack, this was the last thing any of us needed.

I was on her in a flash, bundling her to my chest and tucking her under my chin. Lyssa shivered, a little ball of granite fighting the breakdown with everything she had, and I wished she would just let it out.

Cry.

Scream.

Let go in my arms—because I could *take* it.

Sure, I'd been worried about her since she unleashed literal hell on our rivals.

Since she left a hole in the forest like a crashed meteor.

Since she *ripped* an alpha's heart out and tossed it aside like trash.

Since she healed Lucian's horrific injury and apologized over and over again.

Of course I was scared—a little of her, but mostly *for* her.

First that, then Ewan off to check the sketchy eastern perimeter alone, and now *this*?

Lucian should have known better.

He wasn't usually this selfish. This was more than keeping secrets for the sake of his fated mate.

This was just... a fucking *dick* move.

"I don't g-get it," Lyssa said thickly as she tipped her head back to look up at me, leaving a tearstained blob over my sweatshirt. "Why would he go?"

One arm still slung around her, I finagled my phone out of my jeans pocket with my free hand and tapped around for Lucian's number.

Straight to voicemail.

Jagweed—for *real*.

"I don't know, baby," I murmured, tossing the rectangle on his bed and scooping her closer with both arms. "But... I say we find out."

Arms loosely knotted around my waist, Lyssa leaned back even further, almost like she was checking if I was serious, and her eyebrows shot up. I shrugged, the solution to this new—really stupid—problem obvious.

"I mean, yeah. Let's find him and get answers. This is *his* pack too. He doesn't get to just bail."

The embarrassment from her breakdown sharpened to a raging

wildfire, her cheeks hot and red, her emotions tearing through our bond so fast and hard that my inner wolf whimpered.

"No, no." I hastily brushed her fresh tears away. "I'm not saying *you* bailed, just—"

"Don't treat me like a pup," she insisted before stumbling back and using her slightly too-big sweater sleeves to dry her face and wipe her nose. "I should have just talked to all of you. I thought I was being mature and doing what was best for everyone, because I didn't want to fight and *still* walk away when it was over... I messed up." Her lower lip wobbled. "I messed up so bad."

"We all do," I told her without missing a beat. Seriously. Every single one of us trips and falls—in life, in love, in our own families. It was the getting back up part that mattered; Dad had always said that. "Baby, you came back right away—"

"But my mess caused all *this*." She motioned to the stripped bedroom, to the lack of warmth and wolf touches that had made this Lucian's home for less than two measly months. I gritted my teeth, swallowing the first scathing comment that came to mind, and took a beat to rephrase so I didn't make things worse.

"Don't... take responsibility for *his* choices." We all sucked at talking about our feelings. We sucked even harder at dealing with all the emotional bullshit that happened when you and a bunch of alphas were fated to the same she-wolf, but Lucian was *very* attached to our mate. Even if it was hard, whatever was bothering him—he could have just talked to her about it instead of sneaking out while she attempted to bake a pie *for* him. "Seriously, he's a grown-ass wolf, and he left for his own reasons. Don't have to put that on yourself, or us, or anybody." The second her eyes started to glisten again, guilt pluming in the bond, I grabbed her hand and dragged her toward the door. "Come on. Let's just find out what's happening so we don't drive ourselves nuts guessing."

I mean, right? Enough of the guesswork. Enough spreading the blame around where it didn't belong. Enough misunderstandings. Time made us stronger as a pack, but to really get over the next hurdle, *we* all needed to make moves and just do *better*.

Lyssa followed without hesitation or protest, and when I let go to drag my sweatshirt off, she was right there with me, already tossing her hoodie on the floor, sports bra next. By the time we reached the front door, we were both naked and padded across the front porch on paws, not feet. Even though it was just after five, the sun had set a good half hour ago, Redwood Grove plunged into darkness, winter right around the next corner. Our breaths fogged as we greeted in our wolf forms, the wraparound decking lit up under the motion-activated lights.

Golden eyes assessed me, her wolf form the calmer one between us. Still, she happily took my snuffles and licks along her snout, both our tails slashing back and forth, paws dancing, claws clacking. After a thorough hello, rubbing up against each other, scenting and whimpering and dancing through the reunion, we set off together, determination ringing in our bond.

Lyssa went for the spot Lucian usually parked his jeep.

Which was gone.

I huffed, glowering at the grooves left by the tires. Hadn't even noticed its absence when I got home, honestly, because the busted old thing blended in with the landscape most of the time. While my mate sniffed, her hackles up, tail still, I tossed my head back and howled.

Not for Lucian.

If he was in the jeep—super weird that he would *drive* away— then he wouldn't hear anyway. He would *feel* all this, the confusion and longing coming from Lyssa, the frustration rankling our connection from me, but there was no point in calling out to him.

This was for Ewan. My howl split the night sky open. Clear and cloudless, dotted with winking stars and a full moon, the heavens carried my summoning straight to him, the message clear.

Come home.

This wasn't a leisurely pack howl, the sort you fell into unexpectedly on a run. It was poignant and straightforward, harmonized a few moments later by Lyssa. We sang together on the gravel driveway, calling Ewan away from the eastern border, demanding him *here*, with us, to sort out the next issue.

We were three howls deep when he finally answered. Clear and strong, Ewan replied with a howl of his own, the baritone to my alto and Lyssa's soprano.

Usually that was Lucian's octave.

It was like he *knew* that dick had jumped ship.

Even though we couldn't see him coming, something in the bond said he was on the way. Something unspoken but *deep*, some cozy warmth that told me he was on the same page.

And with that, the song died down.

Lyssa put her talented nose to work, sniffing the route Lucian's jeep had taken as it peeled away from the heart of our territory. I trotted along behind her, alert, my wolf side finally *maturing* now that shit had taken a turn for the serious. Scanning the shoreline, the tree line, the shadows, and the stars, I kept an eye out for danger and an ear out for Ewan and let my mate lead the way.

Because if anyone was going to find the wildest alpha male in this pack, it was her.

4

LYSSA

Nestled downwind in some scraggly thickets, I tracked Lucian's enormous wolf form as he trotted along the snowy ridgeline. All around us, tundra surrendered to winter, the ground varying degrees of frosty, icy, and snowy, dropping in temperature and spiking in brutality the further north we went. I knew the area—vaguely. Beyond that ridge stretched a field of nothingness, then a smattering of tall, thin trees, scarce of game and nutrients this time of year.

My pack and I occasionally wandered this far north in the springtime, but when the winter snows settled, there wasn't really a point. No food. Barely enough shelter. Nothing to protect the yearlings or feed the pups during their first winter.

Wolves knew to move south.

But for one miserable week, Lucian pushed north—headed for the ends of the earth at the tip of the arctic, like he wanted to walk right off it and into the abyss. Still and silent, I watched him, locked on his grizzled black fur, his long stride, until finally he veered right and vanished over the horizon line. Only then did I creep out and stalk after him, cautious as ever, Kira's paws barely making a sound as they glided over the snow, our emotions corked and stuffed deep,

deep down.

One long week of tracking had made me feel more my old self than I had in months. For the last seven days, I was pure wolf. Stalking. Sleuthing. Marching long distances in the daylight and snoozing with one eye open come nightfall, same as him. So far, he hadn't noticed he'd picked up a tail: I made sure of that.

Still no clue why he left, but as I crawled up the ridge, rocky patches slick with ice and dips full of thick, sticky snow, I knew one thing for sure…

My mate was hurting.

All week long, I endured the loneliness rolling off him, the outpouring of heartache—a sickness getting worse by the hour, by the *minute*. Every step a struggle. The further we hiked from Redwood Grove, the worse the sensations got, leaving my throat raw, my chest locked in a slowly tightening snare. At this point, it was a struggle to *breathe*.

Because of him.

Because of *his* hurt.

He could fix it. He could just turn around and come home, but my quiet, brooding, broken mate was being so *stubborn* that it drove me *nuts*. I ached for him, yes, but frustration, anger, and a savage heartache of my own boiled my blood.

Seven days ago, Ewan, Soren, and I got to the northwestern territory line, surrounded by my former pack, who accepted my mates at first glance, and realized Lucian had left. Gone. Left it all behind. Ditched his jeep near his old cabin, shifted, and fled the territory without a word—without an explanation for *any* of us. At first, Ewan suggested we just let him go.

"He'll come back when he's ready," my black-haired mate grumbled. "Let him cool off. He feels… tense."

Of course he felt tense: he was abandoning his family—for *good*, it seemed like. Soren and I had pushed back against that and put our collective foot down. *No.* He didn't get to do this to us. Even when I had considered leaving, I only planned to go one city over and call as soon as I got settled. Lucian had left *everything* behind. No phone.

No bag. No clothes, that day's outfit left in a pile on the filthy hood, the rest of his stuff locked inside the jeep.

No, this was too serious to just let it play out.

In the end, we decided to track him, confront him, and either bring him home—or cut him loose.

And my mates had voted for *me* to do it.

No fighting. No bickering. No roughhousing between Ewan and Soren. They yielded, admitting that I had the best chance of finding him.

They let me go.

Let me cross the territory line alone…

Trusted me.

A few from my old pack followed me past Hampton's city limits, sticking to the thick forest, but eventually they all peeled away.

And then it was just me and Kira. No phone. No clothes. No nothing—same as Lucian.

I picked him up fast. Once he cleared the witchy metropolis, my mate stopped trying to be tricky, to confuse a potential tail, and I locked onto his scent hard. Hunting him was a huge responsibility that I took *very* seriously, not just for the sake of my heart, my love, and our future pups, but for the trust Soren and Ewan had gifted me that evening.

I wouldn't let them down.

And most of all, I wouldn't let *us* down—me and that stubborn jerk meandering across the barren field below.

Keeping downwind and low to the ridgeline, I followed his huge prints in the snow, his oakwood scent spiraling where his paw pads pressed deep. The early afternoon sun inched across the sky, headed for the horizon like it had all the time in the world—but it would set suddenly and soon, plunging the tundra into darkness. Way across the field, Lucian sniffed at the tree line, then eventually decided on the right fir to camp beneath. He nosed around its base, clearing the snow, digging himself a hole to curl up in after the hours and hours and *hours* of walking we had both done today. Normally when he slept, I napped.

Not this time.

Huffing, I hurried down the rocky ridge and into the field, purposefully putting myself in a position where he could *finally* scent me on the icy breeze. I made it halfway across the sprawling snowscape before he caught me, head snapping up, scarred and haggard, surprise pounding through our connection.

Shock.

Joy.

Elation.

Fear and panic and that aching, heavy, *deep* heartbreak that made me misstep and fumble, belly grazing the snow.

All this time, I had submitted to the slow, cautious, precise huntress in my soul. Kira and I had been an unstoppable team for seven long days, cohesive and focused, all the other emotions tucked aside for the sake of *not* losing the scent. Before I dozed off here and there, surrendering to a light, dreamless sleep where Idunn still blocked me from the orchard, I had imagined our reunion.

I pictured something soft and sweet, suitable for the bond I shared with Lucian. Tender. Intimate. Intense with a lot of eye contact.

But as he stared at me from the shadow of that skinny fir tree, his eyes dark gold and his fur missing a few chunks, all that fell away. My pace quickened. My temper spiked. My paws pounded the frozen ground in a fury, all the upset and sadness and ache and longing and *anger* getting the better of me and Kira.

He tentatively stepped into the light as I sprinted for him, then braced, his entire body tensing from nose to tail, when I *charged*.

Slammed into him like a transport train barreling down the tracks, all teeth and snarls and wrath. No softness. No tender greetings and whining and nuzzling. I snapped and bit and bodychecked him, letting him know—as if opening the floodgates on my side of our emotional connection wasn't enough—that I was absolutely *devastated* over what he had done.

While his hackles shot up and he bared his teeth, Lucian only fought back half-heartedly, taking my attack until he didn't.

Until he shifted into a naked god, steaming and dirty, blood weeping from the slash I left along his ribs. Moss green greeted me when our eyes met, but he dropped it just as fast, staggering backward and panting. No. *No.* He didn't call the shots here. Not after what he put me through that day—sulking in front of his locked bedroom door for hours, leaving to make us a nice dinner, and coming back to find him *gone.*

Not just out for the day.

Gone gone.

I lunged for him, shifting as soon as all four paws left the ground, and crashed into him as a much shorter woman, fists beating his chest, shoving my unmovable mountain man with *half* the strength Idunn had gifted me, teeth just as sharp as Kira's.

"What are you *doing?*" My shriek echoed through the pathetic forest behind him, the firs and spruces so sad compared to the lush trees of Redwood Grove. I shoved him harder this time, forcing him back a few paces, shock once again flickering through our connection.

"How long have you been following me?" Lucian rasped, his voice just as unused and prickly as mine. Snarling, I swatted at him, but this time he ducked out of the way and put a few large strides between us, emotions all over the place.

"That's not the point," I hissed, throwing my hands up with another shriek. "How could you just *go?*"

He leveled me with one of his calm, measured looks, the one that said any wolf in his sights was being unreasonable. Now, however, he had turned that judgmental glint inward, every muscle taut, his breath fogging in short, sharp bursts, his spirit absolutely broken.

"Lucian..." My voice cracked and my eyes watered, and my mate just bowed his head. "Please. You're killing me. *Please.*"

"I thought I watched you die that night."

The weight of his grief hit like an avalanche, sudden and severe, pounding into me out of nowhere and burying me deep. The air squeezed out of my lungs. My knees gave way. I scrambled to grab a drooping fir branch, only to miss by a mile and collapse in the snow.

534

Lucian made no move to help me, almost like he *knew* everything burning in him had just jumped to me. Not real—yet so *horribly* real that I struggled to take a breath, hand to my chest, tears streaking my face and plopping into the snow. Kira's howl barely penetrated the sea of pure, uncut *sorrow* filling my head, and when I finally got a grip on it, plugging the dam just a little, I sat back on my heels and gulped the frigid arctic wind, wondering how this man, this wolf, *my* mate, was still standing with all that going on inside.

"I... I couldn't do it again," he admitted roughly, finally buckling and falling to his knees, both of us just kneeling in the snow, steam rising off our skin in subtle waves after the shift. "I-I can't. I knew I loved you, and then I lost you, and... and I fucking *can't*, Lyssa."

I gawked back at him, the tundra's savagery turning the ice in my veins to steel. "W-what? Love is the whole point of this—"

"I've felt it too much in my life," Lucian muttered, hands limp on his thighs—thighs that were always so big and firm and *muscular*, deflated now, our meals this past week scarce. "Too much love lost, and I won't s-survive losing you."

I slumped deeper into the snowdrifts, Kira silent inside, the wind trilling softly through trees. In time it would ramp up to a scream, ghostly and shrill and terrifying for pups. Easy to get lost in, the familiarity of the wild, the natural world beckoning me back to a simpler time when all that mattered was food, shelter, and pack. Shifters were complicated and messy—but so was love.

I chose the mess.

"I guess that's the risk we take, isn't it?"

Normally, Lucian and I were on the same page. We got along best as wolves, his steadfast calm so familiar, so cozy and warm and nostalgic. We rarely argued. Quick to agree and make decisions, we didn't need long, layered conversations—we were wolves of action and intuition.

I expected him to nod at that.

To agree like he always did, even if I was teetering on the edge of *wrong*. He was my patient mate, my constant, my backbone.

He just stared at his hands, nipples pebbled, scars jagged and too obvious against his tanned skin today, the slit across his throat loaded with memories that soured my belly.

In that moment, the journey finally settled on my shoulders. Seven days of walking, trotting, sprinting. Seven nights of Idunn barring me from the orchard, making my sleep less satisfying than usual. Seven twenty-four-hour stretches on minimal food and rest and water.

We were true wolves out here.

And the life of a wolf, as much as I had loved it for the last eighteen years, was one of *suffering*.

We... deserved more than that. Scarred and flawed as we both were, this wasn't the life for either of us anymore, up here at the ends of the world, alone.

"Lucian..." I tipped my head, rooting out his eyes, begging through the bond for him to just *look* at me. He offered a glimpse of the green I adored and nothing more. "I don't know what happened to you in the past, but I know it's bad. I feel it." My weak wave at his various scars, to the gnarled one across his pec, the bite someone had taken out of his side, only made him shut down more. "I know it hurts, and I *know* that hurt too. But I choose love." For the first time in my life, I finally felt worthy of it. "I *choose* love over the pain. Ewan and Soren and *you*. I'll take all of you even if it means I'll have to feel what I used to at some point." Loneliness. Otherness. No self-worth. No love. No family. "I'll take this, *you*, for as long as I can."

Instinct nudged me toward his lap, desperation mounting, the *need* to straddle his thighs and hug him overwhelming. As soon as I inched forward, however, Lucian flinched back, and I stilled on all fours, tensed, waiting, heart breaking.

"I... I can't," he choked out, shaking his head, his inner turmoil battering me from all sides. So harsh. So violent. Flashes of red danced across my line of sight, and I blinked it away, knowing it belonged to him, that he had so much churning in there it had started leaking into our bond—maybe even poisoning it.

"*Why?*" Maybe if I knew, I could make it better.

Honesty was terrifying. The truth, shiny but cold, sharp as silver, could undo any great love story.

But it *had* to be worth the risk.

So said the movies.

And so said my own love story.

Lucian shook his head and flashed gritted teeth. *No.*

"Okay." I sank onto my heels, tears welling. Was this the final chapter of *our* love story? "Okay." *He isn't ready.* I refused to be another person in his life who scarred him. "I just needed to know."

Then, my body acted without my consent. Without thought or planning, I pushed up and trudged away, snow up to my knees. Logically, I knew it was freezing, even to my shifter skin—but I couldn't feel it. Numbness washed through me, muffling Kira's panicky yelps, dulling the buzz in my fingertips.

"Lyssa—"

"I couldn't *wonder.*" I stilled and sniffled, then brushed the freshly fallen damp away with a shrug. An empty field loomed ahead, the ridgeline that final barrier before the long, lonely march home. The view was probably the least appealing I'd ever faced, so I rounded on him, ready to make *one* last stand before waving the white flag. "It's a choice, Lucian." His eyes snapped to mine, gold winking through the green, his inner wolf fighting to be seen. "I know it's fate and destiny or whatever, but it *is* a choice at the end of the day."

Hard as it had been, we *all* made that choice as individuals. Ewan could have chosen his career over the effort it took to make this work. Soren could have found a local girl who knew his history and blindly supported his traditions.

I could have left that first day.

Lucian could have stayed in the woods.

We were fated—but we *chose* this.

And he had a choice to make now.

My mate stared at me for a beat, then folded over with a harsh breath like someone had stabbed him, *bam*, right in the lung. I stood there, trembling, shivering and not from the cold, then steeled myself when the first of his tears peppered the snow. Resignation flowed from him to me, but I pushed back—just this once, even as the ground crumbled beneath me and my heart shredded into a million pieces.

"And if you *choose* to stay h-here, alone, where nothing and no one can hurt you..." Light-headed, I gulped down a much-needed breath. "That's y-your choice." *What are you saying?* "You have a home with me—with us. It's not perfect, but it's ours. You have wolves who l-love you." I stabbed at my chest. "*This* wolf does." His head snapped up again, and I huffed a weak laugh. "You're my mountain man, Lucian. I feel you in my *soul*." From the first day, he touched the deepest part of me with his kindness, his patience, and his *wild*. "But I understand if you... need to protect yourself."

Heck, I should have understood that better than most—but I didn't. Not now. Not with him. Not after everything.

But I loved him enough—apparently—to let him go if that was what he needed.

Arms crossed, I took one last long look at him, at my mate broad and solid as a mountain. At his unkept beard and his dark brown waves. At the mossy greens and the scratches I'd left on his bicep from our first mating.

Goodbye.

As soon as I turned, Kira burst forth. She did it to protect me, to let me fall apart somewhere deep inside, surrounded by dark and warmth and *her* strength. Even though it pained her just as deeply as it did me, she marched away from Lucian, padding across the snow-white blanket, and headed for the soaring rocky ridge. Eyes forward. One paw in front of the other. *Move.*

A sharper, deeper resignation flowed from him to me through the bond, and I *hated* it.

Halfway across the field, however, thunder boomed at my back. No, not thunder. Pounding, crashing, resounding *paws*—

I whirled around, nostrils flared, hackles up, *just* in time to catch the mass of black fur before Lucian in his wolf form bulldozed into me.

The resignation—wasn't to *stay*.

Love flooded the bond, an inferno blazing along the invisible strings connecting his heart to mine, scorching away the sorrow, and he tackled me with a playful bark. We rolled in the snow, nosed at each other, snapped our teeth, and nipped at ears. Rubbed our scents into each other's coats. Licked and pawed and *whined*.

Howled to the afternoon sunshine stuck behind the clouds.

This wasn't a wolf saying goodbye.

It was my mate—saying hello.

And sorry.

We frolicked around the field for the better part of an hour, tired and happy but suddenly brimming with energy. All that untouched white ruined with paws and tails, with charges and sprints and tumbles.

Then, just as darkness crept across the sky, the light sinking into the horizon, we set off together, side by side.

Headed south for Redwood Grove.

Headed *home*—together.

5

SOREN

"Okay, hello." I clapped my hands together and leaned forward, the fire crackling away in the pit on the back porch. "Welcome, everyone, to the bonfire of trust."

Nearly eight o'clock, the rest of Redwood Grove settled into an inky night while we four bathed in flickering orange. The rest of my pack stared from their wooden deck chairs, Ewan to my right, Lucian at my left, Lyssa bundled in cozy blankets on the other side of the flames. While the other two dillweeds had hard liquor piled around them, Lucian constantly feeding the bonfire from a stack of kindling just to keep his hands busy, our girl slurped a hot chocolate loaded with whip cream and caramel drizzle courtesy of yours truly. The pyramid of Belgian brews at my feet remained untouched —but given the heft of their stares, the strain in our bond, I'd be cracking into the top can soon.

A week and a half after Lyssa disappeared into the great beyond, me and Ewan emotional wrecks every day she was gone but forcing ourselves to *trust* in her abilities, she sauntered home with our wayward alpha. Unfortunately, while those two seemed to have come to an understanding, the rest of us were in the dark. The house was awkward again, the tension unbearable, everyone tiptoeing around to avoid the eggshells.

Just... no.

We were better than that.

Over breakfast, I floated this—the bonfire of trust—and once I explained the premise, Lyssa was all over it. Everyone had baggage, and if we got it out, picked it apart, and made the whole pack aware of why we did the shit we did, we could avoid inadvertently stepping on future land mines.

My mate was aggressively for it.

Lucian and Ewan dug their heels in all freakin' day, eventually conceding at dinner for Lyssa's sake.

And now...

Here we were.

Awkward AF but trying.

"This is a judgment-free zone," I insisted, sliding into the role of MC by default. I mean, yeah, I had some stupid teenage angst in my history books, but these three—they had heavy shit to offload, and if *they* led this, they'd cherry-pick information, and then what the hell was the point? "We all know that each of us has something inside that shapes the way we are today. To be strong alphas, we should have as few secrets between us as possible."

Snapping a couple twigs, Lucian rolled his eyes and scooted closer to the pit to toss them in. He then grabbed his fire-poking stick and fussed with the smoldering log arrangement, while Ewan scoffed and chugged another gulp of straight bourbon. Awesome.

"Fuck off, both of you. This is for the good of the pack and our future pups so we aren't a bunch of moody assholes forever," I rattled off, my wolf eyes darting between the pair like a warning. Lyssa, meanwhile, quietly nursed her hot chocolate, already rocking an adorable whipped cream mustache. "This is a safe space." Ewan scoffed louder this time, and, still grinning at my cute-as-pie fated mate, I flipped him off without taking the bait. "And if your past, or upbringing, or trauma, or *whatever* is still haunting you, now is the time to get it out. We're here, as a pack, not to judge or condemn—but to help. As fated mates, we all deserve that kind of peace, right?"

When Lucian and Ewan's judgy wolf gazes slid to me, glinting with firelight, I nodded toward Lyssa. Most of all, this was for her.

And, you know, Lucian had bailed for a reason, something dark and probably fucked-up, and Ewan lost his cool easier than the rest of us...

These two had skeletons piled a mile high in their closets, and if we didn't clear them out now, this pack would stay stuck in this loop, doing the same crap over and over again. Same problems. Same fights. Same results. Same stupid misunderstandings that would threaten our unity as alphas. Nope. No more.

Lucian conceded, grumbling under his breath and sinking into the deck chair that was way too small for his massive body, the wood groaning, and grabbed the unopened scotch by his side. Ewan then surrendered with a long, dramatic sigh, swirling his drink, the ice tinkling against the crystal.

Over the fire, swaddled in blankets, her hair in a messy bun, Lyssa wiggled her eyebrows and shot me a thumbs-up, her eagerness an ever-present tremor in our collective bond. I felt it in my heart, the little wobble, the extra-fast beat every so often.

At least *someone* appreciated my effort here.

"Good, so..." I grabbed the chilled beer can from the top of my stack, then cracked it open with a fizzy *hiss*. "Who wants to go first?"

I then slumped into the chair's ass groove, eyebrows up and waiting. A gentle breeze danced across the lake, water black and sparkly as the sky, and the nighttime chill slipped its icy fingers under my long-sleeved shirt, my sweats. While Lucian and Lyssa had opted for similar outfits, dressed for comfort above all else, Ewan sported a luxe V-neck sweatshirt and pressed slacks—and weird, pretentious boat shoes.

Seriously, this guy.

For a bonfire.

Still, despite his stupid outfit, Ewan was the first to rumble something to himself, breaking the oppressive quiet. He shuffled to the edge of his seat, all the sharp angles of his face, his glass-cutting jawline, warmed and softened by the orange glow.

"Hi." He hoisted his bourbon. "My name is Ewan Quinn."

"Hi, Ewan," Lucian and I drawled like we were at an AA meeting. The joke flew right over Lyssa's head, her brows knit, frown hidden behind the sagging stack of whip and caramel.

"As you know… I'm a Quinn." Another big chug cleared his glass, and the black-haired wolf went for his first refill of the night from the half-drunk bottle at his feet. "I'm the firstborn son and heir to Mason Quinn's drug ring. We operated in the Toronto area for a few generations, knocking off rivals and claiming territory. The family made a lot of money. I was born into it, and…" He capped the bourbon bottle with one hand, eyes never lifting, never flitting between us. A subdued energy settled over him, leaving a void in the bond. "And I've seen some shit. I've had to silence people, bury pack enemies—all while I was just a fucking teenager. My cousins are… fucked. The psychopath gene grows like a weed on their branch of the family. Mom's an alcoholic who I don't speak to anymore. Dad ran the gang into the ground because he turned into a fucking addict…"

His gaze darkened, a thick sourness spilling into the bond, so foul and bitter that the rest of us shuffled and twitched in our seats, my gut roiling at the sensation.

"But, you know, Mason Quinn always stayed *just* sober enough to really beat the shit out of his kids for no reason. The asshole would just… out of nowhere, just…"

He went quiet for a bit. Nobody said a word. Lucian fussed with the fire. Lyssa nursed her hot chocolate, sympathy flowing from her through the connection, all warm and toasty, so much so that I nearly yanked my sweater off and did this thing shirtless. My inner wolf, shockingly, had an issue with some alpha we didn't know knocking Ewan around; he snarled, stalking around inside, pacing, angsty and seething, keen for a fight.

I bit the insides of my cheeks, swallowing the ache for him—for a wolf I'd come to blows with time and time again in the last year.

He didn't want pity; you could see it in his eyes. This was a judgment-free zone... but that made it even harder not to *feel*.

"I abdicated my role as alpha," Ewan remarked after ages of drinking and staring at the fire. "I let the next in line take the title, even though he wasn't born an alpha. I was maybe... twenty? I got out." His words had a gravelly edge to them, deep and guttural and rough—but numb, the wolf protecting the man. "It wasn't the life I wanted. I saw what it did to my brothers and sisters. I saw my cousins dabble in trafficking humans and female shifters. I saw so much... *filth* that it still makes me sick, and I just left."

He zeroed in on the fire, on the embers flaring at its base.

"Dad killed himself with a wolfsbane overdose just before I started my second year of university. I found him strung out on the can with a needle in his arm." Ewan's jaw danced through a clench, and he glowered at his bourbon like he couldn't stomach it anymore. "Cops were closing in, really building a case against our pack. Human cops—they had no idea what they were up against, but a bunch of my packmates are in human prisons now. We aren't immune. They're just... wasting away in a cage."

Shit, man.

Scowling, I shot back the rest of my beer, then crunched the can and tossed it aside.

Those wolves must be losing their minds—literally. If prison didn't drive them nuts, it would break their inner wolves *for sure*.

Then, you know, Lady Fate help the rest of us when they were eventually released...

Wouldn't be surprised if they went on a rampage just to satisfy the innate urge to *hunt*.

Still though. Drugs. Trafficking females—you deserved a cage if that was the life you chose.

"I feel... guilty," Ewan admitted, sharing what sounded like a genuine flaw for the first time since I'd met him, "for being a part of it. I feel like an asshole for not stepping in to help the others—I just bailed and left them to figure it out. I needed to find my own way through this, and... and I think it all still really influences how I handle my anger and my fear."

He brought the crystal up, then paused just shy of it touching his lips. Nostrils flared, he breathed the bourbon in, the hint of caramel rising above the liquor, the faint whiff of honey—a Christmas blend. "School and work were always an escape for me. Putting my head down and focusing on shit outside the pack... It felt *normal*. It made *me* feel normal. Making something for myself separate from the Quinn legacy has been the driving force in my life for almost a decade, and I've kept to it."

Clearing his throat, he tossed back the entire glass, then set it on the chair's wide, flat armrest. Hands threaded together, he leaned toward the fire again with a sigh.

"I'm trying to do better." His coppery gaze slid toward Lyssa. "I *will* do better."

The bonfire crackled angrily, demanding sacrifices, and in the quiet that followed Ewan's promise, Lucian tended to the beast with a deep frown. Our bond possessed a strange energy, messy and conflicted, emotions pouring in from all sides.

Still, this was a *good* thing.

Knowing Ewan's history, what made him tick and why he acted the way he did—it was better for all of us. Alphas rarely let the rest of the pack in. They were untouchable and distant, seemingly flawless, always in control.

But their mate knew the truth.

In our pack, all of us had to know the truth. We had to help each other.

Support each other.

This was how we'd survive.

When Ewan finally risked a glance around our silent circle, insecurity wobbled out of him through the bond. Fear. Regret. Uncertainty. I tried to muster up something that wouldn't sound sarcastic or douchey, because while that wouldn't be the intent, *that* was how he would hear whatever came out of my mouth right now.

Hackles high, on the defense, he was ready to rebuild that impenetrable wall—

But then Lyssa was up and moving. Blankets and hot chocolate abandoned, she padded swiftly from her chair to his, then folded over on top of him in what could only be described as a she-wolf bear hug. Not sensual. Not even really romantic. Just—there. Big and tight, Ewan's face shoved in her chest, her nose in his hair. In that moment, relief swept through our connection, cooling the smoldering ruins of Ewan's past, the impact it had on us as a pack, and just for a few blissful seconds, reinstating *peace*.

When she pulled away, half her face lit with orange, the other in shadows, she cupped Ewan's razor-sharp jawline and kissed him. Again, nothing like I'd seen at the Chalet. No *need* and passion and ferocity.

This was better.

This was acceptance in all its glory, open and raw and glistening in the gold—a promise of forever.

I went for my second beer, throat thick and eyes stinging as their connection, their intimacy, warmed the bond and touched each of us.

"Thank you for sharing that, Ewan," I said roughly as Lyssa drifted back to her chair. Wind rustled through the bare trees on the other side of the house, branches clattering, the air singing through the boughs.

Ewan flipped me off.

I flashed my teeth.

Then, as if we thought the other couldn't see, we both smirked, the venom from the start of our relationship muted—and, *finally*, almost gone.

It took a little while for the aftershocks of Ewan's brutal past to settle. I wanted to delve in, root around, give my opinion, but we had all agreed—judgment-free zone. So, Lucian tended to the fire. Lyssa gulped her hot chocolate. I plowed through another beer, and Ewan went inside to grab fresh ice for his bourbon. Once he perched on the deck chair to my right, an expectant hush fell over the pack, and I cleared my throat, waiting for someone to take charge.

And remembering that someone was me.

"Okay, so, uh, who wants to go next?" Nailed it.

Lyssa glanced at Lucian.

Lucian stared at the fire.

Ewan rolled his eyes.

And I geared up to—

"Hi, my name is Lyssa."

She blurted it so fast that every word strung together, one feeding into the next. It took a small beat for the rest of us to even process what she said, but this time when we all murmured *Hi, Lyssa*, it wasn't a joke. She must have thought *that* was how you started this thing and piggybacked off Ewan. Tension skittered between us, a stone bouncing over the lake before *plunking* to the bottom. No one said a thing when she hesitated, we three males focused on *her*, hanging on her every word, this moment a long time coming.

"I recently learned… through Idunn, uh, that my parents…" Huffing, she readjusted her position in the chair that was way too small for Lucian and absolutely massive for our mate. Mug on the armrest, she fiddled with the blankets, her messy bun, her hoodie half-up and struggling to contain the bronze beehive on top of her head.

She was just buying time.

Fiddling and fussing to put off the inevitable.

No one rushed her.

We waited.

Lyssa had taught us how to be patient.

"So, my dad was apparently this alpha wolf of a New York pack," she finally admitted once there was nothing left to rearrange and tug and organize. Huffing a few loose, wavy strands from her face, she locked onto the fire, losing herself in it, her eyes melting to liquid gold. "He mated with my mom… even though he already had a fated mate." Yikes. Not unheard of, but generally not well received for an alpha to create new bloodlines with anyone *but* his fated after they were mated and marked. "I guess my mom wanted to take the mate's, uh, spot in the pack? Anyway, she got pregnant with me. The secret got out. My dad's mate ran her out of the territory... Hunted her. After I was born, the mate found her and... killed her. The alpha never looked for me. I-I didn't exist to him."

Cheeks hollow, Lyssa grabbed her mug in both hands and slugged it back, then wiped the remnants of her whip mustache on her sleeve. I slowly set my new, unopened beer aside, enraptured, inner wolf completely still for the first time in our life, both of us *needing* every detail like we needed air.

And from the looks on their faces, the intensity in our bond, Ewan and Lucian were right there with me.

"The mate left me at a fire station, which I guess is... something." Hot chocolate gone, Lyssa set the empty mug on the deck next to her foot, then leaned forward, elbows on her knees, to watch the fire. "That was how I got into the human foster system. My first foster parents adopted me shortly after taking me in. Reed and Nikki... I know now that they were fundamentalists, or, uh, at least really conservative in their, uh, religious beliefs. They were strict but fair in their own way from what I remember. We went to church a lot, prayed a lot, missed out on a lot..."

"But, you know, I think they loved me in the beginning. They'd adopted two foster kids before me, and the house was always really busy with more coming in and out. It was loud but not chaotic. We all shared rooms, and we didn't always get along, but we tried. Nikki homeschooled us. Reed worked... somewhere, I dunno. Life was really structured, and we lived in this old farmhouse..."

Her eyes lit up at the memory, the lift of her lips affectionate.

"We had chickens, goats, sheep, and, uhm, *pigs*. Yeah. I loved the animals. I liked the routine. I... I was happy there." The smile flatlined. "I felt safe." Her words turned empty, and I suddenly tasted *ash* at the back of my throat. Ash and smoke and sorrow. "Then I shifted for the first time, and it..." Her voice cracked. "It all came crashing down."

Sniffling, she sat back and dried her eyes, the rest of us so tense, so still, we had basically turned to stone.

Hell, it was like I had to remind myself to *breathe*.

"It was an accident. We were all watching a movie one night, and I just... shifted. Kira popped out, and she was so excited—and everyone was terrified." Lyssa shook her head, eyes narrowing. "They put me in the barn that night, then, when I was a girl again, took me to doctors... but they had no idea what... They couldn't just *say* I had turned into a wolf, so it was all metaphor. Behavior issues. Defiance. Attitude problems—that kind of stuff. Reed refused the prescribed medications, so it was a lot of therapy at first... and prayer."

"Fuck." It slipped out before I could stop it, and I bit my tongue, pissed that *that* word had punctured her story. I mean, the fear of that word came from this time in her life, and she didn't need the reminder.

But as Lyssa stared at me from across the flames, it was like she looked clear through me, succumbing to the memories, stuck in freefall and crashing fast.

"I couldn't control the shift at first, and Kira was so protective." Kira was... the wolf? Her wolf? Cute. My guy had never wanted a name, but *now* he did. "Anytime I was really scared, she came out to fight for me. So, uh, the therapies obviously weren't working. Nikki and Reed got more desperate. I spent days inside the prayer closet asking for God's forgiveness, asking him to please take Kira away, to make me normal. When that didn't work, Reed... he... the belt... He tried to scare the demon out—"

"He *beat* you?" Lucian growled, his every word slow, measured, and brutal. If this Reed guy were here right now, that wolf would have ripped him apart.

Fury whipped through our bond.

I gritted my teeth, a prickling sensation falling through me like an airstrike, and then, *boom*, exploding in my gut.

If he was here, we *all* would take a turn making *him* scared.

"The bruises never lasted, so I think he thought... it didn't hurt?

But he had no idea," Lyssa muttered with a little nod, frowning at the fire. "It was two years of that, and Kira stayed. It was just me and her, and then... the priest came." She cleared her throat as her hand seemed to unconsciously wrap around it. "They tied me to a bed... for a weeklong exorcism. They thought Kira was a demon... that *I* was..."

Glass splintered, and out of the corner of my eye, I caught Ewan chucking his busted tumbler aside with a scowl, the pain of splintered crystal in his palm niggling in mine.

"I thought I'd die there, but I didn't," Lyssa admitted, choking out the confession, her trauma unfolding through our connection like she had finally let go a little. Let it out. Let us really *feel* the terror, the pain, the betrayal.

It made me sick.

Literally.

Bile scorched up my throat, but I swallowed it back down, refusing to puke—refusing to take from *her* hurt and make it my own.

But we all felt it. Lucian had gone a sickly pale, his forehead shiny with cold sweats, and Ewan looked ready to upchuck all that bourbon over the side of the porch and into the lake.

"When it was over, he called me an abomination." She wiped at her face with trembling hands, then hid them in her sweater sleeves, using the thick fabric to stem the constant flow of tears. To her credit, she appeared to be *trying* to hold it back, to come across strong, like she had moved past all that horror—but she didn't have to. Not for us. Not here. Bonfire of trust—judgment-free zone. "I guess he didn't know about shifters, because he said I was an affront to God... Thinking back on it, I'm p-pretty sure he tried to tell Nikki and Reed that it would be a kindness to kill me."

Lucian's snarl came out a monstrous roar this time, and Ewan shot to his feet, then stiffly sat back down when Lyssa's wide eyes drifted in his direction.

I... couldn't move.

Couldn't speak.

Some fucking *asshole* had suggested killing *our* girl? Our fated mate? Just because she was a fucking *shifter*?

Did she have his name?

Was he still alive?

Because, screw it, by dawn tomorrow—he wouldn't be.

"Reed drove me out to the middle of nowhere instead," our girl said hurriedly, flying through the rest as if that might calm us. "He walked me into the forest and told me *this* was where I belonged, that I was too big a risk for all the souls at home. Like I'd... taint them. And then h-he left." Her voice cracked, and her lips wobbled. No stopping the tears anymore. No damming up the floodgates. "I chased his truck, but I lost it. I was y-yelling for him to come back, a-and then it was Kira crying for him... Then I... Then I got lost. And I was so scared and alone, and the forest was so dark and scary..."

"Lyssa, you don't have to—"

"But then Mama and Papa found me."

Mama and Papa.

Ewan and I had met her wolf family before she hunted down Lucian.

Just your standard wild wolves—who clearly adored our girl. So long as they didn't cause a problem for nearby farms or wander inside the village, they could stay in Redwood Grove forever; there was more than enough game to feed them. For now, they made a home in the western woods, riding out winter a brisk walk away from the heart of this pack.

"They were alone too back then," she said with a watery chuckle. "Just two young mates... and I was in their territory. They found me in wolf form, and I was almost the same size as them. They could have killed me—but they kept me. And they raised me. Fed me. Protected me." Her voice lifted, the affectionate memories of pigs on a farm paling in comparison to those two. "Taught me to hunt and trusted me to defend their pups. I stayed with that pack until you guys found me.

"Sometimes I went into towns or bars or whatever. I snuck into movie theaters, stole clothes from drying lines and cabins and thrift stores. Left caches all over the place that I could dig out whenever we were in the area. I spent days in libraries sometimes just so I wouldn't forget how to read. No more school for me. I did my best to, uh, not go full wolf, you know?"

She did a hell of a job.

My girl.

Our fated.

A fucking *survivor*.

Stunned silence smothered the back deck, disbelief echoing through our bond, our collective shock dulling the rage we all felt for our girl—but for how long was anyone's guess. Ewan, Lucian, and I gawked at her. Lyssa lost herself in the fire.

"And I think that, uhm, influences how I handle pack and togetherness," Lyssa insisted, barely squeaking it out, her energy scattered. My inner wolf whined suddenly, a little too affected by the weight of her frenetic emotions in our connection. "I-I don't ever want to be left in the woods again, but I'm trying not to assume that will happen anytime one of you leaves. With my new, uh, *powers*, I feel like that little girl sometimes, like a freak who doesn't fit in anywhere, and it scares me, but I really don't want to l-let what happened back then ruin my whole life—"

Lucian was up and on the move, me and Ewan hot on his heels— only it wasn't a race. It wasn't a competition to see who could reach Lyssa first, who would wipe her tears, who would steal a kiss. No snarls. No growls. No jostling or elbowing or shoving. We all had a place around our shivering mate, Lucian falling to his knees and blanketing her legs with his enormous body. Ewan drifted around behind, almost symbolic in the way he had her back, hugging her with his arms draped over her shoulders.

I crouched by her side, my inner wolf whimpering, whining to get out and lick her tearstained cheeks. I brushed my knuckles over them instead. Shuddering, Lyssa slipped a hand into Lucian's hair, while the other reached back to briefly cup Ewan's jaw, then thread with mine, our fingers weaving together as I came in for a nuzzle. She closed her eyes. Breathed deep.

And we just held her.

Supported her.

As her breathing slowed, the wind rattling through the woods died down too.

The fire still snapped, sure, but with a less aggressive bite.

I nosed at her flushed cheeks, her chin, her neck, not saying a word—because we all spoke volumes in the silence. We found comfort in each other, my leg nudged against Lucian, my hands occasionally brushing by Ewan. No bared teeth. No glaring wolf eyes.

In time, we found our pack heartbeat.

I'd felt it once before, back when Ewan and Lucian agreed we should find Lyssa and bring her home. There was this... *moment*, this wonderful, amazing *connection* that we had never had before. Togetherness. Unity. Allies to the end.

Brothers, even.

That feeling followed us here, whumping between my ears like a pulse, our bond quiet and smooth, calm and collected.

Lyssa's fingers dislodged from mine now and again so she could touch the rest of her mates, and we held our posts, taking a silent vow that she would *never* be a terrified pup alone in the forest again.

Never, ever, ever, *ever*.

One of us would always be there for her.

She wasn't a fucking abomination.

She wasn't a freak.

She was *different* now with these powers, not really a shifter, not a human, not a witch.

Something new and wild and beautiful.

Our girl was perfect. No matter her flaws, no matter the small annoyances you found in everyone, even your soulmate —perfection.

I wouldn't change a thing.

But we would change, of course. After tonight, everything

should be different. Better. Stronger. More cohesive a pack and deeper-connected fated mates.

Our pack cuddle came to its natural end when Lyssa's tears stopped for good, her cheeks dry, her eyes less bloodshot, her hands steady, her smiles big and bright. Each of us kissed her and confirmed she was okay before drifting back to our chairs, and while it all seemed good, the bonfire's flames still sparked in our bond—in the connection I shared with the guys, slowly separating itself from the one we had as a pack and the tether binding me and Lyssa.

I glanced at Lucian, then Ewan, then bobbed my head grimly when I saw it—the *murder* in their eyes.

Anyone who so much as *hinted* that it would be a mercy to kill Lyssa, either because she was a wolf or because she had dead goddess powers...

We'd end them.

Them and their whole damn bloodline, just to send a message.

The queen of this pack was *ours*, and if you messed with her, you wouldn't live to see your next sunrise.

Our collective bond felt strange as we all settled around the fire again. Butts in seats, eyes on the flames, our emotions threaded and twisted together, layered and opposite and so complex it made my head spin. On the one hand, there was that cozy warmth of togetherness, the unification of four wolves who, a few months back, had no clue they weren't alone in this world—that Lady Fate had something amazing up her sleeves. But that heat, that heartfelt *fire*, was also laced with loss and longing, a broken feeling shared by these three alphas knotting in my stomach and leaving a lump in my throat I couldn't dislodge no matter how fast I chugged my next beer.

All eyes eventually landed on Lucian.

He stared deep into the fire, wolf eyes out and golden, just like our mate.

Ewan cleared his throat.

Lyssa shuffled about in the deck chair, her impatience—this

sweet, intense, palpable need for information—zinging through the bond sharp enough that Lucian's eye twitched and his lips thinned.

"My story pales in comparison to—"

I booted him as hard as I could, nailing him in the calf and growling when he glared. Oh no, buddy. He didn't get to skate by on a technicality after Ewan and Lyssa picked open old scars and bled all over the porch. Nope. Not happening.

Just like you treated a stubborn pup, we would *sit* here for as long as it took to get this stubborn dillweed to open up—

"My pack name is... is Hadley." Elbows on his knees, arms hanging, Lucian threaded his hands together and returned that fierce expression to the fire. Hadley. *Hadley?* Why did that ring a bell? My inner wolf stilled, both of us racking our brains, until... "Of the London Hadleys."

Ewan jerked upright, jaw on the floor, and a tidal wave of *holy fuck* pounded through me.

Only Lyssa seemed not to register the magnitude of the bomb that just dropped.

"Who are the London Hadleys?" she asked, innocent and unassuming, fidgeting with the wispy frayed ends of her purple blanket as she looked between us. For a few long beats, no one said a damn thing. Lucian didn't clarify. Ewan just stared at him—and my inner wolf and I debated whether we were supposed to *bow* in front of him now or what.

The London Hadleys...

Holy—fucking—shit.

I had no idea.

Dad would lose his mind when he found out the weirdo hermit wolf who carved bear sculptures out of fallen trees and pissed outdoors instead of building a bathroom in his cabin was—

"Wolf royalty," Ewan declared, blinking those thick black lashes hard like he was trying to shake the shock. "The Hadley pack of London is fucking wolf—royalty."

"You all probably know the story," Lucian said roughly, scratching at his beard with a shrug, "so there's really no point in—"

"*I* don't know." Lyssa's girlish whine was like fire to the wick, setting off a protective urge strong as dynamite through the bond. Her imploring expression, that wide golden gaze, her lifted brows —catnip to Lucian. A siren song he, like the rest of us, couldn't ignore.

Not when she looked so lost and adorable and desperate.

I sank into my chair with a smirk, then went for my next beer. *Good luck getting around* that, *my guy.*

"Little mate," Lucian started with a deep breath, his exhale rustling the bonfire and stirring the embers along the exterior, "my story is…" Fucked. Allegedly. "My story is one of brother against brother." He bowed his head, eyes closed, voice no longer velvety and luxe—but harsh and gravelly, his wolf charging forward… probably to protect him, same as Ewan's had. "I have a twin, you see. Brandon."

Yikes. If I ever spat one of my sisters' names like that, my parents would gut me.

"*I* was born an alpha, but he wasn't."

Lucian rubbed at his crinkled brow with a low growl, his inner conflict, the strife, the *war* going on inside leaking into the bond. I scratched at the back of my neck as I broke out in a cold sweat, his history like ice and snow and sleet dragging you closer and closer to hypothermic shock. Even Ewan tugged his sleeves down from his elbows to his wrists, and Lyssa bundled herself up tighter in the blanket as the wolf continued the tale we had all heard in one form or the other over the years.

A fable.

A warning—about what happened to packs, no matter how established, when we turned on each other.

The London Hadleys: the pack that ate itself alive.

"*I* was destined to rule the Hadley pack. It was my birthright, but not his. We… We're descended from English aristocracy." He focused on Lyssa, as if sensing Ewan and I didn't need the same level of detail. "Our ancestors integrated into the human royal courts, and there we stayed for generations. I ran the family publishing house before all this, but I planned to bow out to take the alpha title when my father abdicated…

"Brandon challenged me for it—in front of everyone, at the alpha ceremony *just* before I started my vows. All our lives, we promised there would be no fighting. He would be my second, my beta, my brother in arms. We would rule *together*, but he… allied with a few of our younger brothers. Our cousins. Anyone who thought he would be the better fit.

"We fought. It split the family in two. London ran red with wolf blood for a long… *long* time." He dropped his head again, his words lifeless, his heartbreak *visceral* and so *real* that it brought tears to my eyes. "Too long."

Across the flickering flames, all of us shrouded in orange and *heat*, Lyssa wiped her eyes, sniffled, but kept her focus totally on Lucian as he folded deeper and deeper in on himself.

"I lost sisters, brothers, aunts, uncles… We fought and fought. Backstabbed and cheated and argued until we were ready to burn the world. We… He… He scarred me."

"How?" Lyssa whispered. Seriously. Shifters could scar their fated mates, but the trauma on Lucian's skin went way beyond that.

"The Hadleys have always allied with witches and warlocks," Lucian admitted with a one-shouldered shrug, his words darkening, the air thickening. He might try to play it off casually, but danger shuddered through the bond, the promise of violence rising. "Brandon had the support of our warlock—and he cursed me. The wounds that cut the deepest, not physically but emotionally, will stay with me forever."

Including the one along his throat, I guess, from the night he thought the Hawthorne alpha had murdered our mate. I set my half-drunk beer on the armrest and ruffled my hair, unable to even imagine wearing the worst moments of my life out in the open, the scars deep and ugly, his skin never shifter-flawless again.

Lucian scrubbed at his face, the wrath in our bond settling, replaced by an exhaustion that made Lyssa's blinks heavy and slow.

"In the end, I left. I surrendered to stop the loss of life, but I was so bloody stubborn about it for the longest time... So many died for choosing me."

His voice cracked. His wolf eyes retreated, that green gaze waterlogged—and locked with Ewan's. Both had lost packmates for one reason or another. To violence and wolfsbane. To something as simple as the hand Lady Fate dealt them.

I... I couldn't...

My sisters, their mates, their pups—I'd throw myself on a grenade for any of them.

"I regret it," the scarred wolf rasped. "Every death ripped a piece of me away—set it on fire. I hate myself for it. I'm terrified of... of *loss*, of feeling as I did back then." He pushed his intensity onto Lyssa, speaking directly to her heart as he added, "To the core— terrified. I can*not* go through what I did before. And I'm sorry, little mate, that it still shapes me. Really, I am. I have to learn to trust and love again, but it's... difficult, I suppose, to form attachments knowing what could happen."

Fuck.

The windows rattled softly to my left, Lyssa's emotions playing through them. The winds shifted and turned, blowing east now. The lake's surface shivered.

And she just stared at him, eyes *so* gold in the firelight, so deep and rich and *ancient* they cut me off at the knees.

Ewan stared too, but probably for a different reason.

I mean, a bomb just went off in this pack—because we had been living with and shitting on and making fun of wolf *royalty* for a seriously long time. The Hadley tragedy crossed the pond maybe ten or so years back, and it made the rounds through North American wolf packs, rumor mill churning, the story embellished.

Not that it needed to be padded or anything.

The truth was bad enough.

Brother against brother—it was Shakespearian, the life Lucian had lived before he hiked into the western woods and hid from the world.

His paranoia, his concerns for safety and borders and always finding an exit...

Ewan's confrontational nature, his intense work ethic, his savagery...

Lyssa's desperation to keep us close, to make herself *perfect* so no one could ever reject her...

It all made sense now.

The tragedy booted my inner wolf over the edge, taking him from bouncy little sunshine derp to *alpha*—still the clown, still the playmate, but not all the time anymore.

"Look, Lucian, I can't imagine what it's like to have a brother turn on you," I started, the words flying before I could stop them— really think them through. His stare burned into my forehead a beat later, and I focused on the fire, letting it fuel me, embolden me. Letting it center thoughts that were usually racing and uncertain and a little juvenile. "*We* are your brothers here. We're the alphas of this territory. It's shared—and it's *ours*. No one is going to turn on the other. Me and Ewan are here for you—"

"And me," Lyssa butted in, shuffling to the end of her chair, her hand up, finger raised, as if we could have *ever* forgotten her. "I'm an alpha. I'm a leader of this pack *with* you—and what happened before will *never* happen here. Not on my watch."

Warmth fluttered in our mangled bond, the connection battered and bruised but *there*. A survivor, just like her.

Just like all of them, actually.

And what had happened to her—*that* wouldn't happen again either.

Not on *our* watch.

Lucian's weak smile told me he didn't completely believe us— and fair enough. He had been burned before. Give it time and he'd see *real* brothers would have his back to the bitter, brutal end. That wasn't the case a few months ago, not before her, maybe not even before tonight, even with the pack song and the heartbeat in our bond...

But that was how it would be from this night onward.

I'd make sure of that.

Slowly, the scarred alpha leveled that thin smile on an unusually quiet Ewan. Across the fire, they squared off, silent and tense. All this time, Ewan Quinn had been talking *down* to Lucian for his taste, his style—for the way he chose to live his life in the woods with no amenities. No creature comforts. No luxury labels.

Little did he realize...

Quinns were new money. His old pack's reputation made it out here to us too, this ragtag Toronto crew who ran the city and the surrounding suburbs.

The Hadleys? The London Hadleys were old as dirt and a thousand times stronger.

And now, Ewan and Lucian's relationship bore the brunt of that imbalance.

Before tonight, that sensation, the unflinching stares—they should have been beating the shit out of each other over the firepit.

Instead, they just stared and stared and stared, Redwood Grove holding its breath...

Until Ewan shattered it all with a teasing grin.

"I think that's the most I've ever heard you talk," he mused. Bourbon bottle in his lap, the tumbler smashed and forgotten, he cocked his head and lifted an eyebrow. "You need to hibernate for a bit to recover, or you good?"

Smirking, I chucked a crushed beer can at him. Ewan caught it, one-handed and without looking, then whipped it across the fire at Lucian, who ducked out of the way.

All of us grinning and chuckling.

And Lyssa looking between us with this expression that just screamed, *Ugh, boys.*

Still, her barely contained smile, the one she tried to hide so it wouldn't distract us—impossible to ignore.

Like me, apparently. I felt her golden gaze a few moments later, and my obvious avoidance techniques blew right over her head.

"Soren?"

Ewan and Lucian finally turned on me as well, and I cleared my throat, cheeks hot and heart beating a little faster under their scrutiny.

"Uh, I… don't have a family tragedy."

Ewan's eye roll declared *Duh* far and wide. My cheeks hollowed, and I squared my shoulders, refusing to give him this one.

"I think my sisters were right all along." I rubbed my hands together, then smoothed the nervous sweat over my pants. "About me being the golden child… I was spoiled—could do no wrong with my mom. I got away with stuff they couldn't. I'm… not trying to do that here. We all have the same expectations—"

Ewan twirled his finger in a whoop-de-do sort of way that made Lucian smirk and Lyssa huff.

"*But*," I stressed, fingers itching to curl around another crushed beer can and lob it at his smug face, "I don't think that's a bad thing." I then scooted forward and looked them each in the eye, letting my fellow males know this didn't make me *lesser*. "Seriously, you guys are damaged. Like, a lot. A lot of messed-up shit has happened to you, and it's honestly horrific. That stuff—it changes who you are, how you handle conflict. Everything."

"Spare us the psychology lecture," Lucian drawled, shooing me off with a lazy flutter of his huge hand. *No.* I refused to let this go. I had crap to contribute to this pack. I wasn't just some goofy beta for them to walk all over.

"What I'm trying to say," I carried on, my wolf injecting a rough growl to every word, the grit catching Ewan and Lucian's attention —making them puff up a bit, their own wolves baited, "is that I'm here. I'm stable. I had a solid upbringing and learned a lot about keeping a pack *strong*, and, you know, comparably healthy and functional."

Lucian bowed his head. Ewan picked at the waxy lid on his bourbon. Lyssa watched me from behind her blanket, eyes shimmering, her affection coursing through my veins—pushing me, encouraging me.

"I'm here to support you guys while you heal and work through this stuff. I'm just… here. I won't judge you. I've got your back. And

I… I'll help us build the same strong, healthy, functional pack I grew up in."

Lyssa's eyebrows arched, and I nodded. *I hear you, baby.*

"But it'll be *ours*. Our own laws and traditions and codes. We build each other up, not tear each other down. We accept each other for who we are, what we are, and what we each bring to the pack as alphas. It's just us now—but we'll have pups soon." Across the fire, our mate went bright red, the sentiment milking a few rumbly growls from the others. "Our strength will attract lone wolves. Redwood Grove *will* have a pack and bloodline that we manage, and we each bring something invaluable to it. We need to sort this trauma out now so no one can ever divide us with it."

Okay.

Yeah, that was good.

Kind of concise. Pretty coherent. Minimal rambling. No silliness.

And Ewan and Lucian *still* looked like they wanted to tease the absolute shit out of me, glancing between each other and me, the bond riddled with the kind of laughter you felt, not heard.

Ewan's lips parted with a soft breath.

Lucian squared off, preparing for the verbal undressing—

"That's exactly what I want."

Lyssa to the rescue.

We all looked to our mate—our teary-eyed, beaming, shining, glowing, *beautiful* mate.

"I want us to be a family," she insisted, shoving her blankets down, shaking them off, and scooting to the edge of the chair. A cozy quiet descended, punctuated by the crackle of the bonfire, the scent of burning wood, and spiraling smoke thick—nostalgic of my childhood, of bonfires under the stars near the maple grove.

"Even healthy families fight." Cue Ewan to pop the bubble. He held up his hands when we all turned on him. "I'm just *saying*. It won't always be sunshine and rainbows and cohesion… is all."

Yeah, well, it wouldn't be overdoses on the shitter and drug rings and trafficking female shifters either—so this was a big step up.

This guy. This fucking guy. Just seize the *moment*. My inner wolf grumbled, his frustration making my hands curl to fists, but once again, Lyssa soothed the rising tension by softly clearing her throat and smiling.

"Well, no, it would be silly to think families *always* get along." She tugged her hair out of the crazy knot on top of her head, that bronze mane tumbling free, then fluffed it out, unleashing clouds of her scent that could calm even the most red-zone shifters. "I mean, wolves fight, but we love too. We make up. We hunt together. We put differences aside. We're *pack*, and from here on out, we act like one." Our mate fixed each one of us with a warning stare—a matriarch laying down the law. "No more running and hiding." She gulped, her own anxieties about that episode flaring in our bond. "No more secrets. We're the Redwood Pack, and we *will* be strong... together."

The Redwood Pack.

Yeah, that should have been the obvious name from the start—but us stubborn assholes refused to settle on anything. In fact, we pivoted and backtracked and steered way around the subject if we could, because before Lyssa, choosing a name, a new banner for us all to run under, made it official.

Permanent.

Forever.

Tonight, it felt natural.

"Agreed," Lucian said roughly, the declaration laced with promise.

"The Redwood Pack," Ewan added, his smile gentle for the first time... *ever*, his wolf gaze a glittering sunset as it sank into the fire. "Ours—I swear it, blue eyes."

He then glanced between me and Lucian, the vow for us too.

And there it was again—the pack heartbeat.

A pulse booming through the bond.

Unity. Togetherness.

I shot up and clapped my hands together. "Let's seal it with a pack run."

No blood oaths. No contracts. No ink and legal language and lawyers. Running as a pack, as alphas, was how wolves did this.

Our word and a run...

No going back.

Lucian and Ewan hesitated, the latter tapping obnoxiously on his bourbon bottle, mind racing, anxiety prickling in the bond—

But then Lyssa leapt up and yanked her hoodie off. Tossed it aside. Next came the bra, her sweatpants...

And the rest of us followed her lead, soon just four wolves howling to the moon, singing our songs, our promises, our oaths— and our love—so loud that even Lady Fate could hear us up there amongst the stars.

6

LUCIAN

I thought I was in the clear—until Ewan charged out of nowhere and bodychecked me so hard into a birch sapling that the trunk *cracked* on impact. Snarling, I snapped at his tail as he whizzed by, Soren hot behind, the pair colliding ahead and crashing into some brambles.

We sealed our pack vows tonight with a run throughout the whole territory. North, south, east, and west—we ran. Together. No leader. No followers. Unity. Equality. Intimacy. Steering clear of humans, we four clung to nature, stopping at one point to rouse Lyssa's old pack from their lazing around my cabin. A few of the braver wolves joined in the playfighting, wrestling with me and the boys, mouthing at Lyssa—desperate for her attention. To them, *she* was their ultimate alpha, and they deferred to her at every turn.

My mate took it all with such grace, never lording it over anyone's head.

I had never felt so bloody *alive*.

All these years, the past haunted me, awake and asleep. Brandon's betrayal. The warlock's curse. My sisters—dead at my feet, all because they supported the *true* alpha in our bloodline.

Chains dragged behind me from London to Redwood Grove, heavy and oppressive and suffocating, forged of pure silver.

Just like that night.

The trauma of my old life seared just as deep as Hawthorne silver.

That night—I'd died when I thought she did. When the bullets hit her—*bam, bam, bam, bam,* four to the chest—it was all over. Nothing mattered anymore. Not that I'd been bested by the savage Hawthorne wolves. Not the territory. Not my past. Not my damaged soul. *Her.* I thought I lost her. She should have *died* where she stood, the silver piercing her heart, snuffing out the most *brilliant* light—our girl should have gone to the stars. She would have been the brightest in the sky, nestled in Lady Fate's crown.

I gave up.

Gave in.

Let the enemy *slaughter* me where I knelt... so I could join her in the sky.

But she came back.

I survived—barely.

Realized I loved her more than life itself. Literally.

And that scared the absolute piss out of me.

I fled north on a whim, hating myself, the loneliness crushing, and expected to die there. Waste away and let the wildlife feast on me in the spring thaws. I couldn't... *feel* that loss again, couldn't shoulder more trauma.

But that was then.

This was now.

Torment hounded *everyone* in this pack—everyone but Soren. Yet that had merit, value, *purpose.* He was a light, same as Lyssa, a beacon to guide us through the darkness and out the other side. Our worst secrets were exposed now. Sure, we all skimped on details. Ewan likely had a great deal more to his story than what he shared at the bonfire, darker and more violent elements edited and kept to himself.

Same as me.

Same as my little mate.

It was our prerogative to disclose that when and if we chose— but the general bollocks would do for now. A solid start. *Just* enough information for the others to flag our behaviors, our destructive tendencies, and our failings when they reared their ugly heads.

So, it was time to stop moping.

Suffering wasn't unique to the exiled Hadley alpha.

It was time to fucking rebuild.

Create the pack all of us had been destined to rule since birth. Fate worked in mysterious ways—and it led me, Ewan, Soren, and Lyssa *here*. To this moment. To a wild, free, primal pack run through the forest and around the lake and up the mountains. Across the nothingness down south and back again, to the maple and birch groves around Soren's old family cabins—to the shoreline in the distance beyond the trees.

Growls and snarls and barks erupted ahead of me, and as I shook off Ewan's playful stealth attack, I caught the pair wrestling in the bushes. Before Lyssa, I would have intervened—because it wouldn't have been for fun. Something like this, Ewan on his back, Soren at his throat, would have been life or death, blood watering the forest floor, our fragile connection hanging by a thread.

Tonight, the pack bond practically glowed. It bloomed with warmth, tender and *new*, the heartbeat we now shared a constant. It had faded to background noise, but we all felt it, this accompaniment to our united pack song.

Above it all, apple blossoms tickled my nostrils.

With a low rumble, I padded through the trees, skirting my roughhousing packmates and heading for the lake.

Because there she was, paws on the rocky shore, nose up, eyes closed.

I turned my attention skyward—to the first snowfall of the season trickling down in fat, fluffy flakes. One landed on my snout, and I snorted, shaking out my coat, flicking the damp away.

The sky had grown heavy throughout the night, a silent, grey promise that we would have our first glimpse of winter soon. For me, however, the north had already given me my snowy fill. Miserable, lonely, *hating* every second of my forced march to the tundra, to the bleak, cold nothingness at the end of the world—I had gorged on fucking *snow*. Deep enough to skim my belly in some places.

Lyssa was no different.

She had followed in my footsteps.

Crested every hill, trekked every valley, weaved through the thinning trees and the emptying landscape—downwind and hidden.

Until she let me scent her.

Until she confronted me. Attacked me. Shouted at me.

Showed me that our love had never been one-sided.

I'd thought I loved her with every bloody fiber of my being *before*.

That was nothing compared to now.

Nothing compared to knowing she had come so far to find me— only to walk away when she thought *I* needed the solitude.

Being there, alone, far from anything and anyone who could add yet another scar to my flesh—Lyssa thought that was what I wanted.

It had *devastated* her to turn away.

I felt it in our bond and in my soul.

But she had been willing to do it for me.

Perfection.

My mate was sheer, utter *perfection* in every way that mattered.

Thank Lady Fate I'd realized all I needed was right there in this little she-wolf with her grey-to-black coat and golden eyes. Thank all the divine entities stuck guiding me through life that I had finally —*finally*—put the fear aside.

It could all still go to pot.

Life was cruel. Love didn't change that.

But I'd be here for it, the highs and the lows, the good and the bad, the love and the loss.

With her.

More growls erupted behind me.

And *them*.

Twats. Frustrating, infuriating, irritating, selfish, pretentious *twats*.

But most little brothers were, right? They drove you mad—and still you'd tear their enemies apart without question.

The good ones, anyway.

Somehow, perhaps in a bit of karmic justice, I finally found myself with two of the good ones.

Two brothers who promised to have my back, who swore it so intensely that it *burned* into our bond—and a mate perfect for all of us.

Shit.

What I would have missed had I stayed in the tundra like a fucking hermit *wanker*.

No more.

Enough of that.

Because I was here now.

I was *home*—watching her—and there was nowhere I would rather be.

Lyssa kept her gaze on the sky, all that luscious gold tracking the snow as it fluttered down. Nothing stayed. The ground was still too warm to hold the blanket of white, but some of the billowing fluff dotted her wolf coat. My little mate shook it off, sneezed, then stomped her paws in a little happy dance, clearly excited to see snow again.

Love hummed in our bond, oozing like syrup on a hot summer's day, and her hackles shot up at the sensation. Still, the stubborn thing kept her back to me, even as I drifted into the breeze, my scent wafting over her. She sauntered back and forth along the lakeshore, snapping at snowflakes, so fucking adorable and exuberant and *mine*.

Eventually, she blessed me with a glance over her shoulder. *Kira*. She had named her inner wolf, and it suited her.

So did those golden eyes, so rich and *deep*, touched by a dead goddess…

Not a witch. Not a warlock. A divine being like Lady Fate who deemed her worthy of all that *power*.

Idunn—she couldn't have chosen anyone better than Lyssa, honestly. It certainly wasn't an accident our mate had become the most powerful in the Redwood pack.

Eyes on me, my little mate wagged her tail and whined for proper attention and company at the shoreline, gobbling snowflakes together.

I had something different in mind.

All that love and affection and warmth went nuclear, an inferno flaring in the bond, *desire* pulsing.

I *wanted* her.

When she found me up north, I needed her. Needed her touch and her voice and her compassion. Proximity. Closeness. *Fate*.

This was different.

We were home at last, the pack united—and there were more ways to cement our vows and promises than a run through the forest.

Her swishing tail stilled when I took a step toward her, slow and precise, predatory and possessive.

Lyssa countered with two steps backward, as was her way from the very beginning. Her black nose twitched like she could *smell* my intensity, my focus, my masculine drive to claim and mark and mate right here, right *now*.

I lowered my head and growled.

She dropped into a fucking play-bow, the cheeky minx, tail wagging again, and barked.

A challenge then, from a she-wolf who had *no* idea what sort of fire she was playing with tonight. We had all been so soft and sweet and loving—but when Ewan and Soren's interest threaded with mine in our bond, their paws tromping through the undergrowth at my back, her demeanor changed.

We changed.

My packmates prowled to my side, fire raging from Ewan to my right, danger dripping from Soren to my left. Lyssa tipped her head side to side, sizing us up. The run had been equal. No alpha. No leader. She easily kept pace with three larger males.

But the dynamic had shifted as suddenly and violently as the wind.

Snowflakes plunged straight down for the earth now, pinging and bouncing off the ground in hard little balls. The lake surface rippled and danced. The trees bowed.

Lyssa snorted again, slowly easing upright, *power* blooming in the air.

This… was all her.

A bluff charge.

Testing the waters.

Daring us to fight back.

To *hunt* her.

Claim her.

Fuck her.

That was her favorite game, right?

Snow decorated her brow like a crown the longer we stared each other down, the tension mounting, the intensity rising—

With another teasing bark, she turned on a dime and along down the shoreline, tail up and scent dragging behind like a comet's tail.

We raced after her, hunting her, as need *pounded* through the bond like thunder.

And our little mate—brave and loyal and *fast*—she just dared us to keep up.

7

LYSSA

So, this was *living*, wild and free and real.

Feeling frisky, melting under the fires of my mates' molten want, I sprinted toward the house with a spring in my step.

All my life, this was everything I had ever wanted.

A pack.

A family.

Creatures who felt like me, thought like me, shifted like me —*loved* like me.

With Ewan, Soren, and Lucian close behind, this was a familiar scene, same as the first night when they chased me through the forest for hours, only now I wasn't terrified and screaming for my wolves. No, now I wore a sharp, dangerous smile, even as Kira, and put them through their paces because it made my heart *happy*. As I peeled around the edge of the lake, on the final lap to home, I caught them weaving and changing positions but always maintaining a V formation, a proper pack hunting the most elusive prey.

Me.

They intended to hunt and claim *me*. I felt it in my bones, right down to my soul. The well trembled deep inside, touched by their desire, and even with my playful stride, my bouncy steps and challenging yips, something about this time was different.

More intense.

More *focused*.

Heavier, the gravity of three males at my back threatening to trip me up and slow me down, but I refused to fall. Refused to falter out here, to make it that easy, so they could pounce and take me beneath the first fluffy snowfall of the season.

Best of all, as I raced down the shoreline, the heart of our territory looming bigger and bigger, the porch lights flickering on almost instinctively at our thunderous approach, I didn't think.

At all.

Not a single thought in my head beyond the moment. No dwelling on my past, now an open wound. No worrying about Ewan's ties to the monsters he had escaped. No *aching* over Lucian's betrayal by the wolf who must have been the closest in the world to him—his twin, a piece of him, a half of a whole.

None of that.

That was for later, in the thick quiet while my mates slept and my heart shattered for them.

Now, it was all instinct.

I veered around the porch, thinking the unlocked front door too obvious, and zipped down the right of our sprawling homestead. Leaping over the wooden stairs at the side of the house in a single bound, I shifted midstride, launching on four paws and landing on two feet. Grinning like a wild woman, naked and sweaty and panting, hair blazing behind me, I whipped around the back deck, careful not to smear my scent anywhere, and went for the sliding glass door. With a quick glance over my shoulder—alone, my mates elsewhere—I bit my lower lip and *eased* the door open as soundlessly as I could, then slipped into a dark, quiet, empty house.

Briefly, I hesitated in our sunken seating area, the same place I had first spilled my guts to Ewan and Soren about Idunn's gifts.

It felt so long ago.

Really, it was just shy of two weeks back.

So much had happened—most in the span of an hour, around the dying bonfire outside in the manmade pit, the embers still flaring but soon to be snuffed by the snow.

Head cocked, I listened for intruders. No bare feet on the tile or hardwood. No doors whooshing open, the knobs turned hard to silence the creak.

Good.

They'd be on the house shortly, but this huge building with three floors and countless rooms offered plenty of hiding places. Even as I tiptoed out of the sitting area, past the dining table, through the open kitchen—I felt it.

Them.

Desire and lust and the need to *conquer*.

It made my thighs tremble. Had me wet between them, my sex growing slicker and slicker with every step. While Kira enjoyed a good game of hide-and-seek as much as I did, she sensed this was so much more. Without fuss, my wolf side retreated, leaving just the woman to fend off my prowling mates—a woman used to predators.

A woman who had been dumped among them a lifetime ago—and now *ruled* them.

A ruler who lost all credibility when she skipped into the foyer and screeched when Ewan barreled savagely through the front door, all teeth and wolf eyes and taut muscles, my fallen angel turning dark and demonic and so, so, *so* terrifyingly beautiful. I sidestepped him with a shriek-giggle, cheeks burning, his powerful invasion of our home actually catching me off guard. My mate lunged with a snarl, determined to capture and claim, maybe throw me to the floor and mount me before the others.

The thought sent chills down my spine and goose bumps soaring over my skin.

But I ducked under his arm, this hunt strangely graceful, a violent dance between mates, and blitzed up the stairs.

Veered right, crashing into the wall, going way too fast for the turn at the landing, and bounced into Soren's bedroom.

Moved swift and silent as a shadow, Idunn's power tingling playfully in my fingertips.

That was... new.

Not the usual buzz.

Just a tingle.

A reminder that it was there, that my intensity and *need* and feelings still brought it to the surface.

But nothing shook or rattled or crashed to the floor. As I slipped inside Soren's huge walk-in closet and crouched in the dark next to a dusty suitcase, the power in me almost seemed... respectful.

Retreating, like Kira, so I could have this all to myself.

With a hand clamped over my mouth, I listened to at least two of my mates prowl around the house, stomping and growling, whispering my name with such *heat* that it made my core clench—made the pleasurable waves surge through me like a riptide. Before, it was Kira—and now Idunn's power—that made it hard to think. Then I met my mates and *their* emotions threaded through me as our bonds forged into something unbreakable.

Now, it was their want, their collective wildfire fogging my brain and lighting my body up like a firework. Usually I was much more creative at hiding, but as the seconds ticked by, it got harder and harder to strategize.

Almost impossible to do anything before I scratched that familiar *itch*. It grew sharper and more insistent, my mates close, the pack's energy making it so much worse that I actually whined and arched and ground my swollen folds against my calf as I crouched, more and more desperate for relief.

Just as I was about to slip my fingers between my thighs and dull the need myself, the closet door flew open, crashing into the shelves on the other side and unleashing a storm of Soren's scent. Usually he was just so cozy, cinnamon and nutmeg and allspice, fresh-spun cotton on a warm summer's day. Tonight, a dangerously masculine musk mingled with his smell, dirt and sky and snowfall and pure, uncut *wild*.

It would have been so easy to surrender to the hulking figure in the doorway, his shoulders so deliciously broad, his torso tight and slick from the shift, muscles out, his expression so serious—*oozing* power.

Instead, I grabbed a handful of hoodies off the nearest shelf and flung them all at him, then dove between his thick thighs, scooted under him, and sprinted for his bedroom door. His snarl made the hairs on the back of my neck rise, made my sex even wetter—and made me giggle, the sound egging him on, begging him to win our game.

Down the hall and around the corner, I caught Ewan scaling the staircase—and I leapt clear off the landing, avoiding it entirely, and landed nimbly on the tile below. Dropping briefly into a crouch to cushion my fall, I scampered off, headed for that little side door at the back of the foyer that opened to the deck, the same Ewan had once hauled my moose kill through on Thanksgiving.

This time, Lucian's enormous body filled the glass door before I could wrench it open. He appeared out of nowhere, forcing another shriek from me, and I reared back with a giggle, ready to make my final stand in the basement.

Ewan caught me before I pivoted all the way around, scooping me up with one steely arm and tossing me over his shoulder. Wriggling and squirming like a little worm, I fought the whole way to the kitchen, then squealed when he nipped at my backside, hard enough to leave a brief indent from his teeth.

The thought made me shiver.

My midnight mate carried me to the soaring stone hearth, then kicked the coffee table aside and dumped me on the beige-and-teal checkered throw rug. The sliding glass door whooshed open, unveiling Lucian's oakwood scent, and footsteps echoed past the kitchen as Soren prowled onto the scene, all of them converging around me.

While Ewan backed off a little, standing tall and proud as his fully erect shaft, I stayed on my hands and knees, sizing my mates up. Analyzing the gaps between them, I tried to gauge who was breathing the hardest—who was my best bet to squirm by for one final chase. Soren by the steps into the sunken seating area. Lucian close to the hearth. Ewan at my back by one of the couches.

One empty couch to my right. It ran the length of the little wall between the living and dining areas, crowned by a black wooden railing.

Easy to scale in a single jump.

I lurched forward, about to tackle the couch in one step, the railing in another—

Ewan snagged my ankle and ripped me back, the others smirking, pure predator as I crashed onto the couch. My black-haired mate then hauled me up by the scruff of my neck, cuffing me like a pup, and left a chastising bite on my shoulder while I tried—hopelessly—to twist out of his iron grip.

But there was no point in trying.

The snare had tightened.

Hunted. Caught. *Fucked.*

That was the game.

All of them just as naked as me, heat coiling between our bodies, need pounding through our connection and desire turning my thoughts sinful, I had no choice but to *watch* as Soren and Lucian stalked forward. One went high, Soren's tongue trailing up my side and over the swell of my right breast; the other went low, Lucian's mouth grazing my inner left thigh, his hands stroking the backs of my calf. Ewan behind me, keeping me here, collaring me roughly while his free hand skimmed my belly, my ribs, then up to cup my breast.

For a moment, I surrendered.

Just a few precious seconds, head lolled back, eyes closed, lips parted. I gave in to the capture, to feeling like the most wanted prey in the whole world—to the blissful suffocation of three males touching me, licking me, teasing me, tasting me.

My eyes snapped open when someone's hand delved between my thighs to gently pinch my clit. *Enough.* No more submission. Lips peeled back, teeth out for them to see, I reached around for Ewan, for the rock-hard dick digging into my lower back so insistently that it was impossible to ignore a second longer. He hissed when I closed my fist around it, my grip harsher than it should have been so early in this dance, mimicking the one on the back of my neck. I held him, reminding him that he was *mine*, then eased up, walking my fingers up his length and stroking the velvet tip, smearing the salty damp around.

All without ever taking my eyes off the steepled ceiling above, off the wood beams and dark finish.

Ewan suddenly disappeared with a growl, all soft and rumbly, full of sinful promises and a whiff of danger. He slipped out of reach, leaving me exposed, but just as I tried to peek back and see where he went, his hands found my hips. Settled onto the couch, he hauled me away from my other mates, the motion sharp and jerky enough to knock me off-balance and send me tumbling into his lap.

He blunted my fall—but only just enough to steer me over his shaft and pierce me to the hilt. My eyes widened and my mouth rounded as he stretched and filled me, my sex so slick with our mingling desires that I eased down with almost no resistance, like my body had been starving for this.

Still, even if my heart, body, and mind *craved* all of them—it was a shock. It came out of nowhere, without their fingers or tongues readying me, and I exhaled a trembling gasp when I finally touched down at his thighs. Seated. Staked. So exquisitely full that fiery little waves crashed through my low belly, again and again, that tingle in my fingertips migrating south.

"Don't act so surprised, blue eyes," Ewan whispered heatedly, one hand grazing my back, the other along my thigh to spread me wider. My eyes snapped open—at some point they had clenched tight, light and color dancing behind the lids—and I found Lucian and Soren watching, eyeing me like they wanted to eat me and share me and pass me around the table. Lips brushed the top of my spine, followed by teeth on my shoulder over Ewan's mark as he rumbled, "We can fucking *smell* you across the house... It's like you're in *heat*."

"And you know what's cruel?" Soren mused, his wolf eyes an amber inferno, his voice rough and low as he strolled toward us.

Stroking his dick, his length so hard it had to *hurt*, he tipped his head and grinned. "Denying a she-wolf in heat."

"One way to get your eyes scratched out," Lucian added gruffly. He paced back and forth behind Soren, prowling, assessing all this with such careful scrutiny that I shivered, desperate to know what he was thinking. Feeling? Want. Need. Desire. Lust. That was easy. It radiated through our bond and jumped from male to male—I wanted to get inside his *head* and hear every filthy word I saw in his golden wolf eyes.

A part of me felt bold enough to ask.

My lips parted—

Ewan's hand fisted in my loose hair and angled my head up, forcing my mouth open wide enough for Soren to thrust into with a groan. My eyes rounded to dinner plates as I took him, our positions from Halloween reversed with him in my mouth and Ewan spearing my pussy.

And Lucian watching, watching, watching—

On the prowl.

My largest mate stalked over and kneeled at my side, one arm resting lazily on the couch cushion as Ewan passed my hair to Soren —handing over the reins of their frisky mare—and took control of my hips again. Slowly, Ewan rocked me, back and forth, back and forth, the pressure so *exquisite* from the start that I whined, the sound muffled by the dick in my mouth.

A dick that retreated, then plunged back in, both of Soren's hands on my hair. Last time, I had set the pace until Ewan took over and fucked my mouth, but even then, he was slow and thoughtful until neither of us could stand it anymore. Something happened when Soren mated.

He turned savage.

Gone was the cheery social butterfly who taught me the shopping cart dance on Halloween, happy to make a fool of himself in public so long as I was laughing.

Here, he became this dark, towering god with gold-spun hair and punishing eyes, thrusting as deep as I could take him every time. I didn't *quite* gag, but nearly, eyes watering, drool dribbling out of the corners of my mouth, and I pushed at his taut abs—as if that might actually do anything.

Like he would *stop*.

He felt the way I enjoyed this—no lying to any of them, not when we shared this bond, but *especially* when we mated, emotions high and feelings out in the open.

Ewan lifted me suddenly, then lowered me back down, changing things up out of nowhere, bucking his hips in time with this new rhythm. I scrambled to keep up with them, to do *something* beyond being used like a rag doll, but all I could do was grab hold and hang on for the ride.

Things went from torturous teasing to downright *cruelty* when Lucian spread my thighs wider and zeroed in on my clit. With nothing more than his fingers, he threw me worst of all, stroking the sensitive bundle, circling the tender nerves, kicking me closer and closer to oblivion.

My eyes drifted shut, mind empty, full of thick pleasure that was about to swell and gather and spiral into a storm—

Whack. The crack of skin to skin echoed through the space, and I squealed, eyes shooting open as pain seared my left butt cheek.

Oh.

Right.

They didn't like it when I closed my eyes—*especially* when I came. My mates liked to enjoy themselves too, liked to watch my pleasure explode in the gold.

Using Lucian's sturdy shoulder and Soren's muscular thigh for support and balance, I did my best to stay *here*, eyes open, glancing between them as Ewan bucked into me from behind and Soren relentlessly thrust into my mouth, over and over again, no mercy, no stopping it.

So—full.

Too much... *fire.*

I smacked at Soren's thigh, but he didn't stop—barely even slowed. Lucian chuckled darkly and picked up the pace between my thighs, rising and falling with the way Ewan handled my hips, all of them frustratingly in sync as they played my body.

Needed a break.

A full, deep, glorious breath.

Needed—

I broke apart when Lucian pinched my clit, his delicate caresses gone brutal. Ewan flicked my nipple as I shuddered and shook and squealed around Soren's shaft. Pleasure blazed through me from top to bottom and back again, settling in my belly, the wildfire way out of control. My explosion touched them too, Lucian's cheeks darkening, his gaze wild. Soren groaned and stilled inside my mouth, holding me in limbo as bliss crashed into me again and again. Ewan cursed and smacked at my backside, this time, maybe, because my sex clenched so hard around him that finally *he* felt trapped in all this.

Suddenly, Soren withdrew, and I collapsed into Ewan with a gasp. Eyes watery. Nose runny. His salty taste lingered on the back of my tongue, my chin soaked with drool, some of it even dribbling down my neck.

"Fucking *give* her to me."

Oh. That wasn't a request.

That was a *demand*.

Stretched on the rough carpet, Lucian made no attempt to claim me himself. No, he stayed there, on his back, shaft hard and intimidating, his eyes dull gold and locked on me. While Ewan didn't move, just smoothed his hands up my thighs so that I wriggled a little on his lap, Soren played peacekeeper, sweeping in and lifting me up. A ragged gasp slipped out of me as soon as Ewan did, my limbs limp from the climax, my head blissfully empty.

Then *alert*, all of me tensing, preparing for the next mate, when Soren lowered me onto Lucian, the pair spreading my thighs again, lining me up to slide down his shaft. I moaned the whole way down, the fullness stoking the flickering embers in my core, just like the brisk wind outside toyed with the dying fire in our pit. While Lucian's cheek twitched and his lips thinned, those huge hands supporting me during descent, he never took his eyes off me—not once. Even when mine rolled back once he speared me fully, I still felt his stare, the gold so like Idunn in a way, so intense and centering and *present* that I could feel him even in the darkness.

A girl might have been insulted to be treated like this, passed from one mate to the other, no agency, no sense of purpose—just lifted and deposited and *fucked*.

I actually kind of liked it.

Not in all areas of our life, but this...

I liked this.

Liked the way Lucian urged me forward, cradling me into his chest before pumping into me. The first time we mated was like this, me on top, riding him, howling to the hidden moon when pleasure tore through me properly, thoroughly, for the second time in my whole life. The first climax came courtesy of his gorgeous mouth and silky tongue, which I kissed now, even with Soren's taste lingering.

Lucian took all of me, kissing me deeply, pounding hard enough that my body jerked and everything jiggled, and my other mates *growled* so appreciatively I thought I might just turn to mist and float away.

"Pause," Soren said roughly—and we did, Lucian's hips stilling with him thrust deep inside me, his huge hand cradling the back of my head. "I... I need... I need..."

Suddenly, Soren squatted in front of me, those dangling balls and bobbing shaft a little too close to Lucian's head given the way my frowning mate flinched. Then, out of nowhere, his eyes pure amber and his grin wicked, Soren swiped his thumb over my bottom lip—then thrust a finger into my mouth. Not deeply, but enough to make me rear back, blinking hard, and wonder what this could *possibly* do for him.

A second joined the first, and I sucked, our eyes locked, Lucian's hands wandering, Ewan's footsteps pacing behind me. Once they were good and wet, Soren retreated and meandered around behind. Soundlessly, my mates manipulated my body again, Lucian cupping my backside, a hand for each cheek, and easing me up and off his length. I went willingly—but a little confused.

What were they—

"*Ah!*" I jumped when Soren's two fingers pumped into my sex, in and out, paling in comparison to Lucian and Ewan's dicks in length and girth.

But he didn't seem there for fun.

All of this felt like it had a purpose. It… He…

What was he—

I squealed much louder this time, shock rippling down my body and coloring Lucian's cheeks. Twisting around, still straddling my mate, I opened and closed my mouth a few times as Soren teased my tightest hole, one no one had ever touched before but plenty of wolves sniffed just for kicks.

Before I could demand to know *exactly* what he was doing, Lucian brought me back to him. His hand found my chin, so gentle and sweet. He stroked my jaw, my cheeks, my lips, then coaxed me into his arms. I settled onto his chest, folded over, arms bent, and tensed when one of Soren's fingers worked inside me *there*.

I sucked in a sharp breath, instantly alarmed.

But then Lucian kissed me. Soothed me. Stroked me and murmured against my skin—no words, just gentle growls and soft rumbles that spoke to the wild in my marrow. Slowly, I relaxed, allowing Soren's fingers to work me, fill me, stretch me. There was some discomfort, some pain, but my mates worked through it together.

"Easy, blue eyes." Ewan knelt by Lucian's shoulder, dick still wet from my arousal and hard as stone. He swooped my hair behind my ear, then steered my attention to him with one firm finger under my chin. "You want to please *all* your mates, right?"

I nodded enthusiastically. Of *course* I wanted to please my mates. I had wanted all of them to mate together for so long, even more so after Halloween. Before I could confirm that, however, Soren retreated—and then plunged into my sex, his dick *much* more satisfying than his fingers. My hands fisted at Lucian's shoulders, nails gritting into his skin, both of us jerking and bobbing with Soren's thrusts. Just like my mouth, this seemed to have a purpose, because *just* as the delicious fire started to throb in my core, he pulled away—and returned to that untouched hole.

"And *we*—" Ewan cupped my chin and forced me to look at him and only him. "—want to please *you*, Lyssa. Always. We'd never hurt you."

"I-I know," I whispered, bowled over by his intensity, by his sincerity flowing through our bond. "I trust you not to—"

My mouth fell open in a silent scream, tensing when Soren started his slow push, testing the hole with something much bigger than a finger.

Okay.

Okay.

They would never hurt you.

I knew that—logically.

This was just… intimidating.

But his fingers *had* felt good with a bit of effort, slowly pumping in and out, stroking my inner walls like the most intimate massage I'd ever had. This—him, big ol' *him*—could be the same. Eyes closed, I sucked down a steadying breath, then a much deeper one, willing my body to relax.

Surrender.

Surrender to the moment, to them, to their love and care and sweet touches.

"Good girl, little mate," Lucian whispered, stroking my cheek with his knuckles, then slowly wending down my neck, my shoulders, my collarbones, and between my breasts. As always, his touch was calming, his presence grounding. Still sprawled beneath me, he barely moved, steady as the mountain he had always been, supportive and *there*. "Good—relax, just like that… Very good."

His praise emboldened me, and I eased forward, sinking into him just as Soren sank into me. Lucian's huge hands soon found my butt again, rearranging my hips, spreading me for my own sake.

"You have to understand, blue eyes," Ewan added, words a raspy growl. When I opened my eyes, I found him on the ground at Lucian's side, slumped over so that he could meet my stare while I cuddled into my mate's burly chest. "No one wants to sit on the sidelines anymore… No one wants to *watch*. We want you. All of you and *only* you."

"But you tell me if you want to stop," Soren insisted, still slowly claiming me from behind. One of his hot hands smoothed over my backside, brushing Lucian in passing, then kneaded my lower back, arching me further, rubbing my still-tensed muscles. "You tell me if it hurts or it's too much."

He'd feel it if that was the case. Sure, it stung a little, but he took his time, allowing my body to make the adjustments it needed. No, it didn't hurt, didn't feel like he was ripping me apart—just that it was a little scary to try something *so* new, with all three mates watching me experience it for the first time. Still, Soren's genuine concern twined with Ewan's heady honesty, with Lucian's care, with all their *want* still pounding through our bond.

My eyes stung.

I clenched them tighter, fighting back the tears that they'd take for pain or fear—not the happiness they symbolized, the adoration and affection and *love* that made my throat tight and my heart so incredibly full.

Despite their desire slamming through our connection like raging floodwaters, they all coddled me. Soren rubbed my back and scratched between my shoulder blades. Lucian cupped my face and rumbled a love letter to my heart. Ewan had the rest of me covered, massaging my calves, my thighs, my arms, occasionally nibbling over my scars from their teeth so that my pulse spiked and my core clenched.

I wasn't sure when Soren filled me completely, but he stayed still for a long time after, his patience making him tremble. Only when my eyes fluttered open and my breath came easy did they all snap into a new routine, lifting me and arranging me and organizing my limbs.

"Deep breath, baby," Soren murmured, mouth right next to my

ear, blanketing me with his body. I did as I was told, filling my lungs, my belly, braced on Lucian's chest. Goose bumps erupted along my arms like my body knew something I didn't. Anticipation whumped through our bond, my mates getting growly again, antsy and desperate. "And... exhale."

I let it all go.

And Lucian nudged inside me.

My eyes rounded and my jaw dropped, both holes claimed.

I'd thought I was full before with a dick in my sex and another in my mouth, but this—

Oh. I folded over with a sharp breath and saw stars behind my clenched lids.

"Lyssa." No-nonsense and firm, Ewan brought my head up, cupping my chin again. "Are you okay?" He added a little pressure, prompting me to open my eyes. "You need to tell us." *Tell* them? I could barely think, let alone speak. My mouth opened and closed a few times, but no words came out. Ewan frowned and scooted closer, Soren and Lucian almost painfully still. "Say something, blue eyes, or we'll stop and try something else. No one will be upset. We can come back to this another day if you—"

"D-don't stop," I finally managed. I didn't *want* to speak. I wanted them—*now*. I wanted to be claimed and rutted into by *all* my mates, right this second. All the fullness from before, from past matings with each of them alone, with Ewan and Soren together—nothing compared to this. Tonight had been all about pack unity, and this felt... groundbreaking. Made my eyes water again, made my tongue tied and my heart soar and my sex slick. Swallowing hard, I grabbed at Ewan's steely forearm, needing him too, and squeezed. "Just... go s-slow."

His thumb tenderly stroked my jaw, wolfish gaze assessing my expression quickly, and he nodded, the promise of protection unspoken and deafening.

Then he turned on Lucian and Soren with *zero* tenderness, just brute strength and raw alpha, a warning in the flash of his teeth and the narrowing of his eyes. My other mates snarled, indignation rippling through our connection.

Tension.

The first signs of it after our vows and promises and secrets—

I whined, redirecting them back to me, and the bubble burst. Poof, just like that—gone.

Whatever Ewan expected—or maybe even feared—was unfounded. Lucian and Soren probably hadn't shared a female like this before, but they moved together, tender and cautious as they loved my body. None of Soren's usual rough, domineering alpha lovemaking showed itself. He was sweet tonight, just for a little while, nibbling at my shoulders, stroking my back, thrusting into me slowly as I adjusted to two males possessing me at the same time —down *there*. Eyes closed, I submitted to all of it.

To the tightness.

The fullness.

The sensation of being well and truly claimed.

They went slow and gentle until my hips decided enough was enough.

Until my body called the shots for me, bucking a little, writhing, rocking between them like I had my own power again. Their growls were music to my ears, my mountain man and my sweetest, silliest mate *fighting* with themselves, their restraint shivering in our connection, to hold back.

I told them they didn't need to without saying a word.

Lucian arched off the rug a little harsher.

Soren followed, pumping hard once, twice, then grinding me into Lucian's body so that my clit got some much-needed attention too. I whined again, this time because I could barely *stand* it.

And because I never wanted it to stop.

Strange—to wish a feeling would go away while also needing it like air.

When we three found a rhythm, rough enough for mated wolf shifters but still clearly gentle enough for my comfort, Ewan joined the group. All this time, his concerned gaze had burned across my body, raking up my sides, across my face, studying me for the first flicker of distress, his energy hesitant and strained.

Now fluid and hot and rich like melted chocolate.

He stepped into the pile—literally, standing over Lucian's shoulders and dragging me up by my chin. As soon as our eyes met, his an inferno and mine a little watery, he stroked my lower lip, then plucked at it with his thumb.

A silent command.

Gazes locked, I obliged with a wry grin, mouth falling open for him, waiting, expectant and eager to involve him in—

He thrust halfway in without warning, his shaft so hard, so desperate for attention, that it felt cruel to deny him. Fingers threading into my hair, Ewan set our pace, pumping slow and steady at first, never deep enough to make me gag—but just enough to make me feel full to bursting now.

I had no clue what to do with my hands. I wanted to put them to work, but the best I could manage was to brace one on Ewan's thigh while the other planted on Lucian's chest.

Goodness, this was a performance.

A dance with so many moving parts.

My three mates were so steadfast and stubborn and alpha—they couldn't have done this before.

I had to be their first like this.

Ewan fucked my mouth in his own time, hands fisted in my hair.

Soren ground and ground and bucked and *oh*, a little harder, *please*.

Lucian cradled me with his body, with his strong thighs and firm hands, arching off the carpet to pound me deeper.

I felt a little helpless in this position, stuck between them, stranded and strung up like a puppet.

But I loved it.

Because even if I could barely move beyond what my mates allowed, I was *safe* too.

Supported.

Cherished.

Loved.

Sure, no one had said it besides Lucian—but I felt it from *everyone*.

They all had to as well, that warmth in the bond, totally separate from the fires of desire and the rivers of *want* in our veins. It was soft and tender and gentle, like golden sunshine on a spring morning.

Like the sky in Idunn's orchard.

And best of all, it was *ours*. Love or not, this was a pack sensation, a feeling just for us, and as I closed my eyes, muscles tightening, pleasure soaring, body aching, I wished to Lady Fate— she *must* be listening, right?—that the heat was here to stay.

Ewan lost control first.

Not that I could blame him.

Because by then, Soren and Lucian had stopped being so gentle and sweet. They took me as wolves, as alpha *men* who wanted to mark their mate all over again. I was lost between them, floating on clouds but firmly tethered to the earth, all my squeals and mewls muffled, mouth always full.

"*Shit.*" Hot, salty jets splashed the back of my throat, and Ewan's dick pulsed as his pleasure whumped through my limbs. I moaned just as Lucian growled and Soren groaned, Ewan's climax touching all of us. My midnight mate hissed, expression taut, his climax *taking* so much from him that he wasn't just my fallen angel anymore, but an actual *angel*, pure and divine, ethereal and stunningly beautiful.

He retreated on wobbly legs, and I sucked down a much-needed full breath, chin slick with drool again, eyes watery, lips stretched in an exhausted smile. My own orgasm teetered on the brink, *right* there, the fires raging, everything inside so perfectly tight that I could just *scream*.

Soren beat me to it. He stilled, thrust deep inside me, and spilled himself with a ragged shout. Another wash of pleasure hit the group, knocking Ewan to his knees and kicking me that much closer to oblivion. I tried to ride it out, eyes boring into Lucian's muted gold, challenging him, *daring* him to outlast me, but that soon became impossible. Soren might have eased out of me, the pressure lessened, my body slick, his seed smeared on my backside, but he wasn't going anywhere.

No, if I was the puppet, Soren became the master whenever we mated. His fingers twined into my hair. He wrenched me upright, baring me to the others, my nipples achingly puckered and my skin glistening with sweat.

Then his hand skimmed down my body, bracing me as Lucian bucked and claimed and snarled.

He found my clit through all the motion, and once he latched on, he wouldn't let go, even as I protested and squeaked and swatted at him.

Because he had a goal, my Soren, and that was to send me kicking and screaming into the black. Body shaking, teeth clenched, eyes shut so, so tight, I tried to fight it, but Soren's fingers combined with Lucian's thrusts and Ewan's burning wolf eyes—

Oh.

No.

Can't—fight—it—

My eyes snapped open when the strings pulled too tight and finally snapped. Fire sparked in the hearth, appearing so suddenly as if lightning struck through the chimney, flames high as the bonfire Lucian built outside. Ewan scrambled away. Soren staggered back with a sharp breath.

Lucian bucked harder.

I screamed, the pleasure so intense it *hurt*. The orange soared higher, devouring the logs that had only been for show all season. The windows rattled. My mates snarled and hissed and slammed their fists into the floor, the walls, the couch, my climax blazing through all of us.

Through the whole house, apparently, Idunn's power beating in my chest like a drum. Not my fingertips. My *heart*, my body pulsing with it, milking the pleasurable waves and pushing them higher.

Lucian didn't stand a chance.

He tried to grind me into him, maybe stoke this climax to new heights, but, really, none of us could take much more.

His release spilled through the bond like the tide, whooshing forward to claim each of us, then dragging us out to sea.

I collapsed onto his chest, panting and gritting my teeth against the assault.

The windows had stopped shaking, at least.

A tentative glance up showed the fire down to manageable heights, fading fast, the wood there unsustainable long-term.

Sweaty, *hot*, I rolled off Lucian—who lay there in a daze, sprawled and staring at the ceiling. The mossy green was back, wolf eyes gone, and he looked about a million miles away, his smile kind of dopey.

Adorable.

As I flopped onto my back, Ewan dragged himself onto the nearest couch, while Soren claimed another all for himself, stretched out, a hand clapped to his forehead and his chest bobbing with every ragged breath.

Quiet blanketed the house.

Peace.

Calm.

Heavy in a way that felt *right*, like the soft weighted blanket Ewan had bought me while I bled last month.

Perfect.

Parched, mouth dry and body pleasantly sore, I rolled over with a *lot* of effort, almost an embarrassing amount, and then pushed onto all fours. No way could I actually *walk* to the kitchen and grab a drink, maybe a couple of beers from the fridge for my mates, but this was good enough.

"Where the fuck do you think you're going?" Ewan growled. Lounging on his side, elbow on the armrest, he arched an eyebrow when our eyes met. A little miffed that he seemed to be recovering faster than me, I sat back on my heels and pointed toward the kitchen.

"I—"

"Get your ass back here and *stay*," Soren ordered, the domineering side of him clawing out as he watched me with bright amber wolf eyes. Ewan tsked right alongside him, both of them chiding me like I had committed a cardinal sin. My blond mate did a lazy sweep of my figure, then flashed a grin worthy of Lucifer himself. "We aren't finished with you yet."

Delight squirmed in my belly. Anticipation fluttered in my chest. The fire snapped and crackled, growing a little stronger as my mates growled and edged closer.

I scrambled off with a giggle, crawling frantically toward the three steps behind Ewan's couch, ones that would whisk me up to the dining area, the kitchen—way beyond, the hunt officially *on*.

But Lucian caught me in a heartbeat, his hand snapped around my calf. Grip like steel, he hauled me onto the carpet, the green swapped for gold, and then flipped me onto my back, suddenly so desperately vulnerable and exposed to all these predators—

Who pounced without warning, more than ready to take me again.

And, frankly, I had never been happier to be *prey*.

8

LYSSA

I knew where I was before I opened my eyes, but something was… different.

Wrong.

The scent of thick, healthy grass. Tree bark and apple blossoms and dirt. A gentle breeze. Temperature so much warmer than Redwood Grove these days. Soft light behind my lids.

All signs that I was *finally* back in the orchard—that despite Idunn blocking me, I had made it in. Somehow. Still no clue how any of this worked, but I wasn't home, in my bed, surrounded by my spent and happy alphas after we mated all over the house until dawn. After we watched the sun rise over a breakfast feast, one we all pitched in on, and squished into a single shower stall together, my belly sore from laughing so hard at three huge males fighting over body wash and shampoo and who got to wash me first…

We fell asleep in *my* bed, just a tangled heap of limbs and snores and scents, covers off, the heat of our pack like a furnace on the cold, snowy morning.

Now I was back here.

And… my neck hurt.

The rest of me should be just as pleasantly sore and stiff as when I crawled into bed.

But I was... fine.

Relatively.

Just the back of my neck was so...

Tense.

Yeah, that was it.

And my *back*.

Like someone had been scratching it for too long, in the same spot, which turned a great thing—*yes*, back scratches!—really uncomfortable.

Sucking down a sharp breath, I opened my eyes and came face-to-face with Kira, her enormous head barely fitting on my lap. She peered up at me with those bright blues, her eager tail-whip whooshing over the grass.

I never woke up like this.

Always on my back, serenaded by the wind beneath a sky trapped in perpetual sunrise.

Yet here I was... under a tree. Against the trunk. Like someone had sat me down and left *ages* ago judging by the stiffness in my neck, my head hanging for hours.

Weird.

"Hey, pretty girl," I croaked, stroking the soft fluff between Kira's ears as I arched into the apple tree. Rolled my shoulders. Tossed my head for a few satisfying *cracks*. Kira whined and nestled deeper into my naked lap, clearly pleased to see me, her heart just as full as mine anytime we met in the orchard.

But she was more impatient today.

Instead of falling into the usual cuddles, Kira jolted up—not in a full sit or she'd tower way over me, but in a tense *down*, her huge head at eye level, her bright blues burrowing into mine.

Still thumbing the ache out of my neck, massaging the base of the skull where the weight must have hung the heaviest, I frowned, then flinched when she frantically licked my cheeks and reared back with a huff.

This wasn't a congratulations for the wild night I'd had with my mates.

Not a celebration for opening up about our past to the three males who would forever keep my secrets.

No joy for our amazing run, for the frolicking with my old pack, for the silly games that turned sinful and rough and *wonderful*.

"You feel it too, huh?" I tugged at her left ear with a sigh, weirdly exhausted instead of relaxed and refreshed, molasses chugging through my veins, then used her sturdy body to haul myself up. Kira braced, her patience fleeting, then slowly rose behind me as I lumbered off—and then rolled my ankle *hard* when I stepped on an apple lost in the long grasses. Squealing, I flailed my arms out, looking ridiculous, but regained balance fast.

Idunn was so meticulous about her apples.

She loved them, her care and attention obvious throughout the orchard.

Why—was this one on the ground?

Kira charged into my personal space, ready to bully whoever made my heart race. She then paused, snout in the grass, no doubt realizing it was just an apple.

Yeah, kind of embarrassing to—

My arms went limp when I spotted the next fallen apple.

Then another.

Another.

Green, red, yellow—a mix of all three. Idunn cultivated tons of apples here, and from where I stood beneath the shady boughs of the tree, a lot of them were... on the ground.

I gulped hard.

So many... overturned baskets, their harvests spilled and forgotten.

Protectiveness lanced through me, the first murmurs of anger tickling my fingertips.

"Idunn?"

Who was *I* to protect a goddess? Even a dead one could probably fend for herself, but as I marched forward, Kira a few paces ahead with her nose in the grass, zigzagging like she had caught the scent, my heart said she *needed* me.

This dead goddess had abandoned a good chunk of her power.

And if someone—or something, the green comet flashing across my mind's eye—was here *hurting* her, then I'd put a stop to it before I woke up in my own bed again.

Kira veered left, then right, then circled the base of a tree and snapped up to peer into the canopy. I jogged to her side, using her like a stepping stool to poke around the leafy branches. Sometimes Idunn hid there when the vampires—*"More than vampires... to touch us here."*—hunted us, their frost, their *darkness*, creeping through the orchard night after night after night.

Nothing.

"Idunn?" I pushed away from the tree and stalked into the middle of the row, squinting down the line toward the endless green horizon. "Where are you?"

"Get *out!*" She had never sounded like that before—never so frantic and breathless. Always calm. Always girlish and sweet and ancient. I whirled around to find the goddess charging toward us, her honey-blonde waves disheveled, a few of the sapphires missing from her shoulder pads. Her hand shot up, and I raised mine too, patting the air, silently pleading with her to just calm down and explain—and to not blast me with that diamond light again, forcing me out of her world and back to my own. Kira whined like a pup about to be scolded by her mama, ears flat, tail low, and slunk toward her. My dead goddess slowed but didn't stop, her golden gaze ringed with fire. "You two can't *be* here. You..."

She jerked forward with a squeak like her bare feet had grown roots, stuck in place, a flustered pink blossoming in her cheeks. Dress in her fists, she twisted and turned and scowled, then looked to me—then up.

Way up.

Eyes widening.

All the color fading.

I stiffened when the breeze died.

Kira padded around, still a submissive pup in the goddess's presence—until she saw whatever made that alluring *hum* behind me, the air thick with it. Those bright blues narrowed, and Kira's tail shot way up, along with her hackles, and she revealed every deadly tooth in her huge mouth with a snarl.

I smelled him before I ever saw him.

Crushed pine needles and sea salt and a strange sweetness. The forest, the sea, a childish humor—all twined together with the distinct musk of masculinity. He cast a shadow, the light suddenly different, like he blotted out the sun I never saw.

I swallowed hard again, Kira's snarls steeling my spine, and slowly turned around.

Then had to look way, way up.

Because—

Goodness, he was *tall.*

Taller than Lucian, but lean and limber—lanky limbs. Not weak. Not bone-thin and clinging to life. No, this *man* had muscle under his dark green tunic, his grey linen pants, his leather boots—the outfit belted like Soren's Halloween costume. Pale. A little freckly. Features so sharp they put Ewan's to shame. Angular chin and narrow nose and high cheekbones, beautiful and ancient like Idunn. Despite smelling all *man*, his looks teetered between masculine and feminine, hair fiery red and wild like a lion's mane, trundling past his shoulders.

Fingers inked with black runes like the ones Soren had buzzed into his hair.

Rings—of iron.

As soon as my eyes landed on his thin lips again, he smiled, revealing straight pearly-white teeth—and dangerous canines. Sharp. A meat eater. Not like a vampire, but more like a wolf in shape and size.

"Hello."

Voice like silk. It was only then I realized I was *shaking*—realized that the grass at our feet had grown thick and long, creeping up our calves, brushing the backs of my knees.

Squaring my shoulders, I forced myself to meet his eyes.

Green and circled in gold.

He cocked his head and breathed me *deep*, nostrils flared, smile not exactly warm, and gaze beyond calculating.

I finally stumbled backward, instinct bellowing like a fog horn to fear him.

That this was a bear I *shouldn't* provoke.

Kira skirted the warning, shooting by me like a dark grey missile, just a shadowy blur she charged so fast—

The man batted her aside like a fly.

She landed in the grass and rolled onto her side, still snarling, still baring her teeth, but he focused on me like the attack had never even happened. Taking a step closer, he ducked down, long, lean fingers smoothing over his thighs as he crouched to meet my eyeline.

"Are you Idunn's vessel, then?" His hand lifted, eyes snapping so *precisely* toward the goddess behind me. The sweet smell was a lie; everything about him screamed predator, and his movements told me he had a lifetime of stalking, hunting, and killing under his belt. "Ah, ah, ah, little one. I gave you the chance to explain things. Your turn is *up*."

Over my shoulder, I spotted a sulking, pouting Idunn, her hands in fists and her cheeks pink again. To her credit, *she* didn't seem scared anymore—more so annoyed, which only made the knots in my belly loop tighter.

"No one ever said the gods were kind."

"Yes, yes…" His heat warmed my cheek, a breath away now and silent as the grave. Gasping, I staggered back, and Kira leapt to her paws, but the man just dipped lower to really get on my level. "Oh, *yes*, look at those *eyes*." He grinned like a wolf—like *the* wolf. "So giving, isn't our little Idunn? So selfless."

"W-who are you?" I gritted my teeth, hating how he latched onto the stutter like Kira might an elk who stumbled behind the fleeing herd, their legs weak, their gait wonky—their time almost up.

He smothered my hand in both of his, eyes never once dipping below my face, never down to my nude body like the Hawthorne alpha had. Instead, this *man* kissed the top of my hand and squeezed hard enough that my bones ground together.

Rough enough that it really *hurt*.

And something told me that was just a taste of what he could do.

"Loki," he rumbled. "You can call me *Loki*, she-wolf." He then wiggled his bright red brows. "All my friends do."

Before I could whisper a name that felt old as time itself, try it out for size, Loki tugged me closer and stared into my eyes, so deep and penetrating that the orchard disappeared and all that was left was *him*—green trapped in gold, like a planet on divine fire.

Tell me, he urged, words slithering around the inside of my skull, his lips still stretched in that dangerous smile, *have you planted the seeds yet? Started your own golden orchard?*

It took all my strength—both the raw shifter power in my bones and the new, godly grit Idunn had poured into my soul—to rip my hand away.

"W-what?"

So assertive. So *alpha*. Ugh. I shook my hand out to get the blood flowing again, then tried to stand taller. With every foe I faced in Redwood Grove, I was always shorter, but I felt ten feet tall when I squared off with them.

Not the case here. Loki was a *giant*, literally and figuratively, his energy choking the entire orchard. No matter how straight I kept my spine or how far I rolled my shoulders back—I was finally just a little she-wolf.

"We were all so worried…" Loki swooped down again, assessing me in that intense, calculating way that made my skin crawl—and not with disgust. This wasn't a male leering at a female because he desired her body. No, this was a higher being deciding whether he should crush me like a bug. He straightened suddenly, soaring to his full height, and I let out a shaky breath, hiding my trembling hands with my arms crossed; the bug lived to see another day. "Our gardener *left*. She died, you see, and we aged without her. No more *apples* for Asgard."

"Loki, don't—"

"And then one day, the apples..." The green in his eyes turned electric, glittering like emeralds in the sun, and then there was that *smile* again that made my knees so, so weak. "The *apples*." He clapped his hands together and lunged after me, and I scrambled back, not stopping until he did, until I'd put at least five long paces between us. Loki flicked a dismissive wave at the apples all around us, like *these* weren't worth his time. "One bite and we were young again. Not decrepit husks—youthful and *alive*. But... they need to be *tended* to, you see."

Oh.

No.

No, no, no, no—*I* made the apples grow. Idunn had said...

And he...

He seemed to like apples.

No.

My lips shivered, and my chin wobbled. *No*, he was going to keep me, wasn't he? Idunn blocked me from the orchard because some apple-obsessed jerk had come looking for her—what did he call me?—*vessel*.

"Oh, little wolf," Loki crooned, a bit of velvet in his tone, soft and calming like a lullaby, "don't be frightened of tricky Loki. He is the *father* of wolves and shapeshifters..." He gestured up and down his figure, a hip cocked, putting all of himself on display for my wide, terrified eyes. "Don't you know your history?"

Kira finally prowled to my side, and as I buried my hand in her fur, a tendril of strength unfurled through me. Just a little one, thin and barely there, a reminder that I was still an alpha, even here—even if he was a god.

Right?

Idunn was a god.

Loki... was a god too?

"Ladies," he drawled with a hand to his heart, "let's be *friends*. Where are you living these days? Not here. No, no, not here." Suddenly he was *right* in front of us again, practically on top of me, and both Kira and I yelped at the magic trick. Loki's nostrils flared as he scrutinized me, then her, then me again, movements fluid as a snake, gaze darting, mind working so fast I swore smoke trickled out his ears. "Midgard, yes, I smell it on you—but *where*, precisely? I *must* drop by and formally introduce myself—"

"Don't tell him," Idunn ordered. I looked back to her for answers —and that was my fatal error.

Never turn your back on a predator, especially one that was bigger, faster, and probably a whole heck of a lot *meaner*.

Pain seared my skull, and I jerked back with a startled cry, but by the time I stumbled around, Loki had put about ten feet between us. Grinning, he held up a clump of brown hair, individual strands fluttering in the breeze that finally swept through the orchard again. Loki's smile sharpened. Kira lunged.

And this man, this god, disappeared—*poof*—in a cloud of greyish-green mist.

Idunn's diamond light struck from behind—

And I jolted awake in my own bed. Gasping, *hurting*, heart racing, and covered in sweat, I pushed up and squinted against the harsh morning sunshine. It spilled through the thin curtains hanging over the glass balcony doors, snow melted, the timber decking outside damp and the panes frosted. All around me, my mates slept on, Soren snoring the loudest and flopped across the end of the bed, Lucian straight as an arrow along the edge, Ewan near the headboard and hogging two pillows—one to hug, one to straddle.

Fighting to calm my breath, needing time to process things before my mates came to, I slowly sank into my spot in the center of the pack. Middle of the bed—all for me, where I had slept through this nightmare in a tight ball, some of the wild wolf habits refusing to die.

Kira whimpered when I settled and winced, my head on *fire*. Shaking, I reached around—and found a few loose hairs Loki had missed.

Then a substantial chunk missing from the *root*, torn out at the base of my skull.

And as I lay there, staring but not seeing, I just knew—even though I was out of the orchard, safe in my bed, surrounded by my fated mates...

I hadn't seen the last of him.

9

EWAN

"Dylan!" A tiny figure crashed into me from behind like a rocket ship way off its trajectory. Somewhere in the crowd milling around Redwood Grove's ice-skating rink, a woman's voice, exasperated as fuck and *so* done with this Dylan kid, shrieked, "Watch where you're going!"

A command hopefully directed at the pup and not me.

Because I'd done fuck all, literally just standing here and minding my own business when her whelp launched a sneak attack on my shins. I peeked over my shoulder, scowling as he used my trench coat like a fucking anchor to fling himself after a pack of other elementary-aged boys zipping through the crowd around the now permanently parked food trucks. A beat later, the woman appeared, haggard and with a little baby girl bouncing on her hip. Coat open, cheeks red, she shot me a mildly apologetic look, which I waved off like it was no big deal—because, seriously, it was, I'd barely felt the hit—and then she was gone, winded and shouting for all of them to slow down.

Yikes.

Just another sprinkle of crazy on an already chaotic day. The first of December marked the reopening of the Quinn Park skating rink in the largest family-oriented suburb of Redwood Grove, populated mostly by locals who worked at the hotels, spas, restaurants, shops—the works. What was usually a huge grassy field now had an enormous rink in the center, permits splashed around for village food trucks to hunker down until spring.

Strings of Christmas lights connected all the truck awnings, the air thick with competing scents, sweet and salty and everything in between. A good two inches of snow had finally settled around the village for good, the last week full of blusters, then soaring temperatures, then wet, then freezing nights and black ice—and repeat.

Until now.

Until the first day of the most magical—and most profitable—month of the year for a village like Redwood Grove.

And I was here for fun.

Fun temporarily sidetracked for a work call, but that was the *only* one I planned to take for the rest of this sunny Sunday afternoon. I'd *promised*. Still, my property group had closed on a stunning waterfront condo—a whole fucking *building* just for us—in Vancouver, and I personally had wanted to hear the news before anyone else.

But, yeah. That was done.

I rolled my shoulders back and scanned the crowds of humans in their winter duds. No more work. Time to be *present*. Here. The adrenaline coursing through my system at the news of this successful acquisition—didn't matter. Not the day for celebrating work shit. Nope. I'd promised to be involved and off my phone.

A promise I broke an hour into this outing—but it was just a *very* brief pause. Back at it. *Let's go.*

Hands in my coat pockets, I sauntered over to an open spot along the rink's exterior wall. It came to roughly hip height on me, while a few pups nearby had to bounce on their tiptoes to watch the skaters inside. With Christmas tunes already strumming from the huge outdoor speakers, humans of all ages skated in a big arcing circle, couples holding hands, parents minding their little ones as they battled the ice.

But in the middle of it all, a much greater battle raged.

Lucian vs. ice skating.

I bit back a smile as the massive wolf tipped forward, then overcompensated and reared *way* too far back, balance shot to shit in either direction, huge arms windmilling and expression permanently pinched. *Fuck*, the struggle was so real for him today—to have teenage girls giggling at his effort instead of swooning over his aristocratic handsomeness must have been a huge blow to the ego.

As a wolf, Lucian fucking *Hadley*—seriously, still couldn't get over that revelation—was what every alpha aspired to be: graceful, powerful, strong, focused, and, above all else, calm. Today, the entire pack learned his greatest weakness: ice skates.

Because from the time we all laced up in the skate rental area to now, he just could *not* get his shit together.

Pretty satisfying, actually.

Then, right beside him, in what had to be the cherry on top of his own personal hell, Soren looked like he came out of the womb wearing a tiny pair of skates, practically floating over the ice. The wolf had a whole bag of tricks up his sleeve, able to do jumps and basic spins; in true Soren fashion, he had already made friends with a gaggle of middle schoolers who tried to teach him more complex moves, which he purposefully botched just to make them laugh.

He skated backward in front of Lucian now, arms out, hands reaching, coaxing the uncoordinated giant forward like all these parents with their clumsy toddlers. In fact, there was literally a couple doing it alongside them with their little girl, using the free space in the middle of the rink to help their pup find her sea legs, and I couldn't help it.

I snorted and snapped a picture, storing it away on my phone for future blackmail.

Sure, we'd all sworn to be united—but I could still tease the fuck out of both those alphas when they deserved it.

Leaving that disaster of a wolf for Soren to manage, I swept the circling skaters for Lyssa, but she was nowhere to be found, her rosy scent just faint enough to set my wolf on edge. Our girl had been a little wobbly on the ice at first, same as me, but she picked it up a hell of a lot faster than Lucian, skating circles around him in no time, her smile bright and beautiful as the sun.

Meanwhile, my frown slowly embodied a shadowy full moon the longer I searched for her. She had been... *twitchy* this week. Still warm and attentive and *thrilled* that we were finally a unified pack, secrets exposed, *real* blackmail fodder—particularly on me—out in the open, binding us together with the sordid details of our past...

But a little distant.

Distracted, maybe.

I eventually found her by the skate rental booth, seated on a bench next to the rink wall, unlacing the final loops on her right skate and tugging her foot free. Rocking a pair of pink leggings and her black winter coat, mittens on strings hanging out the sleeves, Lyssa was the most fucking adorable thing in a ten-mile radius, hands down, especially with that perky ponytail and frost-whipped cheeks. Concern melting away, I headed straight for her, just waiting for her head to snap up when she scented me.

Only she... didn't.

Not until I was right on top of her, human chaos unfolding everywhere else—but the air still around her with that deep-set frown and unfocused golden gaze. She flinched when my ass hit the narrow wood plank, shock leaping from her to me and trickling down my spine.

Odd. Normally, she scented us a mile away; it was annoyingly difficult to sneak up on my mate, but that didn't stop the rest of us from trying, especially around the house, where there was always a dark corner nearby to pin her against and kiss her, *fuck* her until her squeals drew the attention of everyone else.

Since the bonfire of trust last week, that was what our life had become—a whole lot of group mating. Conversations came easier now that we all had some background on each other, a few behaviors explained, others noted and zeroed in on with a hawklike intensity whenever they flared. So far, it was mostly just calling Soren out on being spoiled and tantrumy. I mean, fuck, it was way easier to poke fun at an innocent flaw; my anger, Lyssa's anxiety, and Lucian's scars were *messy*.

And for now, in our fuck bubble, all of us getting along and eating together and Lyssa kissing me at the front door before I left for work and waiting there to greet me when I forced myself to come home for dinner at six o'clock sharp *every* day—no one wanted to rock the boat. No one wanted to deal with *messy*, because that was what we three were: messy as fuck.

Cutting yourself open and spilling your guts was terrifying. Sure, Lyssa was the only one I had really cared about that night at first, the only wolf I genuinely trusted with my darkest horrors, but the others hadn't judged me.

All my baggage. All my bullshit. All *my* scars left by the Quinn legacy—nothing. I had expected some judgment, especially from other alphas, for abandoning the next Quinn generation in that cesspool, but if I had stayed, I'd probably be dead by now.

Or an addict like my dad.

Or in prison like my brothers.

Or a blackout drunk like my mom.

Fate had led me here, to my soulmate and two males who vowed to have my back.

Difficult as it was to trust after the many, many, *many* years of psychotic Quinn bullshit, I preferred this.

I… chose this.

Officially.

Hell, if asked a year ago would I *ever* share a bed with Soren Acker and Lucian motherfucking Hadley, I would have laughed in your face and cracked you across the jaw.

Four days ago, we moved Lucian's king-sized mattress into Lyssa's room, combining hers and his to make one massive bed for all of us to sleep comfortably on.

Honestly: best sleep of my fucking life, surrounded by all of them.

Not just her—*them*.

Sure, we weren't all always there. We shared night patrols, finally putting Lyssa into rotation when she pitched a fit at the initial male-only schedule posted on the fridge. It didn't sit well with any of us, her going out there alone, but she had proven herself time and time again as a strong, competent, *way* above-average wolf shifter. She had tracked Lucian solo. Killed the Hawthorne alpha, his pack silent now, not even a droplet of challenging piss within a mile of our eastern border. She had her childhood wolf pack claiming the western woods, a few even tagging along on her patrols.

She could do it.

We didn't have to *like* it, and if she wasn't there, we three were more inclined to sleep in our own beds—but not as often as I'd predicted.

For the most part, we slept like a proper pack.

Our mate loved it.

We liked it.

Things were *good*.

Except for her frown.

Except for her not even registering my approach until I crashed down beside her.

"You okay, blue eyes?" I nudged her with my elbow, my tone rumbly and deep as my wolf clawed his way up, whimpering for his mate. "Seems like you're a million miles away."

With a weak grin, Lyssa went for her left skate, her right foot resting on top of mine, the wool socks with reindeers on them cute as hell. "I think... Rosa's mad at me."

"What?" Frown back for an encore, I watched her nimble fingers tackle the skate's laces like she did this every day. "Why?"

My mate shrugged, the weight of her *feelings*, mixed and mingled, just a bushel of confusion, seeping into me.

"Has she said something?"

Lyssa shook her head with a sniff, our breaths fogging in the cold.

"Has Ethan?"

The warlock had popped over a few times this week to chat with Lyssa about her powers. Always when I was at work: I usually caught him leaving just as I pulled in the driveway. We waved. Chatted through my open window. He pressed for me to start journaling her progress, and I promised I would.

I hadn't.

Lucian loathed having Ethan Perry at the house—understandable now, given his pack warlock had cursed him. Seriously, if I ever met that magical fuck, I'd happily gut him and toss his corpse in the lake.

Soren seemed to tolerate the conversations, though Lucian told me Ethan liked to show up while *he* was at work as well.

When that happened, Lucian would then whip out his ancient phone and shoot Soren a text.

Soren would rock up five minutes later and wait things out, both of them eavesdropping from the kitchen while Lyssa and Ethan chatted in the sitting room. So far, nothing seemed to have come from the conversations. Ethan asked questions that he insisted were standard for baby witches and warlocks during their first year at their formal academies, and Lyssa appeared to answer as honestly as she could.

Even without him actually *teaching* her, our mate had been learning to control her new abilities just fine. The warlock seemed especially interested in her ability to grow plants from scratch, but we were just happy she felt secure about *us*, growing more and more confident she wouldn't accidentally maim us with vines or whatever. Until she said otherwise, Ethan could ask questions and make suggestions; Lyssa would take what she needed. I trusted her to do that.

Just like I trusted my fellow alphas not to beat him bloody anytime he showed up unannounced.

Sort of.

The warlock hadn't *done* anything, but since mating with all her fated at once, Lyssa now had three hypervigilant, overly protective, growly assholes who would skin a male alive for looking at her wrong.

So...

Probably not the best idea to show up when we weren't there to hear everything, only scent another male's presence around our girl after he'd left. It never made us suspicious of Lyssa—just him. What did he say? What did he do? Did he touch her? Flirt with her? *Proposition* her?

You know, all that awesome irrational, illogical animal-brain-driven bullshit.

I'd seriously have to talk to Ethan about that. We were pals, sure, but the wolf in me, the beast in *all* of us, had really upped the ante now that things were solidifying for the Redwood pack. As feelings and truths and bonds strengthened, all the pieces falling into place, outsiders would have to tread lightly and respect our dynamic—no matter how much we liked them in the human world.

"No, no, not at all," Lyssa insisted. She then grunted through pulling off her second skate and set it beside its twin under the bench. "Ethan's been great. Really sweet and supportive and not pushy..." Squaring upright, she glanced out over the rink, looking past the skaters breezing by us. "It's just a feeling."

Through the gaps, I found what caught her interest: Rosa in her purple snow-bunny outfit, sporting cat-eye sunglasses and right up against the perimeter of the rink. She waved little baby Aster's arm at Ethan as he skated back and forth, the warlock making silly faces so their chubby-cheeked pup giggled and bounced in place. Lyssa was *obsessed* with Aster—a good sign for our future pups, honestly— and the sight of her smiling and laughing should have lightened her mood.

But it only made her frown deeper.

Confusion twisted through my ribs, her feelings like grasping ivy, featherlight but abundant as they wove through me from the bond. I knuckled at my chest, inner wolf instantly triggered again.

"Lyssa, what's wrong?" I arched my brows when she side-eyed me but said nothing. "What's bothering you? I can feel... some of it. Your confusion and uncertainty. Do you know why it's happening?"

And for Rosa Perry of all people. Not only could that witch take care of herself, but she was probably the sweetest female I'd ever met. Almost *too* sweet, the kind of ooey-gooey goodness that would rot my teeth had Lady Fate paired me with a she-wolf like her.

"Not really." Smoothing a few loose wisps of brown behind her ears, Lyssa continued to watch the Perry coven's interactions across the rink. We were all here together, a friendly outing on a Sunday afternoon to enjoy the first skate of the season while the ice was still new, with dinner reservations in a couple of hours at a mountainside restaurant Lucian considered *way* too pretentious.

So far, however, Lyssa had stuck by us, which should have raised a few red flags given her intensity for Rosa *and* Aster. Here, she watched the pair like she couldn't get a read on them—just like I couldn't get a proper read on her.

Fucking annoying, actually, to feel so much and *still* struggle to understand your mate.

"I feel very, uh, protective of Rosa and Aster," she admitted a few moments later, her head bowed, "and I still don't know why, but it's been like that for a while. Like, almost as if I can't control it. My body, my heart, is just telling me—grab them and go. Protect them."

Fuck *me*, was I ever in love.

I'd denied it before, insisted that it was too soon and we weren't ready, but right here, right now, I wanted to hop on this bench and scream it to the world.

"Oh, blue eyes," I murmured, wrapping an arm around her and crushing her into my side, "it's because you're already a mama wolf."

Lyssa snuggled right in where she belonged, but her confusion ripened at the statement, playing out in her expression and through our bond.

"What? I'm not—"

"I mean, you know, in *spirit*," I said lightly. Seriously, this she-wolf was going to be the *best* mom out there, even if all but one of the maternal figures in her life had failed her.

And for all we knew, she *could* be pregnant at this point. All that mating—we'd have no clue who the pup was sired by until they were born and their physical traits leaned in one of three directions, but whatever. Any pups she had were *mine*, and Soren's, and Lucian's, regardless of genetics. For now, however, Lyssa had a maternal streak a hundred miles wide. "You see someone really important to you acting off, or being too quiet, or maybe a little down, and you want to protect her. It's normal."

According to Ethan, Rosa had a whole litany of issues behind closed doors, ranging from insecurities about her body to anxieties about their relationship and her ability to mother Aster, to run a household *and* be a successful salon manager—all that. It wouldn't surprise me one bit if Lyssa picked up on her moods and her fears no matter how hard she tried to hide them.

Our girl was just that good.

"I mean, I guess?" Frowning at her fingers, Lyssa shrugged and took her time to mull things over, curling her socked toes over the outdoor carpeting. "I don't know... I just don't feel like that with anyone else."

My mock gasp had her flinching upright, and I pressed an overly flouncy hand to my heart. "Not even with your *mates*?"

That did it; a grin split Lyssa's face, blooming wider with my every dramatic scoff, until she finally giggled and shoved me, both of us falling into play-wrestling a little too easily out here.

You know, surrounded by all these *people*.

All these humans, this cacophony of scent, sight, and sound, the anxiety of work, work, work on a low simmer inside, always moving, thinking, planning, and preparing for the next step—it all went quiet with Lyssa.

When it was just me and her, the bullshit fell away.

And I realized—every fucking time, as if it hadn't already occurred to me before—that she was the center of my world.

The *real* center.

True north—right here, in her.

While still tangled in each other's arms, Lyssa's legs a precarious inch away from throwing themselves over my thighs so she could then straddle me and claim the upper hand, we settled somewhat when a gaggle of kids blitzed by. Shrieking. Laughing. Shouting to each other about one of the food trucks.

A few long paces behind them—the runt of the pack. Smallest pup of the bunch, he waddled in his swishy snow gear, calling out and begging them to slow down, wait up, give him a second to take off his skates.

Which he ran in now.

Barely.

Doomed from the start, bud.

I watched the scene unfold with gritted teeth, my inner wolf huffing and puffing, totally unimpressed. We both wanted to scoop the runt up and put him with the rest, but that wasn't our place.

It *would* be when we had pups of our own.

Best direct that intensity where it belonged and not on random human snots who plowed through the crowd with no regard for anyone but themselves.

"Look, I really doubt Rosa is upset with you." Hard to imagine what *would* set Rosa off, but I was confident Lyssa wasn't capable of going that dark. "But if you're concerned, why don't you just talk to her?"

After all, Lyssa was great with her words.

Less so with the spelling of them, but that was a work in progress, something she remained *very* self-conscious about.

I glanced across the rink to Rosa and Aster; the witch *had* been a little quiet lately. More subdued than usual, actually. Her smiles weren't as bright, her laughs weren't as big, her clothes weren't as formfitting. Most males wouldn't notice the latter, but Rosa Perry had radiated pure *style* since I met her.

On the rare occasion I saw her since we brought the Perrys into our current pack dilemma, she dressed like Halloween: baggy and unflattering. Still designer labels. Still *chic*. Just… not meant for her body type.

My eyes narrowed as I watched her fuss over Aster's little teal hat with that obnoxious fuzzy pompom on top.

Maybe my mate was onto something.

"I *want* to talk to her, but it's just…" Lyssa pursed her lips, her frustration buzzing faintly in my chest. Arm stretched around her shoulders, I reached down and squeezed her elbow.

"It's just?"

Frustration gave way to worry; if I hadn't felt the shift in my mate, I'd have to be blind not to see it on her face. Sighing, I looked to the witch for one last sweep, ready to make a call for myself—but then Lucian *ate* it, so fucking hard, right in my line of sight.

Just… face-planted in the middle of the ice, his rage pounding in the bond and Soren's laughter howling over the blaring Christmas carols.

I snorted again and dove for my phone, hunting for it inside my jacket's maze of inner pockets, but Lyssa smacked my thigh and shoved a warning finger in my face.

"Don't make fun of him—he's trying something *new*."

Abandoning the phone for her sake, I rolled my eyes. "A *Hadley* does not need to be babied, blue eyes."

Especially Lucian Hadley.

Yeah, I'd creeped the fuck out of him after the bonfire of trust. Sue me.

The internet sleuthing wasn't for anything but to appease my own personal curiosity, and Soren had probably done the same. In the shifter community, the Hadleys had a reputation on a global scale, even more so after rumors spread about brother against brother, about all the aristocratic blood spilled, about the literal *war* raging in London over alpha ascension. A once great pack with a history of entertaining human kings and ruthlessly navigating royal courts—brought to its knees.

Decimated.

Barely clinging to life, even now, well over a decade after the fall.

Lucian Christopher Hadley had attended all the finest private schools. Dripping in old money, filthy rich, born to a family vicious and powerful enough to have *three* private warlocks duty- bound to their bloodline, he had wanted for nothing. Groomed all his life to take over his mother's publishing empire, then step into his father's shoes—he had everything.

And his brother stabbed him in the back.

A warlock he had likely been raised with cursed him.

He watched family and friends and allies *die* in horrific, gruesome ways.

So fucking talented and skilled—and *broken*.

Yeah, my brothers were cocksuckers. Sadistic. Money hungry. They'd stab me in the back too, given the chance, alpha or not, and had done so throughout our childhood. After all, we played pin the blame regularly to avoid getting the shit kicked out of us by Dad; I knew what they were about.

I knew they'd fuck me over the first chance they got over literally anything.

Just one of many reasons why I'd left.

Brandon and Lucian Hadley—that hadn't seemed to be the case. They were human tabloid darlings, and from what I had scoured, they seemed like *friends*.

Seemed to genuinely like each other.

Twins with a soul bond.

And then… the ultimate betrayal.

Lady Fate had been cruel to the Hadleys. Twin firstborn sons— one an alpha, the other not. Devastating.

War had been brewing in their bloodline from the day those two were born.

But now Lucian had us.

Brothers who *wouldn't* turn on him. Even before Lyssa, I had come to terms with the fact that we were in this together—but after fating to one she-wolf, mating with her, *sleeping* together in the same bed?

He was mine now. I had willingly taken on the responsibility, same as Lyssa and Soren, of rehabilitating that surly asshole and bringing him back to the world.

And if someone fucked with him, someone from his past, I'd string them up and bleed them slow in good ol' Quinn fashion.

But I would *also* torment him over the fact that he sucked *ass* at skating.

Because that was what brothers were for, right?

Just as I was about to share that little nugget of wisdom with my fated mate, I found her in that thousand-yard stare again, pushing past Lucian and Soren's theatrics in the middle of the rink for Rosa.

"Blue eyes, just—"

"I want to talk to her *alone*," Lyssa stressed, glancing at me out of the corner of her eye and then nodding pointedly across the rink. Rosa had company again, Ethan back for more kisses with little Aster, more smiles and silly faces and waves.

Ah.

Right.

Girl talk.

Fair.

We had pushed for her to have friends outside of the pack for *this* exact reason, and if she wanted alone time with Rosa, I'd make it happen.

"Okay, sure, grab your boots." I nipped at her ear, then stood and ruffled out my trench, my dangling red wool scarf purely for aesthetic and offering zero additional warmth. "I'll drag Ethan away for a hot chocolate run."

Fireworks erupted in her golden gaze at the mention of her favorite cold-weather beverage, and Lyssa grabbed her skates, skipped over to the rental counter, and traded them for the leather boots I'd surprised her with the other day. Cost a mint. Hot off the delivery truck from Italy for one of the local shops, a style that wouldn't be shelved until January.

But I had feelers out everywhere, which meant when I demanded them, I *got* them, because not only should *my* mate be a Redwood Grove trendsetter, but I *needed* to spoil her absolutely rotten for no reason and with no expectation of anything in return.

Just because.

Since the bonfire of trust, a lot of my actions were just because. No ulterior motive. No ten-step plan to reach the next goal.

Just... because.

Just because everyone in her life had let her down—and I'd spend the rest of *my* life fixing their fucking mistakes.

Once she was zipped up, we headed around the rink together, arm in arm and tactfully dodging the hordes of human families everywhere. By the time we reached the Perrys, Ethan looked *just* about to push off for another lap; I flagged him down with a wave and a grin.

"Snack break," I announced, letting Lyssa loose and leaning on the rink's frosty white exterior wall. "Gimme a hand, will you? My mate is craving hot chocolate *right* this second, apparently."

I then cast my she-wolf a hapless look, and, playing along, she poked her tongue out at me—then turned it on Aster, the little chubby pup in teal huffing out her laughter, smile huge and grabby little mittened hands already reaching for Auntie Lyssa.

Effortless on skates despite being built like a beanpole, Ethan glided back to the wall and drummed his gloved hands on the top. "Well, can hardly have *that*. Cravings unsatiated turn mean." The warlock smirked at his wife as she settled on a nearby bench, already handing Aster over to Lyssa. "Or dramatic."

Rosa waved her man off with a thin smile and a roll of her emerald greens. My mate's protectiveness hit me like a punch to the gut, and a quick check to the center of the rink showed Soren and Lucian frowning, the former pressing at his stomach and searching for the cause. Ethan, meanwhile, skated down to the nearest break in the wall to climb out for our snack run, and I hurried after to offer an arm for the warlock to brace on in his skates. Meanwhile, I peeked over my shoulder as subtly as I could...

And found our girls seated together, cuddled up for warmth, Rosa's smile huge and Aster plopped squarely in Lyssa's lap.

Yeah, no. Not a chance in hell that witch was *mad* at my mate. Not possible. Not from the way they whispered together, breaths foggy and eyes bright, all grins and giggles without their males.

"You think they can make these hot chocolates Irish?" Ethan mused as he hobbled over to a bench, death-gripping my arm and wobbly as a newborn fawn now that he was off the ice. I smirked and nodded toward the truck I had in mind, owned by a good business acquaintance of mine who was currently manning the counter and licensed to serve liquor.

"I think we can figure something out."

"Nice."

As Ethan hastily undid the intricate laces looped around his skates, I did another check on the girls—happy, chatting, cooing at little Aster—and then my fellow alphas.

Soren threw his hands up in defeat when Lucian ate it again, this time landing on his ass.

I snapped another photo.

Lucian's head whipped in my direction at the *click*, and he flipped me off as I laughed.

Then watched a *very* red-faced woman with a line of little pups in tow, clinging to one another's coats like elephants holding each other's tails, unleash holy hell on the poor bastard for using such *profanity* in front of her angels.

Soren immediately bailed, leaving him to fend for himself.

And I decided, after all that, Lucian deserved at least a triple shot of something *hard* in his hot chocolate if he was going to survive the rest of our day.

10

LYSSA

Come *on* already.

Seated on Lucian's knee, his legs spread wide so I could angle into him, I grabbed his left arm and shoved up his sleeve to check the time.

Yeah, just what I thought: *late*.

Lucian rubbed my back, his breath blooming like a foggy cloud, there one second and gone the next. "Bored, little mate?"

"It's late," I grumbled, tapping on his watch with a scowl. The bench under us creaked with even the slightest movement, struggling to hold two sturdy shifters.

"Welcome to pretentious public ceremonies." Behind me, Soren leaned against the brick wall of one of the village square shops, fiddling with his phone, just as antsy as me to get things moving— but probably not for the same reason. "Get used to it, babe. We're gonna do a lot of this stuff for Ewan."

I huffed and tugged Lucian's sleeve down, then scanned the steadily growing crowd in front of us. I wasn't *bored*—I couldn't be bored here. December 6 marked the lighting of the Redwood Grove Christmas tree. This huge square courtyard hosted the farmer's market during the warmer months up until Thanksgiving, then a

Christmas bazaar for two weeks in December; as of today, a massive twenty-foot pine tree stood proudly in the center, and probably half the village had shown up to watch it come alive.

It was *gorgeous*—and not just the tree.

Everything. The whole square.

Not boring.

Stunning.

Lights twinkling in shops windows. Snow on the ground. Christmas carols warbling from somewhere. Wreaths on doors and garland on railings. The tree already looked lovely, decorated within an inch of its life, full of huge ball ornaments and snowflakes and figurines and apples, some of the decorations plucked straight from the rugged wilds of the Redwood Grove valley. At its peak was a beautiful golden star; it would be even *more* spectacular once they turned the lights on.

Not only had little Christmas elves turned the village breathtaking and festive, but Ewan was going to be at the center of it all tonight, the PR branch of his company organizing the setup. Right there, to the left of the tree, on the black stage threaded with shimmery tinsel, was where he'd stand, all scrumptious and handsome and *strong* in that black suit he had stalked out of the house in earlier this evening. The red-and-green scarf I'd found at the thrift store Soren and I had raided on a recent grocery run went *perfectly* with the look, exactly what he needed for the ceremony.

It wasn't silk or cashmere or a designer label, no, but when I gave it to him, Ewan had smoothed it out and handled it with such tender loving care you'd think it cost millions.

I couldn't wait to see him up there, looking so handsome and wearing *my* scarf.

This was the kind of pack outing I *craved*.

But, I dunno—something felt off.

In my belly.

A constant churn that wasn't coming from the outside for once. Not influenced by my pack. Not Idunn's power running amok. No, the low-grade nausea had made itself at home during dinner and still hadn't left.

No idea why.

That salmon had been *awesome*.

Like—so good. Ugh. Soren really outdid himself there, busting out perfectly cooked and seasoned giant salmon steaks all by himself after a full day at work. Lucian and I... We garnished.

And occasionally poked at the asparagus crisping on the stove.

But as tasty as it had been, something must not have agreed with me, because my tummy was unhappy, and Kira had disappeared ages ago for a grumpy nap, the churn rubbing off on her and putting us both in the mood for bed.

Tonight should have been perfect. A snow-covered village decked out for Christmas? All my mates here? A tree coming to life right before my eyes? Yes, yes, *yes*.

Only they were running late.

And my tummy felt weird.

And I kind of just wanted to go home and put on my comfies, then watch a movie in someone's arms and fall asleep halfway through.

Applause suddenly erupted from the *very* human crowd gathered around the tree, their scents and clumsy movements so obvious now—and only making my tummy tantrum worse.

Soren pushed off the brick, fidgety hands finally in his pockets as he peered over the crowd, and I sat up straighter, leaning side to side, looking around heads and grinning when I spotted the ceremony officials taking to the stage.

"Oh, look, *look*, there he is!"

Soren smirked. Lucian *started* to roll his eyes, then stopped when I gave him a chastising tap on the nose. To his credit, he had been willing to *try* more social outings lately, and that was all I could ask of him.

The grump would fade in time.

Hopefully.

You know, once he realized how much fun we could all have together.

Unnecessarily bundled and buttoned in my winter coat, I shuffled to the edge of his lap and sat as straight as I could, totally fixated on my mate. With my scarf the centerpiece of his stylish outfit, outshining even those crisp leather gloves, Ewan loitered at the far end of the stage while an aged human with salt-and-pepper hair and a fuzzy cap—the mayor, according to Soren—stepped up to the microphone and greeted the crowd.

He then launched into a speech about the holiday season, about being grateful for our beautiful community, our supportive locals, our wonderful growth. While I listened, I stayed glued to Ewan—*my* mate looking so powerful and important up there, my dark fallen angel, my divine masculine beauty. He didn't have to say a word, yet he commanded the village square.

Just the sight of him in his element, with the rest of us here for support, made my heart very, very full—and happy enough to quiet the tummy upset, at least for a little while.

The mayor finished his speech by touching on family, on the true meaning of this season. The thought of having my *first* Christmas in over eighteen years with love and comfort and *mates* and belonging and a roof over my head with tons of delicious food in my belly and Soren's parents coming home for the holidays to celebrate us all finding each other and his sisters flying in for New Year's and, and, and…

Well, it brought a tear or two to my eye.

"Here, little mate. Quick so you don't miss it." While he could probably feel my emotional surge, Lucian stayed soft and sweet as he patted my hips with both hands, then nudged me up when the crowd burst into another round of applause. "Stand on the bench so you can see."

Sniffling it all away, I grabbed his hand and let him help me clamber up so I stood head and shoulders above the crowd. Soren drifted closer as Lucian settled in front of me, and I leaned on his broad shoulders, my chin nestling into the thick, lush dark brown hair that I so loved stroking my fingers through.

"*Oh!*" Maybe a bit obnoxious, but I couldn't stop myself from clapping Lucian's shoulder and pointing when the tree finally lit up —because it was so *magical* and beautiful and, ugh, *wow*! The ornaments and tinsel and pinecones were so colorful, but the big bulbs of light brightening the darkness were pure white like stars on a clear night. Stuck at the back of the crowd, a little distance between us and the final row of humans oohing and ahhing over this huge tree, our trio felt... small.

But like we belonged.

Like we were a part of the much larger human community in Redwood Grove. This territory belonged to *us*, and we would defend it—and by default, all these people—with everything we had.

But this was a little too cozy for my emotions, too sweet and picture-perfect, like it belonged in a movie, and the village square swam with the next rush of tears, my smile so wide it hurt, my heart about to *burst* right out of my chest.

Best of all, Soren and Lucian had finally ditched the attitudes, just as infatuated with the tree as me, their smiles genuine and the emotions threading through our bond all positive. The connection between all four of us glowed just as bright as those tree lights, and I snuggled into Lucian from behind, arms draped over his shoulders, chin on top of his head, and really tried to take it all in, every wonderful detail.

Because after this, Ewan would go back to work, bogged down with the next big event of the season.

Lucian was scheduled for patrol, which meant my time with him tonight was also limited.

But it didn't hurt to watch them leave anymore.

They always came home.

As time passed and our connection deepened, we each got just a little more comfortable with the rhythms of our pack. We all came and went. I patrolled the territory borders, same as them, and everything felt more *together*. I knew bits and pieces of their past lives, why Ewan was so quick to anger and Lucian was so desperate to hide, and they knew *me.*

They respected me.

My trauma, my heartache, my disappointment in the way *I* came about—my dad betraying his fated mate for my mom, who had just wanted to climb the pack ladder with no regard for this other female...

Since I learned about all that, I'd feared it would turn them off.

Make them think I was too damaged to waste time on—that I came from a broken line.

But they were here. All three were more patient and thoughtful, more open and talkative, more curious and understanding.

And they *loved* me.

No one else had made declarations like Lucian yet, but I really felt it these days. Nothing in my life touched like this before. Nothing went *this* deep, not even my ties to Mama and Papa, my wolf parents settled into the western woods and fading fast.

This was *real.*

A part of me... still didn't accept it. I still expected to wake up from the fantasy, back in the forest and living with wolves.

Expected Lady Fate might still check her notes and realize, oh, no, she put me with the *wrong* males and rip them all away.

But never mind that.

Be *here.*

Serenaded by Kira's soft snores, I refocused on the tree, on the lights and the star and the decorations, following its sloping line down from the top, then to the sea of excited faces in the crowd. Pups pointed and chattered to their parents. More than a few couples kissed like they were the only ones here, while some of the elderly grouped together sipped their complimentary hot chocolates and teas from the stand across the square.

So lovely.

So many of them, bundled up and warm and basking in the light of the tree—

I suddenly flinched and blinked and sucked in a shallow breath.

Fear slashed at my insides.

There, in the middle of the leftmost crowd by the tree—

Everyone was looking at it or each other...

And Loki was looking at me.

Back to the tree, dressed in a pine-green peacoat, physically shorter than he had been in the orchard, his fiery mane swept back in a ponytail—he stared *right* into my eyes. Unblinking. Unmoving.

Kira snapped awake inside and snarled, sleep making her groggy and unsteady, our heartbeats spiking together. Stunned—*terrified*—I went limp at Lucian's back.

Was this... real?

Lucian threaded his fingers through mine.

"Lyssa?"

So far away. He sounded and felt so—far—away as invisible fingers stuffed thick cotton in my ears, muffling the ceremony while a hive of angry hornets buzzed around my skull. Soren popped into my line of sight with a frown, but his handsome face blurred, the only thing in focus *him*.

Green eyes circled in gold.

Same angular face. Same sharp canines exposed with his bored smile. Same masculine energy with an air of femininity in the way he moved.

I blinked really, really, really hard, squeezing my eyes shut until it hurt, and when I opened them—

Still there.

Loki smiled wider and waved, the gesture small, intimate, and just for me. No one paid him any attention, and he tipped his head toward the tree, then pointed at it with this expression that said, *Huh, this is nice.*

My heart rocketed into my throat.

Kira rumbled out a warning, my vision sharpening as she tried to force the shift right here, right now, desperate to prove herself against the creature who had knocked her aside before like she weighed nothing. All her razor-sharp claws and vicious teeth and raw, brute strength—*nothing*.

No.

I sucked down a deeper breath, filling my lungs to bursting, and shook my head. *No, not here. Not in front of all these humans.*

She answered with silence, then a seething growl that launched acid from my upset tummy, bitter enough that it scalded the back of my tongue and I tasted blood.

Kira wanted to *fight.*

I wanted to flee.

With Loki, we'd probably do both at some point—but not here.

"I-I'm fine," I forced out, my voice miles away, the world a little hazy as I wobbled off the bench onto more solid ground. No more trips to the orchard since that *man* ripped out a chunk of my hair. Somehow, Idunn found a way to block me again. Maybe that had always been the case—maybe I was only allowed in when she decided, and last time had been an accident, a slip of her control.

I wished she'd just let me in already.

Dreamless sleeps made me wake up sweaty and shaky and kind of nauseous, and I would rather there be a clear-cut cause.

For the last week and a half, I'd struggled to parse fantasy from reality. Idunn's afterlife *felt* real when you were in it, but it was something beyond this world. Sometimes I wondered if it was just my brain trying to rationalize things—or if Idunn's power was talking to me, and creating that world with a dead goddess so sweet and informative was my mind's way of making sense of things so I didn't completely lose it.

With no more missing clumps of hair, no more silky chuckles skimming over my skin, and no more green comets—I wasn't sure about Loki.

I'd kept him to myself, Kira tense and growly anytime thoughts drifted in his direction.

But…

Oh.

No.

No, no, no, *no*—it wasn't a dream.

He wasn't—

"Baby, are you sure?"

I blinked and jerked backward into the bench when everything pounded into focus again, startled with Lucian and Soren so close, so *in* my personal space, one crouching on either side and assessing me with narrowed eyes and thin mouths, their concern staticky on the nape of my neck.

"The bond," Soren reminded me softly as he squeezed my shoulder. "We can feel—"

"Something isn't sitting right from dinner," I blurted, barely aware of what was coming out of my mouth as I pushed onto my tiptoes and scanned the crowd. No Loki anymore. No piercing green-and-gold eyes tunneling into my soul. No wolfish smirk daring Kira to strike.

But I smelled him.

Barely.

And that was proof enough.

I shook my head and forced a smile, seeing its strain in my mates' expressions as I glanced between them. "Can we just go home?"

Soren and Lucian swapped looks, a wordless conversation flowing between them and only them—which suited me just fine. Over the heads of those in the crowd, Ewan appeared to be searching for us, loitering at the corner of the stage and completely ignoring the pair of grey-haired women talking at him.

"Uh, sure," Soren said a beat later. "Let's head back to the car, then."

While we all preferred walking, the steadily growing snowdrifts would definitely ruin the nice outfits we'd forced ourselves into for the ceremony. Hard to have fun bouncing through the wild when you had to *look* human and pretend all this icky white wet was just too cold for your civilized senses.

So, after some back-and-forth between Soren and Lucian over whose car we'd take, the three of us had piled into Soren's BMW and driven down, then spent way too long searching for parking on the packed narrow streets, this tree-lighting ceremony drawing crowds from outside the village too.

Arms crossed tight, chin tucked, I headed for the nearby alley that cut from the square to the main road, Soren and Lucian trailing a few paces behind.

Suspicion dripped down my spine like a melting icicle.

Worry buzzed in my chest like TV static.

I sighed and slowed, their emotions in our bond too powerful to ignore.

Finally, I just stopped. Back to them, I frowned, fighting with myself—because this wasn't right. We had promised no more secrets. No more hiding things. No more running away for the sake of everyone else. Squaring my shoulders, I rounded in place, then stepped aside when a pack of teenagers came crashing down the thin corridor between shops, strings of colored Christmas lights crisscrossing overhead, even the dumpster decked in garland.

Once they were out of earshot, I sidled closer to my silent mates, both of them wearing expectant expressions—ones that told me even if I tried to sugarcoat this or pepper in a few white lies, they'd see clear through.

"I need to tell you guys something." *Duh.* My reaction to Loki hadn't exactly been subtle. To assume they hadn't noticed was an insult to both Soren and Lucian, and to keep this to myself was a betrayal of our vows. "I've kind of been sitting on it for a few days, just because, uh…" I swooped my loose brown waves behind my ears, then fluffed the fake black fur lining my jacket's hood just to put this antsy energy to use. "Honestly, I didn't know what to make of it, and I wasn't sure if it was *real* or not until… now."

Neither of them said a word in the silence that followed. No judgment. No exasperation. Soren stood there waiting, his blue eyes soft and warm like the sky on the first spring day, whereas Lucian crowded my personal space again, his golden wolf eyes out and ready to attack.

Not me.

It.

The unseen danger still haunting his every step.

Swallowing hard, I grabbed his wrist for support, my squeeze a little reminder that I was—*technically*—okay and the ground wasn't falling out from under us.

Not yet, anyway.

With a deep breath, I filled my mates in on this Loki character, from the disarray in Idunn's orchard to the way he towered over me like an actual mountain. How he manhandled Kira as if she were a newborn pup and not a full-grown alpha. About Idunn blocking me after the comet—which I now guessed had something to do with *him*, that green the same sheen as his eyes—and her blasting me away the first chance she could.

About Loki ripping out my hair and the lingering pain when I woke up after.

How he asked if I'd planted my own orchard yet, so intense and interested, like he knew so much *more* about my own life that it was embarrassing.

"And I just s-saw him in the crowd," I finished breathlessly, cheeks hot and prickling. "Not a lot actually scares me out here, but he—"

"If it's *he* from the Norse pantheon, the guy is a literal god," Soren insisted as he speared a hand through his hair, glaring through the alley to the village square all aglow with its newly lit tree, buzzing with the hum of the crowd. "I'd question it if you *weren't* scared."

Fidgeting with my coat sleeves, locked on to a little string I'd already picked out of the cuffs, I turned to Lucian for—

Oh.

But he was already gone, stalking down the narrow alley, bulldozing through a herd of humans and vanishing around the brick corner at the end, off to prowl the square without us.

While his expression had warned not to mess with him, that he'd rip out your spine like it was nothing, it wasn't anger rolling off him. No, as Soren smoothed a hand up to my neck, battling with my jacket for skin-to-skin contact, his firm touch and big hand oddly grounding when he cuffed me and held on, Lucian's emotions were stark and obvious in the bond.

Protectiveness.

Stability.

An inner calm and focus that we all envied.

He accepted what I told him, that this Loki was *here*, in Redwood Grove, without question.

Soren too, his feelings prickly and a little panicked but not suspicious or doubtful, even as he tried to shape his expression into the same *chill* that worked better on Lucian.

They... trusted me.

With this.

With something that sounded nuts.

Like a fever dream—*again*.

Everything about Redwood Grove, from fated mates to shifters to witches and warlocks and cursed rivers, had all been new to me. The coffee maker and my sleek phone and credit cards that you just had to tap on the machines.

New.

Different.

Strange and a little exciting.

For the first time, however, I realized it wasn't just *me* wading through all the new, different, strange but exciting stuff. My mates might understand this world inside and out, shifter culture etched in their bones, but dead goddesses and the power to make plants grow, to make the windows tremble, to *heal* Lucian after the Hawthorne alpha hacked his throat wide open...

Ruling this huge territory together.

Sharing a mate like me.

Wild and a little divine.

And now *this*?

I wasn't the only one struggling to keep my head above water—

and that made my heart stumble, trip, and fall head over heels deep into *love*.

This was it, right? It had to be—*true love*, like in the movies, the real deal.

Trust without question.

Affection without expectations.

Protection without hesitation.

"Are you *sure* you saw him?" Soren croaked. Voice rough, eyes amber, his frown deepened when I nodded—and he looked a little scared. My Soren. My savage alpha in the bedroom, my silly wolf in the forest. My *man* in a blue jacket to match his human eyes, jeans forever stained with splatters of stuff he couldn't remember. My happy guy—my worried mate, gaze flitting around the alley, his hand flexing at the back of my neck as he mulled things over. "Okay. Okay." He nodded, cheeks hollowing for a moment, then flaring back out. "Okay, right. Sure. Loki—god of lies and shapeshifting and, uh, probably a lot of other shit... Here. Uh-huh. Right. Okay."

I pressed a hand to his chest, right over his heart, and leaned in. Despite trying to soothe his mate, his posture shielding, his stance defensive, Soren's babbling triggered something protective in *me*.

"Soren—"

"We need to have a pack meeting," he said firmly, shaking off some of the fear with a roll of his shoulders and a *crick-crack* of his neck, head tossed side to side, expression determined. "Figure out the best plan here."

I patted his chest. "Definitely."

"I'll tell Ewan to come home." Still frowning, he dug out his phone and tapped at the screen, then locked it and shoved it clumsily in his pants pocket like he'd only needed to check the time. "No more work tonight."

Yeah, right, that would go over *swimmingly*. My midnight mate had already complained over breakfast about the tree lighting ceremony cutting into his work hours and forcing him to skip dinner with us. As if he needed something *else* to poke at that teeny, tiny inner panic button that made his anxiety spike over another schedule change. "Uh, okay, but—"

"Hey." Soren eased around in front of me and ducked down, brushing his knuckles over my cheeks, all soft and gooey and *exactly* the energy I needed right now. "It's okay, baby. No one's upset about this." His eyes snapped to blue with one blink, then back to amber with the next, like he and his inner wolf were wrestling over the steering wheel. "Uh, I mean, we *are*, but it's a *for your safety* upset, not a, like, uh, upset that this is happening kind of... thing." He exhaled sharply and straightened, humiliation roiling in our bond, the dark and twisty overtaking all his usual gentle vibrations. "Sorry, I'm kind of all over the place right now. Lemme just—"

"It's okay." Grinning, I grabbed at his thick wool collar and tugged. "I get what you're trying to say."

No one's upset about this meant no one was going to boot me out.

He said it like he had to make that clear to me.

Like my drama, my issues and problems and all the baggage that came from drinking Gull River, was a *pack* problem—not a Lyssa problem.

I appreciated the support.

I just wished I felt as confident about it as he did.

While *that* particular fear had its hooks in deep, I let go of the Ewan concerns. My mate had promised to do better, to *try*, which meant I shouldn't dread him having to adjust work for something this important. After all, I'd immediately assumed he would grouse and grumble and groan, which wasn't really fair to him: we were *all* trying to do better lately, and Ewan deserved that chance just as much as the rest of us.

What was the saying about assumptions?

Something about asses?

So, yeah—*that*.

"We'll find a way to keep the pack safe together, right?" Soren murmured as he drew me back to his side and nuzzled at my temple, into my hair, then down to my neck. Goose bumps trailed after the icy tip of his nose, and I nodded, some of his courage jumping to me, strengthening my sense of security, building the wall around us just a few bricks higher.

"I mean, you ripped out an alpha's heart," he added, both of us slowly unraveling when Lucian rounded the corner and stomped down the alley toward us. Soren huffed, his emotions taking a nosedive in the bond, worry clawing at the reins even as he forced out, "I think we can handle some, uh, douchebag trickster."

"I didn't see him," Lucian announced, his words velvety but deep, wolf *right* there, golden eyes brighter than usual like he was on the brink of a shift. Heat rolled off him when he stopped just a few inches from us, like he needed to both shield and watch over me *and* Soren as that gold tore around the alley and up to the rooftops. "But there was this strange scent—"

"Crushed pine needles," I clarified. The scent of all those humans, the tree, the decorations, and the hot chocolates and snacks from the high street booths might have drowned Loki out if you didn't know what to smell for, but at Lucian's stiff little nod, I figured he'd found him without even realizing it. Our eyes locked as I untangled from Soren's side. "And sea salt, and—"

"And something sweet," Lucian added gruffly. I nodded again, glancing between my mates, and Lucian let out a long, harsh breath that was more growl than anything. Soren ruffled his hair, the nervous tic becoming more and more apparent.

"Awesome." My blond mate shifted his weight from leg to leg, rocking back and forth, his adrenaline spike coursing through our bond and making Lucian snarl. I shook my hands out, Kira pacing, all that bottled-up energy a weakness here in the heart of human Redwood Grove.

Wordlessly, Lucian shoved at Soren, who pushed back—only it wasn't the old roughhousing from the start of our story. No, this seemed more like a way to safely and quickly expel some of that adrenaline, the pair punching each other in the arm, wolf eyes out, the air swelling with *heat* strong enough to make a few humans passing by do a double take.

I want in.

Seriously, it was either punch something or run.

I stomped my feet instead, like I was clearing the slushy snow off my boots.

"We should grab Ewan and get out of here," I insisted, the slight wobble in my voice stopping my mates' weird little ritual. While Soren looked like he was about to agree, Lucian shook his head and nudged the blond alpha in my direction.

"You two go home."

"But—"

"I'll tell Ewan to meet you there," he rumbled, peeling off his coat and shoving it at Soren. "I'm going to track him—see where he's been nosing around."

All my courage flatlined. "*Lucian, no—*"

Sweater scrunched up to his elbows, my massive mate scooped me into a hard, demanding kiss, then all but tossed me into Soren's awaiting arms.

"He'll be fine," he whispered in my ear, both of us watching Lucian jog back down the alley and disappear into the crowded square again. Soren might have held me tight, Lucian's jacket bunched between us, his oakwood scent familiar and cozy. His mouth might have brushed my ear with every word, his voice rich and deep and reassuring—but none of that dampened the *fear*. Soren hugged harder, probably feeling my mounting terror, experiencing it as human couples never would. "Lyssa, he doesn't want Lucian. He wants *you*."

Business as usual, then.

Always me.

Always *me* putting my mates in danger.

It should have made me feel just a sliver better knowing that Loki wasn't interested in Lucian—that it had been all about the apples in the orchard.

But someone had already tried to *hurt* Lucian to make me comply with his demands. I'd already squared off with one villain promising to steal a piece of my heart away forever. Shred it right before my eyes. Set it on fire while I screamed. The Hawthorne

634

alpha held a gun to Lucian's temple and placed his finger on the trigger...

One breath, one wrong move, and I could have lost him.

And that jerk was only a *shifter*.

What the heck would a *god* do to get exactly what he wanted?

11

LUCIAN

This god's trail was obvious.

Far too obvious, his contradictory scent smeared all over the place.

Purposeful too, his path out of the village through the mountain slopes and into the western woods clear as fucking neon blazing in the darkness.

Like he *wanted* to be followed.

Like he wanted to be hunted.

And I was more than happy to oblige.

While a little shaky and sporadic in the village itself, humanity tainting my quarry's footsteps, as soon as I left it behind, things were so much clearer. With Ewan on his way home to connect with the others, I followed this unwelcome creature into the wilds, ditching my clothes along the way until I was pure wolf, nose to the ground, to the sky, to the trees he seemed to rub his whole fucking body against like he was quite happy to stay on a predator's radar.

Thus far, I hadn't given my enemy's species a second thought. He could be a titan for all I cared—or Lady Fate herself. If something was a threat to my mate, tracking her from a dead goddess's dream world into reality, he needed to be *gone*—immediately. This was a pack issue, certainly, but if I could bully some trickster out of the territory before things turned violent, I'd take that as a hard-earned victory.

So, I followed his scent into the wilderness, the pine, sea salt, and sweetness a combination that turned my stomach.

No idea why he was here, but clearly Lyssa's new powers attracted unwanted attention, and this Loki villain wasn't the first to come sniffing around her.

Probably wouldn't be the last either.

And if it *scared* her, if it was something Lyssa didn't feel she could handle despite her growing strengths, then it was time for her mates to step in and get the job *done*.

As a team.

In theory.

That was how it was supposed to be after the bonfire, yet here I was traipsing through the western woods alone, old habits refusing to just bloody well die already.

Once the god was dispatched with, I'd refocus on the *other* threat nosing at our girl: Ethan Perry.

The fact that he liked to sniff at her, poke and prod and ask question after question after question without her mates around if he could swing it—my hackles were perpetually up in his presence. Just the thought of him, the mention of his name, triggered the wolf in me, though I struggled to discern if it was because this warlock, Ewan's *friend*, was a legitimate concern or if my baggage still colored the world.

Or was it the third alternative: we alphas simply *loathed* the thought of another male spending so much time with our forever girl.

Our divine she-wolf.

After all, her magic never triggered me—not like the warlock did.

Yet his mousy little witch wife rarely set me off either, which was telling.

Nose to the ground, I slowed at yet another clear set of

footprints in the forest floor courtesy of massive boots *ground* into the rock-hard dirt, Redwood Grove blanketed in snow and ice and frozen grass. Growling low, I tracked the zigzagging path, looking first like he was walking, then possibly skipping, headed into snowdrifts around some young pines.

A soft whine sounded from my left.

I straightened and huffed a cloudy breath, zeroing in on the male alpha of Lyssa's old pack. A large grey wolf—large by *beast* standards, anyway—tinged with a coppery-red undercoat. Yellow eyes. Strong. Agile.

I rather liked him.

We all did.

He calmly led his new pack alongside his mate, the female raised under Lyssa's watchful eye. He never intruded on our business. He really threw himself into play-wrestling whenever we crossed paths but never escalated to aggression.

This one—he'd make a fine alpha for years to come.

Breed strong litters to fill our territory with *real* wolves, my mate's family claiming it for themselves in the natural world, their howls combined with ours yet another deterrent to rival shifters interested in crossing our borders.

Tonight, he poked his fluffy face out from behind a maple, huffed, then whined again. I cocked my head, eyes narrowed, struggling to decipher the nuances of real wolf-speak.

Then, without warning, he turned and scampered into the shadows.

Right.

That was telling.

The wind suddenly died down, the bare branches still, the forest too quiet.

I mirrored that energy, moving like a shadow, back on the trail and following Loki's scent deeper into the trees.

Until it all disappeared.

His footprints in the snow, in the earth itself—gone.

No more pine or sea salt or saccharine sweetness.

Beneath the sprawling bare canopy of an old ash tree, the trail vanished.

"Hello, wolf."

My blood ran cold when a lightly accented but aggressively male voice sprinkled down like a spring mist. Painfully still, muscles taut and adrenaline pounding, I took a beat to compose myself—and then looked up.

There, in the thick boughs of the forest's tallest tree, its bark light grey and rough, was a man.

Just sitting there.

Watching me.

Waiting for me to catch up.

All long limbs in a tailored black suit and a wicked smile—he wasn't what I'd expected.

Yes, even *I* had seen the screen adaptation of the old Norse myths, a performance staged by humans blissfully unaware that the gods in question still roamed the earth.

The real thing was... different.

Lean and strong, masculine yet beautiful. Intense green eyes shrouded in golden rings and kissed by a cruel, childish mirth. Pale. *So* very pale. A shock of long red hair that made Rosa's mane look dull, thick and full and swept into a ponytail that draped over his right shoulder.

He peered down at me, seeming massive despite the heights he'd climbed to settle in that perfect cradle of thick, strong branches.

I bared my teeth.

Snarled.

Fluffed up to my biggest size, individual furs standing on end, hackles trembling, saliva dripping, every fiber of my being ready for *war*.

The old god briefly studied my display, then rolled his eyes and waved me off. "Oh, put those away, child, before you hurt yourself."

Fine. If he wouldn't take my threats seriously in *this* form, let me speak fucking *plainer*.

I shifted from wolf to man in a flash, a primal snarl carrying through the transformation. Steam spiraling, heart raging, hands in fists, I glowered up at him with such ferocity that a lesser creature would have just dropped dead.

Loki cocked his head to one side, then the other, his dark smile a permanent fixture, my threats falling on deaf ears.

"Get out," I rasped, slow and deliberate, vision so sharp and focused that it was a bloody miracle my wolf didn't come flying back out on a whim, "of the *fucking* tree—"

He leapt down and landed *hard*—so hard the world shook, trees trembling and ground shuddering and my knees buckling. Forest critters scampered out of their nearby holes, fleeing across the woods as fast as their little legs and wings could carry them. Scrambling for balance, I staggered back and regained my sea legs fast.

Then rose to my full height.

And still had to glare *up* to meet his eyes.

Rare, to face off with a foe who had several substantial inches on me.

No matter.

Even the tallest tree could fall.

"*Loki*," I snarled, needing him to know I saw him for who he was, that Lyssa had shared everything and he wouldn't catch us off guard again, "you are not welcome in this territory—"

"Tut, tut." He kicked a bit of snow at me, the cold dusting my shins. Tone light and conversational, he *still* wasn't taking this seriously—and that would be his downfall. "Mind your manners when you speak to the father of your species."

I reared back with a snarl, teeth bared, contempt written in my scowl, in the narrowing of my eyes and the tightening of my fists. Folklore and legend in *some* shifter circles, particularly wolves, linked our origins to this ancient god. Until I saw proof, however, his sentiment was just a tactic, a means of control.

Rolling my shoulders back, I bullied into his personal space, sizing him up, *right* in his face so that he knew *he* was the outsider here.

He was the enemy.

And he sure as hell wasn't taking our girl *anywhere*.

Loki took my charge with a sniff, then a sigh and another eye roll. He didn't move, didn't even flinch when our noses brushed and my chest slammed into his much leaner one. I was wider. He was taller—but thin and wiry, like I could snap him in half by accident and call it a day.

Just as I was about to shove him back, physically direct him toward our territory border if need be, this ancient god snapped all by himself.

Caught my throat in a death grip, crushing my windpipe, nails gritting so deep into my flesh that rivers of blood spilled down my body, the wounds catastrophic with so little effort.

Still sporting that savage grin, his face blurring in and out of focus, he *laughed* as he slammed me into the ash tree's trunk, then hoisted me off the ground.

Body slowly going limp, I attempted what should have been a knockout right hook, flesh slick with blood, *heat* spiraling all around us.

He caught my fist and *ripped* it backward, knuckles to forearm, pain screaming through me, bone broken and flesh torn.

Darkness crept in from the corners of my eyes, slow and ominous like a prowling fog, wolf wailing—

And then I was on the ground, snow at my back and the fog receding as I gasped into the starless black sky. My body hopped to, skin stitching and bones mending, pain dropping from an air-raid siren to a smoke alarm to a text alert *ping*.

"I'll give you a second, shall I?"

Loki loomed over me, feet planted on either side of my head, and as I drew a *real* breath through my mended windpipe, he tapped my jaw with the toe of his boot, then chuckled and stepped back.

"W-what do you want?" I forced out, unable to just lie here, silent and aching, underbelly exposed to a predator far beyond my skill and strength. Loki sniffled noisily again, then scanned our surroundings, green gaze bouncing around the shadows.

"Did she tell you?" He gripped his suit lapels and shook them out, the motion followed by a waterfall of soft yellow light ghosting down his figure. As soon as it touched the ground, he was *different*. Gone was the suit, replaced with a simple linen tunic, green—the exact shade of my eyes, actually—and a brown pair of slacks. Bare feet. Hair loose. Runes tattooed over his fingers, his nails like black talons, his features somehow sharper, wilder, and infinitely more dangerous.

He'd taken off the mask, then.

The sort he donned for humans—keep the sheep calm and placid so the wolf could prowl the flock unnoticed.

"Of course she told us," I gritted out. The fact that Lyssa told us less than an hour ago would *not* factor into this conversation, naturally.

Not that it mattered—the god didn't push. Instead, he dropped with a *whoosh* of his mangled scent and squatted at my side, those slightly manic greens boring deep into mine.

"Tell me," he urged heatedly. Strange: his breath didn't fog. Not even a little. "What would you do to protect her?"

I arched up somewhat, abdomen trembling, body still recovering from his attack. "I'd *die* for her."

"Even like this?" Loki pressed, needling me with just his voice, frantic little pinpricks driving into my chest. "Even as she is now? Lyssa isn't a pure shifter, Lucian Hadley—never has been."

"She's my *mate*," I countered without missing a beat, glowering up at him. "Always has been."

The god pursed his thin lips, then bounced a little in place, looking like a monstrously handsome *child* about to rip into the chocolate bar he'd hidden from his parents. Excitement seeped from his pores, and his long fingers danced on his thighs as if he couldn't sit still anymore.

"And the other males?"

Soren and Ewan—I had no doubt either would give their lives for our mate, and Lyssa would do the same. It wasn't a one-sided thing here, where only the males would sacrifice themselves for their fated. If the chips were down and it was between her and us, Lyssa would choose *us* every bloody time.

But if it were up to me, she wouldn't ever get the chance; I'd make the call first and be fucking done with it.

"We'd die for each other," I told him, his energy infectious, riling my inner wolf and coaxing him to the surface. Teeth gritted, I sucked down a few steadying breaths, fighting my own body to stay in control—to not rise to his level. "That's the point of a *pack*."

Chuckles caressed my body like silk butterfly wings, and Loki shot to his feet fast enough to give those bloodsucking leeches a run for their money. Then, much to my surprise, he offered me his hand.

I glared at it, then rolled onto my side and stood without assistance.

Never in my life would I *owe* this creature anything. Manners, politeness, kind words, and favors—all tricks of the fae.

And, no doubt, tools of the trickster.

Unfazed, the god looked me over more thoroughly this time, slow and clinical, assessing my strength, my value, my *worth*, right here and now.

"Relax, wolf," he purred when our gazes clashed, his locking onto mine and holding it. Every muscle stiffened, and, arms limp, I found myself frozen. Unable to move. Blink. Barely capable of *thought*, his voice slithering around my skull, my eyes already watering. "I have no interest in acquiring your *little mate*." He drawled my pet name like he knew—like he had *rights* to the small, personal intimacy I shared with Lyssa. "I'm not here to take her, or use her, or sell her." The golden rings around all that startling green blazed like hellfire. "Consider me a mere observer for the time being—a fly on the wall."

He finally blinked, releasing me from his thrall, and my whole body sagged so suddenly, my inner wolf's cries a distant echo, that I needed to brace on his arm so I didn't outright collapse. Lips peeled, wolf hiding somewhere deep inside, I pushed off him and put some space between us.

"For now," Loki drawled, "I just need to decide if she's worth saving."

My gut bottomed out. *"What* did you just say?"

With one last feral grin, Loki ambled toward the old ash tree, offering me his back—a fucking *mistake*. I lunged, snarling, about to grab on and do whatever it took to pry an explanation from him.

But he shifted at the last moment, going from a giant male to an enormous white snowy owl. Feathers littered the ground at the first beat of his huge wings, a good eight-foot span on either side, and the *force* behind the next flap, the gust like howling winds, knocked me flat on my ass.

And I just sat there, watching him rise into the night's sky, his hoots a taunt...

His final words playing on repeat, *pounding* with every frantic beat of my heart, like a broken bloody record.

12

SOREN

"Hello, *beautiful*."

Homemade sourdough bread. Tangy-as-*hell* horseradish. A mountain of grilled onions. Crisp sprouts for texture. And the pièce de résistance: thinly sliced roast duck.

Ugh. *Yes.* Been waiting for this all day.

Morning.

Technically I'd only been in the office three hours, but this baby had been singing its siren song from the corner of my desk the whole time.

Get in my mouth, you majestic piece of art.

After tearing open my bag of sour cream and onion chips and cracking the lid on my fizzy pop, I slowly, tenderly, and carefully got to work on unwrapping *the* sandwich of the year. Like I was freakin' Indiana Jones handling treasure, I peeled back the tinfoil a bit at a time, basking in the scents as they hit me, my inner wolf drooling, both of us in a food daze as we hunkered down for lunch together.

What can I say? Mondays needed a little extra help, especially when you'd rather be home with your gorgeous mate—and the rest of the pack, oddly enough—but had to put in a few hours here and there to keep on top of crap in the professional world. Yeah, I had awesome guys working under me, but I wouldn't be doing my duty of managing the Acker legacy if I didn't at least manage some overview and answer a few emails and fix some spreadsheets and, you know, other officey shit that drove me nuts but was just part of the job.

Fun.

This past weekend had been all fun. Even with Loki's shadow stretching across Redwood Grove, his scent everywhere but the man himself concerningly absent, I did my best to keep spirits up around the house. We played card games Saturday night and watched movies on Sunday. We all took a dip in the freezing lake and went for a run around dawn.

Best of all: we slow roasted four *stunning* ducks Lyssa and I snagged from the village butcher. Roasted veggies and salads and homemade bread and freakin' *duck*. There was enough to worry about lately, all our anxiety amped after a living *god* showed up last week—kicked Lucian's ass to boot; now and then, we needed some fun.

And with Ewan handling the impending holiday chaos at his various businesses in the village, Lucian and Lyssa lolling around the house, me stuck in my office cabin—this baby was *my* fun for the rest of the workday.

I rubbed my hands together, lording over my masterpiece and sniffing deep. Glorious sandwich gods, *thank you* for this blessing—

My phone shrieked from under a pile of paperwork.

I stiffened.

Side-eyed the stupid thing.

Went back to my sandwich.

But it kept on ringing.

So, with a scowl a mile wide, I rooted through the mess and dug it out—then *panicked* the second I saw Lucian's name on the screen.

"*Shit.*" In my haste to answer, I fumbled and dropped the stupid thing—not for the first time today either, the tough old bird—and winced when it *clunked* on the floor. The ringer carried on wailing, and I frantically scooped it up, butterfingers on high, and finally stabbed the screen and smacked the phone to my ear, a little breathless as I barked, "*Orchard?*"

We had a pack code word now, one that signaled shit hitting the fan. Initially, it was just for the boys, but then Lyssa overhead the conversation when we thought she was in bed and demanded to be involved—which was fair. She had been in on every other conversation regarding this Loki douchebag and how we planned to manage her powers going forward—including what to share with outsiders, Ethan Perry included—so, sure. We brought her in on it, even though the code was really about her.

A go word that told the rest of us to raise hell and slit throats—because our girl was in danger.

"What?" Lucian said roughly, sounding distant and muffled like he didn't have the freakin' speaker end of his thousand-year-old phone anywhere near his mouth. Palms sweaty, appetite dead, I rolled my eyes and tried not to snap as emotion pummeled my insides—and he just cleared his throat like it was business as usual. "Oh. No, not orchard."

A relieved breath whooshed out, taking that huge adrenaline spike with it as I slumped into my chair. "Shit, man. Scared the pants off me."

"Not every phone call is a crisis," the Brit drawled, all dry wit and rogue charm and ugh. Trust Lucian Hadley to sound cool despite being total crap at using a phone.

"Talk *into* the phone, you jagweed—"

"Soren—"

"And can you seriously blame me?" I snagged a chip and popped it in my mouth. "I mean, seeing your name on the screen—should be pigs flying by my window any second now."

"Soren—stop."

I stilled at the shift in his tone, the humor gone and replaced with something… else. Hard to put a name to it, but I suddenly *felt* it through our connection. The worry and concern and apprehension was just classic Lucian, but then *excitement* undercut all that, and I sat straighter, frowning, unsure what to make of it.

"Uh, what—"

"I need you to fetch some pregnancy tests."

Everything inside went numb. My wolf stopped prancing around, his one-track mind already back on the duck now that we knew it wasn't an *orchard* situation, and my mouth suddenly felt like the Sahara.

Pregnancy tests.

Need to...

I nearly dropped the phone again, catching it this time with my shoulder and holding it there while my hands plopped uselessly into my lap.

"Uh"—my voice did a prepubescent crack—"w-what?"

"Lyssa," Lucian remarked, a glimmer of that dry humor back. "She's been sick all morning. Otherwise fine besides a few bouts of vomit, but still a little nauseous—sounds like morning sickness. I'd fetch them myself, but I don't want to leave her alone when she feels like this, so I need *you* to go to the chemist and get some tests. Ewan isn't answering his fucking phone."

I blinked at my computer monitor, the screen bright, the words blurring together.

"P-pregnancy tests? What for?" *You dumb wolf. You big, dumb, blond idiot wolf—* Snapping out of it, I lurched upright and grabbed my phone properly. "Sorry, never mind. Uh. Shit, okay, hold on." Palms sweaty, stomach in knots, I stabbed at the monitor to turn it off, then rolled away from my desk. "Be there soon."

I then hung up, leapt out of the chair, whirled around—and tripped clear over the damn thing. The chair and I crashed the floor, phone flying, curses and growls bouncing around the cabin. Heart hammering, I jumped up, smoothed my clothes out, then booted the chair aside, went for the door—only to sprint back and crash into my desk, soda spilling and sandwich forgotten, to grab my keys.

Then *bolted* out the door, my inner wolf howling for his mate, the maple grove outside blanketed in snow suddenly seeming a whole heck of a lot brighter.

⁊⦚

Twelve long minutes since the pee waterfall stopped behind the closed door of the master suite's bathroom—and I'd basically paced a path down to the first floor. Twirling my phone, tossing it from one hand to the other, I meandered back and forth while Lucian perched on one of the two king-sized beds we had jammed together for pack snoozes. Perfectly still, painfully silent, the alpha waited with bated breath, his energy steadying our bond, calm and patient, while mine was off the charts obnoxious.

Just like my inner wolf.

Seriously, the guy wouldn't shut up, all antsy and yipping nonstop, urging me to bust down the door and demand answers.

I called Ewan again instead.

Straight to voicemail—again.

Yeah, the guy had a million things on his plate, the ski slopes opening this weekend, his hotels inundated with guest bookings, his clubs and restaurants in holiday mode—all that crap. But this was important. And given we had a—according to Lucian—weird, intense, manic god circling our fated mate like a vulture, he should probably be more accessible.

My best guess was that he was in an actual meeting, with actual people, and not just some virtual thing he could mute and step away from.

We still gave the guy a lot of crap, but since the bonfire last month, he *had* been making a serious effort to be more involved. He showed his face for dinner most nights, even if he either went back to the village for a few more hours or out on patrol immediately after. He was cool with my suggestions for Christmas decorations and the tree-cutting trip we had planned for next week. He *tried*—credit given where credit was due and all that.

But…

But…

Ugh. I could have used him here right now, Lyssa's anxiety streaming through the bond from behind that stupid closed door and Lucian just this big block of muscle, really living up to the Mountain Man nickname our mate had given him. I needed someone to bounce off, do a bit of playful bickering, maybe even wrestle to expend some of this energy, and even if it wasn't always friendly, Ewan was my go-to for that shit.

Reaching the wall again, I wheeled around and tossed my phone from my left to my right hand—and way overshot. Lucian growled when the damn thing clattered to the ground for the umpteenth time since I barreled through the front door with an armful of pregnancy test boxes, then slowly peered over his shoulder.

"Soren," he rumbled, golden wolf eyes narrowing as I slowly bent down to grab my phone, its screen one drop away from splintering, "you—are driving me—*mad*."

I shot up and raised my hands by way of apology, and he faced the bathroom door again with a huff, still as stone, silently waiting. No anger in the bond, mind you. A little frustration—which was fair. I wasn't exactly the easiest wolf to be around when I got like this, so fidgety and clumsy. All that fed into our pack connection, the energy muddled and frantic, probably driving Ewan *mad* too wondering what the hell was up.

The bathroom doorknob turned, creaking softly.

Lucian rocketed off the bed.

I bolted to his side, heart in my throat, and chucked my phone somewhere behind me so I didn't drop it again. It bounced off the mattress and right over the side, crashing to the floor.

Neither of us looked back to check on it.

My vision sharpened as the door opened, inch by inch, and Lyssa shuffled out, looking adorably rumpled with her tangled bun, wispy bronze tendrils spilling everywhere. Rocking a flannel shirt and nothing else, she left the bathroom with pink cheeks and a shy smile.

And ten pregnancy test sticks from the million packs I'd dumped on the counter earlier after panic-buying a whole shelf, the cashier looking at me like I'd lost my mind.

"Uh, the box says two stripes means… pregnant."

Her golden gaze flicked between us, between the literal mountain at my side and *me*, slack-jawed and processing way, way too slow.

Two stripes.

Pregnant.

Ten sticks—all two stripes.

Holy shit.

Holy *shit*.

Inner wolf howling the pack song, I whooped and charged right into her. Lyssa dropped the sticks with a giggle, all ten clattering on the floor just as I scooped her off it.

"*Baby!*" I hugged her tight and spun us around, elation buzzing through me like bees on steroids. Her trembling arms coiled around my neck, and I kissed her laughing mouth, her cheek, her chin, her nose—whatever I could reach. If it were up to me, I'd hold her for the rest of the day, just like this, happy and giggly and light as air…

But it wasn't just me here.

So, after taking my fill of kisses and cuddles and nuzzles, I set her down and stepped aside, stumbling a little when Lucian bulldozed by to embrace our mate. While Lyssa and I had been laughter and noise and movement, she and Lucian succumbed to this precious quiet that influenced *me* too. It slowed my racing heart, my scattered mind, my frazzled inner wolf. Lucian held her so that nothing in the world could touch her, their murmurs personal, private, and, frankly, none of my business, their kiss deep and full of longing. Intimate. Intense in their own way, not lesser than my reaction—just different.

I preferred to hoot and holler, honestly, and while I gave them time and space, the antsy feeling crept back in fast. Before I knew it, I was bouncing on the balls of my feet, desperate to dive in there and celebrate our mate.

As soon as Lucian eased away, however, the hulking alpha shot me a warning look, one that ordered me to calm the fuck down—stat. Swallowing hard, I planted my feet and waited, tough as it was, so I didn't overwhelm Lyssa with all this crazy.

"How do you feel?" Lucian rumbled as he swept a few of the stray wisps out of her face, her bun precarious and on the verge of collapse after my roughhousing. Oops.

Lyssa glanced between us again, her expression a little too neutral for my liking—then burst into tears. Just—big, heaving sobs that she hid behind her hands, her shoulders shaking, her breath catching. The concern in our pack bond went nuclear. Shit. Shit, shit, *shit*. This couldn't be good. This couldn't be—

But then she straightened up again and she was *beaming*, her waterlogged gaze pure sunshine.

"I'm so..." She motioned between Lucian, me, and herself, floundering, her sheer *joy* pulsing through the bond like a golden inferno. "We... I..." Our mate then clutched her belly and squealed. "We're going to have a pup!"

I whooped again and pounced, hauling Lucian into the group hug this time because that was what Lyssa deserved. Squished between two much taller males, she happily accepted Lucian hoisting her up and cradling her between us.

"Where's Ewan?" Lyssa tossed an arm around my shoulders, the other just barely stretching along Lucian's. She licked her lips and squirmed as my fellow alpha dried her tearstained cheeks on his sweater sleeve. "Someone call him."

Ugh, *fine*. My inner wolf snarled when I forced myself out of the group huddle, stalking around the beds and swiping my phone off the floor.

Cracked screen.

Yup, seemed about right.

It took a bit of finessing, but I managed to tap around just right to place a call.

Voicemail.

Again.

And again.

I tried three times at Lyssa's wordless urging, her longing and desperation threading through our bond, lacing tighter and tighter every time Ewan didn't answer. On the last attempt, I bit my tongue and refused to badmouth him—refused to darken this beautiful moment. It… wasn't his fault, probably.

He'd hear the amazing news soon enough.

But in the grand scheme of things, our mate being pregnant with the first pup in our bloodline, the Redwood pack's *first* heir—this was big. And he had missed it.

That wolf would never forgive himself, and, yeah, Lucian and I could rip him a new one later, but once he realized what he had missed, no one would be harder on Ewan Quinn than good ol' Ewan Quinn.

After shooting him a text to call *now*, I abandoned my phone and rejoined the group hug. I'd done my duty for Lyssa's sake, but enough. My mate was *pregnant*—and I for one didn't want to miss a single second of it.

13

EWAN

Slumped in high-backed leather, tie loose, dress shirt crinkled and sleeves jerked up to my elbows, I watched the sun set behind me. Over the passing minutes, the light dipped lower and lower on the opposite wall, that big orange ball sinking below the horizon and blanketing Redwood Grove in darkness. Twelve video bubbles rotated around my monitor, filled with the faces of my investor group, an array of other like-minded men and women who shared similar interests and goals. Sometimes we invested in projects together, sometimes alone, but we always went to each other for advice. We all came up in this cutthroat world around the same time, and I considered them brothers and sisters in business arms.

My fingers coiled around the crystal tumbler for the dozenth time in the last hour, smothering the condensation, but again the bourbon went untasted.

I couldn't... bring it to my lips and take a swig like the rest of them, these dressed-down industry titans coalescing at the sunset of another successful workday.

Toasting each other.

Celebrating a fantastic year.

For the most part, we all made solid profits on our investments, and as December inched to a close, it was about that time to look toward the future.

Most wanted to get deeper into charity projects, funneling our profits from the group's collective pot into more philanthropic avenues over the next four quarters.

Great.

Fine.

More than happy to fucking oblige with... whatever they had in mind.

No idea, honestly.

Because I'd barely heard a word of it, snippets of conversation and familiar buzzwords barely penetrating my brain fog.

I just wanted out.

Of the office—not this world or this life or, you know, the game.

Lyssa, Soren, and Lucian were picking a Christmas tree this afternoon. As the sun set and temperatures dipped, they'd all pile in Lucian's rickety jeep and head south to a tree farm the Acker pack frequented over the years. After getting our asses chewed by Lyssa for dismissing *all* his Halloween traditions, we conceded to most of Soren's December activities, especially when our fated mate—our stunning and *pregnant* fated mate—seemed so eager to participate.

They were out there now, hunting for the perfect tree, an axe in hand and Lyssa gushing and squealing and totally in her element with the snow up to her knees and her cheeks fucking wind-kissed pink and...

And I wanted to be *there*.

With them.

With her—my girl.

My she-wolf, who'd learned she was carrying the first in our new bloodline without me.

Four days later, we already had her scheduled with the same witch ob-gyn in Hampton who had delivered Aster, one who specialized in magical and shifter females and came with glowing online reviews outside of Ethan's recommendation. We'd cleared the remaining shit out of Lucian's bedroom and had started the nursery conversion, paint swatches en route, the room closest to the master and the perfect size for our firstborn.

Last night, before Soren's patrol shift, we had all cozied up on the huge couch in front of the crackling fireplace and created our online baby registry, the list of wants already two hundred strong.

I'd buy it all, of course, but Soren had *insisted* we give his pack first crack.

Not only had our world flipped upside down in the last four days—*again*—but we had been inundated with Acker wolves. His parents video-chatted with us from a hotel in Sierra Leone's Freetown, then phoned multiple times a day as they prepared for the trip back to Redwood Grove for the holidays. Most of Soren's sisters had done the same, his phone ringing nonstop, all of them insisting on speaking to *all* of us.

Before this, I had a really basic working knowledge of his immediate family.

I now knew them, their mates, and their kids well enough to identify them by voice alone.

And that was… kind of nice.

Kind of *really* nice.

Because Lyssa, Lucian, and I had no calls from family.

Lucian in Hadley exile—not exactly the smartest idea to let them know a new alpha was on the way. Lyssa had no one but her wolf pack, who seemed to sense something was different about her when a couple came poking around the house the other night.

Yeah, I had a few Quinn assholes who were relatively sane compared to the rest, but nope. I hadn't included any of those toxic fuckers in my personal life since I was nineteen; I wasn't about to extend an olive branch now.

But suddenly—we had family, we three self-made and literal orphans smacked in the face with Acker positivity and enthusiasm.

That was some exhausting shit.

But in a good way.

In a way that had me actually looking forward to Christmas, Soren's parents *much* friendlier now that their son and I were fated to the same she-wolf. Then all the sisters were Redwood Grove-bound for New Year's…

It'd be chaos.

Loud, busy, tiring chaos.

And—probably for the first time in my life, ever since I realized what a fucking shitshow the Quinn pack was—a part of me really wanted that.

Unfortunately, these four busy days had shifted my priorities —*hard*.

Concentration was a pipedream, and planning for the future made me want to pull my own teeth out, my inner wolf an asshole anytime we weren't around Lyssa or the others. Heartburn for *days*.

It had reached peak obnoxious tonight, the burn so scorching I tasted blood, my wolf a rumbly, grumbly *dick* whenever I asked him to just fucking chill.

But he knew as well as I did that they—my pack, my family, my *mate*—were out there, in the cold, at the tree farm, doing cute Christmassy shit, unleashing waves of happiness and excitement and *desire* into our shared bond.

I was here.

Staring at a screen of fellow workaholics, all human except one raven shifter who refused to acknowledge a fellow supernatural creature even though we were both very aware the other existed in our investor pod.

Sitting. Staring. Not drinking.

And definitely not listening.

A firm *tap, tap, tap* on my door shook me out of the misery cloud that had been slowly thickening as darkness crept across my office. Moving like molasses, I muted the video feed and leaned around the monitor as Jocelyn in her white-and-gold polka-dotted jumpsuit nudged her head inside.

"You dead?"

The fuck? Frowning at her, I held up a finger to my investor squad and wheeled down my desk out of sight.

"What?"

"I know your stupid face," my vixen assistant announced, sidling in and half closing the door behind her. She wasn't the only one on this call; all our executive assistants loitered in the background, mics muted and screens dark, there to take notes while their bosses got tanked on a Friday afternoon before five o'clock. Arms crossed, shoulder pads extra aggressive today on her slim fox frame, she swept her stick-straight platinum locks behind her ears, then arched an eyebrow. "You're not here." She motioned to my desk stiffly. "Like, you're just... not."

Still seated, posture shot to shit, I glanced at the monitor, then my bourbon, then my phone. "They're choosing a tree tonight." For all I knew, they probably already had a victim selected and were taking turns hacking it down. "At that farm off the 629 exit."

Everything about her softened, arms no longer crossed but fingers intensely focused on picking at her new silver-and-green manicure. "I know the one."

My phone vibrated with an email alert, and I eased forward—then flipped it facedown and pushed it off to the side. "I don't want to be here."

Much to my surprise, Jocelyn snorted, pure fox sass when I met that tawny gaze. "No shit."

"I-I think I need to..." My frown deepened, the thought striking like a flash lightning storm. "Need to... hire someone... else."

"You think?" Hip cocked, Jocelyn perched on the little bar Lyssa and I had christened what felt like *years* ago—then scrambled off like she'd just remembered I had fucked someone on it. Smirking, pride warming in my chest, I shot up and snagged my jacket off the back of my chair.

"You want a job?"

"Yours?" She crinkled her nose and scoffed. "*Fuck* no."

Just the answer I'd expected—but if she had said yes, I'd give her whatever she wanted. Jocelyn had been by my side from the start. She'd helped build Quinn Enterprises into what it was today, yet she refused all my stock offerings. Refused to accept a *penny* of investment. The stubborn vixen just wanted to come to work, do her job, coordinate my life, and make me suffer a little along the way, then go home.

Drink.

Seduce gorgeous women.

Bury herself in distractions to forget the loss of *her* fated mate all those years ago.

Kindred spirits, me and her.

Whether she ever accepted my offer of executive status or not, I'd care for her, protect her, for the rest of our natural lives.

"Are you sure? It comes with perks," I mused, grinning as I shrugged my jacket on. "Endless hours and lots of stress and literally no social life—"

"I get all that anyway." She waved me off, this manicure especially sharp, talons ready for a fight. Clearly not seeing anyone special these days. "But I'll interview all your candidates—really put 'em through the wringer." She sauntered closer, heels clicking with every step, when I rounded my desk and just about sprinted for the door. Her slim figure blocked me, and she took a few seconds to fix my tie, an expert in making me look softer and more presentable than I actually was, more *civilized* than I ever could be, then smoothed her hands down my sleeves and fixed my lapels. Her smile had a strange warmth to it that didn't suit her—that put me on edge. "We'd need a small army to do what you do—"

"To be clear," I interjected, planting a chaste kiss on her cheek and gripping her narrow shoulders, "I'm not *leaving* or, you know, dying... I just want to pull back a little—"

"For the sake of your future kid and your *pregnant* mate?" she finished for me, brows up, snark back at the wheel. "A mate who's about to get very hormonal and *very* protective? Uh, yeah..." Jocelyn shoved at me playfully, the sister I'd always wanted. "About fucking time, bro."

"Hey." I pointed at her as she drifted toward my desk. "You know how I feel about *bro*."

"Oh my god, just go already." The fox flipped my abandoned work phone over and tapped the screen, her angular features briefly illuminated by the max brightness setting. "You know, before Soren picks some stupid obnoxious tree that won't even fit through the front door." She side-eyed me, smirking, and pressed a delicate hand to her brow. "Oh, the aesthetic *horror*. Your gentile sensibilities will never *recover*."

Headed for the door, I flipped her off over my shoulder. "I owe you one, fox."

"No, you don't." Whoa. Wait a second. Her tone stopped me dead in my tracks, serious enough for me to whip around and find a fox falling apart at the seams. Eyes watering, lipsticked mouth trembling, arms crossed, and hands in such tight fists the knuckles bled white. Sniffling, Jocelyn offered me her profile as if that would hide the flash of sincere *feeling* tearing across her entire being. "You're like my big brother, Ewan, and I know you're my boss first—"

"Categorically false," I rasped, the sudden lump in my throat painful. *Fuck.* Generally she kept the breakdowns to herself, though I knew this vixen well enough to tell if she had spent the night wallowing. Bloodshot eyes and pale skin—paler than usual, anyway. Snippy attitude. Refusal to eat for the day. Yeah, I recognized the fucking signs. Also knew that she wouldn't let me step in and help, balking at my offers to pay for therapy, grief counseling—whatever she needed to heal the gaping wound still festering after that goddamn bear murdered her forever.

As fast as this onslaught appeared, she culled it. Shaking her head, she wiped at her eyes and brushed what I assumed were clammy hands on her thighs, and when she faced me again, there wasn't a hair out of place. No mascara blotches. Bloodshot eyes though.

And if I went over there to hug her, she'd knee me in the balls for sure.

Foxes were no match for wolf strength, but they always managed to land a hit hard enough to escape.

"I'm just really excited for you guys," she admitted hoarsely.

"This is a big step… Anytime you need me to take over stuff here for the day, I got you."

Of course she did.

Jocelyn had had my back for years—then put *her* feelings aside about her lost mate to help me time and time again with mine since finding her.

I stared at her for a long beat, long enough that she definitely suspected some shit was up and fidgeted with her pristine romper, until—

"You know you're my choice for godmother, right?"

Since this fated connection extended beyond a pair, we all had a say in who would care for our pups if something happened to each of us. Highly unlikely, and once the Redwood wolves grew in numbers, we'd probably assign the role to a trusted beta or two.

For now, Soren had his parents.

And I had my fox sister.

Jocelyn blinked back at me, then sucked in her cheeks when her lower lip wobbled again.

"A title that will be *revoked*," I added, lobbing a smirk her way to break the tension, "if you teach my kid so much as *one* TikTok dance —are we clear?"

She nodded, wiping at her eyes, a few tears slipping loose this time and free-falling down her sharp cheeks. This fox played a major role in my world, professionally and personally. There was no one better to take care of my future pup if disaster struck and wiped me, Lucian, Soren, *and* Lyssa off the face of the earth.

Yeah, she'd be the cool, sarcastic, let-them-get-away-with-murder godmother—but Soren's parents would bring balance into the equation.

When she didn't say anything, just gawked at me with teary eyes and a kind of scary, shaky smile, I pointed at the computer monitor to restore our more comfortable status quo.

"Tell them I've got a family emergency and need to step out." I grabbed the doorknob behind me and wrenched it open, a flood of Jocelyn's stale coffee from the mugs scattered around her desk wafting in. "Then make sure they don't shove their heads too far up their own asses and agree to something fucking stupid." I stepped out of my office, paused, and marched back in. "And draft a job post. We'll workshop it and send it out the first week of January."

With my favorite headhunter firm on speed dial, I'd have a handful of competent people to shoulder some of my professional burdens in no time. Some of the higher-ups at Quinn Enterprises were on my short list as well, high achievers nurtured in our corporate culture chomping at the bit to scale the corporate ladder —for a salary bump and a much higher quality of life with a relocation to Redwood Grove.

Housing included.

Yeah, this would be a fucking breeze.

Letting go? Allowing someone *else* to do what I did on a daily basis? Leaving the office and the anxiety of not accomplishing exactly what I had planned in a single day pounding me in the chest like a fucking sledgehammer? Much more difficult—but I had a support system at home to help with that, and a pup in the making who needed someone more serious than Soren but not *as* serious as Lucian around.

Someone to teach them how to fight.

Someone to spoil them and pamper them.

Someone to tell them just how fucking much he loved them, every single day—who would make sure their childhood was the exact opposite of his.

The others would do all that too, sure, this pup guaranteed a surplus of love, but I...

I *needed* to forge a better legacy than the one I escaped.

"Aye, aye, Captain. Now get out of here."

We all had a part to play in raising our pups, we three males and our fated mate—and my allegiance just wasn't to this office anymore.

Not completely.

I mean, I still wanted to build plush trust funds and send our bloodline to the best schools or, you know, whatever they wanted to do with their lives outside this valley.

Someone needed to fund the pack coffers.

But I could do that from home.

And I could do that with hands-off investments.

And…

And I could take care of *my* pack without hibernating at the office.

No more living for my work.

It was time to live for *them*.

After waving Jocelyn goodbye, I set out into the darkness, into the snow and the cold and the *wild*, ready to do just that.

14

LYSSA

"What about this one?"

Soren trudged over, snow pants swishing, the white stuff flying up around his sturdy boots, and scrutinized my suggestion of a bushy Douglas fir. Hands locked behind his back, he crouched and scooted around the tree, then stood tall to inspect the upper boughs before shaking his head and stepping back.

"No, no, look at the holes over there." He pointed out a couple of limp branches. "*Next!*"

Man, it was a good thing I found his intensity and boyish charm so endearing, because we had been at this for forty minutes already, the sun gone, the lamps around the tree farm lit—and no end in sight. With our afternoon schedules cleared, we'd all piled into Lucian's jeep and headed for the southwest side of our territory, which my old pack had avoided originally due to all the farmland fenced with live wire. I'd really been looking forward to this, beyond excited to choose and cut down our own tree for the first pack Christmas in less than two weeks.

Soren turned out to be just as picky about trees as he was his meat cuts at the butcher. Nothing was good enough for my blond mate, but as he marched off to the next specimen, I just smiled.

Because this was adorable.

Unfortunately, I was probably the only one who thought that. Over my shoulder, a groaning Lucian threw his head back to glare at the starry black sky, our rental axe embedded in the snow at his feet, his patience wearing thin in the bond.

"This is getting a bit ridiculous now," he barked when he finally straightened and shouldered the axe, plodding along over the packed trails between the rows upon rows of trees—just another orchard in my life, one that *felt* magical even if it technically wasn't. Dressed in sweatpants soaked with snow where his boots cut off, my mountain man didn't bother to pretend the cold affected him today, wearing nothing but a hooded sweatshirt up top. No gloves. No hat. No scarf. The teenager cashing us in at the start of all this had seemed kind of concerned. My mate breezed by me now, wolf eyes locked on Soren's back, leaving a rich, scenty cloud of oakwood in his wake that I floated after, nostrils flared and smile growing.

"We have to find the *right* one—"

"For fuck's *sake*, Soren," Lucian shouted back, oblivious to the fact that somewhere out here was a family with little ones doing the same thing we were. "They all look the bloody same. Just *pick* one already."

Soren twisted around, strolling backward, his grin like cheeky sunshine brightening up the night. "And this is why *you* are not in charge of tree picking. Onward, pack Redwood!"

I put a little pep in my step, walking twice as fast to catch up with Lucian's long strides, then hooked my arm around his with a barely subdued sunshine grin of my own. He passed the axe over to his other hand, then tossed his arm around my shoulders, tucking me into his side and slowing way down to accommodate for me.

Winter had hit our territory hard and fast, snow falling every other day lately, the ski slopes open and the lake finally starting to freeze over. Even with the scarcer game, my old pack had settled comfortably in the western woods, and as December chugged on slowly, chock-full of activities, Ewan was about halfway through his holiday obligations in the village.

Cold, dark, and cozy, the afternoon was... actually pretty perfect.

We were one of four groups at the tree farm today; the rest stayed near the main building and parking lot where, in theory, the best trees had already been felled and put on display. Soren insisted we'd find the *real* gems way at the back, and so we pushed into the darkness, shifter night vision a blessing with the spotty lamps cutting in and out at random.

No Loki, even if he made his presence known around the village.

In the western woods.

Along the lakeshore.

On our front steps.

He had told Lucian he was just here to watch—to decide if I was worth saving, whatever that meant.

Idunn kept me at an arm's length, so no prying for information in my dreams, and this new god had made himself scarce, his shadow looming but not as threatening as we all predicted.

Still, I went nowhere alone these days, something I was actually in favor of—especially now that I was carrying our first pup.

And nowhere had felt safer for me or this unborn little one than the tree farm with Soren and Lucian. No Loki scent despite the abundance of pines. No Hawthorne howls—nothing from them since I butchered their alpha, in fact, and we hoped it stayed that way.

No other rival markings along our southern borders.

No work out here.

No technology to confuse me.

No Ethan to ask a million questions, to try and persuade me to make something grow from nothing for him.

No Rosa being distant.

No pack drama.

Just pack *connection*. Just the three of us, one missing—but what else was new—and the orchard.

Just the anticipation of finding a tree and the excitement of decorating it once Ewan came home later tonight.

Just snow and sky and crisp, cold air and my mate's arm around me, firm and protective, his scent mingling with Soren's into something strange and new and wonderful.

Something that *didn't* make me throw up.

Because, ugh, my tummy was *sensitive* lately. Fortunately, the internet said it was very normal to experience morning sickness at this point in a pregnancy, though I planned to discuss it in more depth at my upcoming doctor's appointment. Somehow, Lady Fate had decided yet again to bless me—this time with an extended pack of women, Soren's sisters full of advice and stories. Two of them had already had pups, and they, along with his mom, shared a lot of stuff the internet didn't tell you during our calls over the last few days.

It just felt good to know what I was going through was *normal*.

Even if it felt uncomfortable.

Even if it had me running to the toilet to empty my guts at least once a day.

So much had happened in my life, from my first shift all the way to Gull River and its golden aftermath—none of it had felt normal. Always a freak. Always an outcast. Always *different*.

Pregnancy?

Normal.

Fingers crossed, anyway. I mean, I still felt the same. It was way too early to feel kicks or work around a huge belly. For the most part, besides the morning sickness—which came when it wanted and not just in the mornings—I was still me.

All in all, excluding the odd flutter and Kira being *especially* testy when males besides our mates got too close, it still hadn't hit me that I was literally growing another shifter.

The first of our bloodline.

My *baby*.

But that would probably change, right?

Soren's youngest sister Clara, who'd had twins already, said it didn't really sink in until the first ultrasound where there was more than a bean-looking thing on the screen.

So...

I had time, I guess.

Time to fall even deeper in love with the gentle flutters in my belly than I already was.

Lucian, Soren, and Ewan were family. Pack. Fated mates. *Soul*mates destined for the stars. And now we were growing by one more, one more wolf to love and adore and protect with every fiber of my being—

Lucian lilted left suddenly, ducking to inspect and tug at another Douglas fir, and I slowed, shaking my head. Easy to get wrapped up in everything and burst into happy tears—again. It had happened a lot the last four days, on almost every phone call with Soren's family, at every meal, anytime I caught my mates looking at me with hope and wonder in their wolf eyes.

Couldn't let this overwhelm me.

Nope.

Gotta stay *present*—really commit to this tree hunt, because Soren needed someone in his corner.

Packed snow crunching underfoot, I finally came to a stop, then glanced between Soren meandering between the trees on either side of the row and Lucian examining this particular one with more interest.

Then, with a burst of giddy energy, Kira all playful and bouncy from the moment I'd hopped out of Lucian's jeep at the front gates of this farm, I tiptoed off to the side where the snow was less compact. Grabbed a handful. Smoothed it into a perfect snowball.

And hurled it at Soren.

It slammed into his shoulder and exploded on impact, like a snowy firework flying in all directions, and he shot upright, surprise tempered with confusion in our connection. Sighing, I pointed at an unassuming Lucian.

Soren's mouth twisted in a mischievous arc.

He made his own sloppy snowball, all angles and heft, then

chucked it at Lucian as my mate slowly eased up, his tree inspection over—

Bam.

Right in the side of his face.

Lucian dropped the axe, because unlike *my* dainty snowball, Soren's didn't explode and fall away. No, it stuck in my mate's beard and plastered to his head, hanging on for dear life as he peeled it off.

"Soren!" I gasped for effect, hands flying to my mouth, eyes wide and accusatory, grin hidden behind my gloves. "That's *so* rude!"

My blond mate folded his arms, understanding slithering across his features, and Lucian rounded on me.

He cocked his head.

I swallowed hard and dropped my hands, struggling to maintain this mask of shock and indignance. Kira chuffed and snorted, pawing at me, whining—urging me to run, because this alpha looked two seconds from pouncing.

No, I got this. I resisted the urge to glare up at my forehead like I sometimes did to scold her, barely able to maintain eye contact with those deep, warm moss-green orbs.

Which narrowed suddenly.

"Oh, little mate…" Lucian wiped the last bits of snow from his face, a few stragglers clinging to his beard. "You're a *terrible* liar."

"What? *No.*" I stabbed a finger in Soren's direction. "No, no, he… I…"

Shoot.

Axe abandoned, Lucian lunged straight at me, seeing clear through my games, and I bolted with a shriek.

"Serpentine, baby!" Soren shouted, sprinting parallel to us a few rows over. "Serpentine!"

No idea what the heck *that* meant, but I zigzagged around trees, giggling, pushing hard to run in the snow with these stupid winter boots on. Lucian lumbered after me, snarling and growling, the sounds serious but his emotions so beautifully light and carefree in our bond that there was no *way* he was actually angry at me.

In fact, he seemed to purposefully slow down so we could drag out the chase, circling pines and skirting firs and charging uphill toward the far reaches of the farm's property.

Smiling, feeling like a pup again, I peered over my shoulder to get a better read on him, all these lush, happy trees and the barely there wind making his scent harder to track—only to get a front-row seat to *another* Soren-ball pounding Lucian in the face.

Other side this time.

For symmetry.

I heard the thought in Soren's voice and stumbled to a halt, jaw dropping and hands flying up for real when my blond mate plowed into Lucian from behind a pine, tackling the enormous wolf to the ground.

Really in his element here, my Soren, because I suspected Lucian hadn't heard *or* seen the blond wolf either until he was right on top of him.

"Run, baby!" Soren locked his arms and legs around Lucian. "I'll hold him off! I sacrifice myself for the queen—"

"Bloody hell," Lucian groused, and in one swift maneuver, he had them rolled over and Soren pinned on his back in the snow, both of them belly up to the sky. Golden wolf eyes locked on me, my mountain man tried to spring up, only for Soren to grab onto him from behind and scramble around, trapping him in a headlock.

Full of giggles, I sprinted away, refusing to let Soren's heroics go to waste. Four rows over, I peeked around a pine, worried that the fight might get too serious without me—only to catch Lucian and Soren shoveling snow at each other, both on their knees, like two kids in the pool splashing the heck out of one another until one cried uncle.

Adorable.

But of course, I'd never tell them that.

Never tell them that I *saw* them being brothers, alphas and friends and playmates, just two wolves without a care in the world —at least for a little while.

With the boys at my back, I pushed onward and trudged through the rows, hiking up a slope that peaked at a jagged hillside with a steep drop on the other side. The fence stopped me from marching that far into the wilderness, the property line stuck full of metal poles with electrical wire stretched between them. On a whim, I tossed a bit of snow at the nearest one, flinching at the sizzle, memories of tumbling into something similar as a pup making my skin crawl.

It wasn't horrible, all things considered.

Not the worst pain I'd ever felt.

Physical pain paled next to emotional agony, anyway.

Keeping a safe distance, I stuffed my gloved hands deep in my coat pockets, then just *breathed*. Sharp, freezing air filled my lungs. Ahead, natural pines huddled together for warmth; bobcat tracks cut from their depths, down to the fence and back again, like the little guy realized this wasn't the kind of farm you got a fat, full belly from. No chickens or ducks or pigs here—just trees as far as the eye could see, the orchard stretching over nearly ten acres.

If I hadn't walked through a *real* endless orchard, Kira by my side, the horizon always a faraway dream, this place would look like it went on forever.

But a paved country lane snaked along its southern border, the parking lot brightly lit, cars ambling by and little figures milling around the precut stock near the farmer's house, shop, and barn. Here, there was a beginning, middle, and end.

Exhaling a hot cloud, I faced the forest again, the wilds of our territory stunning at night.

For seventeen long winters, I lived out there.

Huddled with my pack. Nestled into Mama's side. Hunted and foraged and warded the pups away from humans when they got curious.

Shivered.

Starved.

Ached for springtime.

Even as autumn inched closer to the first frost this year, I'd thought that was better than *this*—than wearing stupid boots and a winter coat with fake fur around the hood.

I licked my lips and stepped back again.

No more of that.

I was wild in my soul, a wolf at heart—but I belonged on this side of the fence.

Kira whined softly like she agreed, heat pluming in my chest. The forest didn't call to her like it once did.

Me neither.

And... that was a good thing.

It would always be a part of our home, but *real* home was with—

Oakwood tickled my nostrils, and I closed my eyes, ears twitching at Lucian's approach. He made no effort to mask himself; this wasn't a sneak attack. No, my victorious mountain man just stalked up the hill, loud and proud, an enormous pine to my right, an empty stretch of snow to my left along the fence line.

Heavy, deep footsteps crunched closer and closer, my heart beating faster and faster, until two burly arms wrapped around me and hauled me away.

Hid me in the shadows of this huge pine, *way* too big to be hacked down and put in someone's living room.

Contemplative quiet shattered, I tapped into the energy from before, giggling when he whirled me around and attacking the clumps of snow still in his beard.

"Do you know what you started back there?" Lucian rumbled as I brushed the last of it away. I fluttered my eyelashes innocently.

"No idea what you're talking about—"

My mate snagged my wrist and tugged me closer, then threaded my arm around his neck as he bent over me, conquering my space and making Kira *purr*. He hooked my waist with pure *muscle*, all man as he smirked down at me, the cool tips of our noses brushing, breaths mingling, bodies so naturally entwined.

"Little mate, you are what the common folk call... a shit disturber."

I sucked in my cheeks, scowling as he chuckled, then pushed at his chest with my free hand and tugged at the hair on the back of his neck with the other, chastising him as a woman *and* a wolf. "That sounds gross—and kind of insulting."

"I say it with the utmost love and affection," he drawled, voice all grit and gravel and *danger*, his want pounding through our bond so suddenly, so out of nowhere, that I gasped. The teasing fell away at the assault, his tone, his strength, his intensity, his hold on me so overwhelming, even now, after all this time, that when he kissed me, I felt so helpless against it.

Impossible to resist, my brooding alpha mate.

We came together in a tangle of tongues and the clash of teeth, the kiss deep and harsh—but slow. Slow and sensuous, like we had all the time in the world to explore each other, to claim and mark and dominate each in our own way. Lucian was a snowcapped mountain, an unbreakable diamond, steadfast and eternal, sweeping me off my feet with his energy, his aura, his *presence*.

But I was passion and fire, ripping off my gloves to cradle his face and tug harder at his hair and stroke his beard, setting the pace with touch and sound, with moans and sighs and *whines* that had him rock-hard against me in no time.

Footsteps crunched across the packed snow paths, bringing with them Soren's scent, a cozy autumn blend that always set my heart at ease, and then stopped a little way off.

And then nothing for long enough that Lucian and I slowed our kisses way down, wolf eyes burning into us from the side, a dark, sinful chuckle breaking the silence.

"Smart." Soren appraised us with a heated up-and-down sweep, unzipping his coat without ever breaking focus. "This *is* the most logical way to stay warm. Quick thinking, you two."

Cheeks on fire, I beckoned him closer with a casual toss of my head—an invite my mate seized right away, pouncing, at my back in seconds and steering my mouth to his by my hair. Where Lucian had been slow, passionate depth, Soren came at this with a completely different approach, all taunting pecks and sharp nibbles, his tongue a terrible tease as it flickered in and out of my mouth. I chased after him with a growl, really arching back to taste him, snapping at his bottom lip hard enough to make him snarl and fist my hair—to rouse the *monster* inside him.

He came out to play whenever we mated, this mischievous beast, dangerous and unpredictable, a piece of my heart I could never part from.

Today, however, Lucian stole the unpredictable crown right off Soren's head, and while I was distracted with my blond mate, he went for the waistband of my sweatpants—and yanked it down my thighs, dragging my panties with it, skin assaulted by the cold in a way that woke me up.

Made me gasp.

"W-wait," I stammered, tearing away from Soren to plant a hand on Lucian's shoulder. He had already settled on his knees, eyeing the crest of my thighs hungrily, the golden shimmer in his wolf eyes darkening—a warning to others, a beckoning finger for me. Still, as good as it felt to be trapped between these two again, alphas at my front and back, we were in public. There were *kids* here... somewhere. You know, a few acres south. "What if someone sees—"

"I think we'll hear them before they see us," Soren countered, his tone light and airy, his smile pure *devil*. Pleasure pulsed in my lower belly at that alone, at the promise of his skillful lips on my skin, but I couldn't let them see that—either of them.

Couldn't let them think I'd given in *this* easily.

"Fine." I peered left and right, exaggerated and searching, pretending to scope out the landscape for potential humans. "But make it quick."

Both mates chuckled incredulously, Lucian leaning back on his heels, Soren raking his teeth up my temple.

"As you wish, Your Highness," my mountain man growled, his tone dry and his eyes *ravenous*. Soren's wandering hands latched onto my coat zipper and yanked it down, unleashing another blast of cold across my figure, the chill welcome and invigorating.

"Demanding little thing, isn't she?"

"Finally," Lucian muttered before dragging his tongue up my inner thigh and gently spreading my legs wider. He then glanced up, locking eyes with the male behind me, the one fighting with the fake fur around my hood, and arching an eyebrow. "Something we agree on."

Jaw dropped, I was about to interject, my outrage an act because, *oh*, there was something so deliciously wrong and *hot* when they all talked about me like I wasn't here. Not outside of mating, of course, but in this heady bubble, all of us driven by animal instinct, I loved listening to them discuss me like they *owned* me.

However, before I could get one scandalized word out, Lucian claimed his prize, shoving between my thighs and licking me like he kissed me: deep and passionate, his mouth all-consuming, devouring me like this was the last time, the only time. Heat ripped up my core, and I squealed when he circled my clit. At the internet's advice, I'd tamed the curls there, cutting them back with a pair of scissors, trimming and shaping and making things more manageable.

I even went to show my mates when it was all said and done— and of course they rumpled it up right away, shoving and snarling and fighting to inspect my handiwork first.

It should have been old news to Lucian now, my sex, wet and swollen and slick with desire, but he lapped eagerly all the same, his sounds savage and his tongue powerful. Usually Soren was the first to distract me while my other mates tormented my body, but this time, he just held me, supporting me when my knees gave out and my vision tunneled, everything tense, colors already dancing behind my clenched lids long before the explosion.

And what an explosion.

It came out of nowhere, long before I expected and halfway through the climb, my body seemingly primed for a breathtaking climax. Fire sparked over my clit, two of Lucian's fingers thrust deep and stroking my inner walls, his mouth focused on the little bud, and then everything went *black*. I tumbled over the edge, falling, falling, falling, hoping I'd never touch the ground again...

"*Fuck*, baby," Soren hissed, jostling around behind me, the lighthearted seduction gone, the beast taking over. "I love how you sound when you come."

Had I been making noise?

Probably.

Wouldn't be the first time I was totally oblivious to it, lost in pleasure, in the way my body shivered and jerked against my will, just a puppet on a string. When I finally pried my eyes open, the pops and pinwheels of color fading, I noticed the pine that had given us all this lovely privacy had thickened, *way* more needles on the boughs than before.

And I let it go.

Enjoy the extra needles, friend. My gift to you.

Something crinkled at my back—plastic, the tough kind that held its shape even when you peeled it loose. Frowning, I twisted around.

"What's that?"

Soren held up the tiny pocket-sized bottle of clear liquid with a wicked grin. "Lubricant." He then leaned around me when Lucian groaned. "*What?* Always better to be prepared for surprise, you know, *stuff.*"

Those words belonged to my loveable, goofy blond mate, but his tone made me shiver, the beast at the reins, his eyes a startling amber and glowing in the darkness. Much to my surprise—and Lucian's—he then tossed the bottle, forcing my mountain man to scramble back to catch it.

"I call dibs elsewhere," Soren declared before grabbing my shoulders and twisting me around to his open coat and his dropped sweats, black briefs straining to contain his interest. I licked my lips, gaze dropping to his erection appreciatively, and stroked him over the cotton, a damp patch near the tip, my caress making the beast shudder. Lucian, however, seemed to take offense to being told what to do, his snarl making the hairs on the back of my neck stand up, his own alpha beast bellowing through our bond—

Soren flashed his canines.

Lucian shot up, his huge frame looming behind me.

Innocent and casual, I shoved my pants the rest of the way down and yanked them over my boots. My coat came next, adding to the pile of discarded clothing between my growling mates.

Bare legs.

Bare butt.

Yeah, that stopped a fight dead in its tracks.

Huge hands stroked my exposed skin, slipping between my thighs, caressing my folds from the front and the back, and the tension in our connection softened. *Heat* simmered along it instead, my wants overtaking their petty, wordless argument. I gave them each a hand, stroking Soren through his briefs with one, yanking Lucian closer with the other. Eyes rolling back in his head, my blond mate surrendered to my touch for a few moments; behind, the little bottle of lubricant cracked open, followed by a *squirt* that made my face light up with a prickly blush.

Not sure why that embarrassed me, but, you know, here we were.

Soren didn't give me the time or space to sink into the feeling. No, with a low rumble vibrating in his chest, he nudged my hand aside, tugged his briefs down, and stroked his dick. Such a handsome dick, at that, prominent and thick, not *as* intimidating as Lucian's—

But still.

Oh.

Still stretched and claimed when he hoisted me up and lowered me onto it. Shivering, I let him steer me home, steadying myself on his shoulders, legs wrapped around his waist, our eyes locked and lips parted. He stole a lingering kiss, the beast restrained for the time being, the brush of his mouth to mine tender and soft, patient and present. My body clenched around him, pleasure fluttering in my core, and he groaned, eyes trying to roll back again.

Smirking, I clenched on purpose this time.

His eyes snapped open, the amber an inferno.

With the third clench, he fisted my hair and yanked me in for a proper kiss, both of us crashing together, just two alphas tangling for control.

Interrupted by Lucian—one finger, gentle and steady, probing my backside. Then Soren slowed, holding me yet spreading me wider around his torso.

They were always so good about preparing my body for mating. With Lucian, Ewan, and Soren, there was no pain. No tearing like that drunk jerk from the bar. No ripping on the inside. Just *pleasure*.

But, the other hole—it could be tender.

When it came to mating, we weren't exactly built to be patient.

But my mates took their time with me, and lubricant made things a *thousand* times easier. Readied me faster. Had me all whiny and needy quicker. Had me bucking and rocking, desperate for Lucian to join us, to let go—to draw pleasure from my body.

To love me.

Connect with me.

Protect me and torment me.

Unfortunately, Lucian was the least likely to give in to my, as he called it, *puppy shit*. No matter how whiny and demanding I became, he didn't swap his fingers for something *much* larger until he decided I was ready and dripping. Want slicked my thighs. My nipples pebbled so tight it *hurt*. I could barely see straight after all that readying, but then he thrust the tip of his dick in—and the world came back to focus. I sucked in a sharp breath, and he slowed way down, Soren kissing me, murmuring sweet nothings, bracing me until Lucian finally fully took me, inch by blissful inch.

Even then, we just held each other. Protected by the massive pine, we cuddled and nuzzled and kissed. Touched and whispered and grinned. I giggled. They growled and sucked at my neck, leaving temporary bruises that felt just as deep and *right* as their mating marks.

Only when I *begged* for movement did they oblige, and, seeming to enjoy my suffering, Lucian and Soren started at a torturous grind. No amount of whimpering or eyelash fluttering spurred them on. My good-natured swats? Nothing. The snaps of my teeth

—didn't get the results I wanted, earning a chastising smack to my backside from Lucian and a few sharp nips along my neck from Soren.

So, hopelessly trapped and loving every second of it, I gave up—and gave in. I submitted to these two alphas and greedily accepted whatever they offered, whatever pace they set. And it stayed so *slow* for ages.

Until Lucian bucked a little harder.

Then Soren countered.

Back and forth, they upped the ante, almost like they wanted to outdo each other, falling into a competition that I wasn't a part of yet *very* much involved in.

A dangerous game to play, especially when they ignored my cries, saying *something* to each other but all their words muffled and muddled as a thick, smothering cotton plugged my ears.

I came apart between them with a great keening cry, the pleasure explosive, the warmth overwhelming. Scrambling for something to hold on to, I shuddered and jerked in their arms, losing myself in the stars above—*hearing* the pine tree grow at my back.

"Shit, *shit*—" Soren lost it with a snarl, my climax tipping off his, which then reverberated back to me fast and fiery enough that I squealed.

Which meant Lucian was just done for, unable to withstand two pleasure storms tearing through our bond for more than a few seconds. Throw that third orgasm into the mix and my mates lost their footing, Soren collapsing first, me careening down with him, and Lucian barely bracing in time, hands slamming into the snow so that he didn't flat-out crush us.

Pleasantly sore, the aches delicious and fleeting, I flopped onto Soren with a happy sigh, and we lay there for a while after, sweaty and panting, smiling and kissing and murmuring. Lucian broke away, collapsing on his back in the snow, and I slid into the dip between my mates, an arm and a leg for each of them, claiming them for the wilds of our territory to see.

Eventually, however, we moved. Tidied up and fixed clothes.

Helped each other zip things and fluff fake-fur hoods and locate gloves that got lost in the shuffle. After all, we came here for a tree.

The rough-and-tumble mating was just a fun distraction.

Heart full, I sauntered away from the electric fence, away from the steep hills and dark forest, moving along the rows and studying trees with a more discerning eye this time around.

Until a fourth set of boots clomped over the snow, headed my way at a steady clip, Soren and Lucian chatting amongst themselves about six trees behind.

I slowed.

Kira clawed out from wherever she went when I mated, sniffing deep, her breath whooshing, her eyes sliding into mine and making the world so much sharper.

And then—

Rosewood.

I brightened instantly and skipped down the gentle slope, then peeked around a sad, scraggly Douglas fir that I almost wanted to buy as well—just so it got a home—and there he was.

"Ewan!"

With our forgotten axe in hand, my midnight mate frowned and held it up, almost like he wasn't sure why we had left it back there— totally unaware of the snowball fight that led to a beautiful mating beneath the stars. Kira snuffled and yipped, thrilled to see our work-driven mate at the farm, and I bolted straight for him, leaping at the last second and flying into his arms. Ewan caught me with a grunt, axe discarded, and staggered back a few paces as I wrapped myself around him like a bear trap.

"Hello, blue eyes," he murmured through his velvety chuckles, bundling me up in his arms and looking so scrumptious and stylish in the long trench. The thick red-and-green scarf I'd given him made it tough to nestle into his neck like I wanted, eager to drag my cold nose over his skin and make him fuss and tsk, but it smelled like *him*, like rich rosewood and a spritz of the sandalwood cologne I really liked. Spinning us around, he boosted me up a little more, leather-gloved hands cupping my backside, and gave me a little jostle. "*You* smell like you've just been thoroughly fucked..."

I cradled his strong jawline, stroking the sharp angles of his cheekbones, the defined black brows, shivering I was so happy to see him. This morning, my midnight mate had sulked at breakfast while we discussed the best plan of attack for this tree hunt. I hadn't called him out on his mood; work just made him miss *so* much at home, he'd been devastated to learn that we all found out about our first pup while he was in a meeting.

Just some stupid, run-of-the-mill status update discussion with a few of his underlings that made him ignore phone calls and focus on numbers.

It *killed* him.

As I'd expected—and Lucian predicted—Ewan immediately overcompensated by being aggressively nitpicky with my new doctor, who I hadn't met yet but her assistant got an earful from my mate over the phone, and dropping thousands on nursery furniture that first night.

Almost in a panic.

He had missed out on something big...

Now he was here.

He'd left the office to help find our first Christmas tree.

And from the way his emotions bloomed in the bond, he was really happy about it.

"Yeah, you just missed out, bro." Soren flipped him off with a smirk when Ewan's eyes narrowed, the dark hickory tracking him and Lucian over my shoulder as the pair strolled by. "And it was a *good* one."

Shaking my head, I steered him back to me by his dimpled chin. "It's always a good one—and you're here now."

"Apparently you guys *need* me here," Ewan mused as he set me down, scoffing at Lucian as the massive wolf grabbed the axe and shouldered it again. "Seriously, what have you been doing all this time?" He knuckled my chin before I could answer. "*Besides* bathing in orgasms, you cheeky thing."

"Perfection can't be rushed," Soren shouted back, not stopping, only slowing to examine a tall pine before moving on to the next a few trees down. Tossing an arm around my shoulder, Ewan tugged me close and kissed my temple, then glanced back in the direction we'd come from.

Almost like he was trying to see what he had missed for himself —just something else to feel guilty about.

Lower lip snagged between my teeth and Kira egging me on, I ducked down and made another snowball.

Smoothed it into a perfect circle.

Stood. Tossed it between my hands, smirking up at a curious Ewan.

Took position.

Aimed.

Fired.

And nailed Soren on the back of the head—then took off into the orchard with a shrieking giggle, Ewan at my heels already forming our next projectile, the fight *on*.

Our night nowhere near over.

15

LYSSA

"Oh, look, there's Ethan!"

Blasted in the face with a wall of freezing December air, then Hampton Mall's heating system dousing us one last time at the automatic doors, I followed Rosa into the outer courtyard as she swiveled her overflowing shopping cart toward the SUV in the pickup zone. Yup, that was Ethan all right, the behemoth black vehicle rumbling, exhaust pluming out the rear, headlights off but the interiors on.

No Lucian anywhere.

Of course.

He and Ethan had dropped us ladies off around the same time hours ago for what turned into the craziest afternoon of Christmas shopping I'd ever experienced. Back then, Ethan had insisted he and Lucian go grab a coffee—maybe even a late lunch while the, quote, *women of the house* stocked up on gifts.

I'd left my mate to make up his own mind, but from the deadpan expression and the prickliness in our bond, the chance of him taking the warlock up on the offer hovered around zero.

Gripping my own overloaded cart, the brand-new credit card in my pocket linked to Ewan's account officially broken in after hours of heavy use, I ambled after my friend.

My friend who had just been... *weird*.

Aster was her usual adorable self, strapped into the baby seat attached to the mall cart, napping on and off throughout the afternoon, totally oblivious to the hectic holiday shoppers. I'd held her and bounced her in the bathroom after Rosa changed her diaper. I'd made her giggle and huff and squirm with silly faces in mile-long checkout lines. I'd asked Rosa a million questions about pregnancy and childbirth—all that fun stuff.

And Rosa had answered every last one of them, in detail, without hesitation.

We chatted about gift options for my mates.

Christmas lights for the house, which was still dark while the rest of Redwood Grove illuminated come nightfall, neighbors in competition over who had the best setup.

We talked hair and makeup and pregnancy cravings. She was bright, bubbly, and sweet, still the Rosa I knew in some ways.

Only to shut down completely when it came to my powers, suddenly just a husk of a woman.

I tried time and time again to discuss my progress with her, share things I had kept from Ethan just because I trusted her more —because we had been in this together from the start.

Nothing.

Nothing but tense smiles and hurried nods and a change in conversation topic, usually to something nearby, a trinket or *thing* she could grab and redirect my attention onto.

As if I wouldn't realize.

As if I wouldn't notice the change in her demeanor, the tightness around her mouth and the bandages on two of her fingers, or the way she constantly readjusted her turtleneck to hide what I recognized as bruises from a single fleeting glance.

Not just love bites either.

But big ol' black-and-blue *monsters*—from a whole hand, not some nibbling teeth or mischievous suction.

The urge to *protect* had been absolutely smothering from the second we strolled into the mall to now, nearly six hours later, the sun long gone and the night *way* too cold for baby Aster to be out in for long. Kira's hackles rose, tingling at the nape of my neck and down my spine, the closer we got to the Perrys' SUV, and I scanned the other cars in the temporary pickup zone, searching for Lucian and coming up empty.

However, with his oakwood scent cloying around the mall's entryway, he couldn't be far. Frowning, I readjusted my grip on this wayward shopping cart, the rear right wheel prone to locking, and then slowed way, way down as Rosa beelined for the back of the SUV.

Because it wasn't just Ethan in there.

Definitely not Lucian. No, his opposite sat in the front passenger seat. Male, sure, but much older. Weathered and pocked pale skin, his profile sagged a little, his hairline receding but his snow-white mustache as lush and bushy as his eyebrows. The second Rosa opened the trunk, the man basically plastered himself against the window, electric mustardy-brown gaze landing on me.

I stopped completely, using the cart like a shield, and stared back.

Unblinking. Unflinching. A direct challenge.

The driver's-side door opened and Ethan hopped out, his dirty-blond locks bobbing over the SUV's roof as he headed for the back —hopefully to help Rosa, maybe get Aster out of the cold.

But that wasn't really my concern right now, even if my gut *screamed* for me to grab both females and run.

No, it was this stranger shoving the door open and stumbling out in a dusty purple suit and an open grey trench. Thin, frail, he hobbled out and slammed the door behind him, then seemed to almost regain his footing—bad left knee, given the limp, my predatory gaze noting it right away.

His eyes lit up as he hurried closer.

His thin lips bloomed into an unsettling smile.

He felt… wrong.

Electric and *magical*, same as Ethan and Rosa, same as all those females in the bathroom at the Chalet on Halloween—but intense. *Way* too intense, way too fixated on me.

I flashed my teeth with a low growl, hoping this warlock would get the message, Kira set to *murder* as a strange male approached me and our unborn pup. Power blossomed in my chest, warm and centered, a faint buzz tickling my fingertips—just a casual reminder these days that it was there, locked and loaded, same as Kira, and ready to fire on a threat.

The warning didn't stick. Heck, it didn't even land in the general vicinity. This male kept coming, and it wasn't until Ethan peeked around the SUV, he and Rosa still loading bags, that he must have realized his friend was about to get his leering smile scratched clean off.

"Whoa, whoa," he called, hopping the curb and jogging after this ancient, sprightly creature. "James, hold on."

Before I could line my cart up, take aim, and launch it straight at him—like knocking down the last pin at the bowling alley Soren took me to the other night—a much darker, much more dangerous warning ripped through the courtyard.

Humans milling around scattered, either into the mall or out to the jam-packed parking lot. One of the loitering cars in the pickup zone bailed, tires screeching, Lucian's snarl more like a lion's roar, pure gravel and grit and crashing like thunder in our connection. Ethan and this James character stopped dead in their tracks. Rosa stood stock-still with a trio of plastic bags in hand, while Aster twisted around in her baby seat for a better view.

Behind me, my mountain man crashed out from the shadows, like he'd set up shop just around the corner for a smoke, a smoldering cigarette between his fingers. Furious, eyes bright gold and raging, his footsteps fell in great, terrifying *booms* as he prowled closer. Still in the same leather jacket, white tee, dark jeans, scary steel-toed boots as earlier, I assumed he hadn't shifted all this time, super agitated in a metropolis dominated by witches and warlocks yet unwilling to let me tag along with Ethan and

Rosa, *determined* to drive me out of Redwood Grove territory himself.

As he flicked his cigarette in the general direction of a metal garbage can, I almost told him to calm down—then thought better of it.

Yeah, no, this protective mean streak sat just fine with me.

If anything, as he raced to my side, all teeth and wolf eyes, huge hands in fists, I'd do what I could to encourage the attitude.

Rosa said pregnancy made us a little crazy.

Hormones and whatnot.

I guess it turned me into a raging protective she-wolf, because I suddenly had no issue wheeling this cart aside and eliminating the potential threat all by myself.

Lucian could help if he wanted.

"Sorry, sorry," Ethan sputtered, scrambling between the end of my cart and his friend, arms up like that would actually stop two wolves from charging. "I—"

"Apologies." Despite his tiny wrists and thin, spidery fingers, his rounded shoulders and knobby knees visible even under those pressed trousers, James had a strong voice. Confident. Loud enough to rival Lucian's snarl, actually. He raised his hands, then bowed his head a little, his submission a little too phony for Kira. "I forget... with shifters, mates and whatnot... My name is James Bennet."

Like I gave a rat's butt about his name.

Lucian sidled closer, still seething, the air scalding, his wolf *this* close to bursting free and tearing through his clothes. He shouldered in front of me, one hand death-gripping the cart, and tossed his head side to side for two noisy *cracks*, gearing up for a fight.

"I work at the academy," the warlock clarified, opening his trench to reveal a holstered wand. He then pressed a hand to his heart, inching around Ethan and zeroing in on me again like Lucian wasn't even here. Which, you know, fine. Go ahead. I didn't need my enormous mate to take care of business. Something about him though, his eyes sparking with little flashes of white lightning, his teeth almost too big for his mouth—it turned my stomach, especially when he added, "I'm so sorry, Lyssa, to have startled you. I just… I feel like I *know* you."

"You don't know her," Lucian growled, more beast than man now. Ethan fidgeted with his puffy green parka, cheeks flushed, eyes darting between me and my mate like he suddenly realized how much danger they were all in—and like I might actually *stop* it. Behind him, Rosa was back to loading bags, head down, curls obscuring her features. Aster watched on, transfixed, eyes huge and curious. Lucian, meanwhile, nudged the cart to the right, further blocking me from this James Bennet, and then motioned for the warlock to back the heck off. "Step *away*."

"Lucian, if I'd known you were here the whole time," Ethan rambled, his voice pitched slightly higher than usual, his hands gesturing wildly, "then we would have invited you in and out of the cold—"

"Why do you know me?"

Lucian stiffened at my flat tone, my straightforward question. No sense in pretending that James *hadn't* just revealed his hand, probably to pique my interest and start a proper conversation. He and Ethan swapped glances before the much older male gestured for the younger warlock to proceed, easing back and bowing his head properly this time—and still watching me from beneath those spidery white eyebrows.

Like a hawk, this guy: he missed nothing, circling innocently before the big dive.

I stood taller, Kira filling me with strength and savagery, refusing to cower no matter how he made my tummy roil.

"Professor Bennet is a member of my dad's coven," Ethan remarked, seeming calmer now but still tracking Lucian out of the corner of his eye. "Sort of… extended family type thing. He… I've known him since I was a kid, and I've been talking to him about your, uh…" He then scanned the courtyard with a frown, onlookers dispersed, everything business as usual. "About your *situation*."

All the color drained from my face, leaving only a prickly static at the shock of him just... *telling* people about me. Ethan had never asked. He'd *mentioned* that he had associates in Hampton who might be able to help, but nothing like this.

As if sensing my dismay, Lucian snarled, and Kira mirrored his ferocity, just as unimpressed with what *she* deemed a betrayal. Distrust left a lump in my throat, hard and distinct and very much belonging to the wolf at my side. The longer this standoff lasted, the deeper our emotions threaded together, our bond taking a turn for the physical.

Not good.

Great to feel the connection, of course—but a huge distraction when you needed to stay light on your toes.

"Gull River is deadly," James said, diving in before I could muster a response for Ethan. He then leaned further around to avoid Lucian completely, gaze burning into mine. "Yet not for you. And that's fascinating, but, I imagine, also quite frightening."

I sucked in my cheeks, biting at them, and searched for Rosa. Ever since my mates brought me to Redwood Grove, that witch had been my constant support. Always there to cheer me on or cheer me up, I *needed* her.

But she was all the way over there, buckling Aster into her car seat, back to the whole thing like it wasn't even happening. Shifting my weight to one leg, hip cocked, I watched her—Kira howled for her—and waited for her to really feel the brunt of my attention.

Nothing.

As soon as Aster was in, Rosa closed the door gently and bolted around the SUV to climb in the other side.

Which left me with a fuming mate and two staring warlocks, one waiting on pins and needles, stone still and breath bated, for me to say something.

"It was... kind of scary at first," I admitted, but only because Ethan had probably told this professor as much already. I mean, I thought I could share my feelings with him—my honest experience of absorbing a dead goddess's power.

Yeah, that stopped now.

"Uhm, but I'm getting used to it," I added in the strained silence that followed. Grabbing at Lucian's arm and squeezing hard, I was about to tell him we should get going—something about dinner, or whatever—when it hit me.

Pine.

Sea salt.

Sweetness—candy canes and children's laughter and a fresh gust of frost.

Loki.

Both Lucian and I snapped around to the mall entrance, but the arrival of a city bus on the other side of the courtyard meant it was suddenly more nuts out here than inside, shoppers everywhere, kids running and colliding with people leaving the mall with their huge carts.

Still, the flash of bright red hair in the thick of things...

Had he followed us to Hampton?

Why? For *what?*

What the heck was this god up to?

"Yes, yes, so I hear," James interjected. While Lucian moved behind me, as if deciding Loki was the bigger threat, the bushy-browed warlock studied me like I was absolutely *captivating*, and not even my mate's firm hand on the back of my neck could settle my racing heart. "You know, I teach spellwork at the academy, and I'd be happy to assist with the, er, *transition.*"

"Thanks." Nope. Nope. Not happening. Not going anywhere alone with this male. "That's... nice of you."

Lucian's fingers stabbed into my throat, and I elbowed back, scowling. *A little too hard there, mate.* He loosened up with a sharp breath, like he hadn't noticed he was about to cut off my air, then draped an arm over my shoulder and across my chest, locking that steel grip around the shopping cart handlebar instead.

"Well, look," Ethan started, his expression, the way he clapped his hands together and grinned, suggesting that he might finally bring this conversation to a merciful end, "it's miserable out here."

He wasn't wrong—dark and cold, the misery was still brewing, the overcast thick, the starless sky pure onyx flecked with swirling grey. A storm was on the horizon, one I didn't look forward to driving through in Lucian's less-than-reliable jeep.

"We'll let you go." Thank goodness. "And you two can get better acquainted at Yule, eh?"

"*What* Yule?" Lucian demanded, taking the words right out of my mouth. Ethan's smile cracked as he stared my mate down, almost the same height but clearly looking way, way up so as not to trigger him further.

"It... *Yule*..." The warlocks exchanged glances again, almost like *How dare they not know?*, the implication making me and Kira bristle. I knew *yuletide*, the word tossed around in old fairy tales and songs, but just like Samhain, it could all be very, very different—not just some commercialized holiday, but something real, authentic, and ancient to Rosa's community. Ethan, however, cut my wonderings short with a nasally laugh and a hand to his forehead. "Oh, *right*— sorry. I talked to Ewan about it this morning... We're hosting a huge Yule feast on the twenty-first. Big shindig at our place—dinner, fancy dress, yule logs, dancing, music, carols. You know, the whole shebang." He leaned closer and winked at Lucian. "*Lots* of booze."

I peeked over my shoulder. Yup, there was that deadpan, dreadfully unimpressed expression he wore anytime Ethan assaulted our doorbell.

"Ewan accepted on behalf of the pack, so, uh, we'll be seeing you." Ethan fidgeted with the big buttons on his coat, enthusiasm fading when we didn't immediately rise to his level. He then pressed his luck with my mate one last time, totally oblivious to the way his professor friend was *still* staring at me—that he hadn't blinked in the last minute or so, totally transfixed. In another life, another place, surrounded by savagery and danger, I'd poke those eyeballs out and be done with it, but all these humans, the busy hum of *society* pressing in from all sides, kept me civil. "Time to dust off the ol' suit, Lucian, my man."

My mate grunted, his knuckles white around the cart's handlebar, his patience razor-thin and precarious in our bond.

I for one relished the chance to party.

Dress fancy.

Eat good food.

See Rosa's house for the first time...

I sucked in my cheeks, staring clear through her husband to their SUV. Why hadn't she brought this up earlier? We could have shopped together.

Discussed it.

She seemed to enjoy teaching me things, and I was more than happy to learn about what Yule meant to the witch community.

But...

Nothing.

"Sounds like a lot of fun," I blurted, partially to break the tension, mostly because it seemed like the right thing to say. With a wavering smile, the afternoon of Christmas shopping really starting to take its toll, I turned into Lucian's chest and tugged his sleeve. "I need a dress."

The warlocks chuckled amongst themselves—*ha, ha, silly little female*—as Lucian slowly tipped his head down, then sighed. "We'll get you one, little mate." When I whined and tugged harder, fingers really twisting into the supple leather, he cocked an eyebrow with a ghost of a grin. "*Now?*"

I nodded. "Now."

"Seems like your evening is spoken for," Ethan said, chuckling as he saluted my long-suffering mate. "See you two later."

I leaned on the shopping cart, butt jutted into Lucian's thighs, and watched the warlock go—even as James Bennet stood around staring a few moments longer. He snapped himself out of it when Lucian's warning snarl finally hit home, and he dipped into a jerky little bow before toddling after Ethan, climbing into the front of the SUV and *whamming* the door hard behind him.

And then there was Rosa.

Just looking through the window at the back, expression flat and lifeless until the SUV started to pull out of the pickup zone. Then there was the brilliant smile I thought I knew so well—but it didn't reach her eyes. Not by a mile. Her robotic wave and trembling grin made the protective urge explode, and I shoved the cart aside, then caught myself before I sprinted after her. Shaking, I just watched, helpless and confused, as the huge black vehicle wove through the rows of parked cars, eventually disappearing in the sea of chrome, metal, and glass.

"Lyssa—"

"What did you make of that?" I demanded, frowning up at my mate. His golden wolf eyes tracked the SUV over my head, following it left, then right, then way out until it was gone.

"Inappropriate conduct by that Bennet warlock," he said gruffly, his whole being tight, his emotions subdued—barely making a dent in our connection. But that was Lucian: an alpha who went deadly calm in a crisis, unless my life was on the line. "Running up to a pregnant she-wolf like that…" Some of his quiet splintered, teeth bared and voice gruff. "Ethan sharing intimate details about pack business… I don't trust it."

"Yeah." Good. At least I wasn't the only one all that had rubbed the wrong way. Meanwhile, Kira wavered between bloodlust and contemplation—ready to rip throats out *or* pause and weigh our options. "Me neither."

"You sure you want that dress?" Lucian steered me back to him by my hood, then cuddled me up against the back of the shopping cart again, almost like he needed me protected from the front and the back. "I assume Ewan only accepted the invite to be polite—"

"We're going," I said flatly. Usually I enjoyed Lucian's efforts to wiggle out of social events, but not this one. Not after Rosa's goodbye set my teeth on edge—made me want to peel that SUV apart to get her and Aster *out*.

No, little wolf, no.

I stiffened with a sharp breath, heart in my throat. *Idunn…* Squirming free, I ducked under Lucian's arm and searched for her, even just a whiff of her ghostly form. She had been so quiet lately, still blocking me from the orchard even though Loki was very much *here*, in the real world, haunting me and not her.

But that was her voice.

Her words.

Her warning, whispered on the *whoosh* of the automatic mall doors sliding open.

"I smelled him too, but I think he's gone—"

"Something's wrong with Rosa." Loki might be the more pressing threat, but he had stuck to his word: the god just observed. Hovered. Tortured us with his scent everywhere, but he hadn't made any *direct* moves against me or my mates since he showed up in the village square. My mates had a theory he was living in Lucian's log cabin since things had been moved, the ivy I sprouted ripped off the door and chimney, the snow cleared around it, but that was fine; my old pack could keep an eye on him.

Rosa...

Rosa trumped Loki right now.

"Are you sure, little mate?"

"Positive," I told him, still eyeing the doors as they opened and closed with shoppers coming and going, exhaling a blast of heat every time. "She's been off for weeks, and I want to poke around at the source."

Hmm.

Maybe not the *best* idea to tell my hypervigilant mate that I sensed danger and wanted to dive headfirst into it. Nibbling my lower lip, I faced him again, expecting an argument—expecting that I might need to really state my case here.

Lucian just fell deep into my eyes, gold to gold, the dull roar of rustling carts and obnoxious conversations and shuffling plastic bags fading away. He cupped my chin, his big hand so wonderfully warm, and kissed my forehead.

"Let's put all this in the jeep first," he rumbled, jerking his chin toward my haul of Christmas gifts, "and then we'll find you a dress..."

16

EWAN

For fuck's *sake*.

Where the *fuck* were my fucking cufflinks?

Growling, I yanked open the bottom drawer on my rustic accessory cabinet and rooted around *again*, like I'd missed them in this meticulously organized finite space the first three times.

Diamond-encrusted.

Snowflake design with a blue tinge.

Gorgeous, expensive as hell, and never worn—I'd been saving them for the first big pack event of the holiday season. Before tonight, that would have been Christmas Eve, which Soren was already menu-prepping for, his parents landing in Toronto on the twenty-third and trekking to Redwood Grove on their own. Of course they refused my chartered plane; Acker stubbornness clearly stemmed from the head down.

But then Ethan approached me with stars in his eyes and a giddy tremor in his voice, thrilled and honored that his allies in the Hampton coven chose *him* to host Yule this year—and I couldn't say no to the invite. He'd just been so jazzed about it, and he had come through time and time again for my shit, lending a hand on Halloween, always there to support me when I needed the numbers.

Devoting all this time to Lyssa—helping her without asking for a damn thing in return.

I hadn't thought twice about it: the Redwood pack was going to Yule.

Only Soren and Lucian really weren't feeling Ethan Perry lately, and at first I wouldn't have blamed them—just told them to get the fuck over themselves.

He wasn't some random male.

He was a married male with an adoring wife and a beautiful daughter.

A sentiment I'd needed to hammer home to my stubborn inner asshole, who snarled and bared his teeth anytime we scented the warlock at the house.

But then Lyssa threw *her* suspicions into the mix, her uneasy feelings plain as day in the bond, and I finally whacked the fucking sawdust out of my ears and listened.

In her mind, fuckery was afoot in the Perry coven, Rosa's behavior on a downward spiral and strange enough that Lyssa wouldn't stop pushing for us to investigate.

So, the excitement for tonight's feast? Out the window.

Loki, Lyssa's growing powers, and our shifter rivals? Back burner.

Tonight was all about making sure Rosa Perry—and by extension Aster—was okay. That and fostering positive relationships with the Hampton coven on *my* terms, because it never hurt to have allies in magical places.

For Lyssa's sake, anyway.

Ethan had made some serious missteps with this pack in the last few weeks, including bringing a strange warlock into things without my consent. If all was well in fucking Denmark tonight, I planned to take him aside and *really* drive the point home, because my roundabout way of saying *back the fuck off* at our last Friday night Chalet visit, drinks flowing and conversation tougher than usual, fell on deaf ears.

Huh.

Still no *fucking* cufflinks.

I slammed the drawer shut and picked through the four above it, opening the secret compartments and rifling through all the junk I didn't need. In the end, I bailed, leaving my old bedroom behind for the master suite we all shared permanently now. Passing the landing, the stairs down to the foyer, a *crack-hiss* of a beer opening tickled my ears, accompanied by the deep hum of chitchat in the kitchen.

Soren and Lucian—pregaming for a warlock party.

Made sense.

Lucian needed to be at least a little buzzed to set foot inside Ethan Perry's house, and Soren dreaded having to be a bubbly, happy, sunshine puppy for supernatural folk who probably didn't share the Perrys' sense of shifter acceptance.

I left them to it, only slowing when I hit the nursery. A work in progress, four distinct and very different shades of paint samples decorated the north-facing wall, all of us divided on color. The crib had arrived yesterday, still in the box and needing to be built, and the rest of the furniture was set to trickle in over the coming weeks.

At a full stop, I touched the doorframe, cufflinks the last thing on my mind, and took in the shadowy room, the silhouettes of boxes and shelves, the window overlooking the snowcapped forest and the frozen lake.

The perfect space for our first pup.

Easy access for late-night feedings and changing and cuddling, no matter how sleep-deprived.

Warmth bubbled in my chest, and my inner wolf chuffed, desperate to burst through my pressed suit and scent-mark the absolute shit out of here. We had all agreed to wait, however, until the room was ready—painted, furniture set up, plush toys everywhere. *Then* all four wolves could have at it, sniffing and scenting and making it smell like them.

A protective precaution.

A necessary evil so they all knew the pup inside was, without a doubt, theirs to the moon and back.

With a shake of my head, I tapped the doorframe affectionately, eyes narrowed at the paint some careless dick had chipped off the frame while lugging boxes in, and then carried on toward the master suite.

All confidence and power, dressed to impress, hair roguishly swooped and polished shoes clicking, oozing *alpha* in every reflection, I marched in—

And came to a stop just as fast, all that male rah-rah bullshit whooshing out like a pinpricked balloon.

Because...

Holy *fuck*.

She...

Lyssa...

Fuck.

Fuck, fuck, fuck—so *fucking* breathtaking.

Twirling around at the end of the connected beds, she looked up at the last spin, her gown fluttering, her feet bare, her eyes glistening.

"I look like a princess," she announced. Emotion choked her every word, pride *and* insecurity twisting our bond, *feelings* so potent inside this little she-wolf that whatever came my way hit like a truck.

Loosening my tie, I just stared and breathed and ignored the whumping pack heartbeat between my ears.

Because...

Fuck. I loved her.

With every fiber of my being, every thrum of my heart, every cell —*love*.

And in that moment, I couldn't believe she was *mine*.

Couldn't fathom why Lady Fate had chosen such an exquisite, perfect, *stunning* she-wolf for me—just some runaway alpha from a psychotic pack who worked too hard and felt too much but never let it show. Never let anyone in. Never got out of his own fucking way.

Almost like...

698

Like I'd been waiting for her to free me.

Waiting for the princess to slay the dragon's chains and tell him to *fly*.

Princess didn't quite fit for my fated girl—but she definitely looked like royalty tonight in that dress.

Lucian spending four hellish hours at Hampton Mall to find said dress also didn't fit, but definitely worth the torture.

Our mate was a dream in her off-white gown, a divine bride made for the stars. Floor-length, it flowed beautifully down her strong, shapely legs, silver accents throughout the skirt trickling like raindrops on a window. Light glinted off the handwoven designs, the thought and care that went into this dress stunning—for a mall purchase, anyway. A grey satin bow knotted around her cinched waist, the loops at the back droopy, the tails lost in all that skirt. Fitted bodice, solid and structured, with a subtle V neckline and thin straps up top, no sleeves, her arms powerful and deserving of the spotlight.

No baby bump yet either.

Too early.

But he or she was in there, nestled safely beneath gossamer and silk and tulle, their mother a showstopper.

Heartstopper.

Lyssa had even tackled her hair and makeup solo tonight, her mane soft and fluffy, spilling down her back like a bronzy waterfall. The white headband was an adorable touch, and the golden shimmer on her lids suited her complexion. Mascara. A bit of blush. Nude lip.

Perfection.

She stopped spinning, her gown settling, her cheeks darkening, and she fidgeted with the satin sash around her waist.

"W-what?" Uncertainty played across her features, trembling through our connection and making my inner wolf rake up my insides—because I was just standing there like some slack-jawed jackass, mouth literally open and head empty except for fucking dress details. Lyssa moved on to her hair next, pushing it back over her shoulders, then dragging it forward. "Did I do something wrong?"

Still so uncertain with this stuff.

That had to go—because Lyssa mastered all the mundane nonsense I used to care so much about ages ago.

"Blue eyes," I rasped, hoarse and thick, *love* clogging up my windpipe, "you aren't a princess."

She blinked back at me, eyes glossy in seconds, hurt in our bond and on her face. I just shook my head, grinning, wishing she could see herself how *I* saw her right now.

"You're a fucking *queen*," I clarified. Standing taller, I swallowed the painful lump in my throat, my inner wolf easing up on the torture. Then, as Lyssa's brows lifted, I took my time for a very deliberate sweep of her beauty. "And don't ever forget it." Vision sharpening, wolf eyes out, I stalked toward her with a growl, then snagged her hand and lifted it over her head. "Come on, beautiful… Give me another twirl."

Sniffling, Lyssa did as she was told, going slow this time, no longer watching her dress dance with each rotation. On the third spin, she giggled and fluttered her dark lashes up at me, those golden pools beckoning me for a dip. "What's the difference between a princess and a queen? They're both royalty."

"Princesses are in training," I told her without hesitation, knowing *exactly* why my mate would never be my little princess, not when she had been born a queen, regardless of her parents' failings—destined to *rule*. "Their lives are frivolous, all for show— just a piece on a chessboard for their fathers and husbands to play."

I steered her closer, sweeping her under my wing, this snow queen claimed by her black knight, her midnight wolf. Guiding her hand along my shoulder, I tucked her arm around my neck, then hooked her waist and jerked her against me, hips to hips, our rocking rhythm coming a little too easily. Hell, I could almost hear the music, a whole symphony just for us.

Lyssa's lashes danced like butterfly wings. Her breath hitched.

Her sumptuous lips parted, and she *took* me, possessed me, with a single glance.

"A queen *rules* her kingdom," I whispered, struggling to stay present as she swayed to my beat, as the gold filled me up—as she fiddled with the hairs at the back of my neck, so innocent and sweet and gentle. A façade: nothing about *our* mating was ever innocent, never sweet, and rarely gentle. "A queen is power, beauty, strength, and calculation personified." I swept her around the bedroom, nothing more than a basic waltz, and she followed without hesitation, never once stumbling over my feet. When I dipped her, I caught the flicker of her heartbeat in her throat, that pulse point a tease, a bullseye for my teeth. "Remember, love, that you are *not* frivolous. You are not a pawn on a chessboard." I cupped the back of her head, holding her in that dip, bracing, taking her full weight and vowing *never* to let her fall. "You are not something to be played —*you* are the player. You are *our* fucking *queen.*"

Cradled in my arms, I could have stared at my queen all night. Right here. Like this. Frozen in time and space, lost in her watery eyes and her shy smile.

She kissed me instead.

Made her own moves, the strongest player on the board.

According to the timeline I'd drilled into all their heads at lunch today, we were supposed to leave soon. Very soon. Too soon for anything that this kiss might lead to.

Fuck it.

With her fingers twisted in my hair, her body arched into me, I kissed Lyssa with all the ferocity my queen deserved. The makeup, her pretty hair—screwed. We were all hands, tongues tangling, the bedroom filled with an aria of moans and groans in perfect harmony. Steering us upright, my inner wolf retreating but the *beast* prowling forward, I scooped my girl off her feet and dragged her into the pit. Skirted the beds though, those two kings thoroughly christened time and time again since we'd created this pack den.

No, I hauled her into the walk-in closet with all its shelves and drawers. Only then did I break the kiss, when I needed to find the perfect throne, and I swept three neat piles of Soren's sweaters off one of the larger shelves, then sat Lyssa on the edge. She settled with a giggle, feet dangling, legs swinging, lips swollen and cheeks flushed.

The color deepened when I sank to my knees, kneeling before the only she-wolf in my life worthy of my fucking servitude.

"If I'm a queen," she mused, walking her fingers along my shoulder, "are you my king?"

"You have *three* kings, blue eyes," I growled, a wicked grin blooming when she nibbled at her ravaged lower lip. I then gathered the excess material, white and shimmery, silver woven throughout —which felt a bit on the nose for a shifter, but all the little beads and baubles caught the light beautifully. Soft yellow spilled through the walk-in doorway, the lights in here off, the setting so secluded in a house where privacy just didn't exist. At the start, that had royally pissed me off—never having a breather, always someone in my face, in my business. Now, I couldn't imagine it any other way. Always someone to turn to, to tussle with, to *talk* to—or not. Someone to just sit with in amicable silence while we went about our day.

I hadn't realized what I'd been missing until her.

Until all of them.

Not that I'd tell fucking Soren and Lucian that—but Lyssa would know.

If not by my words, then by my actions, in the way I swept her skirts up to her knees and parted her thighs, my growls rough when I realized she had no stockings down here. No garters. No nothing but a simple pair of white cotton panties that already smelled like her womanly musk.

"You remember, love…" I shouldered the fabric, then dragged a finger up the delicate flesh of her inner thigh, smitten with the way it pebbled and her breath hitched. "You are a queen worthy of three kings—*that's* how powerful you are."

In every sense, Lyssa radiated *power*. Not just what she had absorbed from Gull River. No, it went deeper than that. It was in her DNA, her marrow: power and might.

Struggling to contain myself, monster and man battled for control, the man determined to make her squirm with words, the animal inside starving to *claim* her quivering center.

"Ewan—"

"And real kings," I whispered, tugging her panties down and snarling when she lifted her hips to help, "they *kneel* for their queen."

I wrenched the damp cotton over her thighs and down her calves, leaving it to dangle off one foot. With my prize bared, I slipped under her dress and swept my tongue over her slick folds, her taste divine, her squeals music to my fucking ears. Her legs hooked over my shoulders, tightening around my face, and, honestly, I could have died happy here, suffocated but so fucking in love that it didn't really matter.

Only it did.

Poetic, to die between a woman's thighs.

Not very practical in real life.

Smirking, I opened her up just a little, my darling rose, her scent a whole field of them tonight, and ravished her as she deserved.

Possessively.

Deeply.

Intimately.

I gritted into her thighs hard enough to leave bruises, hoping they'd last long enough for her to see just how deeply I fucking *wanted* her. What she did to me—how she made me lose control and set the caged beast free. I lapped at her pussy, fucked it with my tongue, tormented her clit and swollen lips—occasionally with a hint of teeth, just to feel her squirm and jerk and try, *oh, yes, just try and escape.*

I worshipped at the altar until it fell apart.

Until Lyssa clamped those strong thighs around my head and rocked against my hungry, laughing mouth, throwing herself into oblivion with a soundless keen. Her pleasure blossomed in my core, made my dick even harder—like that was fucking possible, every drop of blood in my whole body already gathered inside the needy shit.

All our climaxes hit different. Sometimes a whisper, others a roar—the majority somewhere in between—but they touched *everyone* in this connection. This one was a tidal wave, rocking from her to me and back again, pirouetting along the bond and no doubt hitting the assholes downstairs. It kicked adrenaline through my veins, turned my voice hoarse and savage, desperate for my own release as I reared back and clawed my way out from under her dress, gasping for air and hungry as *fuck* for her pussy.

Desperate to feel it clench around my cock, slick and tight and shuddering through the next orgasm I forced out of her before we left.

Somewhere deep inside, the man who valued logic and control and schedules cried that we should just *go*. Leave it at that—pat her perfect ass and send her on her way.

The beast smothered him and spurred me on as I stood, Lyssa's desire smeared all over my mouth and down to my chin. One hand to her sweaty forehead, the other her heaving chest, she didn't seem to notice me at first—didn't catch on to the predator closing in until it was too late. Her eyes rounded the moment I claimed her waist, and I ripped her off the shelf, then spun her around, gown *beyond* in the fucking way, the walk-in suddenly tight and *hot*, the open door leaving us vulnerable.

"One other thing to remember, love," I drawled, snagging her wrists and guiding her hands to some of the higher shelves. I pinned them there, then waited until she gripped the wood—like she knew she'd need to support herself for the next part of this ride. Once her trembling fingers found somewhere to grab onto, I wrenched open my belt, dropped my freshly ironed slacks, and dug my dick out. "You might be a queen, but we kings..." I then hiked her dress up and prowled closer, smothering her with my body, claiming her right then and there. My lips brushed her ear with every word, my savage tone a warning, a reminder of the beast within. "We kings were made to *conquer*."

Head ducked, Lyssa moaned, the wood groaning under her fists, her submission so fucking *sweet* that I nearly nutted into my hand. Thankfully the man regained some control, and I managed to hoist her dress further and trap all the fabric, her satiny bow, in the dip of her lower back, pinned there between her body and mine.

And then I fucking *conquered*.

I plunged into her heat from behind, lifting her off her toes I pounded home so hard, so fast. *Fuck*, my mate was perfection every goddamn time. The inferno between her thighs was my undoing, and for the first time in my life, I embraced defeat. Wholeheartedly, I succumbed to the wild thing in my chest, to the primal want in my blood, taking without question, grinding and bucking and pumping into her without a care for the rest of the night.

Nothing else mattered.

Nothing existed beyond this moment.

Just me and her, our bodies entwined, our hearts pounding a beat through the bond that only we could hear.

Threading one hand into her hair, careful not to rip or tug or pull too hard, I blanketed one of hers with the other. Held on for dear life, fucking her, mounting my mate and consuming her cries and mewls like a starved wolf at the end of a bleak winter. She was the spring sunshine, the flowers, the streams.

Lyssa was *life* renewed, and with her, I was so fucking *alive*.

Not a corporate zombie.

Not an alpha obsessed with material gain.

Not a brooding introvert who just craved *space*.

She brought out something new in me—and she had no idea.

I'd owe her forever for that. For the rest of our long lives, until our aging bodies turned to starlight.

Her free hand found me, scrambling down my torso and fisting my jacket. Despite the position, she rocked back as best she could, meeting my thrusts, demanding *more*. That gown posed its own set of challenges—namely diving through it to find her tender clit, but damn it, I was a wolf possessed, obsessed with his mate's pleasure.

Battling gossamer and tulle and silk, I slowed way down to a brutal grind as soon as I stroked that sensitive bud.

And then she was well and truly mine.

Just a whimpering, trembling, babbling *goddess* in my arms, lost in the moment, in her rising pleasure, in the heat soaring between us—until she broke.

Lyssa came with a sob, and I gently nudged her head back, wordlessly insisting she rest it on my shoulder so I could fucking *watch* all my hard work play out. She was just so divine when she climaxed, so open and beautiful and *mine*.

Piping-hot pleasure ripped through me, her destruction my salvation, her orgasm triggering mine. Choking her name, I buried my face in her neck, teeth raking her flesh as ecstasy swept through my limbs. First, it was like gasoline, making the fires burn brighter, hotter, and ten times more dangerous.

Then it was floodwaters, snuffing the flames, releasing me from their torment so that a cool calm took their place. I slumped against her. Lyssa folded into the built-in shelves. Both of us indulged in the human and wolf noises in our arsenal, nuzzling and kissing and touching, hot and sticky, until finally she pushed me away.

Not roughly, and not cruelly, yet the caveman side of my brain hated to leave her.

But I went, because she was right: enough now.

Still chasing my breath, I collapsed against the shelves on the opposite wall, Lucian's leather jackets hanging, their owner's oakwood scent just a little too strong for my heightened senses. Lyssa, meanwhile, slowly smoothed her dress, then turned and hopped back on the empty shelf, Soren's discarded sweaters in a heap at her feet.

"How much damage control do I need to do?" she asked breathlessly, all smiles as she finger-combed her wild hair, then righted her skewed headband and tried to correct her smeared lipstick with her thumb. Cock limp and spent, inner wolf dreading going anywhere formal after this, I loosened my tie some more and undid the top button on my dress shirt, *way* too fucking hot suddenly.

"Uh…" My queen looked like a thoroughly fucked she-wolf right now—no point in denying it. "I tried to be careful, but…" I scanned her from the top down, from her sweaty forehead to her swollen lips to her flushed, shiny chest. "Maybe just a quick touch-up?"

"More like a quick shower," she muttered. Then her eyes widened as panic sliced through the bond, and she scrambled off the shelf, pulling her skirts as far away from her body as possible. Yeah, good call. Staining it before she had the chance to show those Hampton coven witches and warlocks how fucking stunning she looked would be a waste.

As soon as she went for that silver bow around her waist, my mind nosedived straight into the gutter again. Wicked thoughts about unwrapping her like a fucking Christmas present trickled in, and my cock twitched, swelling, excited to mount her *one* last time before—

"Did you two seriously just…?"

We both jumped when Soren's voice pierced our hazy after-mating bubble. Dressed in a shockingly stylish three-piece mulberry suit, black waistcoat and socks, hair neatly side swept, stubble freshly shaven, the blond alpha planted his hands on his hips and scowled.

"Come *on*," he growled as Lyssa undid the side zipper of her dress and I tucked my dick away, all those devious plans on pause—for now. Soren motioned between us, then to himself. "We were literally *right* downstairs. Where's the invite?"

"You missed out, *bro*," I sneered, echoing his words from our rambunctious night of tree hunting when I'd shown up just after these three heathens fucked behind a tree. Leaving Lyssa to shimmy out of her dress alone, I strolled toward him and swatted at his chest. "And it was a *good* one."

Soren threw his weight into his shoulder when I tried to shove by, and, my belt still undone, fly open, button barely holding my slacks together, we tussled in the doorway, me trying to get out, him trying to bully his way in.

We both stilled, however, when our very naked mate breezed between us, parting the alpha seas with a hand on each of our arms, her hair over one shoulder and her golden gaze twinkling mischievously.

"Play nice, you two," she ordered, practically skipping to the bathroom so those perky ass cheeks bounced. "We have to go in fifteen minutes."

Transfixed on the sway of *everything*, I just stared, then snapped back to the moment when water crashed to tile, her quick shower underway.

Something I should consider myself, actually, everything feeling a little sticky south of the border.

Before I could join her—for a shower and nothing more... probably—a familiar twinkle caught my eye.

Scowling, I looked Soren over, the suit tailored well to his frame, his tie knot neat for once—and his sleeves crowned with *my* diamonds.

"Are those my fucking cufflinks?"

Soren held both wrists up, preening like some douchey peacock. "Yeah."

"Soren—"

"They match the suit."

"Give me," I growled, "my cufflinks."

He backpedaled, a challenge in his smile, in the slight bend of his knees like he was preparing for an attack. "No."

"We don't have time for this."

"You two found a way—"

I lunged after him. "Give me those stupid fucking—"

"*No.*"

And as eager as we kings were to kneel before our queen, to bow to her every whim, right now, with my cufflinks on the line and Soren's laughter echoing through the house, Lucian's heavy footfalls padding down the hall, our queen's words fell on deaf ears—because we did not, in fact, play nice.

We played cheap and dirty, Soren splitting my lip and me smashing his nose.

Then Lucian watching it all unfold like he was taking bets on the winner, offering cheats and hints to both sides.

We played rough.

We played to *win*.

Most of all…

We played like brothers, who, as our showered and dressed mate sashayed by in her sparkly kitten heels, eventually shook hands and called it a draw, fixed each other's suits, and went on our way.

After a quick scrub myself, I let Soren wear the cuffs.

Because, fuck me, they were only cufflinks.

17

LUCIAN

"Can you at least pretend like you're having a mediocre time tonight?"

I slowly turned my sneer onto Ewan and twisted it into the most manic Cheshire cat grin I could muster—then it was *his* turn to deadpan, staring at me with those dark hickories, his pupils slightly dilated from all the top-shelf bourbon he'd been guzzling since we arrived. The black-haired wolf exhaled sharply the longer I held the psychopathic grimace, then took a long, long swig of liquor and refocused on the party.

Honestly, did any of them expect me to have a *blast* tonight? A rip-roaring good time? Surrounded by witches and warlocks from Hampton and beyond, this was my bloody nightmare wrapped up in a gothic yuletide bow. Here to celebrate the winter solstice, the darkest night of the year, a good fifty of them in sweeping gowns and fitted suits filled the grand room, yule carols humming from somewhere, servers circulating with hors d'oeuvre platters, the cheese and sausage bites outright wolf bait.

But not for mine.

No, mine remained on high alert, insisting we maintain position with our back to the wall so no fucker could sneak up on us.

Scope the perimeter.

Assess any incoming threats.

If I could, I would have swept this huge chalet the moment we arrived, but I suppose that was considered foul party etiquette. Still, the polite thing for our hosts to do would have been to offer a tour so I could at least get a proper smell of the place.

I'd never realized, size-wise, that Ethan and Rosa Perry's home rivaled ours. Safe inside the village's stone walls, the suburbs weren't exactly a part of my border patrols. Enormous, custom-built, decadent to the last detail, their two-man coven occupied a chalet nestled at the foot of the mountain range, tucked away at the crook of a dead-end cobblestone street. Situated amongst the local elite, they had the nicest house on the block. Most expensive landscaping. Pricy shingles and a ridiculous Christmas lights display, with a family of snowmen—mother, father, baby—on the front lawn. Hell, the property looked like it belonged on a postcard. Three-car garage. Electronic front gates.

Perfect.

Too perfect.

And much, much too busy inside, the place decorated within an inch of its life with plants and landscapes and tile and stainless steel, a strange blend of witchy warmth and emotionless ice.

The air was electric, their magical auras fucking *smothering*, and peppered with bursts of roast pheasant and fresh-baked breads, garlicky mash, and sugary sweetness from Rosa's sequestered kitchen.

We were among the last to arrive this evening, despite showing up only ten minutes after the party was set to start—red flag number one.

Rosa had been there to welcome us and take our coats, garbed in some awful emerald pillowcase, looking like an inflated Christmas tree with huge red balls dangling from her poor ears, her makeup heavy and her curls straightened and her smile thin.

Red flag number *two*.

Red flag number three had been ongoing since Ethan escorted us into this domed ballroom with its wall of windows overlooking an ostentatious timber deck and a neat hedge maze. All eyes on us—on Lyssa.

All attention on Lyssa.

Questions and comments and *oh, what lovely eyes you have, dear.*

Not that I could blame them: our mate was the most exquisite creature in the room. Stunning in the gown we chose together. Beautiful with her hair and makeup styled to her preferences by her hand. Effortless with that beaming smile and radiant laugh and gentle gestures, like she had tamed herself for this audience.

Like she was a fucking master at the game.

A society darling in the flesh.

An *act.*

But they lapped it up, desperate for more. Even now, my little mate occupied the center of what should have been the dance floor, witches and warlocks circling her like bloody sharks. The belle of the ball. The star of the show.

Huge red flag.

So big and bright and waving *right* in our faces that I struggled not to charge through all those pretentious twats, toss Lyssa over my shoulder, and get the fuck out.

I held back for *her*—because she hadn't sniffed around enough about Rosa. We all knew her intentions tonight, the purpose of this outing spelled out explicitly, even if Ewan had ulterior motives regarding the Hamptonite power players.

Lyssa was concerned about her friend.

We, as her devoted mates, were all therefore concerned about Rosa Perry as well, who popped in and out at random over the last hour and a bit, never staying for long.

Almost like she had to make an appearance. Smile, giggle, thank everyone—then bugger off.

Unease settled permanently in the pack bond tonight. Gone was the pleasure of Ewan and Lyssa's mating, the brotherhood from Soren and Ewan's playfighting, the *joy* of seeing our girl all dressed up and looking like the North Star.

Apprehension. Uncertainty. *Vigilance.*

Hunger too, even my gut gurgling when the servers wandered too close.

The sit-down dinner started at eight.

Twenty long minutes to go until we trickled into the dining hall next door, the seats assigned, the next three hours of course after course after course, yule logs burning away, bound to be tedious as *fuck.*

Alas.

This wasn't the first upscale gala I had knuckled through, and having been fated to the same breathtaking she-wolf as Ewan Quinn, I suspected it wouldn't be the last.

Ewan rounded on me again, both of us tucked off to the side next to some hideous abstract painting of what I *assumed* was a haunted forest, the trees—maybe those were trees—warped and gnarled and angry, the canvas dotted with gold blotches, and just as his lips parted, our host made a beeline straight for us.

Ethan Perry, dressed in a full red suit, perhaps to complement his wife in green, practically sprinted around the circular hall, eyes on Ewan and phone in hand.

"We need to talk," he hissed as soon as he slammed into our orbit. Lovely. Ewan tossed back the last of his bourbon—conditioned, perhaps, to associate his friend with the bottle because Ethan bloody Perry had been refilling his glass since we got here—then glanced at me, uneasy curiosity prickling between us. The sensation tingled in my palms and coated them in a cold sweat. My inner wolf sniffed deep, this warlock officially on our radar, way higher up the threat priority list after last week's revelations at the mall.

Fuck *Professor* James Bennet.

He had no right to know a damn thing about our mate—even less of a right to pester her tonight, glued to Lyssa's side and fawning all over her.

"What's wrong?" Ewan murmured, tone pleasant, expression neutral, ever the politician in a crisis.

So long as it had nothing to do with our mate's safety, anyway.

Because then he was a complete disaster.

"Vampires," Ethan choked. My packmate sucked in a harsh breath, and everything inside went cold. My inner wolf's hackles bolted upright like we'd been struck by lightning, anxiety and alert and *rage* pluming in my chest and darkening in Ewan's cheeks. Our snarls fed off each other, and Ethan's eyes darted nervously between us, hesitant as he inched closer, watching me like I might peel the flesh off his frail bones.

And one day I might.

This warlock had teetered on the tightrope of my opinion ever since we met, the tether thinning as time passed—until it was but a single strand, taut and trembling, seconds from *snapping* and plunging him into the abyss.

Clearing his throat, shoulders suddenly thrown back and concave chest thrust out, he found his nerve and sidled between us. Yew and mint. Always yew and mint, an obnoxious combination for a scent profile—especially when his wife was so beautifully warm with her amber and honey. Nostrils flared, I fought every primal urge, every bad memory, every fucking *scar* on my body, and *didn't* grab him by the throat.

Focused more on Ewan, the dirty-blond beanpole lifted his phone, swiped the screen, and angled it toward us.

"My security crystals along the property perimeter triggered," he whispered as he revealed a crisp black-and-white video on the screen. Mounted above the detached garage, the security camera faced the winding driveway, and as soon as he tapped the little button in the center, the footage came to life.

I eased closer, canines bared; the timestamp implied this had happened five minutes ago.

A shadow blurred across the screen, reminiscent of those fucking leeches in motion when we hunted them through the territory.

A second joined it, only this time the figure stopped.

A few of the nearest voices died down at my snarl, and Ewan had to brace me, a hand to my chest, when I lurched forward—almost like I could dive into the phone and rip that cunt apart with my bare fucking hands.

I'd torn his throat out once before.

Halloween night, in the back alley, I beat that maggot bloody and would gladly do it again.

Bold twats, those two, slinking into wolf territory again after we made our positions *very* clear.

Such fury pounded through me that I barely felt Ewan's, but with a deep breath, eyes glued to the screen, some of his wrath seeped in.

Swaddled in an enormous black trench coat, the vampire called out to his companion, skin so white it was practically translucent—then looked straight into the security camera.

A swift blur later, the screen went black.

And then Ewan's anger flowed like a riptide, ready to drag you out to sea and bathe in your screams.

"I don't..." Ethan tapped the screen again with a trembling finger, face pale, eyes hollow. While Ewan watched the video replay, I focused on *him*, on the fear oozing from his pores, the undercurrent of panic in his every word. "I d-don't know what to do, but my wife and *baby* are here, and if they hurt either of them—"

"We'll take care of it," Ewan announced, his resolve firming up in our bond—and making Soren's eyebrows raise from across the room, still standing sentry behind our girl.

"Stay with Lyssa," I rumbled. While it would have been faster and easier to take those shits out with three alphas on the hunt, someone needed to watch our mate's back.

Like it even needed to be said.

The reason we were both so bloody fuming was *her* and the pup in her womb, the two most precious creatures in the world right now. Her safety took top priority, and our intensity around her was only going to get worse over the next nine months. Beyond that, we hadn't changed the way we acted with her or around her in the privacy of our own home. After all, she wasn't exactly showing yet.

Not at all, really. At first glance, she was just our mate—but our wolves knew better. *We* sensed the change, instinct taking over, protective drive way over the top and still climbing.

Precisely why Soren hadn't left her alone tonight.

Ewan would inevitably schmooze and network and work the room.

I was destined for wallflower status.

And Soren—Soren was on mate guard duty, a role we all took with the utmost seriousness.

"Perimeter sweep?" Ewan muttered under his breath, to which I nodded. By now, we understood our strengths.

"With Soren." I operated best as a scout, silent and lethal in the shadows, ready to strike at a moment's notice with a very clear idea of the *whole* picture. Soren had proven himself an exceptional tracker the last few months, second only to Lyssa. Ewan, meanwhile, tolerated *others* best; he ought to stay here with the covens, minding our she-wolf, his fake smile the most convincing in the pack. "We'll find the bastards and put them down once and for fucking all."

"Just be quick about it."

"No," I drawled, shooting him a sidelong glance as Ethan devoured the security footage again, "I thought I'd take my time... See the sights, maybe get a quick ski in—"

Ewan rolled his eyes. "I think I preferred when you didn't actually talk."

"Everyone does," I fired back, mirroring my packmate's smirk before stalking off, sticking to the outskirts of the party and headed for the door. With every step, the humor fell away, that moment of comradery fleeting on the outside but lingering in our bond. My wolf had already moved way on, images of the property's exterior flashing across my mind's eye—and Soren's narrowed gaze burning into the side of my face.

I caught his amber eyes, both our wolves surfacing, the bond frazzled and Lyssa's elegant façade faltering, and then nodded toward the door. Poor bastard, stuck there in the thick of it, surrounded by witches and warlocks who hadn't paid him any attention beyond a curt greeting. Usually *he* was the social butterfly, yet I'd watched him fade to the background, his pleasant expression slowly becoming strained the more bright-eyed supernatural figures closed ranks around our mate.

He stayed with her until Ewan threaded through the crowd to take his place, then trailed after me into the empty hallway outside the brightly lit ballroom. Kitchen scents ripened as soon as you passed the threshold, overtaking the perfumes and colognes and bloody *magic* inside. My stomach griped. My mouth watered. My inner wolf licked his lips—but neither of us was hungry for *food*.

No, we'd taste cold, dead vampire flesh before the night was through.

"What's up?" Soren demanded as he breezed out of the ballroom, ditching his untouched drink on a little side table between two pots of thick, thorny ivy. I went for my tie, voice rough and harsh, the shift so near it burned under my suit.

"*Vampires*. Here. Now."

No further explanation needed. Scowling, Soren wrenched his tie loose and ripped open the top few buttons on his dress shirt, both of us jogging for the front door.

And ready to neutralize this threat *permanently*.

18

EWAN

I'd never seen the dining hall before.

Usually Ethan and I just sat on the back porch, watching the sunset and sipping expensive liquor, chatting about all the shit the rest of my social circle wouldn't put up with.

This was… new.

And very, very *heavy*.

Gothic architecture around the slitted windows, the stained glass depicting abstract nature scenes—mostly trees, actually. A dining table to seat fifty stretched the length of the room, made of dark, tough wood and lined with the chairs you'd see in some gaudy historical drama, steepled with dangerously sharp buttresses on each side. A ribbed, vaulted ceiling. Ornate candle centerpieces spread throughout the table scared off the winter shadows, surrounded by holly and pines and acorns and wine on wine on wine, the bottles corked and waiting for these festive supernatural partiers to crack into them.

Place cards on every plate, guest names written in swirly calligraphy, clearly done by hand—Rosa's touch, from the smell.

Mine was at Ethan's immediate left, his spot at the head of the table currently empty.

Guests milled around the room, admiring the architecture, the glass designs, the yuletide decorations scattered across the table. Some sat. Most strolled and chatted and sipped from their chalices. Magic ripened the air the longer the night went on, fucking claustrophobic but not surprising: this was a solstice—and a big one. Magic was the name of the game tonight, especially for Ethan's Hampton guests. A time to celebrate the darkest night of the year. To worship the moon. To beckon the light home.

All that good shit.

I blinked, eyes annoyingly heavy, and set my empty tumbler next to what I assumed was my wineglass, the napkin poking out its top styled like a peacock's tail. Aim off, I clunked the bottom on the edge of the china dishware, a few heads turning at the noise.

A fresh burst of adrenaline struck out of nowhere. My inner wolf howled, desperate to be out there with the boys, right on those fucking leeches' heels, snapping, snarling, seconds from ripping them apart.

But I had to be here.

Had to watch Lyssa.

Had to... take care of all these drunk warlocks and their tittering witch wives.

My mouth watered, the sensations in the pack bond unleashing a storm of goose bumps down my arms.

Hunt.

Out there, Lucian and Soren were free—free from this fucking suit, the constraints of polite society. Free from small talk and fake laughter and the undercurrent of concern over our mate's safety.

Wanted to be with them.

But—

No.

Here.

Shit, gotta piss.

Rolling my shoulders back, I leaned over the table, scanning the few faces with their ass in a seat—not stopping until I hit Lyssa.

My girl.

My she-wolf goddess.

Right in the middle of things, already seated, her adrenaline ramping up, same as mine, same as the whole pack—but she kept her cool, deep in conversation with Rosa, whose name card put her at my queen's right.

Okay. So. She was in good hands, then.

Boys would take care of those douchebag vamps.

Ethan was checking on the first course in the kitchen.

Party guests seemed good and happy and *way* less focused on Lyssa.

Awesome.

I shuffled back, grabbing at my chair when the world lilted to the side.

Uh.

Okay.

My inner wolf rumbled, his gruff more muffled than usual, and I barely felt him rake up my esophagus.

Weird.

Fucking *weird*—

Oh. Wait. I zeroed in on the tumbler again, on the melted ice and the empty glass and how many drinks had I had since I got here?

Social gatherings were a one-drink maximum—had to keep your wits sharp when you swam with sharks.

But…

I'd had more than one tonight.

During that first hour, hour and a half, *whatever*, Ethan frequently injected himself into my conversations for a refill, always a different brand, a different scent, a different herbal sprig to really bring out the *flavor*.

Shit.

Fucked that up.

Good thing I wasn't on the hunt, because…

I gripped the chair harder.

Was I drunk?

No.

No, it took way more than three—six?—bourbons to knock a wolf shifter on his ass, especially an alpha.

Built different.

Built *stronger*.

But I suddenly… *felt* a little—

My bladder screamed when I finally stepped away from the table, loud enough that I couldn't ignore it anymore. *Fuck's sake.* Inner wolf yowling, screeching, bellowing—but so far away. So distant. Barely a whisper.

Shoulders back, I did my best *not* to advertise that I'd become such a fucking lightweight since mating with my fated, bearing her mark on my flesh—gorgeous ol' ball and chain. Around the table I went, steadying myself on the backs of random chairs, then stared at Lyssa until she really *felt* it. My mate scratched at the back of her neck as my eyes drilled holes into her skull, then slowly glanced over her shoulder—then straightened when our gazes locked. The subtle lift of her brow, the curiosity prickling between us, her apprehension—

Bonded wolves really could speak without ever saying a word.

Never like this before, not even with my kin.

I patted the air, then sucked in an exaggerated breath and let it out slowly. *We're good.* Some of the tension eased out of her shoulders.

"Bathroom," I whispered, fully aware that over the din of conversations and clicking heels and music from unseen speakers, she'd hear me. Lyssa tipped her head to the side, so wolfish in her mannerisms, so fucking *beautiful* I could easily toss her on the table right here and now—mount her all over again. Make her squeal.

Do some mating ritual in honor of the winter solstice.

That'd go over well with this crowd, right?

For, uh, fertility and abundance in the… coming spring.

Yeah.

When the message finally landed, she nodded and waved me off; we had both seen the open powder room just down the hall, through the huge doors at my back and literally fifteen steps away.

I'd be back in a flash.

Because with the sheer volume of piss sloshing around inside me, this thing would empty like a fucking firehose.

Still, even if I wouldn't be gone long or far, I waited, watching, studying my mate until I was sure she had settled into her chat with Rosa again, the witch animated and natural, relaxed for the first time all evening.

The *Something is Wrong with Rosa* theory was still up for debate.

I'd seen both sides so far.

Only time would tell.

Okay, go.

After one final hazy sweep of the dining hall, I ducked out through the main doors, two tall, lean panels carved with runes—

Runes like the ones Soren had found on the internet for his Viking costume.

Another piece of the Perry homestead I'd never seen before.

Shaking my head, I ignored the mouthwatering scents wafting from the lower-level kitchen and beelined for the powder room.

Periwinkle-blue walls. Standalone sink. Toilet with a basket of dried apple blossoms on the tank. *This* fit the aesthetic I'd come to expect from their house—not that gothic monstrosity back there.

Toilet lid and seat up, I broke the seal with a long, satisfying groan, bladder emptying with the force of trundling river rapids.

A loud, powerful enough stream that the asshole suddenly knocking on the door should have heard.

I glanced back with a scowl, then checked the little doorknob lock.

Yeah, engaged, shithead.

Another knock, all knuckle, insistent and demanding as I shook my junk dry.

"Just a minute."

The third knock had me rolling my eyes with a snarl. "Fucking..." I gritted my teeth, reining in the inner asshole, and cleared my throat. "Hold on."

"Come on, man," a male's voice whispered from the other side. "You done yet? About to shit my pants out here."

Sounded like a drunk pup.

Not that I had much of a leg to stand on, Ethan's top-shelf booze really knocking the wind out of my sails tonight.

I even zipped my briefs into my trousers, then struggled to wrench the fabric free, scowling.

Shouldn't feel like this.

Could definitely handle my fucking liquor.

Shouldn't sway and—

I staggered shoulder-first into the wall, narrowly missing the hanging towel rack, and finally ripped the silk out of the zipper, then finished fixing myself up. More frantic knocking, that dick apparently in serious need of *this* bathroom when there were like six in this fucking house.

After a quick hand-wash and pants-dry, I unlocked the door and yanked it open, still sober enough to give the impatient twenty-something, lanky as fuck, bug-eyed, pale warlock on the other side a piece of my mind—

When he stabbed me.

Right in the gut.

Really leaned into it, shoving a silver dagger into my abdomen.

I exhaled sharply. My inner wolf screeched.

And this fucker *leered*.

Marched me backward, the silver taking instant sedative effect. Barely felt my fingers. My knees buckled, and I crashed to the tile, *agony* ripping me apart from the inside, blood on fire, shadows creeping into the edges of my vision.

"Can't forget the collar, eh, *dog*?" Giddy, almost salivating, this Hamptonite who probably still had a year to go at his academy groped around inside his jacket, eyes wild, teeth bared.

My inner wolf bolstered me, his snarls breaching whatever had kept him muzzled all this time, and, hands scrambling weakly along the wall, searching for something to grab, I kicked out.

Nailed the fucker right in the knee, then the crotch, and sent him stumbling back into the bathroom doorframe.

Shit, shit, shit, shit, shit, fuck, shit, shit, shit, shit—what is happening?

Weak and fading fast, the silver poison leeching into my bloodstream, I went for the dagger this asshole had used to turn me into a stuck fucking pig.

Only to look up just as my hand closed around the handle—and found the warlock seething at me, slightly rumpled, ashy-brown hair askew...

His wand at the ready.

Offensive posture.

Ethan had told me that term once—taught me about dueling over scotch on the porch.

Cotton filled my ears, really upping the high-pitched siren bleating between them.

Weapon locked, loaded—and when he fired, he did so with a sneer and a smarmy Latin incantation.

Red blasted me in the face.

Red like the cranberries adorning the yule wreaths.

Red like blood.

Red all over.

My wolf howling, screaming, drowning in red light...

And then—nothing but the black abyss.

My body floating.

My mind shutting down.

Shutting down.

Down.

Down.

Down.

Gone.

19

LYSSA

Where is everybody?

Tonight I learned you could feel totally alone in a room full of people.

Because none of them were *my* people.

Forty-seven witches and warlocks had descended on the giant dining table, settled and drinking and chatting. To my right, Rosa's chair remained empty, and the greying witch to my left kept bumping me with her wayward elbows, stinking of red wine, her eyes glossy and her stories so nuts *no way* anyone believed them. On the other side of the festive wreath, through the wine bottles and flickering candles, James Bennet just stared. The guy had been up my butt since we got here—or, at least, he *tried*, Soren forced to physically body-block him—and nothing had changed since we moved rooms.

Rolling my shoulders back, remembering my posture and poise for such a fancy party with such fancy strangers, I grabbed the stupid tiny fork at the end of the row of forks beside my plate—then grimaced.

Snails?

Really?

First course: six snails in their shells on a golden plate.

Apparently they were a French delicacy, but I'd never liked eating them in the wild, the shells too crunchy and the meat too *blegh*.

Plus, they could make you sick.

But everyone else just gobbled them up, experts with this useless two-pronged fork, effortlessly extracting the innards while I just poked at the shells and tried to keep my nose from crinkling.

Kira barely noticed the stupid choice of first-course eats.

No, she was distracted by the fact that Rosa had been missing for about twenty minutes.

No Ethan either, the meal started without our host.

My mates were still out hunting, bloodlust pulsing in our bond, those vampires *toast* if Lucian and Soren managed to sink their teeth in this time.

And... no Ewan.

He'd left for the bathroom ages ago, way before Rosa excused herself. He'd seemed a little unsteady on his feet, toddling off in what should have been a straight line but was more a roundabout loop for the main doors—twin panels that stretched high, high up to the ceiling, elegant as the rest of this room dressed like a fantasy movie set.

At one point, pain ripped into my belly, sharp and visceral enough that I'd gasped, and all the color left Rosa's cheeks.

No telling which of my mates had taken the hit though.

After, it all went quiet, then flared again with the adrenaline of the vampire hunt.

And Kira's suspicions bounded higher and higher.

Because Rosa was still being weird—same as the mall, she operated on an uncomfortable frequency tonight, either giddy and high-pitched or demure and withdrawn.

No in-between.

Only fleeting eye contact with me when everyone else fought to lose themselves in my gold.

And I just...

Where the heck was my pack?

Where were the Perrys?

Why would anyone think *snails* were an elegant appetizer?

Teeth gritted, I gently set my fork down, my six dots of dark snot untouched, and then pushed my chair back. The hairs on my neck stood the more eyes darted my way, witches and warlocks always glancing, then turning away *fast* to whisper like I couldn't put two and two together. Sure, this dress was gorgeous, and Lucian had excellent taste, pushing me to go bold with the white, but it wasn't my outfit that had these vultures circling.

Friendly vultures, yeah. Polite and curious and full of compliments—but still buzzards waiting for me to go down.

The magic in the air felt different from the women's bathroom at the Chalet. Oppressive. Heavy. All-consuming and a little aggressive. Strange to sense a shift in atmosphere, the environment so subtle, the changes probably lost on humans, but *I* felt it—and Kira lived it, absorbing the energy and spitting it back out in her snarls.

I tried to glide for the hall's big doors, not wanting the *clunk-clunk-clunk* of my little heels to draw more unwanted attention. As soon as I slipped through, I made sure to shut those panels behind me, needing to hear the *click* before I moved on.

Needing to confirm that they couldn't see me anymore.

I had to find my people, my pack, and I couldn't do that *well* if I was being scrutinized at every turn.

In the corridor, too bright and much lighter than the dining hall, the dull roar died. No hum of conversations, no tinkling of cutlery, no glassware clinking on teeth or pretentious guffawing laughter right in my ear. No, out here was for sight and smell, the lights in the ceiling *white*-white, the scrumptious scents of pheasant and other meats and breads and desserts spiraling from the kitchen. A wolf without a mission might have followed the food.

I blocked it out.

Tapped into Kira's *focus*, alert and on edge, a huntress on the prowl.

The bathroom I figured Ewan had used was empty—and smelled like bleach.

And iron.

Just a smidge of each, subtle enough that a less sensitive nose would have missed it, but both triggered alarm bells. Kira breathed deep, then snorted and snarled, totally certain now that *something* had happened to my mate.

My mate who had stayed behind to keep an eye on me and Ethan's guests as vampires roamed the snowy wilderness outside —gone.

Scowling, I stalked down the hallway, then stilled, Kira demanding I *stop* when we caught a whiff of Rosa and Ethan. To my left, a shadowy stairwell wound up to the second floor, and their scent signatures hovered there—amber and honey, yew bark and mint, like little gumdrops on the ground...

Leading me to the witch's cottage.

Gnawing at my cheeks, I glanced left and right—then started up the stairs. Slow and quiet, fingers lightly grazing the banister, I stayed on my toes, eyes wide open, nostrils flared, and relied on all my senses to catch danger before it struck.

Power bloomed in my chest.

Baby pup fluttered in my lower belly.

I touched them both, pup first—*Sit tight, baby... Mama might have to rescue one of your dads tonight*—then my chest, massaging the flat, bony plate.

Very aware that I considered it *my* power now.

Not Idunn's. Not anymore.

It had been hers from the start, but if I was stuck with it, I needed to acknowledge it once and for all.

Accept that, like Kira after my first shift, it was here to stay.

That it was a part of *me*.

No one else.

Me. Mine. Not separate. Not alien. Not demonic.

Just another limb, another piece of my soul.

Because if I was about to face whatever had Kira on edge and twisted my belly into knots, it was better to be at peace with the monster.

Me, Kira, and the *power*—we were a singular weapon, and every cog needed to fit together just right.

Greeted by another dark corridor, I stilled at the top of the stairs, all these old wood floorboards a little too creaky for my liking. A lot of the décor disappeared up here, the walls painted and wainscoted but lacking the downstairs canvases. Still on my toes, I scanned up and down the empty hallway, met with closed doors at every turn—except for one. At the far end, just that one stood slightly ajar, white light slanting through the slit.

No sign of Ewan anywhere, not even a whiff of rosewood in the air.

Head cocked, I crept toward that half-open door, Rosa and Ethan's smells sharpening, beckoning me closer—

"What is *wrong* with you lately?"

I stiffened and Kira snorted, the warlock's tone confrontational and patronizing to the max—and so, so different from the soft, dutiful voice he used with Rosa and Aster around us.

"Ethan, please—"

"Don't you want to live forever? Don't you want that for Aster?"

Confusion dragged its icy finger down my spine, and I slipped out of my shoes, leaving them behind, and tiptoed toward the edge of the light.

"You don't have to do it this way," Rosa insisted, voice wobbling, words stuttering like she had to force them out. "W-we can just ask Lyssa—"

The shocking *crack* of skin to skin stopped me dead in my tracks, her strangled cry drop-kicking my heart into my throat, Kira pitching an absolute fit inside. The protective urge that had haunted my visits with this witch flared, violent and white-hot in the pit of my stomach, and my whole body *shook* with the effort it took to stay still, because...

Because...

Had he just...?

No.

No.

No, he wouldn't—

She was his rosebud.

His wife.

His mate.

He would never—

"You have been *out* of control the last few weeks, seriously," Ethan groused, sounding way too cool and collected for what I'd just heard. Bile sizzled at the back of my throat, and my vision sharpened, skin caked in *heat*, Kira desperately trying to force the shift so she could rip him apart. *Patience.* Judging from the scent of leather and old books, we'd stumbled onto Ethan's office—which made it *his* territory. Couldn't just charge in blind. Needed to take a beat, process, and really—

"Why do you make me do this?" Oh. Okay. *That* was how this was going to play out? I tossed my head side to side, cracking my neck each time, and rolled my shoulders. Was he... blaming her? "You think I *like* this? I thought we were past the need for it by now."

Rosa whimpered. "I-I can't just watch you do—"

"Do what?" he demanded, ice and steel, way, *way* more confident than I'd ever heard him sound. "*Say* it."

"Lyssa is the steward she chose—"

"And I'm going to let some wolf bitch take everything, right?"

I blanched, outrage and shock setting my blood on fire. Kira snapped and howled, raring to go, and the monster stroked my rib cage—a reminder that it was there, that I was the wolf *bitch* who tore out an alpha's heart.

Footsteps clipped around the room. "Get up." A beat of silence followed, then the sharp snap of Ethan's fingers. "Fucking *get up*, rosebud."

More scrambling, more footsteps—then a squeal and a *smack*, a crunch and a wail, followed by an explosion of *blood* in the air.

I lurched forward.

"What are you doing?"

And stopped, his voice so dangerous and low that it should have been for me, for the enemy at his door.

Not his wife.

Not *my* Rosa.

"Y-you broke my n-nose," the witch told him. From the thickness of her words, the gargle, the wobble and trembles and *blood* and pain she must have been in—she also sounded a little too calm.

No, not calm…

Empty.

"And, what, because we're having a party, the rules don't apply?"

The rules?

What *rules*?

Fabric rustled and floorboards creaked.

"I c-can't go down there like this-s," Rosa insisted. I knew that wobble—that barely keeping it together before the dams *burst* quiver. "Let me use the spell, please, just once—"

"I'll make apologies for your absence." Ethan sniffed, the sound followed by what I guessed was the buttoning of a shirt—or cufflinks, or *something*, like he was fixing the mask before leaving his rosebud here alone. "Tell our guests Aster's being fussy and you're staying with her."

"Please," she choked. "Please, don't h-hurt her—"

"Do I need to explain myself *again*?"

Rosa squealed for the last time. "N-no!"

And I charged.

Kicked open the door so hard its knob got stuck on the wall.

Red bled across the stacked shelves and the leather office chair, the desk that smelled like oak and the empty black wood-burning stove. Kira battled to break free, clawing up my throat, my skin blazing and my chest heaving, when I spotted Ethan looming over Rosa.

Rosa on the floor.

Blood streaming down her face and peppering her dress.

Her nose visibly deformed.

Her tears falling and her mascara running.

Her eyes *terrified*.

"Get *away from her!*"

Out came the chorus of female voices, me and Idunn and Kira and so many more I hadn't met yet, layers and octaves that had screamed through the forest and felled trees and haunted Hawthorne wolves.

His eyes went wide, the whites like dish saucers and growing by the second as I lunged and tackled him, my snarl a war cry.

A promise.

A vow that he wouldn't make it out *alive* if he didn't submit.

We crashed into his desk, pens flying and computer monitor toppling and wood groaning, then rolled to the floor. Ethan put up a mediocre fight, all long, useless limbs and bared teeth, but I overpowered him in a second. Slammed the base of my palm into his nose just right so that it *crunched*. Blood spurted. Bone broke. The warlock howled and arched, then attempted to curl into a sad little ball at my feet, and I settled back on my haunches, disgusted.

The scuffle had lasted fifteen seconds—*maybe*.

Fifteen miserable seconds and he tapped out.

How many *years* had he beaten his mate?

How many times had he broken her nose?

Enough for her to recognize the pain of the break, at least.

"Lyssa, w-wait—"

"Rosa, go get Aster," I growled over my shoulder, unable to look at her *and* keep Kira inside. My girl was out for blood, snarling and snapping and *fighting* to escape.

Kill Ethan.

Protect Rosa.

Whisk Aster away.

If I fell into those watery emerald pools, bloodshot and miserable, I'd lose control.

"We're leaving," I said flatly, hands trembling, adrenaline *pounding*, fueled by Kira's rage and my mates' hunt and everything in between.

Groaning, Ethan squirmed and rolled over, arms moving—reaching inside his disheveled suit jacket.

Nope.

I pinned him on his back, then grabbed his fingers and hauled them out from under the red fabric before they closed around their prize.

Wrenched them as far back as I could so he wailed, then rooted around inside for—

His wand.

I broke his thumb just because—since no one had taught him, he ought to learn wolves didn't put up with *tricks.*

Then I broke his wand, snapping it in the middle with a wince.

Oh.

No fireworks or smoke or anything.

Kind of disappointing that at the end of the day, it was just a stupid stick.

One I tossed aside, the broken bits clattering over the hardwood.

"Ethan?" He tried to roll away, to wiggle like a worm under his desk. Canines bared, I caught him by the chin and forced him to *look* at me. His hazels darted around, desperate not to make eye contact, but I snared them soon enough; gold would always win. "Listen to me..." Tone civil, I squeezed his jaw, *just* to the point of splintering his mandible, and then smiled. "If I see you near Rosa or Aster—if I even *smell* you in Redwood Grove—I'll kill you. Got it?"

He managed a dismal nod, whimpering, eyes welling with fat, glistening tears.

Tears he didn't deserve to shed.

It all made sense now.

Rosa's bandaged fingers—the way she flinched at sudden movements like her *friend* might reel back and strike her. The random bruises. The high necklines and wrist cuffs on her outfits. The way she deferred to her husband—like he had broken her spirit.

"Lyssa—"

"Rosa, *please*, go get Aster." Her gasp made my heart *ache*, but I needed her to move—to leave the room and take her bloodied amber-and-honey scent with her. Kira was *right* there, just below the surface, my vision so sharp and defined it *hurt*. I sounded just as cruel as he did, probably, savage and brutal but for completely different reasons. Voice low, words rough, I was on the brink of going full wolf and tearing this house apart, so, *please, friend, just give me a second to breathe.*

For once, the power in my chest wasn't causing a scene.

Nothing rattled.

Nothing grew.

It waited inside, patient and constant, a faint tickle in my fingertips and a strength in my heart that I really, really needed on a night like this.

Heels scratched over the floorboards behind me. Clumsy, disoriented, Rosa's gait told me she needed medical care as soon as possible, but I waited, still as stone, eyes on her cowering husband, until her footfalls scrambled out the room and down the hall, then echoed up another flight of stairs, hopefully to grab her pup so we could just get out of here.

Reconnect with Lucian and Soren.

Have *them* track down Ewan—because Rosa needed a guard wolf tonight, and once we walked out the front door, it was Captain Kira reporting for duty.

Yeah, my dead goddess powers would probably fare better against a warlock—if this loser was stupid enough to try and take her from me—but if I didn't let Kira out to assess the situation, lick those tears dry, snuffle Aster's hair to confirm the pup was safe, she would never forgive me.

I waited until short, tentative footsteps clicked across the floor above before I finally let go of Ethan's face. Shoved it aside, actually, hoping it gave him whiplash.

Hoping his horrible brain slammed into his skull and got all bruised and angry.

He deserved way worse.

"I don't think I've ever met anyone this pathetic before—and I've known some seriously disappointing humans in my lifetime." I tipped my head to the side, scanning his snotty nostrils, his watery eyes, his quivering lower lip smeared with blood. Reed and Nikki, the priest, the male behind the dumpster... Compared to them, Ethan Perry was a standout. Anyone who brutalized their mate, who *hurt* the mama of their beautiful daughter, ranked somewhere below scat on the wilderness hierarchy. "I guess you learn something new every day."

So beyond *done* with him, I stood and turned, enjoying the way my skirt flared and smacked him in the face.

But then he grabbed it and wrenched it up.

Dove underneath.

Snarling, I whipped around, about to knee him in the face and break that nose for good—and then *pain*.

Gut-wrenching, heart-stopping *agony* in my calf, and I stumbled away with a yelp, frantically gathering all the silvery-white fabric—

He'd stabbed me.

With a stick.

Sharpened to a deadly point, it pierced straight through the meat of my calf and out the other side, the injury bloodless, the effects of the pale wood *instant*.

My knees buckled and hit the floor. Pain shredded my muscles. Black nudged into my line of sight, creeping like a steady fog. Shaking, strength fading, Kira's screechy yowls much, *much* too loud —I tried to raise my hand. Point it at him. Do *something*.

But I could barely lift it above my waist.

The power in my chest, in my fingertips, in my tingling palms and on the tip of my furious tongue sparked, caught—*exploded*. Fire raged in my veins.

And nothing happened.

Nothing.

"Want to learn something *new*, bitch?" Ethan rasped, on his knees, bug-eyed and manic as he shuffled after me. I folded onto my elbow and tried to scoot back, but nothing responded how I expected—especially when he fisted my dress and hauled me across the floor, my bare skin screeching over the wood. He cupped a hand around his ear, demanding an answer, then chuckled when I opened and closed my mouth—and no words came out. "Yggdrasil is an ash tree. Just a big, big magical tree where all the nine realms sit."

What—

He clamped down on my calf under the sea of white, and I screamed, the pain like a branding iron searing up my leg.

The shriek faded fast—but it still ripped my throat apart. Still ushered in the shadows, my vision narrowing, the world around me muffled, so fuzzy and soft.

Except for him.

"The Norse gods travel that tree, its branches, to visit our world from Asgard," Ethan whispered, easing closer, staying in that darkening tunnel as every blink got heavier and heavier. "And when you stab them with a piece of it..." His throaty cackle made me flinch, that voice new and vile and *ugly*. "It's like sticking a shifter with silver. Not many people know that. Those who do usually don't live to tell their secret, but if you're smart enough not to blab..." He then had the nerve to swoop my hair behind my ears and adjust my headband. "Did you learn something new, Lyssa?"

He patted my calf twice, each smack blinding *agony*, and then stood, looming tall and brutal, hands on his narrow hips.

"Night, night, puppy." The warlock guided my eyelids shut, a finger on each. "Thank you for your sacrifice."

And then, not for the first time—*please, please, not the last*—the darkness finally claimed me.

20

SOREN

When we kicked down the front door and stormed the Perry chalet, Lucian and I expected the blood...

But not the silence.

Not the empty rooms across the first floor, the haunting dining hall with its escargot apps half eaten, wine bottles open but full. Stoves off in the kitchen, meal prep abandoned midway through. The vacant ballroom, scents lingering, a reminder of what this night had been before we bailed to hunt leeches—the music stuck on repeat, stuttering and buffering and obnoxious enough that Lucian flung a serving tray at a speaker in the ceiling just to get some relief.

All that trauma in the bond.

The pain.

The fear.

Then *nothing*.

We'd killed our first vamp when the real tidal wave hit. Deep in the snows, racing east and tailing those stupid, taunting blurs, something nailed me in the gut.

Lucian had slowed.

I'd growled.

We swapped glances as wolves, treachery afoot, but zeroed in on

737

the biggest threat first. Back then, we thought two packmates in this chalet was enough—that Lyssa with her powers and Ewan with his rage could handle a crisis without us.

Together, me and the seething brute to my left, both of us just standing in a silent corridor with its too-bright lighting, lost, sniffing, scenting out what the hell had happened here—we took down a vampire. Having learned from the last hunt, we coordinated a stronger attack, better tracking and a swifter, more violent strike. Once we got a hold of him, the other became inconsequential; he didn't come back for his screaming companion, and together, we tore him apart.

First the throat, then cut clear through the spine.

Head gone.

Arms torn off.

Body savaged, just to send a message.

And then we left him there to rot—or be eaten by the predators circling in the shadows, carnivores drawn to the scent of frigid blood and the sounds of a squealing death.

That second wave of hurt struck so much deeper.

Ripping through the pack bond, someone had been *seriously* messed up here, and we'd arrived at the chalet breathless but ready for war.

And now... this.

All this nothing.

"What *happened?*" I muttered, hands on my hips, chest heaving, inner wolf as silent as the house itself—but primed and raring to go after spilling serious blood tonight.

For the best, all that quiet inside, his readiness for *more*, because if we abandoned the hunt and let the adrenaline fade—it was over. Panic and fear would take over, and then I'd be totally useless to the alpha by my side.

Eyes narrowed, nostrils flared, Lucian scanned the hallway one last time, our search of the first floor effectively over, then grunted and headed up the nearby stairs. I followed a few paces behind, watching his six and keeping an eye out for my own.

Upstairs was more of the same, but we quickly tracked Lyssa's scent to an upturned office, the floor smeared with glittery blood.

Hers.

One hundred percent.

Our mate was made of starlight; it made sense she bled it too.

Shit. *Shit, shit, shit, shit.*

My wolf yowled, panic raking my throat, and I shook my hands, flexing them in and out of fists as I struggled to get the terrified fuzzball under control. Lucian, meanwhile, paced the room, sniffing noisily, then flipped the desk over like someone might be cowering beneath it.

Nope.

Nothing.

"Fuck."

"I can't feel Ewan." Classic brain-mouth disconnect, saying whatever the hell came to mind—but I couldn't. Not in the bond and not in the house. Watching Lucian stalk to the dark windows across the room, I shook my head. "Lyssa either."

"We would… *endure* their loss," he growled, clearly more experienced with loved ones dying. "In the bond—you'd know."

"And feeling nothing at all?"

"Magic," the hulking alpha sneered, ripping the curtains closed and rounding on me. "Trickery and bollocks—"

Floorboards creaked upstairs. Our heads snapped up, my wolf settling now that he had something tangible to focus on, and I tracked the groaning wood, like someone shifting their weight between the panels, then uneven stumbling…

Whump.

Then someone crashing to the floor, solid enough to make the walls shake.

Lucian and I shot off like bullets, tearing down the corridor and zipping up another staircase to the third floor—only slowing to assess the bloody handprint smears on the wall. Not glittery this time, but it had a distinct smell: honey and amber.

Rosa.

Darkness engulfed this upper floor, but smell guided us down and around and around, through a maze of hallways to the opposite side of the chalet.

To a room as big as the ballroom, with a domed glass ceiling open to the stars.

With a cradle and a rocking chair. Bookshelves and wooden storage chests. Stuffed toys and blankets and baby powder.

Aster's nursery.

And Rosa curled up in a corner. The witch gasped when we pounded inside, the sight of two naked, raging, sweaty, bloody wolf shifters in the dark probably terrifying—but I saw her clear as day.

The sight of her—made me want to throw up.

Then *rampage*.

"Rosa?"

A split lip. A busted nose. Swollen cheekbones. One black eye— the other so inflamed it had completely closed over. Her earlobes... torn, like someone had ripped those huge earrings out.

She cradled Aster to her chest, the tiny witch gurgling and staring at us, calm and quiet as always, her wide eyes probably seeing *way* more than anyone gave them credit.

Seriously—*what* happened while we were gone?

Tears parachuted down her bloody cheek with the next blink, and I rushed over, *very* aware that she didn't need some shifter's junk in her face, and carefully crouched beside her.

"Holy shit, Rosa," I whispered, taking quick stock of her injuries. Someone had used her face like a fucking punching bag. As far as I knew, magical folk had an arsenal of spells, charms, and potions to heal wounds—but she just sat in them, her nose clearly broken, potentially her left cheekbone as well given the swelling.

Meanwhile, Aster was cute as a button in her purple jammies.

Except for Mom's fresh blood on her cheek. Without thinking, I wiped it off; Rosa wouldn't want to see it there.

"I'm s-sorry," the witch croaked, hugging her pup tight. Blood stained her dress, but it was her voice that struck the deepest—

hoarse and crackly, like someone had *throttled* her and her windpipe needed time to recover.

"Rosa—"

"What did you do?"

Jaw clenched, I glared back at Lucian. The wolf remained in the middle of the room, standing on a baby blue rug with fluffy white clouds all over it. While concern warmed our bond, he seemed better at wading through this gut punch, headed straight for the jugular.

I mean, yeah, I guess—bigger picture.

Rosa had just *apologized*.

What the hell did she have to be sorry for?

She blinked her black eye back at him, the other puffy and bruised—oozing a little. The protective urge Lyssa had mentioned flared in me, but I pushed back, fighting my inner wolf's desire to shepherd her and Aster to safety.

"Rosa." I settled on my heels, wanting to touch her and comfort her and *fix* this. "What happened?"

But Lucian had the right idea: she was a witness.

Her lips wobbled, but she forced them into a smile when Aster twisted back to her. Little hands went for her hair, and Mom just let her fist and yank, tears falling, breath hitching.

"Ethan's f-family belongs to a specific coven," she started, still raspy but loud enough this time that her words carried through the room. "To me, it's a… a cult. *Gyldent Blod*—g-golden blood. I-I didn't know when we—not until we married, but they've been obsessed with becoming the *new* gods f-for centuries."

My blood ran cold, and I braced on the nearby window frame, needing to steady myself or I'd take off running—on a mission to spill *golden blood* wherever I could find it. When that didn't work, however, I closed my eyes and concentrated on her voice, all the while tapping into the pack bond and drawing on Lucian's steadfastness, on his insane ability to keep cool as the ground fell out from under us.

"Do they worship Loki?" he rumbled, that harsh baritone demanding *honesty*.

"No, they don't worship a-any of the old gods." Eyes open, I found Rosa shaking her head, that frail smile still firmly in place for Aster's benefit. "They just w-want what they *have*."

Huh. You'd think warlocks and witches would be chill with the magic in their souls, but apparently not. Apparently, the grass was *always* greener.

Idiots.

"What does that—"

"Three centuries a-ago, the Blods tricked the goddess Idunn," Rosa remarked, leaning heavily into the storyteller role, almost like she was reading to her pup from one of the books on the shelves. She kept it as light and airy and lyrical as her bruised windpipe allowed, fussing with Aster's hair, stroking her chubby cheeks. "They worshipped her—but only to trap her. Brought her f-from Norway to here. Planned to b-build a new colony and force her to plant the trees."

My eyebrows shot up. Trees? The orchard? Lyssa's dreams—

"Why trees?" I pressed, but Lucian connected the dots faster.

"That's the legend, isn't it?" Arms crossed, he marched the perimeter of the circle rug, one foot in the front of the other, head bowed and emotions in check within our connection. "Idunn grows trees with golden apples. One bite and you—"

"You're young again," Rosa finished for him. "Yeah. You can s-start over in your prime. It's how those gods became immortal. They had long lives to start with, but the apples are key. For centuries, they eat the fruit."

And Idunn gave her powers to Lyssa...

Holy. Shit.

"But she died." The witch shrank deeper into the corner when Lucian's sharp wolf gaze landed on her. "I-I don't know how, but she died in these m-mountains." A shaky wave toward the window guided me to the looming silhouette of snow and stone. "And I guess she left some of her power behind in the water... Ethan was r-raised with the mission, generation after generation watching and waiting for her return, and he brought us here to… I'm not… I *couldn't* be initiated because there are other supers in my bloodline. I'm not a pure e-enough witch to be one of the new gods, and I wouldn't w-want to." She sniffed and grimaced, agony searing across her swollen features. "They're h-*horrible*. No respect for the *real* gods at all—"

"What's happening tonight?" Lucian barked, his snarl ricocheting around the room. Rosa hugged Aster tight to her chest as my fellow alpha stalked toward us, the pup squirming and whining, and I held up a hand—which slowed his wrath but didn't stop it. All teeth, he shoved an accusatory finger toward the mountains. "Will they force her to grow the trees?"

Fuck. No wonder Ethan was so intense about the nitty-gritty of Lyssa's powers—that jagweed had even demanded Ewan track her progress in a stupid diary and *give* it to him. He never had, as far as I was aware, and if we hadn't stopped him the night Ewan shared that shitty tidbit, Lucian probably would have gone full rogue wolf and murdered Ethan Perry in his sleep.

In hindsight—should have let it happen.

Now…

Now she…

They…

It's a trap.

All of it. Realization plunked down my back like some demented water torture, and I pushed away with a snarl, shooting to my feet and pacing the length of the wall just to get some of the steam out.

"Worse," Rosa whispered roughly. I stilled. Lucian looked seconds from lunging and dragging her up and slamming her against the wall.

He handled his shit, thankfully.

Not that I would have let that slide or anything.

"They think they can bring her back," the witch told us, nestling Aster under her chin and cupping the back of her head. "Idunn…" She sucked in a sharp breath, setting off the next teary waterfall. "They think they can p-put her *spirit* back in Lyssa's body."

Violence sparked in the bond, Lucian's rage fueling mine—forcing me to pull a total Ewan move and sucker punch the wall. I blew clear through the drywall, the wood, right out the other side.

Every bone in there shattered.

Damn it.

Scowling, I ripped my hand out—just a limp flesh bag at this point—and held it to my chest, the bitter bite of healing bone, skin, and tissue an afterthought. The outside wafted in, bringing with it a rush of freezing air and a few snowflakes.

"I'm sorry," Rosa whimpered. "When I f-found out about her... After Gull River, I-I thought... If I could just keep it a secret until she was strong enough, they wouldn't be able to..." Her lips wobbled so hard the bottom split open again, fresh blood weeping down her chin. "But then you guys told Ethan, and he was so a-angry." She clenched her one eye shut, shuddering. "And I... He... I couldn't *stop* it."

"Have they gone back to the mountains?" Lucian growled, low and deadly, even his point toward the window aggressive. The witch nodded—and he left. Stalked right out of the nursery and vanished into the shadows. I started after him, then hesitated and stopped. No. *Can't walk away from her like this.* Not only would I never forgive myself if I left Rosa here, exposed and vulnerable and so clearly broken, Lyssa would rip me a new asshole if she found out I had abandoned her beaten, bloody friend in this fucking house. So, even as my adrenaline soared and my wolf howled, *murder* brewing like bubbles on a witch's cauldron, I returned to her side and stiffly crouched down.

"Rosa." I grabbed her shoulder this time, *needing* her to hear me —because I'd only say it once. "Get out of here and go to our place." My head's reassuring bob didn't seem to land when she peeked up, but whatever. At least I could say I *tried*. "The spare key is, like, duct-taped under the back porch. Take it, lock yourself in there, and hide with Aster in the basement, okay?"

She scrambled after me when I stood. "Soren, they'll kill you."

"I don't—"

"This is very *dark* m-magic," the witch whispered frantically, on her knees—begging me to stay? "Please, be—"

"I can't leave Lyssa to whatever fucked-up shit they have planned for her—"

"No, no, I know." She sank onto her heels, Aster on her hip, seeming almost relieved that she couldn't sway me. "Just..." The witch lunged onto my wrist, *magic* pulsing in her palm, her eye electric green. "Just cut her loose... I-I'm sure Lyssa can take care of the rest."

I swooped down to kiss the top of her hand, then the back of Aster's head. "Get the hell out of here—and don't look back."

We held each other's gazes for a beat, then both nodded. I helped her up. Steered her toward a bag it seemed she had already started packing...

Then ran.

Fast as my legs could carry me, my inner wolf tearing free before I reached the front door and burst into the freezing night.

Hot on Lucian's trail up the mountain—*war* pounding with every savage beat of my heart.

21

LYSSA

I greeted the orchard with a scream.

Then another.

And another.

Eyes clenched *so* tight—but the tears still raged like liquid fire down my cheeks.

"I know, sweet girl." Idunn sounded small today, her voice mousy, her words weak. "I know it hurts…"

Gasping, I flailed onto my side and groped at the thick grass bed I came to on, blinking but not seeing past the wall of *agony* tearing me apart from the inside. My gown had followed me into her afterlife, and I yanked it up my legs—

No ash wood.

No stake.

Nothing in my calf to account for the *pain*.

Black veins skittered up my legs, disappearing under the thick layers of white and glittery silver. I groped at them with a sob, balanced precariously on my elbow, my whole body trembling—

Kira unconscious and just out of reach.

Not there to greet me today. No licks and nuzzles and whines.

Just—a lifeless body, limp on her side, eyes closed and tongue poking out the front of her muzzle. Adorable under any other circumstances, just a goofy wolf taking a nap. Her chest rose and fell with every deep breath, and I sank onto my back, crying out, the wildfire under my skin burning me alive.

Kneeling at my side, Idunn fussed with my dress, smoothing it, fixing the sequins, twisting the shoulder straps the right way around, her brow knit and her mouth thin and her eyes molten gold.

No whites again.

No irises.

Just pure divinity.

"Why didn't you *tell* me?" I gritted out. No stopping the tears anymore. No damming the breach. Idunn caught the strays on her finger, sweeping them aside, her lips wobbling through a shaky smile.

"No one ever said the gods were kind," she whispered. I hated that line. *Hated* it. Of all the beings in this world, she ought to be kind to *me*.

"Did they..." *Oh, stop—please just stop!* I arched and hissed, the ripping sensation scorching up my thighs and into my belly. "Did they p-put the ash in you too? Is that how you died?"

Am I dying?

One hand clenched at my tummy—at my pup, who deserved a better start than this.

"I died by my own hand," Idunn murmured, tucking my hair, fixing my headband. "I never wanted this for you." The world suddenly darkened behind my clenched lids, and I snapped them open to find her *right* over me, hovering, face-to-face, nose-to-nose, gold to gold. "Sweet little wolf, my Lyssa... You *are* my steward. My vessel."

I tipped my head back, starting to go numb to the pain, to the gentle breeze—to everything. My lips buzzed and my fingertips tingled, but not with power.

No, like I was...

I was...

I blinked at the sky.

Dark blue today.

Streaked with mauve and deep, dark shades of red.

Sunset in the orchard.

Never seen it before.

Always sunrises—

"I willed my life and my power into that river with a *condition*," the goddess whispered, pinching my chin and steering it down again. "Only the worthy may take it on. The grove is *worthy*, nature in all her glory. I still feed the valley—make it strong, make it blossom." Her nail stabbed into my skin when I started to fade, eyes drifting shut, and I snapped back to the moment with a sharp breath. Idunn tipped her head left, right, and then descended, our noses nudging, her lips brushing mine. "From my bones, the earth thrives. But so much power—so much potential. *You* are its keeper." A sleight of hand and she cupped my jaw, shaking me, trapping me in her gold. "Do you understand?"

"*No.*"

"You don't desire it," the goddess stressed, her voice splitting in two—one inside my skull, the other in the orchard. One a whisper, one a deep, guttural monster that sang to my wild. "So you will have it." Her forehead pressed to mine, her breath cold as it fanned my lips. "You are *proven*. You have endured, Lyssa, and, listen…"

Then she slapped me.

Just as darkness clawed into the corners of my eyes, spiderwebs stretching, making themselves at home, Idunn *struck* me hard enough to scare it all away. With a strangled wail, I pushed onto my elbows, heart about to leap from my chest, the pain suffocating— and still I *breathed*.

In a prim kneel, posture perfect, hands on her thighs, sapphires on her shoulders, Idunn nodded.

"My girl, my darling wolf—you will endure *again*."

Face scrunched, I bore down, fighting the burn.

Maybe I didn't want to *endure* again.

Maybe I just wanted it over and done with.

Maybe I was sick of always falling flat on my face and struggling to get back up—

No. My heartbeat stopped that train of thought before it left the station.

No-no. No-no. No-no.

Faster than usual, yeah, but a constant rhythm, a reminder that I was very much *alive* no matter what they threw at me.

Of all the creatures who drank from Gull River—I was built for this.

Survival.

Steel snapped around my wrist, *squeezing,* and I clawed at Idunn with a whine, the pain so jarring and cruel and *sharp*—only then noticing the black snaking up my arm, her grip the one thing stopping it from spreading further.

"They *tricked* me," she hissed. "Trapped me. Stole me across an ocean so I would make *them* gods." She then hauled me up and shook my arm, her knuckles white, her talons slicing into my wrist. "There are no gods but *us,* Lyssa. Do you understand?"

Us?

I wasn't a goddess.

I wasn't Idunn or Loki or whoever else—I was just *me.*

"I..."

Black dribbled from my veins to her skin, like she was leeching out the poison—letting it pitter-patter into her orchard. Idunn pressed harder, bleeding me faster. "I spared the world their cruelty. Do it again. You are *worthy...* Remember that, my sweet wolf. In *your* bones, you are the answer to the bargain I struck with your realm. My power, my blessing, in exchange for a steward who could keep it. Who they couldn't *control*—warriors at her back, loyal to the end."

I shook my head just as she shook me. No, no, no, *no.*

Yes, yes, yes, yes, the goddess echoed back, her voice on the inside again, sweet and soft as morning dew.

"The world waited so long." Her grip finally loosened, and black blood puddled between us, sprinkling my gown and hers. "But it had to be just right. *My* choice. My wishes. My declaration as I poured my life into the river. *You* made the apples grow." When she cradled my chin this time, it was so gentle. Idunn sniffed, her full gold eyes welling, and *I* caught the damp spilling down her cheeks. "I am dust, Lyssa. I am shadow. You... *You*..." Taking a breath, she beamed at me through the tears, and through the *agony*, her love soared. "You—"

Oh, youuuuuuu...

Masculine chuckles sprinkled down my back. Fluttered in my ear. *Licked* my neck.

Fingers tiptoed across my skull—then a *rip* like he'd gotten ahold of my hair again, tearing me from the gold, from the sunset, from *her*...

And back into the black I fell, screaming all the way home.

22

LYSSA

"Welcome back, wolf."

Ugh. So *sick* of waking up in strange places—

But this wasn't strange.

No.

My nostrils flared with my first gasping breath, absorbing the mineral tinge of damp stone, the scent of honey water, the clash of light and dark behind my lids.

I've been here before.

Kira groaned and lifted her sleepy head inside, drugged and dazed, her energy so heavy it was a fight to open my eyes and keep them that way. When I did, my head slumped to the left, neck stiff and grumpy—and I tumbled straight into *green* circled with gold, blazing bright. A straight nose. Thin, seductive lips that peeled back like curtains on a stage, opening to dangerous canines and straight pearly whites.

Loki.

Grinning, the god tapped my nose with—

Oh.

Oh.

With the stake he must have pulled from my calf, the ash wood slick with glittery blood, its end razor-sharp. I flinched when it touched down in a gentle *boop*—that was the source of the pain, the fire burning me alive in Idunn's world. Right there, in his hand.

My body still ached, but more so from whatever hard surface I was currently stretched across. The longer I stared at him, the more my senses settled into reality, smells clearer, sounds sharper, running water coursing behind Loki's crouched figure.

He was... below me, somehow.

Hunkered down like a frog, chin resting on—obsidian.

A smooth, cool obsidian table.

"I think," he whispered, trailing a finger in a wobbly line through my blood on the stake, "you're worth saving." He then slapped the ash to my lips when I tried to move my thick tongue—tried to murmur *something*, everything still waking up and shaking off the poison—and pressed the wood closer like a finger to keep me quiet. "*Don't* make a fool of me."

Kira rumbled and huffed, mildly insulted that *we* would embarrass *him*, then stretched inside. The twist and flex of her muscles rippled through me, and I followed in her footsteps, rolling my ankles and shoulders, bending my fingers, working my jaw as I rolled away from Loki and stared straight up.

To the roof of a cave.

The cave—the place where it all began.

Gull River.

Perfect.

Awesome.

Always wanted to come back here for some dramatic showdown with the baddies, just like the movies.

Voices murmured somewhere nearby, volumes spiking at random but the words incoherent, and I finally let my head fall to the right.

Ewan.

I jolted, flailing the rest of the way over onto my side, eyes wide, heart pounding.

There, beside me on what I now figured was an altar—my midnight mate.

In chains, silver crisscrossing his body, an ornate collar clamped around his neck. Blood oozed from the open sores, the silver burning, my dragging senses finally recognizing the smell of burnt flesh. Naked and unconscious, he lay beside me with his eyes shut and his lips parted in a pained grimace, the rise and fall of his chest slow.

Too slow.

Too jerky, stuttering every other breath.

Someone had left a knife in his gut—maybe the same jerk who had carved all those symbols across his body, the strange alphabet copied from the silver collar.

Kira attempted a howl, her song hoarse but determined, like she could reach our mate from all the way inside—wake him like Sleeping Beauty.

Loki *sighed*, the sound long and luxurious, and when I glanced back, he stretched the length of the altar, arms out in either direction, his chin on my thigh, his hungry gaze on Ewan.

"A blood offering—to the gods." Another huff, then a big eye roll and a click of his tongue. "Pity. Been *ages* since I've got a proper one."

Biting the insides of my cheeks, I stared at his stupid, handsome, disappointed face.

Then smacked my whole hand against it and shoved him off.

Just—so not in the *mood* for another dramatic male in this equation, honestly.

"Take *me* instead of her."

Soren? My heart tripped over itself for the next few *whumps*, and I pushed onto my elbow, finally taking a proper sweep of a cave that was empty last time. Yeah, the same spotlights were still here, holes in the mountain so perfectly round they had to be god-touched— three, two in the walls and one in the ceiling, bringing in a flood of white light. Gull River cut across the space, trickling down the soaring stone behind me and coursing to the opposite wall, then disappearing, headed deeper into the mountain and off to feed the valley.

"From my bones, the earth thrives. But so much power—so much potential. You are its keeper."

But the crowd of witches and warlocks in sweeping golden cloaks?

New.

The obsidian altar?

Definitely new.

Torches around the exterior, a worktable with a big shallow bowl and bunches of dried herbs, the slitted entrance that you had to crawl through replaced with a huge ugly hole—*very* new.

I knew this crowd.

Even with their simple black masks, profiles and backs to me, I *knew* them.

They'd asked questions all night, pretended to be so interested in me for me.

Hampton Coven.

And behind the table with its tools—knives and ice cream scoopers and crystals—stood the most pathetic man I'd ever met.

Ethan Perry, all fixed up from my attack, still wearing his bright red suit like he was Lucifer incarnate, his golden cloak splayed open to expose all that fine tailoring.

And—*ugh, come on.*

A crown on his head.

A literal golden crown with sapphires and a shiny apple in its center.

Yeesh.

Panic clenched its cruel fist around my throat when I finally noticed my other mates.

Lucian and Soren, swathed in silver chains, naked, on their knees in front of that table and all its ritual horrors.

Beaten and bloodied—but still holding their heads up high.

I should be screaming.

Wailing.

Begging.

Fighting.

Instead, an unfamiliar calm swept over me—a golden river without the treacherous rapids. Even Kira dipped her toes in, hackles up and teeth bared but heartbeat calm. Beating, beating, beating with mine, my vision sharpening, both of us one voice, one being, assessing the situation with a calculating eye and an unfrazzled mind.

Power bloomed in my chest.

Anger.

Rage.

Only nothing shook. The world stayed still. No one gasped or whipped around as the *feeling* centered me—made me strong.

No.

Not this time.

It all lived inside now, safe in my chest, in that bottomless well, fueling the forge.

"I don't *need* you," Ethan sneered, adopting some weird lofty accent suddenly—unless that had been his normal voice all along, but it sounded like a cheap imitation of Lucian. "I need *her*. Have you got a goddess inside you? No? Then fuck off with your offers, mongrel."

Wow.

Wow.

I am so gonna murder this guy.

If, you know, Lucian and Soren didn't get to him first, so close and yet so far from his throat draped in all that silver, their wrath crackling in our bond like an unchecked wildfire.

But it didn't really touch me.

I *felt* them, yeah, but for once I could… set it aside. Accept it, but not let the raging emotions of my fated mates drive me.

"The goddess will feast on your hearts," Ethan continued, rising to his full height and sounding so snooty it made my skin crawl. The golden crowd chuckled as my mates snarled, and their conductor gestured for them to get *louder* with a wave of his hands. "Yes, yes, *that* is the only thing you're good for now."

Okay—enough.

Shaking my head, I reached over Ewan and grabbed his thick collar. Silver sizzled into my fingers, my palm, but I'd felt worse pain in every way, this ache like a sunburn on a bad day. With a few good jerks, the collar broke free, spurting a fresh, hot wave of Ewan's blood up my arm, and I sat up properly, tossing the filthy thing in the river.

"Hey…"

The jeers and laughter died down when one of the witches caught me, pointing with her wand, and I sniffed dismissively, all eyes on me as I sat there and kneaded out the kink at the base of my skull. Scrambling around the ritual table, Ethan skirted my mates in a wide arc, a new wand clutched in his bony fist, and then slowed, struggling to raise it when his wide eyes soared past me.

"Who… are you?"

Over my shoulder, Loki loitered around like a mildly entertained bystander, one hand in his pocket, the other twirling the ash stake. Dressed in a svelte three-piece suit, black like his nails, like the runes inked in his fingers, he kept it casual with his flaming-red hair in a loose ponytail, wispy bits flaring around his face.

Yeah, probably pretty jarring to find a strange god crashing your…

Uh…

Whatever this was.

Loki flashed one of his scary smiles, full of teeth and malice, then held up the bloodied stake—shook it a little to steer Ethan's attention there. A few golden cloaks bolted, their footsteps echoing through the mountain passage, out to the caves covered in bat poop.

"You know me, warlock," he drawled. "We've met in your nightmares."

Before I could get a read on Ethan's horror, really commit his expression to memory, Ewan groaned, then gulped down a breath.

Slowly, his bloodshot eyes fluttered open, and I crouched over him, stroking his face and blinking back the wave of tears.

Okay, so I'd managed to keep my cool for the most part—a little slipup when my mate showed he was *alive* got a pass.

"L-Lyssa?"

"I'm here," I whispered with a nod, my smile wobbly, my next blink dropping a tear onto his forehead with a *plop*. "I've got you. You're okay."

His blinks were labored and uneven, left eye opening more than the right, gaze totally unfocused as it whizzed around.

"I love you."

But that was clear as day.

My heart skipped a beat again, and I showed him just how much *I* loved him by peeling the silver chains from his chest, ignoring the cloying melted flesh stretching from him to the links, the scent of blood and trauma.

"I know, brown eyes," I murmured, tossing this set off the altar, the burns on my hands sealing in a flash, the pain temporary. "Me too."

"*Stop.*" Ethan's bellow bounced around the cave, making the crowd shuffle and whisper. My kneeling mates, meanwhile, were already subtly and stealthily working to free each other from the silver, but their agony cut straight to the bone. My gaze flitted between them and this warlock on the verge of a tantrum, hoping they felt my resolve in the bond—that I was coming for them no matter what. All this was just a blip in our love story. *I swear*. Ethan, meanwhile, had the balls to march a few feet closer and level his wand at Loki's chest. "Stop all of this!"

Lips pursed, Loki glanced at the ash stake—then lit it on fire with nothing but his mind. Power *pulsed* in the air like the invisible shock waves of an explosion, ruffling my hair and sending a few more of Ethan's flock running. I shielded my bloody mate with my body, bowed across him, a hand over his eyes to protect them from the swirling debris.

Flames gobbled up the stake, my blood—turned it all to real ash, just black dust that Loki sprinkled on the floor with a scowl.

"All this..." Ethan licked his lips, gaze darting, gears turning. "All this is for *you*, my lord. Loki, father of wolves and monsters. King of lies. It's for *all* of you." He motioned to the river, which I suddenly remembered smelled like sewage to everyone else. Sulfur and filth. Urine and vomit. To my senses, it was still honey, still shimmering starlight and glittery diamonds—because it was *made* for me. "Idunn must return... for the apples, of course. For *you*. I'll put her back in her physical body, and she—"

"Ah, but you see, there's a hiccup." Loki held up a finger, silencing Ethan's sputtering before it got any traction. "I'm afraid... you're just not *skilled* enough to do any of that." Head cocked, his pleasant tone vanished. "Who are *you* to speak for a goddess? Little Idunn is quite happy where she is now—and we've a new gardener."

All eyes on me again, huh?

Something in the way he said that...

We've a new gardener.

Poof, connection sparked between us. Me and Loki, wolf and trickster, like we were... on similar footing.

Definitely not *even*, but closer than before.

I didn't trust it for a second, of course, but if he considered *me* pack—I'd take it for now.

Stares boring into me from all sides, I slid off the altar, the leg that took the brunt of the ash stake tender for the first few steps. Stretching side to side, I gave Kira a little extra *pull* in her muscles, her adrenaline and mine entwined but settled.

The calm before the storm.

"We... You..." Ethan adjusted his lopsided crown, that vigorous headshake knocking it off its perch—and then the idiot fired a shot at a *god*.

Bang. Red light whizzed like a shooting star and nailed Loki in the chest, exploding on impact, his lesser magic flaring over the black suit.

Gone in a flash.

The warlock met my gaze fleetingly, and I smirked as I peeled another chain from Ewan's limp, bloody, naked body. *Idiot.*

To my left, Loki slowly looked down at where he'd been hit. Smoothed a hand over the supple fabric and readjusted his tie. Across the cave, more golden cloaks fled, as if sensing they were *not* at the top of this food chain.

Because, totally unharmed, suddenly Loki *laughed.*

It started with a slow build, soft chuckles to rough barks to savage *howls.* Humor didn't touch him, didn't so much as flicker in his eyes, the gold around the green like dancing hellfire. Demonic and guttural, the sounds boomed off the walls, layered and rich like *ten* Lokis stood there cackling. Many in the crowd covered their ears. Ewan grimaced, trying to block the noise with his shoulder, and Lucian and Soren huddled into each other, riding out the assault together.

The kinship sharpened between us, my own wrath similar, full of voices and harmonies, good *and* evil ripping up my throat.

As Ethan scampered back to his stupid table, picking through herbs and rearranging crystals, I delicately peeled the last of Ewan's restraints away, tossing them onto the pile of silver at my feet. Then, my gown speckled with mud and blood, I wrapped both hands around the hilt of the dagger in his belly. Our gazes locked. I arched an eyebrow, and Ewan closed his eyes tight, then nodded.

He bellowed when I ripped it out, his pain affecting all of us in the bond, Lucian and Soren snarling, Kira whimpering.

I chucked that in the river too, my skin mending, and swooped in to help my mate sit up.

"Easy," I murmured, Loki's laughter finally fading, half the scattered torches extinguished. Looping an arm around his broad shoulders, I gently eased my mate's legs over the edge of the altar, then braced him when he lurched hard to the side. "Easy, love. Take your time."

Defiance flashed in his gaze, half hickory, half a sunset on fire, his wolf struggling to take over. Jaw gritted, Ewan tried to shimmy off the obsidian himself, but I forced him back, taking an exaggerated breath that he had no choice but to copy.

"You're healing." Cupping his strong jaw, stroking all the sharp, beautiful angles of his face, I smiled and nodded to the once open wounds, now just waxy pink memories. "Give it a minute at least."

Only four golden cloaks left when I went for Lucian and Soren —and one sprinted off when our eyes clashed. Ethan, however, had the nerve to get between a she-wolf and her mates, leveling his wand at my chest with a tsk and a scowl.

I raised my weapon in kind, arm outstretched, palm up, and drew from the well.

Power tingled in my fingertips.

Visions danced across my mind's eye.

And his new wand sprouted black rose heads at the tip—thorns along the shaft. The warlock dropped it with a hiss, little red droplets blooming on his palm.

Soren and I made eye contact briefly, my blond mate studying me over Lucian's heaving shoulders. My mountain man stayed locked on the threat—but I nodded to Soren, and his head dipped back, understanding flowing between us.

Concession.

Acceptance.

He was ready to just let me do my thing.

And I *would*.

Shoulders back, I stared down the three remaining golden cloaks, then tipped my head to the side, daring them to *do* something with those trembling wands. No one said a word, the cave silent except for the crackling torches and the ever-present *rush* of running water. One found his nerve, his lips parting—but I took a single leisurely step forward and they scattered like headless chickens. This way and that, knocking into each other, throwing elbows, *fighting* to get through this new door first.

I flinched at the *thunk* of a giant tome landing on Ethan's ritual table, disrupting the herb bunches and knocking over the crystals. The warlock shoved his shallow bowl aside—to collect blood and guts, maybe—and wrenched the book open, then frantically peeled the thick pages apart, most of them sticking, his fingers shaking.

Searching for answers in the faded ink.

I turned my attention elsewhere, to the thunder of fleeing footsteps. Slowly, calmly, I sank to my knees, then smoothed my hands over the cool ground. Closed my eyes. Drank *deep* from the diamond well. Asked Kira what we ought to do—let them go... or punish them.

Punish them.

Or they'll never learn.

Mouth quirked, I splayed my fingers wide and let the power flow, like tugging the cork out of a bottle and tipping it on its head. The dark winding corridors played out like a movie reel, memories flashing, my awareness of this wild space so much *better* than theirs.

Shrieks erupted far away.

Screams echoed through the mountain.

I saw it unfold like it was *right* here in front of me—the thorny vines like booby traps, dropping from above and twisting out of the ground. Roping around ankles and snaring around throats. Tightening, tightening, tightening, strangling the life out of them, Loki's laughter haunting the corridors—just like those golden cloaks *laughed* at my bleeding mates, at the silver slicing their skin, at their pained growls and desperate pleas.

My eyes snapped open.

Lucian and Soren studied the doorway, torch flames a good three feet high on either side. Ethan had his nose in that book, teeth bared in a fear grimace—because not all smiles in the animal kingdom were *happy*.

And the screams...

Oh, the screams.

Even if one or two escaped my thorny beasties, the local covens would *know* not to mess with the Redwood wolves.

Because there was a goddess in their midst, and she didn't take kindly to jerks hurting her mates.

Speaking of which—

"P-please understand," Ethan croaked, backing away from his table, his herbs, his book, his crystals, as I hurried over to Soren and Lucian. "I did this for my daughter—"

"You did it for yourself," Lucian countered, snarling when I peeled the silver from his shoulders, carefully unwinding it all the way down to his bound wrists. "*New* god."

"If she can be a new god—" Ethan jabbed a finger my way as I moved on to Soren, my skin flayed, the pain nothing. "—why not me?"

Before any of us could answer, Loki snorted. All eyes darted in his direction, and I found the god hovering next to Ewan, squinting at the waxy skin on his abdomen where the carved symbols once sat, healing fast and his overall color perking up.

"Because you can't even *cast* properly. Do you know what you spelled here?" He tapped Ewan's torso, jabbing at one of the last sigils to fade away. My midnight mate twitched and flashed his teeth.

Loki *winked* like it positively tickled him—like Ewan was just a pup throwing his newfound strength around.

Then he rounded on Ethan with a sneer, his venom splashing throughout the cave, all these males wilting.

It made me stand just a little taller, the last of Soren's bindings gone, my flayed skin knitting back together.

"You Golden Bloods have always thought yourselves so *clever*, but this is power beyond your reach." Loki took a menacing step toward Ethan, and the warlock scrambled back a good five, tripping over his own feet on the sixth and tumbling onto the banks of Gull River. He rolled away fast, gagging, and pushed onto his hands and knees. Loki stilled, appraising this mess of a man with his hands clasped behind his back, his head cocked, his movements wolfish enough to spark recognition in the pack bond. "The gods didn't *choose* you, Ethan Bernard Perry. It's as simple as that."

Lucian and Soren loomed behind me suddenly, on their feet and healing, prowling, eyes locked on prey that was barely worthy of the title. A hand curved over my shoulder, and I glanced at my sweetest mate, Soren's amber eyes blazing, his gaze catching what was left of the dancing firelight around the cave. A slight lift of his brow, and I heard him in my head.

Are you okay?

Smoothing my hand over his, I gave him a little squeeze and a nod.

Because I was.

This wasn't the chaos of killing the Hawthorne alpha.

The fear.

The terror of what I'd just done, blood-soaked and panicked.

This was a calculated hit—neutralizing a petty threat before it did something stupid.

Said threat shot up and sprinted for the doorway, but I beat him to it. An intentional wave of both arms, hands fisting the air, *dragging* down like pulling out a projection screen—and the doorway was no more.

Just a wall of thick, spiky branches threaded together, strong and unbreakable.

Ethan whipped around *just* before he crashed into the deadly points, then raised his hand.

"Don't make me hurt them, Lyssa."

Lucian shifted by my side, soaring over me in his scarred wolf form, deadly teeth out, saliva dripping, *hungry* for warlock flesh.

"I don't need a wand to cast," Ethan added, nervously eyeing Lucian, then a shifted Soren—then way behind me, the cave a sauna now that all three of my mates had let their wolves free. "My magic m-might not work on *him*, but it does on them. Just let me leave and we can forget all this."

Soren lunged, but I caught the tip of his tail.

Didn't pull, of course, but that slight contact stopped him dead in his tracks. Claws clicked over stone, and while I waited for Ewan to join with the others, I lifted my hand—a silent request to *wait*.

Not a command.

Not an order.

I wasn't their mistress with these powers.

We were still *equals*.

I just needed to…

Kira needed to…

Licking my lips, I gathered my bloody skirts and strolled closer, swaying with every step, watching the fire glint off the sequins. Wordlessly, I walked right up to this warlock who had tricked us— who had been welcomed into our home, into our *pack*, with open arms.

Who beat his wife.

Who wanted to rip Idunn from her paradise.

Who planned to sacrifice my mates and feed her their hearts— her in *my* body.

"Seriously," I said, keeping things light and conversational as this stick insect trembled before me. I looked him up and down, then sighed. "I've never met *anyone* this pathetic before."

Kira huffed, her bloodlust soaring, our adrenaline spike resonating in the others sharp and visceral enough that they *snarled* and snapped their teeth.

Smiling sweetly, I reeled back—and punched him as hard as I could in the throat.

My knuckles shattered his windpipe, and Ethan Perry crashed to his knees, gasping. He clawed at his neck, eyes wide, mouth gaping like a fish out of water.

And I turned my back on him for the last time.

As I strolled away, my mates attacked.

All three prowled in as a unit, low to the ground, ears back, the cave serenaded by a symphony of growls and snarls—and then screams.

On my way to Loki's side, I closed Ethan's weathered old book. Brushed the herbs on the ground. Tossed the crystals into Gull River.

Knocked the ritual table on its back and kicked that ceremonial bowl across the stone.

The old god watched on, smile manic again, his greedy gaze drinking all this in. His tongue flicked out, a snake tasting the air, and as soon as I stood beside him, both of us facing the carnage, he dug into his suit jacket and groped around.

Then tapped the top of my hand.

I raised it, palm up, and there he placed golden seeds in clumps of three—nine total—and closed my fingers over to protect them. Kira sniffed deep, her interest in the little golden droplets making me shiver.

"Plant them here," he rumbled, our eyes locked. "Protect the fruit. Eat it. Feed it to your mates and offspring if you want. Live forever."

Green and gold slid to the bloodbath, sparkling with wicked delight as my pack tore Ethan Perry apart. Slowly. Thoroughly. In all the ways that made his suffering *last*, his wails gargled and thick now, his insides on the out but his heart still beating.

Loki then ducked low, swooping right in my face, his breath frosty. "You'll be seeing more of us in the future."

Us.

Gods.

Gods who needed the golden fruit from the trees these seeds would grow to stay young for all eternity.

I swallowed hard, cradling the seeds to my chest, and watched him amble off—dip the toe of his fancy leather shoe in Gull River, then eye the bright hole in the ceiling.

"Tell my fellow gods," I said over my pack's brutal chorus, needing to catch this trickster before he disappeared again, "that they are more than welcome in Redwood Grove." Loki went deathly still, his profile severe, his eyes locked on the light above. "That they can eat the fruit anytime—so long as they keep the peace."

Loki slowly looked at me, eyebrows up, then laughed, his silky chuckles fluttering around the cave like butterflies in grotesque contrast to Ethan's death rattle, and vanished into thin air.

23

LYSSA

Seated on the last of the basement stairs, I clinked the two chilled bottles together, waiting. One sparkling cider, one champagne, they looked nearly identical with their wax seals and fancy labels—easy to get them confused.

Important that I didn't.

This pup in my belly was too young for champagne.

Laughter erupted upstairs, explosive and warm, fueled by liquor and New Year's cheer. Kira tippy-tappied around inside, impatient, eager to get back to the hoard of extended family, footsteps crashing from one side of the house to the other as teeny Acker pups stayed up way, way past their bedtime. I tipped my head back, grinning, and tracked the movement, gauging how heavy the footfalls were— light for the kids, thunderous for the adults wrangling them.

Kira snorted and nosed at me, adrenaline prickling my limbs, coaxing me to sprint up these very stairs and join the fun.

"Be patient," I muttered, scowl directed at my forehead. The basement was the only quiet place in the house, totally off-limits to guests, from the cinema room to the wine cellar to—

A door opened at the end of the hall.

To Rosa's temporary bedroom.

The witch slipped out, rocking a silver sequinned dress that hugged her curves, leggings transparent and heels high. Curls extra aggressive tonight, she slowly—*so* slow and quiet—shut the door behind her, crouched down by the knob, both of us holding our breath...

Click.

Closed.

We waited another ten seconds before she straightened and rounded on me with a groan, dramatically wiping the sweat that wasn't there off her forehead.

Her face perfect again.

No broken nose. No shattered eye socket. No busted cheekbone or split lip or ugly black bruises.

For years, her mate beat her. After we trudged home from the mountains, bloody but together, safe in each other's arms, my mates and I found Rosa cowering in the cinema room, Aster asleep in her arms.

There, on the couch, through tears and grief, she told us *everything.*

Every horrible, disgusting, *pathetic* thing one mate could do to another.

It began with demanding expectations and harsh corrections if they weren't met just after they got married.

Then verbal abuse.

Mental, emotional—sexual.

The beatings started roughly four years ago, the rest a slow build, escalating eventually to *that*, and by then my friend, this beautiful soul, was so damaged that she had just accepted his cruelty.

Accepted that she wasn't allowed to use healing spells or creams —because whatever he had done to her, no matter how brutal, had been *deserved.*

Scum.

Absolute *pond* scum.

We'd left his bones in the bat cave, amongst the sticky white droppings and twittering chirps, for the vermin to pick clean.

"Okay," Rosa *Marcus* whispered, her ex-husband's last name ash on the wind. "I think she's finally asleep."

Then, she plopped the plastic silver tiara on her head while I grinned. Soren's mom had handed them out after dinner—tiaras for the girls, crowns for the boys, tonight a very special night indeed. Nothing fancy. Just dollar store trinkets. Every last wolf, witch, and fox in this house had put theirs on, even my midnight mate, who would have thought something so cheap might damage his skin just a few short months ago.

More crashing footsteps boomed upstairs, and we both stilled, eyes following the direction of the chaos, then looked back at the door.

Nothing.

Not a peep.

Goodness. Little Aster was the star of the show lately, Acker wolves just as obsessed with pups as me, and she had been spoiled rotten for days. Tonight, however, she refused to go down. No matter how tired and whiny, no matter how many of us rocked her, she just would—not—sleep.

Until now.

And now Mama Rosa was *free*.

In more ways than one.

No more Golden Bloods in our territory.

No more Ethan.

No more vampires hired by the warlock to kidnap me on Samhain—brought back for an encore to distract my mates on Yule.

Rival packs had also backed way off, almost like they sensed something bigger and badder protected Redwood Grove these days.

"Here," I whispered, passing the champagne bottle and shuffling over to free some space on the stairs. Rosa accepted with both hands and hunkered down beside me; one swish of her wand and a soft murmur had the red wax curling at the ends of both bottles, making it way easier for us to tear into these babies. She just knew, without me saying a word, that I'd want to keep mine as a souvenir, a memento of the best holiday season *ever*.

One that had started rocky and terrifying, bloody and brutal —sure.

But after that?

It was everything I'd ever wanted.

"Cheers." Rosa offered her bottle, and we clinked their long necks, then drank. Bubbles tickled the back of my throat, the cider *very* appley and maybe a little on the nose—but it was way too delicious for me to care about that anymore.

Apples were about to become a massive part of our lives going forward; might as well embrace them now.

Just like Rosa embraced her champagne, old habits dying hard; only now that Aster was out for good, motherhood responsibilities on the back burner, did she indulge. Hopefully, time would help with that—time, and the sale of the Perry chalet. She put the house on the market Christmas Eve and planned to buy something small in the village.

But Ewan put his foot down.

No. She'd have a custom cottage for her and Aster *here*, near us— near her pack.

Because my mates had offered her the position of Redwood Pack witch. Just like Lucian's old pack, she now had a formal title, vows exchanged to protect *us* and our bloodline with her magic.

In turn, she had four wolves—one with goddess-level rage—to watch over her and Aster for the rest of their days.

Soren had roughed out a patch of land in his family's old maple grove. Blueprints were already underway, permits drafted for city planners to approve, construction set to start in the spring. By fall, she would have her *own* home, the heart of the new Marcus coven.

Until then, she had a spacious guest room and an en suite bath and big ol' house at her disposal.

A wolf who loved her like a sister.

Males who would rip literally *anyone* apart if they threatened her.

And, you know, all of Ethan's businesses. One thing she *didn't* need from us was money.

Protection. Support. Space.

All her scars were on the inside now, and if anyone understood working through trauma one step at a time, it was our pack.

"Oh, gods." Rosa lurched forward, champagne dribbling down her chin, her emeralds wide. "What time is it?"

"No idea." Another burst of chaos from upstairs had us both glancing up, little feet pitter-pattering, then squeals and a *whump* and laughter. Chuckling, I grabbed her hand and got us both to our feet. "But that sounds like our cue."

Fingers loosely threaded, each of us clutching a giant bottle just for ourselves, we jogged upstairs together—slower than Kira wanted from me, but Rosa's heels did *not* lend themselves to sprints. My stockinged feet, meanwhile, slipped all over the place tonight, my New Year's Eve dress the golden twin to Rosa's silver. At this point, however, my feet and ankles were a bit swollen—thanks, pregnancy, for some serious bodily nonsense—and I just couldn't be bothered to put on shoes when the party was happening in my own home.

We stumbled out the door at the top of the stairs and, *boom*, crashed right into Soren's dad on his way back from the nearby bathroom.

"Come on, little ladies, or you'll miss the fireworks," Tomas Acker chided, smelling like the lavender soap I'd stocked there and sounding like the sweet, soft, aging wolf I'd met in person just last week. A wolf who looked like Soren with more greys and lines, his skin a little leathery after vacationing in Europe and Africa for most of the year…

Who had scooped me into the biggest bear hug when I'd gone for a handshake that first night, trying to not overstep my boundaries. Who hugged me tight and said I could call him Dad if and when I wanted.

Who really *felt* like a dad, his energy calm and comforting, his patience endless, his humor dry and his inner wolf more like Lucian than Soren, preferring to hang back and watch over his pack—even when most of his pups had packs of their own now.

Mari Acker, meanwhile, was a little more particular. Soren's mom had swept into this house under the impression that she was here to *fix* everything, rearranging cabinets and moving furniture, until Soren reminded her that there was already an alpha she-wolf.

And she didn't want to get on her bad side.

From there, the older matriarch slowed down and backed off— but then charged full steam ahead whenever I went to her with questions.

Which I did a lot.

Because it seemed to make her happy to teach me both wolf and woman things. The wolf stuff I had down by now, but I still smiled and nodded, my heart full because *she* was in her element mothering the rest of us.

Fortunately, her intensity shifted elsewhere once Soren's sisters arrived a few days ago, shacking up in the village with their mates and pups but very much *here* for the last night of the year.

Giggling, Rosa and I let this huge wolf usher us toward the kitchen—where the noise *really* ramped up, full of Ackers and their mates. Young pups raced around, dressed in their nice clothes just like the adults but most of them taking after their uncle with some serious food stains on shirts and pants.

Shifters spilled from the kitchen-dining area into the sunken living room, the fire going strong despite each one of us burning like a walking furnace. Six Acker she-wolves. Six of their mates. Five pups, all under the age of ten. Soren's parents, with Tomas veering off to separate two of his grandsons when their brawl under the dining table got a little too rough. Jocelyn on the couch with Soren's mom, chatting away, drunk as a skunk and very cheery.

Lucian at the island talking meat temperatures with one of the she-wolf mates—Brian? Alan? Hard to keep so many names straight these days.

Soren whizzed around everyone, his energy manic since his siblings showed up, his niece perched precariously on his shoulders and squealing up a storm, arms out like airplane wings.

Last night, the chaos had been out there, across the eastern forests and into the mountains, all of us on a massive multi-pack run. Twenty-three wolves—and one fox. Bonding. Connecting. Meeting as wolves, the rest acknowledging me and my mates— respecting the authority we had regardless of age and bloodline. Our pasts didn't matter. To them, *we* were the Redwood wolves, and our word was law.

I'd never experienced anything so beautiful.

And to know I had finally found my pack, my *people*, my friends and family—

It still brought a tear to my eye.

Spurred by Kira's loving howl and all these stupid pregnancy hormones, I turned away, just for a few seconds, to wipe off the damp and compose myself, and when I faced the mingling crowd, full of laughter and conversation, every surface covered in *food*, I spotted Ewan at the back door.

Sliding it open.

Stepping inside.

Cheeks rosy and four buckets of chilled champagne bottles, one for each adult, waiting by his side.

Thumb and finger to his lips, he whistled, the sound shrill enough to quiet even this rambunctious crowd.

"Okay, Ackers, Redwoods..." He gestured dramatically for the open door. "Grab a bottle and *move out!*"

Five minutes to midnight, everyone abandoned their drinks, most of them just as tipsy as my midnight mate, and filed out to the back deck, grabbing an unopened champagne bottle on the way. Unsurprisingly, Ewan had dropped a small fortune on the good stuff; it wasn't enough to just have a flute of champagne for *this* midnight celebration. No, no, everyone needed a full *bottle*.

I stuck to my cider but still snagged a new bottle from the fridge, then trailed after the shifter herd outside, Rosa in front of me, Lucian closing in behind, his hand settling protectively on my hip, his cozy oakwood scent enveloping me and making Kira rumble. Once out in the icy December night, one of the Acker she-wolf mates—Arjun, pretty sure this one was Arjun—gave Rosa his giant sweater, her teeth-chattering turning everyone's heads and putting *all* these wolves on protective mode. Flushed, the witch thanked him, and I held her champagne while she tugged it over her head and righted her tiara.

With the fireworks set on a timer across the lake, there was plenty of space out here to ensure everyone had the perfect view of the display Soren and his dad spent almost all day organizing. I, however, went for the far end near the shoreline, wanting the pups and our guests to have the best spot in the house. Lucian followed, and after Soren passed his niece over to her dad, he joined us. Rosa and Jocelyn huddled together closer to the middle, taking advantage of the pack body heat for Rosa's sake. Pups stood on our patio table, jostling and elbowing their cousins, determined not to miss a thing, and the adults frantically loosened their champagne corks, ready for the big midnight moment.

Nestled between my two mates, I joined the countdown when it started twenty seconds out, shouting and counting, smiling and laughing, bouncing on my toes and bursting at the seams.

"Three!"

Ewan sidled up behind me, arms around my waist, chin on my shoulder.

"Two!"

Soren wiggled beside me, readying his champagne.

"*One!*"

Lucian kissed me, hard and full on the lips as the back deck erupted in cheers and whistles. Rosa had prepped me for the midnight traditions, and while it would have been so easy, so *simple*, to get lost in Lucian's kiss, I owed all my mates a kiss before the sixty seconds were up. First kisses of the new year were just so important: slow but deep with Lucian, rough and biting from Ewan, and playfully sweet from Soren.

"I love you, baby," he murmured against my lips, and I snapped at his smiling mouth, plagued with happy tears again.

"I love you too."

"And I love *errrybody*," Jocelyn boomed, crashing into our huddle and raining sloppy, drunk hugs on me and all my mates. Rosa followed, the kisses my boys had for her chaste and on the cheek. We then navigated the Acker pack for hugs and celebrations, all of us shouting and pointing, clapping and whooping, when the first of the fireworks erupted. Bright yellow and red lit up the sky, explosions of light and sound erupting all around the valley, ours not the only fireworks to ring in the new year. Green and blue pinwheeled through the fading blasts, the set timed to last for the next fifteen minutes.

Ten minutes in, my mates and I broke away from the group. Back to our little nook at the far end of the deck, they cuddled around me to watch the show, Lucian to my left, both my arms curved around one of his. Soren to my right, leaning into my personal space, our hips together, our smiles identical. Ewan behind me, holding me, hugging me, his rosewood scent grounding me in the moment.

But not for long.

Not when I spotted a familiar figure a good fifty feet down the shore, seated on a rock, his silhouette unmistakable.

Loki.

Long limbs and an outfit of soft, airy linen, hair wild and loose, he watched the fireworks with an oddly peaceful grin on that sly mouth of his, and when he glanced my way, I lifted a hand for a shy wave.

And he waved back, just like that, civil and friendly, two of the females from my old wolf pack by his side, one sitting upright so he could stroke her ears.

The wolves wandered closer over the holidays, grieving the loss of Mama and Papa with me. We found them Christmas Day on a pack run, having died in their sleep and living way longer than wild wolves should.

I broke apart, of course, the knowledge that they had gone peacefully, asleep and together, only a small consolation.

Ewan and Soren dug a grave for each.

Lucian disappeared at the time—then returned with *that* god right there sauntering along behind him.

No one had said a word.

No one asked a *thing* of him.

And he turned Mama and Papa into starlight right before our eyes. Magic older and deeper and far more powerful than mine filled the western woods that afternoon, and now they were twin constellations grounded over Redwood Grove, living together amongst the stars.

Why he had stayed—no one knew, and I seriously doubted he would come right out and say it.

Probably waiting for me to plant the golden seeds hidden in the drawer of my bedside table.

And I would.

This year.

Soon.

Once family went home and life found its new normal—I'd plant each seed in the mountain, somehow, and grow an apple orchard of my own.

"Happy New Year, blue eyes," Ewan rumbled against my neck. I cozied into him, leaving Loki for now, back to watching the bursts of color against a black sky.

"Here's to a year of firsts," Soren added, holding his half-drunk bottle in front of me. Lucian clinked his against it, and Ewan ducked down to grab mine and his, both lined up against the railing so they wouldn't be in the way.

"Cheers," Lucian growled, all their wolf eyes out, our pack heartbeat just a little louder as we toasted each other. After a long sip of sparkling cider, all warm and fuzzy inside, Kira content and our first pup fluttering for attention, I pressed a hand to my belly, then glanced between my three fated mates.

"Happy New Year," I whispered, all eyes on me as mine welled with joy, "and here's to many, many more…"

THE END

AFTER THE END

TEN YEARS LATER

Ten years after The End, the Redwood wolves remain in Redwood Grove as the village grows and flourishes, its natural and man-made riches fueling the whole territory.

Ewan continues to value his career, but only focuses on work at Quinn Enterprises three days a week. Jocelyn is still his second-in-command and rules the office with an iron fist, an official unofficial member of the local wolf pack, single and godmother to the pack's firstborn.

Soren manages the Acker properties, pubs, and rental cabins as head of the property group, but is only physically in the office two days a week.

Lucian is responsible for pack security and shares *some* border patrol with his fellow alphas, but prefers to handle it himself. If he isn't stalking the territory perimeter, he is home with the pups and his fated mate.

Lyssa grows the golden apples for the Norse gods, who visit every so often with Loki as their guide to take a bite of her harvest and become young again. Outside of her sacred duty, she brought life and growth back to the southern wastes, now owning a family-run orchard there, the produce sold at local farmer's markets.

No one has taken a bite of the golden apples for themselves yet, but they will, one day, when they're ready.

Collectively, Lyssa, Soren, Ewan, and Lucian agreed that even though packless lone-wolf shifters flock to their territory looking to join them, drawn to their strength and resources, the Redwood wolves is an immediate family affair. The golden apples remain a secret, and they want to keep it that way.

If the secret *does* get out, the pack witch is there with a memory modification spell. Ten years on, Rosa and Aster Marcus still live in their lakefront cottage, very involved with pack activities.

While all four alphas foster their own professional goals, pups are their top priority.

Ten years on, the pack has grown by four, each of them alphas in their own right. Avery, aged ten, is the firstborn son and currently crushing hard on Aster. Twins Viktor and Marcus recently turned eight and are a dangerous combination of brains and brawn, wild little terrors at their Hampton elementary academy for shifters and witchfolk. Little Celeste, aged six, is the first and only she-wolf of the lot and is deeply bonded to her mom. Shy, quiet, fiercely protected by her big brothers and her three dads, Lady Fate help the idiot who dares break her heart.

The Redwood pack lives a quiet, stable life in their territory, growing, loving, and bonding as a family. Lyssa and her mates are best friends and soulmates, deeply in love and aggressively protective of their pups.

For now, they enjoy living a fairly normal life, just separate enough from the humans in their territory to let their inner wild soar, while also involved in the community so that they feel rooted to more than just the natural world.

Of course, it isn't sunshine and roses all the time. Parenting has a steep learning curve, especially with four alphas involved, but over the ten years, the pack found its rhythm. Lyssa and her mates complement each other, using their strengths and weaknesses to raise the most well-rounded pups they can.

So far, each male has fathered pups, all of them taking after their dads as black wolves when shifted. Firstborn Avery is Ewan's little twin, though he acts more like Soren with a love for cooking, movies, and lazy Sunday afternoons around the lake. He's his mama's sweetheart and is always happy to help manage his younger siblings if she has her hands full and no mates around to step in.

The twins hail from the Hadley bloodline, highly intelligent and generally bored in school. They've taken after Lucian with a love for patrolling the territory and learning about the nitty-gritty of the world around them. Marcus, a nod to Rosa's maiden name, is the more dominant of the pair, while Viktor has mastered his dad's calm steadfastness better than any of the pups so far.

Celeste is Soren's, through and through, her eyes like Lyssa's old grey-blues and her hair sandy like his. Quiet, docile, observant, she's the baby of the pack and secretly loves the attention that brings. While she is bonded to Lyssa on an almost spiritual level, she always goes to Ewan for cuddles.

None of the pups have inherited Lyssa's golden eyes, but they show signs of being *more* than shifters, the forest perking up under their paws, their strength superior to their peers.

While each of Lyssa's fated mates technically has one (or two) pups to call his own, they belong to everyone. Ewan is Dad. Soren is Pops. Lucian is Father.

Ewan is pushier about academics, but he also spoils each of his pups rotten. They want for nothing, including his time and attention. While still a business shark, his investment folder huge, he remains very determined to *never* be like his dad. He's soft but firm with the pups, eager to teach them right from wrong, and always lets Celeste fall asleep in his lap during movie nights.

Lucian is the rock, there to listen deeply and dole out advice. He is a protector, quiet and alert, but will get goofy when the pups demand it. Of the three, he puts up the biggest fight when Celeste wants to paint toenails or braid hair, but he's also always the first to fold. Soren isn't enough of a challenge for their little girl; it's Lucian or bust when it comes to embarrassing Halloween costumes and dressing up like Santa.

Lyssa and the others worried Soren might end up being too much of a friend to the pups, but over time he grew into the parent role. He's always up for games, hiking, boating, hunting, fishing, and dollies. Still the pack cook, he preps most meals, does the grocery runs, and manages the pack vegetable garden alongside his mate. However, when a fight breaks out, he's the first to break it up, especially in wolf form, while Lucian and Ewan then sweep in for the verbal discipline and time-outs.

Last but not least, Lyssa. This she-wolf adores her life, all the ups and downs, the good and the frustrating. Her pups are her world, and she would do anything for them. Her mates are her soul. Her golden apples are her legacy. She has a blast running the family stand at the summer farmer's markets, and even sells jams and apple pies in the village during the holidays.

In the future, the Redwood pups will eventually grow up and leave. Find their own mates. Start new bloodlines.

Lyssa and her mates, aging slowly but obviously to the Redwood Grove human population, will retreat into the wilds of their territory. Build themselves a new home for the four of them with space to spare for grandpups.

And when the time comes, they'll eat the golden apples for themselves.

Become young again.

And again.

And again.

Living. Loving. Growing. Tending to the valley as stewards and protectors.

Until they're ready for Lady Fate to take them to the stars—and a new she-wolf in Lyssa's bloodline is worthy to drink from Gull River and grow the golden apples herself, with mates strong and protective enough to keep the pack's secret alive.

Now and for always.

ALSO BY RHEA WATSON

ॐ

All the Queen's Men Series

Paranormal Romance Standalones

Same World

Reaper's Pack

Caged Kitten

Bloodline Trilogy

Lily of the Valley Series

Paranormal Romances inspired by the Hades/Persephone Mythos

Surrender: A Free Short Story

To Love a God

Cronus Society

Secret Society Paranormal Romance Standalones

Bride of Shadows

Kiss of Death

Standalone Romances

Smoke and Mirrors: A Royal Sci-Fi Romance

Magpie's Song: A Leviathan Smutvella

Root Rot Academy Trilogy

The Dragon's Omega

Sacrifice: A Tiger Shifter Omegaverse Romance

RHEA WATSON WRITING AS EVIE KENT

Rhea and Evie have now merged, and all future Evie titles will be published under Rhea's name. Pre-2023 titles will stay under Evie Kent on Amazon and Kindle Unlimited.

ABOUT THE AUTHOR

Rhea Watson is a Canadian paranormal romance author who writes lone wolves and found family, fated mates and forever love. She dreams about living in a cottage in the woods that would make any fairytale witch jealous, and wishes every day was Halloween.

In her spare time, Rhea babies her herb garden, watches hilariously bad horror movies with her own hero, bows to her cat's every whim, and flies through Netflix shows like it's her day job.

Rhea writes MF, MFM, Reverse Harem / Why Choose, and (paranormal) omegaverse.

Rhea can be reached directly at:
rhea@rheawatsonauthor.com
authorrhcawatson@gmail.com

Want to keep in touch with Rhea about her life, writing cave shenanigans, and upcoming releases? Opt into her monthly newsletter here.

FACEBOOK READER GROUP
WEBSITE

www.ingramcontent.com/pod-product-compliance
Lightning Source LLC
Chambersburg PA
CBHW051052030726
47504CB00006B/1585